THRESHOLD

Unbound Book Five

NICOLI GONNELLA

MOUNTAINDALE
PRESS

This is a work of fiction. Names, characters, places, and incidents either are the products of the author's imagination or are used fictitiously. Any resemblance to actual persons, living or dead, businesses, companies, events, or locales is entirely coincidental.

To the Papermates.
Longtime friends, D&D players, and a constant source of encouragement and love. You folks rock.

CHAPTER ONE

Within the Foglands, summer blossomed.

Golden sunlight shone from a cloudless blue sky, laying a thick blanket of warmth along the strong branches of a massive forest. Beneath those boughs, creeping through the emerald shade, flora and fauna thrived on the abundant life Mana that pulsed beneath everything. Cautiously, creatures of all stripes stepped from their dens and warrens and burrows, sampling the quietude in the air.

A'zek padded into a sun-dappled clearing, sniffing. The sleek, patterned fur on his head and shoulders shone in the morning light, ripping with his lithe musculature. In fact, it was just as glossy as the scales that covered his hindquarters, sweeping toward a long, barbed tail. He was a Chimera—a harnoq, to be specific—and he did not like the silence.

For the first time in years, the Mountain Below did not rage.

A'zek had hunted his valley for decades, growing greatly on its bounty, and he knew how to spot a trap. The Mountain Below, the Domain that dwelled beneath the western range, was not quiet. It was waiting.

For what?

This was the question that plagued him—and his Companion, though the old man would not admit it. The danger posed by any Domain was great, but most were content with the resources they generated. They were self-contained, until they weren't. Eventually, they fell apart, weakened by overpopulation of their horrors or drained of power until the shell around them collapsed. A'zek had dealt with two such Domain breaks before, and though the latter was simple to deal with, the former was a nightmare. A rush of monsters—even ones weakened by low Mana resources—was a threat to be taken seriously. And the Foglands had changed.

With the unraveling of the fog, then the death or retreat of the Twisted Ones, their home had become both safer and unfamiliar. A'zek, who procured the food his Companion needed to survive, had delighted in the change at first. Prey was plentiful, but so, too, were the predators. The mortal Races had once again begun to hunt his land, Humans and Goblins and Orcs and Dwarves, all of them searching for treasures and meat.

Qzik claimed it was but the natural progression of the flow of causality, and that the Endless Raven would provide. A'zek was not too proud to admit that such explanations were lost on him. He was a creature of action, and he would not wait to find out why the Mountain Below had stilled. If it were to break, then he would be there to deal with it. He was a Guardian, after all. It was his duty.

The harnoq had secured food and safety for his Companion and set forth, crossing the wilds until he had come to the very foot of the western mountains.

He did not have to wait long.

From the calm morning, a storm erupted above the peaks as a blood-red disc rose into the heavens. Dark clouds appeared as if conjured, crackling with summer lightning and the promise of a cold deluge. A'zek would not have flinched at that, for the wilds were capricious at the best of times. No, instead his ear was fixed upon the Domain that shook the earth below.

Vibrations he could sense more than feel shook the wilds. Birds scattered into the sky, prey and predator alike howling in fear and challenge. A'zek spread his legs and pushed his Affinity deeper, down into the dusty brown darkness, where the orange heart of fire pooled.

Wing and claw! A'zek gasped. *It cannot be.*

In a chamber of ice and fire, a golden giant raged.

Standing atop a plinth of dark metal, forged from the heart of the volcano he had called home for millennia, a figure in immense golden armor sagged. The Archon panted in exhaustion.

Reforged ruined, Marked beasts slain. Four of my Arcids reduced to scrap. The sour contempt he held within his false breast boiled. *My plans of easy conquest, denied.* He looked up, the eye-fires within his gleaming metal helm narrowing with concentration. *But still...*

The Archon hurled his Will against his cage, and the Domain screamed. It was not a scream for mortal ears, but one of Spirit and Mind, the locked Aspects of reality itself that bound Domains in place. The wall between the Archon and freedom was never thinner than it was now, and he would not be denied.

The Bloodmoon still rises!

A door appeared in molten lava, one larger and grander than any he'd manifested before. It rose from the liquid death as a black sentinel, an impossible barrier that had taunted him for centuries. The Archon was trapped within his Domain, imprisoned by Nymean precursors he barely recalled to live in darkness until the end of time. But the Archon refused. He had recovered his shattered Mind and Spirit, took claim over his constructed Body, and began to plan. And all of his schemes and machinations had led to this moment, when the Bloodmoon rose high in the sky for the last time, when the power of the Goddess of Tides could be stolen.

"Your power! Give it to me!" the Archon demanded, activating an array. A concussion of sound ripped through the volcano's heart, cracking the walls and sending stone splashing into the magma. Elaborate lines of maddening script illuminated along the plinth and up the sides of the chamber, twisted sigils that were focused all upon a single glyph beneath the golden warrior. He had learned much from the Labyrinth's ruins.

"*Siphon!*"

A'zek cowered as a spear of crimson energy dropped from the sky. A moon he had never before seen created a dark bridge of power between the heavens and the peak of the tallest mountain. A wash of ineffable music nearly swept him away, so powerful that it was all the Chimera could do to hold onto himself. His senses howled in joy and pleasure, countered only when something *else* emerged from the mountain.

A yellow-red radiance that grabbed onto the divine light. Dissonant pain cut through the pleasure, a sound that devoured the other with an unending appetite. Tendrils of yellow-red grasped with gluttonous abandon.

It felt like one of the Twisted Ones, and the thought of that shook A'zek more than anything else. The power that threatened the Domain was not starved or weakened. It was monstrous.

The carmine energy surged through his array, funneled into the glyph at his feet and into the Archon. Power untold flooded his forged channels, filling his core nearly to the brim. Had he not built the array, he would have died then and there, cracked open from within.

"Domain!" he bellowed, and the mountain shook. Tendrils of power spread out from him, threads that converged upon the massive, black portal that towered from the magma. "I command you!"

Blood-red light suffused the portal's frame, lighting up sigils upon its surface that had been invisible only moments before. More and more pulsed from the Archon, only barely ahead of the flood that surged within him.

"BREAK!"

A flash of blinding *nothing* filled the volcano's core, as if the Void itself vented into his sanctum. His armor corroded under its onslaught, and he felt the death of over two dozen wurms behind him. The Archon screamed and unleashed the remains of his stolen power, fashioning it into a sword and shield. The light bent around him, and his Will thrust directly into the center of the black portal.

ERR-0R!
Domain Failure!
Countermeasures Deployed!

Script circles flared to life around him, hundreds of them, *thousands.* They dragged at his limbs with the weight of mountains and tore at his Spirit and Mind with vindictive might. Warnings and error messages cascaded across the Archon's vision, but he ignored them all, cutting through them with the dregs of crimson power.

Domain—!
Shell Integri—!

The Void shattered into blinding light, and thunder subsumed them all.

When the light cleared and the echoes died away, the Archon stood upon his ragged plinth and beheld glory. The magma beneath his feet had cooled and hardened, darkening the interior of his volcano, but a brilliant new illumination speared into the space.

Sunlight. The Archon strode forward, hand outstretched. He could barely touch the rays that cut through the dust and darkness of his Domain. *No. Not Domain. I am free.*

FREE! howled the Voice inside of him before devolving into mad blubbering.

"Arcids! To me!" he commanded.

Behind him, the grinding of stone indicated an opening door. His servants had hidden behind bulwarks for their safety, and only the most stalwart of his wurms had come along to aid him without fear. He allowed that perhaps his Arcids were wiser, as fully a third of his wurms had perished. *You will be remembered, my children.*

"Master!" a chorus of voices greeted him as his eight creations burst through the opened doors. The Arcids were a variety of shapes and sizes, a side effect of their anomalous genesis. They were his lieutenants, built to serve him and no other. All of them went to a single knee before him, while glorious sunlight lit his golden form like fire.

"Master! Are we to rally and attack the city?" Number 55391 asked. Its pale armor all but glowed in the breeze that flowed through the sundered mountain.

"No. The Nym remains there, and he is… potent," the Archon said. He was not happy to admit it, but the boy presented a danger to his plans that he could not predict. "A Master Tier aids him. A Chanter of the old magics."

He could tell by their confused silence that they had no clue what he meant, but the Archon didn't care. Explanations were for those who were required to think, and these existed to take orders.

"No, we shall speed up our timeline. Seek out the waterfall and the Temple it hides." He spread his arms wide, and yellow-red vapor rose from his charred and battered armor. "For the first time in Age, I am free. Let the mortals cower in their city, for these lands are mine."

A'zek blinked to awareness among the branches of a tree. At first, he thought that he'd somehow been knocked out and lifted into the air, but the answer was simpler than that. As he stood on shaky legs, A'zek saw that all of the forest around the Mountain Beneath had been torn free of the earth when the base of the mountain itself had detonated. All around him was devastation on a scale he had never before seen.

How? He looked up to the terrifying moon, but it was gone. As if it had never been. *The Domain...is broken. Endless Raven save us.*

Creatures began to pour from the darkness, things with chitinous sections and too many legs. Wurms that slithered through the stone itself and enormous figures in icy armor, breathing a vivid purple-white vapor onto the sundered earth.

There was nothing he could do, not against them. Though it hurt his heart and ferocious pride, A'zek fled.

The Henaari needed to know about this.

CHAPTER TWO

"Intent and Resonance are both important to any grand working. But it is Affinity which defines the result. Keep careful watch over it."

-Landrus k'Nand, 1458, Second Age

Zara Cyrene was late.

She was not in the habit of being late. The Grand Harmony was built upon exacting intervals of time, and the Cantus Sodalus had long stressed that its Chanters emulate its benign punctuality. Trailing Felix as he worked upon the Territory Quest had helped her hone that ability, but it had also strained her in ways she had not expected. She had been sent to find the Unbound, gather them, and educate them, but she hadn't expected to care. His near encounters with Primordials and the Divine—impossible as it seemed—had put her Will to the test. She had nearly intervened.

Compassion was not always a virtue. Not in this.

The wild days following the Inquisition's defeat and DuFont's death had since occupied much of her time. From teaching the young ones more about the Grand Harmony to giving what aid she could to the new Lady of Haarwatch, each and every moment had been filled with the fervor of enterprise. It was an invaluable opportunity for the Cantus Sodalus to gain influence on a rising ruler, and one with true System Authority? Even stunted as it was by DuFont's unwise expenditures, it was a powerful tool for any ruler.

Already, Quests had been issued, and not by the System, but by Lady Boscal herself! It was a revelation to Zara, a way of interaction with the System that none but the Hierophant enjoyed. Evidently, true System Authority holders could issue Quests in relation to their Territory. Though, so far, the only ones they had been able to access were requests for raw materials like ore, monster cores, stone, and lumber. The people had gotten to work quickly, but it was a long haul toward getting Haarwatch on its feet.

Still, Zara had great hopes for Cal and for their continuing alliance.

That exuberance had led to her current quandary. She had become wrapped up in the new challenges Cal faced and had lost track of time. So now Zara rushed, flitting through the rain-soaked streets on a late summer's evening, headed for the quarters she had long thought destroyed. The walls remained standing, however, as well as the expensive glass at the front. Above the door, a nine-pronged star greeted her, a decoration from an older tenant, yet it had proven strangely prescient. Who would have guessed the Unbound would have come to her as a Nym, albeit one on his way to something far stranger?

She passed inside.

There were no books within—they had long been moved to another location—and the inscribed sigils upon the walls had long faded in potency. She caressed them as she passed, igniting them with a minor effort of Will, and was greeted by a rustle of phantom feathers. The rafters above her head filled with close to two hundred birds, varied in type and level to a casual Analyze, though harmless enough. As she passed the counter, one specific avian, a small but fluffy owl, landed atop the weathered surface.

"Sing the song of passage, milady," it chirped in the common tongue.

Zara smiled, lips over her sharp teeth, and let out a short, melodic whistle. From her lips came the sound of thick paper turning in calloused hands, and the creak of cured skin, bound with glue and thread. The small owl let out an appreciative hoot and flitted back up to the rafters.

"Keep an eye on the door," Zara murmured before moving into the back room.

Hidden along the side of her office was a second door cleverly built into a false wall. No magic or music hid it away, just tricky engineering. She tripped the disguised latch and entered, closing it behind her.

Within was a long, narrow room that smelled of sage and must. At the far end, to which she hustled, there was a basin of water atop an elegantly carved wooden stand. The basin was made of beaten copper, and it was empty. Another whisper of Will set aquamarine power flowing down Zara's fingers and into the bowl, until the liquid Mana began to swirl rapidly in a counterclockwise motion.

A note escaped Zara's lips, a sound that reverberated in the narrow room as if it were an amphitheater. Blue and gold briefly flashed in her vision as the System noticed her song. But soon the aquamarine increased, and the swirling Mana rose out of the copper basin. All at once, it formed into the shape of a skull. It was followed by tendons and muscle and skin forming over the skull, layering over itself until it formed a facsimile of a floating, withered head.

"You're late," the head accused.

"Forgive me, Mauvim, it has been a busy day," Zara said with a bow of her neck. "I have been advising the new Lady of Haarwatch, guiding her in the power she now finds within herself. It is remarkable what power true System Authority grants a person."

"Babysitting nobility, newly made or not, was not your task. What of the Unbound?" Mauvim's voice was sharp as a whip, and Zara thought she heard a note of worry. "Is he ready for what is coming?"

"He is..." Zara let herself trail off, her Spirit tracing the faint connection she had with the boy. He stood somewhere to the west, most likely the Wall again. "There is still work to be done."

Mauvim hummed to herself, her jowls quivering. "Then you must push him. Things are changing quickly. Word of more arrivals has spread along back channels and secret messengers,."

"Did our people find them first?" Zara asked, and it was as if a fist clenched her heart.

"Unclear. Silence has taken hold. The Hierocracy received word of a 'great threat' to the south and has sent its Paladins to seek them out. Three entire battalions into the Expanse." Mauvim shook her head and continued. "Early word from Isla is that the Unbound has taken the form of a Minotaur, of all things, but I've not heard from her in weeks. Regardless, if the Expanse doesn't kill the Unbound, the paladins will."

Zara frowned. The Paladins were worse than the Inquisitors, and far stronger. "Does Isla request aid?"

"She wouldn't even if she could. You know the scrutiny she faces in the sands."

Zara did indeed know. The Scorched Expanse was nearly as anathema to Sorcerers as the Hierocracy, if for different reasons. "And of the others?"

The tiny head of her mentor *harrumphed*. "Little is known. To the north, we've heard rumors of a Gnome with strange powers, and the east is as quiet as ever, but that is to be expected. The border lets little through, even information on the strains of Song." Mauvim fixed Zara with a single, unblinking eye. Rendered of Mana and catalyzed Spirit, it was far more elastic than her true face, which the ancient Sorcerer only used to enhance her meaning. "Your experiment. Is it through? He is truly Nymean?"

"Yes." Zara nodded. "Things and information have changed since last we spoke, however." She swallowed, a bit nervously. Though she had reported the results of the Territory-Wide Quest, she had not gone into much detail in her last missive. When last she had fully reported in, Felix had just arrived back in Haarwatch. With quick words, she explained the events that had unfolded the past several months. Mauvim, for her part, listened with increasingly boggled eyes.

"...And that brings us to now. We have the city under control, and we're attempting to shore up defenses before any more redcloaks arrive or the threat of the Archon manifests once again."

"Two cores? Divine and Primordial?" Mauvim muttered to herself. Her Spirit lashed wildly from fear to hope and back to terror. "And his Race...he has become a Primordial? But what of the infection? The curse all Primordials suffer under?"

"Entirely absent," Zara said, though she couldn't quite believe it herself. "The Maw's influence nearly ruined this region, but when Felix absorbed the last of it, all of those changes were nullified. Somehow, the boy is free of the Blind Gods' curse upon Primordials, though we have not yet dared to experiment with his blood."

"Remarkable," Mauvim breathed. "Denied a god, a Lost one no less, and fought off an invasion. He is the greatest candidate yet, Zara. We must bring him in. The others need to meet him."

"That is the plan, but...the dangers here are not to be ignored. There is much to do before he can access the interior of the Continent." Zara could feel the wounds in the city where the Archon's Mark had cut into the ambient Mana. "The Archon must be dealt with, once and for all."

"Very well." Her mentor sighed. "Little is known of your true situation in the west, at least as of now. But word has spread of the Foglands opening up for the first time in recorded history; that would have been impossible to hide. The Inviolate Order was clearly suppressing it before, but now the news spreads like wildfire among the merchants. Talk is of rare resources the likes of which we've never seen. Your little town will be awash in new presences sooner rather than later. You do not have much time to get him out of there before things get complicated further."

Mauvim drew herself up, for all that she was a projected head of Spirit and Mana. "The Order is making moves. Your dispatch of the Master Inquisitor was felt, even here, though the Grand Inquisitor has not yet taken action. She sits within the Enclave, still. As long as she remains far from you, you can remove your threats with time enough to secure the Unbound." Mauvim paused again. "I feel a quiver in your Spirit. What is it?"

Zara grimaced. "A few redcloaks survived, and they ride for Setoria with news that Haarwatch has fallen to a Primordial."

"What!?"

Zara bore witness to a great many curses and off-color phrases, ones she had never before heard in her long life. So many that the ancient woman eventually ran out of languages and merely sputtered in rage.

"I will see what can be done about Setoria. But we run short on time, all of us," Mauvim managed after a while. "We cannot tarry.

Events are pushing forward faster by the day. Is this Felix worthy? Will he serve?"

"The boy has made questionable Choices, some of which he hides. But I believe he is worthy, yes," Zara nodded to herself, letting conviction swell within her Spirit. "I believe he will serve against what comes."

"He must. They all must. The darkness on the horizon has begun to blot out the edges of the Song. It is faint, but the fledgling seers all speak the same. Ruin advances."

Mauvim fixed Zara with ageless eyes. "We must all be ready for the war to come."

Felix stood upon the battlements of the Wall, peering again into the darkness of the forest. The sun had set, and three moons were hovering before him, two blue and one silver. The Twins and Siva. He glanced at them, his Perception enough to make out their pocked faces and empty seas. Other than their color, they seemed so very similar to the moon of his home, yet his Affinity tingled.

Vellus was chained to her own moon. Are the other gods the same? He chewed his lip. *Am I staring at more gods?*

Pit let out a derisive note as he flew by, buffeting Felix with wind and making him laugh.

"Yeah, I'm not a fan of the gods either, at this point," Felix said to his Companion. "Makes me wish I could go back to being an atheist. At least then it was just other people trying to screw me over."

"What was that?"

Felix looked up and saw Hector Ty'nel stepping out of one of the Wall's many enclosures. A Human of middle years, he was around the same height as Felix and bore a well-groomed goatee. He was wiping a series of styluses on a rag that sparked in the dark.

"Oh, just complaining," Felix said. "Pit's a good listener, even if he won't sit still."

On cue, Pit dropped from the skies with a clatter of claws and eight hundred pounds of muscle. The orichalcum battlements rang like a gong as he hit, each claw striking a different tone. Pit pushed against Felix, nuzzling his giant head against his chest in a way that was at first endearing then quickly annoying.

Treat?

"You big pig," Felix muttered and pulled out a ream of jerky he'd scrounged up earlier. Pit snagged the whole of it, gulping it down in an instant. "Hey! Some of that was for me."

Pit put his head down, feigning regret, but Felix could feel the jerk's Spirit. He was happy as a clam.

"I've got some food from my wife, if you want to share, Felix," Hector offered. Felix happily took him up on that, giving Pit a squint and grimace.

Pit trilled out pleased birdsong and leaped into the air, already taking laps again.

Pit's Flight is level 42!

Hector laughed. "He's a handful, that one. Still can't believe you've tamed a Chimera, though."

"Tame is not entirely accurate," Felix said with a smile. "It's more of a partnership thing."

"Aye, a Pact. People've been talking about it since you saved the city," Hector sat down and pulled out a large, hard-bottomed satchel. He pulled out various cloth-wrapped items, and Felix's mouth watered. "I've heard quite a few have gone looking for their own Pact to make."

Felix sighed. "Yeah, those idiots below are all clamoring for me to tell them how to do it. They don't particularly care that it has drawbacks."

"Ah, the Fiend's Legion," Hector laughed and handed Felix an unwrapped sandwich. Felix's Voracious Eye took it in: roast avum, onions, some sort of lettuce knock-off, and thick brown bread. "You can't really blame them. They see you, how powerful you've become, and they want to emulate that. Kind of flattering, I think."

The Fiend's Legion was the name of the self-styled defenders of the city. They had taken up watch over the massive hole left in the Wall by the Apollyon and were preventing any monsters from entering the city. There hadn't been many in the past week.

"You deal with it, then." Felix groaned and took a bite. "Oh holy crap, this is good," he said around a mouthful.

"I'll pass the thanks along to the cook," Hector said, beaming. "Nea hasn't had much time to cook, what with all the brewing and concocting she's had to do. Been living on what I could scrounge from the grocer down on Echo Lane, but Nea got mad when she heard. She went all out for tonight."

Felix smiled as Hector spoke. His voice was warm, and he could literally hear the love he had for his wife in his voice; it rippled across his Spirit with such clarity that it humbled him. Felix and the Alchemist hadn't always been on the best terms, and it was interesting to see another side of her.

"How's your kid doing with all this? Amaya, right?" Felix asked. "Hard as this is for us adults, I can't imagine dealing with it so young."

"She's handled it well, though mostly that was because we found your camp so early on." Hector shook his head. He stared out over the battlements, back toward the city. Lights were picked out among the dark shapes of rubble and ruin, but far too few. "The first few hours after the tower fell? It was a nightmare. Things are coming around now, slow as it is."

Felix nodded. He'd been unconscious for a large portion of those early hours, but he'd heard enough tales to last a lifetime. Revenants rampaging across the city, the Eyrie collapsing, people across the city dying in droves. He couldn't help but feel guilty about it. So much of what happened had been—well not his doing exactly, but he had been involved.

Guilt didn't have to make sense.

Hector and Felix talked and ate, weaving between topics of sigaldry and his family life. Amaya was a cool kid, a bit precocious, and reminded him of Gabby. His sister, the one he'd left on a boat with her hurt friend.

God, I hope they're both okay. That mom is okay and isn't missing me too much. The thought made him sad, enough apparently for Hector to notice.

"Sorry, I can go for days when I talk about my kid, ya know?" Hector smiled and wiped his hands. He began picking up the discarded cloth and replacing them in his satchel. They had worked through the large spread very quickly, but that was to be expected of folks with Journeyman Bodies. He could go a long while without any food, but when he ate, he *had* to eat. They needed the energy, anyway, especially if they were gonna work all night again. "You ready to get back down there?"

"Yeah, might as well get back to it. There's a lot to do." Felix stretched and tried to think happier thoughts, like all the Skill levels he'd gained since he'd begun this project.

"We're a bit away from the foundational arrays, but you're learning fast. We should have this Wall working again in a day. Two at most." Hector patted Felix on the back and walked back into the enclosure, where a set of spiral stairs led down into the guts of the Wall.

Felix hung back, looking at the sky. Stars were spread across the cloudless night, more than he'd ever seen in his life, and he could pick up a dark shadow flitting across them.

Back at it, Pit. Keep an eye on those dorks down below, yeah?

A single, hawk-like cry cut through the dark, and affirmation thrummed across their bond. Felix nodded to himself and got back to work.

CHAPTER THREE

Theurgist of the Rise is level 65!
Invocation is level 42!

Felix had been learning a lot in the past few days. While part of his retreat into the Wall had been to escape the... consequences of notoriety, it was also to sate his curiosity. When initially surveying the Wall for major issues, Felix and his team had encountered more than the giant hole in the center. Sigils had been burned out, and entirely new sigaldry had scored itself into the magical metal.

It was Profane Sigaldry, the Archon's own creation, and it was a perfect opportunity to advance his sigil Skill. Theurgist of the Rise was a combination of Sigils of the Primordial Dawn—according to Zara, a sort of ur-script, a precursor to modern work—and the Archon's Profane Sigaldry. Toge,her, they interacted in the strangest of ways, which meant standard modes of sigil training had limited effects for him.

Hector was more than happy to study a new inscription style, as were Atar and Alister. They were somewhere nearby, likely on the other section. Hector and his team of eight Iron Rank Inscriptionists had made it to the lower levels of the Wall, where the more complicated arrays were housed.

"Felix, look at this," Hector said, four hours after their evening meal. He pointed to a circular array of sigils molded into the orichalcum panel. Felix's eyes flickered across it—his Skill humming as he did.Names and connections spooled out in his Mind, as much his own memory as the Skill boosting him. He recognized maybe forty percent of what he was inspecting at any given time.

"Strengthening array with a... kinetic buffer," Felix said. "Same as all the rest on this level."

"Not that, this," Hector clarified, pointing at the diagonal slash of scorched markings across the array. Profane Sigaldry. All of the arrays had been marred in some way by them. "It's not just the sigils used here, it's the positioning. Look," Hector traced his finger along the scorched line, twisted, inverted magical markings describing a path across the majority of the original array. "The way it cuts into each major glyph is intentional. The only thing I can't figure out is the language itself."

Felix pointed at the Profane Sigaldry. "I told you. It's inverted. The runes take up the negative space the standard stuff doesn't occupy."

"Runes?" Hector asked, eyebrow raised.

Felix rolled his eyes at his own lapse. "Sigils. It's a name from—nevermind." He traced out a symbol near the glyph—a combination of sigils to form a centralized symbol—for the kinetic buffer. "This is the inverted symbol for *force*. It's... huh. It must be directly countering the array it crosses. Wow. That must have taken some serious effort to do."

Hector blinked at him, and Felix realized his assistants were as well. The Inscriptionist stroked his goatee. "Serious effort. You aren't kidding. There is no possible way this could have been done by an enemy leagues away. Either we're dealing with a genius savant with powers *far* beyond us—in which case, we should simply run—or this was sabotage."

Felix's mind flashed to the Arcids, the three that had infiltrated Haarwatch and had caused so much damage. "Sabotage makes sense. But I wouldn't push magical bullshit off the table just yet. If I've learned anything the past few months, it's that the Continent has an unending supply of it."

That got a few chuckles, weak humor though it was. Felix was preaching to the choir a bit; having their Guild and town pulled down around them by a super monster and its spawn had left its impression.

Felix left Hector to his work and walked along the interior chambers of Haarwatch's Wall. Everything glowed faintly, suffused with Mana that coursed through the simplest inscriptions and the ones that were damaged the least. Cal had sent power to the fortification with her Authority, but she hadn't much to spare at the start. Even a week later the resources that Haarwatch had operated on were too depleted to do much more than power a few defensive constructs. It wasn't enough to fight off another monster horde. Not yet.

He meandered down another set of stairs, accompanied by that red-gold glow. The Guild had been pretty Spartan about their decorations: there was a tapestry every hundred yards, but that was about it. The tapestries depicted the Guild logo, a spear and sword crossed over a shield. The subdued architecture was interesting despite the drapery, done in a style that Felix recognized from below the city and a few other places. Nymean architecture, he supposed.

Speaking of Nymean craftsmanship...

Felix's hand found the wire-wrapped grip of his Crescian Blade, and a firm tug pulled it free of its sheath. It was hooked, supposedly made by the Nym to have a curve in the center so that the blade resembled a sickle. It was a slightly longer version of what, on Earth, was called a khopesh and was useful for hooking onto an opponent's shield or arms during battle. Felix chuckled to himself. He had spent an entire evening wracking his brain about where he'd seen a similar sword before; it had been supremely satisfying to put that thought to rest.

He flipped the blade, inspecting its bronze-like metal. Crescian Bronze it was called, which made sense in a boring sort of way. Zara had told him it was an excellent medium for enchanting, held onto magic for years without decaying, and that it was a rare find. It was the same metal that the Essence Anchor was made of, back in the Labyrinth. A glyph was etched into the base of the blade, just above the crossguard, and it was surrounded by hair-thin secondary and tertiary sigils. They dealt with things like direction and heat; ancillary things. The glyph, however, was one he'd recognized from an unlikely source. Though the Archon's Profane

Sigaldry was a twisted, inverted version of the common variant, Felix could still read the outline.

Siphon. It explained the sword's ability to cut through spells, as demonstrated by DuFont several times. Unlike the Archon's version, it didn't suck up Mana like a sponge. Instead, it redirected it, turning a spellform back into vapor and dispersing it to either side of the blade. Felix's Manasight could pick out other arrays within the blade. Unlike the Siphon array, they weren't on the surface, but buried in the metal. He hadn't a clue on how it was done, and he didn't recognize what they meant. Neither did Hector, when he had asked.

Felix had completed a Hidden Quest involving the sword, and had a Title as a reward.

Hidden Quest Completed!
Inheritor of the Key!
You've proven yourself worthy in a trial by combat with a Master Tier existence! The Key is yours by Right and Might! Seek out the Temples to discover its true purpose and unlock its power.

New Title!
Inheritor (Unique) (Evolving)!
You are the master of the Nymean Key! Evolve this Title by seeking out Nymean Temples!

Which led directly to yet another Hidden Quest.

Hidden Quest Discovered!
The Door Of The Lidless Eye!
Seek out the Temple you once took refuge within, Ascendant. Dire secrets dwell within, awaiting the Inheritor. It is your duty to prevent the darkness from escaping into the light. Do not tarry, for the Archon is close and the darkness closer.

There were mysteries around that sword, and returning to the Waterfall Temple would begin to solve them. But...

The Archon is out there, and this city isn't ready to defend itself. There is so much left to do. Felix slammed the blade back in its sheath, set alongside a blue-metal bone. He took a slow, calming breath. *It's about time to go help in the city center, but...I suppose I should go check on them before I go.*

Felix didn't want to, but it was his...was "duty" the right word? Responsibility, maybe. He shook his head and braced himself as he unlatched the ground-floor gate, which came right up to the large hole in the Wall. Beyond a set of red-gold metal stairs were a few men and women of a variety of Races and ages, though leaning heavily toward middle age. They were clad in patchwork armor and a motley collection of cloaks. It would have been entirely unremarkable were the cloaks not emblazoned with a glyph in bright blue paint. It looked like an open eye that was also on fire.

They've got a logo now? Felix tried to hold in his groan, but it was hard. *I can tell it's supposed to be a glyph of* eye, fire, *and* lightning, *but they're stretching their artistic license quite a bit there. It's barely legible.* He padded down the stairs, his new boots relatively loud on the metal. He hopped onto the flagstones, moving just far enough ahead to see around the jagged rent in the metal. Felix stopped dead.

Oh no.

They were...fighting over his sword?

There were fifty of them, and three distinct groups had converged at the center of the gap in the Wall. Between them, sunk into the flagstones, was a large, eight-foot blade shaped from the fang of the Ravager King. His Blade of the Fang was what happened when a lance and a greatsword had a baby; it was way too big to carry around with him all the time. It kept getting caught on low doorways and stuff, so he'd thrust it into the ground with the intent to get it back later.

"The Fist were here first," one of them growled at another. Closer now, Felix could tell their group were all wearing heavy metal gauntlets. "So back off!"

"What right do you have to this spot? You don't even fight with a weapon!" said one of the opposing members. They were the largest contingent, and all of them had some sort of sword strapped to their bodies. "This is clearly a spot the Fiend meant for the Blade."

"You're all idiots. It's not meant for any of that. It's the line in the sand, you see?" The third leader stepped forward, hands out. Behind her were just as many folks as the sword guys, except all of them had hammers and clubs. "It's the point where we crush the monsters that come for us. So clearly it was a spot of honor for the Bone."

Oh god, Felix palmed his face. *They formed gangs.*

Before things could devolve further, Felix cleared his throat. His Journeyman Body and stupidly high Vitality (or was it Endurance?) let his "*ahem*" practically boom out into the open space. A few of the closer members of the Legion actually fell down.

"The Blue-Eyed Fiend!"

He wasn't sure who said it, but every one of them turned to gawk. And then—to Felix's eternal embarrassment—they *saluted.* Fist to their cores, about six inches above their navel, then out again. The two men and woman that had been leading the arguments stepped forward.

"We were simply, ah," the one with gauntlets stumbled. Felix briefly Eyed them all. His name was Oskar. "Do you have orders for us, sir?"

"Have uh, have you seen any monster activity? Either here or at the tree-line?" Felix asked, grasping for something pertinent.

"No, sir. Do you wish for us to send out patrols?" Oskar perked up hopefully. "We can do a sweep of the—"

"Sounds good. Just leave enough people here to protect the gap, I guess," Felix said. He walked past the line and grasped the handle of his Blade of the Fang. He directed a stream of Essence into the weapon, and the markings on it hummed to life. It pulled from the flagstones easily. "Don't fight anything too high above you, right? How many of you have Analyze?"

A few hands went up, mostly among the gauntlet group. "Good. Analyze is important. Don't start a fight you can't win. Doesn't matter what weapon you're using if you die before you can lift it."

Felix's Affinity thrummed as the threads of connection between him and the Legion vibrated in chorus. Every one of them looked at him with serious eyes and gave some variety of solemn nod. Felix repressed a sigh. He was at a loss as to what else to say. "All right. I'll be back, then."

Pit, he sent. *We're leaving.*

Back to friends? came the reply, filled with a surge of warm emotions.

Yeah, back to friends.

Adamant Discord!

Ensuring he was far enough away from the members of the Legion, Felix flared his newest Transcendent Skill. Blue-white lightning crackled around his body, and those who were closer stumbled back, though the electricity never strayed far from him. Steel-like cords pushed to the forefront of Felix's awareness, lines of connection, not to people as Affinity sensed, but to everything. With a significant effort of Will, Felix *pulled.*

With a crack of thunder, he shot from the earth, up at an angle and through the topmost portion of the Wall's gap. He heard a gasp from behind him, but no one was hurt, so he put it from his mind as he soared up and into the air.

The ache in his Aspects started immediately. Felix still hadn't fully recovered from his wild fight against DuFont, and Adamant Discord put a strain on his Aspects in a way he couldn't really quantify. It was like his entire being was contracting with every activation, just like a muscle. So at the apex of his leap, Felix let the song of his Skill cut out, and he fell.

Right onto the back of a swooping Pit. Felix laughed as Pit let loose a happy shriek and cut a tight loop in the air.

Alright, bud. City center.

They took off like a shot.

"We need to clear this area!" Vess shouted, and people scrambled to obey. "I hear more people!"

The area she stood on had been trampled flat by the Apollyon, that gigantic Arcid. Buildings had collapsed and shattered, so she and a few other teams had been working day and night to clear them all. They had thought the buildings empty, but each new structure brought the chance of someone trapped, and Vess' increasing Perception and Affinity could seek them out rapidly.

A team of Untempered citizens and Iron Rank fighters focused on Strength and Endurance shouldered up the foot thick slab of stone. It was propped up at an angle, leaned against a horizontal wall, and created a pocket below. That was where Vess could hear movement, soft whimpering, and the whir of fear.

Spear of Tribulations!

Two silver spears manifested from her Mana, appearing just above her shoulders before swooping forward to prop up the slab. The Iron Ranks were having trouble holding it up, but the strength of her spears was directly proportional to her considerable Intelligence. The spears flexed slightly as the stone rested upon them, but they held, and the workers all groaned in relief.

Gaze of the Unseen Hunter!

Vess' sight shifted into a different spectrum, one of heat that depicted the stone around her as a cool shade of blue. Within the darkness, however, she could see three shapes picked out in reds, yellows, and oranges. Two were shifting about, larger men perhaps, but the third was eerily still and awfully small.

Gaze of the Unseen Hunter is level 56!

"It is all right. We have come to help," she said into the dark space. "Can you walk? Do you need assistance?"

There was no answer, just the sound of shifting rock. The sense of fear increased. Vess frowned.

"Are you injured? I promise you, we are here to save you," Vess said, attempting to inject as much calm into her voice as possible.

Without warning, a shape leaped from the shadows, and Vess nearly gutted it. But it was a child, dirty and bloody, and trembling with fear. "Twin's teeth. Are you okay, little one?"

Someone screamed, and Vess looked up to see two man-sized Ghostfire Simians tear out of the dark.

"Monsters!"

"Fire!" Vess commanded, grabbing the child and pulling them clear just as the Iron Ranks around them let loose a barrage of Mana bolts. Shadow, flame, ice, and stone, each only held the strength of Iron Rank, but all together, they tore one of the beasts apart.

A third spear manifested in Vess' left hand, and she spun it once before impaling the lead Simian through the face. It's head exploded, and Vess kicked it in the chest to free the weapon, holding onto the child with her other hand. "Clear the slab!"

Workers fled. More warm shapes surged up from below, and she waited half a heartbeat to let them draw a bit closer. Just as they reached the edge of the opening, she hurled her third spear and clenched her Will.

"Seven Tribulations!"

Her spears burst into a storm of air Mana, tearing through the lead monsters and dropping the slab with an earth-heaving crash.

The child in Vess' arms whimpered, and she hugged tight to the heiress' pauldrons. Vess' heart ached at the fear she saw in the girl. "Shh, shh, you are safe. I promise."

You Have Killed A Ghostfire Simian (x5)!
XP Earned!

Vess waved away the kill notification in irritation. She had thought they were done with these creatures. They hadn't encountered any beyond the first two days. Hopefully, these would stay trapped, but she doubted it. The city was honeycombed by tunnels and sewers that would allow them to escape in some way. That meant it was time to take care of them, now.

"Break into teams; look for more openings," she ordered. "Do not enter any openings. Send up a signal. And someone take this child to the Manor. Go."

The Iron Ranks and Untempered alike jumped to task, one of them rushing forward to gingerly take the weeping toddler from Vess' arms. The Manor had begun housing a great many orphaned children in hopes that the parents could be found soon. Part of her ached to see the child in such pain, but the rest of her was filled with an immutable fury at the monsters, at DuFont, the Guilders, and the Inquisitors.

A crash of thunder broke in the sky, and she spotted dark wings flying far above. A haze of familiar song passed by briefly, like a strident concerto from one of Pax'Vrell's finest amphitheaters. Vess took a sharp, measured breath.

Felix is done with the Wall for now, I suppose. She looked back at the crumbling ground, that fire in her belly still burning. *I will meet up with them later.*

There were monsters to kill, and she had fury to spare.

CHAPTER FOUR

Pit's Flight is level 43!

Pit's wings propelled them through the dark skies, spotty lamplight, and torches below and a sea of stars above. The moons had set, leaving it all the darker. For once, Felix regretted his advanced Perception. Without it, he would have felt suspended in the inky blackness of outer space. As it was, he could easily pick out the rooftops and streets by the limited light of the stars.

At least I can enjoy the wind on my face, Felix thought with a deep breath. They were flying fast, eating up the distance between the Wall and the city center. *Being up here is nice.*

Pit trilled in agreement but said nothing else. He was focused on flying.

Honestly, he was impressed the tenku could hold them up this long. Felix had gained a significant amount of density when he'd hit Apprentice, and yet again when Journeyman Tier came and went. Pit's Stamina was dropping pretty fast, but he could manage a couple miles at the very least.

They didn't have that far to go.

Flickers of activity below caught his eye, where the search and rescue teams were still excavating portions of the city. Felix had helped with that for several days before being persuaded to use his powers for more pressing tasks. Any survivors found or monsters encountered could be handled by the Apprentice Tiers below. There were always at least a couple high Apprentice—those closing in on Journeyman—fighters among them for support. A chittering scream cut into the night, followed by a familiar swirl of air Mana. Felix almost had them swoop down, but the scream was silenced instantly.

Vess is still out there? As far as Felix knew, the Heiress of Pax'Vrell had been working non-stop for the past three days. She took breaks, but only to help Cal with some piece of statecraft. The woman was a machine; it was as impressive as it was worrying. *Her Endurance isn't high enough for all this. She's gotta sleep.*

Felix leaned into Pit's back, and the tenku replied with a burst of forward momentum. He resolved to speak to Evie, get her to talk some sense into Vess. They were all driving themselves hard, but everyone had limits, even if some of them liked to pretend otherwise.

The two of them landed in the city center not long after that. It was among the worst affected by the sundered Domain and subsequent infestation of Primordial Spawn. The area was terraced as each Quarter rose higher and higher as it reached the heart of the city. Once, the apex hosted the Eyrie, the Protector's Guild tower and highest structure in all of Haarwatch. That had changed when the Ravager King—and Felix—had collapsed it from the inside out. Most of the tower had fallen on the Crafters' and Wall Quarters, but a substantial amount had savaged the richest part of town.

After that, it had been host to the majority of the Revenant horde. Felix and his friends had eradicated them, but signs of their presence lingered. Claw marks on stone and trees, statues that had been utterly defaced or even decapitated. Like the one with the Human stepping on a Chimera; that one had ended up sliced into pieces somehow. Pit let out a pleased rumble in his chest, and Felix snorted.

Not a Revenant, then. Felix patted Pit's flank. *Good pig.*

Still, he imagined he could smell them, but it was just in his head. All that they were, Primordial Spawn, was now in him. He wasn't exactly happy about that, but he'd made peace with it. Mostly.

Felix dismounted, and the two of them walked the cleared thoroughfare. Though it was something like four in the morning, the city center was bustling. Men and women of all Races hustled through the streets, carrying stone or lumber salvaged from the surrounding structures. Inns had reopened, turned into massive kitchens and temporary housing for as many as they could fit.

The city was rebuilding, and far faster than Felix had expected.

It was odd to him. The civilization level was roughly around what Felix would call medieval times (admittedly not a subject he knew a lot about), but it was also incredibly advanced. The existence of magic changed the game, leading to the code-like sigil arrays and complicated enchantments. Add in the fact that anyone with half a Temper to their name could do the work of ten people back home, and their speed made sense.

That didn't even factor in Skills like Architecture and Construction (among many, many others) that Felix had only recently learned about. Construction, to his knowledge, had been long considered a base Skill, not worth learning or mastering for those who would compete for supremacy on the Continent. Felix found it fairly wonderful that the Dusters, long considered the dregs of Haarwatch society, were now valued more than the richest noble.

The sound of hammers on metal drew his attention. On the other side of the square that had once held the Eyrie's lowest floors, a tall, six-story building of granite had been newly erected. Felix could tell it was new because, in a space that was certainly prime real estate, both spots next to the building were completely empty. Much of the square was in ruins, with only some of it rebuilt. A sign had been hung out front, formed of more granite and carved with a series of letters he recognized as the common tongue of the Hierocracy.

Coldfire Smithy, Felix read with a smile. An image of flames had been engraved above the letters, too. *They got it open. And in a good spot, too.* He was sure some noble was mad about it, probably complaining to Cal right now, despite the hour. Felix let himself smile just a little bit more. For the most part, he was happy he didn't have to shoulder the System Authority, if just to avoid scenarios like that.

Hammer on steel and the faint wash of heat he could detect meant the smithy was up and running, too. No one was wasting any time. Their friend, Oveh, must have done most of the construction work, because the front of it was a beautiful, geometric design filled with complicated square knotwork. She was one of the few people he'd met who also knew Stone Shaping, and she had grown impressively. Felix could handle more volume, undoubtedly, but the Dwarven woman was deft and creative. Her work was beautiful. Felix's style was more brutalist. Big, chunky, and hopefully useful.

"Felix!"

A soft pulse of his Spirit let him recognize the voice before his memory caught up, fast as it was. Elle, Dwarven armorsmith and proprietor of the Coldfire Smithy, strode from around the corner. She had a hammer in her hand and soot on her cheeks, but her smile was wide.

"Hi Elle." Felix waved, stopping Pit with a touch. The tenku warbled and pawed at the earth. "Sorry about him. I think he was excited to see the kitchens at Cal's."

Elle shook her head, but her smile didn't stop. "Chimera or not, he's just a big puppy, isn't he?"

"The biggest and best," Felix agreed. "How goes the arms business?"

"Busy as can be. We've been making orders nonstop, even had to hire some more apprentices and runners to get the volume out. Even so, we're still fighting to keep up with the volunteers to Cal's new guard."

Cal—Vess, really—had put out notice that the new Lady of Haarwatch needed a new guard to protect the city. It was made clear that this wasn't the Protector's Guild, though some Guilders had found their way into the ranks. He heard Cal had Bodie and Vivianne checking on everyone who applied. There was always the chance someone with a grudge might try to get even.

Felix had kept clear of the whole mess, though.

"How's your wife? Rafny still foaming at the mouth that she's making Apprentice Tier weapons?" Felix inquired with a smile.

Elle laughed, a husky noise that fit the beautiful smith. "She's champing at the bit, ready to do some 'real work' again. You know, she's still mad she couldn't modify those weapons of yours." Elle gestured to the bone club at his side and oversized sword strapped awkwardly to his back. It had to sit almost sideways to not drag on the ground, which made walking in a crowd a bit hazardous.

"Tell her the Revenant leather grips she added have been holding out great," Felix said with a grin. "But, I've been inspecting this thing for a while and can't find out much. Can you bring it to Rafney? Tell her it's a challenge." Felix took his Crescian Blade—sheath and all—off his belt and handed it to Elle.

The smith's eyes widened, and her Spirit danced in wonder. "Crescian Bronze, really? When do you need it back?"

Felix looked at the Eyrie, rising again brick by brick. Most of the reconstruction work was to rebuild something as the new center of town, and it was already a solid eight stories tall. He idly wondered if she were building a new tower.

"Soon, most likely. Things won't stay peaceful for long," Felix said, his mood falling.

Elle considered him with a tilted head, a full foot shorter than him but still a dominating presence. "Always more fighting to do," she agreed. "I'll make sure Raf gets this back quickly. When we do, I have some things I've been working on, too. Hopefully these don't break when you use them."

"Thank you. A lot. But I don't think I need it; I've got my scales." Felix patted his chest. His Skill—Sovereign of Flesh—allowed him to form thick armor plating out of his skin and Essence, transforming them into scales harder than metal. "Anything that's going through my scales is gonna shear through armor, even if it is Journeyman Tier."

"Oh I'm aware, Felix. You live a dangerous life," Elle said but pointed her finger at his chest. "But what if your Skills aren't working? Slap an elision collar on you, and you're gonna get run through, just as easy as any slob off the street."

Felix half-shrugged. "I mean, my Body is really strong, I think—"

"There's always someone stronger." Elle poked him in the chest, hard enough for it to hurt a little. "Always."

He didn't really have anything to say to that.

Evie sat among chains.

Her Mind was still and her Spirit as calm as the ankle-deep water she sat within. It was cold, but she ignored that. Chains shifted, twisting, slithering in the air above her.

A clinking had started—had always been there—and her Spirit quickened.

Is that—?

Rain dribbled onto her, and Evie swiftly reasserted her calm. It had gotten easier, clearing her Mind like this, but it taxed her in ways she didn't like. She'd wake up later with a killer headache. Still, she pressed on. She was close.

Shapes were formed above her, twisting, moving things of clanking sounds and shifting links. If she gazed upward, Evie would see a complex web of spiked and bladed chains, all of them meeting and separating in a chaotic jumble. She had been trying to make sense of it all for weeks now, ever since Harn had helped her truly visualize her core space. It was hard, but Evie had made considerable progress.

Her core pulsed, a tower-sized chain coated in ice and radiating a deep, unending cold. It continually froze the chains and water at her center, which only broke apart after it drifted far enough away. Something about the cold—the ice—filled her with strength and surety. Evie felt powerful underneath the pulsing chain, but her job wasn't just to bathe in her core. She had to *rearrange* it.

Evie pitted her Will against the cold, exerting influence over the cold and the chains both and could feel them shift and the ice crack. The converging knots of links slipped and loosened, moving a span at a time. Chains fell away, looping outward and clarifying the knot she worked upon.

I think this one is… Acrobatics. More ice broke, and some massive links fell away. Evie felt a surge of energy hit her, and golden-blue light pulsed from her center. She grinned. *Yeah, definitely Acrobatics.*

The water around her began to move. Icy cold touch lapped at her thighs and knees, rising higher. In the distance, beyond the clinking, she heard the pitter-patter of raindrops.

Blood and ashes. Calm! No smiling.

Her Aspects had grown and strengthened, her Mana clearer and more intrinsically tied to her chosen elements. Water and ice swirled within her core space, just as her chains formed the bulk of it, all of it a representation of her power. But the issue wasn't strength, it was control.

Evie needed control.

The roar of oncoming rains increased, no longer held back by the tentative force of her Will. The water rose with it, until it was a racing wave headed for the center. For her.

Calm!

The wave hit.

"AH!"

Evie exploded into motion, rising from her meditative crouch already swinging her limbs, and struck a wall. She rebounded and fell flat on her butt before she recognized her quarters around her. Her cot was against the wall—pushed there along with everything else to give her more training room—and a nice, woven rug was beneath her. The wall she had hit, however, wasn't a wall at all.

It was an arm.

"Taking more naps, Evie?" Harn grumbled. He was wearing normal clothes, civilian clothes, and his busted and scarred face stared down at her in faint amusement. "Did I interrupt your beauty sleep?"

"Get bent, old man," she muttered back, though not with any heat. "Feels like someone split my head like a log. Where's your armor, anyway? It's weird seeing your face."

Harn pulled his thick arm back and folded both across his chest. The jacket and trousers he wore barely contained the man's bulk, though he wasn't much taller than Evie herself. A handspan or so shorter than Felix, even. He usually wore his armor everywhere, which wasn't unusual for Guilders or general adventurers, but it made him stick out, regardless. It wasn't huge or crazy complicated, and other than the weird helmet, it wasn't all too different from regular old platemail. But she'd seen it expand and grow, shifting its shape to protect the man. It was weird.

Harn grunted—in amusement, she thought. "Get dressed; Cal summoned us."

"Oh? Summoned, huh? What has Her Lordship's knickers in a twist that it can't wait 'til morning?" Evie frowned out the window, feeling at her tender head. The sky was black and dotted with stars, which meant it was only half as black as her mood. "*Proper* morning. I was *this* close to a breakthrough."

"Quests."

That shut her up. Evie smoothly extended her legs and stood. She was at the door before Harn even turned around.

"What're you waitin' for? We've been summoned!"

CHAPTER FIVE

Felix left Elle with a promise to visit her before long, though she just about twisted his arm to extract it from him. She was as relentless as she was strong. He was just glad she liked him; Felix wouldn't want the city's premier armorsmith as an enemy.

Frankly speaking, Felix didn't want anyone to be his enemy. He'd had enough of those to last a lifetime.

He reached the steps of the new Haarwatch Manor, home to the new Lady of Haarwatch and its fledgling government. The steps were steep, leading up another terraced hill that must have been three hundred feet higher than the square he'd just left. At Felix's insistence, they had built the steps with several different gaits in mind: the larger steps for Humans, Elves, and Orcs, and two inlaid segments of shallower steps were for Gnomes and Goblins and others who had a shorter stride. Oveh had done the work perfectly.

He could have jumped his way up the steps, or flown on Pit, but along with a rejection of governance, Felix didn't want to draw attention to himself. Landing in the new local government building on the back of a Chimera was something of an eye-catcher. Instead, he walked up quickly, taking the steps two or three at a time with an easy grace. All that Agility and Dexterity really paid off. He reached the top in seconds.

A wide-open area had been excavated to house the base of the Manor, though to Felix's eye, it was more of a tower. The thing took up as much as a city block, after all. The stonework was rough so far, without Oveh's deft touch. Maybe Cal would let him play around with the outside of it? It was roughly circular, with tons of pillars and porticoes that framed a courtyard filled with wide expanses of dark soil. Greenery was to be planted there, he had been told. That architect they'd saved the other day was really proving his worth. The place looked...regal.

"C'mon, bud," Felix nodded at the entry. "Should be plenty big enough for us both."

Pit warbled.

The main entry was big enough to let Pit in, despite him being bigger than a horse now. Most of that was wing, which he could tuck up, but it was nice to see his friend not having to duck anywhere. Pit felt a little sad he wasn't small anymore, especially whenever they went to sleep. Little man loved to cuddle, and now he was too big for beds. Felix sighed and scratched his Companion behind the ears.

The interior of the entryway was tiled and spare, with two sweeping staircases leading to an exposed balcony and areas beyond. A few guards dotted the area, each of them dressed in half-plate armor with a sword and axe at their sides and their faces completely visible. Cal's office was located on the second floor, at least for now. The two of them walked swiftly across the floor. The tiles were covered with dirt and rock dust, despite the valiant efforts of a few Untempered servants. It felt like walking across a freshly mopped hallway right in front of the janitor. Felix pulled an apologetic face, but the servants didn't even look at him, and neither did the guards; their Spirits all shivered in fear.

Oh, right. He was the Fiend, and he had a giant Chimera with him. No wonder they were afraid. *Faster, Pit.*

They fairly flew up the stairs, bounding up five steps at a time. Felix was careful not to break the stone behind him, but his footwear was really taking a beating. He'd have to replace the simple leather boots in the morning. He nodded at the guards along the path, and they let them through without comment.

On the second floor, they passed several empty rooms, most

devoid of even furniture. The sound of a ruckus grew louder the farther along he went, however. At the far end of the hallway was a larger chamber, practically a ballroom, and this one was filled with people. Inside was a crowd of Half-Elves, Orcs, Dwarves, Goblins, Gnomes, and Humans. He thought he spied another Race or two mixed in there, like one of the birdlike Korvaa, but the press of folk was too tight. There had to have been three or four hundred people in there. Everyone was lined up before two large tables, and most of them were armed and armored.

Felix spotted the Regis and Holt—former Elders of the Protector's Guild before the Master Inquisitor destroyed their Charter—they were behind the tables and speaking in measured tones to each applicant. Because that's what this was, he realized. They were all applicants to Cal's new city guard.

"Next!" Holt announced, as the Human before him walked through another door on the far wall.

Interesting. Felix wondered why the two of them were allowed to stay on in positions of authority. As far as he knew, those with Guilder connections were given the greatest scrutiny. Too much bad blood. They moved on.

Cal's office was not much farther, secured behind a large double door that looked like it was made from a whole tree. Each door was easily fifteen feet tall and six feet wide, made of a dark-stained wood but otherwise curiously blank. Four newly appointed Haarguard were standing there, two to a side of the large double doors. One of them held up a gauntleted hand. It was shaking.

"Civilians are not allowed into the Lady's offices. Please take yourself and y-your Chimera—"

"Poul, no. That's the Fiend, man," one of the others whispered. Felix didn't recognize any of them, either from their camp or around the city. "And that's Pit."

The guard, Poul, looked between his friend and Felix in horror. "Oh, sir! I'm—I'm sorry to—I didn't mean—"

"Hey, don't worry about it," Felix said. "You're just doing your job. I'm just going to visit Cal—uh, Lady Boscal—real quick."

They all moved aside, but their eyes never left him or Pit. He could feel a mixture of shame, awe, and no little fear in their Spirits. Felix frowned. His Affinity was useful, but against folks who had zero defenses against it, he had to pull back on the reins a bit, or else he started swimming in their emotions. For now, he waded through it, and the two of them entered Cal's offices.

It was a large room, one of the few that had been actually furnished. Expensive-looking couches and tables dotted a seating area near an unlit fireplace, while pieces of framed artwork had been hung sporadically from the painted plaster walls. There was even a chandelier. The wall opposite the door was composed entirely of windows, and it looked out over the city. Specifically, in the direction of the Wall. A massive desk sat before it, currently overflowing with parchment and scrolls. A woman with short, tawny hair and dark eyes that looked tired sat at the desk, her hands gesturing as if manipulating the pages of an invisible book. His look lasted all of a second before she perked up, a wan smile on her lips.

"Oh, Felix! I had just sent a messenger for you," Cal said as she stood and stretched a kink out of her back. A stack of papers threatened to topple, but she stopped it with a quick touch. "Are you finished at the Wall?"

"For now," Felix groaned. He sat down heavily in an armchair. He regretted it when the thing creaked ominously. "Hector and his team are moving steadily through it, removing the Archon's influence and getting things up and running. He thinks the basic arrays will all be functional by the end of the night."

Cal looked relieved. "Good. We'll need it."

"Why? What's going on? Why did you send a messenger for me?" Felix asked. Cal's Spirit was more guarded than others. He wasn't sure if it was a Skill or just a very good control over her own emotions, but he couldn't really read anything deeper than surface exhaustion. Pit sat on his haunches beside him, piping inquisitively.

Cal smiled at the tenku's tilted bird head. "I'll explain in a moment. We're waiting on the others."

"Alright." Felix drummed his fingers on his lap, unsure what to do with the extra time. "How've you found the Authority? Is it a burden or freeing, being in charge of everyone?"

A snort ripped from the older adventurer, a mixture of amusement and exhausted disdain. "Being in charge is nothing new to me, just the scale's a bit bigger. The Authority though, *that* is incomprehensible. Truly, I've never dealt with an aspect of the System that was so obtuse. It speaks of songs and vibrations, but it gives no solid answers as to what should be done with them." She sighed. "As much as I… appreciate the responsibility and power, I'd much rather you'd have kept it, Felix."

"Oh no. The Authority tried to kill me. Or restrict me so much I might as well be dead, anyway," Felix said, waving his hands as if to ward away the very idea. The functions of Authority, or parts of it anyway, didn't much like Unbound.

"Hm. Well, it is useful, at least in some ways, and the Seat and Seal aren't too complicated to understand." She caught his confused expression and gestured at the floor, where a series of sigils began to glow ever so slightly. It described a simple spiral, composed of many, many sigils piled atop one another in an ever-tightening line.

It ended beneath Cal's desk, directly under her in fact, where some sort of complicated glyph was etched out. "The source of Authority for each Territory. This is just a relay, a control point in a more practical location, as the real Seat and Seal are deep underground. Inconveniently so. It's also a touch more complicated than the few I've seen in other Territories, which might explain the oddness." She shrugged, and the sigaldry faded until it was indistinguishable from the other floor markings, a clever disguise. "I'll leave any more answers for everyone's ears, eh?"

The wait was relatively short.

"—said 'keep up' not 'kick me off the stairs!'" There was a distant grunt. "That does *not* qualify as training."

Evie finished the last bit as she walked into the room, followed by a smiling Harn.

"Everything is trainin', long as you do it right," he said and laughed. The man wasn't wearing armor, but some sort of jacket and pants. Pit warbled in delight and bounded over to the two. "Oh, Pit's here."

"Felix! You here about the Quests, too?" Evie said excitedly.

"Quests?" Felix looked at Cal, who only smiled, waiting. *Hmm.* Felix drummed his fingers on the arm of his chair. *Quests, huh?*

Quests weren't easy to find, typically. Felix had gotten a hold of quite a few, but most were hidden by prerequisites and accomplishing specific tasks first. Your average adventurer wouldn't see three Quests in five years, according to what he'd learned. It was no wonder Evie was excited. Quests were a way to gain rewards of gold, Titles, or even new Skills. Apart from all of that, they also awarded Experience, which was always needed to advance in the Continent.

Felix eyed his own Quests, the new and the old.

Quests
Home Sweet Home! - 3 of 5 Threats Eliminated
Shrines of the Broken! - 1 of 7 Shrines Found
The Proving! - 0 of 5 Spells at Adept Tier
The Door of the Lidless Eye! - Unlock the Door

Quests. More trouble than they're worth, I think. Felix poked at his first —and oldest—Quest.

Home Sweet Home!
You have found a safe place in the wild Foglands, an ancient Temple long thought lost. You are charged with securing your ancestors' Temple from all threats. Be wary, young Nym, for your trials have just begun.
3 of 5 Threats Eliminated
Reward: Title, Home, Variable

Threats:
~~**Seven Legged Orit**~~
~~**The Risi**~~
The Archon
~~**The Unending Maw**~~
Unknown

An impossible task. One of the threats was a Blood Beast created by the Maw, another was an incursion of five hundred Frost Giants. Then the defeat of a Primordial older than any civilization on Earth. He'd managed all three of those things, though not without mishap. The Archon was a continuing threat, one that would be just as challenging as the Maw had been. Not only that, but there was another entirely unknown threat out there, too. Felix shook his head. Maybe he'd get it done one day, but he'd rather stay away if the threat curve kept moving as it had.

If only the Archon agreed.

The door opened again, letting in a towering mountain of muscle and armor. The man was nearly seven feet, half that wide, and was wearing armor similar to the Haarguard's, if...fancier and covered in rock dust. Behind him were two other men, both in identical armor, though much cleaner. Felix saw the guards outside the room saluting to them as the door closed.

"Bodie, Yan, Kelgan. Thanks for making it here so fast," Cal said. Her voice was as exhausted as ever, but Felix heard life returning to it slowly.

Yan, a bald man with a sharp goatee, elbowed Kelgan in the side. "See? Told ya the girl'd get here before us."

"Unfair. Harn hadn't even told her two minutes ago." The spearman rubbed at his ribs, but gave Yan a small handful of copper stones and silver swords—local currency. "We had to hoof it across the whole burnin' tower."

"Ain't a tower, numbskull," Yan corrected as he walked far enough into the room to claim a seat. "Haarwatch Manor. It's more stately."

"I see a big, round building, I call it a tower," Kelgan groused.

Smart dude, Felix thought with a smile.

"Wouldn't miss something so interesting." Bodie laughed. The big man gave Harn a handshake and nodded across the room at Felix. "Felix. How's the Wall?"

"I was telling Cal. Hector thinks it'll be ready by morning, for the basic protections, at least," Felix said, then gave him a lazy salute. "Captain."

Bodie rolled his eyes. "You call me that here, and I'll have to use your title, Blue-Eyed Fiend."

"Oh, still using that one? I prefer the Titan Slayer," said Evie. She'd found a couch and balanced on the back of it. "Has more punch, ya know?"

"Nightstorm."

"Stonebreaker."

"I heard someone calling him Thunderbird just this mornin',"

Yan said, before tapping his chin thoughtfully. "Though that mighta been for Pit."

The tenku preened under the attention, but Felix groaned. His Tempered skin flushed so hard it felt like a fever. "Okay, okay, I give up. You win."

Those merciless bastards laughed and laughed.

"Hey, did I miss the joke?"

Felix peeked over to see Atar and Alister walk into the room. They were dressed in battle robes made of some sort of silk and hardened plates of enchanted fabric. Very expensive-looking, and each one well-tailored; purple with orange accents for Atar and a deeper blue for Alister.

"You're late!" Evie said. She'd gotten food from… Felix looked around and didn't see any out. Did she carry it with her?

"Thought you two were at the Wall?" Felix asked instead.

"We were, hours ago. Some of us sleep, Felix," Atar said. "Wait, were all of you up?"

"Meditating."

"Rubble reclamation," Bodie said with a shrug. That explained the dust.

"Arms training with the fellas downstairs," Yan said, and Kelgan nodded.

Harn grunted.

"Absolute madmen, all of you," Atar said. "At least Alister had the good sense to..."

Alister winced in feigned chagrin. "I had some ideas on array designs for the new waterworks."

"We have to inscribe for seven hours tomorrow! You're going to make me do all the work?" Atar's perfect coif was already becoming undone at the prospect of labor.

"I'm sure he'll be up for the task, Atar," said a new voice. Zara had slipped into the room, apparently behind the two mages, and was busy pouring herself a glass of water from a pitcher on a side table. "But I believe Lady Boscal has some news for us."

"Oh, Zara. Have you seen Vess?" Cal asked.

"She was mopping up some monsters in the rubble. I passed the word, and she'll be along when she can," the Naiad said.

"Good enough, I suppose," Cal said and motioned at the door. A shine of sepia suffused the thing, revealing a glyph taller than

Felix. He picked up *silence* and *wall* from the thing before it faded. A muffling ward. "Now that you're all mostly here, there are a few things we all need to discuss." Cal stood and swiped her hands through the air. A blue box bordered in gold filigree chimed as it rotated into view.

New Territory Quest!
Enemy of the State!
You have a hostile neighbor that threatens your Authority. End the threat.
Rewards:
+10 Levels
+Increase in Authority
+Title
+1 Gold Chest

"Noctis' tits," Evie breathed. "These rewards."

"Ten whole levels? That'd be a boon and a half," Kelgan said. "Hard enough earning any once you cross level fifty."

"Levels are nice, but I'm more interested in that Gold Chest." Yan grinned and rubbed his hands together. "Lieutenant Yan needs a new sword."

"Funny, Portia was telling me the same thing," Kelgan laughed. Yan shouted and shoved the spearman, which only made him laugh more.

"Hm, 'hostile neighbor' sounds suspiciously like 'Archon,' to me," Harn grumbled over the two bickering. "How come it doesn't say?"

"Quests aren't known for being helpful," Cal said with a sour twist to her lips. "Haarwatch's got two neighbors: Setoria down the Verdant Pass and the Foglands. We already know the Archon wants us dead. The problem I got is that I don't know if Setoria does, too."

"Why would they?" Yan asked, distracted from the punch he was trying to throw at his friend. "We're all part of the Hierocracy, right?"

"Because a contingent of Inquisitors fled over a week ago," Zara said. A shocked hush fell over everyone, and Felix stood up.

"Fled to Setoria? To do what?" he asked.

"To report that the city has fallen to a Primordial," Zara said. Neither her face or Spirit betrayed anything as to what she was feeling. "They go to call on the Grandmaster Inquisitor."

There was a beat of silence before the entire room erupted in chaos.

CHAPTER SIX

"Grandmaster!"

"The head of the Inquisition is headed here? Now?"

Everyone shouted at once, all of them in different varieties of alarm and anger. Bodie, Yan, and Kelgan all reached for their weapons, the rhythm of fear wafting palpably from their Spirits, while Harn simply grimaced. Evie leaned back on the couch, patting her chest. She'd nearly choked on her sandwich.

"We're gonna have to fight *more* of them?" Evie asked with a cough. "You think they'll tell that I blew up a bunch?"

"You mean *I* blew them up," Atar said distractedly. He sat heavily in an armchair opposite Zara. "We're all dead."

Felix held out his hands. "Hold up. I need this explained. Who is the Grandmaster Inquisitor?"

"Leader of the Inviolate Order of Inquisition, the second most powerful branch of Hierocratic rule. And one of three Grandmasters in the entire Hierocracy," Cal supplied. She gripped the hafts of her long daggers. "What I need to know is why this wasn't reported to me earlier."

Zara frowned, just slightly. "I have eyes on them. Those who left were Acolytes led by a handful of Initiates—normally more than enough to handle any troubles along the Pass, but no longer.

They have been waylaid this past week, barely able to move beyond the Iron Gate."

Cal, and everyone else, relaxed slightly. Felix cleared his throat. "Iron Gate? I've never been through the Verdant Pass. How long is it to reach Setoria?"

"Bronze Gate is about a quarter of the way to Setoria. After that, you got the Iron Gate at the halfway point and the Tin Gate a bit after. Takes a month, easy," Evie said. She set aside her food and leaned forward. "That's merchant time, though. Redcloaks shoulda been movin' faster. What's the holdup?"

"Monsters," Zara said simply. "The wards that protect the Pass are maintained by Haarwatch and Setoria, each handling their end. Haarwatch hasn't bothered with its wards in weeks. Not since the Eyrie fell."

"Which means beasts from the Wilds are likely flooding the Pass," Cal said. "That's a spot of luck I hadn't expected."

"And it means we can stop them," Zara said.

"If they get to Setoria, what then?" Felix asked. "Is the Grandmaster there?"

"Blind gods, no. She'd have no reason to be," Cal said. "But there is a Waystone, and with that, it will only take a single sunrise to send word to Amarath."

"A Waystone?" Felix asked.

"Magical doohickey, sends coded messages to other Waystones. Big bastards, too," Evie provided. "Not gonna find one of them in every city though. Expensive to make, I hear. Pathless' folk just keep them in cities they care about." She gestured around her. "They didn't care much about Haarwatch before."

From what Felix had gathered, the Hierocracy worshiped the Pathless as a sort of state religion. Unlike the missing gods that the choristers worshiped, the Pathless was a deity that seemed to delight in ignoring its faithful. Their god's creed was something akin to benevolent disinterest, though the Orders had congealed around three particular tenets. Felix had heard most of it from others, but the gist was that they sought Order, Strength, and Purity. Not in any particular sequence, but that's what everyone harped on about.

They were taught that all have a place in society, violently discouraging social climbing, and that all places were secured with strength. Those who were strong rose to the top to provide for their lessers and be supported in turn. Order and Strength. The last one, Purity, was best exemplified by their zealous hate of anything regarding Sorcery, the magic of the Chant, and the Grand Harmony. He didn't really know why they hated it, except that it was outside of the hierarchy of the System. Maybe that was all the reason they needed.

To Felix, it was a system to keep things the way they were. The haves and the have-nots, same as on Earth. Except on the Continent, people could bend steel bars with their bare hands and—if they advanced enough—lived for centuries, so keeping the lower class weak was almost a death sentence, especially once monster attacks were factored in. The Pathless seemed like a dick.

All things considered, however, an absent god was his favorite kind these days. Last thing he wanted to do was get tangled with another one any time soon. Felix had reservations about anything so powerful. Gods, Primordials, or otherwise.

He had Vellus—the Goddess of the Storm, Blood, and Tides—to thank for the current strangeness to his core. *Cores, plural,* he corrected himself. *Though she had help.* The Unending Maw was just as involved.

"So, Grandmaster, is that a Tier or a title?" Felix asked.

"The leader of the Inquisition is always the Grandmaster, and below her are three Master Inquisitors. I believe you met one," Zara said, giving him a flat look. "However, their Tier does not have to be Master or Grandmaster to earn those positions. Unfortunately for us, in this case, she is both."

Felix felt his gut drop. There were basic Tiers of advancement on the Continent, as he understood it. Beginner was between Skill levels 1 and 25. Apprentice Tier was 26 to 50. Journeyman was 51 to 75. This was followed by Adept and Master Tiers, each with increments of twenty five separating them. Beyond that, Felix had a hazier grasp of things, but it kept going.

"A Grandmaster's existence is miles above even myself," Zara admitted. "In the Hierocracy, only the Hierophant is of a Tier higher than her three Grandmasters."

"You think she'd actually come out here?" Yan asked, his face serious. "I mean, the Primordial isn't even an issue anymore."

"They don't know that. But they do know that the Master

Inquisitor was killed here. That alone should be enough for her to take interest," Cal explained with a dark look. "How do we stop it? Can they be stopped, even waylaid by monsters?"

"There is the threat of the Grandmaster coming, but it is not yet assured," Zara said. She sipped her glass of water calmly. "And I have...methods to catch them. But it requires that I ask a boon, Lady Haarwatch."

Cal raised an eyebrow. "A boon."

"Indeed. I would have left already, had the city been in a state that it could be abandoned. Now I am ready, but I need a few strong arms and skilled fighters. Can you spare me some volunteers?" Zara looked to Cal as well as Bodie.

"Why would *you* need help for some low-level Inquisition?" Cal asked.

"The Verdant Pass has grown strange. I can hear it in the night's songs, and I… worry. If we do not catch them quickly, they will reach Setoria, and I will need allies to stop them all." Zara sighed, a musical lilt to her voice. "The ratcatcher cannot secure her prey without a proper net."

Cal inclined her head. "Fair. Bodie?"

"We've some to spare, but how many will you need? What's the plan?" the big man asked. "I'll not send my people into a fruitless battle against the redcloaks. Not again."

The ward on the door faded as a light knock sounded. Moments later, a woman wearing half-plate armor stepped into the room. She was covered in dirt, dust, and a little blood—she grimaced as everyone turned to look at her. The door shut behind her, and the wards reappeared.

"My apologies for my late arrival," Vess said, her grimace turning to a rueful smile. "There was work to be done."

"Didn't miss much. Just planning on how we can ambush some redcloaks before we're all killed," Evie said cheerfully.

"What?"

"The path we seek is not for those faint of heart," Zara continued, looking back to Cal. Felix saw Evie pull Vess aside and begin to whisper. "News spreads slow in the wake of our tragedies, but as I said, the Verdant Pass grows dangerous. What I will ask of them is neither safe nor wise, but it is the only way, if we are to head them off before they reach Setoria." She took another calm sip of water. "We will traverse the Dark Passages."

"Madness," Cal hissed. "You will lead men to die."

"They will be protected," Zara said, tapping one of a number of amulets strung around her neck. The woman wore a flowing gown intermixed with hardened plates of armor. Battle robes. "I have enough to furnish seven, aside from myself."

Man, I'm getting tired of not knowing all these terms, Felix thought. Lessons in Chanter magic had continued, but his knowledge of common subjects remained lackluster. *Waystones, Dark Passages?*

"Okay, so we need a team to go after the Inquisition," Felix said as he stood up. "But there's no way to know if the hostile neighbor is Setoria or the Archon. So, we also need people to head into the Foglands. Right?" Felix started pacing as he spoke.

"I've already begun sending teams into the treeline to secure lumber and herbs to renew our stock," Cal said. "The minor Quests I'm allowed to issue have given rise to many volunteers. But few have gone farther than a mile beyond the edge, and our scouts have not yet returned."

"So we don't know if the Archon is doing anything, then?" Kelgan said. "I'd think another beast horde would be easy to spot."

"Nothing's been seen, and the treeline has been quiet this whole week," Felix said. "The...Legion haven't had to fight a thing."

"I mean, would they notice?" Evie asked. "They're all green with a single battle under their belts."

"They're vigilant, I'll give 'em that," Harn said. "Standin' watch at the Wall all hours of the day."

Felix stopped pacing and turned to Cal. "Do we have enough people? To keep Haarwatch running, repair the Wall, and carry out two simultaneous missions?"

"I assume you'll be going into the Foglands, Felix?" she asked.

"I—" he touched where the sword usually hung at his waist. "I have to. Got a Quest of my own, after all." He'd already shared the particulars on his Quests with Cal and a few of the others. "I'd need a team of my own, though."

"Good," Evie said with a stretch. She slung an arm around Vess' shoulders, both of them smiling at Felix. "We're gettin' bored here, anyway."

Atar stood up. "If they're going, so am I. I'll not turn away a chance to grow stronger."

Alister sighed. "Fantastic. I suppose I'll come along."

"We'll work out the details in the morning," Cal interrupted. "But yes. We can make this work. The city has enough people working to replenish its stores. I'm told the mines are starting to produce ore again, and not just iron. My concern, however, lies with what must be done. The threat in the Territory Quest could refer to either the Inquisition or the Archon. Neither are forces a small group could fight against, not directly. All of you risk your lives on these missions."

"Haarwatch and the people inside it won't survive if the Inquisition or the Archon come for us again," Zara said. "It is either attack or run away entirely. Abandon the city and the Authority."

"You know that's not an option," Cal said.

"Then we attack. If we stop the messengers, we will buy enough time to further secure the city," Zara said. "Our course of action seems clear, yes?"

"Good. Then those of us who need it, sleep. The rest?" Cal looked at Felix. "Get to work."

Cal gave out her orders to everyone, and like that, the meeting was over.

"Felix?" Zara called. "A moment, if you will."

He met the gazes of Evie and Vess as they left Cal's office and gave them the handsign message for "see you in a bit." Felix turned back to Zara, who was still near the overloaded desk with Cal. Everyone else filed out.

The doors closed on their own, and the sound ward re-established itself.

"What can you tell me about this Waterfall Temple?" Cal asked as he approached them. "That's where you're going, right?"

"Yeah. It's located deep in the Foglands, past the city of Shelim and the Labyrinth. I'm not entirely sure how far, because I didn't travel back here in the normal way." Felix's mind flashed back to the Void. "It's not a path I'd recommend."

"The city of Shelim is about two weeks' travel by foot," Cal said. "We walked back from there after you'd cleared the fog. It's treacherous ground out there and filled with dangerous beasts. We ran into only a few, but you'll have to be careful. Who knows what's changed since the fog lifted."

Felix nodded. The Foglands had never been safe, though the Razorwing Skinks couldn't threaten him anymore. "The Temple is hidden behind a waterfall, and I've got the only key. I'm not concerned much about the Temple so much as what's inside it. The Quest only describes it as darkness, and I can't say that language fills me with excitement."

Cal barked a laugh. "No, I'd have to agree. It may even be the hostile neighbor my own Quest indicates."

"To get to the Temple, will you pass over the Archon's Domain?" Zara asked.

"Yeah. I think his is below the mountain range to the west of Shelim. I went through a cave system below it, which is why I ended up in the Domain originally," Felix said. "I'll keep my distance, unless he's managed to break his Domain already. Then the whole plan goes out the window."

"You think he knows about the Temple?" Cal asked.

"The Quest indicated he was close, and I know he was aware of a Nymean Temple because, ah," Felix flushed slightly. "I may have told him."

"What?" Zara said, and he could actually feel her Spirit shake. "How? Why?"

"Coercion, when we first met. But I don't think he knows exactly where it is." Felix recalled the Archon knowing *of* the Temple, but he had tried to get Felix to reveal the location. "Like I said, if the Archon is free, my whole plan will change. Based on what the Quest said, the last thing we want is the Archon reaching the Waterfall Temple first."

"Why not remain here? You hold the key to this Temple, so how will the creature reach it?" Zara asked, but Felix saw through the question. The Naiad always seemed to be baiting him, asking leading questions or… testing him. He still didn't know why.

"He doesn't strike me as the type to take no for an answer," Felix said. "Who's to say he couldn't force the lock? I've no clue how powerful he is, other than he threw me around like a rag doll when we met. I've grown stronger, but the only other thing I've seen break a Domain was the Ravager King, and I only defeated that because of its connection to the Maw."

"Then, the plan?" Cal asked.

"Get in, find the Temple again, stop whatever my Quest says is threatening us, get back out." Felix grinned through the sour roil of his belly. "Easy peasy."

CHAPTER SEVEN

After Cal's meeting, Felix and his crew—Vess, Evie, Atar, and Alister—all put their heads together to determine what they would need for the journey ahead. They quickly decided that they'd each put together a pack, enough for several weeks, as well as whatever weapons and armor they needed. Felix had less experience in this particular venue than the others, so he took their suggestions earnestly and made a mental list. Thrilled by a confusion cocktail of fear and enthusiasm for the Quest ahead, he had wanted to go out and secure his supplies immediately. But it was, like, four in the morning. While many were awake and bustling, that did not include everyone or even most.

So the six of them all went their separate ways for the night. Pit had warbled and left through the nearest floor-to-ceiling window (of which there were several), telling Felix that he was going to fly about town. Evie said she had to go "sit in a wet room" and left, whatever that meant, while Atar and Alister both went back to bed, the latter mumbling about the arrays he'd devised. Atar nodded, annoyed, all the way down the hallway.

"They are nice together," Vess said. Felix turned to see her watching Atar and Alister turn the corner. "Alister is good for him."

"True. I can't imagine anyone else putting up with Atar's...

Atar-ness," Felix agreed. His smile turned into a real chuckle when he saw Vess laugh. "I'm glad he moved on."

"Moved on? From whom?" she asked, brows tilted.

"From you?" Felix said, a note of surprise in his voice. "You never noticed?"

"Oh." Vess put a hand up to her mouth. "No, I never realized. How did you know?"

"He told me," Felix said. He laughed. "Actually, no, I guess he didn't. But he'd glare daggers at me whenever he saw us talking. Pretty easy to read between the lines there."

"Oh," she repeated.

Silence stretched in the spare Manor hallway. Felix was acutely aware of her Spirit singing out, but he dampened his sense as best he could. It felt like… it felt rude, with her. Felix could tell she was nervous, but then so was he.

"I suppose we ought to go to sleep," Vess said after a while.

"Probably," Felix said. "I haven't slept in… four days? I think."

"Four days? Felix, you need to take better care of yourself," Vess admonished. Felix shrugged—a little guiltily, he admitted.

"There's been so much to do. After the Arcids and monsters were eradicated, all the tasks have been..." Felix let himself trail off. "Compared to fighting off giant monsters and gods, fixing a wall and moving rubble feels good. Achievable, sorta. Over all that, we've got this golden jerk." He ran fingers along a beveled edge on the seamless stone wall. "So there's a timer. Everything always feels… I've been moving from crisis to crisis since I arrived here, with barely time to breathe. Sometimes, it feels like, if I slow down, I'll..."

"You'll what?" she asked.

At some point, Vess had moved closer. Or he had. But they were close. Inches close. Her dark brown eyes were ringed in gold. Felix forgot his words for a second, distracted by her… everything. She smiled at him gently, her cheek dimpling.

"Felix Nevarre. Primordial. Unbound. Hero. I know what it is like, having the expectations of others on your shoulders. The weight of it all." Vess poked him in the chest. "But you will kill yourself if you keep going like this, Unbound or not, you're not immortal."

"The Archon, the Grandmaster Inquisitor. It never stops, Vess."

Felix looked at her, only a few inches shorter than him. "I know I'm not immortal. I'm not perfect. I just… how many would die if I took a break? How long will I last against either of those threats as I am now?" Felix grunted in frustration and took a step back. "It's about survival."

Vess looked at him, head tilted and the collar of her gambeson undone. She was sweating slightly, and her soft brown hair had a sheen to it.

Felix closed his eyes and breathed. "But I will sleep. I need it. You're right about that."

He turned to leave, but a soft, musical sigh had him glancing back.

"All you are doing is surviving, Felix." Vess smiled again, that dimple deepening. "Try to live, once in a while."

She walked away and, despite himself, Felix watched the whole time.

In the face of his preparations and the… agitation Vess had introduced into his life, Felix did go to sleep for about three hours. It was all he could manage. He tried to go back to sleep for twenty minutes after his body had become suddenly, inevitably awake—to no avail.

Energy churned within him, Essence and Mana ebbing and flowing within his cores like a stormy sea. Flaring his Fire Within Skill, he visualized his core space all around himself.

It felt like dropping into a dark, endless ocean. It was pure, unrelieved black in all directions, much the same way the Void had appeared. Except his core space contained a vital potency to it, a latent energy that always felt poised to burst alive. With the barest thought, convoluted patterns etched in light manifested all around him, arranged in concentric circles that were sparse in the outer and inner edges but grew dense in the middle distance. At the center blazed twin lights of crimson-gold and blue-white.

It resembled nothing so much as a solar system. The patterns of light even rotated and revolved around the twin suns, moving at a sedate, celestial pace. Each pattern was a Skill, a representation of his abilities that had been carved into his core space by the

System. As they leveled higher, moving closer and closer to the next Tier, the Skills moved inexorably nearer to the bright center. The twin suns were two rings of liquid power, flaring and fluctuating as they spun against one another and generating a deeper darkness within their joined centers.

There had been little progression with either of his cores ever since they'd evolved into a [Thunderflame Core] and a [Cardinal Beast Core], the first touched by the Divine while the other was filled with Primordial power. Ribbons of light extended from each of his cores, wrapped tightly around the bright prominence of the nine Skills he'd Tempered into Journeyman. As those Skill revolved, the ribbons twisted, braiding beneath the stacked cores like a maypole made of light. He'd been told his core was in the Weaving Stage, which meant his Skills and cores were adding to one another, combining and folding together in a new, powerful way.

If I were normal, this would lead to the Weaving Stage of core development. Zara had given him a crash course on the advancement process. But not even the wise Naiad knew how his new named cores would affect things.

On top of that, the Weaving Stage often altered the combatant in unforeseen ways. The consequence of folding your Skills into one's Aspects. It was like Tempering, which formed a specialized Body, Mind, and Spirit (the Aspects) out of the Skills one used to Tier up. When Felix had reached Journeyman, he had formed all three from strong Skills and potent Essences.

Body: Calamitous Dawn (Journeyman)
Mind: Fatebreaker (Journeyman)
Spirit: Rising Sovereign (Journeyman)

The result had pushed his being further and further from the human he had once been. That didn't bother him as much as it once had, not even the fact that he was a Primordial now. Life was strange, and Felix's was stranger than most; nothing exemplified it so much as the tree-like object that grew from between his stacked cores. It shined with a colorless lightning, much as his [Thunderflame Core] sparked with a blue discharge, but it also exuded a heavy, oppressive weight. The tiny branches of it quivered—resembling nothing so much as veins devoid of a body—and were it not growing out of the dark, hungry abyss between his two cores, Felix imagined it would have collapsed his entire core space.

It was a piece of Divinity.

The smallest, tiniest shard of it, but a piece nonetheless. Zara had confirmed it, though she was flabbergasted and confused as to what it meant. As amusing as that would have been otherwise, Felix hadn't enjoyed it. The piece was stolen—eaten—from Vellus, the mad goddess who had tried to do what so many in power have wanted to accomplish: steal his will and enslave him. Felix found zero enjoyment from the idea that a piece of her had been lodged within himself.

Fire Within is level 66!

Felix sat up with a frustrated sigh. He wasn't going to sleep again.

Might as well train.

Pit hadn't gone to sleep. His flying had continued through the early morning. Felix could sense, roughly, where his friend was, and with a flex of their bond, he could see from the tenku's eyes. Pit was hurling Wingblades down on Ghostfire Simians that the search and rescue teams had unearthed. Vess had revealed more monsters in the sewers, she had said, and now groups were busy hunting them down. Pit's Wingblades made short work of the half-starved monsters, ending nearly all of them by himself. A cheer rose from the Iron and Tin Ranks below, and Pit *reveled* in the adoration.

Felix snorted and dimmed their connection. He felt a desire to join his Companion and help, but Pit had things under control. Other things required his time this morning, preparations and the like, but many wouldn't be up for hours. To keep himself busy and to satisfy his curiosity, he went to train.

Previously, Cal said they'd found a cache of old training tools in the ruins of the Eyrie. So many for the lower Tiers, but a few higher-Tier ones, too. In the past few days, they'd also found and reestablished a training area in the lower levels of Haarwatch

Manor, mostly just for the guard, but they'd been told they could use it as well. Felix had been too busy with the Wall and search and rescue before that.

He was curious as to how he stacked up against the Guild's standards. He knew he was strong and fast. Faster than Evie by a good margin. Reaching the Second Threshold and his two named cores proved to be a distinct advantage, providing him explosive power. Time and again, his stats had given the advantage in almost every encounter he'd found himself in. But through training and experience, his skill was growing, too. Finally. He hadn't sparred with Evie again, but he imagined he'd be able to suppress her with skill alone now.

Though, I heard she evolved a Skill in battle. Hmm, Felix rubbed his chin. *Might be fun to fight sometime soon.*

He took the steps three at a time into the basement levels. The air grew cooler against his skin, beads of moisture clinging to the walls. Within a minute, he found a tiled passage leading to a thick metal door guarded by two bored-looking Haarguard. Felix braced for the inevitable "oh, you're the Fiend!" but they let him through without a word, though their Spirits rippled in recognition. He smiled in relief as the thick door slammed shut behind him.

Ahead was another corridor, though this one was wider, at least thirty feet across, and lined along either side with thick glass. Four distinct chambers were beyond the glass, though two of them were dark. The other two had a number of arrays glowing on the glass and within the chambers proper, though only on the walls and ceiling. Felix's brief study of them revealed them to be simple enchantments for lights, sound transmission, and...something to control doors inside the chamber. A single attendant stood by either room, studying the goings-on in both. Her hands hovered over the arrays, and Felix's Manasight could pick out the vapor that lingered around them, held ready.

Controlling the rooms? Felix looked within. Inside the first there were three people in guard uniform fighting off two wooden mannequins that moved about with a jerky speed. The guards were equipped with shields, short swords, and a mace, and they utilized all of them to fend off the things. They fought well, for Tin Rank, and two of them were approaching Apprentice Tier. Still, the Wood Golems struck hard and fast, too fast for the guards. One was struck to the ground and the others raised their hands up in the handsign for "surrender."

Immediately, the attendant let her Mana flow out, engaging the arrays. The Wood Golems stopped moving immediately, falling to the ground as if their strings had been cut.

Ooh, interesting, Felix cooed. *The arrays control the Golems, too? That's very cool.*

Show over, he turned to the other occupied chamber. Within was a full squad, five people each equipped with the usual Haarguard complement of weapons and armor. They were moving in better coordination with one another, and all of them were over Apprentice Tier. Iron Ranks, pushing closer to Bronze, maybe. The guards looked well acquainted with their weapons, and Felix didn't doubt they were once Guilders. He could pick out some of the sword forms Rory had taught him, things Felix hadn't been able to put to good use yet. He'd gotten better with his weapons as well since evolving his martial Skills with one another. It cost him Mana to fully utilize that new expertise, but it was worth the increased capability.

The guards were fighting against four Clay Golems and a single Steel Golem. Felix knew the former was a magnitude greater in speed and strength than the Wood Golems, but seeing them in action was impressive. They all had wooden spears that were nearly as tall as the six-and-a-half-foot-tall Golems, and they looked like they knew how to use them.

They still move weird. Jerky like the wooden ones. A result of the delay between their Spirits and Minds? Felix mused. Hector had talked to him a bit about Golem construction, but it had mostly been over his head. He understood that people created a complex sequence of arrays that mimicked a Spirit and Mind in order to have the Golems react to specific stimuli. Like magic AI, except extremely limited.

Felix had asked about them because of the nature of the Arcids; from the Memories Felix had extracted, he knew the Archon had built the Arcids from scrap and the remains of other creatures. Most recently the Frost Giants. Hector had gotten an opportunity to study their Bodies too, but said he had no clue how they were actually made. "This is entirely beyond me. I can't even understand the edge of this complexity." The Archon was smart as well as strong and tough.

Just my luck.

The guards struggled against the Clay Golems, but two of them caught the constructs' weapons in walls of ice, while the others shattered them with their maces. The blunt weapons—built to exacting Apprentice Tier standards by the Coldfire smiths—were more than enough to destroy the relatively fragile baked clay.

"How easy is it to fix those?" he asked the attendant. She looked at him in surprise, clearly not noticing him until now.

"Blind gods, you startled me," she said, yet the Mana at her hands never wavered. *Impressive control.*

"Sorry about that. Didn't mean to." Felix pointed the Clay Golems, now piles of scrap at the guard's feet. "You can fix those?"

"Oh um, yes. Wood and Clay are easy. Steel is harder, though," she said.

The guards now faced the single Steel Golem, which had seemed to wait while they had fought off its lesser brethren. The construct carried a longsword and large shield, and it knew how to use it. It was taller than the others, easily seven feet, and it moved with a fluidity the Clay lacked. Strike after strike was turned by the construct, the five guards no more effective than children. In less than ten seconds, every single one of them was laid out, and the surrender sign went up again.

"Fast," Felix noted. The attendant only nodded. Within the chamber, the lights flashed once and a door on the far side opened. More attendants rushed in, swiftly collecting the pieces of the Clay Golems and wheeling the untouched but unresponsive bulk of the Steel Golem away. The guards collected themselves and limped back the other way, toward Felix.

"Shoulda covered us better, Vyne," the lead guard complained as they walked through a gate into the corridor. He was Human, with a thin mustache and a serious black eye already forming. "Damn thing shouldn't have touched us!"

"I Taunted it, Kylar and it came for me. It was too strong," a Human male with a large shield said. Vyne, Felix's Voracious Eye agreed. "We're not ready for Steel, yet."

"Twin's teeth, man! We're Iron Rank! Steel should be easy,"

another guard, Nevia, said. She was a Dwarf and dressed in the mage variant of the Haarguard armor.

"But it isn't," said the fourth member, an Elf named Kikri. "And your ice magic was basically useless, Nevia."

"Can it, Elf. I didn't volunteer for the guard for sass from a twig."

"Hah!" laughed the last of them, an Orc.

Felix suppressed a smile at their conversation. Annoyed as they were, they seemed to like one another, if their Spirits were to be believed. Plus, they were twenty feet away and talking quietly. It was a societal nicety in a world with people who could hear a pin drop down the block to at least pretend they couldn't, most of the time.

Instead, Felix turned to the attendant and gestured to the first chamber. The Tin Ranks had come and gone without much fanfare, and he was very curious about these Golems.

"Can you send me the toughest Golems you have?" Felix asked the woman. She stared at him a moment, frowned, and looked harder. Felix could feel her Skill trying to peer at his details, but his Veiling Amulet wouldn't let her. "Don't worry. I can handle it."

"Very well," she said and gestured. The gate to the first chamber opened, and Felix entered.

"Who's that?" Vyne asked. He'd set his shield onto the ground and was rubbing his shoulder with a salve.

"Who?" asked Nevia. She followed Vyne's gaze and saw a lone man enter one of the chambers. "Dunno. We just got back into town, right? Think we'd know everyone by now?"

Kikri squinted at the man. "New recruit, maybe. Not wearing the uniform yet. Why?"

"He just requested the toughest Golems they had," Vyne said in disbelief.

"What?" Kylar laughed. "Does that idiot have any idea what he's doing?"

"New recruit? Probably trying to look good for the attendant." Davum smirked. His tusks jutted at the woman in question.

Kylar put his hands on his waist. "No way this fool will get through anything, not by himself without armor or even a weapon," Kylar said loud enough that Vyne was sure the attendant could hear. The man had a thing for the mage, he'd been clear on that in the past. "Not when *my* team couldn't get past the Steel." The man looked at Kikri and whispered. "Think she heard me?"

"Idiot," Kikri muttered. "Let's watch the moron fail and get out of here."

CHAPTER EIGHT

The chamber door shut behind him in relative silence, and Felix was faced with a large square area. Approximately two hundred foot square, by his estimation, it seemed designed for larger battles than just squad versus squad. The floor and walls were tiled with whitestone—imported, he surmised, though Voracious Eye didn't say—which was apparently highly resistant to physical and magical damage.

Interesting. Must be expensive, or else they'd make more things out of it.

It was all pretty impressive. Felix suspected that they had been excavated from the rubble as opposed to built from scratch. The sigaldry lacing the walls and floors spoke to that as well. Inscriptionists could push out sigaldry fast, but to do something like this while everything else was being done? He found that unlikely.

Felix was considering going back out and asking the attendant about it when a door opened on the far side of the chamber. The door slid up, revealing an unrelieved darkness, and out stomped six Steel Golems.

Voracious Eye!

Name: Steel Golem
Type: Construct
Level: 55

HP: 6600/6600
SP: 5400/5400
Lore: Golems are constructs built in the image of the mortal Races and designed with complex sigaldry to mimic them further. Most Golems have a measure of autonomy, as dictated by their sigaldry, but are almost always under the ultimate control of a mage.
Strength: They do not feel pain or fear and are highly resilient.
Weakness: Limited cognition.

Felix's Voracious Eye had grown stronger, and his own analytic prowess had advanced in lock step. It had taken him a bit to realize it, but the details of an enemy's Strength or Weaknesses had more to do with his own ability to read a target rather than any magic.

The Golems walked forward, moving far more fluidly than their Wood or Clay counterparts. They looked basically like mannequins—as he'd noticed before—oval, featureless heads and slender bodies that operated on ball joints. The Steel, however, had some extra heft to their frame in the form of rivets and raised ridges. It gave them the illusion of having armor in addition to the steel shields and longswords they held in either hand.

Felix quirked an eyebrow. *Are they the strongest she has?* He doubted it. *Guess I'll find out. Let's start slow, though.* There was a reason he'd left his weapons in his rooms. *No Skills. Just stats.*

The Golems closed in.

"Look at him, he's frozen with fear," Kylar said with a laugh. "Move it, newbie!"

"Six Steel Golems," Kikri said, her voice a mixture of fear and amusement. "It'll be over before he can move."

Vyne looked at the attendant. She was roughly his age, though Tempering made that hard to tell. Her face was serious, and the sigaldry of the controls glowed beneath her fingers.

Was she trying to kill the guy?

"Oh, Night," Davum said with a laugh. "Did anyone tell him the surrender sign?"

Nevia cackled, leaning against her staff. "Absolute nitwit!"

They *definitely* moved quicker than the Clay Golems.

Felix ducked beneath one blade and deflected the next with the flat of his hand. The longsword clanged and smashed into the whitestone floor, sending up sparks. Another thrust forward, this time going lower in what Felix recognized as the Second Form of Crane Style.

The Golems know Sword Forms? Felix thought as he twisted around the strike. It wasn't fast enough to hit him, but the surprise of seeing even a basic sword kata meant it had cut the front of his tunic. *That's* amazing.

Felix kicked backward, putting distance between himself and the Golems. The lithe steel constructs followed on stuttering limbs. They were faster, but their movements weren't anything like a normal human combatant. They came at him fast, but he exploded forward.

The ground shattered behind him.

Pushing his Agility, Felix tore through the intervening space, flexing his Dexterity and Strength as he jumped up and through the wide swing of the lead Golem. Still mid-air, he kicked outward, connecting with its featureless steel head and using it as leverage to spin. Felix's entire body rotated while his arms and legs lashed outward in a storm of strikes. Flesh met metal, again and again, until he slid through the gap he'd made and landed cleanly on his feet.

Behind him, the bodies of five Steel Golems burst apart. They collapsed, no more than silvery scrap.

Hm. I didn't have to push myself at all with them. Felix frowned. He'd have to tell the attendant to give him better constructs.

A mighty clang filled the air as Felix caught the descending blade in his bare left hand, his fingers tight around its sharpened edge despite the last remaining Golem's attempts to pull it free.

"You're very loud," Felix said. "Stealth isn't really an option for you."

The Golem suddenly let go of his sword and brought his shield around to bash him, but Felix had already moved. He spun, letting his entire Body gather behind a massive backhand. The impact was like thunder, and the Steel Golem flew backward. Right into the reinforced glass, sending cracks spider-webbing across its surface.

"I thought I said 'tough'?" Felix said aloud, looking to the attendant. The woman simply stared at him, as did the guards who had stuck around. The Steel Golem slipped to the ground, its shield and torso completely sundered. He frowned.

Can she hear me?

"Blind gods..." Nevia hissed. She touched the cracks that had formed on the thick, enchanted glass.

"Did you—did you see what he did?" Vyne asked.

"No, I missed it. I blinked and they were all on the ground!" Davum grunted in surprise. "Was it a Skill?"

"I didn't see any Skills," Kikri said. "That was just him. Blighted Night, how?"

Vyne looked to Kylar, but the man had gone absolutely pale, and his fists were wrapped tightly around the handles of his twin swords. "Ky, did you spot it? He had to use a Skill, right?"

Kylar didn't answer; instead he looked over to the attendant and licked his lips. "Who—who is that?"

The mage glanced at their group and Kylar in particular. "Someone I should have listened to," she muttered. She flicked a sigil, and Kylar heard a hum of energy. "I am sending the strongest in now, sir."

"Sir? Who—Wait, the strongest? Truly?" Kylar stared at the attendant in shock. "He—I don't care who he is, he won't survive!"

"You tell him that," she shot back and activated the array.

"I am sending the strongest in now, sir."

Felix smiled and nodded at the attendant. She'd heard him, after all.

The Steel Golems hadn't ever been a real challenge. Though

they had known some Sword Forms, the constructs hadn't been fast enough or strong enough to take advantage; Felix had destroyed them before any of their moves could matter. While it felt pretty cool to tear through an enemy, all Felix could think about was the bill he'd owe Cal by the time he was done.

And the attendant said fixing the Steel ones was trickier than Clay. Felix groaned and looked at the gleaming metal parts scattered around him. *Maybe I can fix a few? Might give me a chance to see their insides in a more… constructive way.*

Felix was poking at a glimmering piece of sigaldry when the far door opened again. This time the darkness disgorged seven more constructs, each a head taller than the seven-foot Steel Golems. Those in the lead were made of a translucent material filled with a haze of bubbling vapor. They were broader across the chest and arms, with thicker legs and wider feet. They stomped into the whitestone room, multi-hued Mana vapor boiling within their frames, swords and shields in all of their hands.

Voracious Eye!

Name: Glass Golem
Type: Construct
Level: 72
HP: 7100/7100
SP: 5400/5400
Lore: Golems are constructs built in the image of the mortal Races and designed with complex sigaldry to mimic them further. Most Golems have a measure of autonomy, as dictated by their sigaldry, but are almost always under the ultimate control of a mage. Glass Golems are made of glass imbued and tempered with Mana vapor.
Strength: Need more information
Weakness: Need more information

Glass Golems? Magic glass, clearly. Felix watched them file into the room, neither rushing nor dawdling. They prowled and spread out, as if they considered him dangerous. His Affinity pinged off of their Aspects, a strange music returning to his senses. *Advanced*

Minds and complex Spirits. Their Bodies feel strong, even from here. This—ooh, what is this?

As the group spread, a Golem in the rear stood out. It was made of a similar transparent material, except with large plates of red-gold metal formed to its body, almost like armor plating.

Voracious Eye!

Name: Orichalcum Golem
Type: Construct
Level: 76
HP: 7904/7904
SP: 5900/5900
Lore: Golems are constructs built in the image of the mortal Races and designed with complex sigaldry to mimic them further. Most Golems have a measure of autonomy, as dictated by their sigaldry, but are almost always under the ultimate control of a mage. Reinforced with orichalcum, this style of Golem is a powerful combatant.
Strength: More information needed
Weakness: More information needed

"Now this is more like it," Felix said with a grin.

The enemy engaged.

The leading Glass Golem reached him in seconds, and Felix slipped aside of its vertical chop. He pushed off the ground, cracking it and sending his knee hurtling into the Golem's midsection. He felt it crack, but the construct's only reaction was to smash Felix with its shield. Felix dropped low, the tall Golem missing him by over a foot, and launched a right jab into its knee. The joint bent, shattering like the glass it was and letting loose a boiling steam of Mana. He would have done more, but his Perception twinged, and Felix threw himself into a forward roll, narrowly evading another glass sword.

He rolled to his feet and immediately parried the blows of three more glass blades. The Golems had lagged behind on purpose, choosing to surround him instead. Felix dodged what he could, but several of the glass longswords cut through his tunic and trousers, and one left a thin gash on his right thigh.

"Tch," he hissed. They were strong enough to break through his Armored Skin. "I guess I have to take you all seriously."

Unfettered Volition!

Felix moved like a whirlwind, slipping between their thrusts and slashes in unerring precision. He reached out and grappled with one of the Golems, grabbing their left arm at the bicep. Flaring his Strength, he tore it clear off. Glass tinkled and purple-blue vapor billowed out. He spun, still holding the arm and the shield attached, using it to block three oncoming strikes before hurling it into the face of the fourth Golem. It stumbled back, unbalanced and cracked from the impact.

It never recovered.

Felix leaped atop it and decided to attempt the Chant again. Within his core space, a symbol gleamed with blue-gold light, and Mana streamed from his core into his channels. Sounded by his Affinity, Felix's Intent shaped the Mana into the pattern he desired. Virulent green vapor burst from his hands, mingling with his fists as they lifted into the air, propelled by the techniques Zara had taught him. It all took less than a fraction of a second before Felix brought both of his fists down on its chest.

The Glass Golem exploded beneath him.

Corrosive Strike is level 49!
Corrosive Strike is level 50!
Journeyman Tier!
Congratulations! You Have Reached Journeyman Tier with Corrosive Strike!
You Gain:
+10 STR
+10 PER
+10 END

Corrosive Strike is level 51!

Yes!

He had finally, properly activated a Skill without using the

System. Felix had fought off and on, trying to utilize his Intent and Affinity to achieve that result. He'd only managed weak versions before, unable to access the entirety of his Skills' power. This time, instead of fizzling out, the Skill felt stronger than ever before.

Distracted by his victory, he was caught off guard by a Glass Golem as it tackled him.

"He's going to die!" Vyne said. He'd watched the man fight through the press of the Glass Golems, but it was hopeless. He was fast and strong, but their blades moved too fast. Vyne already saw crimson staining the whitestone. He didn't want to watch a man perish because he didn't know his limits. "Stop the Golems!"

"He called it on himself, Vyne," Nevia said. She was scowling at the pile of Glass Golems. They couldn't even make out his figure anymore, so tightly did they press him. "Not her fault if he dies."

"This is a training facility, not an execution chamber," Vyne grumbled before marching himself to the attendant. The woman was sweating, busily tweaking shining parts of the array before her. Each touch sent shimmering trails of magic into a part of the array. "You have to do something. Stop this."

"I can't," she said. Her eyes flicked between the glass and the array. "He asked and—and don't you know who he *is?*"

Kylar looked up at that. "Who?"

Beyond, the chamber filled with a sudden, brilliant, blue-white fire.

Okay, he thought. *Okay, not quite as easy as I thought. Skills time.*

Influence of the Wisp is level 45!
Influence of the Wisp is level 46!
Influence of the Wisp is level 47!

The Golem had brought him to the ground, only to be joined by every single other one in a massive dogpile. He'd had to Enthrall them to get out, kicking all the way. The blue-white flames flickered and faded after only a few seconds, but it was enough time to get to his feet.

The Golems followed, a little scuffed, but mostly unharmed.

"Fire doesn't do much to magic glass, huh?" Felix asked them. Maybe if he could get it hotter? But then, the Glass Golems were far more resilient than their Steel brothers. Each time he hit them, they regrouped and came back for more, moving faster and faster. He saw none of that jerky, puppet-style movement. Even the one without an arm and the other with a busted leg moved fluidly. They all dropped low, shifting into what he recognized as Boar Stance.

Felix copied them, setting his body low to the ground and spreading his arms wide. Rory had taught him this, though he hadn't tried it out in a fight. It was a Stance that preferred quick, full-frontal assaults and charges, prioritizing finesse for direct lethality. They came at him, an onrushing tide.

Affinity. Intent.

Focus on Adamant Discord...

One of the largest patterns within his core space lit up with power, and Mana poured into his channels. Far more than before. He shaped it, sounded it, Willing it to do as he intended. Sparks crackled across his limbs, brilliant, blue-white bolts hotter than any flame. Cords of invisible steel tightened across his chest, and Felix let loose.

The light sparked weakly ahead of him, barely gouging the whitestone floor and leaving the charging Golems untouched.

Great, he grumbled. *Back to failure.*

Unfettered Volition!

Felix leaped straight up, unassisted by his Skills, soaring thirty feet over his enemies.

Shadow Whip!

A single tendril of shadow Mana manifested in his grip before splitting in two with a flex of his Will. The two pieces whipped down, latching onto a single Glass Golem and redirecting Felix's considerable bulk back down into the fray. With the speed of a falling boulder, Felix crashed into the back of the Golem.

Corrosive Strike!

The Golem broke beneath him, his weight and blow too much for its enchanted glass. Felix only had moments as the Golems recognized his presence and twisted around. He threw out his hands, and purple-white Mana flooded outward until it enveloped all of them.

Mantle of the Long Night!

The ground flash-froze as frost crawled up the Golems' bodies, slowing their movements by the tiniest fraction. Felix ducked and dodged, sweeping their legs out with kicks and well-placed punches. Glass shattered, and Mana vapor swirled. There were no screams, no roars of pain, just his own heavy breathing and the relentless onrush of Glass.

It was *fantastic.*

"Haha!" Felix laughed, bursting another Golem's smooth-translucent skull. "Hahaha! Keep 'em coming!"

———

"Is he… laughing?" Kikri asked in disbelief.

"What is he?" Davum asked. His face was all but pressed to the glass. "All those Golems..."

Kylar was pale as he repeated his question. "Who? Who is that?"

———

Mantle of the Long Night is level 44!

...

Mantle of the Long Night is level 47!

Shadow Whip is level 41!
Shadow Whip is level 42!
Shadow Whip is level 43!

Five down. Two to go.

Felix cut off his Mantle, letting the arctic winds die down. They were helpful to slow the Golems, but after a while, all they did was create a fog that made it annoying to fight in. He could hear their Spirits—after a fashion—and his Perception could pick them out alongside his Blind Fighting Skill. But, after a while, it all became interference that took more and more concentration to separate.

The fading fog revealed the last Glass Golem already swinging at him. Felix caught the blade with a hastily shaped column of whitestone. The rock was tough, but the glass blade still cut halfway through it. In the moment it was disarmed, Felix juked around its shield and kicked a hole into its pelvis. Hips shattered, it listed to the side and threw its arms down to balance itself. Felix's uppercut took its head clean off.

Okay. That just leaves.... The fog swirled and cleared. The Orichalcum Golem stepped out, perhaps a hundred feet away, still bearing its sword and shield. Felix squared himself against the construct, considering his options. It had been faster than the Glass Golems, moving out of his reach every single time he had retaliated. It was likely stronger. But was it stronger than him?

Let's find out.

The Orichalcum Golem charged, shield up and sword held to the side. It was fast, and its long legs ate up the ground between them.

Adamant Discord!

The ties that bound him and all things to the world vibrated. Invisible cords of unbreakable metal stretched between them, Primordial and Construct, and Felix gripped them tight. And *pulled.*

Lightning burst, an orb of electricity that flowed along their connection as the Golem's entire body was lifted off the earth. It merely reoriented itself, raising its red-gold sword and shield.

He pulled harder.

Wild Threnody!

Mana surged, filtering through the pattern of Adamant Discord before pumping through his looping channels. The power spooled out onto his fists. Electricity and undulating waves of distorted force swirled atop his knuckles. Felix screamed wordlessly, and the Golem screeched, a sound like distressed metal.

They hit.

"Down!"

Lightning and thunder boomed outward, cracking the floor and walls and ceiling. Dust kicked up in an expanding ring, and the thick, enchanted glass blew out completely. Vyne braced against the stone lip at the bottom of the observation window, his shield held above him and Kikri. Still, the crackle of power nearly threw it from his grasp.

"Are you all right?" he asked the Elf.

"Y-yeah," she said, before wincing. A shard of glass had cut a line across her cheek. "What in Siva's name was that?"

"That... that isn't something that should happen, right?" Davum said from beside them. He'd already stood up and was staring into the training chamber. Vyne helped Kikri stand and looked himself.

"Twin's teeth," Vyne whispered.

The entire room—a room constructed of *whitestone*—had been split in half. A massive crevasse had formed across its expanse, and pieces of pulverized whitestone were everywhere.

And in the center, amid a field of scrapped constructs, stood a single man with eyes that burned like blue flames. Completely unharmed.

"No. That's impossible," Kylar said. "That's—"

"That," the attendant interrupted, stepping forward with awe and fear on her face. "That is the Blue-Eyed Fiend."

Felix looked around him and sighed.

"Cal's *really* gonna be mad about this."

CHAPTER NINE

Felix returned to his rooms with mixed feelings. The training session had gone well—he'd earned a number of Skill levels and had even successfully utilized his Intent and Affinity to activate a Skill without the System. But the destruction at the end had put a damper on things. Plus, he'd ruined his clothes again.

He stripped his sliced tunic off and discarded his pants and boots. All had been broken in some way, though his boots had taken the worst of it—the soles had burst entirely, presumably from his kicks at the Golems. He hadn't anticipated ruining his outfit so quickly, but he was still prepared for it. Life on the Continent was not clothes-friendly, he'd found. His Health was at full, but still Felix checked himself over for cuts or bruises. Getting tougher skin and a more powerful constitution was great until you realized it meant that minor things went unnoticed for longer. Last thing he wanted was to change his shirt and stain it with a bunch of blood.

Felix gazed into a full-length mirror he'd had installed in his bedchamber. It was one of the few things in it, aside from a very big bed he rarely used and a six-foot-long steamer trunk. He looked at himself, inspecting his unblemished skin and lithe figure. Less lithe than previously perhaps, since he'd gained a fair bit of bulky muscle with his advancements, but far different than what he'd entered the Continent with—the changes wrought by skyrocketing stats were a magic all their own.

Add in the effects of Tempering his Body, and he barely recognized himself. His hair was black and shaggy, his eyes were blue, and his face was still his own, but that was all that was the same. He'd been de-aged as his Vitality increased, and Tempering into Apprentice and Journeyman Tiers had suffused him with vigor. Felix hadn't been ancient—not even thirty—but he looked barely past twenty now. From what he'd gathered, it was likely he'd look the same for decades if not more. Zara, for instance, was Master Tier, and she looked positively ageless.

What will I look like in fifty years? A hundred? Vess told him her father, only Adept Tier, was nearing his three hundredth birthday. At Journeyman, he was looking at over a hundred, easily. Yet the question loomed. *Will I even survive that long?*

The Archon awaited, and the threat of the Inquisition was not to be ignored, either. Brooding, Felix quickly got dressed.

He had gone training to clear his mind and test himself—to see if his Skills were improving at all. Felix was certain they had, but was it enough? Zara had begun teaching him how to use his Harmonic Stats—Intent and Affinity specifically—to activate his Skills, claiming it was stronger than relying on the System's shortcuts. It was hard, however, and he'd had a small handful of successes over the course of a month. It wasn't a tool he could lean on yet, not reliably, at least. Many of his Skills lagged behind in Apprentice Tier, and he needed to work on those more, and that meant the quick activation through the System's process. The gains to his stats and overall strength was another step toward evening the playing field with his enemies. He checked his Status.

Name: Felix Nevarre
Level: 49
Race: Primordial of the Unseen Tide (Lesser)*
Omen: Magician
Born Trait: Keen Mind

Health: 3450/3450
Stamina: 3374/3374

Mana: 3142/3142

STR: 968
PER: 842
VIT: 700
END: 594
INT: 664
WIL: 1212
AGL: 622
DEX: 775

BODY
***Resistances*: The Song of Absolution (L), Level 70**

***Combat Skills:* Dodge (C), Level 53; Heavy Armor Mastery (C), Level 1; Blind Fighting (R), Level 45; Corrosive Strike (R), Level 51; Wild Threnody (E), Level 56**

***Physical Enhancements*: Armored Skin (R), Level 72; Unfettered Volition (E), Level 55**

MIND
***Mental Enhancements*: Deception (C), Level 22; Meditation (U), Level 54; Negotiation (U), Level 15; Bastion of Will (E), Level 69; Deep Mind (E), Level 57; Manifestation of the Coronach (E), Level 45; Ravenous Tithe (E), Level 70**

***Information Skills*: Alchemy (C), Level 27; Tracking (C), Level 19; Exploration (U), Level 44; Herbalism (U), Level 29; Voracious Eye (E), Level 51**

SPIRIT
***Spiritual Enhancements*: Dual Casting (U), Level 50; Mana Manipulation (U), Level 51; Manasight (U), Level 50; Manaship Pilot (R), Level 22; Etheric Concordance**

(L), Level 64; Sovereign of Flesh (T), Level 60; Unite the Lost (T), Level 8

***Spells*: Abyssal Skein (R), Level 36; Cloudstep (R), Level 33; Fire Within (R) Level 65; Influence of the Wisp (R), Level 47; Invocation (R), Level 42; Mantle of the Long Night (R), Level 47; Oathbinding (R), Level 34; Shadow Whip (R), Level 43; Stone Shaping (R), Level 55; Wrack And Ruin (E), Level 45; Arrow of Perdition (L), Level 39; Theurgist of the Rise (L), Level 65; Adamant Discord (T), Level 58**

Unused Stat Points: 34

Harmonic Stats
RES: 220
INE: 280
AFI: 344
REI: 208
EVA: 180
MIG: 143
ALA: 355
FEL: 282

Felix's stats, as usual, were off the charts compared to his level and Tier. According to Zara, Cal, and Harn, on Strength and Endurance alone, he could go toe-to-toe with many Adept-Tier warriors… while also slinging spells against Adept-Tier mages. Unlike either group, he was well-rounded and had more options in a fight. Each of his Primary Stats—meaning everything but his Harmonic Stats—had risen above 100 and then 500, pushing him beyond the First and Second Thresholds. Each Threshold was a sort of convergence of power, where his Primary Stats reinforced one another to a greater degree than before. For example, it meant his 928 in Strength was effectively higher than the number indicated, but the System didn't tell him how much.

Ultimately, it meant he was powerful. None of his friends

doubted that, and Felix had come to recognize it himself. Still, his power was a candle flame against the bonfire of a Master Tier existence, let alone a Grandmaster.

Felix chewed his lip, flicking through his Skills. He had twenty-one Skills below Journeyman Tier, and while some of them might not be particularly useful in a fight—Negotiation and Manaship Pilot for instance—he didn't like to see any of his Skills lag behind. Not only because of the skill-grinding gamer he had once been, but because each Tier offered boosts to his stats that pushed him further along his path. The Third Threshold, which he assumed was at the one thousand marker, loomed close.

That said...Felix concentrated, mentally allocating his thirty-four unused stat points. There.

STR: 928
PER: 814
VIT: 700
END: 624
INT: 664
WIL: 1212
AGL: 664
DEX: 775

Split into Endurance and Agility to get everything above six hundred. Thankfully, he had a number of modifying Titles that made each point count for more than normal, so thirty-four had stretched to seventy-two. Felix leaned back against the footboard of his king-sized bed. The wood creaked ominously, and he had to ease off the majority of his bulk. *Being faster and sturdier will help with some of my dumber battle decisions.*

Felix knew he wasn't a genius at fighting, though he wouldn't say he was an idiot, either. His stats and increasing Skill levels frequently carried him, typically ending fights before tactics and form were an issue. It was something he was working on: it had been proven to him several times now that proper training almost always beat out stats, unless those stats were monstrously higher.

More than that, he thought with a glance at his Skills list again. *Having the proper Skill to respond to a threat was key.*

Felix had a lot of Skills, enough that he sometimes forgot to use them all. He needed to rectify that, instead of simply leaning on his stronger Skills for everything. Sovereign of Flesh and Unfettered Volition were powerful, but he had to incorporate it all into his fighting style. Down below, he'd used Shadow Whip and Corrosive Strike to devastating effect. Combining Adamant Discord with Wild Threnody was a new, on-the-fly decision, and it had caused a surprising amount of destruction. It was definitely a Skill combination he would try again.

The damage to the training area, however, was regrettable and a little embarrassing. It had been excavated and restored to working condition only days ago, and now they'd have to close a portion of it. He had offered to fix what he could, and even said he'd help fix the Golems—as best he could—but the attendant had all but shoved him out the door. Her Spirit had vacillated between alarm and awe, as had the other Haarguards who had lingered to watch him. That, more than anything else, had made Felix uncomfortable, and he left quickly.

Felix shook his head. He was running in circles again. There were preparations to be done and—

Someone knocked on the door. Felix extended his Perception and Affinity, feeling for details. What he sensed made him raise his eyebrows before he paced for the entrance. He threw open the doors and peered at Elders Regis and Holt, the latter having just lifted his hand to knock again.

"Good," Felix said. "I was gonna come look for you later. Come in." He gestured into his chambers, and the two mages shared a look. "I have some questions that need answers."

Vess hadn't been able to sleep after she and Felix had spoken. She was left feeling restless and energized by her own outlandish behavior.

Smiling at him like that? What was I thinking? She alternated between pacing atop her fine, plush rug and sitting uneasily on her four poster bed. Something about the man always put her off-balance, and the heiress still didn't know how to feel about it all. So, she had spent the majority of the morning planning.

Such a task was not something nobles of her rank would stoop to, but Vess had been without servants or aides for the better part of a year. Ever since she joined the Protector's Guild, she had striven to prove to everyone—herself included—that she could manage without the trappings of her upbringing. Arranging supplies for their entire crew as well as simple transport for the forests and ravines that dotted the Foglands was an act of rebellious autonomy she relished.

Vess poured herself into the details. She didn't expect they would be on foot the entire time, though she tried to account for that as well. There were an uncounted number of unknown dangers in the unveiled Foglands, and it was best to attempt to cover all of the possibilities one could prepare against.

However, as the morning wore on and the sun rose higher in the cornflower blue sky, Vess realized she was also putting something off with her marathon of laborious organization. Namely, a conversation with the only man capable of knocking all her carefully laid plans awry.

As Vess stepped into the cool granite expanse of the third floor, she frowned for several reasons. The Healer's Ward always smelled of astringent solutions and a fetid undertone she refused to contemplate, but now there was something else among the scents. It was flowery and too sweet, like fruit on the edge of rot. She kept her distaste from her features, however.

Diplomacy is level 63!

There were a number of robed apprentices in the reception hall of the Ward, all of them busy pushing medical carts and taking rapid notes on reams of parchment. Vess passed them by without a word, and though she sensed confusion and even a few motes of anger in their Spirits, no one stopped her. She didn't wear her rank on her person like most nobles, but the weathered armor of a former Guilder spoke volumes.

The Ward was far larger than the ramshackle hut they'd operated out of in camp, though Portia still ran the place. She had more help now, clearly; Vess spotted at least ten other apprentice healers as she traversed the hallways. That extra help and the medical supplies they had requisitioned from the Sunrise merchants had been an almighty boon for so very many people in Haarwatch. It made Vess feel good about teaching Cal how to leverage her Authority while still keeping good relations with the greedy traders.

Vess had spent some time helping Cal settle into her new role, as her lifelong position as Duchess-in-waiting gave her a certain insight to the management of a large Territory. She had years of lectures from her father and his aides to pass on, countless hours that had been drilled into her head until she could recite them all from memory. There was much to convey, though not everything was applicable to how Cal would run her new Territory, or feasible with their current lack of… pretty much everything.

Yet Vess had chafed at the hours wasted on conversation. Every moment she wasn't helping clear the rubble and search for survivors was one that weighed upon her conscience. She had not spoken idly to Felix on the burden of power; it was a yoke she had labored under for many years. Only recently had she grown strong enough to bear it in new, different ways. Now that she could enact change with her own two hands, Vess felt it a waste to sit in throne rooms and leave the dirty work to others.

This visit felt much the same. She would rather be finalizing her packing or hunting down the last of the monsters in the sewers, but instead she was forced here. To see *him*.

Except he wasn't in his bed. The sheets were mussed and the series of tonics on his bedside table were half-drank.

The healers did not come for him, else he would have been forced to finish his tonics. No signs of a struggle, though the sheets were tossed back rather thoroughly. Vess narrowed her eyes, and they filled with a tingling warmth.

Gaze of the Unseen Hunter is level 58!

She spotted a lingering smudge on the ground where unshod feet had pressed against the cool stone. The faint heat haze strengthened as it progressed, turning to true footprints once outside the room. They were simple to follow, and even simpler to guess why he had left his bed. He was headed toward the inner courtyard.

The inner courtyard was a very small garden—a mere hundred

strides across and twice that in length—and one populated more by dirt than greenery. The area had only been sparsely planted, its priority lagging behind the care of the city's citizenry. When Vess arrived, she could spot the lingering heat traces of her quarry, though his Spirit was a careful blank to her Affinity. She clucked her tongue and pushed forward over the shrubbery covered hills.

In the center of the garden, in an area that had been tamped flat, a large man practiced his sword Forms beneath the morning sun. Vess frowned as she saw him, covered in bandages that were stained with a mixture of sweat, dirt, and some sort of oily solution. Darius Reed, Chosen Hand of the Duke of Pax'Vrell and her anointed protector moved well for a man so recently on the verge of death. His breathing seemed easy, and his eyes clear, if distracted by the whirling dance of his wide, double-edged blade.

"You are supposed to be resting," Vess said suddenly. The Hand halted mid-swing and smoothly pivoted to sheathe the blade at his back. Vess frowned, annoyed that he didn't even look guilty.

"Lady Dayne," he said, his baritone voice smooth despite the flash of… was that anger in his eyes? "I am merely reacquainting myself with my capabilities. I shall need my fortitude replenished if we are to make good time."

"Make good time? Where, perchance, do you think we are going?" Vess asked. *If he heard about Felix's Quest, I will strangle those chatty lieutenants.*

The Hand, however, tilted his head as if the answer were clear as day. "We are returning home. Your Lord Father has demanded your presence."

That stopped her cold. "What do you mean, he demanded—? Are you in contact with my father?"

"No, but it was a contingency within his original orders," Darius explained. "I was to protect and aid you while you recovered from your time in the Foglands, and once you Tiered up into Journeyman, you were to be brought home to rejoin his court." He said it all with a stoic, expressionless face. "Since you hit Journeyman during the… recent troubles, we only had to wait upon my convalescence."

Vess shook her head, her mouth suddenly dry. "That is impossible. There is so much work to be done here. My father—"

"—Does not care about this Territory. His only concern, and

thus, *my* only concern is your well-being." The Hand shook his head and took a single step closer. "This city has proven itself more trouble than it is worth. After their defeat, the Inquisition will undoubtedly dispatch its forces to purge the Territory. I cannot withstand what the Inviolate Order will send." He put his large, calloused hand out, palm up. "We must leave. Today."

CHAPTER TEN

"I was surprised you asked to speak with us," Elder Regis said as she walked into Felix's sitting room. She was slight, an inch or so over five feet tall, and rounded with age despite her unlined face. Her eyes roved around the room before locking back onto Felix. "I'm sure you don't like the Guild very much."

"Hah! Why should he?" Beside her, the older Elder Holt laughed. He was taller than Felix by six or seven inches, with his long, auburn hair held up in a ponytail. His long beard was streaked with five precise lines of gray. The laugh wasn't jovial, though he tried to force it. "What exactly has the Guild done to endear him to them?"

Felix motioned for them to sit in the armchairs that were the sole decoration in the room. His chambers were a collection of three rooms: sitting room, bedchamber, and a private bath. He'd asked the two former Elders to speak with him because of who they once were; as Elders of the Protector's Guild, they must have had access to reams of information.

"'Them,' huh?" Felix asked. "That makes it sound like you've both officially cut ties with the Protector's Guild."

"Because we have," Holt stated. His mustache made for a powerful frown. "I'll no longer truck with a guild that puts power ahead of its people. What we did, that business with the Domain? All of it stank to the heavens. Had I known—"

"But you didn't, and neither did I, not until it was too late," Regis said with a sad upturn of her brows. She reached out and put her small hand on the older man's before looking at Felix. Her eyes were steel. "We are not perfect. We have chased power as anyone else, but it was always to raise up our people. The Protector's Guild is called such for a reason," she said before sighing. "Once upon a time."

"And now we atone with Lady Calesca's new government," Holt rumbled. He pulled his hand free from Regis' and straightened his dark robes. Much like Atar, they both wore reinforced and enchanted cloth in preparation for battle. "Which brings us back to the reason why you requested a meeting. What does the vaunted Fiend want from two lowly ex-Elders?"

Felix smirked at the feel of their Spirit: a mix of dark humor, resignation, and actual curiosity. Neither attempted to hide what they were feeling, and Felix wasn't sure they could anymore. Both of them had been damaged by the touch of Primordial Spawn, though they had suffered far less than the choristers of Yyero or Siva. The former Elders simply had their foundations damaged, reducing their advancement to High Adept, perhaps permanently.

"I wished to pick your brains on three subjects. I'll start with the most pressing." Felix folded his arms before himself. "What do you know of Primordials?"

He felt a flare of panic from both of their Spirits before they mastered their emotions. Holt spoke first. "Why would you wish to learn more of them? Haven't we seen enough of their kind to last a lifetime?"

"Indulge me," Felix said.

"Zara, ex-Archivist that she is, would be far better suited for such—"

"Zara is busy with something else right now, Regis. I'd appreciate it if you could tell me what you know while I wait on her," Felix said with a smile.

Deception is level 23!

"Oh. Of course." Regis cleared her throat. "According to

legends, Primordials were birthed at the dawn of the First Age. They have been around for longer than recorded history. *Any* recorded history: Elven, Dwarven, or otherwise. As you saw with the dragon-like beast that attacked the Eyrie, they are gargantuan forces of nature, and they seem to serve no purpose but to end life wherever they find it."

"End it or infect it," Holt added. "We had doubted the last, but the Revenants and their ilk demonstrated the truth of it. A Primordial spreads like a disease, and everyone affected is dead, even if they don't know it yet." He looked at Felix, and this time it was appraising. "But not here. All infections have vanished as if they never were, and even the Revenant corpses we've encountered are all listed as 'Manawarped Humans' and the like."

"Lucky for us," Felix said. He ignored Holt's gaze. "So, there are other Primordials? Harn told me of one in the sea somewhere to the east of here."

"Yes, that is another strange detail about a Primordial's appearance in our midst. They are believed to be a sea-dwelling Type, as only the vastness of the oceans could hope to contain their bulk. The few that have come ashore live on in horrifying legends, and their mere presence has ended kingdoms in mere days. The attack Harn spoke of was the last known sighting of a Primordial, to my knowledge, and it was half a world away." Regis paused and steadied her breath. Anger blossomed within her Spirit. "Those men and women we sent to claim the Foglands must have encountered something out there, a hidden Primordial that spread its infection into our city. Had he shared his findings with me, perhaps this could have all been avoided."

"The Guild was headed down a dark path long before Teine lost control of his experiment," Holt said gruffly. "Our action was required years ago, but we were blinded by the good we could accomplish." The old man—large and physically fit—seemed to wither and diminish before Felix's eyes. "I count my blessings that we are even still alive when all the rest have fallen."

Regis went quiet at that, and Felix let them have a moment. He didn't care for the head of the local Guild branch. His Mind flipped through what he'd been told and what he'd learned.

"What are their powers? Are they all the same?" Felix asked.

"Again, you ask us about legends as if hoping for facts," Regis said with a sigh. "If a listing of Primordial powers is extant, I have never seen it. I would hazard a guess to say none living have experienced the might of a Primordial and lived to tell the tale."

"Until now," Holt added. "The Primordial you fought in the sky had breath of fire and the capability of flight, despite its preposterous proportions. You would know more of its capabilities than we do."

"Hm," Felix grunted. Likely, each Primordial had different abilities, and the Ravager King had been a corrupted amalgamation of the Maw and whatever the Domain-Core had been. It was not a good example of their power. The Maw, on the other hand—Felix blinked as a thought occurred to him. "If the Primordials are so dangerous, if they infect everyone around them, why didn't the Inquisition do something?"

"A solid question, and one I've been worrying at," Regis admitted. "The standing order in most nations is to kill all living things that have encountered a Primordial. Mortal, animal, plants. Everything. That the Inquisition did not is evidence of their incompetent leadership."

Holt snorted. "Not surprising, considering DuFont was calling the shots. She was always a greedy little cuss. So hungry for power that she must have ignored all the warning signs. If the true leadership of the Inviolate Order arrives, they will not do as DuFont. They will raze the city in fire and ice and not stop until all of us are gone."

Felix felt a pang in his chest as he thought of the zealots currently racing to Setoria. It was clear the threat was enough that the Grandmaster would come herself. "They'd do that?"

"Without hesitation," Holt said. He laughed again, yet this had more humor than bitterness. "The only thing more universally feared than a Primordial is a Demon of the Void."

"Demon—?"

"Don't they tell those tales anymore? It was all we could talk about when I was a boy," Holt looked at Felix in surprise. "I suppose the names change. Dark Terrors, Demons of the Void, Unbound. If one of them appeared, the entire Continent would go to war."

Deception is level 24!

Does he know? Felix kept his face studiously blank and his Spirit as calm as possible. *How could he?* The former Elder's Spirit did nothing to give him away, though. Felix's biggest secret was safe… for now.

"The Fiend didn't call us here to talk about nonsense, Holt," Regis said with a slight edge to her voice. "The Primordials, much to my regret, are not a children's myth. But that is also all I know on the matter. What were the other subjects?"

Felix began to pace again, organizing his thoughts. "What do you know of Omen Keys?"

Both of them suddenly sat up like they'd been shocked. Their Spirits buzzed with a curious combination of excitement and trepidation. Felix wasn't surprised. The item—which he had received as a reward for completing an insanely difficult Hidden Quest—was related to his Omen, a sort of class designation that granted leveling bonuses to your stats and was supposedly tied to your destiny.

Felix had Revealed his Omen shortly after his arrival on the Continent—The Magician—and it had served him well by giving a boost to his Willpower, Intelligence, and Perception with every level earned. The Key itself was a mystery, however, though its item description hinted at its powerful nature.

Name: Omen Key
Type: Path (Enhancement)
Lore: Omens are our destinies unveiled, hints at futures yet to come and strength yet to unlock. Not all attain their destiny, but all meet their Chosen Fate. This is the Key to your Path. Walk boldly or not at all.

"I see you recognize the term," Felix said slowly.

"How could we not?" Regis said with a soft voice. "We ran a Guild branch, after all. Our primary concern has always been advancement and training. An Omen Key… why do you seek such knowledge?"

"That's my business, I think," Felix said before repeating himself. "What do you know?"

Holt gestured to Regis, who was clearly going to press Felix. "The boy has saved our lives at least twice. I'll not begrudge him some information, Olivia. An Omen Key is the first step beyond your Reveal, one that opens your Path."

"My Path," Felix repeated. "What does that mean?"

"Your Path is unique to you, and it must be walked to unveil the true power within your Omen," Regis added.

"Amazingly, that's still not really an answer," Felix said with mounting frustration. "Omens aren't unique, right? There are only twenty-two of them, so why so much mystery built around them?"

"Thus the importance of one's Path. It elevates one's Omen beyond the standard twenty-two, pushing one to greater heights of power," she said.

"Okay, so more power. More stats? Skills?" Felix asked.

Holt leaned forward. "One's Path is a personal thing, not shared among anyone, even your loved ones. Who you are shapes, directs, and guides it, and the destiny you find is the one only you may grasp."

Felix sighed. "That's pretty vague."

"Much of the System *is* vague, Felix," Holt said, but his smile and Spirit conveyed a sense of sympathy. "It does not hold our hands as we pursue power, nor does it warn or defend us from the consequences of our own actions."

Felix took a breath through his nose and nodded. That sounded like the System he knew. No free meals. "Okay, so an Omen Key enhances your Omen. If, hypothetically, one had received such an item, what should be done with it?"

"It should be used as quickly as possible, but only if you are ready for the challenge it presents," Regis said. He could hear her heartbeat speed up as her Spirit danced with anticipation. "If you fail, there is no second chance."

"Challenge? What sort of challenge?"

"We said it opens the Path, yes? That is not a metaphorical statement. It is a Key, and Keys open Doors. It is their purpose, their own destiny. You open your Path, and you walk it," Hold said. "The challenge within is wholly dependent on you."

"So like fighting my shadow self or something?" Felix muttered to himself.

"What?"

"Not important," he waved off the question, though he realized they had heard him perfectly. He would have to cross-reference some of this with Zara later, to see if they were misleading him, but he suspected not. "I appreciate the information."

"We appreciate being appreciated," Regis said with a half-smile. "There was something else, yes?"

"Ah, yes. Below the city there were Nymean ruins, and you said a curious thing: the city of Haarwatch was built by the Nym. This is true?"

"To all our earliest records, yes," Regis said. "The foundations of Haarwatch are built upon an ancient Nymean city, and the deepest parts of the sewer system touch upon their ruins. As you saw."

"That's surprising. I thought they were a Lost Race," Felix said. "Doesn't information on Lost Races vanish?"

"You are correct. When the Ruin takes something, all written records of them will be erased as well. Like the Unbound, I suspect the Ruin is just a name history invented to account for peoples lost to time and disease and monstrous violence." Regis shook her head, a light frown on her face. "However, there are a number of Nymean ruins, mostly in the north of the Continent. They're all, without exception, packed with dangerous magic and traps to kill the weak or unwary. Most have been picked clean, so seeing that chamber below the city was a real treat. I was quite distressed when we learned the Belais Crystal and the statuary were destroyed."

"You and me both," Felix grunted. It had exploded on top of him, after all. "I saw the traps below the city, but I was curious whether these ruins contained more than that. Special magic, maybe? Doors marked with stars?"

"I am familiar with the general rule of Nymean ruins: count the stars. All the ruins have them, and the more points a star has, the more dangerous the traps," Regis said. "But that is the extent of my knowledge."

"I've seen such doors," Holt added. "I was just a boy, though, and that time has long passed. What I remember is deep within a ruin near Levantier, there was a door. It was through a gauntlet of traps, enough to kill dozens of men. We were young and foolish, and we pressed on, despite our casualties. The promise of riches was too much."

Holt leaned onto his knees, his fingers steepled as he regarded the bare stone floor. "We reached the door, one marked with a ten-pointed star. We knew what that meant, of how dangerous it was within. I knew we shouldn't open it, but we'd just survived traps that so many didn't. We were drunk on the immortality of youth. We opened it."

Holt took a long, surprisingly shaky breath. Felix heard his Spirit quiver.

"Something got out, something that...it killed three of us before we even started running. It was *fast*, so fast we couldn't see it. I only survived because our team leader threw me from the ruin into the sunlight that it couldn't abide." The man clenched his jaw and twitched his beard. "This is all I know of the Nym. Maybe you'll get treasures from their ruins, but that's incidental. The Nym weren't hoarding gold beyond their doors, Fiend. They were hoarding *monsters*."

In the distance, a series of bells began to ring. One, then two, then more as the ringing grew closer. All three of them jolted to their feet.

"Attack," Regis said with a gasp.

"On the Wall," Felix snarled.

CHAPTER ELEVEN

Felix raced out of his chambers, and though Regis and Holt both started running, he soon left them behind. They might have been Adept Tier, but he had more Agility than both of them put together. The bells were ringing louder, but Felix needed to get outside. So he headed to the roof.

The hallway outside his rooms took a hard right turn, and Felix kicked off the stone wall and redirected himself. Stone broke behind him, but he flared his Skill.

Stone Shaping!

The cracks he made flowed back together, healing behind him.

Not sure how much I trust those two, Felix thought. The former Elders seemed earnest in their desire to fix what their leadership had ruined, namely the city itself. But was earnest desire enough? Felix wasn't certain, which was why he had almost immediately regretted mentioning his Omen Key. *The looks on their faces when I brought it up… it was like I'd mentioned a steak dinner to a starving man.*

Felix burst through a side door and onto the stair landing. Steps led up and down. He surged up them, taking steps four at a time.

He hadn't gone to Zara with his Omen Key yet. That part was true. The Naiad had been acting increasingly distant, involved with Cal and other things she wouldn't explain. Felix wasn't the center of her world, and didn't expect to be, but the training she had promised was slow in coming. Their group of three had only a single proper lesson in the last week, the rest having been independent study of a sort.

Something was going on with her.

So, he wanted to get another's opinion on his questions. Primordials, Nym, the Omen Key. The first two were important to figure out before he made it to the Waterfall Temple. Who he was, who he had become, was increasingly pertinent to the Quests that kept getting shoved in his lap. The Omen Key, meanwhile, seemed like a perfect power-up. Unlock the power of his Omen? More bonus stats per level? Other… stuff? But it sounded dangerous, as well as time-consuming.

Feh, before I leave, I'll pick her brain. See if what she says matches those two.

He kicked open the door on the last landing and found himself amid a number of offices. The stairs stopped short of the roof by two floors, apparently. People had started poking their heads out of their doors, folks in robes and tunics of a nicer sort than Felix usually saw. The Manor's own bells had started ringing as well, sounding awfully similar to a fire drill from back home.

"An attack?"

"The Fiend!"

"What's happening?"

He didn't answer their shouted questions, instead focusing on racing past their doors. But the warren of corridors didn't lead to another set of stairs that he could find. Frustrated, Felix chose the next best thing. The end of the hallway had a huge window, facing southward and letting in a large amount of morning light.

"Out of the way!" he shouted.

People dove from his path as he rocketed down the hallway, straight for the massive window.

Sovereign of Flesh!

Scales erupted along his body, coating him in dark black armor marked by glowing cyan markings along his arms, shoulders, and chest. The last to form, a tight, featureless helm slipped over his face and skull, though his vision was unobstructed.

Unfettered Volition!

Faster than a car, Felix shot down the corridor, the sharp talons on his fingers meeting the glass first. He slashed his arms to either side, slicing through the window an instant before his entire body barreled through it and into the empty air.

KRASH!

Adamant Discord!

Blue-white lightning kindled around his body as the steel lines of connection hurled him straight into the sky. His heart soared as he did, the exhilarating thrill of defying gravity better than even a good fight. Once he was high enough, he flipped his body and braced for pain.

Adamant Discord!

With a strained lurch, he was redirected westward, toward the Wall.

Mervin Cors rang the bell again before relinquishing it to a Tin Rank member of the Blades. "Remember! Ring three times, pause, then ring two times! That's the signal—"

"I know! Go! They need everyone!" the boy shouted back. Mervin frowned at the new recruit's lip, but couldn't deny the kid was right. They wouldn't have brought on a *child* if they'd had anywhere near enough forces to man the Wall. He jogged down the steps, quickly exiting the Wall's interior and unsheathing his longsword. His shield was already on his right arm.

We can do this, he thought as the bell sounded again.

The Rent was wide and deep, a massive tear through the heart of the Wall filled with scraps of twisted red metal and masonry. It was barely filled by the Fiend's Legion, even bolstered by a few dozen Haarguard. They numbered close to a hundred, all told, each of them battle-tested and *most* of them with a single Temper under their belts. They were ready as they could be for what was coming.

We can do this, he repeated to himself. *Right?*

The scouts had reported monsters only a mile beyond the tree-line, and as Mervin pushed through the poorly ordered ranks, he spotted the trees shaking in the distance. He sidled up to his team, themselves set a bit aside from the others.

"About time," Garin groused. He leaned against his spear and stared at Mervin as he approached. "Your Blade buddies keep you?"

Mervin grunted in annoyance. He had passed the Legion's tests and was allowed to join the ranks of the Blades, considering his tentative skill with his side sword. The others hadn't, and Gerin at least was still a little sour about it. "Something like that."

"Well, don't let us distract you—"

"Shut up, Garin," Piotr said. His voice was thin, but the command was unmistakable. He had withered a bit after their failed excursion to the Nest. Something had stolen his Vitality, leaving him weakened but otherwise capable. He gritted his teeth and held his own spear in a white-knuckled grip. "We're here to fight, not bicker."

"Yeah. The Legion is just one way. Don't got no archers either, but I'm not bellyachin'," Lars added with a grin. He hefted his longbow and nodded into the distance. "Looks like the Unarmed Mastery guy is doin' a speech."

"Don't you mean the *First of Fist*?" Garin snickered. "Dumb name."

Mervin turned and saw Oskar Akales step ahead of everyone. He was the leader of one of the factions of the Legion and probably most outspoken among them all. Like everyone else, he was wearing piecemeal armor, but his hands gleamed with steel gauntlets of quality make.

"The monsters come! Remember your duty to the city and to our benefactor! We have rung the warning bells, and the Lady has heard it. We have but to hold the line." Oskar pointed at a literal line that had been carved into the rock and debris. It was uneven, stopping and restarting in several places. "No monsters enter the city. Not on our watch."

A strong cheer from half the crowd rang out, as men and women of all Races lifted their various weapons into the air. The Haarguard, each armed with sword and shield, like Mervin, merely shifted their feet. All eyes were on the treeline. Mervin swallowed his fear and mastered his jitters. He was a member of the Blades now, those Legionnaires who had devoted themselves to mastering one of the weapons used by the powerful Blue-Eyed Fiend. Mervin hadn't joined out of devotion or whatever it was these folks had for Felix, but because they were continuing to protect the Wall. All of them still wished to serve, to do their duty. The Guild was no more, at least in Haarwatch, but this place was their home.

Oskar raised his voice once the cheering stopped. "As the Fiend before us, we seek power to protect those without it! By Fist and Blade and Bone, we are the line in the sand!"

The last was echoed by every Legionnaire in the crowd. It was everything Mervin had wanted when he left his father's farm. Honor. Glory. To grow stronger and use that strength to protect what he loved.

And right now, that meant fighting monsters.

He was ready. Mervin had lived through too much to be afraid of another monster horde.

Without warning, the treeline exploded with motion and noise. Branches snapped and emerald leaves burst outward as creatures the size of small hounds tore through the air. Mervin's Perception, his highest stat, could pick out their vibrant yellow plumage and cruelly hooked beaks. Their wingspan was about as wide as his own outspread arms, and they were *fast*.

"Birds?" Lars shouted in disbelief.

"Wynhawks!" Piotr rasped, loud as he could. "Analyze confirms it! Average level is 24! Tier 0 beasts!" Tiers were roughly similar to the Guild's Ranks. Tier 0 was the equivalent of a Tin Rank or someone who hadn't Tempered themselves yet. The word spread like wildfire around them.

"Keep your guard up; we can take them!" Oskar shouted. "Focus fire!"

Sparkbolts, Ice Arrows, and Shadow Jaws shot outward, slamming and bursting and snapping into the dog-sized flying creatures. Most shots didn't kill them, but the barrage steadily dropped their Health. Beside him, Lars fired arrow after arrow, each imbued with a piece of his sound Mana so that the missiles screamed as they flew. The Wynhawks fell, only thirty strides before they would have swarmed their line.

"Is-is that it?" Garin asked, his spear at the ready. He sounded disappointed. "I didn't even get to try out my new Skill levels."

Sentinel's Regard is level 42!
PER +2!

Mervin's rare Perception Skill—Sentinel's Regard—flared with a low tune that quickly turned fluting and rapid. He spun toward the trees. "There are more," he hissed before shouting. "More! More are coming!"

This time the trees literally ripped apart, their trunks shattered as a fleet of charging avians swept through. They were all twice as big as an avum—fully half again as tall as Mervin himself—and were covered in coarse brown feathers and had thick, muscular necks surmounted by sword-like bills. Razorstorks. Dozens of them. Their feet pounded at the earth, too heavy to fly, but were followed by hundreds—*thousands*—of smaller bird-type monsters. They flew ahead of the charging horde like a living cloud, screeching in clear challenge.

"They're all Tier I!" Piotr gasped. His hands shook on his spear. Tier I was the equivalent or Iron Rank—*their* Rank. "All of them!"

Too many! Mervin quailed, and his sword dipped in his grasp. *We can't stop this—!*

SKREEEAAAW!

From above, a veritable forest of purple-white spears dropped from the clear blue sky. Avian monstrosities were run through, split apart, and otherwise horribly maimed as a dark shape swooped down from above.

"Thunderbird!"

Chimera! Mervin goggled. "That's Felix's Companion!"

The beast flew above them, spinning in a tight roll as distorted waves shot outward from its body. The avians flew after the Chimera in a shifting flock of wild colors and enraged screams. Those waves, however, cut through them like they were nothing more than Tier 0 beasts.

Yet the Razorstorks continued their charge.

"Rally! Rally!"

A haze of Mana and Stamina wafted down the line, and Mervin saw a regeneration boost Status Condition appear in his vision. Fenwick, the First of Blade, lifted his greatsword and pointed at the enemy.

"Charge!"

A charge? That's idiotic! Mervin thought with panic. *They'll die!*

Yet the Legion didn't even question the order. They swarmed, gauntlets, swords, hammers, and maces gleaming in the morning sun. The largest of the avians—brown-colored Razorstorks—dropped their heads and put on a burst of murderous speed. Mervin hung back, his own crew taking potshots at the creatures from afar.

"*Get back!*" someone shouted, a voice that boomed across the field like thunder.

Lightning followed.

The front line of the Razorstorks was launched upward as bolts of jagged, blue-white lightning danced across their huge forms. The entirety of the Legion flinched back, some of the closer ones thrown from their feet by the impact. Razorstorks struggled to their feet, flailing with wing and talon, as the back lines continued to approach without stopping.

Until a figure rode a bolt of lightning down from the sky itself, crushing another Razorstork with feet shaped as talons and a body covered in dark scales. The Fiend. *Felix.*

Beneficial Condition Applied!
Status Condition: Rallying Cry

Rallying Cry
For the next minute, all Health, Stamina, and Mana regenerations are doubled. Chance of Frightened Condition reduced by 50%!

Mervin gasped as the effect washed over him, along with everyone else in sight. It was like a beam of golden-blue light had shone from above.

"No!" the figure shouted, and more blue-white lightning crackled around the man's shoulders and head. "No more deaths! Not today!"

A force of swirling blue-white light pressed down on the horde of monsters, and those nearest him stumbled onto their bellies. The Fiend, meanwhile, was hurled into the sky where he sparked with brilliant arcs of lightning that all but outshined the sun.

At the same time, the earth rumbled. Across the breadth of the battlefield, a rippling tide of devastating stone thorns erupted, each the size of a man. Monsters were skewered by them, the earth beneath their feet transformed against them. As they went, the spikes gathered into larger shapes, jagged hooks and spears thicker than the tree trunks in the distance. Dusty brown Mana poured from the Fiend's now-floating body, a tempest of power that beggared belief.

How much Mana is he using? It was more power than Mervin had seen anyone wield, apart from the Elders themselves. *Just how strong is he? How could one man do all of this?*

In the space it took Mervin to think those words, the battlefield had been cleared. Entirely. It was littered with massive spikes of blue-gray stone and the remnant corpses of hundreds of monsters. Some had even skewered those avians flying above.

The Fiend landed once again, his dark form hitting the ground like a cannonball.

"What the hell is he?" Piotr said, a quiet awe in his reedy voice.

"Strong," Garin said. "He's like a monster himself."

That wasn't strong enough, Felix thought with annoyance.

He had landed amid the monster charge, intending to stop it and kill them in one fell swoop. But his Adamant Discord wouldn't do what he wanted it to. He'd tried to crush them all to the ground, but he'd instead pulled them *up*. Along with a significant chunk of the earth. In his panic, he'd lost focus, and his grasp slackened. He was lucky the Skill still had its lightning aspect, otherwise a significant portion of them would have survived his landing.

Tch. He had to cast Adamant Discord *again* to get the grounded enemies immobilized, and that had sent him up into the air. *Must be something like counterforce or balance. I push down, I get pushed up.* He tapped his lip with a dark talon, careful not to split his own skin. *The Stone Shaping took care of most of them, at least. They were weak. A lot weaker than I anticipated, really.*

You Have Killed—

Felix waved off the notification, letting it pass through him but otherwise ignoring it and the many others like it. He looked around him at the corpses of monsters that were slowly fading into a greasy black smoke as they decayed. In the sky above, Pit wheeled after the last clusters of bird monsters, trilling a happy song through their bond.

Need any help? he asked.

No, came the immediate reply. *Having fun.*

Wingblades and Frost Spears shot out, but not nearly as many as he'd expected. Instead, his Companion lit himself on fire and chased after his prey with remarkable grace. He managed to keep them all outside of the city. Felix was seriously impressed; his little tenku had come a long way.

The portion of his interface that was Pit's notifications flickered into view.

Pit's Wingblade is level 61!
Pit's Frost Spear is level 64!
Pit's Poisonfire is level 45!

Wow, yeah. Keep at it, bud. As long as the tenku kept making gains and wasn't hurt, Felix was happy to let him hunt.

Manifestation of the Coronach is level 46!
Adamant Discord is level 59!
Stone Shaping is level 57!

His own gains weren't bad, especially that level of Adamant Discord. He must have been onto something with the opposing forces.

"Sir?"

Felix turned to find an older Human woman standing at attention only a few feet away. She was wearing a hammer at her waist and had a crude symbol stitched on the right side of her tunic. The woman hadn't snuck up on him—he'd heard her footsteps scrape clumsily across the ground—but he was surprised. The other Legionnaires were too timid to come so close.

"Yeah?"

"Captain Irina Kovalt, sir. First of Bone." She saluted with her fist to her chest, right over that embroidered symbol.

Oh, now I see it. It's a femur. Felix restrained the sigh that wanted to slip free. "How can I help you, Captain?"

"Help? Sir, you've more than helped already! You damn near

wiped the monster horde out completely! Alone, no less." The woman was probably in her fifties, but she had the excitement of a schoolgirl as she looked out at the jagged battlefield.

"Yes, right. So you don't need anything?" he asked. He really wanted to get back to the city center and finalize his preparations.

"Oh, we just wanted permission, sir."

"Permission for what?"

"To loot the bodies, sir. We've a number of butchers on hand that can make use of the monsters before they go bad and recover monster cores."

"Oh!" Felix could have slapped himself. "Yes! Do that. Send all monster cores to the Lady Haarwatch, please. There are a number of ongoing City Quests for monster cores. Make sure you all take the Quest before turning them in, though."

"Yes, sir!" Captain Kovalt saluted again and gave a series of sharp handsigns. At her signal, the Legionnaires eagerly ran forward, several with long, glowing knives in hand. With a nod from Felix, the captain also went off after the nearest bird monster, gutting it in two quick movements. Their knives would stem the rot, allowing them to harvest what they needed from the corpses.

Huh, monster cores. I should have thought of that. Felix shook his head as he walked back toward the sundered Wall. *Cal will need all she can get to fuel the city, and it'll get these folks some steady experience.*

Felix had sensed the captain's incomplete Temper through his Voracious Eye, similar to many in the field. A few had pushed entirely through Apprentice Tier, but they felt... flimsy, somehow. He wasn't sure where the certain came from, but his Eye hadn't lied to him yet.

He'd almost made it through the Wall when a wash of aquamarine vapor announced the sudden appearance of his mentor. Zara flowed up to the Wall, riding a wave of her own power, one that gave off a steady, sparkling sound like wind chimes and soft marimba music. It faded as the wave vanished.

"Zara," Felix greeted her. "You're too late. The monster attack is all over."

The Naiad looked beyond Felix, at the Legionnaires as they picked across the battlefield and carved into the monsters nearby. She turned her ice-blue gaze on him. "You cannot coddle them forever."

"What are you talking about?" Felix asked. He felt his mood sour at the tone in her voice. "I saved their lives. Those monsters were too strong for them. Too many."

"Perhaps. But you robbed them of valuable experience, both System granted and not," she pointed out.

"They're out here because of me, Zara." Felix surveyed the sweaty, laughing soldiers. Their Spirits were jubilant, a stark difference to what he'd felt as they began their doomed charge. "I'm responsible for them."

"No you're not," Zara said with a sharp look. "They're—for the most part—grown adults. Many have been making their own decisions for decades before you arrived."

"That's not what I mean," Felix said. "If I hadn't—"

"Inspired them?"

"*Misled* them," Felix growled. A few Legionnaires perked up at his tone and quickly moved farther away. "They're chasing after my accomplishments, and they'll die because of it. I asked Cal to disband them, but she refused. I tried talking to them, to convince them to stop, but their Spirits *sing* when they think of protecting their town." Felix scrubbed his hands over his face. "So while I'm still here, I can at least protect them."

"Felix," Zara said, her voice softer and quieter. She put a hand on his shoulder. "They have chosen this path. All of us, them included, have to live with the consequences of our decisions. Choice and Consequences are sacred and cannot be taken by another. Not unless we let them." She let go of his shoulder and turned back to the battlefield. "Danger abounds on the Continent. You do them no favors by protecting them from it. That is how it always has been and always must be."

Felix frowned. "Maybe you're right, Zara. But, just because something has always been, doesn't mean it should be."

CHAPTER TWELVE

Felix left Zara behind as he prowled the line of the Rent. The Legion gave him lingering glances as they hustled back and forth, dragging severed wings and piles of salvaged feathers. Felix let his Sovereign of Flesh relax, dismissing the dark armor in favor of being slightly less recognizable, but he wasn't really paying attention to them.

Why now? A monster attack only hours after they decided to head after the Archon. *Is it a coincidence? Or was Hector right?*

Did they have a spy in their midst?

Felix spread his awareness outward, his Perception spreading to its limit. He could hear and feel and see *so much*, enough that, without his powerful Journeyman Mind, he'd have fallen to pieces from the sheer volume of information. Tempered twice over, Felix could at least sift through it—like tuning past radio stations—moving across the white noise for anything that stood out. Blood and stink and frustrated grunts as monster flesh fought back against butcher blades. Mundanity, or as close to it as it came on the Continent where attacks like this could happen whenever.

But they didn't happen whenever. Right? Felix had heard the monster attacks were escalating ever since he had come to Haarwatch for the first time. Before that, they'd had a strange amount of beast activity in the Foglands. Then, after they'd defeated the Archon's forces, it had stopped. For a week, not so much as a peep. *Now this. What's the connection?*

"No, I need to speak to him, Akales!" someone shouted from Felix's left. Fenwick Cole, according to his Voracious Eye.

"You've no business that can't wait," Oskar Akales replied, another familiar face. "I must ask him about the allotment of these cores. Sir!"

Felix withheld a groan as he turned toward them. It was like dealing with unruly children, for all that both of the men were at least middle-aged. Fenwick's hair was mostly gone, except around his ears where it gathered wildly.

"Don't you cut me off, Akales—"

"Gentlemen—Firsts—I apologize, but I think the Fiend has already told us where the cores are going," another voice cut in, and Felix was surprised to see another familiar face. Mervin Cors, the first person he'd met after returning from the Void. He'd gotten stronger, he could tell, and there was a confidence to his voice that Felix was surprised to hear. Mervin inclined his head to him. "I heard you speak to Captain Kovalt. We're to bring them all to city center and the Lady Haarwatch."

The two armored men stopped short of Felix's side and stared at Mervin. He could see as well as feel the consternation coming off them both. Fenwick glared at Mervin, then cleared his throat. "Sir, those cores could push our soldiers' own power further if they were allowed to use them."

"Given to the Blades, you mean?" Oskar said. He laughed and clanked his hands together in a mocking clap. "Very good. Meanwhile, the Fists were the first into battle. If anyone deserves them, it is us."

"If I may, Firsts, there are several outstanding Quests for monster cores held by the Lady Haarwatch. There are so many cores here; all of our people could rise in levels in a short time." Mervin looked between the two of them. "Is that not a better use than clogging your divine-given power with monster cores?"

Felix was impressed. The young farmboy had grown up. Last he'd seen him, Mervin had been wracked with nerves and no little fear.

"Mervin's right," Felix said, defusing the anger gathering on Fenwick's face. "Using monster cores to strengthen yourself is a shortcut that can hurt your growth. One or two are fine, but more than that, and your core and channels will never amount to much." *Or so I've been told.* "You'll get more bang for your buck if you go to Haarwatch Manor and take the Quests."

"Bang for your—?" Fenwick started, before shaking his head. "Very well. If that is the truth of it, then I'll not gainsay the Fiend."

The bald First of Blade stomped away, followed only a moment later by the First of Fist. At least Oskar gave him an apologetic look before returning to his soldiers.

"Apologies for intruding, Lord Fiend," Mervin said.

Felix put out a hand, stopping the kid from talking. "Man, no. Don't apologize. And don't call me that. Not like we're strangers, right?" His hand tilted until it was held out in a handshake. "Mervin, right? Been a while."

Mervin tentatively took Felix's hand, and they shook. "Oh ah, yes. It's been some time… Felix."

Felix smiled. "Yeah, there you go. I honestly can't stand the titles these guys keep throwing at me. Kind of exhausting, actually."

"I suppose I can see that," Mervin allowed, though his Spirit rippled with confusion.

"Don't worry about it. Glad to see you're doing well, though. Already..." Felix let his Eye linger over the kid. "Level 22 and in the early stages of Apprentice Tier. Good job."

Mervin flushed with pride. "It has been a… challenging time. Strength was the only option." His expression faltered for a half second. "Guild gone, Wall broken, city… but we're here. Ready to serve."

Felix's gaze caught on the patch sewn onto the kid's jerkin, a crude sword. He regarded Mervin in a different light. He'd clearly been through a lot, more than some in the city perhaps, and he'd come out the other side all the stronger. Tempered.

Was Zara right? Should he have left these monsters for the Legion to fight? Let survival of the fittest decide who was worthy of life and who wasn't?

"Sir, er, Felix?"

"Hm?"

"How can I get stronger?" Mervin asked nervously. He looked out at the battlefield, littered with dead monsters. "I am… I am not enough."

Felix huffed a breath from his nose, more in consideration than annoyance. It was exactly what he was thinking: how to keep them safe without continually putting himself between them and danger. Still, it wasn't exactly a straightforward question. Levels and good, high-rarity Skills were important, but so was a solid foundation and Tempering. But so much of what constituted strength on the Continent was a product of luck or—he blinked—insider knowledge.

Of course! Felix thought on what everyone had taught him since his arrival, from Harn to Magda to Cal and Zara. And what he had learned himself.

"What're you good at?" he asked.

Mervin didn't hesitate. "My Perception is my highest stat, and I—"

"No, not your stats," Felix said as he waved a hand. "You. Do you have something you're good at? Like a hobby?"

"Oh ah, hm," Mervin thought a moment. "I do enjoy whittling."

"Whittling." Felix scratched his jaw. "Okay, yeah. How do you think about your core?"

"My—it is a ball of light, pushing the divine gift of the Pathless through me to strengthen my flesh and mind and spirit."

Yeesh. Right, he's a Pathless guy. "Okay, so just a ball of light? Nothing else?"

"Should there be?" Mervin's earnest confusion confirmed a lot of what Felix had been told. People weren't given knowledge in this world. Not without strings attached. Felix frowned, remembering his earliest days, when his own core was nothing more than a spark of fire in his gut. That was also when his Perception picked up that all the butcher work had stopped around them. He had become an island of calm as the Legionnaires listened closely.

Good. Listen up.

Felix cleared his throat and spoke just a touch louder. "Think of it like this: your core is a hunk of wood. Right now it's just sitting there, doing its best at being what it is. Simple wood. You have to carve it down, shape it into the form that fits you." Here he stumbled, unable to articulate exactly how he'd figured his own core space out. "Your core space responds to what you believe it to be, sorta. Your channels are the same, linked to the process. So if you carve say—"

"A plow?" Mervin provided.

Felix paused and smiled. "Yeah. Yeah a plow works, especially if it works *for you*. Maybe for someone else it's a bird, or a castle, or a giant wall with a hole in it," he said, gesturing around them. A few soldiers laughed before stifling it and pretending to work. Felix grinned at them. "Find out what makes you *you*, and you'll find that strength follows."

At least, that was what worked for me, he thought. Yet he kept the sentiment to himself. Certainty from authority could work its own kind of magic, he'd found, and the basics were solid. Tentatively, Felix felt those around him with his Affinity. It felt like a wave of refreshing water and the sound of early morning birdsong.

What he sensed with that Harmonic Stat wasn't always straightforward, like rage or fear or admiration, and sometimes it pushed its way through his other senses by way of explanation. A type of synesthesia, combining senses to suggest a greater whole, much how Manasight often worked. His Affinity sensed that the people around him were affected by his words, and the impression Felix got was that it was positive.

Hopefully, it helps them grow. They'll need it if more hordes are coming.

"I see," Mervin was saying after staring at the ground a moment longer. "Begin with the core."

"Begin with the core. Yeah," Felix said with a smile. "From there it's just a matter of—"

"Run!"

Felix's head snapped up, instantly taking in the explosive charge of an injured Razorstork. It had apparently been stunned, but not dead, and a Legionnaire stumbled back with a skinning knife held out. The big bird hurled the Iron Ranks in all directions as its deadly bill struck through flesh and armor alike. The Legionnaire fell back with a cry, and the Razorstork charged. Its eyes were vivid and maddened by pain and… fear. Felix felt a flash of its Spirit across his Affinity, a blade of light that scraped against his eyes and shuddered against his ears. Felix gasped.

The avian stank of blood and burning ozone, and at first, he thought it was because of him. Residue of his own lightning spell. But no. It was a signature stain that he'd recognize anywhere, perfect recall or not.

Vellus.

Felix's Affinity trembled, and half-seen strings, threads of connection between living beings spun outward into the Foglands. Unreasonable fear had overwhelmed these creatures. They were running from something.

From above, Pit squawked in warning, but Felix leaped into its way. It was like a prehistorically sized cassowary and just as terrifying, were it not so weak. Felix held out a single hand and tried something new.

Stop. You are in no danger. Wielding his Intent like a scalpel, he severed the connections that drove the avian. It stumbled, as if he'd cut something vital, but the charge did not stop. It was too far gone. *Stop!*

It screeched at him in challenge, and Felix's mouth thinned.

Wild Threnody!

His Blade of the Fang leaped to his hand as unattributed Mana poured into it. The off-white tooth turned a luminous white, and Felix made a single, powerful downward slash.

You Have Killed A Razorstork!
XP Earned!

The Razorstork was severed in half by the glowing Fang, and it fell into two wet piles to either side of him. The smell of cooked chicken and boiled offal assaulted his Perception; only Felix's powerful Endurance let him withstand it without gagging.

Eugh. No. Not Vellus. Not directly. That connection was too weak to be her, but it tastes like it, only without the bite. As if someone had channeled the mad god's power near these creatures, and they fled it. *Smart bird.* He looked at the corpse again. *Sorta.*

Fortunately or unfortunately, depending on how you looked at it, the list for culprits was short. Felix was pretty certain who had terrified an entire forest of monsters away from the Foglands. It was the only creature that had previously utilized the Goddess of Blood, Storm, and Tide's power before.

"Goddamn it."

Congratulations!
You Have Tempered Your Spirit!
You Have Formed: the Ashen Reach Spirit!
+10 INT
+30 WIL
+20 DEX
+10 PER
+5 VIT

"Burnin' *finally*," Evie hissed. Her voice was a raspy croak from all of the screaming, but it was a small price to pay for finally achieving Journeyman Tier. Everything about her ached as a result of her strained Aspects, and she felt wrung out like a dirty dishcloth.

With a flicker of Will, she brought up her new Formation.

Body: Boreal Gyves
Mind: Unshaken Thrawn
Spirit: Ashen Reach

With Cal and Aenea behind her, Evie had been able to get her hands on some good Essence Draughts for her Tempering. Her Spirit and Mind were Rare, with her Body being a touch better than the rest at Epic rarity. Distilling a chain Essence had been a find and a half, and not for the first time, Evie resolved to kiss that Alchemist when she had the chance.

Evie stood up, her muscles as wobbly as a newborn chick, and she tentatively felt at her core. Tiering up didn't necessarily advance one's core stage, but she'd been working on both all this time. The chains around her icy core had spread out, pushed into a complex web of convoluted links. Mana thrummed through it all, the same as freezing rain and inexorable chill. There was more work to be done before touching on the Ring Stage, but she was close.

A knock interrupted her musing.

"Yeah?" Evie rasped. "What do you want?"

A muffled voice sounded from beyond the wooden door. "Ma'am, the supplies you requested have arrived."

"Yeah, yeah, yeah," she snapped. *You're gonna call me 'ma'am'?!* She hobbled to the door and threw it open. A young boy stood there with three other porters. Several lumpy packages sat against the ground, each one wrapped in oilcloth to protect them from the elements. "All here?"

"We visited every storefront you asked, ma'am," the boy said again. Evie opened her mouth in annoyance, but then another voice interrupted her.

"That's a lot of stuff, Evie," the voice said. She turned to see Atar walking swiftly down the hall, his thin metal stave in hand. "You carrying that all yourself, ma'am?"

"It's for all of us, Sparky," Evie said, narrowing her eyes at the mage. She gave the porters a couple silver swords from her purse. "Thanks, lads."

The porters palmed the money and scurried down the corridor, gone so fast she was half-certain they'd Tempered their Bodies.

"You look a wreck," Atar said, coming to a stop near her door. "Didn't you get any sleep?"

"Not a wink. Been pushing into Journeyman all night," Evie groaned. "Just made it."

"About time. You'll need it, too, if the Foglands keep spitting out monsters," Atar said. "City just pushed back another horde."

"What? I missed the fighting?" Evie growled. "Noctis' tits."

"We'll all get our chance for more, you can be sure of that."

"You heard somethin'?" Evie asked, hopeful.

"No," Atar shook his head. "I just know our fearless leader. I'm fairly certain Felix can't get through the day without facing a horde or two."

"It's been quiet the past while, though," Evie pointed out.

"Exactly what I'm worried about," Atar grimaced. "Come. Coldfire sent me to get you and Vess for a final fitting. They've got some new armor for us all."

"Right, Elle's been working on somethin' for me." Evie closed her door and followed after Atar. The packages could sit for a bit. "We goin' to get Vess now?"

"Already tried her. She's not in her rooms," Atar shrugged. "Haven't seen her since the meeting."

"Oh, well, hopefully she'll already be there."

CHAPTER THIRTEEN

Felix scoured the battlefield for more evidence of Vellus or the Archon. Now that he had the scent, it was easy enough to find traces but no more than that. Whatever had compelled these creatures to rampage had touched them briefly, if at all. The threads of connection were fuzzy and almost completely faded.

Mervin followed him, helping as he could. Eventually his friends came along, moving monster corpses so Felix could inspect them. The stone spikes he'd left in the field made the going slower, and after the skinny one—Piotr—said the spikes would get in the way of ranged attacks from the Wall, he happily dropped them back into the earth. All it cost was a bit more Mana, barely worth mentioning.

Felix caught up a bit with Mervin, learning a smattering of what had gone on in his life since their parting. The kid wasn't exactly a friend, but he *was* friendly and seemed to genuinely want to help the people of Haarwatch. Compared to DuFont and Teine, Mervin was a breath of fresh air.

His friends were similar in demeanor, though Garin had something of a chip on his shoulder. Something to do with Mervin passing the Legion's tests while he didn't. Felix hadn't even been aware there were tests or that they were recruiting. That both annoyed him and put him at ease. More people would mean better protection, but it also meant more folks flocking under "the Fiend's" banner.

Felix explained again about their core and how to proceed from their current points of advancement to better strengthen themselves. Garin, Piotr, and Lars took to it well enough with a few questions, while the rest of the Legion crowded close by, attempting to be inconspicuous. Felix had shared everything he thought pertinent for their advancement, things that had been hidden from him due to forced ignorance and compartmentalization of knowledge.

Mervin's friends were… interesting. All of them had a weirdness about them that Felix hadn't been able to place, until Mervin had revealed they'd all Tempered with special Essences Teine had distilled. Then he recognized the nascent connections between himself and each of them, threads that were crimson-black but faded. Washed out.

Two guesses on what the Essences were from, he sent to Pit. The tenku screeched in annoyance. *You said it. Glad he's dead. Well, mostly dead.*

Teine was currently sipping food out of a straw up in Portia's magic hospital. Temper shattered and power scattered, the man's core was all but snuffed out by whatever the Arcids did to him. It was brutal, and less than he deserved. He may have helped destroy the Nest—Mervin had confirmed it was Teine who blew up the Belais Crystal at the end—but Teine had caused the Primordial infection in the first place. Felix could still see the effects of his idiot experiments, most evident in the emaciated form of Piotr. That guy had definitely been affected by the Primordial's power in a greater way than the others. Maybe the Essence was too potent or… it didn't matter. Felix couldn't sense the Maw's power—his power—in the man, but his Aspects had been affected. Felix didn't have a fix for it, though. Hopefully, the help with their cores would be of some use.

The defenses for the damaged Wall were still not online, which was concerning, but problems happened. Hector had stuck his head out for a bit to say the repairs were taking longer than expected.

"If you could tell the Lady Haarwatch to divert more power to our defenses, that would be appreciated," Hector had said. "This Profane Sigaldry is taking a significant amount of our power to eradicate, and we've little to spare for activating some of the more elaborate arrays."

"I'll pass the word," Felix promised. And, after ensuring that the Legion was following his orders regarding the monster cores, Felix and Pit left the Wall.

Their flight was relatively quick, despite the miles of city below them. Pit's levels in Flight and rising Strength proved their worth as much as his Agility and Endurance as the Wall Quarter flashed beneath them. Felix hugged tight to his friend, the feel of his silky smooth fur and glossy feathers a balm to his worried mind. Things were changing, again; his friends and allies were splitting apart to take care of the urgent issues that threatened them all, and Felix bemoaned the loss. While the last week hadn't been a vacation, it *had* been quiet.

He was gonna miss it.

Pit warbled his confusion at Felix, clearly feeling the melancholy that hummed inside of his Spirit. By way of explanation, Felix shared his recent memories in a flurry of sense images and impressions and emotions. In response, Pit did the same, relating his time spent hunting more monsters in the sewers. It wasn't something they did often, as they were typically together all the time, and it tended to gloss over details, but it was useful.

"You've had a fun morning, then," Felix said.

Hunt bad is good, Pit sent back along with a rumble of contentment. *We hunt bad again? Soon?*

Felix considered the Foglands retreating behind them. "Yeah, very soon."

They entered the city center, and it was chaos. So much so, in fact, that Pit immediately decided to converge and hide within Felix's Spirit for a time. The flash of light caused its own minor kerfuffle in the square, but it passed soon enough. Felix fell about thirty feet but landed with a light flexing of his knees.

Didn't even break the flagstones, he noticed. *I'm getting better, I think.*

Pit chirruped encouragingly.

Whenever his stats jumped significantly, Felix had a hard time adjusting to the increases. It was part of the reason he had gone overboard with the Golems that morning. And again with the monster horde, though that had been more intentional. Since his Tier up and… other changes… Felix had taken the entire week to finally get his balance again.

Which was good, because while he'd managed to land in a less occupied corner of the square, the area at the base of Haarwatch Manor was wild. Humans, Orcs, Goblins, Races of all sorts rushed everywhere in such numbers that had Felix remembering that Haarwatch was a city. A decimated one, but the population was still huge.

A particularly large contingent of Orcs and Hobgoblins were hauling several wagons the size of city buses with the help of a team of avum. The wagons were built like tanks because they bore entire trees, sheared of branches and ready to go into storage, in their beds. Normally gathered east of the city, in the Verdant Pass, these logs would have traveled down the Ianus River until they hit the collection point about midway through the city. Teams then had to lift the logs out and bring them to either the sawmills or to storage. It was the same with ore and stone being mined along the edges of the mountains. All of it was being brought here to the city center.

There were Quests to be had, after all.

Felix Eyed the people around him, checking on their Aspects and levels, noting for the first time that the vast majority were pushing into the twenties. That was a real change from his previous observations, where only those with professions or Guild ties found themselves with enough experience to get out of the teens. A good number were even half a step into Apprentice Tier.

"War is good for society," a voice behind him grumbled. Felix's senses washed outward and Skills began to hum within his core space, but he simply turned. Calmly. Ish. Behind him was a Dwarven woman with dark hair and darker features, made more so by the soot that streaked her face. Rafny Coldfire, weaponsmith extraordinaire and wife of Elle, the armorsmith. "Strengthens a people."

Felix let out a breath. "You really think so?"

Raf shrugged, studying the crowd. "People die in wars. Kill. It's stress and opportunity, the two things you need to advance in this world." She hawked and spat onto the flagstones, narrowly missing a Gnomish man's wide-brimmed hat. "Hierocracy says strength is good. Can't say I don't agree. War is good for my pocket, too, so take it with a grain of salt."

"They are stronger," Felix allowed. "The ones who survived. But—"

All you are doing is surviving, Felix. Try to live, once in a while. Vess' words flashed back to him, perfectly recalled thanks to his Born Trait. Pit cooed comfortingly in his Spirit.

"But what about the rest?" Raf asked, tilting her head up to look him full in the face for the first time. He'd never noticed the smattering of freckles on her face, or the lines that had been worn around her eyes. "I think about them everyday, Felix. I lost… we all lost friends and family because of the Guild's burnin' dumbassery. Because of greed. There's not a day that goes by that I don't wish they had all survived; and there's not a moment that I don't thank the blind gods that Elle wasn't one of 'em."

"They deserve more than this," Felix said, gesturing to… everything. "Seek strength, sure. Go after power if you want, but that shouldn't be the line that decides if you live or die. Right?"

"That'd be nice, Felix. Real nice. You tell me when you figured out how to make it work, and I'll be first in line for your little utopia." Rafny smiled wryly at him. "Meantime, I got gifts."

For the first time, Felix noticed a growing number of boxes that had been stacked up behind Rafny. They were fairly close to the Coldfire Smithy, and apprentices were busy lugging out more crates for the pile.

"What's all this?"

"What'd I say? Gifts, you daft Fiend," Rafny said as she ran her hands over some of the crates. She popped open one such crate to show fifteen steel shields nestled among straw. "Well, gifts implies I don't get paid, and that's plum not true. More like… civic offerings. Lady Haarwatch keeps us safe, we give her enough metal to outfit an army. Got armor and shields and simple weaponry galore. All Apprentice Tier. Even a few Journeyman-Tier items for the officers."

"Very nice," Felix said appreciatively. His Eye picked out details on the shields and they were solid. He wasn't entirely clear on the smithing process, but apparently they folded Mana into the items to bring them to the appropriate Tier strength. An Apprentice-Tier shield meant it could stop a similarly Tiered Skill until the material degraded. Using a Beginner Tier—aka normal—shield to block an Apprentice Tier Ice Arrow would be as useless as taping a sheet of paper to your arm. "I saw they were increasing recruitment, but this is a lot. I'm impressed that so many people want to protect their communities."

"More like they want two square meals a day and a place to sleep," Rafny said, closing the crate with a grunt. "But aye, probably some community-minded folks among 'em. Maybe. A lot of this is for the mission you're all trekkin' out on."

"Mission?" Felix asked, his heart-rate ramping up. Their Quests and plans should have remained a secret.

"Yeah, headin' out to the Verdant Pass, aren't you?" Rafny asked with a squint. "Yan and Kelgan been walking around town talkin' about it all morning, tellin' everyone about it who asked. Some that didn't, actually."

Those idiots. Why would they... No. They're not that *dumb.* Felix looked around, fully recognizing the assortment of avum and a surprising number of armored Haarguard. *It's a misdirect,* he realized.

"I figured you'd be heading with them," Rafny continued. "I heard it was dangerous and important and—sorry to say—you're probably the most fearsome Haarwatch's got."

Felix grunted noncommittally and nodded to the pile again. "Got anything for me and my friends in there?"

Rafny smiled. A twinkle immediately shone in her eyes. "Oh aye. First, though, I'll return this." She pulled his khopesh and sheath from the pile and handed it over with extreme reverence. "I wasn't able to tell much from the metal or the strange shape, but I do know it's unnaturally sharp. There's no sharpening array, no durability glyph carved into the blade or handle. Just the one, tiny array etched at the base, and that just siphons and diverts Mana."

Felix took his Crescian Blade back from Rafny and strapped it back onto his belt. It joined the Femur of the Envoy on his opposite hip and the Blade of the Fang on his back. "I know about the siphon array, but there's more in there, I know it. Thanks for taking a look."

"My pleasure. Since you're leavin' today, I gave it back; I'd much rather keep it and take the whole sword apart," Rafny's eyes gleamed as she stared at the khopesh again. "The ancient smiths knew secrets we've long lost, and I think some of them are bound up in that blade. You let me know if you learn anything more, yeah?"

"Not a problem," Felix promised. "You said there was more?"

"Ah, aye, hold this." She shoved a box into Felix's hands. Something inside clanged around, probably armor, and it weighed hundreds of pounds. Luckily, Felix was plenty strong and simply set it aside. "Aha! Here you are!"

With a flourish, Rafny produced a pair of boots. Greaves, really, as they were made entirely of a dark grey metal and designed to cover him from the knees downward. Heavy, reinforced plates lingered at the knees, top of the foot and toe, as well as thick soles with a serious tread. They easily weighed sixty pounds apiece.

Voracious Eye!

Name: Greaves of the Fiend
Type: Armor (Enchanted)
Lore: Built by Eldrunna Coldfire from the remains of a powerful construct, the unique metal is stronger than mithril and extremely resilient. They were designed specifically for Felix Nevarre, Blue-Eyed Fiend of Haarwatch.
Self-Repair VIII - Ambient Mana will be absorbed to repair any damage to the Greaves.
All Terrain IX - The soles are enchanted to retain a sure grip despite the terrain.

Felix raised his eyebrows. Mithril was a step above steel—a metal imbued with a natural magic much like orichalcum—and was extremely expensive. To use something stronger than that...

"Is this made from the Arcids?" Felix asked, and Rafny shook her head.

"Of course not. It's made from the Apollyon."

Felix laughed. "Well, at least it turned out to be useful."

"It did, at that. Those constructs have given my craft a significant edge. I've gained six levels!" Rafny almost crowed in excitement. "I don't know what the metal is or how it's been made so receptive to Mana, but it's remarkably good for advanced weaponry."

Felix chuckled and strapped the Greaves onto his feet and lower legs. They felt good, perfect even. Their weight was almost a comfort, and it made him think about how much damage a kick would do now.

"How do they feel? Fits like a dream, yeah? Elle does quality work." Rafny grinned. "Now you can stop wearin' those pathetic hobnails."

"I have missed nice boots, that's true," Felix agreed. "What else do you have?"

"For you? Just one more thing. Another gift from Elle." She produced two circular bands, thick as a wristwatch and completely smooth. "Put these on."

"What are they? Bracelets?" Felix took them and slid them onto his hands. Immediately he felt them hum, as if an electrical current was passing through them. To his Manasight, they began to glow with flows of orange and silvery Mana.

"Twist them, right here," Rafny pointed.

Felix did so, and with a soft metal-on-metal sound, the bracelets expanded into full on vambraces. From wrist to elbow, he was sheathed in segmented metal, and those flows of orange and silvery Mana only increased.

Voracious Eye!

Name: Vambraces of the Fiend
Type: Armor (Enchanted)
Lore: Built by Eldrunna Coldfire from the remains of a powerful construct, the unique metal is stronger than mithril and extremely resilient. They were designed specifically for Felix Nevarre, Blue-Eyed Fiend of Haarwatch.
Self-Repair VIII - Ambient Mana will be absorbed to repair any damage to the Vambraces of the Fiend.
Smoldering Lash X - An array inscribed on the right Vambrace allows the user to manifest a whip made of fire Mana.
Conjure Blade VII - An array inscribed on the left

Vambrace allows the user to manifest metal Mana to produce a single blade no longer than ten inches.

"Whoa, Skills?"

"Indeed. The Tier of this new metal let us inlay a couple actual Skills. It's typically a higher-level technique, inscribing actual Skills, but I've just begun to scratch the surface of those levels now." Rafny grinned so hard Felix worried her head would fall off. "Skills are limited to the level I was able to scribe in, so they're both only Apprentice Tier, but they'll at least be useful in a pinch. A surprise, at the very least."

"This is amazing," Felix said with real glee in his voice. He conjured the blade, and it formed in the air before dropping half an inch into Felix's left palm. The fire whip was similar, except it unspooled from the vambrace itself and onto the ground. It was hot to the touch, but nothing his Body and resistances couldn't handle. He dismissed both effects. "I especially like how they collapse."

"That was a trick and a half to figure out, but with your transformation Skill, Elle figured you'd need a way to get any armor off quick. Last thing she wants is for you to ruin more of her good work."

Felix grinned at the light jab and laughed when Rafny showed him how to collapse the boots in the same way. They shrank down into a pair of thick anklets, which was entirely too cool.

"And last, but not least, we made this together," the smith said, pulling a large leather bundle out of a crate. She set it gingerly on top of another and spread it out. It was a saddle made of cured skin and segmented pieces of rust-red metal. "A custom set of barding for Pit, along with a saddle and sheath for your Fang."

There was a flash of light, and suddenly the horse-sized Pit pushed Felix out of the way to inspect his new gift. Felix laughed and let the tenku shove him aside. Pit cooed appreciatively over the design and style of the barding, which was basically armor for the Chimera to wear. Rafny was soon helping to strap it all onto the tenku, testing and checking the straps as she went.

Why hadn't I thought of armor for him?

"You've outdone yourselves this time, Raf," Felix said as the smith stepped away from his Companion. The barding covered

Pit's head, chest, and forelegs with segmented plates of metal that looked almost like—"Are these made of Scales?"

"Aye, the Scales of the Ravager Queen you gave us," Rafny continued. "Elle figured that, since you refuse to wear armor, at least your friend can. And—" she gestured Felix to come closer. She pointed at Pit's chest, to a symbol that looked like an open eye that was also on fire. "We've added your new crest and enchanted it. Those Scales are special, a lot like the construct's metal. Let us add in a Spiritbinding on armor that is still technically only Journeyman Tier."

Felix ignored the crest, the one he'd noticed on the Legion's cloaks, and furrowed his brows. "Spiritbinding?"

"The barding can be bound to Pit, to his Spirit. It's advanced stuff again, but the Scales are such high-quality material that we made it work," Rafny pointed again at the crest. His crest. "Just put both of your blood on the crest and Will it to be bound to Pit, and the barding will stay on him even when you do your little disappearing act."

Whoa. That was huge. Felix quickly cut himself with his Crescian Blade, and Pit provided his own blood. They both smeared it along the crest and, together, they leveraged their Willpower. *Bind!*

Felix felt a soft, distant echo as if something heavy had dropped nearby. Pit staggered, just a moment, but then straightened. With a flash of light, both Pit and his barding vanished. Seconds later, Pit reappeared, still wearing his armor.

Okay, that's rad as hell.

"Don't you got anything better to do?" Atar shouted at him. The olive-skinned mage was leaning heavily against his metal stave, sweating and breathing hard. "How about you-you help us out and carry some stuff, eh?"

He was quickly followed by Evie and Alister, both of whom were wearing armor and packs of similar size to Atar's. Neither was even sweating.

"Sparky, I really think you need to start lifting," Evie suggested. "Maybe Harn can help you with some Endurance training?"

"No, no, no," Atar said with an abrupt, plastered-on smile. He stood straighter, and Felix could see veins in his neck popping into sharp relief. "I'm perfec—perfectly fine."

"Atar, it's fine," Alister said. "I can carry your pack, too."

"No, I have this," the fire mage stated and marched closer to Felix. "What're you standing around for? Don't we have places to be?"

Felix grinned and took the spare pack Alister handed to him. It was fully stocked with food, water, and basic adventuring supplies, as they had planned. However, Felix noticed a third pack being carried by Evie.

"Where's Vess?"

Evie frowned. "Not sure. Haven't seen her all mornin'."

"*Hiyahh!*"

A carriage rolled into the square from one of the busier thoroughfares, led by four matched avum and a driver wearing the armor of a Haarguard. It was followed by no less than fifty or sixty Haarguard marching in sharp formation. The crowd in the square cleared, giving them room to maneuver, and the carriage came to a halt just shy of Felix's position.

A tall man in a pale green doublet and yellow half-cape stepped from the carriage. Parts of him were obviously bandaged, but it didn't seem to inhibit his grace as he turned and let a beautiful woman step out after. Perhaps it was the gown or the styled hair, but Felix didn't immediately recognize her.

"The Hand?" Alister asked in disbelief. "He's not nearly as hurt as I expected."

"Wow," Atar said, his face flushing. "She's beautiful."

"Oh, blood and ashes," Evie cursed. "This can't be good. Vess hates dressing up."

Vess? Felix blinked in surprise. *Wait why's she—*

Vess took her guardian's hand as she stepped out and did not relinquish it.

Oh.

CHAPTER FOURTEEN

"What's with all the floof?" Evie asked.

Vess blushed and twisted slightly as she looked down, inadvertently making her skirts swish to the side. "This… My father—"

"His Grace, the Duke of Pax'Vrell, has decreed that Her Grace, Lady Vessilia Dayne return to his Territory immediately," intoned the Hand, smoothly interrupting Vess.

Evie's expression soured even further.

"Vess? What's going on?" Felix asked. Vess opened her mouth, but the Hand cut her off.

"We shall accompany you all into the Verdant Pass," the Hand continued. Vess wouldn't meet their gaze, and her Spirit felt muddled. "From there, we shall request passage from Setoria via Manaship."

"Very good! We're all here."

Felix glanced over and saw Cal walking down the steps, flanked by Bodie, Yan, Kelgor, and even Thangle for some reason. More Haarguard followed. He even saw Karp and Vivianne among them, the archer and inscriptionist both wearing sharp uniforms of a different shade than the guards. The Lady of Haarwatch moved over the ground like oiled silk, her Body giving her a supernatural grace. Soon, she was climbing the crates laid out by Rafny's apprentices as if they were steps to a stage. Twice as tall as everyone else, Cal turned to take in the entire square, whose steady business had stopped under the weight of so many people of interest. She spread her hands and gave everyone a smile as wide as it was fake.

"Excellent! With this assemblage, there is no threat we cannot vanquish," Cal said loudly as the crowd gathered closer. Felix felt a flicker of unease from her Spirit, rising in time with the curiosity of the masses. "We have been fighting ever since the Eyrie fell. Fighting the Revenants, fighting the redcloaks. All to simply live. Now, as we begin the bare steps toward prosperity, another threat emerges. The brave Haarwatch goes now to face it in the Verdant Pass, alongside our greatest of champions: the Blue-Eyed Fiend!"

Cal gestured to him, and Thangle sent a stream of Mana out of his hands. As if a sunbeam had emerged from behind a cloud, a ray of light suddenly hit Felix like a spotlight from above. The crowd's curiosity and rising fear burst into full-blown excitement, and Felix's exceptional hearing picked out more than a few thrilled voices talking about him. Felix did a half wave. As usual, his Affinity picked out a ripple in the harmonies around him as people's Spirits were moved by his presence. Just as Cal intended.

The spotlight pivoted, focusing attention back on Cal.

"We shall mount up and take our forces into the Verdant Pass and protect our city and Territory!" The crowd cheered, but Cal pushed onward. "All of you are strong and growing stronger, and Haarwatch will never forget what each and every one of you have done to bring us from the brink. Tin or Bronze, Untempered or Journeyman, you are, all of you, heroes."

All at once, the Haarguard stomped their feet and saluted their Lady, and the crowd went wild. Felix was thankfully separated from them by the line of guards that encircled the stack of crates—not because they could have hurt him, but the waves of their emotions battered against his Harmonic senses. He pulled back, closing it off for a moment as Cal climbed down from the impromptu stage.

"Thanks Rafny," she smiled at the smith.

"Don't mention it; you wanted a stage, I can make a stage," Rafny said with a snort. "Plus your equipment's in there. So, have the big guy pass it out."

"Bodie? You hear the lady," Cal said.

Bodie smirked and saluted. "All right, boys and girls! Line up!"

While the big man tossed out breastplates and shields, and Cal returned to talking to her guards, Rafny gestured over to the others. At some point, Elle had come out of the smithy, and she was smiling at the lot of them.

"Evie, Atar, Alister," she said with a nod. "I see you've already picked up your armor. That is good. How do you find it?"

"Comfortable," Atar said, admiring his new battle robes. They were the same black and gray as before, but they were cut slightly differently. They looked reinforced across the abdomen, shoulders, and upper legs. "And the protection built into them is fantastic. I thank you, smith."

"You are very welcome, young mage," Elle said. "And you, Lord Knacht?"

The force mage smiled broadly at the smith. "Alister, please. But yes, my robes are exceptionally well-fitted, and the dueling armor is exceptionally light. How did you make it so flexible?" He opened his blue robes to reveal a pair of greaves, a metal chest piece, and armor going over his right shoulder and arm. It was etched with interlocking lines on each segment and was far more metal than Atar ever wore. The rapier and long dagger at his side reminded Felix that Alister was more a duelist with magic than a wizard.

"All thanks to those Arcids," Elle admitted. "The alloys they were built from were remarkable. The same metals went into your battle robes, Atar, and your set as well, Evie."

Evie tore her eyes from Vess long enough to give the smith a nod. She ran her hands down her leather and metal armor. It looked strong—but was noticeably thinner than say Harn's—and was segmented for flexibility and mobility. She moved her arms a little and pulled a waterskin from her waist. "It's a touch heavy, but I'll get used to it. Damn sight better than my last set."

"I'd hope so; that metal all of you are wearing is likely worth thirty crowns per dram, and the labor twice that," Rafny said.

Evie spit out a mouthful of water. "*Pfaw!* What? How much?"

"Burn me," Atar said, looking at his battle robes. "You charged us so little. Why?"

"Perks of being heroes, I suppose. Though, if you wanna pay full price..." Rafny said, and Elle put a hand on her upper arm.

"Stop teasing them. We were happy to make them, for the

experience if nothing else. But," Elle gestured to her wife. "We have some more for you two."

"Eh, Alister here already got his new sword and dagger. He put his order in a while back, actually, and didn't make me work all night." Rafny reached into a crate that had been set aside, this one far longer and more rectangular. "Here we are."

The Dwarf pulled out a thin metal stave made of dark, umber-colored metal. It was perhaps five feet tall, long enough to assist someone walking but not a staff or anything. She handed it to Atar, and the fire mage's eyes just about popped from his head.

"Highest flame," he whispered. He looked between the stave and Rafny with awe in his expression and Spirit. "This...an earth array?"

"It'll replace that stave you lost, collapses just like the other one, too," Rafny demonstrated, and the five foot stave was suddenly a foot long. She extended it again with a snap of her wrist. "The tip is enchanted with the output of the earth array. Now it can act as your stylus, even on stone or wood."

"Remarkable," Atar said, before regaining his composure and giving the weaponsmith a stoic nod. "My thanks."

"Ooh, ooh, me next!" Evie said, eyeing the item in Rafny's other hand. It was clearly a chain, bladed as her others, and made of a green metal with traceries of silver. She took it gingerly from Rafny and cooed. "Oh it's gorgeous. Does it—?"

"Aye. Made it from that thin construct Felix blew up," Rafny said. *Skeleton?* The thinner Arcid he'd fought had commanded serious strength and a sizable amount of life Mana. Felix peered closer at the chain. "It's a mite shorter than you're used to, but that's just good design. Affix your Will on it."

Evie narrowed her eyes, and the short chain let out a series of clanks as links appeared out of nowhere. She almost squealed in joy, and Felix stared with his Manasight at full burn. He just barely caught a series of glyphs that activated within each link, letting them expand and collapse, similar to his own greaves and vambraces.

"Oh Twin's teeth, this is exciting! Can't wait to try it out!"

"You'll have about twice the range you're used to, at the expense of more weight. I'd suggest practicing a bit more with it —" Rafny explained, but Evie waved it off.

"Just more mass to throw around, far as I care," she said flippantly before grinning. Her Spirit was a bubbling, plucky tune to Felix's ears. "Ooh. Oh, perfect!"

Evie slipped past Felix and leaned into the long crate. She came back up with a set of engraved plates connected by chainmail and leather. "Ouf, this is *heavy*."

"Fool girl, that's why I didn't ask you to pick it up," Rafny grunted, taking the set of armor away from her. It was enameled with white, silver, and blue across the chest and pauldrons. "This is for the Lady Dayne, forged from the Apollyon's flesh and the last of the Scales. As is that."

The last was directed at Evie as she picked up a long, eight-foot long spear. She immediately pivoted and handed the spear to Felix. "Here. Take this and the armor and go fix this, Felix."

"What?" Felix asked as the armor was thrust into his arms as well by the weaponsmith. She was smirking despite the small shoulder slap her wife gave her.

"Fix it," Evie repeated, before turning him around and pushing him toward Vess' carriage. The young woman was surrounded by a few minor nobles who had wormed their way through the crowd, and the Hand was looming nearby.

Fix what, exactly? Change her mind?

Arms full and caught off-guard, Felix let himself get shepherded toward Vess, eventually shrugging off Evie's arms. "Okay! Fine. I'll go talk to her."

He walked the rest of the way, un-pushed but inexplicably nervous.

Why? I'm just talking to Vess. His hands felt sweaty beneath the armor, and the spear wobbled a bit in his grip. *Why is she leaving, though?*

He walked up to the small knot of nobles and tried to keep his face calm and Spirit calmer. Vess at least could hear it. The minor nobles turned, and while the first instantly dismissed him—likely for the common cut of his clothes—the others quickly pulled them and others aside and out of Felix's way. He felt their Spirits quiver and quail under his steady gaze. For once, Felix enjoyed his bit of notoriety.

"Vess, hey, uh." Felix stopped awkwardly in front of the heiress. She was decked out in an ankle-length gown with layered skirts and elegantly embroidered bodice. It—were those sigils? The entire outfit was stitched with an array. *Fascinating.*

"Usually people stare at my face when talking to me, Felix," Vess said. Her gentle tone had a smile in it, but her Spirit was oddly flat.

"Oh sorry. Hey," Felix said, shifting his grip on the armor. It wasn't heavy; it just kept sliding against itself. "So what, ah, what did Reed mean about you leaving? Is he serious?"

Vess hesitated a moment, her eyes flicking back toward the carriage. Darius Reed, the Hand, sat atop it. He wasn't looking at them, but at his level, he certainly didn't have to; the Hand likely had Perception similar to Felix's, if not better. "As my father's Heir, I have duties. Duties that I have not been fulfilling while I've been stuck out here. Duties to my father, and to the people I'm bound to serve."

"What about yourself? What about what you want?" Felix asked.

"I'm nobility, Felix. To be selfish is the path to Ruin. I'll not be another DuFont."

The last was said with the steady sort of conviction he'd come to expect from her. Felix couldn't really argue with her logic, not without sounding like a jerk, so he held out the armor and spear to her. "Rafny and Elle made these for you. For our, ah, expedition."

Vess' gaze lingered on his eyes before glancing at what was in his hands. She gasped, softly.

"Truly? They are Journeyman Tier?" At Felix's nod, she took them from his hands and began inspecting them closer. "Marvelous."

The armor was amazing, Felix agreed. As she laid out each piece, he saw that the plates were heavier than Evie's but not quite the juggernaut thickness of Harn's set. They were inlaid with white and blue enamel, with the silver metal shining through as well in intricate, scrolling patterns along the edge of each piece.

For all of that, other than its durability and protection, it offered little else. The spear, however, was something special. It was marked with twisting dragons along the haft in blue and white, and had a long, leaf-shaped blade at the end. There was an enchantment on it, according to his Eye, an array that focused air Mana atop the spear's edge, letting it stab and slash all the faster.

"It's made of Archid armor and some of my Scales of the Ravager Queen," Felix supplied. He felt a bit more even-keeled talking about weapons instead of feelings. "They both are."

"Reminds me of you," she said.

"The… spear?"

"Straightforward. Effective. Deadly," Vess said as she ran her hands down the haft. "But spears are more than instruments of death. They are tools. They bring food from the hunt." She placed a hand on his. "They protect."

"I—"

"We will be moving soon. Thank the Coldfires for me. I am not to leave my carriage for the length of the journey. It is unfair but—well, it is difficult. Leaving." She met his gaze, and he could see the freckles across the bridge of her nose, almost hidden by her skin tone. Her eyes were warm, like tilled earth, with a ring of gold around the center.

"This is goodbye, then?" Felix asked. He wasn't sad, he just felt an ache. Probably something he ate or—

"Not goodbye," Vess insisted. She smiled, that dimple showing again. "Until we meet again, Felix."

Felix managed a smile. The ache lessened a little. "Until then, Vess."

Without an idea of what else to do, Felix turned and walked away. He only made it a dozen strides, barely halfway to his friends before another presence appeared beside him. The yellow half-cape was hard to mistake as the Hand put two fingers against Felix's shoulder.

"She was never meant to stay here, Fiend," he said. His voice was calm, and his Spirit was without blemish. "Training and her Reveal. The latter is done, and the former I will handle. She leaves for better things, a greater destiny."

Reed met his eyes, and there wasn't any real hatred there. Just conviction.

"For once, Felix, make the smart decision: let her go."

The way down from the city center was uneventful, and the only sound louder than the tap of claws on the road was the clinking of rubble being shifted by dozens of workers.

Evie and the others had pestered him for details, but Felix didn't feel like talking. Within minutes, the call had come to mount up and ride east, to the Sunrise Quarter. Felix had mounted Pit and the others all hopped astride their own avum, and their train of sixty-some men and women rode down the steps into the easternmost Quarter.

The streets weren't clogged with people so much as debris, the terraced platforms and once-exquisite stonework marred by massive gouges, burn marks, and jagged slashes—the evidence of a violent, Skill-fueled brawl. Still, people were out and about, all of them either working to transport materials up to the storage houses or working on excavating the homes all around them.

Felix felt a slight twinge of guilt when he saw the rich mansions on this side of the city, now little more than hovels due to his direct involvement. They had at least been empty when an empowered DuFont and Felix had crashed through them, and later when the Elder-turned-Inquisitor had set fire to the whole city block.

The guilt vanished when he realized none of the people picking apart the fallen mansions were present. Instead, liveried servants leveraged stones bigger than they were, sweating under the summer sun and mounting heat. All of them were dusty and dirty and quite a few were bloodied, as well. Meanwhile, Felix had no doubts that the nobles that owned these plots were sitting comfortably down by the Sunrise Gate, which had been fortified against all the worst the Primordial then the Archon had to throw at the city.

Nobles, he scoffed. He hadn't met many, but the few he had gave them a bad name. Lilian. Dabney. The Hand. Sure, Alister was a good enough guy, had even risked his life for Felix once or twice. And Vess—

Vess is something else entirely. Evie was clearly annoyed that he hadn't told her how their talk went. What did she want him to say? Vess had made her choice, and Felix couldn't really fault her. Wasn't he trying to do the same thing? To be responsible, to protect those who couldn't protect themselves? How could he punch holes in that argument?

People stopped and stared as they passed, like they were in a parade. Fear turned to curiosity, which transformed back into fear when they realized this sizable force was heading into the Verdant Pass. Felix could almost see the gears turning as they regarded the east and the wide, vital fields that stretched beyond the Sunrise Gate. From their heightened position, Felix could just make out the dark woods that enveloped much of the Verdant Pass. The sound of claws on stone increased as a large, piebald avum sidled up next to Pit.

"Talk to me," Evie begged, struggling a bit with her reins. "She comin' with us or not?"

Felix held back a groan, and Pit let out a warning growl that made Evie's avum squawk in alarm. *Stop that. It's fine.* "I don't think so," Felix said. "She's going home."

"Home? To what? Sit in her castle and die from boredom?" Evie squinted her eyes at Felix. "What'd you say to her?"

"What? Like it's my fault?"

"Usually is the man's fault," Evie said.

"True," Alister added.

"Like I said, you should have asked to court her *weeks* ago, Felix," Atar said while rubbing his hairless chin. "She didn't want to wait any longer. Clearly, you missed your chance."

"My—okay, it's not like that. And even if it was, it's not your business," Felix said through a flush.

"Of course it is! Friends meddle in each others' love life. That's what friends are for!" Atar said with a chuckle.

"Oh? How's it going with you two, then?" Felix said, pointing between Atar and Alister. "Have you picked out an apartment together yet?"

"I—I don't know *what* you're talking about!" Atar said indignantly. "We are simply—"

"No, not yet," Alister said, smoothly. He grinned at Atar's incensed stare. "Property values in Haarwatch are a bit shaky right now. Maybe after the Lady has the Territory under better control."

"*Alister*," complained Atar, now flushing himself.

"Oh come off it, Atty," Alister laughed. "It's not like we're trying to hide it, are we?"

"Well, no, but—"

"And clearly, they already know," Alister added. Atar looked at Felix and Evie, who both grinned and nodded. "See?" Alister turned to them and said in a stage whisper. "Atar comes from a backwards place, it seems. Courtships aren't usually announced until the half-year mark down in the Expanse."

"It's simply proper etiquette!" Atar all but screeched, which sent Evie into a fit of laughter.

"Hey, Atar," Felix said, reaching over to pat the man on the back. "It's what friends are for."

They moved quickly, approaching the Sunrise Gate at a solid clip. Felix had to slow Pit down several times as the rambunctious Chimera tried to overtake the avum before them. Merchants crowded near this part of the Quarter, their stalls filled with expensive trinkets and novelties that few had the coin to buy. Folks were far more interested in food, water, and shelter than what silks or spices were brought from the Continental Interior. Still, there were those who browsed the stalls, enough that the makeshift bazaar was a mess of sound and smells. The clatter of talons and jangle of harnesses barely cut through the clamor, yet still their procession was met with the same gasps of excitement and worry.

The Sunrise Gate came into view, a massive metal behemoth, equal to the Wall's own. It was, however, decidedly less magical. His Manasight could pick out agitated flows of power through the structure, overlaid atop the regular flows of the metal and stone itself. Everything being made of Mana made identifying spells trickier, but Felix was getting better and better at it. He could see a few defensive works, such as a shield to protect from minor projectiles and a few more complicated arrays whose purpose weren't entirely obvious. It was made of simple granite and steel, which accounted for its limited enchantments. The material typically defined how many arrays could be inscribed and always determined their potency. As they approached, two burly Hobgoblins in dark Haarguard uniforms began turning a massive winch.

The gates groaned, slipping open as the huge wheel turned. Chains rattled slightly, and the gates—engraved with mountains and a rising sun above them—swung open. Beyond was a continuation of the stone-lined road, following the curve of the Ianus River that breached the wall here as well. It had its own gate, a portcullis that kept the water flowing but prevented anything bigger than a baseball from entering. With a rattling bang, the gates fully opened and revealed a Naiad astride an extremely ugly-looking avum the color of mud.

"Follow," Zara said before wheeling her mount around and trotting into the meadow.

They did, Harn and Kelgan close behind at the head of the procession. The meadow just outside the city was filled with lush grasses and gentle knolls—flat enough for defenders to see across—before it terminated at a line of dark, temperate trees. As they moved, they picked up speed until their convoy was fairly flying across the expanse.

Felix could smell the waters of the Ianus, the wildflowers and crushed grasses beneath them, and the wide, swirling scent of the wind itself. Evie, despite Vess' decision, was grinning at the speed and thrill of the run. Alister too, though Atar was barely holding onto his own. Felix took a deep breath as Pit stretched his legs in a run that more than matched the avum. It had been too long since either of them had been out of the city, and the world felt alive in a way it never did around tamed stone and wood.

Tamed—? Where did that come from?

From out of the sky, just at the edge of his Perception, a brightly-colored bird swooped down. Faster than Felix could blink, it had alighted on his forearm: a jewel-colored kingfisher that regarded him with a single, wide eye.

"Keru," Felix greeted one of Zara's familiars. Companion, maybe, though she'd never confirmed it. "What's up?"

The kingfisher hopped several times until it was atop Felix's shoulder. "I've a message from Zara: you are to break away at the treeline," it said in a piping voice just loud enough for him to hear it. "Utilize your Stealth and cover your path. Good luck, and may the Harmonies smile down on you."

The bird flew away without another word.

Felix exchanged glances with Pit before quietly relaying the message to the others.

Darius sat next to the carriage driver while they were within the city, watching for dangers from her "friends." The Hand hadn't yet been able to anticipate the wild things she had grown close to, especially not that chain-wielder. The Fiend was less of a concern, but his power alone made him a threat to be considered. Darius believed the boy understood and accepted the way things had to be; he wasn't an idiot, despite the Hand's original opinions.

He has accepted the will of fate. Darius let out a pleased rumble from his chest as he climbed off the coachman bench and down onto the side of the large carriage. They had reached the forest now, and with the cover of the trees he let his guard diminish just a touch. If anything were to attack now, it would be monsters or perhaps redcloaks; nothing the Apprentice Tiers couldn't handle.

He opened the carriage door. "Destiny rolls onward, Lady Dayne. In a few short weeks we shall see the spires of Setoria and then—"

Darius' eyes widened, and his powerful Body began to shake. He wasn't sure if it was anger or terror.

The carriage was empty save for a neatly folded dress.

CHAPTER FIFTEEN

Up close, the forest of the Verdant Pass spoke well of its name. It was lush and green, filled with ferns and fronds and all manner of plants. The trees themselves were huge, thick, tall and crowded close together. Felix could see green-gold life Mana coursing through their trunks, descending deep into the ground. Into the underbrush, the grasses, and moss. Only the stones of the roadway, farther and farther away, only they were quiet. Dull.

Strange.

His senses could also pick out various small creatures, insects and rodents mostly, all well below level ten. It was a divergence from the Foglands, where the lowest level creature he'd ever encountered had been level thirteen, and the average was closer to twenty.

Does that mean anything? In games, there were areas of maps that were higher-leveled than others, but that was because it was all designed by people to be that way. According to everything he'd been told, the Continent and the System existed together organically. So why were some places more dangerous than others?

Mana, he abruptly realized. *More Mana, higher levels, stronger monsters.* Mana was just a different expression of the System's own energy, a byproduct of the Harmonies that created and maintained the universe. At least according to Zara.*There's a lot of Mana here... but was there more in the Foglands?*

Felix shook himself. None of that mattered. Not at that moment. Their group had drifted toward the back of the procession, letting the guards and Vess' carriage move on further ahead. Once they hit the rear, Felix concentrated.

Abyssal Skein!

Some of his friends had Stealth as a Skill, but not all of them, and there was little to be done for the giant bird mounts they rode. Instead, Felix activated one of his least-used Skills, one he'd earned in the Void.

"What is—" Alister started, but Felix shushed him.

<Let it wash over you and keep low,> Felix ordered via handsign.

The Void crawled out of his core, so very unlike the burning song of his Mana. A feeling of nothing swept between him and the world around him, neither cold or hot, light or dark. Despite his Willpower and Alacrity—the Harmonic Stat for mental feats of strength—the Skill fought against him.

Abyssal Skein is level 37!

Felix buckled down until he felt his Skein wind its way around Pit, following the course of their bond. In a fit of inspiration, he extended it along the threads of connection between himself and his friends. The oaths they had sworn him.

Abyssal Skein is level 38!

Power surged, the song of the Void a hungry quiescence that swallowed them all whole. Atar gasped. Ahead, a Haarguard looked back in alarm, but his eyes slid over where they stood. He turned and kept moving forward.

Felix felt his Abyssal Skein slithering over his friends and even their mounts, blending them into the environment. The Void stealth Skill wasn't active camouflage or a light distortion, though he'd thought it was at one point; instead he suspected the Void was acting as a thin barrier that faded them from the Corporeal Realm entirely. He could hear it, the Void, a familiar non-song that roared like the silence between dusk and dawn.

Abyssal Skein is level 39!

...

Abyssal Skein is level 43!

And there's the confirmation that I'm on the right path, Felix smiled to himself. He gestured to his friends.

<You're under my Skill. Keep close and move slowly> he signed. He couldn't speak, having to hold his breath to keep Abyssal Skein active, so it was the best way to communicate. His perfect recall and increased Intelligence helped a lot in shoring up his communication skills, even if he wasn't completely sure how to say everything in the Continent's version of sign language.

The four of them headed north as Zara led the rest deeper east. At first, it was simply putting distance between their two groups, but then he spotted the bright form of Keru flitting through the leaves. The kingfisher wove through the branches above, stopping every few feet to stare at them pointedly. Felix got the message and followed.

Before long, they reached a craggy cliff face where several others were waiting in the arboreal shadows.

"Harn!" Evie said, disrupting the Abyssal Skein and causing the entire Skill to unravel. The Void slipped back into his core with a slimy lurch, and they were revealed. Felix pulled in a long, gasping breath as the Skill punched into him.

Harn was unfazed, but the others with him were less stoic.

"Gah! Where'd they come from?"

"Blighted Night! That's the Fiend!"

"Hush, you idiot! We know!"

The five others were each wearing the dark uniform of the Haarguard. They lingered, unknown for a half second before his Keen Mind provided the answer. They were the guards he'd met at the training center, the ones who had failed to defeat the Steel Golems. The lot of them goggled Felix and crew, each atop their own mount, fully kitted out and packed with supplies.

"Harn?" Felix said, question in the name.

The warrior shrugged a single shoulder. "I told Cal I'd be going with you, and she insisted on sending...reinforcements to help with your Quest."

"Fodder," Evie snorted.

"I figured you'd stick with Zara," Felix said, ignoring Evie's outburst. He hopped down off Pit's back. "I'm glad to have you, man."

"Just don't go falling into any death mazes again, eh?" Harn grunted. "I've sworn off death mazes."

"Blue-Eyed Fiend." The leader of the Haarguard group bowed. He was a Human named Kylar, sandy brown hair and thin mustache offset by a lingering black eye. "It is an absolute honor."

"Oh, no, no," Felix grabbed the man by the shoulders and straightened him. "None of that. I already have to deal with it from these guys. Call me Felix."

Atar and Evie smiled at each other. *How nice, coming together to mock me. Glad I'm a unifying force.*

Surprisingly, anger flashed across Kylar's face and Spirit but was quickly suppressed. "Very...very well. Felix. We were sent with you to assist on your mission, whatever that may be."

"Sure. Glad to have the help," Felix lied. He'd rather have his core group alone, but he'd been outranked, apparently. "You're all fully recovered from your training bout this morning?"

Kylar stiffened slightly, and the shield warrior Vyne rubbed surreptitiously at his shoulder. "We are in perfect fighting form, sir."

"Right," Felix turned to Harn. The man stood in front of the craggy cliff face, inspecting it. "What's the plan here?"

"Plan? Easy." Harn grunted. "We skirt the city and use the mines." He waved something in his hand, a cast metal object that fairly shone with Mana. "Cal gave me a ward key. Gonna get us into the mines and out again just shy of the Wall Quarter. Easy as kickin' a Chimera. No offense."

Pit raised his hackles at Harn before turning his nose away in clear offense.

"This is the mine here? It's hidden?" Felix asked, and Harn nodded.

"Not a mine, though. Just a hole in the ground the mines linked up to accidentally. Wards keep the riffraff out and the city secure, especially now that Cal's got 'em back online." Harn waved the object in his hand, and the impression of rock faded, revealing a wide open hole, perhaps twenty feet tall and fifteen feet wide. Felix's eyes picked out a path leading farther in, his Manasight tracing the darkness easily enough.

Atar looked into the dark, eyeing it with some trepidation. "We'll all fit? Mounts and everything?"

"Eh," Harn shrugged. "It'll be fine. Or it won't. No use worryin' about it."

"You instill me with the greatest of confidence," Atar deadpanned. Harn clapped him on the back, nearly sending the mage sprawling.

"Glad to help, Sparky."

"All right, then let's get going," Felix said. "Everyone, off the mounts, we move quickly."

The Haarguard were already dismounted and they simply moved closer to the cave entrance, while his friends clambered down. Packs were loaded onto avum, and Pit gave Felix an excited headbutt in his shoulder. It was time to begin.

"Leaving? Without me?"

Felix looked up, confused and surprised. A figure emerged from the forest shadows atop a pale avum, wearing enameled armor and holding a blue-white spear. A dimple creased her cheek as their eyes met.

"Vess! How—?" Evie exclaimed, moments before a voice like thunder shook the trees around them. Literally shook them.

"*FIEND!*"

"We should flee," Vess said and her smile turned a tad brittle. "Now."

The cavern was completely dark and the ground rough and uneven. Neither feature stopped them, as most of them had Night Eye, a Mana Skill that allowed them to see in the dark. Aside from Vess and Felix, all of their eyes burned a bright, chemical green in the black. Vess utilized her Elemental Eye, which made her irises swirl with a combination of Mana colors.

For Felix, his Manasight served a similar purpose. With it, he could see the strings of Mana that composed everything in the world. Rocks were collections of earth Mana, threaded with various metal Mana types, and even the air and shadows swirled with their own magic. It was everywhere, but it wasn't uniform.

For one, even strands of the same Mana type varied in their coloration. Potency and concentration of Mana meant the colors were richer, more saturated. For earth Mana, that meant where the rocks touched, they were a deeper brown, and where the stones were exposed, it faded to a dustier hue. Even the air was a mixture, white-green swirls interspersed with fainter blue motes and—at least in here—undercut by thick wafts of gray-black shadow.

Despite the chaos of color and movement, Felix had grown used to his Manasight. It let him look at the world as a series of contours and lights, reminding him every time that he was in a world of magic.

"So you gave him the slip?" Evie asked Vess. Her voice was low, but it couldn't help but carry in the caverns.

"Is now really the best time for this conversation?" Atar asked, pointing all around them. "What if the Hand hears you and comes after?"

"Caverns are warded against sight and sound, Atar," Harn said from the front. "No one outside the caves are gonna hear you."

"Oh, well—"

"It's the monsters inside here that you should worry about," Harn continued.

"Something up ahead!" hissed one of the Haarguard. *Kikri*, Felix thought. *The Elf.*

"Name, Type, number, and level," Harn demanded.

"Water Beetles, Insect Type," she reported. "At least twelve of them. All level thirty plus."

Small bits of water, life, blood, and earth Mana congealed into the form of chihuahua-sized beetles. Horns jutted from their faces, and their bodies were covered in a dense exoskeleton. They skittered forward along the ground, quickly closing the distance.

"Stone's own, those are strong bugs," Nevia hissed. Purple-white Mana swirled atop her staff as she turned in the direction Kikri faced.

"Atar, Alister," Felix said. "Take care of them."

The two mages nodded and stepped forward, the latter unsheathing the thin silver rapier at his waist.

"Just two? That's a lot of enemies for—" Kylar started, but was interrupted by two brilliant bursts of fire and force. Felix watched as the Water Beetles were annihilated by Imbued Sparkbolts and kinetic lances. It was over in seconds.

"You conjured those quickly," Alister said in approval. "No Crown?"

"This many Sparkbolts is simple now, even without the Crown of Ignis." Atar tilted his nose into the air. "I noticed your blade work has improved as well."

"Kind of you to say, though I think I only got six of them."

"Five," Atar corrected, his face shifting to a grin. "I took care of the rest."

"Tch."

The Haarguard were clearly impressed, but they didn't waste time. The team kept moving forward, stepping nimbly through the charred and smeared remains of the Water Beetles.

"Are there many monsters in here?" Felix asked Harn.

The man shrugged. "Some, same as any place. The ward on the front doesn't stop things from coming in, so who knows. But we won't have to worry about 'em for long."

The further they walked, the colder it became. While above it was the height of summer, now it felt like a clammy cellar, cold and wet. It also grew darker. The Mana was being leached from the grounds, not in huge amounts, but enough to dim the threads of vapor that thrummed through everything.

"Mana is thin here. I assume we're close?" Atar said. The others were all panting hard, though it hadn't been a tough trek. "It's like the air's too thin to breathe."

Harn grunted and pulled out the crest. It was like a flashlight in the dim surroundings, small enough to fit in his palm and stamped with some shape. Felix caught a flash from a point farther down the path.

Wards.

"We're close. Come," Harn said and led the way.

Soon enough, they came to a clear demarcation in the cavern. The rough floor gave way to smoother stone, and a few cross-braces were visible in the gloom. As the ward key in his hand passed near it, the invisible barrier became a riot of colors, like an oil spill. Reaching into his pouch, Harn pulled free a piece of jerky and held it up. When everyone was watching him, he threw it into the ward, where it was burned up in a vivid rainbow display.

"Don't touch it," he warned. Then, he tossed a loose rock at the ward, and it passed through without effect. "Keyed to living creatures, or once-living. Keeps the monsters contained." Full helm and all, it was impossible to tell if Harn was smiling, at least for the others. Felix—and likely Vess and Evie—felt his Spirit spark with amusement as he looked at their faces. "I got the key, so c'mon."

Another wave of his hand, and the rainbow shimmer parted like a curtain. Felix sent the Haarguard first, followed quickly by the mages and Evie. Vess lingered a tad as she passed him.

Pit cooed at her and nuzzled against Vess' shoulder. She smiled and scratched his jawline, which made him coo all the more.

"I am sorry for the deception, Felix," she said. In his Manasight, her eyes swirled with color, but they still clearly pinched at the edges as she gave him a nervous smile. "It was necessary. Darius is a… dedicated servant. He would have discovered—"

"Listen, it's okay," Felix said, finding himself unable to stop his grin. "I'm, uh, I'm just glad you're here."

The Heiress of Pax'Vrell, daughter of the Duke, vanished for a moment. In her place, Vess smiled deeper, her cheek dimpling. "I'm glad I'm here, too."

"Alright, enough jabberin'. Can't keep the wards down all day," Harn complained. The four of them—Pit and avum included—moved through the curtain of light, followed swiftly by Harn. "Let's keep movin'. And no talkin'. Can't have you wakin' up all the monsters down here."

"Wait, there's more?" Kylar said with surprise. "I thought we were inside the city mines?"

"Yeah. Didn't I mention it?"

"Monsters are everywhere; we can deal," Felix said, moving to the front again. "Harn, is it a straight path back to the surface?"

"Eh, more or less. Can be confusin' at times." Harn shrugged.

"Sure. You take point with me, then. Evie and Vess, cover our flanks. Pit, Atar, Alister, take up the rear. Keep the mounts in the middle, and the Haarguard can cover any other angles from there." Felix pointed at each of them in turn before spinning back around. "Eyes open, ears sharp."

Despite the danger of mine and monster, as he walked to the front, Felix had a big, dumb grin on his face.

CHAPTER SIXTEEN

"Where? Where is she!?" the Hand demanded. He loomed before Zara like a bull ready to gore. The procession of guards and warriors had ground to a halt in a low dell to the south of the official road through the Verdant Pass. Everyone shied away, pulling back from the unsheathed power of the Hand of Pax'Vrell's core. His potency crackled in the shade. "I know you have her, Sorcerer!"

"Calm yourself, Darius. I do not have your ward," Zara said, careful to keep her Spirit veiled by layers of her Intent. She gestured around herself, clearly indicating her person and the empty emerald dell.

"But you know where she's gone?" he asked.

"Only that she is safe," Zara said as Keru alighted on her shoulder. The blue and yellow kingfisher fluffed his feathers at the burly Adept Tier, and Zara raised a finger to calmly stroke his breast. "I would think that is your only concern, no?"

"The Continent is wild, and this corner is wilder than many. I'll not have her gallivanting with that—" Darius stopped himself and took a steadying breath. "My charge has gone missing, and there is no safety if it is not with me. That is my duty."

"Your charge left of her own free Will, yes?" Zara asked.

Darius narrowed his eyes.

"Perhaps she enters dangerous waters, but that is her Choice, as well. You can best protect her by preventing the Grandmaster Inquisitor from coming down on her head, eh?"

"Grandmaster—?" Reed glanced back, then at Zara. "Damn it, Sorcerer. You'll answer to the Duke if she is harmed."

"Were we not all staring down the gullet of a Chimera, I would find that compelling," Zara scoffed. "As it is, the retaliation of the Inquisition will dwarf any vengeance your liege may levy."

"You speak truly? A Grandmaster is coming here?" The slight tremors of fear had finally begun to invade the rhythm of his Spirit. "To avenge its fallen members? That is not the province of a Grandmaster."

"It is when the Master Inquisitor is killed, and a Primoridal has run amok as a result," Zara said, putting some fire in her words. "It is when the last of the Inquisition races to contact her. She is coming, and there is but one thing stopping her." She tapped a finger on the Hand's chest. "Your Choice, here and now. Do you choose to help or to obstruct, and by so doing, doom your ward to a sure death?"

Darius Reed's expression was a thunderhead. He stood there, looming over her for several moments, before receding ever so slightly. "You put me between the blade and block, Zara Cyrene. I'll not forget it." He gestured imperiously for her to continue their journey. "I will end this threat, and in turn, you will promise that Lady Dayne will return with me to Pax'Vrell. Agreed?"

"Agreed," Zara said, careful to keep the triumph from her Spirit. "Everyone! We have arrived."

There was some murmured confusion, and no few sidelong glances at the Hand, but the guards returned. Zara stepped closer to a small hillock at the center of the dell, covered only by long grasses and wildflowers.

"I don't understand," Vivianne said. She was a dwarf with dark red hair and hard lines. A suit of mail and leather covered her despite the series of styluses at her waist. "We are chasing the redcloaks. They are leagues ahead of us."

"I suggest we let the lady speak. Everyone! Form up and listen!" Kelgan said. The guard shuffled forward on their mounts, arranging themselves in a semi-circle around the hillock. He leaned on his dark spear in its stirrup sheath. "Zara?"

"Thank you, Lieutenant Kelgan," Zara said before gesturing to the hillock behind her. "The redcloaks are ahead of us, and though the influx of monsters has slowed them, they have still passed beyond the Iron Gate. It is too far for us to catch them. At least, without help."

A song welled from her core, one that had been drilled into her for decades but never used. It spilled out into the dell, drifting hauntingly through the thick, shadowed forest. Shock and awe flowed around her as the song touched each of the guards, sweeping through their senses like an invigorating breeze. The song parted around the obstinate boulder of disdain that was the Hand, but it was no matter. The song of earth and ancient, Lost ways still served its purpose.

The hillock split apart.

Two stone plinths rose from the broken sod, no higher than a span, graven idols of a man and a woman at their tops. They were broken and cracked by time and weather, worn so smooth that all features were gone. Between the plinths, the earth sundered, splitting from itself until only a yawning, diagonal fissure remained. Ten feet long and two men across, it belched air scented with the deep secrets of the earth.

"We're going in there?" Kelgan asked. He clutched his spear tight and his reins tighter. "Avum won't fit though."

"Everyone dismount," Zara ordered. "And take the binding cloth from your saddlebags. You must cover their eyes and walk your mounts for the duration."

"Blindfolds?" Karp asked incredulously. He tugged nervously at his ginger beard. "What's in there?"

"Danger, among other things," Zara said, leading the way. Grouse, blindfolded and calm, followed behind her until the darkness swallowed them both.

"Damn Sorcerers," the Hand muttered before he descended.

Slowly, one-by-one, they all followed.

They trudged through the dark, navigating the winding tunnels of the deep mines quickly but not without caution. Their line of sight was limited—even with Night Eye—due to the many blind corners. Felix, not possessing the Night Eye Skill, was at a bit of a loss around the wards, but once they were far enough beyond them, the ambient Mana returned to its former levels.

The wards, and their key, fascinated him. They were clearly built with a way to pull ambient Mana into their formations, though Felix wasn't able to find their hidden sigaldry. It was likely buried by shaped stone or something similar, and he hadn't the time to search. Regardless, it was an interesting detail, as few workings in Haarwatch utilized an ambient Mana siphon. The Manalamps in the streets relied on a steady flow of tiny monster cores to function, which was why the lamplighters went about turning them on and off each dusk and dawn. Even Hector's incredible work required cores. The few places Felix had seen siphons were on either antique creations or the Archon's workings. He shook his head. The Archon was a special case and was working with a totally different form of sigaldry.

The common thread of antique constructs and creations was interesting, however. Was the technique hard to reproduce? He had seen it on the orichalcum Wall, and that was clearly a product of an ancient precursor civilization—the Nym. But Felix had also noted a simpler siphon array on the brass lamps in Zara's mansion. Were they ancient relics as well? Or more limited reproductions? If they *could* reproduce those effects, why not use them in the Manalamps on the city streets?

"It's about the expense," Alister explained softly and a little breathlessly when Felix asked. They were wading through a wide underground river, knee-deep and extremely cold. "It-it would cost the city thousands upon thousands of crowns to have each of their Manalamps properly inscribed, not to mention the... intangibles." He took a shaky breath and kept moving, the cold clearly affecting him. "The array you're speaking of is one learned only by the upper echelons of the Inscription Guild, and they do not accept money in the traditional sense. They trade in secrets and knowledge."

"Okay, I guess that makes sense," Felix said. For him, the cold was invigorating, likely coming from some glacial source higher in the mountains, and it barely impacted his Song of Absolution. Pit was not a fan. His Cold Resistance, on the other hand, had jumped by two whole levels during their crossing.

We have to train that up with my Mantle sometime. He thought about all the things he needed to do. *We haven't had a lot of time to train together, huh? Soon as this quest is done, we'll focus hard on that.*

Pit trilled in dimmed enthusiasm and sent sense images of his freezing limbs.

It's good for you. Makes you stronger and puts hair on your chest.

Pit looked down at his own chest, his horse-sized head batting into his breastplate. Felix smiled and ruffled the Chimera's ears. "Then those brass lamps were expensive, huh?" he said to Alister.

"Un-unimaginably so, if you saw so many," Alister agreed, teeth chattering. "Unsurprising, if Zara is as old as she seems. A Master Tier and a Sorcerer to boot, she's likely stockpiled quite the collection."

"Too b-bad the Master Inquisitor blew it all up," Atar said bitterly through his own chills. His dark robes were dragging low, making it even harder for him to move. "I would have loved to see her library—Ah! Something touched me!"

A series of explosive splashes followed as Atar hurled no less than seven Sparkbolts into the water. Fire Mana was almost instantly quenched by the water and ice Mana that flowed deeply in the river, but in the light show, a few yard-long shapes slithered around them.

Voracious Eye!

Name: Veelo
Type: Beast
Level: 17
HP: 244/244
SP: 189/194
MP: 77/77
Lore: Born in freshwater rivers, Veelo revel in glacial streams when younger. As they grow older, they require greater room for their massive sizes. Their scales sharpen with age and level, becoming deadly once they have pushed beyond level 30.
Strength: More Data Required
Weakness: More Data Required

"They're just veelo, guys," Felix said. They were basically big eels. He'd fought some before, when they were a lot larger and meaner. "Level 17. They're harmless."

"Ah! One just bit my leg!" Atar cried out. His voice echoed loudly in the cavern and his avum squawked in fear.

"Maybe because you just threw fire at them, you idiot!" Evie snapped, just as loud.

"Quiet, all of you," growled Harn. He was a bit shorter than Felix, and the water was pushing closer to his middle thigh, but it didn't slow him a whit. He waded through the swarm of Veelo and released a single pulse of his near-Adept Spirit. The Veelo scattered. "You think a few Veelo are all you have to worry about?"

Pit's Cold Resistance is level 29!

The Haarguard, through all of this, were remarkably even-keeled. They seemed entirely too nervous to contribute much to the chaos, which was for the best. The mines passed with little else in the way of excitement, though grumbling between Evie and Atar was always at the edge of breaking into another fight. Alister and Vess acted as buffers, more often than not.

"How'd you do that pulse thing? With your Spirit," Felix asked Harn as they navigated the sloping tunnels. The ground was growing more even, better-traveled. They were close to the entrance. "I've noticed some powerful people have these auras to them, where their Spirit Aspect is affecting the world. I just can't figure out how to do it."

"Hrm," Harn pondered. He ducked below an overhang, pulling short on his reins to have his mount do the same. It was a dark bird, perhaps forest green in the daylight, but in the mines it looked dark as Pit's face. "Hasn't Zara been teaching you?"

"Some, but not enough," Felix said. Pit growled sympathetically. "She has been busy with other things, apparently."

"You sound frustrated," he said.

"I am."

"Too busy. Huh. Of all people, I'd figure she'd be bendin' over backwards to help you," he mused, his strange, frog-mouthed great helm tilted to the side. What was left unsaid were the words: *to help an Unbound.*

"You'd think so, yeah. I dunno. I'm strong, and my Skill levels are high, and my combat training has only been getting more and more involved." Felix had kept his voice low, but he lowered it further as he and Harn took more of a lead. "But am I enough to face the Archon?"

"Are any of us?" Harn grunted right back at him. Felix's head tilted back. "You're takin' too much on your shoulders, kid. You're not alone. We may not be enough by ourselves, but we've proven several times now that we're damn hard to kill all together."

Felix laughed at that.

"As for the Spirit stuff, let's go over that once we're outta the city limits," Harn suggested. "It's a tricky technique to use, let alone perfect."

"That's fair," Felix said. "Thanks, Harn."

"Don't mention it." Harn stopped him with a hand on his shoulder. "Truly. Don't mention it in front of the squirt. She's on my case about her core enough as it is."

Felix grinned and crossed his heart with his finger. "Secret's safe with me."

Harn rapped on his chest with a gauntlet and kept walking. Soon after that, they emerged into the upper levels of the mine and quickly found their way into the late afternoon sunshine. The mine was located at the very edge of the Dust, relatively close to their old warehouse base, but not where he'd fought the Inquisition weeks ago. It also had the benefit of being inactive and fully warded. Harn's ward key let them pass out of the mouth of the mine with another parting of shimmering light.

"Ah, blessed sun! Glorious heat!" Atar whisper-shouted, spreading his arms and robes out beneath the summer sun.

"Gotta admit, I'm happy to get outta the dark," Evie said, and Vess murmured in agreement. The heiress met Felix's gaze briefly before turning back to inspect her saddle.

"Where to now?" Kylar asked before being shushed by one of his companions. "What? I can't ask?"

"Now, we get moving," Felix said and pointed westward. "We're headed for the Wall and the forest beyond."

"The—" Kylar started before choking on the word. "The *Foglands*?"

"Exciting, right? Bit less interesting since the fog went away, but

I hear a lot stronger monsters have started popping up," Evie said with a sharp smile, and the majority of the group paled.

"Enough," grunted Harn. "We're moving."

They moved through town as quietly as a bunch of folks on giant birds could, keeping to back streets and ruined byways as the sun tilted west. The shadows grew longer by the minute, which was helpful, as was the near-abandoned state of the Wall Quarter. Only a few, centrally located shops, taverns, and inns were functioning after the Apollyon smashed them apart like a kaiju movie reject. It was a far greater challenge, however, to cross the Wall unnoticed.

The Fiend's Legion were stationed around the Rent, all but filling the gap and carefully patrolling on the other side. Felix watched them for nearly an hour, realizing they were taking things far more seriously since the monster horde attacked. He would have been almost proud of them had they not been in his way.

"Okay, so what's the plan?" Felix asked. "The floor is open to suggestions."

"Can we go...over the Wall?" Davum asked, his chin jutting out at the glowing orichalcum. "You can fly right? That's… that's what I heard."

Felix nodded. "You're not wrong, but it's pretty flashy. I wouldn't be able to get everyone over the Wall without being seen. I could use Abyssal Skein, but with so many eyes and bodies clogging the Rent, I don't know if we'll get through without bumping into someone."

"Ah."

"What about your rocks?" Evie suggested.

"My rocks?" Felix asked.

"Yeah, the scripted rocks you made," Evie said, miming as if she were carving into a stone. "The boom rocks."

"Oh. *Oh*," Felix said, catching on. *She means my grenades.* Felix had a number of his crude, inscribed grenades in his pack. Perhaps too many, but they'd been useful before. Felix still hadn't figured out a way to make them in a way that anyone could use one; as much of a tactical advantage that held, Felix was almost glad. The idea of everyone having access to explosives was… disconcerting at best. For now, each grenade took a significant amount of Mana to "arm" then a thread of said Mana to follow it as it was thrown, to ignite it. That meant the Skill Mana Manipulation was necessary for anyone who wanted to use them. In the group, Atar, Alister, Harn, and Felix had the Skill, though he'd been trying to teach Vess and Evie.

Of the new folk, he wasn't sure. He made a mental note to get their full list of Skills and general capabilities.

"Okay. That's a good idea. What's your plan, though?" he asked.

Evie laid it out, and no one had any real objections. Soon enough, she had dropped into Stealth and all but ran up the Wall. Her ability to alter her own mass let her do some pretty amazing things, despite not having the stats or Skills to run up a wall. While she ran, a grenade was tucked into her bandolier of knives, and Felix maintained a stream of Mana vapor connecting him to the grenade despite the distance. It took a huge amount of Mana to manage what they were doing but, well, Felix had it. Why not use it?

Through the thread, he could feel when she hurled it off the top of the Wall, angling it to the north. Felix gritted his teeth and held on. His Mana dropped dozens of points by the second, but it was holding. Barely.

So far away, he thought. He had to keep the vision of his thread constant, letting his Mana pulse from his channels at a steady rate. Felix felt like taffy, pulled and twisted as it flew, until he felt the scripted stone land with a dull thud. Evie landed at his side only moments later, and he relaxed.

The vapor thread twisted, igniting the sigaldry.

A muted boom sounded in the near distance, followed by a crackling, secondary discharge of violent force and lightning. The Legion exploded in a flurry of activity that was almost comedic. A large portion of them stumbled over themselves, caught absolutely flat-footed by the detonation and rushed toward the source of the disturbance without a single look back.

"See? Easy," Evie said.

Distracted, the Legion was easy to slip past, especially with Felix's Abyssal Skein covering most of them for good measure. He left Evie and Harn out of it, the two of the most capable at stealth in the group—ironically, considering Harn's big, bulky armor.

The treeline was simple to reach at that point.

They had begun.

CHAPTER SEVENTEEN

Stepping into the Foglands was like walking into another world. Again. Magic swirled around him and thrummed beneath his feet, as if the Mana composing the world was alive here. Every tree shone brighter than even those in the Verdant Pass, every rock and flower and crawling vine—

Corrosive Strike!

A Vinesnake, level 26, splattered against the trunk of a velbore tree. His acid ate into the remains and the tree itself with a loud sizzle, boring a handful of uneven holes.

"Watch yourselves," Felix cautioned the rest. "There's likely a lot more where this came from."

His party nodded and kept moving forward through the trees. The Haarguard exchanged looks and began working as a five-man team, sweeping ahead and clearing their path before advancing. On top of that, they were leading the avum as everyone else had dismounted once they had hit the denser parts of the forest. Felix was impressed. His friends, meanwhile, walked with the casual grace of the strong.

Strong enough to handle everything the Foglands throws at us? He doubted that, but his friends didn't exactly share his concerns.

"Place is so weird without the fog," Evie was saying. She had climbed another velbore tree, distinct with its dark purple leaves and smooth brown bark. "I can see so far."

"You've been here before, right?" Alister asked from the base of the tree. He was poking his rapier at a bush with blue flowers and red thorns. "Right before the fog lifted?"

"Yeah." Evie hopped down off the high branch, turning in a neat flip before landing with a flex of her knees. "Before and right after. Didn't get to enjoy the walk back much."

Felix winced. That was right after her sister Magda died. Saving him.

Vess walked by and clasped the chain fighter around her shoulder and squeezed, once. "Let us keep moving. There is not much light left."

"Truth. And we don't wanna get stuck in the open after dusk," Harn growled as he plowed ahead. He was by far more familiar with the Foglands, and they were following the path they had taken from Shelim previously.

"What happens after dusk?" Davum asked nervously.

"It gets dark," Harn grunted, disappearing into the underbrush.

The Orc paused, unsure whether the warrior was joking or not. Atar passed close by, leaning on his metal stave.

"Dark is when the *real* monsters come out," the fire mage said with a gravelly voice.

Davum paled and looked back at his friends as Atar walked away. The mage's Spirit rollicked with amusement. Felix rolled his eyes and focused ahead.

Harn wasn't lying when he said the dark was worse, and Atar wasn't wrong about the monsters. Felix had spent many nights out there, hiding in trees and hoping nothing noticed him while the sun had set. He was far stronger than he was the last time he was in the Foglands, and he had an entire group of people at his back. They could do this.

They pushed an hour farther into the woods, the trees stretching taller as the ground became more and more treacherous. Ravines tore up the land, narrow defiles and shallow gullies at first, but the breaks would become chasms in a few more miles, according to Harn. He had scouted some of the area during his exodus, though that had been low on his priority list at the time. They had to get past the ravines, up through one mountain range, down through some more forest before hitting another mountain range. Shelim, the ruined city, was in the valley beyond that.

And the Temple is beyond yet another *mountain.* He shook his head. *If the trek is this difficult now, no wonder people got lost when the fog enchantment was active.*

"How long until Shelim?" Felix asked as they crossed another narrow gully. The avum, to his surprise, took to the rocky ground without issue.

"Eh, three weeks, if we take it slow? There's a lot of forest mixed with these mountains," Harn said. "Without the monsters, it'd be a sight faster, but who knows what's out here. This much magic condensed into an area and the number of manifestations and evolutions that are possible seem endless."

"So Mana level does affect monsters?" Felix asked.

"Of course, why—" Harn stopped himself. "Right. Yeah, more Mana in an area, the weirder the beasts get."

"I've noticed it's thicker here than in Haarwatch, the Pass, or the mines." Felix observed. "Do you know why it varies?"

"Gods? I don't know, kid. I'm just a man with an axe," Harn said. He used said axe to cut through a thatch before him, clearing the way with a single chop. "Leave the postulatin' to Zara and the other quill-pushers."

Felix pondered the energies around him, so vivid the time of day barely mattered. He could get lost in the flows of it, and distantly Felix could hear the song that sat beyond it. The Grand Harmony, the timeless vibration that animated the whole of the universe, according to Zara.

It was beautiful, complex, and all-encompassing. The vibrations reverberated through everything, including himself, and Felix could hear strains of it in his core. There it was countered by an atonal, arhythmic droning, an… anti-music that seemed to be everything the Harmony was not. Both sounds had taken root deep within him, opposing songs that sang with every spin of his ring cores.

And then he felt an echo of that same opposition, what he called Dissonance.

It was faint, but it was there. In the Foglands.

Vess watched Felix as he prowled through the dense forest, his shoulders tight and his concentration on something she couldn't sense. She could, however, hear echoes of him in the air. He left them wherever he went, like footprints of sound from his Aspects. It was a heady music, both harmony and something more dangerous.

+1 AFI

They passed trees and moss and stone upthrust from the earth, each humming with Mana to her Elemental Eye. It was limited, far more so than Felix's own Manasight, but unlike Manasight, it did not obfuscate the surface she looked at. According to Felix, it had been very easy to get lost in the flows of Mana, enough that actually seeing objects became difficult. Elemental Eye allowed her to see the traces of magic upon the surface of the world, the elements themselves. Typically, they simply glowed, traces of wind and water and fire tangling and separating in complex patterns.

In the Foglands, however, the elements *burned.*

"Shelim?" Kikri, the Elf, whispered to her Dwarven friend. "Do you know what that is?"

The two of them stood a dozen strides from Vess' position, but she could hear them clearly as though they were whispering in her ear. They had fallen to the rear with the mounts, letting the three men take point. Smart, and not specifically asked of them. An archer and mage would do well with some distance from any enemies they encountered.

"Not a clue," Nevia replied, struggling with the reins of their mounts. "Sounds foreign, though. Certainly not Underspeak. Ugh, move, you blasted chicken!"

"It is a city, ruined in the Second Age," Vess explained, stepping forward to help Nevia with the recalcitrant avum. The Dwarf looked at her in a mixture of relief and surprise. "We visited it when last we walked these mountains."

"Second Age... truly?" Nevia said in wonder and mounting excitement. "A treasure such as that is rarely found!"

"Truly," Vess said with a thin smile.

"Then that is our goal? This Shelim?" Asked Kikri, clutching tight to her lacquered bow. "Are we looking for artifacts for the Gui—I mean, the Lady Haarwatch?"

"I suspect Felix will share our purpose soon enough. For now, know that we head in the city's direction." Vess pointed west toward the slanting sun and the rising earth. "Conserve your Stamina as best you can. The way only grows rockier."

Those words were proven true as they reached a particularly wide chasm, perhaps thirty or forty spans across. It was not something their low-grade avum could leap, and Vess had some doubts about the Haarguard. Luckily, there were a number of floating trees along the ravine, each rooted in an earthen mound that had somehow come unmoored from the ground.

"Fascinating," Atar was saying as they approached. "We didn't see these before. It's a new type of growth, buoyed somehow on… air Mana?"

"That's what it looks like," Alister confirmed. He was crouching and peering at the underside of the nearest tree. "The root system looks intact, too."

"Orphale Trees," Felix said, and Vess felt the guards near her jump. Their Spirits tickled against her senses. "Apparently, they feed on earth and air Mana until they incorporate it into their trunks. Once they hit critical mass, it just..." Felix made a floaty gesture. "Very cool. But now it's time for a bridge."

Felix gestured at the ground beneath their feet, and Vess watched with fascination as the ground softened ahead of him before stretching, taffy-like, into the ravine. With her Elemental Eye, she could see the dusty brown Mana that flowed out of Felix's hands and feet, vapor that soaked into the earth and gave it the power to bend and twist to his Will. It was… beautiful.

But, when the forming bridge reached the floating Orphale Trees, the Mana was sucked away rapidly. Felix grunted in surprise then concentration as a veritable flood of Mana poured from his channels. Stone flowed like liquid, pushing outward along the bridge… until it, too, was sucked away. The edge of the shaping crumbled and cracked, devoid of its animating force.

"Huh," he said with a slight pant. Vess shook her head. All that Mana used, and he was barely winded. "The trees are eating my Mana."

"That's not good, right?" Evie asked, idly spinning her new chain. "I assume that's not good."

"No it's not good," Atar said with a waspish frown. "Without his Mana, we can't get across this chasm, not unless you can carry this many avum on your chain."

"How'd you like a quick ride across it right now?" Evie threatened, whirling her bladed chain up into her fist, held only a half span from Atar's face. The mage flinched back before his Spirit ignited with orange Mana.

"Stop it, both of you," Felix snapped. "There's other ways to..." Felix trailed off as he looked up and down the ravine. "Hm. Maybe. Maybe. How much can they hold, though?"

"What is it?" Vess asked.

"The trees," Felix said. "We can use the trees."

"You thinkin' of jumpin' across them?" Evie asked. "That's a tall order for some here."

"Not jumping, walking," he explained. "I could ferry everyone else across, unless the trees want to eat my other magic. But I don't think I could lift the birds without hurting them."

"And findin' a way down and then back up would add hours to our day," Harn said. "It's better than nothin'."

"Why do we need the mounts, anyway?" Kylar asked. His little mustache quivered when he noticed he had everyone's attention. He rallied as his Spirit sparked with something like pride. "We are moving faster on foot right now, and the way is getting more mountainous. Shouldn't we abandon them?"

"We'll need the birds for after the first range." Harn grunted. "They stay."

Matter settled, Felix instructed them to bring the trees closer. Vess sent her floating spears out to shepherd a number of them, which was more difficult than she had expected. The trees fought back, in a way. The flows of air Mana in and around them pushed back against her spears—made of mostly air Mana themselves—and wanted nothing more than to sit where they were. At least they didn't eat away at them like they had with Felix's Skill, though their resistance was frustrating to her.

Felix took this as encouraging, for some reason, and began to help. Tendrils of shadow whipped from both of his hands, each one securing a single tree, and he hauled back. Strong as he was, it was only a matter of time before he brought them to the cliff face. Evie and Vess grabbed the rest.

"Oh, they're fighting back," Felix said, a slight note of strain in his voice. His tendrils were wrapped now around the outermost layer of Orphale Trees, split into eight or so thinner cords of shadow Mana. The trees steadily bucked against being grouped together like that. "Like similar polarities on a magnet," he said, another one of his meaningless phrases. Something from his home, she assumed. "I wonder if—"

Felix's face twisted in pain, and Vess stepped toward him. "Felix what—"

Then she felt it.

A presence. It was oppressive, jabbing at her senses like a blade. Vess' heart thundered, and her brow dampened. The others were feeling it, too, she saw, in varying degrees. The guard simply looked confused. Vess looked around, searching for the source.

"There!" she gasped.

Across the chasm came the sound of snapping branches and crashing boulders as a horde of monsters barreled toward them. They were huge, running on four legs and covered in rocky armor. Wide, mad eyes and drooling fangs stared and snapped at them from a quarter league away. That oppressive, dangerous presence only multiplied, honing itself to a razor's edge.

"Defensive line!" Harn shouted, and the team staggered to their places. The Haarguard followed, far slower as they fought with the mounts. "Release the mounts!"

The avum ran off, all of them, nearly yanking Kylar's arm from his socket.

"It's too many!" Vyne shouted as he brought his shield to bear. "Nevia!"

The Dwarven mage looked to Vess for instruction. She nodded at Harn. The gruff warrior raised a hand as the beasts thundered down the slope. They were almost upon their position, and the beasts were even larger than Vess had thought. The chasm would pose no problem for them.

"Walls!"

A spray of jagged ice shot up around them, solidifying into a dense wall of ice Mana that covered about thirty span in an arc.

Vess was impressed. It had even grown around the struggling Orphale Trees, locking them in place.

"Great job!" Felix shouted, dropping his shadow whips and giving Nevia a thumbs up. "Now me! *Stone Shaping!*"

The earth rumbled beneath them all as dusty brown Mana exploded outward. Then there was a mighty chorus of bellows, and two of the enormous hulks tore through the ice.

Vess whirled her new spear, heart hammering and core singing.

Finally. A proper fight.

CHAPTER EIGHTEEN

Shelled Aurochs, level 28, Tier II beasts, Felix noted as two shattered through Nevia's defensive wall. *Too strong for them!*

His Mana sank into the earth, ready to shape a series of spikes to stop the Aurochs, but Vess beat him to the punch. She exploded from his side—cracking the ground and the tree behind her with the force of her leap—and met the two Aurochs head on. Her new spear gleamed in her grip, striking in a flurry of lancing blows that blasted huge divots from the ox-like monsters' hide. The Aurochs both bellowed and floundered among the ice, dead before they hit the ground.

Hell yeah! Felix engaged his Will once more, sounding the etched patterns in his core space with blue-white Mana. It spun outward, through his channels, and into the world at large, transforming the rock beneath the soil and roots at his command.

Stone Shaping!

This time, he formed thick, horizontal columns from the stone, supported along the bottom and sides by sloping ramparts. Six wide-nosed rams thrust outward, meeting the thunder of the Shelled Aurochs' advance with the percussion of the monolith. The beasts were many in number, but his creations stopped several in their tracks and forced the rest to either leap atop his constructs or go around.

"Form up! Mages inside, melee on flanks!" Harn shouted. His twin axes were out and bisected the nearest Auroch with a solid strike. Like a boulder in a river, the majority of the beasts stampeded around them and into the forest. "Mages! Everything you got! Loose!"

Sparkbolts, Ice Arrows, literal arrows, and bolts of kinetic force all speared into the Aurochs. The beasts' thick hide—the rocky shell they had—prevented most strikes from felling them, but the sheer amount took many down, anyway. Atar's fire, in particular, was nasty once it caught the Aurochs' shaggy hair aflame, hair that was located around their necks and underside. Alister's bolts of force were also good, as they often cracked open the beasts' shells and allowed the others a vulnerable target.

Felix didn't understand why they weren't huddling up defensively at first. That had been his plan, after all, and why he'd created his fortification. His team, at the core, were safe for the moment. Then it came to him.

Free experience. Experience that, in his case, would be drops in the ocean.

Felix held back, letting his friends and the Haarguard take their turns attacking. Considering the experience penalty Felix was under, even Harn could garner more benefits from them than him. Instead, he inspected that oppressive feeling he had felt when the horde descended.

It felt bloody, much as the force that had frightened the avian monsters at the Wall. It *was* of Vellus, that Felix was sure about—he wouldn't forget the goddess any time soon, unfortunately. His Born Trait ensured the memory stayed fresh and utterly visceral for the next three weeks, but even after that, he doubted he'd be rid of the sensation of floating in that dark place while the goddess of storms and blood tried to—Felix frantically pulled away from the Memory, which threatened to all but transport him back there.

Bastion of Will is level 70!

That *hasn't happened in a while,* he panted. He had thought his Willpower and mental defenses had long grown beyond the power of a wayward Memory. Then again, his Mind had been strengthened as well. It would make sense if the blade of it were double-edged.

Double edged… opposite. Yeah. That makes sense. The Dissonance he was feeling, tinging the Harmony of the Foglands: it was here, built into this bloody force. He'd long ago noticed Dissonance as a major component to the Archon's Profane Sigaldry, which was part of why it hurt people to view. *So he had, what? Used his Profane Sigaldry to...utilize the Bloodmoon?*

That had some merit. The Archon had made use of the Bloodmoon—a rare celestial occurrence—to empower his forces during the invasion of Haarwatch. What was stopping him from using it in other ways? Like—*Shit.*

Like to escape.

The Aurochs came at them, masses of pure, unfeeling destruction. It was all Vyne could do to protect himself, let alone the rest. Were he to Taunt even one, that would be the end of Vyne Pallas.

Still, the fight was invigorating. Seeing the Fiend in action again, even though it was only a single spell… *what* a spell! Stone battering rams, summoned from the earth itself! They effectively split the stampeding horde in two and gave everyone enough breathing room to fight. A single, powerful movement that determined the flow of the entire battle. Vyne hoped to be half so capable in the future.

You Have Killed A Shelled Auroch!
XP Earned!

You Have Gained A Level!
You Are Now Level 33!
You Gain 3 Free Stat Points!

That capability was coming faster and faster now that they were seeing battle. Vyne was not an offensive powerhouse, not compared to Davum or Nevia, but tagging them with his hammer and shield dealt at least a little damage and got him contribution credit, even if one of the Fiend's Companions did the real killing.

His Chimera was especially good at attacking large swaths of enemies, all at the same time, with its blades of air Mana.

"Down!"

Vyne ducked, pulling his head below his tower shield as a rain of icy spears rained down on a wounded Auroch. The beast bellowed in pain and tried to turn toward them, but was instead trampled by its fellows who never even slowed.

"Yes! Another level!" Nevia cried. According to her proclamations, she had benefited the most from this fight so far, but she was also a mage. Mages lived or died on their Mana.

"Almost out, though, huh?" Kikri said with a sharp smile. "I'll keep you in mind as I reach level forty first."

"Listen here, you sap-drinkin' twig tosser," Nevia started before suddenly losing her balance. Vyne leaned forward and caught her with a single hand.

"Easy there, Nev," he said in a low voice. "You're nearly drained."

"Night," the Dwarf cursed. "You're not wrong, hammer face. But it doesn't mean I gotta like it."

"Fair."

He helped her to feet and reset his shield before him. Kikri had wisely moved on. In part, he suspected, because she actually cared for Nevia, but also to reach another tree.

"Green Shaping," she hissed, and from the trunk of a nearby tree came perfect, fully formed arrows. Her quiver filled with them, and the tree groaned as if in pain. "My thanks," she muttered before plucking out a projectile and letting it loose.

The arrows were made entirely from wood, but something about the process strengthened them. They could punch through iron armor, given the right Skills, and Kikri excelled at ranged offense.

The arrow—and the four others she loosed besides—all ignited with a swirling blue and yellow vapor. Suddenly, they burst forward, now glowing with an intense heat, and impacted two of the nearest Aurochs hard enough to shatter small holes in their shells.

"One more for me," she crowed, a little breathless, before following up with another six arrows. How she fired them so fast, Vyne was unsure. He believed she was layering multiple Skills, but that was hard, and it showed in her slowing reaction times. Her Stamina was starting to drag, and it was murder on her Mana as well. Yet she pressed on, just as frantic as the rest of them to make an impression.

Davum swung his greataxe into the fray, letting his poisonous blade spin in a whirlwind of toxins that he swept off into the horde. Each of the Aurochs' breaths weakened them, and the Orc chased after them with murder on his mind. He was one of the few who could deal considerable damage to this foe, as a result of his specialization toward Strength alone.

Kylar, meanwhile, focused on quick, precise attacks with just enough power to create a wound. His dual-sword style was a popular one back in Setoria, but less so in Haarwatch. That was because, in Haarwatch, they had to deal with this sort of thing coming out of the Foglands.

"Die, damn you!" he shouted, swords clanging off their rocky hide. "Die!"

"Kylar! Focus on their eyes and mouths!" Vyne said, shouldering his shield and rushing to his teammate's aid.

"I know my business, Vyne! Mind your own!" Kylar screamed as he hurled himself at yet another Auroch, none of them staying still long enough. His blades sent out sparks with each rapid-fire attack—three or four hits in the time it'd take Vyne to strike once—but the amount of blows mattered little when they could not penetrate. "Why won't they die?"

The shield warrior merely rolled his eyes and took a single, solid step forward. Vyne's tower shield, as tall as he was, smashed into the Auroch and sent it stumbling a single step to the side. It was enough to slow it down so that Kylar's swords found purchase in the beast's neck. The Auroch let out a pained bellow before throwing its head back and smashing the warrior off itself.

"Ahh!"

Kylar landed in a heap just beyond Vyne, and the armored beast turned on them both, snorting in anger.

"Blind gods," Vyne swore, before he planted his shield into the earth and began stacking his Skills, one by one.

High Bulwark!

Carapace of Steel!

Stone Thews!

Mana and Stamina drained from Vyne's Body and Spirit, while the metal and earth Mana burned through his channels. Vapor swirled and settled into and around his Body, transforming his skin to pebbled stone and his blue armor to a dull gray metal.

"Kylar! Behind me!"

The Auroch charged.

Once it was clear the danger had truly passed, Vess instead used the rampaging creatures as an opportunity to test herself.

Dragoon's Footwork!

She flitted between the enormous beasts, feet and spear constantly moving as she carefully thrust and sliced into the Aurochs' necks and eyes. One after the other fell before her, its body soon trampled by the press of its fellows and increasing the difficulty all the more. Yet Vess persisted.

The Haarguards were sending out their own attacks, but they were easily sidestepped. Each step was a lie, a false perception that twisted around the horns of an Auroch or the bursting heat of an enchanted arrow. Friendly fire was always a concern on the battlefield, and Dragoons had to be able to enter the fray regardless. Vess pushed herself, blurring faster and faster, each foot breaking earth and stone and trunk as she launched herself through a brutally graceful kata.

She thought on her father, on his disappointment. She believed that he had ordered her return; he had not wanted her to train so far from home in the first place. His Chosen Hand was but an extension of that feeling—brute though he was—and Vess could admit to herself that she also longed for the sun-kissed streets of Pax'Vrell. To go home… it was a siren call she could not give into. She had a duty here, a responsibility. Friends.

Her father had long stressed family as the utmost importance. To honor the family was the highest calling, and doing her duty as his heir was so much of her life for so long. Her mother often repeated something else.

Ain't no family like the one you forge, Vessi.

Soon, Evie joined her in her own dance. Where Vess' techniques made her difficult to predict and utilized her Strength and

Dexterity to confuse her opponents, Evie simply relied on speed itself. Her Agility was high, pushed well beyond five hundred points, and her Dexterity was similarly elevated. Her friend swayed between the beasts, a frown on her face as her chain twirled around her arm, shoulder, neck; all the while, it sliced and punched into armored hide with a weighty finality.

That frown, Vess knew, was not from concentration. They were both feeling that blade of Intent, one that lingered on the beasts like a foul stench. It fouled Vess' concentration, again and again, crashing over their Affinity. But it was just another distraction, another foe on the field.

She would master it, as well.

Dragoon Footwork is level 66!
Grace is level 58!

"The avum!"

Vess spun toward the voice, nimbly stepping aside from lowing beast to see the mounts running free. She felt their limited Spirits, brief flashes of wild fear, before the birds were trampled by the onrushing tide of Aurochs. The guard who cried out, Nevia, was on the ground after trying to restrain at least one of them. Vess leaped to her, helping the Dwarf up.

"Are you well?" she asked.

Nevia sucked in a sharp breath and cradled her arm a bit. "I'll be fine, but—Vyne!"

Vess followed the Dwarf's gaze, landing squarely on the two guards that looked most alike. Swordfighter and Shieldbearer, and a maddened Auroch charging at them.

Pierce the Skies!

Vess fairly flew into the air, her powerful legs and Born Trait sending her speeding into the branches of the high trees. She twisted, shaping her body and spear so that not a single leaf touched her, before coming back down in a guided arc.

Dragon's Descent!

Vess landed spear-first on the charging beast, stabbing through its toughened head and forcing it into the dirt. From that height, her spear—the Partisan of the Blue-Eyed Dragon—cut through the Auroch's earth-spelled shell without missing a hitch. For good measure, she wrenched back and twisted it, turning the monstrous creature's body to the cowering guard.

Well, perhaps cowering isn't giving them credit, she thought.

The shieldbearer, Vyne, had seemingly utilized every defensive power he had available and stood his ground. His shield was planted properly, even angled in the right way so as to deflect the charge rather than meet it head-on. The swordfighter, Kylar, was much less impressive.

"You idiot! That would have killed us! And you just stood there?" Kylar scrambled to his feet and gathered one of his two swords. Somehow, it had been tossed aside. "You're worthless, cousin!"

"Enough," Vess said and yanked her partisan free. A gout of pale yellow blood followed it, and the swordfighter blanched. "Return to the center. You are both too weak to be fighting these directly."

Vyne sighed in obvious relief. "As I suspected. Thank you for saving us, your Grace." He bowed his head.

Vess inclined her own, just a touch. "You are quite welcome. Now—"

"Kylar!"

Kikri leaped from above, having taken refuge in the trees at some point, and landed with cat-like grace. She straightened and looked at the swordsman and, belatedly, the shieldbearer. "You all right?"

"I'm fine," Kylar snapped, his face regaining some color. In embarrassment, Vess felt. "The—the Lady Dayne saved us."

Above them, Pit swooped down, sending a spray of icy spears down into the Aurochs and driving them further from their group. Vess raised a hand in appreciation, and Pit shrieked in joy.

Without warning, the bloody Intent that hovered around the Aurochs shattered. Another sound supplanted it, plowing through its core before scattering it to the winds.

Felix's song.

It was… alluring and dangerous, a solemnity hiding teeth. Vess shivered and looked over to find the man atop a stone pedestal he'd created, overlooking the still-stampeding monsters. His face was tight with concentration, but it slackened as the oppressive, bloody sensation passed.

"Wow," Kikri said with wide eyes and a slightly slack jaw. "He's *beautiful.*" Vess looked down her nose at the Elf, which made Kikri blush. "No disrespect intended, your Grace."

"...Indeed. Focus on helping your friends," Vess ordered, sending the Elf back toward her team. "And find those avum."

CHAPTER NINETEEN

Felix blinked as the Intent vanished. It had been far easier than he expected. His own Intent had broken the honed edge of it into harmless pieces that dissolved into the ambient Mana. The Aurochs, however, neither stopped nor even slackened their pace. They thundered by, still stampeding away from whatever had so frightened them.

The Tier II beasts were being taken down, but there were so many. At least four hundred, all of them rampaging east, through the forest and… into Haarwatch.

You cannot coddle them…

Perfect recall let him almost hear Zara's voice again, and Felix scowled. This was the second horde he had fought, the second heading east for the city. It was unlikely to be a coincidence, not with how his summer had been going. No, Haarwatch should expect to see more and more of these, unless someone stopped them.

An Auroch ran by, a little too close to the group, and Felix flared his Adamant Discord. The beast was hit by a blast of kinetic lightning, forces that lifted and hurled its shelled body up and over its own herd.

You Have Killed A Shelled Auroch!

XP earned!

A soft trilling sound rippled through his Affinity, and Felix saw the Haarguard flash with a brief pulse of System energy. The Grand Harmony was swirling around them all as they leveled up from this encounter. The sharper pings of Skill levels cascaded like chimes coming from his friends as well.

Strength from adversity, huh, Zara? Felix clenched his jaw. *But too much adversity doesn't grant you strength. It kills you.*

He wanted the Legion to grow stronger, but what would they do against so many Tier II beasts? More than just the Legion was at risk now. They would surely die, and the Aurochs would end up within the city, where they'd kill even more. The Aurochs would annihilate what little remained of the Wall Quarter. Unless they completed the Wall and restored its reserve of power, Haarwatch was practically undefended.

If I have the power to stop it, I'll stop it. No more deaths.

Influence of the Wisp!

Stone Shaping!

Mana poured from Felix, a torrent to dwarf the amount he'd used to build the battering rams. Colored violet and orange, it swept outward in a flash, leaving behind a blue fire on the Aurochs. They were instantly Enthralled, their Willpower overwhelmed by Felix's, and they froze in place. A second wave of dusty brown Mana sent a series of stone spikes upward, piercing their skulls in a single, precise casting.

You Have Killed A Shelled Auroch (x342)!
XP earned!

Influence of the Wisp is level 48!
Influence of the Wisp is level 49!
Stone Shaping is level 58!

Not today.

"Blind gods," the Orc whispered. Davum, according to Evie's Analyze. She was bad with names. His tusks, at least, were neat. They were white and shone in the dappled sunlight. "He killed them all with a single spell."

"Two spells, actually," Atar said from some distance away. He glanced over his shoulder at the falling monsters before looking to his wrist, and Evie bet he was using some weird mage Skill. "Fire, earth, and… augmentation. Yes."

"Interesting," Alister added. He had sheathed his rapier and was shouldering his pack again. "Didn't know he used augmentation magic."

"Kinda makes you feel pointless," Nevia panted, and only her friend Kikri kept her standing. She was particularly slender for a Dwarf, Evie noticed, and seemed to have low Stamina as well. "How does he even have that much Mana? I'd keel over tryin' to affect that many targets."

"He cheats," Evie said with a crooked smile. Not really an answer, but good enough by her estimation.

"He isn't cheating, Evie," Atar said in his professor voice. "In fact, I think I've figured out how it works. See—"

"Twin's teeth, I'm bored already," Evie complained, before pointing the guards at something else. "Ooh, look!"

The Auroch corpses that littered the trampled forest turned to sudden, sparking vapor. It was very different than the usual black smoke of a monster decomposing. If Evie were forced to describe it, this was...it was like a house fire, smoke and all, trapped and funneled. It sped toward Felix and just… vanished.

"Did he just—" Kikri started.

"Yeah."

"How di—"

"Don't worry about it," Evie said with a smile and a shrug. She slung her arm around the Elf. "We'll never get to use it, anyway. We're not cheaters, yeah?"

"Right," Nevia said in a distracted sort of way. She looked from Evie to Felix to Atar. "But wasn't that Mana? And what was—"

"Good at questions. Not so good at listening," Evie said with a dramatic shake of her head. She looked at the Dwarf and Elf with the patient eyes of an elder, for all that she was easily five to seven years younger than either of them. "Trust in my years of wisdom.

Nothing good comes from asking Atar to explain stuff, anyway. At best, you'll just fall asleep."

"Hey!"

Evie perked up. "Ooh, bridge is up!"

They continued onward, though Atar and Alister took cuttings of the Orphale Trees. Felix admitted they were super interesting, and regretted not having the luxury to really investigate all the strangeness in the Foglands. From hidden monsters, house-sized mushrooms, and carnivorous plants, the place had it all. And that was just in the first few miles.

Another hour passed, and the ground got increasingly rocky, with trees growing more and more sparse as the land rose and dipped. It was easy going for Felix and those that were more martially inclined, but the mages were puffing fairly quickly. Harn set a steady pace that kept them going but didn't lay them out. Last thing they wanted was to run into something and have people with spent Stamina.

Atar bemoaned the loss of the avum, and Felix certainly wasn't pleased, but they could roll with it. Despite the Stamina waste, it was still faster to climb directly instead of picking their way up game trails. He tried to enjoy the relative ease; the Foglands was sure to throw more curveballs soon. Felix had no doubt of that. He let Harn take the lead and lingered in the rear with Pit where he could oversee the entire team.

Pit's Bite is level 51!
Pit's Rake is level 52!
Pit's Wingblade is level 62!
Pit's Frost Spear is level 65!
Pit's Flight is level 44!

He checked and accepted all the Skill gains for his Companion, and Pit chirruped in pride. The little man had done a great job on the field, effectively keeping the Aurochs from hitting their relatively weaker allies. Their weakness did raise a few questions for

Felix, though he would be the first to admit his sense of power was a bit skewed. Maybe he—

"Felix?" Harn called from the front of the line. "Come take a look at this."

Felix scratched Pit's neck and walked ahead, pushing his Agility and Dexterity just a touch so that he could pass through the others quickly. It was getting easier, using varying levels of his stats instead of going all out every single time. It was one of the things Rory had harped on during his training. Control. Power was the currency of the Continent, but without control, you were no better than a monster.

Felix had been a monster long enough.

In seconds, he reached the head of the line, coming abreast of Harn as the man stood atop a rocky lip over another shallow ravine. It even looked familiar, though they had passed a dozen such furrows so far.

"What's up, Harn?"

The man had taken off his helmet and held it under an arm. "I think you want to see this. Come on."

Harn called a halt and the two of them went down the steep side of the defile. It was easy for them both, and in short order they stood at the bottom, near a tumbled-down cliff face. A single, triangular obelisk jutted through the uniform stones and weeds. Felix sucked in a breath.

"Shrine of Vellus," he growled.

"Hm, thought as much. I spotted this obelisk glintin' in the sun. Seemed to match your description of the place." Harn walked closer and kicked a few stones.

"Careful, I don't know—" Felix stopped as if he'd run into a brick wall. Two steps in, and his body has all but seized up—he was unable to get closer to the Shrine. "What is this?"

System Alert: Access Denied
Bearer Of The Thief of Fate Title Is Barred From All Divine Locations
Primordials Are Barred From All Divine Locations

"Whoa," Felix gasped, reading the gilt-edged notification that dominated his vision. It came with a sound like a holy choir calling down judgment, thunder and horns and fury.

Harn spun around. "What? What happened?"

"Notification," Felix croaked, before stepping back. He took a breath, now that his body was no longer seizing. "I'm barred from getting any closer."

What does that mean for my Find the Shrines quest? It was still there in his Quest log. *Is it unable to be completed now?*

Harn stepped back, giving the Shrine a dangerous look. "Because of what you did?"

"Yeah, I'd guess so." He'd earned the Thief of Fate Title when he had stolen a piece of Vellus' Divinity in a last ditch effort to survive. She hadn't liked it. "My Race, too."

"Hm, makes sense," Harn grunted. "Primordials—most of 'em, leastwise—are nasty customers. Makes sense that holy grounds are forbidden."

Felix tilted his head and flared his Manasight. There was a... strangeness to the Mana in that place. Like it was slowing down, freezing. The flows eddied in odd ways as they moved across the ground and breeze, each of them swirling and churning through the space, moving close to but not touching the Shrine itself.

Something inside of him stirred, and Felix placed a hand on his chest.

"What is it?"

"My core space... hold on, let me check," Felix said. He dove his senses down into his core, where his stacked rings of flame spun in opposition. They looked fine, as did the Skills revolving around him, and the ribbons of light braided beneath it all.

The growth, however, the piece of Divinity that he had stolen from Vellus, that quivered. Felix pulled himself closer. It resembled roots or veins and was a dark crimson, threaded through with pulses of colorless light. It shook, pulsing like a heartbeat, while those lights flowed up and down its branches in a slow and steady pace.

The Shrine, he realized. *It's reacting to the Shrine.*

The growth felt... heavy, a significance he hadn't appreciated before. Seeing it matched up against the destroyed Shrine, the way Mana was flowing, it weighed on him. He flared his Adamant

Discord and could feel a pull, as if it were exerting a strange sort of gravity. It meant... something, he was sure.

Maybe it's just a Geiger counter for divine radiation? That made sense. At the very least, that made avoiding such Shrines in the future easier.

He returned to the real world.

"Well, I can't get closer to it, and I'm not sure I want to try," Felix said. "Better to leave god stuff to the gods. Right?"

Harn chuckled. "A good attitude to have, were it several weeks ago. Bit late for that, kid."

"I can't argue with that." Felix smiled, though he didn't feel it. "Regardless, we should move on. I don't want any of the others stumbling on this. I've no idea if that bloodgate works both ways or not."

Not too long ago, the bloodgate was what brought him out of the Void. He'd hate to find out later that it could send folks *back*. No one deserved that.

They traveled only a bit farther after that. When the last rays of the sun dipped below the mountains they had started to climb, Harn called it. They found a shallow cave, one that smelled of nothing more than dirt and the bare wind, and started to unpack.

"Why not press on through the night?" Alister asked, echoing a sentiment from the Haarguard. They seemed somewhat annoyed to be stopping with so much ambient light still available. "I was told this Quest is somewhat time-sensitive?"

One of the guards gasped, and Felix could almost hear their Minds start whirring.

"Time's not on our side, that's true enough," Harn rasped, giving the noble a hard look. Alister grimaced and inclined his head in apology. "But the dark ain't friendly, least of all here. I'll not have you all caught unawares in the night, fog or no."

Setting up camp was extremely simple when everyone was vaguely superhuman. The ground was easier to sleep on, and everyone required a bit less sleep, anyway. To give himself some space, Felix used Stone Shaping to dig a bit deeper and added a hook to the tunnel so that they couldn't be seen directly from outside the cavern. He wanted to close off the cave completely, but was thankfully stopped in doing so when Evie pointed out they'd all probably suffocate. Harn had brought a few wardstones to obscure their presence, at least a little, so it was largely unnecessary, anyway.

No fire was allowed, the usual precaution for exploring hostile lands. They had trail rations with them, though, so food wasn't an issue. A sort of salted meat, bread, and plenty of water. It wasn't particularly tasty, but then, Felix didn't need food that much any more. He still needed *some,* of course, but his Vitality made him extremely resistant to both hunger and thirst, so for the moment, he left the rations for the others. He'd also eaten all that Mana and Essence from the Shelled Aurochs, so his needs were met.

While the others ate and settled in, the guards continuously cast pointed looks at one another. Felix noticed it early on and knew why. When it didn't stop, he decided to nip the gossiping in the bud.

"Is something wrong?" he asked.

Kikri and Davum, who were trading glances above Felix's head, started in surprise. They looked at Felix, then at the others sitting nearby. Davum nervously tapped his tongue against his tusks. "There is a Quest?"

Exactly what I thought. "Yes. It's my Quest."

"Quests are both rare and almost always difficult," Kikri began. She too looked nervous. "We—"

"We weren't told it was a Quest," Kylar whined over the Elf. Well, not whined exactly, but it felt that way to Felix. The man had a definite sulk to his voice. "I—we would have appreciated some honesty."

"Honesty's got nothin' to do with it. You're guards, yeah?" Harn grunted. When the swordsman nodded, Harn leaned forward. "Silence means less lips to flap the truth of things. You weren't told because you weren't trusted."

Kylar tried to surge to his feet, but his cousin, Vyne, held him down. The others just looked like their parents had yelled at them.

"The plan was always to tell you once we'd made camp," Harn continued. He jabbed a thumb at Alister. "Knacht just spilled the beans a bit early."

Evie clapped the noble on the back. "Good job, fancy pants!"

She looked at everyone else and sat down among them. "Now that no one can go runnin' back to Haarwatch, and all the snoops have been left behind, how's about we talk about that Quest, then. Eh, Felix?"

Felix smirked. *Leave it to Evie to vaporize tension just by being herself.*

"It's dangerous, I'm not gonna lie," Felix began. "But that's on me. I don't expect any of you to take on those dangers, not fully. It's my Quest, and I'll see it through."

"That a load of guano, Felix, and you know it," Evie said, and was echoed by Atar of all people.

"We're here to help, not sit in the back while you investigate an ancient magical artifact alone." Atar brushed a stray lock from his forehead.

That made a lot more sense.

"Atar means well," Alister said, only to receive a sour stare from the fire mage. Alister merely patted him on the head. "But yes, we are here for you, Felix."

Vess merely met his gaze and nodded.

Felix coughed, clearing his throat for some reason, and smiled at all of them. Even the Haarguard. "Right. Well, then let me explain."

CHAPTER TWENTY

Felix outlined the gist of his Quest. He told them they were looking to reach an ancient ruin before a powerful adversary. And that said adversary was potentially at large in the Foglands.

"So, we're walking into enemy territory?" Kylar asked. His mustache twitched. "How many? Levels and Temper?"

"Tier II and III, from what we've seen, but there are some unknowns," Felix answered. The swordsman clenched his jaw at his answer. "As I said, it's dangerous. I believe the bulk of their force is familiar to all of us. Many of the Reforged were killed, but many more remain."

"Wait," Nevis said, an edge of excitement in her voice. "The ice warriors that attacked the city?"

"Yup," Evie said with a languid stretch. "Big bastards. Ice armor. Used to be Frost Giants."

The ice mage's eyes shone in the waning light. Her compatriots were less enthused.

"We—" Vyne choked a bit on the jerky he was eating but muscled through. "—we are from the Setoria branch of the Guild, sent months ago on a transfer to Haarwatch. We ended up assigned to a merchant caravan to make the journey, only arriving after the Inquisition barred the gates. We didn't experience the fighting first-hand." He shuddered. "But we saw the aftermath."

“A true shame,” the Dwarven mage asserted. “The little I’ve seen of their corpses was remarkable. I'm eager to truly experience their power this time.”

“You're in the minority on that,” Atar said with a grimace. “They’re damn strong, and whatever ritual they performed during the Bloodmoon made them stronger.”

Felix nodded. “We killed around two hundred of them during the battle, which means there are close to two hundred left. That is not a battle we want to walk into without preparations.”

“Two hundred,” Alister breathed. “Blighted Night.”

“Not to mention the Wurms, sundry other monsters we can only guess at, and the Arcids,” Vess added. “And the one leading them all.”

“The Archon,” Felix said with a quiet intensity.

There was silence for a time. Word had spread of the Apollyon and its conversation with the Blue-Eyed Fiend. Even the Haarguard seemed aware of the name.

"This Archon seems… trouble," Davum said, sounding the words slowly. "He seems a bear in his cave."

Kylar pointed at his friend. "I agree. Why're we going to poke him?"

"Because the alternative is to let a known hostile power seize control of magical secrets," Atar said. He sounded scandalized. "What other option is there?"

"Running away seems a solid option," Evie said through a mouthful of bread. She swallowed with a swig of water. "I hear the desert is great this time of year."

"No, it isn't," Atar said with a frown. "My home is wracked with storms in the summer months."

"Right, right." Evie snapped her fingers. "It always sucks."

Atar sputtered.

“The Archon is stuck in his Domain. He cannot escape,” Vess said. She cut off the squabbling and gave Felix a searching look. They knew too well how Domains could break, given the right circumstances. "Correct?"

Felix smiled and hoped it at least appeared confident. “Right. The worst we’ll have to worry about are his forces, which he’s clearly able to send outside the Domain. He’s searching for the ruin, same as us, and is closer to it. We'll have to pass by his Domain on the way, however."

Yet the Archon might soon escape, could have already, in fact. He refused to voice it, at least at that point. It was a bit superstitious, maybe, but he could hold out hope for a little while longer. The Archon was locked away, even if his forces weren't. They had to be the ones driving out the monster hordes they'd seen. What else would put such fear into them?

The conversation thankfully moved onto their projected path, with Harn taking the lead. He had the most experience with the Foglands, Mind-altering mist or no, and knew many of the dangers. Many, but not all. The lack of fog had revealed the Foglands to be a changed landscape. Where the paths were once dizzying and misleading, and the flora and fauna rotting and vile, now it was green and fecund. But no less hazardous.

The going would be slow, by necessity, unless they wished to die. Between Nymean Temples to ancient cities and divine shrines, Felix was increasingly certain that the Foglands held far more than anyone knew. A small part of him was excited to explore it all, while the rest of him considered the cold worry that nestled in his heart.

Would they all survive what they found?

Karp was certain they were going to die.

"Keep to the Path!" Zara commanded, and her voice was like a whip crack. "Eyes forward! Do not stray!"

Entering the Dark Passages had been a trial, as each and every one of their blindfolded mounts had bucked the instant of arrival. It took some doing, but calming touches and a firm hand kept most of them in line, enough to keep anyone from losing a bird. When that chaos cleared, however, Karp had found out *why* the avum had gone a bit mad.

They had emerged into a darkened… chamber, of sorts. The area ahead of them was barely illuminated in a ghostly, green-blue light centered on the Sorcerer herself. The Naiad was practically glowing with it, as if whatever spell she'd wrought created the very floor they walked on.

She had quickly led them forward, through twisting tunnels whose sides they couldn't even see, just the stone and wood they trod. All of it glowed with Zara's magic. The Dark Passages weren't real, or they were, Karp was a bit confused on the matter. *Zara and Vivianne called it a lim—a limin—ah, screw it. Something about being "between Realms," whatever that tripe meant.* All Karp knew was that, if the Passages had a face, he'd have put an arrow in its eye hours back.

Those dark and twisty pathways continued as they led their mounts deeper and deeper. He could barely see his own two feet, and what he could see around him made Karp regret waking up that morning. The shadows around them *writhed* in a way that was both unnerving and nauseating. Things were in that darkness, and no matter how often Zara told them not to look, Karp couldn't help himself.

It was too faint, even with his Journeyman eyes, like shapes in smoke. Forms danced in and out of focus, color and distance so hazy as to be impenetrable. Fleshy, wobbling appendages slid past, mottled things covered in hooks and barbs. They undulated, Karp thought, twisting up, over, even under them. As if… as if the path were nothing. As if—

The ground opened up beneath him. A yawning tar pit. It pulled at him with dark, clawing hands. Karp howled, clutching tight to his mount's reins, but his Strength was not enough. He fell.

"Karp!" A soft but unyielding hand gripped his chin and forced him to look away. "I said, eyes forward."

Karp gasped, finding himself standing once again on solid ground, and his reins torn off in his hands. The path had become stone once more, and he ran his calloused fingers across its polished surface. Stone. Marble. He pressed it, and found it firm, even to his strong Body.

"What...what in Avet's name was that?" he asked.

Zara knelt before him, arranging her black skirts outward and glowing with that soft, ghostly light. "Avet has no hand in the Passages, no god does. We walk between worlds, Karp, and the path does not always move how we expect." She stood again, drawing him up with her. "Keep your eyes forward, off the dark. Focus on the way ahead." Zara turned to the rest of the company, and Karp realized everyone had halted to stare. "That goes for all of you! Watch not the shadows! They will lead you astray!"

Karp felt the urge return—to flick his gaze, just for a moment —but he mustered what little Willpower he possessed and tensed his neck muscles. The wordless whispers clung to him for a prolonged moment before fading. It was a compulsion, truly, encouraging him off the path.

"What are they?"

Zara looked into the dark, ignoring her own advice. "They are remnants. Pieces of the Realms, caught in the nothing between."

Vivianne hustled from the front, grabbing Karp's cuirass to help him remain standing. "The nothing?"

"The Void," Zara said simply before turning back to the front. "We move. There is not much to go."

They walked. On and on, one foot in front of another. Karp felt the Void calling to him again, scratching at his Mind, but he shut it out. He practiced a trick he'd used on the battlefield, a simple technique to keep his mind busy instead of worrying before a fight. Karp broke down his bow in his Mind, the wood, the horn, the lacquer, all of it. Then, he thought on the craft to build it once again. On his father, who had made his first bow when Karp had been no more than ten years old. The memory brought peace as well as grief, as his father had long since passed into the Ethereal.

But it kept his Mind busy, noisy, too preoccupied to pay much attention to the scraping tentacles of the creatures.

Time passed.

Karp was unsure how long they had been down there, but it felt like days when the ghostly green turned to brilliant, blinding white. Then, with a rush of wind and sun and air, they emerged. A green forest greeted them, and beyond that, a blue sky touched with soft oranges and yellows along the scudding clouds.

They had made it.

"We ride a short distance, perhaps ten leagues, then we make camp for the evening," Zara said, already atop her ugly avum. The bird snapped repeatedly at a large buzzing fly, unable to catch it. "On the morrow, we make our attempt."

"Camp? There are still hours of daylight left," Kelgan argued. "We already lost days on your route, we can't afford—"

"Lost, Lieutenant?" Zara said with a raised eyebrow. She smiled, and Karp shuddered at her sharp teeth. "We've lost nothing."

Karp looked up, sighting the sun through the emerald canopy. It was a touch thinner here than farther down the slope, and the terrain was dense and uneven as anywhere else in the Verdant Pass. He sighted the sun, its position, and the mountains looming north and south of them.

"Blind gods," Karp said, loud enough for the rest to overhear. "We're nearly at the Tin Gate."

"What?"

"Impossible."

"The Sorcerer already told you all. The Dark Passages are a shortcut," the Hand said with a sneer. "That vile jaunt was for a purpose, fools. We've spent perhaps six hours to travel a hundred leagues."

Zara's smile was thin-lipped, and her eyebrow raised at the Hand, but Karp saw her nod imperceptibly. "So we have. A few more leagues, and we'll be at the Gate, where we can attempt to cross into the next section of the Pass."

"Attempt?" Kelgan asked after he picked his jaw up from the ground. "The Gate is simply that. There is no chance of failure in riding through it."

"In normal years, I would not argue the point. But this has not been a normal year," Zara said, putting her heels into her mount. The ugly bird squawked and took off at a light canter. "We ride. Now."

Karp checked his bow and climbed atop his bird. He took the time to truly look around him, appreciating the forest for what might have been the first time. Karp glanced back at the low mound covered in unbroken grass. No evidence remained of their passage, no cave or crevasse.

Karp rubbed at his temples and shuddered.

They rose early the next morning, well before dawn. Both Harn's and Felix's senses could detect no roaming beasts nearby. In fact, it seemed most nocturnal predators had gone to sleep. No wonder, as Felix had spent much of the night listening to their terrifying roars and howls. Some sort of battle had even occurred just below their cliff face, and when they emerged the next morning, it was to find a pair of gigantic claw marks on the stone itself.

Now without their mounts, they made faster time along the rocky terrain. They had covered many miles before the sun even started to light up the sky, in fact, with not even the mages putting up much of a fight at the pace. The forest and ravines of the day previous had become rocky foothills in short order, and soon even those were left behind as they ascended the shortest of the mountain peaks before them. Forests covered the slopes, but as they neared the top, it became rockier and filled with tangled vegetation.

Frankly, Felix didn't miss the mounts. The avum were capable creatures, and would have likely helped his friends, but the exertion was an excellent way to push their Body Skills. Not to mention, it was easier to prepare for the inevitable attack by roving monsters. He wasn't ashamed to admit he was a bit biased; he'd never earned a Riding Skill. Even on top of Pit, it always felt more than a bit awkward.

Pit, however, continually bemoaned the fact he wasn't allowed to fly.

You'll be a target, bud, Felix explained for the tenth time that morning. *You have to walk, just like us.*

Pit warbled in a decidedly sulky tone and stomped ahead. Felix could only sigh and roll his eyes.

"Kids, huh?" Evie said.

Felix gave her a half smile. "Hey, Evie."

"Damn, did I make noise that time? Step on a stick?" Evie looked behind her where the path of tumbled stone and exposed roots comprised their ascending path. The majority of their compatriots were struggling with the terrain, though Vess breezed through it gracefully. Kikri and Kylar were moving well enough too, the both of them having apparently invested moderately in Dexterity.

"No, you didn't step on anything. You're just not good enough to beat me," Felix said with a grin.

Evie scoffed. "Just you wait, cheater. I'll get you when you least expect it."

"I'm sure you will," he said. Something shimmered ahead. It seemed like a reflection, but the sun hadn't yet risen above the horizon. "What's that?"

"What's what?" Evie said. She squinted where he pointed. "I dunno. Your Perception is better than mine. If you can't tell?" She shrugged. "Let's go look, though. Atar!"

The words were more stage whisper than shout, but Atar heard her nonetheless. He had progressed well ahead of them, closer to Harn, surprisingly, and when he saw where Evie pointed, his gaze immediately sharpened.

"Oh Highest Flame, that is intriguing," Atar gestured and held up a wrist. It was a common enough Skill called Mana Gauge, allowing folks to get a rough estimate of the types of Mana prevalent in a small area. "Earth, shadow, air, yes yes," he dragged his hand across his wrist and the collection of colors there. "Oooh, higher than anticipated metal Mana. Either there's a powerful vein nearby, or that's made of refined ore."

Felix's interest was only increased, and he hurried up the path, Atar and Evie close behind. The incline steepened, but that didn't stop him. Felix merely vaulted the last thirty feet, landing with both feet atop the sharp tip of the lowest peak.

Beside him, now gleaming in the newly risen sun, was a blade.

Three blades, actually, and not real blades. They were ten feet long and angled so they stuck out of the mountain at a forty-five degree angle to the west. Each one was bronze, and the wide, leaf-shaped blades were covered in a dense, inert script. They were lined up next to each other, same angle and everything, but one of them was snapped off halfway up. It was a clean cut, as if something had sliced through it at some point.

Voracious Eye!

Name: Essence Relay
Type: Structure (Enchanted)
Lore: Built to accompany the Essence Anchor, the Relays work to amplify and spread the true purpose of the Anchor.

Heavy breathing behind him followed by the clatter of stones announced Atar's presence, but Evie had slipped up beside him only moments later.

"Twin's teeth, those are big… things." Evie ran her hand over the discolored bronze. It wasn't pitted or damaged, simply a bit dirty. "What're they for?"

Atar gasped, having hit his shin on a boulder, then he gasped again at the sight of the devices. "They are beautiful!"

"Essence Relay," Felix said, noticing the distinct similarities between them and the massive Essence Anchor he'd once thrown himself upon. They were a fraction of the size, but even some of the script seemed the same. "It's like we thought, Atar. The Essence Anchor I destroyed, the one responsible for the fog array here, was being amplified by these."

Atar wiped sweat from his brow and put his hands on his hips. He took several long, shaky breaths. "There must be more. An array that affected nearly the entire Territory had to have been supported by dozens of these." He held out a hand and, after checking Mana levels, he placed that hand onto the Relay. There was no reaction, and tension bled from the mage's shoulders. He began tracing his fingers along the carved sigils on its surface. "Remarkable."

Evie glanced over the side of the peak, where Harn and the others gathered and a narrow trail moved around the tip. "As much as I'd like to stay and watch Atar fondle his blade," she snickered, and Atar turned beet red. "I think Harn's movin' on."

"Yeah, go down and tell him. We'll be down in a few seconds," Felix said. Evie nodded and hopped down, likely reducing her weight and floating. "Atar? You have paper and charcoal?"

"Hm? Oh! Yes!" The fire mage fished both items out of his bag, and the two of them quickly made rubbings of the sigils on the Relay. Each of them had the same series of sigils, so they only bothered with the one. Still, that took them several minutes to fill up and annotate each page.

Felix didn't necessarily need to make rubbings; he'd remember the pattern and layout of the sigils with little effort. But this wasn't just for him. If he wanted to talk to someone about all this, he needed his friends on the same page, as it were.

Just as Atar was spritzing some alchemical liquid on the pages before packing them up, Felix saw something else. This time, it was in the distance, to the west. The forest stretched onward for endless miles, even to his acute vision, but this was close. Located between the blunted peaks just a mile or two down, there was a structure. A man-made structure, as close as he could tell.

And from the top, smoke was pouring out.

CHAPTER TWENTY-ONE

"It's an outpost," Harn muttered under his breath. "Look, you can see the fortifications."

"Made with ice," Nevia said in wonder.

"No." Vess pointed. "Covered in it. This place was attacked."

They had descended the peak, making their way silently toward the smoking dwelling. From a distance, all Felix's Eye could identify were pieces of the whole: a wall, a roof. It wasn't until he got closer that they could see what its function might be, as well as the size of it. Up above, it looked like a simple dwelling, but it was clear now that several structures lay within, built up with stone walls that rose half their height.

The ice was a new addition, as were the signs of combat. Splintered wood and gouged stone proliferated, speaking of an assault from the west. The ice had been grown up and over the walls that originally existed, and the smoke they had spotted was the black stink of rotting monsters.

"This was clearly designed to defend against something from the west," Vyne pointed out. "If something came from Haarwatch, they could descend as we did, bypassing the walls entirely with a few Skills."

"Most Tempered aren't stopped by walls alone," Harn grunted.

"I'd expect any fortification worth its weight to have a few wards. And this one seems full of 'em."

"Why? It looks like whatever did this didn't leave anyone alive," Atar said. His eyes flickered between the ice and columns of black smoke that dissipated only thirty feet above the walls. "Why defend a place you've abandoned?"

"No clue. I suggest we find out. I ain't leavin' an unknown at my back." Harn pulled his axes from his belt.

"Harn's right. We need to find out who did this and who exactly even had an outpost in the Foglands," Felix said, getting a few nods of agreement.

"No one should be out here," Alister agreed. "Haarwatch is the only way into the Foglands, and it's been closed off for months."

"Not the only way," Vess pointed out. "The Risi made their way from the Hoarfrost. There are likely many ways into the Foglands for the determined."

"We'll find out," Felix said. "Keep close together, standard formation. We're moving."

Abyssal Skein!

Voidstuff boiled from his veins, spreading out of his channels and into the air. Felix gripped it with his Will and Intent and sent it coursing around the connections he'd formed with all those present. His friends and even the guards soon vanished under its influence.

"This feels… unpleasant," Davum said.

Kikri rubbed her hands together. "Like bathing in thick, cold oil."

Abyssal Skein is level 44!

The pattern of the Skill pulsed in Felix's core. Ripples undulated across the entirety of the Skill, but luckily, only he could feel them. It was true, the Skill was unpleasant. It reminded him viscerally of traversing the Void. Still, it was useful considering most of their company had no Stealth Skill.

They moved ahead, approaching the outpost from an angle. They were still slightly above the structure, and had he been alone and uncaring about stealth, Felix might have dropped into it from above. As it was, the sparse slope was drenched in the mountain's morning shadow and provided at least a little coverage. Abyssal Skein did the rest.

The gates of the outpost were open, but not broken, as if whoever had been within had just left them open. Evie and Harn took the lead, creeping low and faintly humming of power held in abeyance. Felix followed right after, less cautiously as his Perception swept the area. A slight fissure passed through him as they passed the gate, and Felix clenched his fists, but nothing followed. It was there and gone in an instant, and his Manasight spotted no other wards in the walls. Neither his Primary or Harmonic senses could pick out anything other than ice and death.

He was proven right as they entered a courtyard of packed earth, around which were three large buildings. Laying at the center of the courtyard was an enormous body, easily twelve feet tall, blue, and covered in jagged armor made of ice.

"Reforged," Felix said.

The former Frost Giant was clearly part of an assault. Its body was riddled with gashes and arrow shafts that had broken even its powerful ice armor. Its head was half-severed, and the wounds were all pouring black smoke up into the air. They had found the source, at least.

Harn sucked in a breath, but waved off Felix's concerned look. "Spread out. See if there are any survivors, Reforged or otherwise," Harn ordered. "Take care. The wards were dispelled on the walls, but there's no saying they'll be dispelled elsewhere."

There was little else to the outpost, which didn't surprise him. The entire place felt… temporary, despite the clear skill required to make the buildings. Felix had expected log cabins or something like them, but all three of the structures were built with an eye to detail and ornamentation. Delicate designs surrounded doors and windows, organic shapes that wove into complex patterns across the lintels. The roofs were steeped and formed with tile, and glass was set into the windows.

The Construction Skill existed, but what combination of Skills would be required to fashion an entire house in the wilderness? Or had they carried all the materials with them? Both options seemed far-fetched, yet here it was.

Pit, go around and check the back. See if there is another entrance.

His Companion chirruped in agreement and trotted off while

Felix slowly walked toward the central structure. He climbed the steps and swept his senses through it all the while. There was nothing but stone and glass and wood, nothing except—

What is that? To Pit, he sent: *I'm going in.*

Pit warbled back at him. *I wait.*

Felix opened the front door, one built for people a good deal taller than him, and saw a wide, empty area. Polished floorboards, simple plank walls, and thick joists, all surrounding what Felix could only describe as an altar.

Is this a Shrine? Felix stepped forward carefully, watching for the moment when he'd be stopped. The altar was filled with circular shapes, elaborate interconnecting round lines that all converged at the top of a carved and stylized plinth. A series of pebbles, shiny and dull, were arranged atop the plinth and at the feet of a statue of a bird carved of a dark wood. Its wings were outstretched, as if it were expanding, and its eyes gleamed. A trick of the light, clearly, as it was definitely an inanimate statue.

Probably.

Felix kept walking, though, until he came right atop the altar itself. The System didn't deny him access or call him names at all.

"What does that mean, though?" he asked himself.

Voracious Eye!

Name: Shrine of the Endless Raven
Type: Shrine (Urge)
Lore: Built to venerate the Endless Raven, it was designed with the Urge's favorites items and shapes. Offerings of items discovered in exploration are placed upon the altar, in hopes of gathering the favor of its dark munificence.

An Urge? Not Divine? Felix scratched his jaw. *What's the difference?*

Felix walked around the altar, looking for something, anything to answer his questions. More feathers and beads and shiny stones, things Felix would imagine would please a raven, but precious little else. Until his hands found a slight depression at the rear of the plinth.

"Ooh, what's this?" Felix ran his fingers over the depression and found a faint ledge. He pulled, and a small drawer popped out. Felix was delighted, feeling a rush of discovery.

Exploration is level 45!

Huh. Felix tilted his head at the notification. He didn't normally gain levels from opening something. He turned to the drawer again, and found within it a single, palm-sized book. Manasight revealed nothing more than the staid flow of harvested wood Mana and the clinging tendrils of shadow. No traps or wards, at least not of the magical variety. He lifted out the book and immediately recognized the script.

"Henaari," he whispered. The foreign script was mostly illegible, but he immediately fished his own battered notebook out of his satchel. The latter half was filled with his own messy scrawl, but the first part was chock full of notes in the hand of the Henaari he had found dead just outside the Waterfall Temple.

"This was a Henaari encampment," Felix said.

"Aye, so I feared," Harn stated. He walked into the shrine, followed by Atar and Vess. "The architecture said as much, but I had hoped to be wrong."

"Why?" Felix asked. "Aren't they just explorers or something?"

"Because the Henaari follow the guidance of their *godling*," Vess said with a grimace of distaste.

"Godling? You mean Urge?" Felix asked. He pointed to the altar. "When I analyzed the shrine, I got info on the Urge called the Endless Raven, but I've seen mention of it before."

"Your luck is its own kind of endless, Felix," Vess stated. "The Henaari follow the guidance of their dark godling, and it always, *always* leads them into trouble."

"Of one sort or another," Harn agreed. "Doesn't surprise me to find them in the Foglands, but it likely means things are worse than we hoped."

"We already knew that, though," Atar said. He had walked further in and was running his hands over the halo of circular carvings behind the shrine. "We're following Felix, and worst-case scenarios follow him like they're tied to his waist." He gasped as he came to the bird carving. "This is beautiful."

"Profane," Vess said with a grimace. Felix sometimes forgot she was fairly religious herself; her family had a long history of devotion to the old gods.

"What's the difference between an Urge and a god, then?" Felix asked.

"Passingly little," Atar said offhandedly, but Vess' huffed a breath.

"A great deal, in fact," Vess said. She also walked closer to the altar, though her hand was firmly around her partisan. "The gods live within the Ethereal, where all souls go when we depart the mortal world. The...Urges live among us, defined by the facet of belief that forged them, fueled by the blood and sweat of their slaves."

"*Slaves*?" Felix asked, alarmed.

"Slaves is a bit much, Vess," Atar said. "It is merely a mutually beneficial contract of power. The Urges are an embodiment of an... archetype, and there are those who bind themselves to them for access to that potency. The Henaari are among them, a nomadic Race dedicated to the tenets of the Endless Raven: exploration and bringing light into the dark places."

"Slaves in all but name, tied to the Will of a being none can fully trust." There was a real heat to Vess' words, something Felix had only heard rarely from the heiress. She typically got along so well with everyone that it was kind of jarring.

"Either way, Henaari on our same path is a bad sign," Harn interrupted. "We need to move. I feel like your Quest ain't gonna go as good as we hoped."

Felix sighed.

Just his luck.

Felix could tell Nevia wasn't pleased to leave. She had already cast a number of spells, judging by the amount of purple-white vapor that hung around her hands and shoulders, and seemed intent on prying the icy armor off the Reforged.

"Just a touch longer! I've almost discovered how the armor is generated!" The Dwarf pleaded with Harn, but the man was as implacable as ever.

"We are tight for time, mage. Wrap up your investigation in ten," he ordered before doing a final sweep of the outpost.

Furious, the mage soon lost control of the spellforms she had built up, and a blade of ice sheared right through the meat of the Reforged's chest.

"Tch! Now I can't see the attachment," Nevia growled and yanked back on the armor, revealing a grisly wound that was belching more of that black smoke. "I—" Beneath her fingers, a series of yellow-red symbols flared to awful life.

Her knees buckled, and everyone within eyeshot fell to the ground with a pained groan. Everyone, that is, except Felix, Atar, and Alister. They all had plenty of experience with Profane Sigaldry. At most, the two mages flinched, but it passed quickly. Felix didn't even do that, though his core space quivered in response to the dissonance of it.

Felix leaned over the smoking corpse. He saw the edges of some sort of array, likely involved in creating the Reforged in the first place. Felix was aware they were a lot like Golems, except built from living things, but the process was far more complex than that. He only knew enough to recognize he didn't know anything about it all. "Hm. Atar, Alister, you've got half a glass. Scribe as much of that as you can."

"Good idea," Alister said, and the two mages pulled scrolls and inkwells from their packs. "We won't be able to get much before it finishes decomposing, though."

"Anything is better than nothing. Nevia," Felix called out. The woman looked up at him, frustration clear on her face. "You've got the same time to check out its armor. Make it count."

She pursed her lips and nodded, returning to the body once again.

"Everyone else, prep to leave. And keep an eye out for anything else."

The time passed rapidly, and none of the mages found what they wanted. Atar and Alister had pages of confusing scrawl, while Nevia hadn't been able to find the connection between the ice armor and the Reforge's snuffed Spirit. The latter was clearly impossible to do after death, and the Dwarven mage had latched onto the idea of capturing one of the monsters alive next time.

They moved on, descending the mountain into the forested

foothills just below. Vegetation was thicker there, and though the ground was far less rocky, the going was far slower. Strange, Mana-fed flora and fauna abounded in whichever direction Felix looked. Even the insects he spotted were leveled in the teens.

The trees and thick undergrowth were so numerous and hearty that they had to cut a path. Harn took the lead there, wielding his silver axes with deadly precision. Vinesnakes, Thorncrawlers, Emberflies, all died as his axes bisected the trees and shrubbery they hid within.

"Alright, you five, take point," Harn grunted at the Haarguard. They looked at each other in confusion, having spent much of the journey nestled between Felix's friends. Harn gestured impatiently. "C'mon, I ain't got all day. There's a lot of XP floatin' around this forest, and you're all higher-leveled than it. Clear the way and earn your keep, eh?"

The lure of abundant XP was enough, and Kylar soon led the way into the forests with both of his swords flashing as best he could.

"Is that the best idea?" Felix asked Harn as they followed in the Haarguards' wake. "They're competent, but what if they run into something really tough?"

Harn shrugged. "Reason Cal sent them was to bolster our numbers but also to train up a team she saw some potential in. She told me they beat a clutch of Clay Golems and almost fought off a Steel, too."

"Oh," Felix said, remembering. He hadn't thought it terribly impressive. "That's true."

Harn snorted, the sound echoing through his helmet. "We ain't all Unbound, Felix. That's pretty good for a team with little to their name. We can't all break a training room and fight down an Orichalcum Golem."

Felix winced. "She told you about that?"

"Told me? She damn near shouted the attendants outta the Manor when she found out." Harn chuckled. This was probably the most pleased Felix had seen the man. "Told 'em you weren't allowed down there without special permissions. 'We don't have anything to challenge the Fiend,' she said."

Felix was a bit crestfallen at that; he'd just wanted to test himself, after all.

"Ah don't worry about it, kid. Cal's all bluster now that she's too busy to use those knives of hers," Harn patted him on the shoulder. "Look at it this way: she doesn't want you to waste your time. Plenty of challenge here in the Foglands, though, once we get deeper. Were it not for the doom n' gloom of your Quest, I'd be right excited."

"Still worth gettin' a *little* eager though," Evie added. She idly spun her chain, making sure to keep it clear of the considerable foliage. She was practicing, Felix realized. "Can't wait to put this chain to real use. Those Aurochs were fine and all, but I want somethin' fast and mean. Like—"

"Tier II! Tier II!" Vyne shouted out, and the earth quaked beneath them all.

Evie looked up at the sky. "Huh. Is this what it's like, bein' religious?"

"Not exactly, Evie," Vess said with a faint smile. She eyed the branches above them. "Race you to it?"

Evie immediately lassoed a branch with her chain and hauled herself into the canopy. "Hmm? I couldn't hear you over me winning!"

"Leave somethin' for the Iron Ranks to fight!" Harn barked after them.

CHAPTER TWENTY-TWO

"Surge! On your right flank!" Kelgan shouted. "Wall up and volley!"

"Stonewall!"

"Sparkbolt!"

"Ice Arrow!"

Wave after wave of monsters crashed against their defenses, but the Haarguard turned them aside. Kelgan panted with exertion. His spear was a blur, each thrust dispatching one of the putrid things. He hadn't expected to find undead in the Pass, but it was clear they were raised from a plethora of Tier I beasts. A half-rotten dire wolf dashed for their defenses, but only made it past the first volley of Mana bolts. It didn't survive the physical arrows their second row fired.

Spear Mastery is level 70!

The Tin Gate loomed above them, so close he could touch it, but the doors were barred by the black-green signature of necrotic Mana. There was a necromancer nearby, controlling this minor horde, but Kelgan couldn't spot them.

Thankfully, his allies had better eyes.

"There! Atop the crenelated tower!" Karp shouted out, swiftly followed by an arrow that exploded with green-gold life Mana. The archer's life Mana had proven to be essential to the fight, with each of his imbued arrows eating into the necrotic Mana and dropping undead puppets by the dozen. Atop the tower, a bubble of black-green Mana vapor bloomed, clear even to Kelgan's Mana blind eyes. "Necro is holed up!"

"Karp! Can you break that shield?" Kelgan shouted.

"Yeah yeah, just gimme a moment!" The red-bearded archer loosed six arrows in less than a breath, his fingers a blur. The dome of necrotic Mana flared again and again, but cracks of green laced the predominantly black cloud.

Around them, the horde went into a frenzy. They'd cut down their numbers, but there were still around a hundred of the smaller creatures, and they were very hard to pin down. Only their wall magics let them keep the noxious beasts at bay, while the few mages in their ranks dropped area of effect bursts of fire and earth.

Where's the Hand? Or Zara? The noble warrior could have slaughtered the necromancer faster than any of them, horde of undead minions or no, while the Sorcerer would have ended it before it began. *Why aren't they helping?*

A muted *boom* sounded above their heads, and the black-green dome shattered into pieces.

"Everyone, fire on my target!" Kelgan shouted before hurling his spear. "Amplified Strike! Kinetic Brace!"

His Stamina and Mana drained precipitously as the two Skills surged from his core and wrapped his spear, even as it left his hand at a speed his Perception couldn't track. The crenelations atop the tower exploded into stone dust as his powered spear struck true, and something cried out. A spell half formed in the thick vapors of Mana—

—and was snuffed out, as three dozen Mana bolts converged on the necromancer's spot.

You Have Killed An Unknown Necromancer!
XP Earned!

Thrown Weapons Mastery is level 45!
Kinetic Brace is level 61!

The remaining undead puppets fell limply at their feet as the Mana that animated them dissipated into the Ether. Kelgan panted through his thick, curly beard and wiped his sweat-slick hair back from his face. This fight shouldn't have been this annoying, but necros turned everything on their head. They were illegal for a reason. They'd had to pull out the stops to push this one mage back, and he'd even thrown his favorite spear.

Kelgan grunted in annoyance, watching his men and women slump in exhaustion. He dreaded the thought of climbing that tower to retrieve his weapon. They were all tired, but damn if he wasn't gonna make the most of his position. He turned to an Iron Rank guard, one he knew specialized in Dexterity.

"Go get my spear."

From their vantage point atop the Tin Gate, Zara and Darius saw the end of the battle. The necrobeast wasn't even a real threat, though its tendrils of necrotic Mana did a passable impression of true necromancy. The guard was never in any danger, not from them. Zara was on the lookout for something worse.

"There," Darius pointed. "The rat has chosen to run."

Below them, on the far side of the Tin Gate, a figure in white armor and a bright red cloak dashed out into the forest. Zara's Analyze caught him just as he escaped the Skill's effective range. An Acolyte of the Inquisition. He was running quite fast, having clearly focused on his speed.

"Better than hiding. If they had sent a stealth user, this would prove far more difficult," Zara said. She hummed slightly as she spoke, and Mana coalesced between her outstretched hands.

"How do you do that?" The Hand asked her. "The humming while you speak."

"Practice. I'm merely subvocalizing the Chant while still speaking. A simple enough technique." A swirl of aquamarine Mana spun faster, tightening into a harpoon made of glistening power. "Go."

The harpoon exploded forward as if thrown by someone with incredible Strength. The projectile ripped through leaves and branches and vines as if none of it was there, until they both heard the distant sound of impact. A muffled groan of pain drifted on the breeze, and Zara smiled.

"Simple enough," Darius muttered, and Zara let her grin widen. It unnerved many Humans to see a Naiad's teeth. She found that to be a useful fact.

"Let us go visit our crimson-cloaked adversary, hm?" Zara didn't wait, but rode a cresting wave of Mana down from the Gate and into the forest proper. She didn't bother to worry about Darius. The Hand could keep up.

Soon enough, she had traveled the quarter league distance and found the Acolyte. Her harpoon had pierced him through the left leg and into the trunk of a fallen tree. Darius appeared only seconds later.

"Pathless forfend," the boy cried out. "The demon!"

Darius looked at her. "I assume he means you."

Zara raised an eyebrow at the Hand, before walking toward the Acolyte. "What was your purpose at the Tin Gate, boy?"

She crouched, just out of his reach, and the Acolyte swallowed in fear before clenching his jaw. Zara could feel him gather all the anger he had in order to drive his terror away. "I'll not speak to you, witch!"

"Just to watch and report, then," she said, humming in contemplation. She felt a flicker of triumph in the boy's Spirit. "They wouldn't dare give anything more important to an *Acolyte*, after all."

The boy, barely out of his second decade, trembled with unrestrained fury. His Spirit quivered in kind as that sense of triumph and fear battled against one another.

"Darius, kill him. He's of no more use to us." Zara wiped her hands and stood, but the song of her words still spun through the trees. The Acolyte's fear spiked, overwhelming all else. His Spirit caved as her song took root.

"No! No, please! I'm to report the result of anyone attempting the Tin Gate, but also to recover the lures we used!" The Acolyte's expression crumpled as the weight of his terror overwhelmed all else. "Please! Let me live! I've done as I've been ordered! I've only killed Sorcerer spawn! I walk in the Pathless' light!"

"Lures. Used to draw in beasts and monstrosities," Darius growled. "They're restricted constructs."

"You have these lures on you?" she asked, letting the song fade.

Darius shot her a look Zara couldn't be bothered to parse at that moment. "All of them?"

The boy nodded.

"Good. You've done well, redcloak." Zara loomed over the Acolyte as his induced fear finally ebbed.

"So you'll… let me live?"

Zara bared her teeth.

The Arboreal Serpent was strong. Easily Tier II, it was likely close to being classified as Tier III. That meant it could compete with all but the strongest Journeyman Tier combatants and perhaps might have destroyed them had they come upon it unawares. The creature was a hundred feet long, thick as a tree trunk, and *mean.* It toyed with the Haarguard before Evie and Vess arrived, which was likely the only reason they survived. But even Evie couldn't quite keep up with its lightning-fast strikes.

The Haarguard weren't without their moments, however. Kylar engaged in a furious dual parry, deflecting the dancing tail strike from the Serpent before ducking out of the way for Vess to take over. Davum struck where he could, and his Strength was mighty, but the Serpent too fast. It took Nevia's ice magic and Evie's Bindings of the White Waste to hold it in place for more than a few seconds. In that time, Davum, Vyne, and Kylar all took their pound of flesh. Kikri was a standout, threading her shots through the Serpent's dizzying movements and even pinning its tail against a tree for over twenty seconds.

Felix was impressed. Harn was right; they were a good team, if a bit weak. Ultimately, Evie dispatched the beast with her new chain, trapping the Serpent between trees as she decapitated it.

All of the Haarguard gained a level from its demise, and his friends all said they'd progressed a sizable way toward their next. Felix tried not to feel jealous. He'd killed almost four hundred Shelled Aurochs, a Tier II beast, and had barely gained a fraction of his next level. That XP penalty was killer.

They kept moving.

The Haarguard learned quickly that everything in the Foglands was trying to kill them. They engaged those they could, but avoided the rest to the best of their ability. Vyne was proving to be extremely capable in that regard, a reliable bulwark against enemies that might have normally ended the rest of them. His defensive-heavy Skill set was remarkably effective even against tougher monsters. It put Felix's Mind at ease and let him quit focusing so much on their protection. As a result, they moved all the faster through the foothills and forest, until they encountered a wide, grassy plain.

"A plain? In a mountainous forest?" Felix asked. "I'm pretty sure that doesn't make geological sense."

"Geo-what?" Evie asked, before shaking her head. "Who cares? It's probably magic."

She had a point there.

"This is where I said our mounts would be handy," Harn grunted. He twisted off his helmet with a muted hiss and peered across the terrain. "Last we came through here, we found dozens of monsters had nested in burrows beneath the grass. Made the walk hazardous, but not if we moved fast enough."

Felix walked a touch closer, Pit at his side. He panned his senses over the grasslands, looking for any evidence of monsters.

Tracking is level 20!
...
Tracking is level 23!

Dozens of tracks littered the grasslands, but the ones that glowed under the effect of his Beginner Tier Tracking Skill were long, thin furrows. Felix flared his Manasight, a Skill that was always working at a low burn, and spotted the flows of green-gold life Mana as it flowed through the grasses. Dusty brown earth, black-gray shadow, and the golden shimmer of the sun's light Mana abounded. But most curious of all were the streamers of orange that smoldered low to the ground, virtually hidden by the long, tangled grass.

Voracious Eye!

Name: Kaltraps
Type: Insectoid
Level: 42

HP: 789/789
SP: 843/843
MP: 3488/3488
Lore: A giant insect that feeds upon the life and Mana of all that step atop it. Uses explosive fire and earth Mana offensively to surprise and kill their prey.
Strength: More Data Required
Weakness: More Data Required

"I see them. They're not so little anymore," Felix said. He pointed out the nearest one, and after a moment, the rest spotted the dun-colored exoskeleton poking up from the dirt. "We step near them, and they use fire and earth to kill somehow. Since this is the Foglands, I'm guessing they pop up and explode before eating our still-burning corpses."

"Gruesome." Kikri recoiled. "And they're level 42? That's on par with the Arboreal Serpent."

"How many?" Harn asked.

Felix hesitated, sweeping his senses across their immediate vicinity again to be sure. "At least thirty for the next hundred yards. Sorry, three hundred strides. And more beyond." Their common measurement for distance, best he could tell, was roughly equivalent to a foot back home. People were fairly loose with actual measurements on the Continent. "They're grouped tightly together, and I imagine, if we set one off, it'll set off the rest. There's no chance of everyone moving fast enough to evade them."

He left it unspoken that he and possibly Evie and Vess could make it across with little issue. Harn, too, probably. The mages and the Haarguard wouldn't make it more than twenty steps in.

"Can we go around?" Atar asked.

"Not unless you have three days to spare," Harn said. He pointed to the north and south, where the grasslands extended into the horizon. Only the blue haze of mountains in either direction suggested they stopped eventually. "Which we don't. As it is, the crossing here will take at least six glasses."

Felix let out a breath. "That takes out the option of Pit and me ferrying people across. Pit might be able to carry a single person across for that time, but he'd be exhausted on landing." Pit bobbed his head in confirmation, his armor rustling slightly. "My own Skills wouldn't last a portion of that time. We'd fall right into the center of them all."

"What about blowing them early?" Evie suggested. "Throw a rock at 'em, make them blow up, get them all tired and we go through."

Vess didn't wait, but scooped up a cantaloupe-sized stone and hefted it. Eyeing the distance, she shot-putted it forward and it struck the first right on its exposed exoskeleton. There was a long moment where they all watched it, but the creature didn't even move.

"Seems they know if their prey is alive," Vess said with a frown. "Fairly intelligent, then. Which means their Mana manipulations will hit all the harder."

"Night," Alister cursed.

Stone Shaping!

A series of stone spikes lanced through the earth, aimed at the nearest of the Kaltraps. But just as the earth Mana reached it, there were a series of muffled *thumps,* and fire Mana flared beneath the ground.

"What was that?" Kylar asked.

"Tried something," Felix said and rubbed his chin. "The Kaltraps countered my Stone Shaping with targeted explosions. None of them reached the monster."

"Make that very intelligent," Vess amended.

"Seems we'll just have to get clever, then," Felix said. "I have a plan."

"Oh no," Atar groaned.

CHAPTER TWENTY-THREE

It was one of his better plans, Felix had to admit. The Kaltraps didn't respond to sound, and only acted defensively when approached with magic attacks. He could drop grenades on them, but he didn't have nearly enough. They would only properly attack when they sensed something living cross them. So what to do?

Send someone with excellent footwork.

Vess darted across their grey-blond carapace, each footstep a deception that the monsters fell for hook, line, and sinker. The Kaltraps burst from the earth behind her, popping into the air like kafkaesque landmines. They were thick as barrels and possessed many segmented legs ending in grasping claws, half of which propelled them up into the air, and the other half attempted to grapple the heiress. Yet her Dragoon's Footwork meant she had already moved on before they felt the impression of her step, leaving them exposed for a few seconds.

Exactly as planned.

"Bindings of the White Waste!"

Chains of ice stabbed through their hard exoskeletons, entangling the living landmines. Their forms lit up as orange Mana vapor surged through their chunky abdomens, but the purple-white haze fought back the rising temperature. They wouldn't hold long, especially with so many secured at once, but they didn't need to be.

"Pillars of the Domineering Sentinel!"

"Imbued Sparkbolt!"

Beams of blue kinetic Mana slammed down from above, crushing the Kaltraps onto their sides. While they wriggled in crushing pain, red bolts of searing fire slammed into them, one after another. It all happened so fast the creatures barely had time to react, but they were Tier II beasts. As the Imbued Sparkbolts hit them, every one retaliated by releasing an explosive cloud of orange fire Mana. Grass charred, and dirt flew as the detonation tore everything around themselves, including the icy chains that held them. The discharge ripped into the earth, creating dark, loamy pits that the monsters immediately burrowed back into.

"No you don't!" Felix shouted.

Adamant Discord!

Lightning exploded from his hands as he gripped the ineffable lines that connected him to each and every one of the Kaltraps. A piece of him recognized it as a connection of bestial animosity, of conflict, and his power surged down those lines. The eight Kaltraps that had been pulled free immediately seized, their bodily control wrested from them as electricity singed their nerves, and Felix hauled back. His Aspects, all of them, twinged in pain as he leveraged their collective bulk from the earth. They fought back, keeping their lower ends still in the ground, but unable to stop him completely. His Skill was fueled by his stats. Unable to hide in the dirt, the monsters stood no chance.

"Pit! Now!"

Pit screeched and thrust his wings forward. Green-white Mana flowed out of his pinions like a dense liquid, changing into near-invisible crescents of hardened air as it cleared his wings. Faster than bullets, they keened as the crescent blades hit the Kaltraps with a hurricane of deadly edges.

Kaltraps shrieked in high-pitched, alien voices as their visible legs were severed. Yet Pit did not relent, and blade after blade hit the insectoids. The creatures were strong, but even its Tier II exoskeleton couldn't keep it safe from the tenku. Their armor buckled and sundered, each piece bursting with green ichor.

Adamant Discord!

Felix flared his Skill, letting the electricity flow through him. Through those that dared to cross him; to make him waste so much time in this meaningless place. The air shuddered and snapped, and burning ozone assaulted his nose, but Felix didn't relent. The Kaltraps began to smoke and curl, their bodies pulling completely free of the earth. They were *incredibly* heavy, and his connection to them felt... slippery, almost. It was hard to maintain his grip. Still, he lifted them higher and higher, until they were more than ten feet from the cleaved grasslands.

Suddenly, the closest creature exploded into an inferno. A storm of fire Mana and impotent earth Mana swept outward from it, as it became a living pyre. As the inferno hit the others, they also burst, until the field went up in a billowing cloud of furious flame.

"Noctis' tits!" Evie stumbled back, just clearing the firestorm. She poked at Atar. "A little warning next time, huh?"

"That wasn't me," he said with a significant look at Felix. "I think you hit a Mana bladder on the bug, Felix."

"Most likely on the tail end," Alister said. He pointed at a charred and blackened form inside the fire. It was still alive and twitching, but not for long. "They kept their rears planted in the earth the whole time. Likely to prevent something like this."

"Hm," Felix said through his teeth. Holding his Skill so long made him feel like things were tearing inside him. "Then... let's try something... else."

Adamant Discord is level 60!

Felix sent his senses along more lines, following the still quivering connections between his Kaltraps to those that hid nearby. The threads were shaky, tentative, bonds of Type and shared drives. But it was enough.

Adamant Discord!

Felix screamed, but the air cracked as blinding bolts of electricity erupted from him. One, three, five, eight more Kaltraps were hauled wholesale from the earth.

"Felix, you're bleeding!"

"Twin's teeth," someone whispered. Kikri, he thought.

Felix thrust both of his hands forward, his Body quivering and his Mind and Spirit screaming. The incandescent blaze in his Skill's grip launched into the seizing Kaltraps.

Wind and sound flattened the grassland for dozens of feet as they erupted into a pillar of fire and fountaining earth. His friends leaned into it, but several were knocked on their asses by the force, and Evie had to increase her mass just to keep her feet.

You Have Killed A Kaltraps (x16)!
XP Earned!

Adamant Discord is level 61!

Felix stumbled forward as his chest and arms and legs all felt as if they'd been shredded. He slammed his hands and knees into the ground, breaking it open with his sheer weight as his Body trembled. Sound was a keening wail in his ears, and his Spirit reverberated with the strain. A string quartet surged across his senses, but it was distorted and burred with atonal riot.

Something wet dripped onto his hands.

Felix lifted an arm and wiped away blood. From his nose and his eyes.

"Blind gods, Felix. What did you do?" Vess leaned down next to him. She reached out to touch him but stopped inches away, as if unsure. "You're bleeding. Where did you hurt yourself?"

"I'm fine," Felix gasped. He muscled down a scream as he straightened up. His muscles felt knotted tight, and it was like bending steel as he stood. "I'm—it's just some internal bleeding."

"Oh, is that all?" Evie said. "You had me scared for a moment, there."

"Felix, take my potion. Stabilize yourself," Vess said. She pressed a teardrop-shaped vial into his hands and closed his fingers over it. "You—"

"Incoming," Felix rasped. His Spirit might have been quaking, but his eyes still worked. The grassland around them waved as if it were in a storm, but the wind wasn't blowing. "I think… we might have disturbed some new friends."

The surrounding grasslands came alive with the skittering voices of hundreds of beasts, all driven to terror or anger by their sudden attacks. A medley of creatures rushed at them, a flood of horns, too many legs, too many eyes, long ears, and sharp fangs.

Harn recovered first. "Tier I! Haarguard! Front and center!"

"Taunt!" Vyne shouted, and purple Mana streamed from the

man's feet. It snagged well over half of the monsters' attention, diverting them away from Felix and toward his massive shield.

"Ice Wall!" Nevia intoned, her voice dropping an octave as purple-white vapor sprayed the ground, leaving jagged barriers of ice behind. She formed a tight funnel, catching the monsters Vyne's Taunt missed and forcing them toward the shield warrior. "Kylar! Davum! You're up!"

The thin swordsman and hulking warrior took place beside Vyne, and they met the monsters with measured violence. Kylar's twin swords flickered and slashed, dispatching the Tier I creatures with carefully placed strikes, while Davum's greataxe reaped them in swaths of bloody mayhem. With Kikri firing her arrows like an Elven gatling gun, it was like watching a blender in action.

"Damn," Felix said. Something seized in his thigh, but he braced himself with a sudden conjuration of a stone column at his side. "They're… better than I thought."

"I told you," Harn said. The onrush of Tier I monsters had slackened considerably. "We'll move ahead once we've all had a chance to rest," he added with a significant look at Felix.

Felix nodded and raised a hand to forestall the man. "I needed to see my limits. They were each heavier than I assumed," he said and checked his status. His Health was still above 60% and both his Stamina and Mana were recovering extremely quickly. "I'm fine."

"Hrm."

They rested for an hour after the battle, despite Felix's protests. He was eager to continue, his Health reduced but climbing, and his Mana and Stamina long since topped off. But Felix couldn't deny that the others needed at least a little rest to recover themselves. Vyne had suffered close to a hundred points of damage as well, though the lesser salves and poultices they'd secured from Aenea were swiftly patching him up.

"Tiny little teeth." Vyne grimaced as another poultice was laid atop his shoulder. The lacerations weren't particularly deep, but the risk of a Status Condition was high. "Rather face an axe to the face any day."

"So you say now," Davum laughed as he ran a whetstone along his weapon's edge. "When you've recovered from your scratches, we can test that."

"Why wait? I'm feeling stronger already, thanks to that level up." The shield warrior flexed his hands, obviously relishing his increase in stats.

"Dumped it all in Strength again, huh?" Nevia asked. "Why not more in Willpower?"

"Endurance and Strength are my mains, you know that. Willpower is a close fourth behind Vitality." Vyne hissed as his cousin slapped on a new poultice. "Careful, Ky!"

"Don't get bit up then, Vy," the swordsman muttered. He smoothed down his thin mustache in irritation. "You shouldn't have kept Taunting them. Between the four of us, we had 'em fine."

"That's the job." Vyne shrugged before wincing in pain. "Lord —uhm, Felix, sir?"

"Hm?" All this time, Felix had been sitting atop a small stone he'd shaped out of the bedrock. It was considerably higher here than in the city, though he had other stone sources to work with back there. His senses were extended out into the wilderness, watching for enemies as the sun stretched toward midday. "What's up?"

Vyne flinched as he met his gaze, and Felix guessed his eyes were glowing again. He wasn't entirely sure why that kept happening. It took the shield warrior a second to recover and speak up.

"How did you decide to allocate your stats?"

Felix could feel the Spirits of the guard increasing into the tight, rapid tempo of guarded curiosity. Even his own friends were drawn by the question. Harn just smirked, his helmet off as he shoved a quick meal into his gullet.

"I mean, did you focus on Strength? Or Endurance? Or Intelligence? You've got that lightning spell that… lifts things, somehow. I'm just—" Vyne looked at his friends, who were chuckling. "What? I'm curious!"

"My method… is not really that useful," Felix started before he sensed the shield warrior's sudden dejection. He cursed. Felix was really starting to dislike his Affinity. "Why?"

"Well, you're strong, too strong, really, and I can't imagine what your Vitality is to put up with as much punishment as I've heard—

and you didn't stop, haven't stopped, to rest. I can speak for all of us when I ask: how can we get to where you are?"

"Kill a couple Tier III and Tier IV monstrosities and live through it," Evie suggested through a mouthful of trail rations. She swallowed and coughed, banging on her chest. "Eugh. That kinda abuse does wonders for stats and Titles, eh?"

Vyne traded looks with Kylar and Davum, but Nevia shot them down. "Don't be planning anything idiotic, you three."

"If they want to charge off and fight some Tier III, they're more than welcome," Kikri said with a wave of her hand. "More XP on this Quest for me that way."

Atar laughed and nudged Alister. "I like her."

The noble patted the fire mage on his knee and rose to his feet. "As fun as this conversation is, we should move. I'm back at full, and I imagine the rest of you aren't far off."

A chorus of agreement met his words—begrudging in some cases—and Felix was happy to be back on the move. He was more happy to be away from that conversation.

Suppose I should come up with better answers for stuff like that, he thought. His capabilities were becoming more and more common knowledge, and the source of his power would likely come to light eventually. Sooner rather than later, if he kept his answers so sloppy. *Hopefully that'll stop the questions for a little bit, though.*

The chain reaction of explosions Felix had caused had cleared the area for nearly a half mile, but beyond that, the Kaltraps thickened throughout the plains. On top of that, there were some flying buzzard-like creatures that kept swooping at them, and a number of antelope-adjacent beasts that kept standing menacingly in the distance.

This is gonna take longer than six hours.

They progressed a half-mile at a time, and soon the process became so routine that they started pressing their Skills harder and harder. Finding the limits of their abilities was the fastest way to progress, after all, and add in the stress of escaping literal explosions meant Vess' Dragoon's Footwork and Evie's Acrobatics and Bindings of the White Waste rose fast. Even Atar and Alister saw several Skills jump two or three levels, despite their slower use.

The Haarguard, Iron Ranked as they were, benefited the most from the repeated assault by Tier I monsters after each successful Kaltrap defusing. They each gained three levels by the end of it all, though their Skill levels were where they shined. Even better, the two groups were working a touch better together. At least, Felix now knew what he could expect them to handle in a situation.

Lure out the monsters, explode them, survive the retaliatory wave of Tier I beasts. Rinse and repeat.

Felix was right, though. It took them most of the day and into the early night before they even saw trees on the horizon. Another four hours had them within spitting distance of the dark canopy, and Harn called it for the night. He had Kikri fashion a quick and dirty shelter from the long grasses all around them, and they hunkered down for a night's rest.

It was perhaps two hours before dawn when Felix woke from a short-lived sleep. Pit was a warm bulk along his one side, but Felix felt uncomfortably cramped. With care he climbed out of the tenku's embrace and out of the grass-shaped hut they all shared. Out in the pre-dawn dark, he breathed a deep breath of cool air.

Damn muscles, Felix complained. His Body was still getting used to the punishment his Adamant Discord put it through. His Mind and Spirit, too. He had a splitting headache and a sense of… tedium? Like someone took his drive and motivation and burned it all up. The latter might have been the monotony of getting through the grasslands, but Felix doubted that. It had gotten repetitive, sure enough, but there was always a part of him that thrilled whenever he used his magic.

I mean, it's magic. He shook his head. *I'm never not gonna get psyched over it.*

But all of that wasn't what kept him from sleeping. Instead, it was a question, one that plagued his subconscious so much that he woke with it on his lips.

That lightning spell that… lifts things, somehow...

What exactly was Adamant Discord? Felix pulled up the Skill information.

Adamant Discord (Transcendent), Level 61!

You have reclaimed power once Lost to the turning of Ages. The Pull of Significance accumulates with every step. Greatly increased power, control, and precision with each Skill level.

It made no mention of what it did, other than the hint about the Pull of Significance, nor what it cost to use. He'd learned both quickly enough, but it was one of the strangest Skills he owned. It was tied to another of his mysterious Skills, Unite the Lost, which seemed to restore things in some way. The indication was that Adamant Discord was "reclaimed" by Unite the Lost, which resonated with his Divine and Primordial Spark that were absorbed into his two cores.

While he used it, he felt those steel-hard lines of connection between him and all things, from dirt to people to the clouds above him. He could sense them even now, without activating the Skill, like words in the back of his Mind. The lightning was clearly a carry over from Reign of Vellus, and Felix liked to think it was the result of his Skill manipulating whatever energies it accessed. Because it wasn't Mana; Adamant Discord touched neither his Mana nor his Stamina. It fed directly on his Aspects, and that might have been the most confusing bit.

How? And how do I get it to stop hurting so much? He'd figured repetition, like weight lifting, would eventually strengthen him. If it was working, he hadn't seen any results, but it hadn't been very long. His Aspects all felt whole, if strained, so no permanent harm had been done. *Yet.*

Felix groaned as he stretched, massaging his shoulders and chest as if to work the strain out of them. It would pass, likely soon, but he couldn't take a break. There were challenges ahead that he had to be ready to tackle. Despite Vyne's words, his strength would not be enough.

Felix began a series of katas, Forms dedicated to his various fighting styles, moving through them at a glacial pace. His perfect recall could almost recreate his trainer, Rory, standing at his side and guiding him.

Like this, lad, he had said. Felix adjusted his stance, matching it to the memory. He began again. Slowly. Carefully.

Yes, lad. You'll get it. Eventually.

CHAPTER TWENTY-FOUR

Herbalism is level 33!
Meditation is level 55!
Arrow of Perdition is level 40!
Cloudstep is level 35!

Tracking is level 25!
Apprentice Tier!
You Gain:
+3 PER
+3 END
+3 AGL

<Harn, why won't you show me the Spirit trick?> Felix used handsign to ask as he ducked beneath a low branch.

<Why so insistent?> Harn signed the equivalent of a grunt—somehow—into the hanging moss beside them. He crept forward with entirely too much silence for a man in full plate armor. His metal bits didn't scrape or clank in the slightest, even in a low crouch. <Careful. Wind might shift at any moment.>

Felix nodded. It had been two days since the grasslands, two days of constant, quiet intensity as they dodged between packs of wild beasts, all of them increasing in level until there were barely any Tier I enemies at all. It was either fight every ten feet or exercise some caution. As much as his friends wanted to test themselves—to push their Skills—neither Felix nor Harn wanted to advertise their location every second of the day.

Felix sharpened his gaze, peering through the tangled undergrowth with more than sight, sensing the three two-ton pigs covered in crystalline spikes. They glittered in the emerald light of the late afternoon, facets shimmering with every snort and snuffle as they rooted for food.

Voracious Eye!

Name: Glitterhog
Type: Beast (Greater)
Level: 55
HP: 9422/9422
SP: 7355/8119
MP: 343/343
Lore: Glitterhogs eat the crystalline deposits that form on the roots of many trees in the Foglands. These crystals are digested and metabolized into their armor, which is highly resistant to magical effects. Their tusks are also made of the same ultra-hard crystal, equipping them with mighty weapons.
Strength: Charging; Defense Against Magic
Weakness: Bludgeoning Attacks

They had run into three packs of these beasts and had even fought a pair of them a few hours back. That was how they found out about the anti-magic armor and sharp tusks. Alister nearly lost an eye. They had put it down with a lot of swearing and bashing. But those were simply Beast Types; these were listed as Beast (Greater).

<What's Beast (Greater) mean?> Felix signed to Harn, and was rewarded with the man silently cursing.

"Means you're up," he replied.

Felix turned just in time to avoid getting gored by a bright pink crystal tusk. The Glitterhog squealed in a basso roar that shook the nearby leaves, but Felix didn't flinch. He pulled the Femur of the Envoy from his waist as he spun out of the way, releasing a streamer of Essence into the weapon. It grew rapidly, flaring with a normally invisible script, and Felix brought it down.

Dodge is level 54!
Unfettered Volition is level 56!

You Have Killed A Glitterhog (Greater)!
XP Earned!

Weak against bludgeoning, he reiterated to himself. The giant pig's car-sized body had been smashed in just below the neck, bisecting the beast and driving his club into the ground itself. He freed it with an annoyed mutter while the ground shook beneath the charge of the second. As the first, it moved faster than a sedan-sized pork chop had any right to, but a single horizontal swipe dashed its crystal-encased head on the forest floor.

You Have Killed A Glitterhog (Greater)!
XP Earned!

"Greater Beasts have better senses than the rest of their Tier," Harn said as he flicked a piece of crystalline gristle from his pauldron. "They made us as soon as we got close. Shoulda spotted that."

"No harm done." Felix shrugged. He slung his club over his shoulder. "Didn't even have to use my transformation."

"Not the point, kid. You know why we're bein' careful. I can't have them know we're comin'." He pointed to the two Glitterhog corpses. "Dispose of those."

Felix saluted lazily and breathed in.

Ravenous Tithe!

The monsters both burst into sparkling black smoke, streaked with bits of pink, green-gold, and blood red. The Essence and Mana that made up the Glitterhogs coursed through his channels and settled into his core, joining a nebula of crackling energy that was slowly being eaten up by his core rings.

He had been packing more into his core space in the past few days than he'd ever had during the invasion of Haarwatch. The Skills rarely appeared—likely due to the abyss at the center of his core space—but bestial Memories kept intruding into his dreams as he slowly processed the stolen power. They were unnerving but relatively tame in comparison to some of the Memories he'd experienced, so he had no hesitation to stockpiling Essence whenever he could.

He could always find a use for it, after all.

"You didn't answer my question, Harn," Felix said after a while. The clearing was empty of enemies and other than the hundreds of insects and small Tier I reptiles hidden in the foliage, they were not threatened. "Why haven't you taught me the Spirit trick?"

"Too strong," Harn said as he hefted one of the Glitterhog's tusks. It was jagged like a lightning bolt or a kriss blade. "You practice pushing your Spirit, and there goes our element of surprise. The Archon'll hear you from across the Foglands, kid."

"Okay, that makes sense. But that's no reason not to show me the general process," Felix argued. "I don't have to use it."

"Hah! You want to dance the axe edge? By all means." Harn set the crystalline tusk on his shoulder. "Close your eyes."

"Alright."

"Envision your Spirit."

"Envision my… what's it supposed to look like?" Felix asked.

"Dunno. Different for different folks."

"Oh, so it's like my core space? I need to visualize it as something pertaining to the space?"

"Maybe. Like I said, different." Harn hawked phlegm out into the woods. "You envision your Spirit, then you spread it out around you, like a big cloak, and press it down." He dusted his hands off. "That's it."

"That's it?"

"Yup. Stone simple, I'd say."

"So if I—"

"Ah ah, no practicin'!" Harn warned him.

Felix lifted his hands in a gesture of surrender. "Okay, okay. Got it." He shook his head. "Envision my Spirit, huh?"

Where to begin?

Vess dropped onto the fallen log with a grateful sigh. Her armor was just the slightest bit charred, though it was quickly cleaning itself. Self-Cleansing was an enchantment woven into every piece of clothing and armor she'd ever owned, and always would be. The hassle otherwise was beyond comprehension.

Especially in light of days like today, she thought with a sour grimace.

The monsters had been tough and numerous that day, a multitude of Tier II beasts in the ground, trees, and the air. Vess had pushed herself to the edge time and time again, which had proven fruitful for her Skills. Many of them were progressing quite well into Journeyman Tier, and even a few of her ancillary Skills were reaching that benchmark. She closed her eyes briefly and visited the temple atop her inner mountain, where the wind of the frozen peaks howled. Her Skills dotted the nearby mountains, many of them growing higher than she had anticipated.

With a flex of her Mind, she returned to the Continent and to all of the aches and injuries she'd briefly ignored. Vess was not unique in that. All of them were battered and exhausted. Even Evie slumped onto the log next to her, having barely adjusted her mass at all, so she hit with a bone-bruising *thonk.*

"Food," she said and made hands at a pack that was almost empty. Their stores could only be stretched so much. "Gimme."

Vess handed over some trail rations and a waterskin. "Go easy. We will need to replenish soon."

"And that's burning difficult without a fire," Atar groaned as he settled in across the way. The stones and logs were in a rough circle, though all that was between them were weeds and limp wildflowers. "I wish Thangle had come with us instead of Zara. At least then we could Obfuscate a fire and cook some damn meat."

"Eat something before you get so cranky you wake up the mountain," Alister said as he passed. His armored robes were torn and bloodied, and he pulled out a whetstone and inspected his rapier. He sighted down its length, checking for nicks and burrs in the edge. "How're the guards doing? I've noticed they've turtled up behind that defender of theirs."

"They have adapted their tactics in the face of enemies they stand no chance against. It is admirable," Vess said. "They proved themselves against the Tier I monsters we've encountered in the past."

"Doesn't really mean much when it's all Tier II. They're a bit of dead weight," Evie said between bites. She sprayed crumbs before washing it down with another swig of water. "At least they can be meat shields."

Vess frowned at her friend, letting her Spirit rumble with displeasure. Evie choked on her water as her fledgling Affinity picked it up. "Gah, sorry. It's a joke," she muttered, a touch sullenly.

"They only lack proper leveling. Their teamwork is very good, far better than my last team," Alister said. Vess felt his own Spirit dip into a brief dirge before evening out.

He thinks of his cousin, Vess realized. *We never did find her body.* Lilian Knacht had opposed them on multiple occasions, and at the last had been overwhelmed by a tide of Revenants. *Not all of it, anyway.*

"Forget them," Atar said with a dismissive wave of his hand. "Either they'll make it or not. What do you all think about this Quest?"

"Felix's or Cal's?" Evie asked.

"Felix's. Cal's is simply that *something* is hostile toward her city. But our Primordial friend is bound to uncover a magical ruin unseen for Ages. I'd burn down this entire forest if it meant we'd reach it immediately." Atar's eyes gleamed, and Vess' Elemental Eye caught the flare of orange Mana through his system.

"Temple or not, this has been a good trip so far," Evie said. "Got some levels, and my Skills have been getting the rust knocked off. Too much time *thinkin'* back at the Manor. It's good to get bloody again. *Ooh,*" she interrupted herself to reach behind the log and carefully pluck something from the ground. It was a curling frond with pink and green coloration. "Solid. I've been bonin' up on Herbalism as a side gig. Turns out Aena's willing to pay a lot of money for a bunch of dirty roots, plus those city Quests were too good to pass up."

Vess nodded. She, too, had started a collection of rare materials to turn into the Manor when they returned. For them, the rewards of those Quests did not offer immense amounts of XP, but every bit mattered.

"What I can't stand is the idea that this Archon might reach the Temple before us," Atar said. "We all saw the Reforged back at that outpost. What are the chances the creature hasn't broken free of its Domain?"

"Breaking a Domain is hard, and even then, the monsters end up Mana-starved, normally," Vess said. "But Haarwatch feels like it was a test run of sorts. If the Archon has not broken free, he will do so soon, and I truly doubt he'll emerge weakened."

"The sigils on the Shrine of Vellus and the Essence Relays we retrieved have proven fruitful," Alister said. "Atar and I are learning a lot from them. I hope to have something to lean on other than brute force when we face these Reforged again."

"Good luck. This is Felix we're talking about," Evie said.

"In his defense, brute force is much more appealing when you have so much of it," Alister amended. "But perhaps we'll uncover more at the Temple, as long as we can reach it first."

"Outrageous. Whatever is inside that Temple belongs to us—him. Felix," Atar corrected himself. "Bring on the ice warriors. I'll melt them all."

"We'll be ready," Evie said, placing a hand on Vess' arm. Warmth clumsily thrummed from her Spirit, and Vess smiled. Awkward or not, the attempt to soothe her was endearing.

Felix kept his word and didn't actually practice leveraging his Spirit. However, he did keep trying to envision his Spirit, but it was difficult to settle on what he wanted. His core space was an imitation solar system, so should he mimic that in some way? Was his spirit a burning star? A sparkling nebula? Felix didn't like any options he came up with and set them aside. He'd rather not have the ability than to settle on a subpar visualization that didn't work for him.

He had plenty of distractions, of course. Their progress through the wild Foglands continued, slowing down considerably as they avoided more and more monsters. The Reforged were around somewhere, and while they couldn't avoid everything, they did a pretty good job of it. Of course, that still meant they fought a *lot* of creatures, all of whom were extremely aggressive.

Pit's Skulk is level 48!
Pit's Etheric Concordance is level 66!
Pit's Cry is level 51!
Pit's Cold Resistance is level 34!

Pit showed good progress, though he ached to fly. Smart enough to know why, he instead took his frustrations out on the monsters around them. Felix, meanwhile, used their bond to guide him toward the worst of the beasts, fighting as a team. During their evenings, Felix had been using his Mantle of the Long Night to help train up his Companion's Cold Resistance. If they were going to fight the Reforged, he'd need it.

Eventually, his friends came up to him to discuss tactics and Skills. All of them wanted to move faster, and what better way than to work together more efficiently. They'd had a few conversations in the past, but Felix was excited—it made his Mind spin as the possibilities unfolded before him.

Control the field. Destroy the minions but focus on the big bads. Classic tabletop strategy from a long time ago, when he'd rolled dice and pretended to be a mighty mage. With the array of Skills at their disposal, though, Felix finally saw how he could accomplish that.

Bindings of the White Waste, Stone Shaping, and Influence of the Wisp were all ways to shut down or guide a battle. Fields of Flame, Pillars of the Domineering Sentinel, and Spear of Tribulations were excellent high-damage area-of-effect Skills. Evie even had her Breaking Wheel, which was a bit more limited but still devastating, especially with her new chain.

In fact, all of their new weapons proved themselves over and over again. Alister's rapier was strong enough to drill holes into the hardiest Tier II monster hides, each strike leaving basketball-sized divots that dropped their Health rapidly. Atar had his stave, which he found could channel his Sparkbolts, amplifying them just a little as he laid the shots out like a Gatling gun.

Vess' spear and Evie's chain both had proven their worth, able to lay down the hurt with considerable more intensity than before. The two of them were whirlwinds on the battlefield, mowing down enemies at a pace he'd never seen from them. They couldn't be touched, even by the rare Agility-focused monstrosity, too fast and too skilled.

On the fifth day from the grasslands, they encountered the Reforged.

It was a squad of them, numbering at least ten, and all were equipped with heavy, ice-forged mauls. They were impossible to miss, as the smallest were fifteen feet tall and the largest more in the realm of twenty or thirty feet tall. Still, despite their massive dimensions, the Reforged they encountered were clumsily combing through trees and undergrowth, their blue skin and icy armor carelessly leaving a wake of devastation in their path. Even worse, they had a number of canines the size of horses with mangy fur and complicated metal additions.

<Siva's Grace,> Vess signed. <Are those Hoarhounds? What did they do to them?>

The Hoarhounds once looked like giant wolves draped with an icy aura of power, but now they were… sickly. Their blue-white fur had largely fallen out, replaced instead with metal panels bolted into their bones. Their forelegs were replaced completely with dark metal claws, and their jaws were like bear traps as designed by H. R. Giger. Felix's sharp eyes picked out Profane Sigils across the metal portions, flaring like steady heartbeats. Felix grimaced. They hadn't been nice creatures, but this felt… obscene.

<Can we not study them longer?> Nevia asked, her thick fingers twitching with anticipation. <That ice armor is so advanced. It's articulated!>

<No. Move. Quietly,> was Harn's terse response.

Felix extended his Abyssal Skein over the group, a task which felt easier than ever yet still utterly unpleasant. They ghosted through the forest, descending into a dry gully to keep a low ridge between them and the Reforged. Felix guided Pit across the ground, ensuring his Companion had Skulk activated as they took a wide circle around the enemy.

The question remained, however: what were they searching for?

Their column jerked to a sudden stop, and Felix swept his senses ahead of them. His Body was ready for violence, but the sight of the tube-like creature before them put his Mind on pause. It looked like a six-foot-long snake with rocks for skin, no eyes, and was half-buried in the solid stone and soil of the ridge. The thick, four-foot-diameter creature wove back and forth like it was... searching.

Pit almost tore from his grip, but Felix hauled back, and his claws only flashed out at empty air.

Pit! Stop! Bad idea!

The creature was a Wurm, looking much like an earthworm with armored hide, four-way jaws, and the ability to tunnel seamlessly through the earth. When they got big, like this one, they could also breathe fire. All in all, not a great monster to encounter in a gully with a bunch of giants behind them.

It lifted its eyeless face, rearing up and spreading its jaws to reveal the wet, purple flesh inside its maw. Dribbles of burning spittle oozed to the rocky ground.

Felix understood his friend's fury, though. The Wurms had captured Felix and Pit when both were far weaker, intending to eat Felix and experiment on Pit. The tenku had been put in a cage and beaten until his wings had broken. All of that history boiled through Pit's Spirit, legible to Felix as if it were written in front of his eyes.

We'll get them back for it, bud. But not now. We have to choose our time, okay?

By cajoling and bargaining, Felix pulled his friend back from the edge of disaster. Perhaps they could have taken the Wurm, but it would bring the Reforged down on them. And even then, they could probably kill them all. But what then? Fight another army to get to the Temple?

We're being quiet, *Pit. The other option doesn't work.*

Pit silently snarled before he dissolved into a flash of light. Thankfully, Abyssal Skein covered that, because the Wurm didn't even react as Pit converged into Felix's Spirit.

Thanks, bud. Just hold tight. His words were only met with meaningless, warbling grumbles.

<They're blind, but they can sense through the earth,> Felix signed to the rest. <Abyssal Skein should keep us clear, but Alister and Vess, ready your Skills.>

The two nodded, each limbering their respective weapons as they crept beneath the creature's questing head. Its jaws pulsed, opening and closing as if it were breathing or maybe tasting the air.

Abyssal Skein is level 45!

They slipped by it, just barely skirting its craggy hide, though they had a close call as it began to move again. The Wurm arced over their heads and into the earth on the other side of the gully, where it undulated through the ground. The lot of them breathed a sigh of relief as it swam away.

That relief lasted until Felix exited the gully, finding a hooked spear inches from his face.

"Who do you serve?"

The voice was melodic, almost painfully so, but her face was elongated with sharp cheekbones and large, almond shaped eyes. She—and it was clearly a woman—bared her wide, flat teeth at them all.

"Answer or die."

They had found the Henaari. And she could see them.

CHAPTER TWENTY-FIVE

Thadeus Thangle pushed through the blowing wind, peering into the snow-like accumulation for his target. His wild thatch of white hair was tangled with sticks and leaves, but he hadn't put mind to his appearance in weeks. Illusions, after all, covered many things, and he'd had more important things to worry about. Now, he clutched at the enchanted rock in his fist, praying to the Twins that its *gale* inscription not fail. It held, for now.

Twin's praise for small blessings.

Around him was a forest of giant, oozing mushrooms. They formed a second canopy beneath the trees, stretching thirty or forty span ground to gills, while the tops soared higher still. The expedition into the Verdant Pass had encountered it two days after emerging through the Tin Gate, and with them came the humanoid mushrooms called Lamellans. They varied from Gnome to Human to Ogre-sized, and no two were alike in appearance. But all of them were violently opposed to the company's intrusion. Even worse, they had control over the larger tree-fungi: at their command, spores would rain down from above like snow.

The spores were the true killers.

The efforts of the wind mages had made it safer for their company, but it had taken them two deaths to realize the danger. Those two scouts—Twins have mercy—they had died when the spores rooted in their chests and began to grow. In seconds, the poor fools were more mushroom than man, and they were dead. No measure of healing could save them. Now their mages expended themselves to keep the spores away from their teams, but their Mana would only last so long.

The Lamellans were many, but the true threat was the monster lure at the center of their horde. The steady supply of undifferentiated Mana was enticing and enraging the local beasts in turn, driving them into a frenzy and fueling the nonstop production of their spores. The Hand led a charge against the Lamellans, personally taking down hundreds of them. But still they came, their unnatural procreation more than a match for an Adept's killing fury. Zara may have been able to find and destroy the lure, as well as the entire forest of monsters, but she had gone ahead. Doing what, only the Sorcerer knew.

That left him. A tiny Gnome against a fungal horde.

His target ducked behind a thick stalk of fungal flesh, swift as a hare in a winter storm. Through a haze of violet Mana vapor, the Gnome could only make out the dim flash of crimson and white metal. Thangle would have been impressed if he wasn't so annoyed.

Damnable redcloaks. How dare they touch my precious illusions!

He had spotted the redcloak moving through the army, covered in a Seeming spell. The spell itself was similar in kind to his Obfuscation in that it was an illusion, but where Obfuscation confused the senses, a Seeming simply showed you what you expected. In this case, a small, weaker Lamellan carrying a heavy rock. Their size and threat were dwarfed by the ten-foot monstrosities that swarmed around them, and even the monsters themselves were fooled. Not the Terrific Thadeus Thangle, though. He spotted the violet haze of augmentation Mana in an instant.

Thangle ducked beneath a thicket of fibrous strands, his small size a boon as he moved alone through the horde. Aside from the wind stone in his grip—enchanted by a harried mage—that ensured the spores kept away from his face, Thangle was slowly rotating his own augmentation Mana in deft circuits. Each pass turned Lamellan senses away toward juicier, extant targets.

Obfuscation is level 62!

"Nine Sundered Serpents!"

That cataclysmic shout was all Thangle heard before the forest around him *buckled*, and the flash of silver and deep blue Mana surged out in jagged streams. Trees crashed to the earth, followed by mushroom spears that sprayed fountains of snow-white spores into the air. Those spores were caught up in the storm of Mana and dissolved instantly. Those streams, nine of them, extended from the greatsword of the Chosen Hand and bisected legions of the Lamellan all at once. The man stood at the head of the guard, his Spirit a riot of power that hurt Thangle to even look upon, even as his Skill threatened to cut the Gnome in half.

Blasted fool! Thangle danced backward, taking cover behind the ten-span thickness of a tree. *Can't he see I'm out here?*

Of course he couldn't, that was the point of his illusion. But Thangle only saw that as the man's failure. If Felix were there, he would have spotted the Gnome right off the bat.

I should have gone to the Foglands, too, he whined. *But no, I decided to help the city guard instead!*

The earth shook again, but this time, it wasn't the Hand's attacks, but the fungal horde's response. A creature, birthed from the glistening gills of a downed mushroom, was the size of one of those ice warriors. It was easily twenty span tall and just as wide, a solid, damp knot of mindless violence. It charged the moment it gained its feet, bashing through trees and fungal forces alike on a beeline toward the Hand.

Analyze!

Name: Lamellan Titan
Type: Mycid
Level: 72
...

Thangle pulled his attention away from the beast as soon as he realized it was well beyond him. Instead, he poured more of his concentration into his Obfuscation, even as the earth bucked again. Ahead, the redcloak had been slipping like an oiled shadow between mushroom and trees, but the roaring charge of the Titan threw him to the earth. The stone he'd gripped fell and, with a flicker, escaped the reach of the redcloak's Spirit.

No!

The unremarkable boulder turned instantly into a shining green gem the size of a Human head. It was unpolished except along two sides where gold script was barely legible. The moment it escaped the redcloak's Seeming, the monsters in the area went absolutely insane.

Zara considered the site of the next Passage. She had cleared the area with some difficulty, as the fungal growths were impressively resistant to magical forces. She found the trick of it soon enough, however, and now the low mound of their next pathway was razed. The last thing she wanted was one of the Lamellan creatures entering the Passages after them. It would be… unpleasant.

"My lady!" Keru shouted from above. Zara looked up to see him bobbing atop a thin branch, feathers fluffed in alarm. "The Mana purity just rose an entire twelve percent!"

She felt it. A lingering coolness on her senses like mint on the tongue, but strangely tasteless. *Undifferentiated Mana.* She whipped her head back to the battle happening half a league behind her. *The lure is potent, more so than the last.*

"Wait here, Grouse," she mumbled to her avum. The ugly bird chirped urgently, and Zara rolled her eyes before tossing an opened bag of feed at its feet. Grouse cooed in delight before ignoring her entirely. "Keru, lead the way."

A wave of power lifted her from the clearing, carrying her behind her familiar at speeds not even her mount could match. The fungal forest reemerged around her, filled with their horrid spores and dominated by the press of thousands of fibrous, glistening bodies writhing atop a single point. Her people were just beyond, valiantly trying to cut through the mass of violent Lamellan, but each one killed was met with another two emerging from the woods.

"Ten Sundered Serpents!"

The Hand's Mana surged forth, cutting down an enormous specimen in a single blow. A wave of Mana bolts, arrows, and conjured spears followed, with little result.

We haven't the time for this. Zara raised her hands and poured power from her core. It gathered in her hands where she shaped it into a spellform that was half-sung into existence.

Full Stop.

Thangle hurled himself over an errant line of metal Mana, barely clearing it before it carved a Gnome-sized chunk out of a Lamellan warrior. He might not be seen, but those Mana blades would kill him just as easily as anyone else. Easier, in fact. The illusionist never put much into Vitality, after all.

He pushed up from the ground, careful not to breathe in the spores that had fetched up between roots, and stumbled onward. At least, until a wall of blue-green Mana screamed into existence, visible to even the most Mana-blind. With a gasp, he put a massive tree between him and the power and erected the paltry defensive magics he knew. The power swept through him, unconcerned with his attempts, and Thangle's senses heaved.

Next thing he knew, he was twenty strides away, upside down against the burning remnant of a giant mushroom.

"You're alright, Thad?" Karp called from across the clearing. The red-bearded archer was covered in soot, and his footsteps kicked up piles of ash. Thangle managed a weary nod before righting himself. "Good. We've got enough injured."

"The… the lure?" Thangle rasped. His body felt curiously dry—parched, even—as if he hadn't had a drink in days. "Where's the lure?"

"Lure? Oh, the rock?" Karp gestured toward the easterly end of the clearing. "Zara and the Hand got it after they killed the rest of the shrooms."

Thangle gritted his teeth. He'd been trying to get the lure because no one else had noticed it or listened to him when he pointed it out. He—he let himself breath outward, releasing tension from his Body.

They got it and stopped it. That's all that matters.

If they hadn't, the fight would still be raging. In fact, the entire forest had nearly been struck down, as all the vegetation in hundreds of strides had been rendered to crumbling ash. Nothing but their people had survived, and even then quite a few were looking haggard. The danger, however, seemed to have passed. Thangle could appreciate no longer being in mortal danger. After the battle for Haarwatch, his appetite for large, involved battles had grown thin, and it had never been large in the first place. There was a reason his physical stats were as low as they were; combat was not for him.

An icon wiggled in his vision, and Thangle raised his eyebrows in surprise.

Obfuscation is level 64!
Mana Shield is level 22!
Turned Blade is level 19!

You Have Earned a New Title!
Warrior of the Fungal Forest (Uncommon)!
You have proven yourself in combat against the legions of Lamellan! +3 to VIT, END, and WIL!

You Have Gained a Level!
You Are Now Level 39!
You Have Earned +3 to INT, +2 to AGL!
You Have 2 Unused Stat Points!

System energy punched into his core, churning through the frame of a spinning gyroscope before spraying outward in streams of inky violet that sent his affected Skills and stats rising ever higher.

Years between levels, and now I've gone and gained six in as many weeks. Thangle pushed through the knee-deep layer of ash and hobbled toward the rest of the company. *What are you doing, old man? War, at your age? Pfah!*

And yet he was but steps from attaining Journeyman Tier. Thangle could not help but feel a little eager for the next fight, so long as it pushed him further. If he continued to improve, he might see his two hundredth birthday yet. The thought warmed him as he picked his way down the hill, joining the groaning procession on their march toward the next Gate.

When the path diverged from an easterly direction, Thangle's stomach fluttered in nervous fear. When Zara led them to another low hill surmounted by stone pillars, his blood went cold.

Again?

With a sing-song word, the Dark Passages beneath the hill opened once again. A crack like the maw of a dread beast opened up, and the fetid breath of the earth filled the area with a faint miasma. Or perhaps that was his imagination.

Perhaps.

Thangle had seen and heard monstrosities in those dark pathways. Karp was not the only one to nearly fall off, nor the only one to hear the insidious whispers of those… things.

"We must hurry," Zara was saying to the company. She held up a green stone that shone dully in the sunlight. "The road ahead of us is littered with more and more of these lures. For all their illegality, the Inquisition seems intent on limiting all pursuit however they have to, whether that upsets the delicate balance of the Pass or not. Or even puts two cities in mortal danger."

She shook her head and stored the stone. Thangle could tell she'd done something to muffle its influence, but he could still feel the bright feeling of its Mana. "They have shown themselves prepared to do whatever it takes to destroy us, our city, and all that lives within. We must likewise be ruthless in our chase. I know many of you fear the Dark Passages, but they are a necessary risk. I will protect you all. Just stay close, focus on the path, and do not stray."

Without another word, Zara disappeared into the unnatural darkness. The Haarguard, despite grumbling and anxious glances, all followed behind. Thangle was among the last to enter, along with Karp, and the pair of them traded nervous smiles.

"I truly dislike this place," Thangle said.

"Then let's get out fast," Karp said. His jaw clenched spasmodically. "Swift as an arrow, true?"

"Let's."

The earthen portal consumed them, soon followed by the blue-green light of Zara's power. It blanketed them and illuminated the path forward so that they all appeared ghostly. The magic didn't unnerve the illusionist—in fact it fascinated him—but the fact that he could feel it made him truly fearful. Whatever place the Passages traversed, they numbed his senses in a way that made him feel almost Untempered. He couldn't even work his illusions within the Passage. Zara had mentioned the effect was worse the higher your advancement, but Thangle couldn't imagine that.

"You good, Karp?" he asked. The archer was gently pulling on his blindfolded avum, who remained fixed in place. He began tugging with greater intensity.

"Soon as I get this blighted bird moving," he grunted. "C'mon, what's wrong? We're gonna get left behind!"

"Wark!"

The avum's call was aggressive, and its crest feathers stood on end as it stared back the way they had come. Thangle looked into the dark without thinking, but instead of some slithering abomination, he saw a very surprised man in white armor and a crimson cloak.

"Wh-what is this?" he moaned in horror.

The scout survived!

"Redcloak!" Karp shouted, yanking his bow free and loosing an arrow in the same breath. The redcloak brought an arm up, and the arrow shattered on his plate armor.

"Heretics, all of you. You have taken me into a place of demons!" The redcloak, clearly an Initiate, surged forward on powerful legs in a serpentine pattern to avoid Karp's ceaseless arrows. "Free me!"

"No one asked you to come along!" Thangle hissed. He turned back to Karp. "We need to run! Now!"

"What? Why—?" The archer cut himself off as he noticed what Thangle saw, and the both of them retreated. Karp gripped the lead of his mount, and with a final tug, it began to trot after them.

Beyond the Initiate, the path had begun to sag and fray, and in the dark...

"Run!"

The four—mage, archer, avum, and Initiate—began a mad dash toward their company and the brighter green-blue glow of Zara's magic. Behind them, the path fell apart all the faster, as if spurred on by the redcloak's frenzied screams.

"Heresy! Sorcery! Vile betrayal!"

"Shut up!" Thangle shouted back as they reached the edges of their group, who were just now turning back toward their altercation. "A blighted redcloak got in!"

"How?" Zara shouted as she pushed to the back, before she waved her question aside. "Night! I'm barely able to hold your fears in abeyance, let alone his!" Groans from around them shook the path even under Zara's direct influence, until it started feeling decidedly tacky underfoot. The Initiate charged at them with madness gleaming in his eyes. "Fine. Everyone be ready to run when I say."

An exhalation of thick Mana vapor poured from all of Zara's channels at once, and Thangle watched in awe as she wove them into strands of incandescent power, each one an enchantment that found their way onto the Initiate. Despite this desperate speed and reflexes, the enchantments layered upon the man until he froze in place, unable to even lift a foot. Spinning her hands, Zara seized the redcloak in her remaining strands and hurled him bodily from the path.

Into the dark.

Where *something* opened an eye the size of the Sunrise Gate, and the man vanished into a mouth made from the stuff of nightmares.

"Now run. Bloody ashes, run!"

Never before had the Gnome been so thankful for military training, as the Haarguard moved with both speed and what precision they could wrangle from the jaws of their terror. Because, all around them, the Passages became a maelstrom of dark horrors, spindly limbs and hooked tentacles writhing around the dwindling protection of Zara's magic, while lamprey mouths flashed in and out of view, twisting among the throng of abominations.

Screams of the dead, the damned, of all their regrets called to them. Thangle heard voices he'd not put mind to in decades, centuries in some cases, but they slithered through his ears with agonized howls. The path wobbled and softened all the more as fear took hold, but he couldn't spare the concentration to keep track of who they lost. Avum, certainly. More than a few squawks were cut short. They slung spells at the beasts, but Zara only cursed at them for their efforts.

"You waste your Mana and merely draw more! Focus on the path! Only the path!"

The Sorcerer's magic bathed them all, but it waned the further they ran. She was clearly expending herself against the abominations, against the Passages themselves as they began to *squeeze.* Thangle felt it like a hand at his neck, and his meager Spirit could do nothing about it.

"There!" someone shouted.

A portal of aquamarine light blazed into existence, perpendicular to their path. With a scream of effort, Zara *twisted* the path, and all of them stumbled. When Thangle regained his feet, the others were already running again. Karp grabbed him by the back of his robes, undignified certainly, but he wasn't about to complain.

The path collapsed behind them, and the darkness pounced, tearing into guards around them. Thangle pulled power from the purple tome in his chest and threw it out of the channels at his feet, shaping the lot of it into spears of augmentation Mana. *Things* snapped it up, twisting about themselves in their frenzy.

The portal flickered with each guard who passed. Dimmed. They reached it.

They leaped through—

—and directly into something warm, wet, and eagerly lapping at his face and chest and—

A lake, he realized. *Water.*

Thangle let out a strangled sort of laugh as visceral relief rushed through his limbs. He rolled over, letting himself soak in the shallows he found himself within. He felt weak, his core almost empty, his Body an exhausted sack of flesh. Men and women were standing all around him, shouting, cursing, but Thangle simply stared up and praised the Twins that he still lived.

Until he noticed the sun. It was...on the wrong side of the sky.

It was dawn only two glasses ago. And we traveled in the Passages for less than a quarter glass. How is that possible?

Because the sun was now lost in the west, nearly about to set beyond the mountains. They had lost nearly an entire day in the Passages.

"Blighted Night," Zara said from nearby. "We've barely moved five leagues."

"How?" the Hand rumbled. Thangle sat up, his gut protesting.

The two of them stood close, and the guards were all picking themselves and their mounts from the edge of a wide lake.

"Our plight forced my hand. Either create an exit or die." Her bright kingfisher alighted on her shoulder and whispered something to her. She shook her head. "We may die either way. The Inquisition has passed the Iron Gate. Our chase just became more desperate."

Thangle laid back down in the water and closed his eyes. *Madness.*

CHAPTER TWENTY-SIX

Voracious Eye!

Name: Wyvora
Race: Henaari
Level: 68
HP: 2434/2434
SP: 1189/1233
MP: 877/877
Lore: Henaari are a nomadic, matriarchal people that are known for their dedication to the Endless Raven. They excel at physical Skills and have a mild aptitude for the magical arts.
Strength: More Data Required
Weakness: More Data Required

Voracious Eye is level 52!

"Answer me!" the Henaari woman hissed. They were so close to the Reforged, to the damn *Wurm*. "Who do you serve?"

Felix held his hands out to the side, eyeing the hooked polearm in his face. The woman—*the warrior*, he corrected himself—was tense and ready for a fight, and her stance was strong. His Voracious Eye flickered across her armor, boots, the pendant hanging from her neck. Most of it was Journeyman-Tier crafting work, and the pendant spoke for itself.

Name: Farwalker's Finder
Type: Necklace (Enchanted)
Lore: Made from the first stone found by a Henaari Farwalker on their first excursion, it has been enchanted to lead them to interesting places.

He'd seen its like before. Had even worn one for a while, before the Archon took it.

"We're here from Haarwatch," Harn growled. He kept his voice low enough that it barely echoed in his helmet. "On a Quest."

Wyvora's stance softened, just slightly. She jabbed her polearm an inch or two closer to Felix. "Prove it."

"Felix?" Harn asked with a grunt. It wasn't his Quest to share, after all.

Felix looked at the Henaari's eyes, the set of her mouth, and listened to the beat of her Spirit. It was tense aggression and impatience. He had a solid idea what would happen, even if he showed his Quest to her. This woman wanted to fight.

"No," he said.

Wyvora burst into motion, her spear going from zero to a hundred miles an hour in less than a blink. Felix slashed his arms up and down, expecting the strike. But she didn't attack him. The point of the polearm hit Harn instead, denting his chestplate and sending him sprawling to the earth with a clatter of steel.

"Imbued Sparkbolt!"

"Grand Impetus!"

"Bindings of the White Waste!"

Chains of ice Mana slipped harmlessly off the warrior, unable to find purchase as she became a literal blur and disappeared moments before crimson fireballs and a ram of kinetic Mana tore through her former position.

The Henaari flashed ahead, pulling Evie's legs out from beneath her with the hook of her spear, before pivoting and smashing Harn on the helmet for good measure. Vess leaped forward, her Dragoon's Footwork and Grace passive Skill almost blinking her across the intervening space. She led the way with her blue-white partisan, all of her Strength balanced at the tip of its blade.

Wyvora deflected it down with a whirling parry that sent a spray of dark feathers at the heiress. Vess flinched back, unbalanced, as her spear hit the rocky earth hard enough to split it apart, and a thunderous crack tore through the air.

"RRRUUUAAAAAAGH!"

"Great job!" Felix shouted at the Henaari. "You wanted a fight? You got one!"

Unfettered Volition!

The woman had lunged for the mages who still tried to pepper her with ice, fire, and force bolts. She had a solid twenty feet on him, was already running, and he was at a dead stop.

It didn't matter.

The earth concaved beneath his feet, but he was already gone, flowing across the gully like the wind itself. Over seven hundred points of Agility and near equal amounts of Dexterity meant when he moved, truly moved, it was like everyone else was standing still. Rocks and soil exploded beneath his heavy tread, his greaves creaking with the strain of his movement.

Felix spun Mana up from his core and into his left palm. A tendril of shadow manifested before splitting into two, and he slung it sideways at the warrior. They hit the hooked polearm and immediately bound it fast. The Henaari drew up short, her spear stopped feet away from Atar's chest.

"How—You—!"

"Me," Felix growled, and hauled back, *hard.*

The spear was pulled back, but Wyvora didn't let go. She flowed with it, her surprised expression quickly turning to a fearsome concentration. Fast as he moved it, she flipped, reorienting herself on the haft before pulling a long dagger from her waist. The Shadow Whip vanished just as she reached Felix, but he caught her blade in his bare hand. And stopped it.

"What?"

Felix didn't answer, but he squeezed, and the dagger snapped in half.

Wild Threnody!

Felix's Adamant Discord vibrated as Mana boiled out of his core and into his channels, shaped and sped along its way by his magical melee Skill, pumped into his bare fist. His left hook caught the Henaari in her right shoulder and hurled her backward powerfully. She hit the ridge with a muffled thunderclap, lightning still crawling across her armor.

"Reforged! Incoming!" Evie howled.

The ridge erupted into a cloud of jagged debris and dust, and the Henaari was buried in it as a half dozen bulldozed it over in their frenzied haste.

"RUUAAAGH! Kill wanderers!" the lead one bellowed. None of his people gave them the time to breathe, however. Quick as a flash, the lead Reforged was met with dozens of wooden and icy arrows, enough that they had to lift an arm to see through the barrage...and enough time for Harn to set his twin axes ablaze.

"Raze!"

They flashed with silvery Mana, and the Reforge's leg was severed completely. It screamed as it fell, but that only put it in range of Harn's axes once more.

It didn't scream a third time.

"No! I hate this Skill!" Atar shouted. Purple-white Mana vapor surged all around them as the Reforged activated their Mantles, a Skill they apparently retained from their former lives as Frost Giants.

Then flares of brilliant orange beat the purple-white back, and Atar dropped a field of near-liquid flame onto the three closest. They screamed, but were not cowed and charged the defenseless mage. He gasped, finding himself entirely too close to run.

Pillars of the Domineering Sentinel!

Six vertical pillars of blue, kinetic Mana slammed into the earth, right atop the three charging Reforged. It stamped out the flames on their bodies while simultaneously staggering them for a brief second. Long enough for Alister to drag him out of the way of their mauls, which slammed into the ground hard enough to split it wide open.

"My savior." Atar smiled.

"Don't be daft next time, Atty," Alister growled. "Maintain distance."

"I know that!"

Unfortunately, one of the three recovered quicker than the rest. Without a sound, it lunged for them both.

"High Bulwark!"

An Iron Rank sped ahead of the strike, slamming his shield into the earth. There was a scream of tortured metal as maul hit shield, but Vyne barely screamed at all. "Be-behind me!" Vyne gasped, before his own Mana rose up. "Carapace of Steel! Stone Thews!"

Atar stuttered to his feet, furious. "I'll not be saved by some *Iron Rank*! Crown of Ignis!" A triumphant, multi-tined coronet manifested entirely of flames. Orange Sparkbolts tainted by a deep crimson snapped around him, motes that became bowling ball-sized orbs of flame. "*Burn*."

The other six Reforged did not sit by and wait while the meat shield and mages made their stand and instead stampeded across the dry gully toward the nearest targets. In this case, that meant the Haarguard.

Blind gods, Evie groused. Her chain gathered at her waist, and she lightened her mass with her Born Trait. Lighter, she fairly flew across the battlefield, weaving between the savage burning fields Atar was creating. She was too far, though, and the Reforged too fast. Meanwhile, the guards had stopped to make a burning *stand*, of all things. *They're gonna die.*

Arrows of enchanted wood and ice hit the Reforged hard, but it barely dented their Health. Kylar zipped ahead, meeting one of their charges alongside Davum, their weapons blurring with Strength and Agility behind them.

"Kata of the Butcher Bird!" Kylar shouted, and his already speedy longswords became looping whorls of enchanted steel. A heavy maul struck down at him, but he danced aside, letting his whirling blades turn it aside with a surprising amount of skill.

"Poisoned Breath!" the Orc bellowed before a venomous green

cloud sprayed outward to envelop the Reforged. Its power was not inconsiderable, and it withered some of the less hardy plants close by.

The Reforged were not even inconvenienced by it.

"Wanderers die!" they screamed, vowels thick in their mouths. "No eyes! No wings!" They swung their mauls, and their Mantles of ice Mana redoubled, quickly coating the ground in a thickening frost. Davum slipped and caught a maul across the back, smashing him into the earth and deforming his armor.

"Davum!" Kylar shouted. "You—!"

Whatever Kylar tried to say was lost as a Hoarhound pounced on him from the clouds of ice fog and rock dust. Its horse-sized body carried Kylar fifteen feet before they landed with a sickening *thud.*

"Kylar!" Kikri howled, unleashing a bombardment of arrows twisting with heat and force Mana. The projectiles hit the Hoarhound in the flank, sending it stumbling aside before it angled its metal-mangled head in the Elf's direction. It bit the next volley of arrows out of the air with a snap of its false jaws, their magic doing nothing to the sigils that burned bright across its face.

Kikri reached for another arrow, but she was out. There were no trees in the gully to fuel her Green Shaping. She backed up, nerves clearly fraying, and tripped over a stone outcropping. It wasn't much, but it was enough.

The Hoarhound lunged—

—and had its snout bashed in by a bladed chain. It tried to howl in pain or dismay, but the chain twisted, altering its direction to wrap around its jaws before it became so damn heavy it sent the hound's head slamming to the earth.

"Bad dog," Evie puffed. "Lie down. Ice Spike."

A literal spike of ice formed in Evie's hand, molding over her fist like a frozen dagger. She punched once, twice, three times into the Hoarhound, but its hide was too thick. The creature scrabbled at the earth, pulling at its weighted head with incredible strength. It stood on shaky legs, and its eyes blazed with madness.

"Damn, I'm a bad matchup for ice monsters," she said, shrugging. The former frost wolf lunged again, leading with Evie's bladed chain. "She isn't, though."

A blue-white partisan exploded out of the Hoarhound's belly as

Vess landed atop it, pinning it completely to the ground. With a savage twist, she ended it. The mutilated creature fell, its organs turned to chopped salad.

"Come. We will end the Reforged together," Vess said before leaping away, her Born Trait sending her soaring through the air.

"Yeah sure, right behind you," Evie groaned. With a flick of her wrist, her chain came untangled and snapped back to its shorter length. But she barely took a step when the ground around her grew suddenly soft and treacherous.

"Shit."

"Ah, burnin' Night! We got Wurms, too!"

Felix's gaze was drawn from the battle to see Evie spiraling her chain around her body, defending from something that was leaping about her so rapidly it was a faint blur in the dust.

"How many?" Felix shouted out.

"Two? Three? They're movin' so fast, I don't know!"

"Christ, it just keeps getting better," Felix hissed. One Wurm he was confident in fighting off, maybe two, but more than that he wasn't sure. Everything was happening so fast, seconds crowding on top of one another. Two of the Haarguard were down, Harn was still grappling with the one-legged Reforged, and he didn't even know where the Henaari went. He hadn't gotten a kill notification for her, so she was still alive. "Hold tight!"

Felix took a run up and blasted across the field, spinning his Mana through his channels in a familiar pattern, sounding the Skill with the Chant.

Stone Shaping!

The rock around Evie loosened, turning to that pudding-like consistency before Felix shoved his hands roughly apart. Mana Skill met his Willpower and Strength, and he leveraged the hell out of both of them until the ground around Evie was ripped entirely free of the earth. Two Wurms dangled from the chunked and disrupted stone, disoriented and disadvantaged but not for long.

"Hit them hard!" he shouted at his friend. Her chain shifted from defense to offense in a blink, blades and spikes twisting like the weapon had a life of its own. It coiled and struck, wrapping around one of the Wurms. The creature bellowed, thick orange spittle oozing from its maw.

Influence of the Wisp!

His Will and Alacrity latched onto the both of them, pushing as hard as he could.

A Wurm (x2) Has Been Enthralled For 2 Seconds!

Blue-white flames ate viciously at both Wurms as they hit the ground hard. Felix didn't let them do much more than hold them in place, however. His hooked blade severed their heads in the space of a heartbeat.

You Have Killed A Wurm (x2)!
XP Earned!

"Damn, Felix," Evie wheezed. "How fast are you now?"

"Not fast enough," Felix said, looking at the two Haarguard on the ground. Harn had finished his opponent and had drawn away the rest from the Iron Ranks. Kikri and Nevia had pulled the two of them away from the conflict.

Before she could offer him false words of comfort, Felix moved on. Pit called to him from above, pointing out another target.

Wyvora lifted herself from the rockslide she found herself within. For a panicked moment, she couldn't find her *aphim*, but the hooked spear was simply a stride away. She stood and through the settling rock dust, Wyvora saw a wild battle.

They're... fighting them off? The Humans were facing off against several of the Reforged monstrosities, and to her surprise, they were holding their own. The abominations were a lot to handle, even for her Journeyman fighters. A few of their number had fallen, but many had not.

Then she saw *him.* Their leader.

Not the one encased in metal, the one with the angry Spirit and burning axes. No. The other one. The one that shone like the sun to her senses.

He moved fast, faster than anyone she'd ever met below Master Tier. Perhaps the Farwalker could compare, before—but no. He summoned that tendril of shadow and large orbs of acid, each spell finding a target and either reaping a life or opening up a Reforged so that one of his warriors could do the deed.

He cannot be allowed to reach the camp. She hardened her resolve and touched upon the thread of power, flooding her Spirit with a dark potency. *Raven bless me, for I need the strength to oppose our enemies.*

Blessing of the Raven Received!
The Urge Hears Your Prayers!

Her wide eyes filled with darkness, and Wyvora let herself smile.

The mages were spent, Evie and Harn injured, the Haarguard useless. Still, the Reforged raged. They and the three remaining Hoarhounds howled as they barreled toward Felix and Vess with all the subtlety and cruel strength of a tidal wave. They came from both ends of the gully, leaving Felix nowhere to run if he wanted to protect his friends huddled between him and Vess.

Felix and Vess found themselves back to back, her with partisan and he with khopesh and club.

"Brings back memories, eh?" he laughed nervously.

"If only it were storming and dark," Vess panted. "It would complete the portrait."

The remaining Hoarhounds and Reforged converged. They charged.

"Well, I can't do anything about the sun," Felix said and spun up Mana from his core. It crackled through his channels until it surged up and into both of his weapons. "Let's see about the storm."

Wild Threnody!

Adamant Discord!

Channeling the Transcendent spell through his weapons, Felix thrust them both forward until he felt the invisible notch that was his connections to his enemies; it was wide and well-trod, and a link caught fast. He poured his Mana into the spell, bracing himself for the pain of what he was about to do.

Lightning burst outward, slamming into the three Reforged and Hoarhound that charged from his side. It seized their bodies. They fought back, but Felix screamed and brought his Strength, Endurance, and stupidly strong Willpower to bear. Things tore and burst, and a concerning wetness trickled somewhere inside of him, but Felix didn't stop.

He lifted them. All of them.

With a roar, he hurled himself in a semi-circle, dragging them with him until they collided with the Reforged on the other side of the gully. They hit with the sound of thunder and crashing metal and stone and ice, and the gully detonated with the force of it.

"Spear of Tribulations!" Vess shouted over the cacophony. Felix staggered as her seven silver spears shot out into the dust cloud, exploding into whirlwinds of razor-sharp air Mana. The whirlwinds dissipated the clouds of stone and dust, revealing mangled flesh and oozing blue ichor.

You Have Killed A Reforged (x7)!
XP Earned!

You have Killed A Hoarhound (x3)!
XP Earned!

"Siva's Grace," Vess hissed. "You're bleeding."

Felix grunted. "From where?"

"Everywhere," she whispered. Her hand hitched before grabbing his shoulder. "You did too much. Again."

Felix coughed up something that he didn't want to think about. His Aspects felt absolutely abused, his legs shaky and his head pounding. "I did what I had to. Just what—"

"SKKREEAAW!"

Pit screeched from above, releasing a wave of air Mana that tore up the earth just behind Felix. Just close enough that Felix could twist and pull Vess out of the way of the Henaari's spear thrust.

His Companion had flown high above them and kept an eye out all this time for the Henaari's reemergence. Felix didn't know if he would have noticed her in time. Even now, looking straight at her, he couldn't sense her presence.

Pit! Now!

Pit swooped low and twisted his body, dropping the greatsword strapped to his saddle. Felix caught it and brought it to bear in a single, fluid movement. The massive blade stopped a hairsbreadth from the Henaari's charging face. "Now. Let's talk."

Her eyes widened, if that were possible, and flicked between him and Pit in the air. Without warning, she dropped to her knees and... slammed her forehead on the ground.

"Beg mercy, Pactlord!"

Felix traded a glance with Pit as he landed next to him.

"What?"

CHAPTER TWENTY-SEVEN

Felix looked at Vess. "What did she call me?"

"A Pactlord," Vess confirmed but looked just as confused as he was. "I have never heard the term."

"It is one who has formed a Companion Pact with a creature of a higher Realm," the Henaari explained, though her voice was a bit muffled from the dirt.

Felix looked at Pit, who had started cleaning mud from between his toes with his beak. Then he turned back to the heiress. "Okay. Vess, please check if everyone is healing. The guards got hit hard, and I'm not sure about the mages."

"Right away."

Felix glared down at the Henaari, who still hadn't lifted her head. "Why'd you try to kill us?"

"This one apologizes profusely, Pactlord." She pressed further into the ground, somehow. "If you wish, this one shall end this one's life now."

"What? No, don't be stupid," Felix said quickly. He was really getting annoyed. "Explain. Now. And lift your head up."

The woman—Wyvora—tentatively lifted her head but wouldn't meet his gaze. "This one is an apprentice. This one's people have been hunted, chased by the demons in ice for many nights now. This one was protecting."

"Protecting what? Your people? We're not after your people." Felix rubbed the bridge of his nose, trying to cover up the nosebleed that had started again. His Aspects were shaky as all hell, but he shored himself up with Willpower. "Why attack us?"

Wyvora nodded at something behind Felix. "The demons in ice are sometimes accompanied by *things* all in metal. Made of metal. Things that looked like *him.*"

Felix turned to look, still keeping a portion of his senses on the warrior. Behind him, Evie and Atar were pulling Harn up onto a broken stump. His helmet had been knocked off, and his face was sliced open in three places.

"You mean the Arcids," Felix said.

"This one knows not their names. They have slaughtered dozens of us, and their information eludes even our greatest Minds." She seemed more disturbed by the latter than the former, and her surprisingly powerful Spirit trembled in fear. "This one feared the worst, and—and when—"

"And when I didn't answer how you liked, you went on the offensive." Felix sighed. He could sympathize with her position, as long as she was telling the truth. Still, he gestured angrily at the smoking corpses of monsters around them. "Pretty stupid. Had you been right, you'd have been killed. You pulled every damn monster in the area."

"Better to die in service than in fear," she said with a hint of her former steel.

Fifteen feet away, Harn grunted in reluctant approval.

"Vess, what's our situation?" Felix asked.

"No one died, praise Siva, but four are in poor or worse condition." Vess pointed to three other prone forms on the dry gully bed. Felix's Eye picked out Vyne, Kylar, and Davum, each with Health below one hundred. Nevia and Kikri stood over them, worry and fear etched into their faces. Kylar was Bleeding, and Davum had several Status Conditions, none of which were great. Vyne had broken his arm, several ribs, his femur, and his tower shield looked scrapped beyond repair.

Evie glanced up from fussing over Harn—himself with a Concussion (Mild) in addition to his wounds. "I got a few potions left for them, but it's cutting hard into our emergency supplies. What they need is a healer."

"I'll be fine," Harn growled and tried to sit up, but Evie dropped her chain on his chest. It knocked him back to the ground.

"Don't be stubborn. You'll take a potion, and you'll like it," Evie insisted.

"Save 'em for the kids."

But Atar and Alister were already administering vials as they spoke. It wouldn't heal broken bones, but it would elevate their Health until their regeneration could catch up. Felix didn't feel great himself. His regenerations were kicking in and would soon top off, but his Aspects were strained in a way that had nothing to do with his Health and Mana.

"If you require healing, this one humbly offers it."

Felix snapped his attention back on the warrior. She was no longer kowtowing but still knelt. "You're a healer?"

"No. This one's only gifts lie in the hunt. But the Matriarch is a healer of renown."

"The Matriarch. You're saying you'll take us to your camp?" Felix asked.

"Yes. It is the least this one may offer to redress the damage this one has caused." She kowtowed again.

Felix looked to Harn, who shrugged with a pained expression that said "*up to you.*" Evie said just about the same with less. Vess, however, tightened her mouth and fixed the Henaari with a narrow eye.

<I don't trust her,> she signed.

<Not sure I do, either,> Felix signed back.

"How can I trust you, Wyvora?" He asked out loud and noticed the Henaari twitch.

"This one does not know."

Felix made a show of rolling his options over in his head, but he'd already decided. His first responsibility was to keep his people safe.

"You lead, then. But if I notice any tricks—and I will—I won't warn you. I will end you." Anger heated his skin and prickled the back of his neck. Anger for lives that could have been lost, and for those who were hurt in a fight they had no business in. "Understand?"

Wyvora swallowed, and her Spirit shook, but she nodded. "This one understands."

Wyvora found herself at odds. As a Henaari, she had an unshakable pride in her Spear Mastery and in the unrivaled gifts her god granted her, but this one called Felix had countered her so quickly, so *easily* that her pride had all but shattered. The others, she could have bested, even the heavily armored one, if she had enough time. But the longer she stared at this man's features, the more sure she was of her defeat.

Even with the Blessing, she thought. Fear curdled her stomach. *This man would tear me apart.*

And he's a Pactlord! I assaulted a Pactlord! Shame rolled through her, tensing the skin of her scalp and arms, and she wanted nothing more than to hide away for all time. But that was not an option. Wyvora would take them to the clan, secure them healing, and her honor would be… not restored, but certainly mended.

"Oh wait, we don't want to announce what we did." The leader stopped their procession almost as soon as it had begun. "Gotta get rid of the evidence."

He wasn't wrong. The smoke of all of the monsters would draw scavengers, as well as the eye of the Others. Those from beneath the mountain.

"What—"

Her words died in her throat as Felix thrust an arm into the air, and every single corpse burst into dark, greasy smoke streaked with brilliant flares of multi-hued light. The smoke rose up before defying its nature and twisting horizontally… directly toward Felix's open mouth. All that they were, devoured in seconds.

"Alright. Ready?" he asked.

Wyvora could only nod.

They quickly traveled from the blood-soaked clearing. Though there were no more corpses to draw other Reforged to them, Felix wasn't taking any chances. Those who could, walked. Those who couldn't were ferried on Vess' conjured spears.

Vess didn't complain once, no matter that Vyne and Davum likely weighed three hundred pounds—at least—with all their armor. She did, however, shoot the Henaari a number of sharp, angry looks. Her spear's aim did not stray from Wyvora's back.

Kylar was supported by both Nevia and Kikri, and they managed to make good time despite his injuries. Harn, meanwhile, trudged along, refusing help in any form, despite Evie's less than gentle cajoling.

It began to rain not long after they'd left the gully, and no calm spring drizzle. This was a summer storm, complete with black clouds laced with lightning loud enough to shake the trees around them.

Sheets of rain drenched them and made the footing treacherous as they descended toward a river, of all things. The water had forced it to swell over its banks, frothing the currents into fast-moving rapids. Regardless, Felix still caught the gut-clenching sight of jagged fins and barbed spines threading the water.

"We're crossing *that*?" Atar asked over the storm.

"Our destination lies on the other side, yes." Wyvora's voice was matter of fact, as if the thought of fording the raging river was nothing more than a stroll across the room. "We will have to ford it at its most narrow, which is several leagues upstream."

"Joy," the fire mage deadpanned.

"Think of it this way, Sparky," Evie said with a companionable slap on his shoulder. "You're already soaked. Can't get worse!"

A winged insect the size of a big dog buzzed across the river, barely audible over the wind. Without warning, two long, narrow jaws snapped it deftly from the air. Both creatures disappeared with a splash.

Atar groaned, and Alister swallowed audibly. Even Evie looked disturbed.

"Nothin for it," Harn said. He ambled to the water. "Let's kill us some fish."

"Ah, but this is too deep?"

Harn didn't pay her much attention, and other than a smirking shrug from Evie, no one else did either.

The river was perhaps five hundred feet wide and only ever got to seven or eight feet deep at the center. Certainly not impassable, but very annoying and likely deadly had this been Earth.

Fly? Pit inquired.

These winds are too strong, bud. Felix watched several trees get nearly bowled over further down the river. The sky was black. *You'd get swept away faster than the river.*

Pit grumped but stayed put.

Felix walked up to the river's wild edge. He sent his senses questing through the waters, past large, writhing fish monsters and into the bedrock. His Mana followed after, lifting from the two rings burning at his center, until red-gold and blue-white light poured from him like water of his own. It sank into the earth in a blink, turning it to gel until Felix's Will and Intent took hold.

And then pillars speared up from the river.

"Blessed darkness," Wyvora whispered.

"Right," Atar tapped his stave on the rocks. "Forgot he's a big bag of Mana."

Once several feet above the churning surface, the tops of the pillars began to spread and widen, forming into a walkway three feet across and extending in an arch over the entire five hundred foot span.

Stone Shaping is level 59!

By the end, Felix had burned through around half of his Mana but had produced a structure that would, at first glance, impress any engineer at his old firm. He was certain it wouldn't last long, however. The supports and design would hopefully be enough for their crossing, but the rampaging monsters and violent weather on the Continent would bring it down in months, at best.

He stepped forward and tested it with a foot. It neither wobbled nor creaked, and Felix risked putting his full weight on it. It held, remarkably. At his last estimate, Felix was clocking in somewhere around six or seven hundred pounds, thanks to his Journeyman Body.

The guard quietly marveled at the feat of magical engineering, and Wyvora wasn't as good at hiding her surprise as she seemed to think. His friends, however, were a different story.

"Couldn't make it a bit roomier, huh? I can barely swing my chain in here," Evie complained.

"Could've done with a roof. Be nice to get out of the rain," Alister said.

"Right?"

Felix rolled his eyes and followed them across, Pit right behind him. Other than a couple jumping Snapjawed Pike, the crossing was uneventful. Vess and Alister dispatched the few aquatic monsters that attacked with ruthless efficiency.

Ten minutes later, they were across and no worse for wear. Felix nodded to the Henaari. "Where from here?"

Wyvora licked her lips. "We progress through there and up the winding crevasse." She pointed to a darker portion of the forest ahead, where it butted up against a set of pale cliffs. "This one must… must express her dismay, Pactlord."

"Hm?" Felix said. He didn't fail to note the tension rising on her Spirit. Behind her, Vess loomed, partisan leveled.

"This bridge is a wonder, but it will allow this one's enemies that much closer to this one's people." Her wide eyes and elongated head threw off Felix interpretations of her expressions, but her Spirit didn't lie. She was terrified of what she was about to say. "I would ask that you—that you destroy it."

Again, she didn't wince, but she may as well have. She'd even forgotten to do that annoying "this one" thing. It made Felix feel like a bully, for all that she'd tried to kill them earlier. He nodded.

"Not unreasonable. I can do that," he said.

It took less Mana to destroy the bridge than it took to create it, which made sense. Felix knew it had several weak points, and he simply dissolved the stone at those sections, letting the entire thing collapse on itself.

It did, however, give him a terrible migraine and a sudden despondency that worked between the cracks of his mood. The bridge fell, but it felt like it didn't even matter. If he could cross the river, so could his enemies. It was a delaying tactic, nothing more. The Archon would come, and they'd all die. Nothing he made would last.

No.

It felt like shifting the weight of a mountain, but his Willpower grappled with it. The mood moved, inch by inch, lifted by pure force of Will and bullheadedness. It was insidious, but he had spotted it. That was half the battle. Once he had recognized what was happening, he could fight it off.

Oof. He literally panted from the mental exertion. *Mind strain* and *Spirit strain. Worse than ever before.* Felix stared at his shaking hands. *Way worse.*

To the others, and especially the Henaari, he simply nodded as the rushing waters consumed the stone bridge.

Control. Maintain control. He clenched his fists. *Don't let them see you sweat.*

"Keep moving."

The cliff led through a winding crevasse and into a box canyon completely filled with snakes.

"Are you kidding me?"

This time, the outburst was from Evie.

"How many obstacles are there?" she demanded.

"Beyond this there is one other." Wyvora walked forward, into the snake pit without hesitating. "This is the easiest of them."

She stopped in the center of the canyon. A few snakes lunged at her, but she didn't move her long limbs at all. Eventually, the snakes gave up and ignored her.

Felix narrowed his eyes and flared his Manasight. Violet Mana clung tightly to the ground, shaped so exquisitely that he'd never have noticed it if he hadn't looked directly for it.

"Illusions," he said.

Wyvora inclined her head to him.

They moved on.

The canyon fed out into another forest, though this one was encased in tall cliff walls and the beginnings of mountains ahead. The last range before they reached the Archon's Domain. From Felix's vantage, however, all he could see were the thick trunks and dark foliage of the forest.

"This way, if it pleases you," Wyvora said.

Up through the forest, they followed the ghost of a trail that switchbacked up an increasingly steep incline. Felix flexed his Tracking Skill, hoping to spot something of their hosts. All he found were animal prints and scat, tree markings and bird nests. Of the Henaari, he saw nothing, and had he not watched Wyvora walk ahead of him, he would not be able to find her footprints, either.

High-level Stealth or some woodcraft Skill? And do they all have it? A handy Skill to pass down for a nomadic community that, if Vess' reaction was any indication, wasn't well-tolerated. *So, I guess the entrance to their camp is gonna be camouflaged and hidden. No one goes to all this trouble to just hide in the open.*

The path curved around a high cliff, and when they rounded it, Felix gasped.

Wyvora gestured. "The last obstacle is one few can match. The Matriarch praised the Raven for three entire days when we found a place such as this. Only truly ancient ruins can do justice to the Raven's munificence."

Before them, perched on the edge of a cliff, was a face. It was overshadowed by a forest of redwood-sized trees, but the darkness only made the Mana of its form glisten. Wyvora raised an arm. "A ruin of the ancient—"

"Nym," Felix said. Wyvora looked at him askance. "We've seen something like it before."

"Truly?" Her voice lifted, and curiosity sparked in her Spirit. She nodded to the massive, moss-coated head, through whose mouth a wide, dark cavern could be seen. "That is remarkable. Few may hold such an honor—"

"Oh no, another one of these?" Alister said. "Last one almost took my head off."

"Let's hope there's no crystal for Felix to drop on us this time," Evie said, slapping Felix on the back.

"That just means he will get creative," Vess added with a dimpled smile.

Felix smirked, and Pit trilled a bright laugh. *Yeah yeah, laugh it up.* He let the smile drop from his face and tried to scrub it from his Spirit. *Game face on.*

They all entered the cave.

CHAPTER TWENTY-EIGHT

Just inside the literal mouth of the cave, Wyvora stopped them.

"This one would ask that your Companion hide within your Spirit. For a time," she quickly added.

"How do you know of that technique?" Vess asked. Her partisan prodded the Henaari in the spine. The warrior only sucked in a tight breath but didn't break eye contact with Felix.

"You are not the first Pactlord I have met," she said simply.

Interesting. Felix and Pit shared a brief moment of consideration, but both decided at the same time. It shouldn't be an issue. The mages climbed off Pit's back with minor groans, and Pit disappeared in a flash of light. *Nothing we can't undo at will.*

Pit chirruped in agreement.

They pressed farther into the cavern. After ten steps, the darkness was complete, prompting the others to ignite their sight Skills. Brilliant green eyes lit the dark, though Vess' shone with a kaleidoscopic variety of colors, red and yellow predominant. His shone a sharp, cold blue, while the Henaari's did not glow at all. In fact, they all but dripped darkness of their own. A thread of strangely colored Mana trailed from her eyes, but the edge of it disappeared into nothingness... or to an unseen external source. The power Wyvora called on was not her own, that was clear.

The way was relatively relaxing, for all that they were within a

Nymean ruin that was bound to be trapped. Felix spotted a star with only two points etched low along the wall, indicating the threat of the ruin. Not as high as the ruin below Haarwatch, which was a comfort, but not a place to get complacent. In fact, while they were still in the "throat" of the giant Nymean face, Felix sensed metal and acid Mana woven together in the walls to either side. Waiting.

"Careful here. There is a pressure switch that spans the length of the floor," Wyvora warned. She pointed out a perfectly unremarkable section of rock and had all of them step over it. Now that Felix knew where the trigger was, he could sense the dense packing of sigiladry that underlaid the stone. It wasn't really a pressure switch, not exactly—there was no movement or mechanical action. Instead, the ground was laid with a script that somehow detected the weight of people above it, and once it did, blades of forged acid and metal would violently eject from the walls.

No, that's not right. Felix thought as they moved deeper into the cavern. *It wasn't weight. There was a glyph I'm not familiar with at the center.* He pondered its shape as they walked.

Wyvora guided them through the cavern, which opened up considerably after the "throat" portion, pointing out traps laid either by the Nym or her people. The Nymean hazards were extremely sophisticated, as Felix had grown used to seeing, but the Henaari ones weren't half bad, either. Easier to spot, certainly, but clever. If he were relying on Night Eye to navigate, as the majority of his team was, he would have stumbled into many of them. In fact, Evie nearly did, and only her exceptional Agility kept her from harm as bolts of light burned her night vision while poisonous thorn roots tried to entangle her legs.

"Noctis' tits," she muttered. "Warn a girl next time."

"This one tried, but you insisted on walking ahead of—"

"Stop. This conversation's pointless. Keep movin'," Harn grunted. "Evie, watch your step. Keep an eye on the Iron Ranks."

"...Sure."

The way wound forward and downward. Aside from the traps, it was nice to get out of the rain. If he concentrated, Felix could hear the thunder outside, but the layers of earth and stone insulated them from much of it. The path seemed… intentional, as far as Felix could tell. Felix's Manasight could pick out all the details around him, and the eddies of earth and air and shadow Mana all seemed remarkably orderly. He was growing better at peering through the chaos of it all, even as each level of Manasight only increased the noise he could perceive. Still, he recognized that the staid progression of earth Mana was a touch more rigid than normal, and even the normally chaotic swirl of air Mana flowed back and forth through the cavern.

Almost like the statue is breathing in and out, he thought with a shiver. *I swear, if we're in some giant stone golem, I'm gonna be real mad.*

Pit let out a worried trill.

Of course we'd be alright. We're tough, Felix said to his friend while attempting to mask his own worries. It was hard to hide things from someone who shared your Spirit. Pit *qwarked* at him, a clear rebuke. *Okay, I'm a little worried. But we'll make it though, however this shakes out. We always do.*

Pit's attention shifted to those behind them. *Friends,* he sent.

Yeah, that's got me anxious, too. He could protect himself and Pit. He'd done that plenty of times. But everyone else? What, exactly, were they walking into?

After only a few more minutes of narrow crevasses and low ceilings, they all emerged from darkness and into a faint, half-light. A massive cavern spread out before them, so wide Felix couldn't see the end of it and so deep the bottom was nothing short of an abyss. Stalactites hung from the ceiling, each the size of the massive redwood-like trees outside, but even they were dwarfed by the size of it all.

"This is the part where you must trust," Wyvora said.

"Trust who?" Felix asked.

Wyvora simply bowed her head.

Vess' partisan flashed, the blade beneath Wyvora's chin before she could blink. "And why would we trust you?"

"Yeah, get her. I'm really liking this angry side of you, Vess," Evie said from the back. Vess' face colored.

"Why do we have to trust you?" Felix asked, ignoring all the rest. His eyes bored into the Henaari's own, leveraging his Willpower. He was a stone, not to be trifled with nor moved by lies or threats. At least, he hoped that's what he conveyed. "Where do we go from here?"

There was no path. The ledge merely ended, and the abyss began.

"Down," Wyvora said, pointing over the edge. "This is where you step off the path."

"You're kidding," Atar said. "Tell me she's kidding."

"This one is entirely truthful. It is the only way."

Harn peered over the edge and whistled. "Thats, *unf.* That's a long way down. Can't sense farther than fifty span, though. Somethin's blocking me."

Alister held his hand up. "I suggest we push the Henaari down the hole first."

"Ooh, I like that. The nobleman with the plan!" Evie chortled. "What'dya say, lady? You first?"

"If that is what the Pactlord wishes," she said, deferring to Felix.

"Twin's teeth, she's got a thing for you, huh?" Evie whispered to Felix. Her whisper was about as loud as a shout. "*Pactlord* this and *Pactlord* that—"

"Evie," Felix said and gave her a look. She raised her hands and rolled her eyes. "Wyvora, if this is the way forward, then I will trust you." Her Spirit was steady and serene as she had spoken. She was either telling the truth or was the best liar he'd ever seen. "You and I will go first, however."

"Very well," she said and stepped closer to the ledge. "A jump side-by-side would be best. This one would rather not dash herself on the rocks."

"...Right." Felix looked back at the others, who were each staring with varying levels of concern. Vess switched between glaring at Wyvora and looking worriedly at Felix. He made the handsign for <I'm fine> and stepped to the edge. "Together on three?"

"As you wish."

"Three."

Felix grabbed her and stepped into the dark.

Vess clutched her spear as Felix and that woman disappeared over the edge. Had it been made of inferior metals, she would likely have crushed it.

"Relax," Evie said. She sidled closer and toyed with the chain around her waist. "Felix can handle her just fine. Plus, if it's a trap, he'll probably just fly back up here with his lightning-whatsit."

"That is true," Vess admitted. She let a piece of her worry go, breathing the stress out along with some of her anger. The Henaari woman got under her skin so easily. And she had to admit it was not only because she tried to kill them all. "I am more concerned of their Urge's unpredictable powers. You saw some of what she did, yes?"

"During the fight? Yeah. I noticed her Skills seemed… weird." Evie bit the inside of her lip. "Thought I saw a black feather or two a couple times, actually. Not sure what that was."

"Manifestation of a compact of power," Atar said from where he was talking with Nevia and Alister. "She's been drawing on her god this whole time."

"That is what worries me." Vess chose to ignore Atar's incorrect use of the term "god." "All of us are strong, but not even Felix can live through a knife in the heart."

"Dunno," Harn said from the ledge. He had sat down on it with his legs dangling above the dark. "Kid's been through a lot. He's got this."

Vess hoped so.

Rushing wind and shadows. Felix clenched his gut, close to activating his Adamant Discord. Wyvora had tensed as he'd grabbed her, probably not expecting it, but she relaxed as they dropped. Felix tried to take that as an encouraging sign.

The wind whipped up at them, and Felix flared his Manasight to its limit. Green-white steamers flowed by them interspersed with a miasma of black-gray clouds and a spinning cyclone of dusty brown. It was beautiful and hypnotic, but Felix couldn't lose himself in it. Like Harn said, he could sense nothing below fifty feet, as if the Mana simply disappeared. He had to prepare for the worst.

They hit. Something tore.

And Felix was standing atop a grassy hill while sunshine filtered through wide, emerald fronds above him. He blinked and turned. Behind him was a cliff carved to show a fierce creature rearing up. It had the scales of a lizard and features of a big cat. A cave was bored out from between its hind legs, the wind sighing softly as it wafted in and out of the opening.

"Holy hell. That was," Felix struggled with the words. His Perception flared, quickly finding Wyvora standing in the woods to his left. He also could tell the entire hilltop was devoid of monsters, even the tiny, insectoid kind. "Why are you so far away?"

"The wards choose the placement of arrivals," she said with a shrug. "A Blessing of the Raven that prevents undue harm."

That... makes sense. Felix started walking back to the cave, which was only twenty or thirty feet away. "Okay, then we need to tell them it's fine to come through."

A hand brushed his shoulder, as if Wyvora was nervous to even touch him. "You cannot. If they are worthy, then they will pass through on their own. If they are not, then they will not."

"What? That's stupid. And you didn't mention that before," Felix growled. "My people stay with me."

Felix stomped to the entrance of the cave, only to find the opening had vanished... and two Henaari had appeared out of nowhere to level their spears at him.

"Who is this trespasser, sister?" one asked. She wielded the same sort of hooked polearm Wyvora used, but looked a great deal older. Iron gray strands threaded through her braids, and there was an ancient depth to her wide eyes. The other was younger, but no less steely in her regard. "Why have you brought an outsider within this place?"

Felix's anger and worry flared up, their careful wrappings beginning to smolder as he regarded the Henaari around him. Pit shrieked, his own fury on the pyre.

"Peace sisters, peace!" Wyvora put her hands up, palms out. "This is an outsider that I encountered in the forests, one of great Skill and power. He—"

"Has he confused your Mind, sister?" the younger one asked, edging forward. The spear closed in on Felix's ribs.

"No, but the—"

"Outsiders are not allowed. What if the enemy had seen you?" the younger said. She was clearly older than Wyvora in addition to being familiar with the woman. "You should have killed him."

"She tried," Felix said through his teeth. He hadn't fully transformed in a while, but the way they were talking made him want to bare his fangs. "Where's the cave gone? I can't sense it."

One of the hooked spears jabbed at his arm, slicing through his shirt and leaving a bloody cut.

"You will speak only when spoken to, outsider. Your kind is not welcome in our camp," the younger guard hissed. "Speak out of turn again, and it'll be your neck that I open up."

Pit screeched in offended rage, and for a moment Felix was tempted to release the Chimera on them. That smolder burned brighter. Yet Felix bit back his immediate response and tried to consider things calmly. Carefully. The younger guard was level 43, while the older was level 55, and both of them were in upper Journeyman, according to his Eye, though the elder one seemed stronger than that.

Likely, she had a couple Skills already Tempered into Adept. Their weapons and armor were built to match their power and were plenty sharp enough to cut him, though the wound on his shoulder had already healed. He shifted his body, presenting neither of them with a good angle.

"You must understand, Ifre, he—"

"He shall go before the Matriarch," the elder guard said before turning to finally address Felix directly. "You will step away and follow. If you dare to step out of line, I will gut you myself. Do you understand this?"

"Yeah, no," Felix said, and unleashed Adamant Discord.

Lightning burst from him in all directions, hitting Wyvora and her two friends, while the connection between him and his targets hardened into steel. He hurled them into the cliff face. Stone shattered, and their bodies bounced off and onto the ground. Wyvora took the hit the best, using some sort of Skill to blunt the impact. She stumbled to her feet, only to find Felix's khopesh at her throat.

"Now open that cave before I tear it apart myself," he snarled, and Pit cried out in fierce triumph.

Vess ground the haft of her partisan into the stone again. She had created an impressive dent already, and if the wait continued, she'd likely bore straight through the ledge.

"What—What's going on?" Kikri asked.

Vess glanced in the Elf's direction, only to notice the area around them was suddenly brighter than before. Far brighter. Vess stepped to the edge, where Harn was chuckling.

"See? Kid's got this."

The once infinite-seeming cavern had become a narrow chute, and fifty spans below them, an opening let in a large amount of sunlight. Among all that light was a man with eyes that flashed a brilliant sapphire.

"C'mon down. Things have gotten complicated," Felix said.

Vess grinned.

CHAPTER TWENTY-NINE

"The storm must have passed," Atar noted, blinking into the bright sunlight. It was edging toward sunset, but the sky was almost blinding after the dark caves.

"Summer storms," Alister mused. "Here and gone."

Felix looked up at his friends as they exited the shallow cave mouth. Moving the cave had proven to be an illusion, but a vividly convincing one. Felix had even felt the stone beneath his hands. Whatever magic they were using was far, far stronger than anything Thangle had used. However, once Wyvora had explained what it was, Felix's Willpower, Perception, and Intent were able to muscle past it. The illusion shattered into pieces. The Henaari's shocked expressions had been satisfying, at least.

"Uh, what happened?" Evie asked. She pointed at the bodies currently cocooned in stone restraints, leaving only their noses free, and at Wyvora who was merely standing aside with a conflicted expression on her face. Harn just chuckled. "Who're they?"

Felix frowned at the Henaari guards. "They tried to capture me and leave you in the tunnel. So I… convinced them otherwise."

"Does this change our reception?" Vess asked, ever the eye on the ball. Her impromptu floating gurney of spears still carried Davum and Vayne behind her. They hadn't woken up the entire journey, and their Health had deteriorated again.

"Wait, what? You said you had healers!" Kylar rounded on Wyvora and grabbed the hilt of his swords. "My team needs a healer!"

"Quiet, oaf," Kikri said. Kylar actually listened, which was surprising to Felix. "Let the Fiend answer Lady Dayne's question."

"It might," Felix answered, ignoring the outburst. "But I didn't hurt them too badly. What do you think, Wyvora?"

She opened her mouth to speak, but Evie snorted. "You're asking her? Didn't she just attack you?"

"Not her, not this time," Felix said. "Still. What do you think?"

Wyvora wet her lips with the tip of her tongue and darted a glance at the rest of his team. When none of them interrupted, she dropped once again to her knees and kowtowed three times. Each time she hit her forehead harder against the earth. "This one apologizes profusely for the actions of this one's sisters. This one begs that you do not kill them."

"Kill them? They didn't try to kill me, why would I kill them?" Felix asked.

"It'd save time later," Evie muttered, but Atar elbowed her in the ribs. She frowned until Atar gasped in pain and clutched his arm.

"This one does not presume to understand the intentions of a Pactlord," Wyvora said.

Felix wanted to pinch the bridge of his nose. His Aspects weren't quite recovered from the fight previously, and he'd had to strain them again. "Enough with the—Look. Honest opinion. Will your people try to murder me and my own if we walk in there with your sisters all," Felix rolled his hand. "Stoned?"

Wyvora lifted her head slightly and peeked up at him. "This one… believes it will be seen as an act of aggression. Even from a Pactlord, such treatment would not be forgiven easily."

Felix grunted. "Yeah, figured as much. Okay. Let's just bind their hands? Evie, Alister, you're on prisoner duty. Harn, are you bleeding again?"

Harn shrugged.

"Great. Let's move, then. How far is your camp?"

"It is two leagues south, along the river."

Felix altered the Stone Shaping around his prisoners, letting them stand up and move their feet, but bound their hands behind their backs. Wyvora took possession of their spears and numerous knives they had hidden around their persons, and they were marched ahead of everyone else.

"You'll follow quietly, or my friends will be more than happy to gut you," he said to them as calmly as he could manage. Still, he couldn't help the edge in his voice. They glared over the top of their stone muzzles. "Yeah, the irony is a bit much for me, too. Let's all just walk calmly back to your camp, okay?"

The journey was simple enough. They traveled downhill into the lush forest, walking along an ancient path of laid stone that was heavily overgrown with moss. More of those massive ferns, easily tree-sized, and tons of hanging vines and brilliantly flowering buds. It reminded him more and more of the area where he'd first woken up. Once or twice, Felix thought he saw carved stone monoliths in the deeper greenery, but they were quickly swallowed by the tree cover and their rapid pace. He would have stopped, had his people not been hurt.

They soon came to a river, though it was more of a wide stream, and they took the time to slake their thirst and refill their stores. Tempered Bodies might not need sustenance as much as Untempered, but they needed *some,* and it had been a while since their last resupply.

Felix noted several crocodile-like creatures on the far bank, disguised by their moss colored bodies and utter stillness. There were even a few in the deeper portions of the water, and those were all a mottled gray-blue-green color. His Eye called them Veiled Aquabbar, and they were all Tier II creatures bordering on Tier III.

Voracious Eye is level 53!

A few swam closer, but Harn stepped forward and flared his Spirit. The crocs milled in place a moment, as if considering their chances. Harn only stood there, resolute, and eventually the crocs turned back toward easier prey.

"Predators are cowards," Felix noted.

"Always are." Harn grunted.

They walked along the ancient causeway, more of a ground-eating jog really, as it paralleled the river. The ground around them rose and fell, hills and dales all covered in old growth forests that stretched just as high as those outside this odd mountain valley. Further in, Felix could now spot cliffs to every side, as if they were in some sort of giant crater.

What's in the center, then? Felix wondered.

A few short minutes later, they had arrived. "We are here," Wyvora said simply.

Felix looked about, but the path seemed to end at a thicket of dense thorns that stretched over his head and choked off the undergrowth beneath the trees. The river continued onward, unhindered, but unless they wanted to wade in, the path was hidden.

"Another illusion?" Vess asked from behind the tip of her spear.

Wyvora hesitated, looking to the muzzled guards before nodding. The guards jerked in their bonds, clearly angry.

"Open it up, if you please," Felix said. No need to anger anymore people than he had to, and they were in a hurry. She'd likely bypass their protections faster than his team would tear them apart.

Wyvora, hesitance gone, stepped forward and ran her hands across the maze-like bramble. The plant life shuddered and twisted, curiously folding in on itself until it vanished completely. Without warning, a thick flock of small, dark birds burst from the thicket. Felix jerked back as they tore upward, fists blazing with sudden acid before they simply vanished again.

"What was that?" Atar asked, his voice strained a bit.

"Looked like birds," Kylar offered. Evie gave the swordsman a look. "What?"

"You may pass freely now, Pactlord," Wyvora said. Felix's Perception twinged as he spotted the guard's expressions, which had turned from apoplectic to confused.

"I appreciate it." Felix led his team through. "Tearing it down would have taken too much time."

Passing through the thicket was more than crossing space, as he felt the distinct tremble of passing one of their strange wards again. Once through it, the Mana of its construction was evident in the myriad flows of violet, green-gold, and white-green vapor all twisted and bent into a complex array of magic. His team flowed past him as he stopped and stared at it.

It's an array… but made out of Mana itself, he thought with a shock. *No stone or wood to act as a medium. That's like the 101 on Inscription. How'd they do this?*

"Felix?" Alister called out, and he pulled his attention away from the warding array. "You should see this."

Felix walked to the front of the group and found themselves atop a slight rise, while below them an encampment filled a bowl-shaped valley to the limit. Dozens of Henaari walked to and fro, passing beneath free-standing archways of elaborately carved wood and stone. Buildings abounded, interspersed with many large trees, all in the vein of the outpost they had run into a few days prior, wood and stone constructed with a distinct skill and style.

Most interesting, though, was that a large, ruined tower lay in the center, complete with flying buttresses and mounds of ivy. A tree grew up inside the tower, breaking through and expanding out of one side, and its branches hung heavy with a bright blue fruit.

"Wow," he breathed. "You made all this?"

"The Dawncrafters are the greatest artisans on the Continent," Wyvora said with pride.

"The tower, too?" Atar asked, squinting. "That is a tower, right? Kinda far to tell..."

"No, we did not make that," Wyvora's voice was steady, but her Spirit echoed with something like sadness. *Why?*

"Incoming," Evie said and unlimbered her chain.

The encampment—village, really—had finally noticed them. Tens of Henaari warriors poured from nearby buildings, each armed and armored in much the same way as Wyvora and the guards. They moved fast, too, a lot faster than a lot of Guilders he'd met, including some of his friends. His team started to draw their weapons, but Felix held out his hands.

"Stop. We don't fight unless we have no choice," Felix said.

"And if they make that choice for us?" Vess asked, her voice a touch heated.

"Then we make 'em regret it," Harn growled.

The Henaari stopped advancing when they were about twenty feet out, separated from Felix's team by the grassy decline and about four feet of wood and steel. A ripple passed through the crowd, and a tall figure in elaborate, layered robes in red and orange stepped forward. She wore a headdress of delicately carved, polished quartz that depicted a raven in flight. Her hair was piled in a curious braid atop her elongated head, both of which only added to her height. Two extra sets of eyes were expertly painted on her long forehead with makeup, and she regarded them with a deep sneer.

"Matriarch," Wyvora gasped quietly.

The Matriarch pointed a hand covered in rings that glittered with Mana vapor. "Who are you? Why have you come to us and harmed our own?"

Voracious Eye!

Felix swept his Eye over the assembled warriors, counting sixty-four including the archers hidden just beyond the closest house. They were all solidly within Journeyman Tier, though the Matriarch was an Adept. And those rings weren't just for show; each of them was enchanted with a single, potent spell. He still had trouble sometimes with Eyeing individual items people were wearing, so he couldn't tell more than that. Either way, this was a kettle he didn't want boiling over.

"We are traveling the Foglands from Haarwatch. We encountered your warrior in the wood and saved her life," Vess said, gesturing to Wyvora. The Henaari's cheeks colored, but she didn't deny it. "In recompense, she promised our team access to your healers."

The Matriarch fixed her furious gaze on Wyvora, who seemed to quail under the attention. "The promises of the Farhunter are worth little, especially here. Yet, you invade our sanctuary, intruding on our sacred space, and take my people hostage. This is an act of the conqueror, not one of peace."

"We are not looking to fight," Vess said. Her voice was smooth and resonant, a lilting bell tone to her every word. Felix could almost see the Mana coursing through her channels as her Diplomacy passive worked through her. "But that does not mean we will not answer force in kind. Your people attacked ours, and we showed mercy in not killing them outright. That makes three spared in only a few hours." She spread her hands, her spear planted to the side. "We do not seek conflict with the Henaari, but the ones you call 'ice warriors' have given us little choice but to take refuge with your people."

A ripple passed through the crowd, and Felix could feel their collective Spirits turn from their slow, strident beat toward something more hesitant. Not all of them, but many. Henaari exchanged quick glances with their neighbors, and spears dipped fractions of an inch. The Matriarch, however, drew herself up to her impressive six-foot-five height and scoffed through her golden facepaint.

"That is precisely the reason why the Farhunter should never have brought you here. We are hidden from the ice warriors by virtue of our goddess, and you are not welcome."

Vess paused. "You are saying you will not aid our injured?" Felix could practically feel his friends' hands creeping toward their weapons. Atar stank of fire Mana.

The Henaari bristled, their spears and bucklers lifting, and something like the sound of flapping wings flitted across Felix's senses. The Matriarch curled her lip. "I am."

Felix flexed his hands. He wasn't looking forward to fighting an entire community, but he wasn't planning on dying, either. *What a fine mess you made this time, Felix.* He wracked his brain for something, anything to get him out of this. His memory, one of his greatest assets, flickered through ten thousand moments since arriving in the Continent. His Mind parsed it all, sorting and cataloging and rechecking everything he knew about the Henaari. About conflict. *Think!*

A flash of memory surfaced, of a bloody, underground garden and the words of a golden giant.

"Matriarch!"

Everyone turned to him.

"We claim the Right of Wander," he declared.

A gasp went up among the crowd, and the Matriarch's snide expression twisted into a delighted, cruel smile. Yet, before she could speak, another figure darted through the press of bodies. As for the Matriarch, the warriors parted with exceptional deference, until a panther the size of a pony slinked forward. Its fur was black but patterned with faint shapes, and its hindquarters were coated in dense scales, all ending in a powerful-looking tail equipped with a deadly barb.

Chimera, he thought, and within him, Pit squirmed in excitement.

Harnoq, Pit provided.

The Chimera—*Harnoq*, Pit corrected him again—walked until it was level with the Matriarch then sat. The woman's expression had soured, her cruel smile turning brittle. "A'zek. To what do we owe the pleasure?"

A'zek casually licked a paw before answering, but it simply ignored the Matriarch. "The Farwalker wishes to speak with you, Felix Nevarre."

It can talk?

"It can talk!" Evie whisper-shouted.

"Did you not hear the boy?" The Matriarch threw a hand at Felix. "He claimed—"

"We are aware of what was claimed. All in due time," A'zek said. It's voice was soft and smooth, and deeper than he expected from a big cat-lizard. "Gather your healers, Matriarch. We are to give them all courtesy due a guest in the old traditions. As the Raven wills."

"...As the Raven wills," she echoed back.

Things began happening quickly, but the armed warriors put up their spears and left without another word. Apparently the orders of a harnoq were worth a lot here. Soon, Henaari in robes of pale green and blue stepped forward and beckoned to Felix's team.

"Those are the healers," Wyvora explained needlessly. "They will take care of your allies."

"And we're just supposed to trust you people now?" Evie asked. "After all that?"

"The Farwalker's Companion speaks with his Voice," she said, as if that explained everything.

Companion? Things began making sense. *The other Pactlord she was talking about. It's the Farwalker.*

"Go with them," Felix said to his friends. "Get everyone the help they need, but keep an eye out. We don't know the lay of the land yet." He looked down at the harnoq, A'zek, who was waiting patiently for him at the base of the hill. "I'll be back soon, I think."

Vess gripped his hand for a brief second before releasing it. She spun toward her floating spears and nudged them toward the healers. Nevia, Kikri, and Kylar were close behind.

With a thought, Felix broke the stone bindings on his prisoners and let them back into the village. They rubbed their wrists and necks, but their eyes seemed to consider him in a new way. He didn't like it.

"Keep an eye out," he whispered to Harn. The man grumbled and slapped Felix on the back.

Felix stepped carefully down the hill, his eyes on the harnoq and his senses spread out around him. Wyvora walked with him, obviously heading to the same destination.

“Don’t do anything I’d do!” Evie shouted from behind.

CHAPTER THIRTY

As his friends were led toward the center of the encampment, Felix followed close behind the swaying tail of A'zek and the prowling form of Wyvora. He was careful to maintain a healthy distance from them both. He didn't *think* either would attack him, after all that, but Felix had been wrong before.

Caution, Pit chirped. Felix couldn't agree more.

Voracious Eye!

Name: A'zek
Race: Chimera - Harnoq
Level: ??
HP: ????/????
SP: ????/????
MP: ???/???
Lore: A chimeric beast, harnoq are solitary creatures without need for mate or pack. They excel at taking down large prey, attacking with claws, jaws, or their barbed tail, which contains a potent toxin.
Strength: More Data Required
Weakness: More Data Required

Protected, he noted. There was a sense of resistance around A'zek, similar to the Inquisition but far stronger. It felt more like how his Veiling Amulet functioned, but several steps removed and not quite like anything he'd experienced. *A spell or something, maybe.*

"Is your curiosity sated, Felix Nevarre?"

Felix started, finding A'zek looking at him with a large, slitted eye. It was a dark black in the gathering gloom, but flashes of newly lit torches cast earthy highlights across his irises. A'zek looked amused, though Wyvora at his side was less so.

"Hrm," Felix said. "You're blocking me."

"And you're not using Analyze," A'zek said, and this time its expression morphed into worry. "A… hungry Skill, your Eye. And it's not the only strangeness about you, Pactlord." Felix only inclined his head, and the harnoq snorted. "You can release your Companion now."

Felix took a sharp breath and looked at Wyvora, but A'zek had started walking again. "It's considered rude to hide in polite company."

"I did not tell him," Wyvora said.

Pit trilled in interest, and Felix agreed. In a flash of light, the huge tenku emerged from Felix's Spirit. This time, A'zek was surprised, spinning and leaping backward in alarm.

"By feather and claw," the harnoq cursed. "You're an ox!"

Pit merely tilted his head in confusion before warbling at the smaller Chimera. Pit was at least twice his size. *I am tenku. Beast of Harmony. Child of Guardians.*

A'zek paused at that, gaze flickering between Pit and Felix. Wyvora simply stared, confused. "Indeed." He turned and continued on the half-sunk path of ancient stones. "Follow."

Felix and Pit followed silently, with the tenku trotting closer to the harnoq. Felix was quiet, however. The words Pit had used were familiar. He'd said them weeks ago, after Felix had begun to fix his Bastion of Mind Skill, but *why* had never been explained. Pit didn't even remember, but to Felix they were tantalizing. Important, somehow.

The sun had dropped behind the mountains by the time they reached a small, unassuming yurt off to the side of the encampment. It was far from the center and the ruined tower, where his friends had gone, and Felix was curious about that. Clearly, the

Matriarch and her retinue were all in the center, the most interesting part of the area.

So why's this guy way out here? Felix had a feeling politics were involved. Clearly, the Farwalker had pull enough to order the Matriarch around. It wasn't someone he wanted to piss off... at least not yet. So, when Wyvora opened the wide wooden doorway of the yurt, Felix stepped through, Pit fast on his heels.

The interior was round, spacious, and heavily festooned with furs and cloth that swung low from thin wooden rafters above. There were no windows, but lanterns made of paper hung throughout, orbs the size of his head lit with small, flickering flames, illuminating the whole space with a warm, buttery light. Felix stood easily in the yurt, but Pit had to hunch uncomfortably as they entered.

"Whoa," Felix said.

In the center of the room, above a shimmering brazier, there hovered a complicated construction of what appeared to be white-green light. Felix's Manasight identified it as air Mana... but not vapor or even liquid, as Felix's often appeared. It was rigid. Solid-seeming. Crystalline. As he watched, it created several rotating shapes of strange invention, each expanding and shrinking in time to a beat he couldn't hear. It was hypnotic, and it took the harnoq's deep voice to shake him from his trance.

"We have arrived, Farwalker," A'zek intoned. The harnoq pushed between Felix and Pit and stepped forward into the center. Wyvora lingered somewhere near the doorway. "I have brought Felix Nevarre and his Companion."

On the far end of the room, half-obscured by gauzy draperies, a figure moved. Felix clenched his jaw and kept his hands at his sides, but it was a close thing. The figure leaned, shifted in what looked like an oversized chair made of wood and bone. His face was in darkness, but the lanterns shone on his legs and torso, revealing a soft body draped in suede and silk.

I can't sense him. Felix flared his nostrils. *It's like he's not even there. Pit?*

Nothing, Pit agreed.

"Thank you, A'zek. Was the Matriarch much trouble?" His voice sounded strong. Confident.

"She abided by your wisdom," the harnoq said. The Farwalker snorted in amusement.

"She merely listened to the winds. Now, she waits for them to turn in her favor. Bah," the Farwalker scoffed and adjusted himself. The chair suddenly rolled forward, and Felix realized it was on wheels. "Enough talk of her. Release me, Raven. Let me see this *Pactlord* for myself."

With a curious rush of wind and faint cawing, the darkness around the Farwalker's face vanished completely, and Felix beheld an old, old man. A Henaari, clearly, as the Farwalker's head was elongated with a high forehead and cheekbones sharp enough to cut. The man smiled, displaying a set of white, even teeth and a nest of taut but wrinkled skin.

Voracious Eye!

Name: The Farwalker
Race: Henaari
Level: 94
HP: 244/5984
SP: 112/177
MP: 6332/6481
Lore: Henaari are a nomadic, matriarchal people that are known for their dedication to the Endless Raven. They excel at physical Skills and have a mild aptitude for the magical arts.
Strength: More Data Required
Weakness: More Data Required

Unlike his Companion, the Farwalker hid nothing from Felix's Eye. He felt none of the odd resistance, and he could perceive him easily now that those shadows had fled. The man was an Adept Tier or perhaps more; unlike others, his power felt fuzzy and ill-defined.

"Your name is 'The Farwalker'?" Felix asked.

The Farwalker smirked. "It has been for many, many years. A consequence of a task well done, I'm afraid."

The old man rolled himself forward a touch, letting more light fall onto his features. "You, too, seem cursed with a competency above your station."

"Not if you ask my friends," Felix said with a half-smile. "Why did you want to talk to me? I appreciate the access to your healers, by the way."

The Farwalker waved his hand. "That's no matter. You spared the life of my neophyte when she most assuredly would not have spared yours. That is worth a great deal to me."

"Neo—Wyvora," Felix said and looked at the woman. She was kneeling beside him, forehead pressed to the ground. More details connected. "She's your apprentice? A… what's it called—a Farhunter?"

He smiled, and his dark eyes crinkled with a web of fine lines. "Indeed. My people are nomads, wanderers. This is our tradition. Yet, there is a duality to my people, Journeyman Nevarre. We wander around the Continent, but each place we stop, we build as if we'd lived there for years. Often, we stay a long time as we search for that which gives us purpose."

"I noticed this place looks very… permanent," Felix said.

"Our encampments can be built in a night, owing to our great Skills and Blessings," he said. "When we choose to leave, they are designed to return to the Great Wilds within a fortnight."

"That's really impressive," Felix said, eyebrows raised. *So the outpost we found might already be gone. Interesting.*

"Your praise is quite gracious." The Farwalker inclined his head. "To answer your unspoken question, Farhunters are those who seek out and find threats to our people before they may come upon us. It is a… difficult calling, but one which Wyvora takes to with vigor."

"So I've seen," Felix said. The Farhunter's Spirit thrummed with delight and shame in equal measure. *Weird lady*. "She risked the wrath of the Reforged—the ice warriors—and their allies to attack us."

The Farwalker frowned, a stark change to the mildly pleased expression he'd maintained so far. Wyvora's Spirit quailed. "She grows incautious. That is..." He closed his eyes. "I apologize on her behalf, Felix Nevarre. I have ensured your people have the healing they require, but I would offer you another boon for the trouble this one has caused you."

"That's… really kind of you," Felix said carefully. "We're really only passing through. We have business at the other end of the Foglands. I'd ask—"

"Think a moment," the Farwalker said as he rolled himself closer to the center of the room. To the glowing brazier and crystalline Mana lattice. "I'd rather your boon not be asked for in haste."

"Okay..." Felix let the word draw out, his Mind turning. The guy was right. Better to make the most of this favor. "You've been attacked by the Reforged."

"We have."

"Why? And since when?"

The old man rubbed his jowls with a calloused hand. "Nearly a fortnight."

Felix frowned. That was after the attack on Haarwatch. Which meant either some had survived long enough to escape, or the Archon was sending more out. "How many have you seen?"

"Is this your boon? Information on the ice warriors and their Master?" the Farwalker asked and nodded when Felix's eyes widened. "I know of them, of him that dwells beneath the mountain."

Pit growled, and at first, Felix thought he was mad at the old man. He had almost chided the tenku when the door behind him was thrown open.

"Farwalker! We have come to speak!" The Matriarch swept in, now wearing embroidered blue and gold robes. A series of gilded combs of bone were in her elaborate hair. She was followed by a coterie of Henaari, each dressed far more modestly in pale greens and blues.

"You honor me, Tava. It is not often that my home is blessed by the presence of the Matriarch and the Synod." The Farwalker bowed in his seat, but Felix noticed his face—and his presence—was once again hidden. Felix could see the man and his chair, but it felt like, if he stopped looking, the Farwalker would simply vanish. It was unsettling.

One of the Matriarch's people bowed in return, a woman with steel-gray hair and fine lines on her face. "Farwalker Qzik. We apologize for barging in unannounced like this—"

"Quiet, Fyszal. You do not answer to *him*," the Matriarch said. "We have come to claim satisfaction for your… *guest*."

The darkened head of the Farwalker tilted from one side to the other. "Truly? Why?"

"Because it is tradition," she crowed, and the Synod bobbed their heads in agreement. "These Humans have accosted our people, and what's more, this boy has claimed the Right of Wander! A Right only those chosen by the Endless Raven may invoke! I would that he face punishment for such a bold action. I demand it."

Murmured agreement filled the yurt, and Wyvnora even sat up from her kowtow. Her face was nervous. A'zek, however, laughed loudly. Several of the Synod jumped in fright.

"Ridiculous. The Raven does not pick and choose those who follow her. All are welcome, for all may seek to bring the unknown to light." A'zek bared his panther-like teeth at the Matriarch. "All who do so may invoke the Right."

"Tell me, Felix Nevarre, have you brought the hidden to light? Have you looked into the dark corners of our world and emerged anew, filled with knowledge and purpose?" The Farwalker's voice was hypnotic, perhaps due to his odd stealth ability or something else. Felix flared his Bastion of Will, but nothing was assaulting his Mind or Spirit. Felix decided, then, to simply answer truthfully.

"I have."

"That means little!" the Matriarch insisted. "How could one honor our Raven without knowing of her blessed existence?"

The lady seemed hell-bent on punishing Felix, and he really doubted it was because he'd bound and gagged a couple guards. *More politics*, he thought. *Great. Where's Vess? She'd know how to get outta this.*

"Felix Nevarre. Did you know of the Endless Raven before you ventured into the dark?" the Farwalker asked. Intoned, was more like it, as if it were part of a ritual.

"Uh, yeah. I found—" Felix stuttered, his mouth about to utter "a Henaari corpse" and he swerved away from that. "I once found a ring called Gathered Light, crafted by the dawnspeakers."

Several of the Synod looked surprised, but the Matriarch scoffed. "Likely looted from the dead."

"That is valid before the Raven's eye," the Farwalker stated. "You, of all, should know this."

The woman turned a very interesting shade of purple as a vein throbbed at her temple. The Synod were suspiciously quiet. Felix desperately wanted to roll his eyes. He wanted nothing more than to avoid the undercurrents he had begun to sense.

"I'm not looking to inconvenience anyone," Felix began. "My team and I are on our way through the Foglands, and we plan to continue as soon as possible. I'm… sorry I restrained your guards. They were rude, though, and one of them cut my shirt." Felix fingered the small rent in his sleeve. "Once my people are healed, we'll be on our way."

"...meets the requirements..."

"...not without a Blessing, he..."

Felix got the impression none of them were listening. This time he *did* roll his eyes. Pit just glowered at the Matriarch, who glared right back, nose raised.

"He must face her himself," she said.

The Synod's conversation ground to a halt, all of them looking at the Matriarch with worried expressions. Wyvora too. The Farwalker merely looked… bored.

"All in favor?" The Matriarch pushed her decision further, scowling at the other women around her. Slowly, one hand after another rose into the air, until it was unanimous save for the Farwalker himself.

"Are you sure, Tava?" he asked quietly.

"Oh, I am," the woman said. The gilded combs in her hair gleamed as she tossed her head back. "This Felix Nevarre will face the Endless Raven herself."

Felix blinked. "I'm sorry?"

CHAPTER THIRTY-ONE

It wasn't long before Felix found himself in the center of the encampment, surrounded by Henaari and staring at the darkened opening of the ruined tower.

"I feel this has been a bit rushed," he said to Pit. The tenku blew a sharp breath from his nostrils and rustled his wings. Concern wafted through their bond.

Tower… smells wrong, Pit sent.

"Wrong how?"

Wrong season.

"Wrong—?"

The crowd of Henaari shifted, the warriors and craftsmen moving aside to allow through Vess, Evie, and Atar. They found him easily, and Evie shoved her way forward.

"Outta the way, string beans!"

"Why are you all here? Where's Harn and everyone?" Felix asked.

"Still getting patched up. Alister is watching them," Atar said and jerked a thumb over his shoulder. "But a couple dour-looking friends of yours came and ordered us here."

"Said you'd gotten locked into a trial?" Evie raised an eyebrow. "A little early to be breakin' laws, Felix."

"What is happening? And what is *that*?" Vess asked, pointing at the tower. Her eyes flashed with Mana as her Elemental Eye activated. "Something dark and cold lives in that place, Felix. Please tell me you are not entering it."

"Well..." Felix scratched the back of his neck. "Funny story—Hey!"

Vess had smacked him across the shoulder. It wasn't a hard hit, at least not to him, but it was surprising regardless.

"Do not joke. Why do you have to do this?" Vess asked.

Felix sighed. "Sorry. They have information we need for my... task. And... and I think, if I don't, they're not gonna heal our people anymore. Honestly, I think they might attack us if I try to walk away."

"Two-faced jackals," Atar hissed. "Let them try."

Felix pushed down Atar's fists. "I like the enthusiasm, man, but I'd rather not fight an entire town."

Vess shook her head. "Better we fight than have you face what I suspect is in there."

"Wait, why? What's in the tree-filled safety hazard?" Evie asked.

"The Endless Raven, I think," Felix said. Evie and Atar shared a look before staring at Vess. The heiress had clenched her jaw so hard he was worried she'd crack a tooth.

"You don't know what you are facing. It is an Urge, Felix. They are defined by what they want. Extremely so. But they are also unstable. Erratic." She pushed her dark brown hair back, out of her face. Quite a few strands had escaped the simple tail she'd put it in.

"So the Raven just wants discoveries, then? That's its deal, right?" Felix asked. "So I just tell it how a washing machine works, and it'll leave me alone?"

"A washing machine?" Atar asked.

"I don't know how those work, now that I think about it." Felix considered things for a moment, his Mind working quickly. "Huh. I don't know how much of *anything* worked back on Earth."

He was stalling and distracting himself, he knew. His friends knew it, too.

"Perhaps you can appease the Urge, but I do not know. Death follows the Raven and those who follow it. *That* is known." Vess swallowed and looked away, at the tower. "This is a foolish risk."

Felix's expression softened, and he gave Vess a smile. "I'll be fine. It's just another god. What's the worst that can happen? Ow!"

Evie had smacked him right on the top of his head. Metal-backed gauntlets and everything. "Don't be dumb."

Felix rubbed at his skull and took a deep breath. All of them were gazing at the tower now. "No promises."

With little warning, guards, replete with hooked spears and bucklers, stepped forward to push his friends back into the crowd. Felix moved to stop them, but Vess waved him down even as one of the Synod spoke up.

"All penitents are allowed to give final goodbyes to their loved ones. Now, they will witness your Trial." The woman, almost indistinguishable from the rest of the Synod, waved her hands at the guards. They continued to push his friends back.

"I don't like this a whit," Evie said. "You touch me with that spear, and you'll find it somewhere you really don't like."

However, all three of them didn't fight as they were pushed to the sidelines, though Atar had his fists clenched and his Mana on the cusp of ejecting from his hands and feet. Vess calmed him with a whispered word, yet she looked little better.

"You must leave your weapons behind, outsider," the Matriarch said from among the Synod. She hadn't done a costume change, but he wouldn't have put it past her. The lady seemed preoccupied with appearances. Or maybe it was just her own pride. "The Raven tolerates no blade in its presence."

"No," Felix said, loud enough to be heard over the casual mutter of the crowd. The gathering went silent, even as it gained new members by the second. "Is your god threatened by a mortal's sword?"

The woman sputtered. "No, no of course not! It is tradition!"

"Don't care." Felix walked to the tower's yawning opening, Pit trailing after him. The Matriarch didn't follow, though she whispered something furiously to a member of the Synod.

The Farwalker and Wyvora were both waiting for him at the entrance, the former in his elaborate-looking wheelchair and being pushed by the latter. Felix could feel that chill wind against his skin, like an open freezer compared to the summer's heat. The Farwalker looked at him—he was pretty sure but it was hard to tell with the magic face shadow—and nodded.

"You who have claimed the Right of Wander shall enter the Realm of the Raven. As do all Henaari, you shall seek a Blessing from the Endless Raven, or else you will be forced to revoke the Right of Wander, the consequences of which are dire."

Yeah, I get it, Felix thought. *Fail, and my team's not getting outta here.* "Is it too late to ask for that boon now?" Felix asked over his shoulder.

"No," said the Farwalker, voice wry. "Let us save some surprises for later." He gestured to the crumbling opening in the tower. "Hold fast to your Spirit, for the dark is not a place for weakness."

Cool, cool, cool. "Do you guys practice ominous phrases?"

"Are you ready, penitent?" Wyvora asked, clearly ignoring him.

"Nope, but when has that mattered?"

The Farwalker's face was shrouded in that darkness, but he swore the man smiled. "Then enter. And may the Raven walk with you."

Ready bud?

Yes, Pit chirped quietly from his side.

Let's do this, then.

Felix and Pit entered the tower expecting all sorts of nastiness, yet they found only rock and root. Tumbled-down blocks of weathered stone covered the floor, and had the sun not set several minutes ago, the holes they left above would have filled the space with light. Instead, Felix only saw shadow, dust, and the gnarled roots of the big tree that grew up the center. The corridor led him to the left.

"This is anticlimactic," Felix complained as they walked farther in. "For some reason, that makes it creepier, though."

Pit trilled in agreement.

Felix had little trouble navigating the detritus-strewn floor. His Manasight, as always, was a useful tool for the dark, though he had to focus to see beyond the cloying vapor of shadow Mana. The cold breeze continued fitfully, bringing with it the scent of wet and salt. Odd, but not unpleasant, and it brought streamers of color to interrupt the shadows.

The path wound around, spiraling through ruined arches and half-crushed lintels, but that huge tree was always in the center. Up close it looked dead and desiccated, riven with deep cracks like a dry riverbed. Yet green-gold life Mana pulsed through it. As he came around the final corner, he saw why.

The tree was six or seven feet wide and filled up a good portion of the interior. A series of spikes were driven into the trunk, around which the tree was lively and not dead. Green-gold threads pulsed from the metallic spikes, each one glowing painfully in his Manasight. The threads spiraled up through the trunk, pushing toward the branches high above and fueling the emerald leaves he'd seen earlier from afar. Without his Manasight, the spikes were curved and silvery, with whorls of green-gold etched into their sides.

Voracious Eye!

Name: Talons of Mzal
Type: Artifact (enchanted)
Lore: Dawncrafted Ages past, they are spikes that channel life Mana into whatever they are thrust within. When removed, they leave no mark. Other effects unknown.

Artifact? Never seen one of those before. And Voracious Eye can't even see all that it does. That alone cemented what his senses were already telling him. The Talons were dangerous.

That breeze started up again, but this time, it was coming directly from the tree itself. Pit lifted his head and sniffed. The wind had a bite to it, like deepest autumn, and smelled of rotting leaves, cold rain, and winter on its way. Pit nudged him.

See? Wrong season.

"Got me there, bud," Felix said and reactivated his Manasight. "But isn't this interesting? This isn't air Mana."

The wind blowing past him was not white-green, but instead thick strands of purple, black-gray, and deep blue. All of them were woven together somehow. Braids of Mana undulated around him, flows of liquid that turned solid as he perceived them, just like the solid working in the Farwalker's yurt. The Mana then surprised him: it collapsed onto the tree between the Talons of Mzal, and with a flash of dark light, the trunk disappeared.

And so did everything else.

"Shit," Felix cursed, hands lighting up with acid Mana. "Stick close, Pit."

The darkness faded swiftly, but as it passed, it revealed a new landscape entirely. They were in an autumnal forest, filled with fiery colors turned soggy with constant storms. Misting rain and cloying fog rolled between the trees, while somewhere in the distance, there was the roar of breakers against the shore.

"Is this an illusion? Or are we really here?" Felix quested outward with his senses, but everything he touched felt extremely solid. They had either been transported, or it was the best illusion he had ever seen.

The trees were sparse all around him and the ground was covered in wet, burgundy leaves. Yet patches of the earth still smoked as if fires were banked beneath the damp debris and twisty columns of hazy smoke rose up to join the dark clouds above. Among the trees were things that Felix originally mistook for large boulders, but which turned out to be alive. Giant Fire Beetles ambled about, each as big as Pit, huge but content to leave them both alone for now. They made sure to keep their distance.

What do we do? Pit asked.

Felix shrugged. "Look around. Keep an eye out for any birds, I guess."

As they walked, the forest thinned even more until it was clear the way ahead stopped at a promontory. From a distance of five hundred yards, Felix could make out the spray from the pounding waves below, but the ocean before him wasn't half the noise he was hearing. The sky was alight, if faintly, and crackling thunder chased every crash of the sea.

The beetles were more numerous here, for whatever reason, and the thinning tree cover left Pit and Felix little option but to pass slightly closer to them. The Giant Fire Beetles, however, did not like that. The first one they came near turned and charged at them immediately, its shell lighting up with all the radiance of magma. Pit lunged forward, using Rake across its exoskeleton and rupturing whatever Mana process was going on. The creature exploded in a burst of orange vapor and thick, scalding offal.

"Klikkikikikik!"

Another two charged at them, incited by the first explosion, and Felix summoned a Shadow Whip into each hand before bringing them down, hard. The tough tendrils smashed both beetle faces into the soggy ground before the whips exploded into black-gray vapor, expended. It was followed by two delayed detonations as the beetles expired.

Pit grappled with another, and a fifth came at Felix from the cliff edge. A ball of molten orange Mana formed between its mandibles as it ran, but Felix wasn't interested in getting burned.

Unfettered Volition!

Bursting forward with all the grace and speed he could muster, Felix slammed into the car-sized Giant Fire Beetle foot-first as he kicked it directly under its abdomen. There was a brief moment in his Perception where Felix was unsure if it would explode or not before the entire beetle lifted from the ground and shot into the sky, trailing orange Mana like a comet.

From out of the smoke and clouds, a massive, jagged beak caught it.

And swallowed it.

A third sound emerged, one masked by the storm and surf. The sound of screeching avians. Millions of birds materialized from the dark, forming around the massive beak as it swallowed the Giant Fire Beetle. Magpies, crows, starlings, and ravens swirled and swarmed, dark feathers meshing until they formed a creature equal to the hungry beak.

"The Endless Raven," Felix whispered.

Its head alone was the size of a city bus, and its body was more like a jumbo commercial passenger plane. Except its wings trailed off into the dark and smoke, as if it truly had no end. It undulated its head and throat, and the faint light of the Giant Fire Beetle vanished into the creature's gullet before it twisted and fixed Felix with a single, house-sized eye.

OFFERING?

"Uh..."

SHINY?

It's...just a big bird? Felix was dumbfounded. He'd expected...well, he wasn't sure what he expected, but not this.

OFFERING?

Right. What do I offer? It likes found things, and apparently shiny things. Felix wracked his brain. He recalled the stones and small objects arrayed around the Shrine they'd found, which brings up another memory. He fished around in his satchel a moment longer before pulling out the small book he'd found at the abandoned Henaari camp, beneath their shrine. He held it out.

"For you."

The Raven tilted its head and pushed closer. It was still in the sky, hovering somehow, but also its head pressed forward until it took the book from Felix's fingertips, snagging it with its massive beak.

CAW! it screamed, and Felix jumped. Pit's feathers ruffled at the sound, half his body puffing up. The Raven flapped its wings—once—and vanished.

"Okay?" Felix said after a moment. *Was that it? How am I supposed to leave, then?*

CAW!

With another trumpeting call, the Raven descended from the cloud cover, and somehow Felix could tell it was pleased. He chalked it up to being bonded to a half-bird for months. The Raven stooped again and shoved its beak into Felix's personal space.

MORE OFFERING?

MORE SHINY?

"I don't have anything," he said. *Not anything I'm willing to part with...*

Pit nudged him, then clawed at the ground.

"What?"

Stones are shiny.

"Oh. *Oh*," Felix said. "Will that work?"

Find out, Pit replied.

Stone Shaping!

Felix poured his Mana out of his channels in a torrent of dusty-brown, and the ground before him turned to mush. Flexing his Skill, Felix pulled rock around, shoving dirt and stone as he delved. Deeper and deeper, sensing the types of rock layers beneath the earth. Loam and clay and limestone, followed by a number of rocks he couldn't name but could *feel*. They felt hard and flat, unimpressive. He moved on.

Felix had never done this before, and the process of it felt awkward at first, but his high Intelligence and Willpower helped him push through the unusual application. He sorted through layer after layer, all while the enormous Urge stared at him with something approaching annoyance. It was taking too long. Then, somewhere perhaps forty or fifty feet deep, Felix felt stone he hadn't before. Crystalline, almost.

With a final surge of his Skill, Felix gripped all he could and brought it up, up, up onto the surface. The soup that had become the ground before him split and parted before the oddly gelatinous arrival of a large crimson and brown stone. More than large, it was fifteen feet wide as he shaped it together again, sloughing off sides and leaving them smooth and polished.

Stone Shaping is level 60!
Stone Shaping is level 61!
Stone Shaping is level 62!

The Raven, far from being annoyed, looked elated. It bobbed its head excitedly, each motion followed by a blast of stormy winds that sent the sparse trees swaying. It picked up the stone and tipped its head back, swallowing it.

YOU HAVE DELVED AND REVEALED, FELIX NEVARRE. WE ARE PLEASED.

"Oh, whoa. Okay." Felix jerked in surprise at the Raven's sudden diction. "I'm glad you're pleased."

YET WE SENSE MORE IN YOU.

"More—?" Felix held his hands out. "I have nothing more to give, Endless Raven. Pit?"

The tenku shrugged and shook his head.

YET MORE REMAINS. THERE. UPON YOU.

Felix followed its gaze to his hip, where his satchel rested next to his Crescian Blade. Felix opened the top of his satchel and rooted around for a moment, looking for something, anything. He touched on jerky and trailbread, a change of clothes...nothing that would interest a demigod or whatever Urges qualified as being.

Felix's hands touched something else, hidden in the bottom of his bag. It was cool to the touch yet sparked in his grip, and Felix swallowed nervously before withdrawing his hand. Glittering in the muted lightning, he held a key made of a clear, faceted gemstone.

Omen Key.

The Raven's eyes glittered.

CHAPTER THIRTY-TWO

"You… want this?" Felix asked, holding the Omen Key.

Pit squawked in outrage. *Not yours!*

The massive Urge merely cocked its head, and it crowed in a voice of ten million birds.

WHY?

"Why...what?" Felix asked.

WHY DO YOU OFFER AN OMEN KEY?

Felix was confused. He gripped the translucent key, too hard he feared, but a Strength that could bend steel did nothing to it. "I… have nothing else to offer," he said slowly. Nothing he wanted to part with, at least. The Omen Key would have hurt, but if the Raven really didn't want it...

INTERESTING. The Raven hopped about, leaping from the titanic swells beneath it and up on to the cliff ledge itself. It landed with a deafening *whumph* and a rasping caw. **AN OMEN KEY IS NOTHING TO US.**

"Nothing?" Felix looked at the Key. "Isn't it valuable?"

THERE IS NO PATH FOR US. URGES DO NOT HAVE OMENS. WE COULD NOT EVEN SEE THE DOOR SUCH A THING MAY UNLOCK.

Felix gratefully put the Omen Key back into his pack. "So you only take things that are of use to you? That isn't my understanding of your… motivation."

WE SEEK THAT WHICH IS HIDDEN OR LOST, THOUGH THAT WHICH SHIMMERS DOES HOLD GREAT ATTRACTION TO US. YOUR OMEN KEY WAS NOT HIDDEN OR LOST... IT WAS GENERATED BY THE SYSTEM FOR YOU DIRECTLY. A RARE OCCURRENCE, BUT NOT WHAT WE SEEK. WHAT WE NEED. The Raven leaned in closer again, and its huge beak nodded at Felix's side again. A talon formed of ten thousand feathers arced from the sky, and it took all of Felix's Willpower not to flinch. Instead of cutting him in half, it merely tapped against the hilt of his Crescian Blade that hung next to his satchel. **THIS IS DIFFERENT. LOST FOR SO VERY LONG. YOU FOUND THIS, CLAIMED IT. WE SENSE... DEATH.**

That was no better in Felix's mind. He'd done a lot to get that sword back, and it was tied to the Temple. He couldn't give it away. Felix didn't say that, instead gripped its handle. "I've killed a few things with it, yeah."

KAAW! A FAMILIAR DEATH. YES.

Felix's memory flashed back to the Henaari corpse he'd found. The sword had been beneath its bones, tangled in wildflowers and grass stalks. The Raven rotated its head until it was looking at Felix almost upside-down.

YES. OUR FAVORED DAUGHTER. LOST TO US. YOU FOUND HER?

"I suppose I did," Felix admitted. He watched those talons, those wings and beak. A single strike might not kill him outright, but it would be very bad. Pit, easily able to feel Felix's tension, spread his stance.

HMM. YOU FOUND HER. YOU WATCHED. YOU SOUGHT OUT THE PREDATOR THAT KILLED HER. THIS IS GOOD.

Felix nodded slowly. He had found the Henaari and buried it—her—when he could, but he didn't recall fighting her killer. There were so many monsters around the Waterfall Temple. How would he have known? Unless...

"It was the Orit that killed her?" he asked.

The Raven cawed, its voice multitudinous and louder than the surf that roared below. **THE TWISTED ONE. WE SENSE ITS BLOOD ON YOU, SPILLED IN BATTLE. MORE.**

"I mean, I killed the Orit and the two Bloodtainted Guardians," Felix said. The Raven didn't seem impressed, just... distracted.

WE SENSE OLD THINGS COME TO ROOST. YOUR BLOOD. IT SMELLS OF... LOST THINGS.

The Raven's head tilted upright, and it hopped closer. Nearly fifty feet closer. Pit growled at it, and the Raven regarded the tenku with its blank gaze.

GUARDIAN BEAST. THE SECOND WE HAVE SEEN. WE ARE NOT INTERESTED. It sniffed, the sound of bellows. **WE NEED MORE. TELL US.**

TELL US.

Felix felt gripped by a certainty that the Raven would not let him leave without another offering. By habit, he tried to feel at the Urge's Spirit, but flinched away from a screaming maelstrom of black feathers. He sensed neither emotion nor Intent from whatever composed the godling, only overwhelming *noise*. Felix jerked back, cutting off the connection and unsheathing his Crescian Blade. He held its bronze blade aloft, letting the dim light gather against the edge. The Raven tilted its head again.

Felix brought it down and sliced open the palm of his hand.

OOOH.

Blood pooled, thicker and more viscous than Felix remembered it being. He squeezed his hand, and the blood spilled outward and onto the earth. The Raven lunged and shoved the tip of its gargantuan beak into the stone and soil, tearing up the blood with a squelch of mud. It snapped its head back just as quickly, undulating its throat until the mess of dirt and leaves and rocks slid down its gullet.

KAAAW! KAW!

Felix barely held his ground as the Raven screamed. The giant bird trembled, the surf crashed, and thunder crashed hard enough to shake the leaf-strewn earth. The Raven flapped its wings, once, twice, kicking up gale force winds that Felix had to lean into in order to keep his feet.

UNBOUND! NYM! PRIMORDIAL!

Its voice was again the million-throated cry of dark birds, and the storm above them intensified. The wind streamed, no less intense, and trees were starting to topple around them. Leaves flung into the air, wet and half-rotted, but Felix kept his eyes on the Raven. Its beak was wide as it screamed, as were the burning mouths of thousands of others in the darkness of its breast. Fear flared along his bond, but so did determination. Neither Felix nor Pit were going down without a fight.

And then it was all gone.

The storm quietened, the wind died, and even the surf went silent. It felt like Felix had gone deaf; he almost checked his Status Conditions, had he not noticed that the Raven had gotten closer once again, cooing all the while. Its eyes were calm and devoid of anything but an animalistic intelligence.

DO YOU KNOW YOUR ROLE, UNBOUND?

"My role?" Felix narrowed his eyes and kept his blade between them and the Urge. "I don't—what's that?"

WE ROSE FROM THE URGE TO SEEK, TO FIND, TO UNCOVER AND LET SHINE. WE ARE MIGHTY, BUT NOT ALL-POWERFUL. WE HAVE A ROLE IN CREATION, AS DO ALL.

Interesting to hear, but Felix couldn't help but feel some emotional whiplash. He didn't know what to expect from this creature. It seemed to have something of an intelligence, even if it was just a lot of birds mushed together. "I don't have a role. I'm just… I'm here. Surviving."

ALL HAVE A ROLE, FROM PRIMORDIALS TO GODS. EVEN THE RUIN.

That caught his attention. "The Ruin," Felix repeated. "I've heard that before. A force that ends civilizations, that wipes out entire Races, even destroying records of them. How?"

CREATION IS FILLED WITH GREAT AND MIGHTY THINGS. TERRIBLE THINGS. THE RUIN LIMITS, FOR THAT IS ITS PURPOSE. ITS ROLE. IT IS THE MOST PRIMAL OF URGES. AN URGE OF FEAR. OF JEALOUSY.

No one had ever given him this much information. Felix pressed. "Not destruction? Isn't that what it does?"

DESTRUCTION! CAW! DESTRU—DO YOU KNOW THE CONSEQUENCES OF POWER?

"The what?"

THE PATH TO MASTERY. OF TEMPERING YOUR MORTAL FORM.

"I've been told it's something of a quest for immortality," Felix hazarded. The Maw had said as much.

KAHAW! KAW! IMMORTALITY! YES. SIGNIFICANCE BUILT INTO YOUR BEING WITH EACH AND EVERY TEMPER. A SOLIDITY, A RIGIDITY THAT EVENTUALLY CANNOT BE DENIED. TIME AND AGE WILL NO LONGER TOUCH THOSE UPON THE PATH TO POWER, BUT THAT IS A SIDE EFFECT! The Raven hopped again. **IT IS ABOUT FINDING YOUR ROLE! THE URGE THAT DRIVES YOU! ONCE FOUND, YOU FUEL IT WITH SIGNIFICANCE!**

Felix could almost hear the capitalization of the concepts the Raven was crowing at him. "The Urge that drives me? Wait, significance. I've heard that before." Zara had explained it as a solidity, an… affixing of one's self as they grew more powerful. The result of Tempers and the choices one made along the way, just as the Raven said. "What is it, exactly?"

IT IS THE CESSATION OF WHAT COULD BE AND THE SOLIDIFICATION OF WHAT WAS AND ALWAYS WILL BE, the Raven squawked. **IT IS MEANING TURNED TO POTENCY, AFFIXING ALL THAT YOU ARE AND MAKING YOU *MORE*. NO LONGER MORTAL. A NEW YOU, CHANGED, TRANSFORMED.** It cawed twice at an almost deafening volume, now that the world had gone silent. **ONLY THE GREATEST REACH SUCH HEIGHTS.**

ONLY THE GODS.

Had lightning crashed dramatically as the Raven said that, Felix would not have been surprised. *I always suspected. Vellus called me ascendant, traveling the Broken Path… that is where the gods came from? They just reached the peak of the mountain?*

"Not you? I've heard many call you a god," Felix said. He still didn't know what the Raven wanted from him, but maybe he could get more answers from the thing.

WE ARE BUT AN URGE. POWERFUL, YES. STRONG ENOUGH THAT WE COULD END YOU, UNBOUND. PRIMORDIAL. BUT WE WILL NEVER BE MORE THAN WHAT WE ARE. IT IS THE ADVANTAGE OF MORTALITY, WEAK AS YOU ARE. The huge bird shook itself, and smaller forms took flight from its back, fleeing into the dark sky. **WE FOLLOW OUR ROLE. IT IS PATH ENOUGH.**

AS UNBOUND, YOU ARE UNTETHERED TO THIS WORLD. UNMOORED FROM CREATION ITSELF. IT IS A CURIOUS THING. A BLANK SPOT IN THE WEAVE OF POWER. A PRIMORDIAL'S ROLE IS FAR DIFFERENT. ONE OF THE UNSEEN TIDE HAS NOT BEEN SEEN IN MANY, MANY LONG YEARS.

"What do you know, Raven?" Felix asked.

DO YOU FEEL THE THREADS, UNBOUND? the Raven asked. **THEY ARE THE TIDES OF THE INVISIBLE SEA THAT SURROUNDS YOU. IN AN ANCIENT AGE—BEFORE THE ADVENT OF HUMANITY OR THE ELVES, BEFORE EVEN THE NYM—THE PRIMORDIALS ROAMED. ALL OF THEM HAVE THEIR PURPOSE, A ROLE, EVEN THE ONES GONE MAD.**

"Aren't they all insane?"

ARE YOU?

Good point.

THINK ON YOUR ROLE, FELIX NEVARRE. THERE MAY COME A TIME WHEN THE ANSWER WILL SAVE YOUR LIFE.

"Can't you just tell me?"

KAW! KAKAAW! KAW!

Felix watched for a full half-minute before it dawned on him that it was laughing. At him.

WE ARE PLEASED, FELIX NEVARRE.

"What?" he asked. "Why?"

YOU BRING TO US SECRETS. YOU CARRY THE BLOOD OF THINGS ONCE LOST. IT IS FAR ABOVE

WHAT WE REQUIRE FROM THOSE WHO SEEK OUR BLESSING. WHO FOLLOW OUR ROLE.

Felix considered not speaking, but found he couldn't help himself. "I'm not following you or your role. Like you said, I don't know my own yet, but it's my own. No one else's."

KAW! KAAAW! GOOD!

"Good?"

THOSE THAT FORGE THEIR WAY WILL DIE, OR THEIR VERY PASSAGE WILL UNCOVER WHAT WE DESIRE. WHAT WE NEED. The Raven shook itself, its shaggy throat feathers wobbling. **WE SENSE A GREAT MANY UPHEAVALS IN YOUR FUTURE, UNBOUND. FELIX NEVARRE, HE WHO IS LOST, WE ARE PLEASED.**

Without warning, the Endless Raven lunged at him.

Unfettered Volition!

Felix blurred, moving fast enough to tear the air and earth around him, lifting his blade into the Second Sword Form while his offhand shoved outward to stop its advance. Yet the Raven snaked past all of his defenses, arriving almost instantly to drive its beak into Felix's chest.

Instead of being pierced, Felix was thrown backward, hurled all the faster by the intense renewal of winds from its wings. Pit squawked in alarm.

BE LOST NO MORE.

Darkness consumed them both.

He heard the chirping of birds.

Felix surged to his feet, lightning crackling along his arms. Vision came shortly after hearing, but it was too bright. Golden sunlight shone sideways through rents in the stonework and directly into his eyes. He groaned and blinked rapidly, his bleary eyes slowly adjusting. The birds had stopped, spooked maybe, but Felix could see now. He wasn't in the Raven's Realm any longer. He was back in the tower.

And it was dawn.

"Pit?" Felix turned once, then again. His heart hammered until he found his friend snoring softly in a darkened corner. "Jesus. You scared me. Hey! Get up!"

Pit warbled groggily at him but got to his feet.

"Yeah, I know you're tired." Felix rubbed at his face with his palms. "I'm more tired than I've been in a while. Whatever that big bird did to us knocked me on my ass."

The soreness he'd felt in his Aspects was worse than before. Felix felt like he could sleep for days ,if he let himself, but he hadn't the time. They'd lost enough of that already.

Who knows what they did to our team while I was away. Felix hoped the Henaari wouldn't attack his people during this whole ordeal, but he really didn't trust the Matriarch. *Be ready to fight, Pit.*

This time, the tenku let out a chirrup that was almost mean-sounding. Felix was impressed.

When they emerged from the minor labyrinth of the tower—now far easier to navigate in the morning light—Felix found a changed sight. The camp-wide crowd had dispersed, likely hours prior, and only eight Henaari guards and his three friends were nearby. All three of them were asleep, Atar and Evie leaning against one another while Vess had her head cushioned on Evie's lap. It was almost sweet, had the armed guards not loomed over them like executioners.

"You've returned!"

The voice caught Felix utterly by surprise, earning a squawk of fear from Pit and a flinch from him. It was the Farwalker, face still drenched in shadow despite the rising sun. He was in his rudimentary wheelchair, and Wyvora was behind him. Both of them looked fresh as daisies.

"Didn't feel as long as it was," Felix said while he lowered his clenched fists. Wyvora flinched, only just noticing he'd spun on them. He imagined he moved a bit too fast for her to track. *Hah, take that for sneaking up on me.* "That big—Raven was a big talker, though."

"She *spoke* to you?" Wyvora asked. Her wide-set eyes looked ready to pop out of her sockets. "With...with words? I—"

"Where is he?!"

To the side, there was a grunt and clatter as his friends half-woke, while before Felix, the Matriarch emerged from a large, ornate structure. Despite the finery on her body, she looked haggard, as if she hadn't slept at all. She was flanked by the Synod, as well as a number of armed guards, all of which converged on the tower and Felix.

"You're awake, Tava," said the Farwalker. He tilted his hooded head at them all. "I trust you slept well?"

"Enough of your banal pleasantries. We are here to pass judgment on your… *guest,*" the Matriarch said with open derision. "He has entered the tower and gone to see the Endless Raven. What, if anything, does the boy have to show us?"

"Felix?" Vess' voice cut through the chatter. He looked over to find all three of them up and pressing closer, though their guards' spears were bared. Vess looked relieved. "You are unharmed."

"See? I told you they'd be alive," Evie said with confidence.

"You said, 'I bet he eats the bird in half a glass,'" Atar said.

Evie shrugged. "I mean, it's a safe bet."

"Eats the—" the Matriarch's face was a thunderhead, and the Synod all looked horrified. "You dare joke of such things!"

"Wasn't really a joke," Evie muttered, glaring right back at her.

Felix, meanwhile, had noticed something. "I did see the Endless Raven. We spoke for a bit, and it sent me back here." He raised his hand. "With this."

Everyone turned to look at Felix as he revealed a foot-long feather. It was dark and glossy, and it radiated equal parts of gentle inquisitiveness and avid interest. Henaari gasped.

"A Feather of the Raven!"

"He brings back such a treasure!"

"An outsider—!"

"Impossible!" the Matriarch cried. The diadems in her woven hair wobbled as she stepped toward him. "That is—you are—!"

"Here," Felix said, holding out the feather. "Analyze it yourself." He knew what she'd find.

Name: Feather of the Endless Raven
Type: Favor (Urge)
Lore: Granted only to those the Raven approves, a Feather is a visible sign of regard from the Endless Raven. Other purposes, if any, are unknown.

"It is true," she whispered. It was like someone had stolen the wind from her sails, as she practically deflated. "How?"

"Not only a Feather," the Farwalker said. Wyvora rolled him closer to Felix, and he reached out a wrinkled but steady hand. "May I?"

"May you what?"

"Show them what you've earned," he said. "It is harmless."

Curious, Felix nodded. The Farwalker touched Felix's chest, and lights burst upward. A series of bright stars poured from Felix's chest, each accompanied by a staccato bloom of blue-white and red-gold light. Around them, his friends and the Henaari both stumbled under a sudden, indefinable pressure. Even Wyvora and the Matriarch abruptly strained against an invisible weight, though Felix felt nothing except a heaviness in his chest. The Farwalker, for his part, merely looked astonished before he did something and stopped the sensation.

"That was—"

"—Spirit of a beast!"

Above them all, the stars that had escaped resolved into a series of shapes. Patterns of light both like and unlike Felix's Skills formed in the air, all of them unfamiliar. One surged to the fore, however, and it resembled nothing so much as a pair of wild, outspread wings.

"The Raven's Mark," members of the Synod whispered.

"Impossible," the Matriarch repeated. Felix was starting to think it was her favorite word. Her tired face had gone pale, and her ringed hands shook as they covered her mouth.

"He is worthy of the Right of Wander," the Farwalker stated. His voice had a slight resonance to it, one that Felix was sure carried to the very edges of the camp. "Felix Nevarre and his Companion Pit are protected by the Endless Raven."

The Henaari all bowed their heads.

"As the Raven wills," they intoned as one.

"Night, that's creepy," Evie said, loud enough for him to hear. Atar elbowed her again, and this time he got the softer part near her armpit. She hissed in pain, and Atar looked inordinately proud of himself.

"It is time, I think, for us to talk," the Farwalker said in a normal voice.

Icons in Felix's vision began to blink and flicker, and he nodded. "Yeahhh. We've got some things to discuss."

But first, Felix sent to his Companion. *Looks like we have notifications, Pit.*

Pit trilled in pleasure.

CHAPTER THIRTY-THREE

"Give me a moment," Felix said to the Farwalker. The man nodded and had Wyvora roll him backward and out of the way.

Felix strode forward, heading toward his friends. They looked tired and a little rumpled, but overall in good spirits.

"Felix! What took so long?" Evie asked as Pit shuffled toward her. He shoved his giant head into her hands and enjoyed a series of nice scratches.

"So you met the Endless Raven?" Atar asked, clearly excited. He looked at the foot-long feather in Felix's hand. "What was that like?"

Vess said nothing, only putting a hand on Felix's forearm. "I'm fine," he said.

"Good," she said. "What happened?"

Felix opened his mouth to tell them, but realized it would take longer than he wanted. "We talked. I gave it some stuff, and I learned a few things." He waved his hand to dismiss the questions he saw in their faces. "Later. I've gotta handle these notifications."

"Fine. But we'll hear it later," Atar said with a frown. He turned back to the Henaari guards that stood close by. "I need to get back to the healers. Take me." He started walking, and the guards gave each other consternated looks before splitting up. Two went with Atar while the rest stuck around, clearly more at ease with Felix's group since he'd earned the Raven's favor, but not enough to leave them alone entirely.

"I should go check on Harn, too," Evie said, then gave Felix a sly smile. "Did you eat the bird?"

"What? No!"

"Evie," Vess admonished.

"I'm just saying, Felix has a track record," Evie said, but put her hands up in surrender. "Fine, fine. You tall guys wanna take me to the healers, too? There's a shellfish I gotta check on."

That left only a single guard to watch over the both of them. Felix didn't like that they were still being guarded. *Why?*

"Thanks," Felix said, meeting Vess' gaze. They seemed lighter in the morning sun, a golden brown. "For waiting like this."

"Of course," she said and plucked something off his shoulder. It was a wet leaf, colored a bright autumnal orange. "From the Raven as well?"

"Something like that. It wasn't nearly as bad as you feared," Felix said. He smiled at her raised eyebrow. "I promise, I'll tell you all about it as soon as I can. Probably once we've left this place behind."

Vess nodded, satisfied. "Something we should do soon. I feel... uneasy here. And not just because of the Urge. There are things under the surface here, and our presence is stirring them up. That Matriarch and her council, the Farwalker. I am unaware of the currents at work, and I detest that."

Felix eyed the guard and shifted slightly so that Vess' body was between them. He moved his hands quickly and as subtly as he could manage. <Think you can look into it?>

<Perhaps. I will need time.> she signed back.

<I'm going to speak with the Farwalker,> he signed. He'd literally combined "distance" and "walk," but it got the point across. <You've got a little bit.>

"Then I shall leave you to it, Felix," Vess said out loud. "I will go and see how our friends are faring."

Felix watched her go. Vess was a pro at intrigue, so it was likely she'd get to the bottom of things before lunch. And, if things went sideways, well, she also kicked ass. The guards might be a problem, but they'd been reduced, and Felix sensed many among the encampment were either still asleep or just waking. He was still looking, thinking, when something hit the back of his knee, hard.

"Wha-hey! Pit!"

Notifications, Pit sent. *Stop staring.*

Felix looked between his Companion and Vess, who just then disappeared among the buildings and odd, free-standing arches. "I'm not staring."

Pit just looked at him.

"Shut up."

He called up his notifications.

+10 FEL
+10 EVA

Voracious Eye is level 55!
Manasight is level 56!
Exploration is level 47!
Negotiation is level 21!
Unfettered Volition is level 57!

Dang Raven hit me hard, Felix thought. He rubbed at his chest, but his tunic wasn't even ripped.

Etheric Concordance is level 67!
...
Etheric Concordance is level 69!

"Oh, nice," Felix said, and Pit chirruped in agreement. Each level made understanding each other just a touch easier, as if they grew more and more inseparable.

Pit's Skulk is level 49!
Pit's Bite is level 52!
Pit's Rake is level 53!

New Title!
Stigma of the Chosen (Legendary)!
You have borne the Marks of three beings above the

bounds of mortality! Greatness awaits you, whether you like it or not! You can now see Marks of all Tiers on yourself and, with some practice, others. +10% MIG, EVA, ALA, FEL

That's it, then. Those were *other Marks.* Felix grimaced. He had a pretty good idea where most of them came from, but he'd seen five patterns of light, not just three, as the Title said. *Hm, but I can see my Marks now, and other people's too. Handy. Title's got a nice boost, though, and to my Harmonic Stats.*

Harmonic stats were confusing at the best of times. He made use of Resonance and Resilience to boost his regenerations, but little more than that. His Intent and Affinity were his most-used Harmonic Stats, allowing him to influence the world around him with the former and sense an empathic connection with the world through the latter. His Might and Evasion had to do with feats and defense of the Body, while Alacrity and Felicity dealt with feats and defense of the Mind. All four of them doubtlessly came in handy, but unlike his Strength or Willpower, they were not stats he'd ever felt "go active."

System energy course through both of them as the new Title modified their stats. As always, a colorless wave of light rolled into his core space, hitting his two rings and converting to surging beams of golden-blue radiance. Unlike previous times, the light ricocheted between his [Thunderflame Core] and his [Cardinal Beast Core] before partitioning. Some flew outward into his core space, while the rest flowed down the ribbons that connected his cores to his Tempered Journeyman Skills.

That's new. His awareness floated closer. *Wonder what it means?*

"Pactlord."

Felix resurfaced to find Wyvora standing a respectful distance from him. He raised a questioning eyebrow.

"The Farwalker would like to speak with you."

Ready, Pit sent. He was digging his beak into his covert feathers but had stood up.

"All right," Felix said, and the Henaari started walking away. Pit followed, and Felix was about to when he spotted something on the ground. He bent down and picked it up. It was the leaf Vess had plucked from his clothes. It looked like any other leaf, if out of season, but what caught his eye was the small wisp of purple Mana that had started to leak from its edge.

Why not? Ravenous Tithe.

The hand-sized leaf burst into dark violet smoke, streaming from his hand directly into his mouth.

"Pactlord?"

"Hm? Coming."

Wyvora led him back to the Farwalker, who sat in his wheelchair, lightly stroking A'zek. The giant cat regarded Felix with fierce brown eyes that flashed in the morning sun. Few others remained nearby. The Matriarch and the Synod had all retreated, and the guards had followed them, save for the one or two he could sense nearby, watching him.

"So," the Farwalker said. His face, cowled and hooded, was still a nest of unnatural shadow. "You have met the Endless Raven. How did you find the experience?"

"Unique," Felix said with a thin smile. "That portal thing though, that's interesting. Talons of Mzal, huh? How do they even work?"

"A bit of ancient magic. Urges, you see, operate slightly differently than you or I. Whereas we live our lives in the Corporeal Realm, Urges dip between all three. In order to visit an Urge, one must either be invited into their territory, be taken, or you get extremely clever."

"Uh huh, and I assume you did the latter," Felix said.

"Not I, but a Matriarch of old did, yes. The Talons are used to form a sympathetic bridge between its material and where the Raven roosts. Affinity and Resonance established with a leading Intent, and the Raven's own power fuels the rest," he said.

"A bridge. How? Wait." Felix crossed his arms in thought. "The Urge's role. Finding things in the dark, bringing them to the light. Is that the connection?"

The Farwalker leaned forward. "Exactly it. The influx of life Mana upon the dying tree is enough of a beacon to attract the curiosity of the Endless Raven. Where did you hear of roles?"

"The Raven was pretty chatty," Felix said. "Wouldn't stop talking, once I gave it some rocks."

"Rocks?" Wyvora said, and by her tone she was aghast and confused at the same time. "You gave our god rocks?"

"In my defense, they were pretty shiny," Felix said. Wyvora sputtered while the Farwalker laughed.

"You've found the way to the Raven's heart, Felix Nevarre. I am impressed."

Not like it was hard. The bird kept shouting "shiny shiny." You'd have to be an idiot not to figure that one out.

Aloud, Felix merely smiled. "I try."

"You succeed. It is something I am quite curious about. Come, walk with me." The Farwalker gestured, and Wyvora began to push his chair along a stone path. It was broken by stretches of earth, as it was not something the Henaari had built but found, along with the tower behind them. Still, the chair barely jostled, a testament to either Wyvora's care or the chair's craftsmanship. "How did you find your Companion?"

Felix raised an eyebrow, and Pit let out a deep chuff of air. "That's a bit of a story, but I saved him from a monster that was trying to eat him. Here, in the Foglands."

"Eat him—?" A'zek looked disgusted. "Who would even dare?"

"The Seven-Legged Orit."

The harnoq stopped in its tracks, though the rest of them kept walking. "Truly? You bested a Twisted One?"

"More than one, by my count," Felix said. "If I'm guessing right on what you mean by Twisted One, Pit helped with the last two."

A'zek growled. "A creature touched by madness, twisted in shape by the blood of the Teeth Below."

Felix's mouth thinned, and he nodded. "Yeah, we're talking about the same things. Blood Beasts. Primordial spawn."

A firm, insistent grip grabbed at Felix's forearm. It was the Farwalker, and his body language was taut as a drum. "Primordial. It remains in the Foglands?"

"...No," Felix said. *Not as it was, at least.*

The Farwalker didn't release Felix's arm. "It is unlike a Primordial to simply leave, not without terrible consequences for those left behind. Many Henaari have been lost to their kind. Are you sure?"

"I'm positive. The Maw is gone." That was absolutely true, and Felix didn't even feel guilty saying it. He wasn't the Maw, after all. "It was trapped beneath Shelim in a labyrinth built by the Geist. We… I found it. I ended it."

The Farwalker held onto him a heartbeat longer, staring up at

Felix's face from the darkness of his hood. Then he let him go. "You speak the truth. Remarkable. Impossible."

Felix snorted and tried to downplay it. "Less impossible and more just very, very annoying. Pit was essential in surviving it. I'd be dead if it weren't for him." Pit pushed out his chest, and pride for Felix thrummed through their connection. Felix ruffled the enormous bird-dog's head. "How did you and A'zek meet?"

"He stepped on me," the harnoq said in a flat tone.

"I did not. I stepped on the ground, and the ground fell apart," the Farwalker said.

"And then you stepped on me," A'zek insisted. "I remember it quite clearly. You've Tempered your Mind too well to keep the memory from me."

"Bah!" The Farwalker motioned to have Wyvora push him a bit faster. Felix walked beside him, passing beneath a number of ornate, free-standing archways. "Regardless, he was skin and bones when I found him, and I fed him until he was returned to full Health. As payment, I asked that he help me find an object I was hunting here in the Foglands."

"Mm," the panther-like A'zek hummed. "We never did find it."

"No," the Farwalker said and sighed. It was wistful and a little amused. "Just all those snakes."

A'zek shuddered.

Huh. You'd think a half-lizard would be fine with snakes.

"Our meeting is emblematic of my people," the Farwalker continued. "We wander, we search, and in the doing, we find that which was Lost, hidden, or otherwise forgotten. My Companion Pact with A'zek was the first in our clan's history, and though we keep only oral records, they reach far. We know that, though our Urge guides us, whispers her Blessings, we have roamed long before we discovered her holy purpose. Why has long been forgotten, though I have… guesses."

Felix remained silent. This felt less like a conversation and more like a lecture.

"To see another Companion Pact established not only nearby, but both Chimeras? Though our pacts were established centuries apart, it is a curious parallel. The Endless Raven teaches us that coincidences are rarely without meaning, even if it is not a direct connection."

They had come to a circular intersection where the archways opened up into a wider area of tamped down dirt and half-submerged flagstones. Several Henaari in robes and armor walked around, all of them taking a moment to bow before the Farwalker before giving them all a wide berth. He ignored them. "I noticed that you were surprised at the sight of your Marks."

"I've never seen them before," Felix admitted. "Though, I have a good idea of who gave them to me."

"Oh? That is unusual. Most Marked remain unaware of their status until it is revealed to them," the Farwalker said. "Do you mind if I bring them up again?"

Felix looked around at the crowded intersection. "Here?"

"Before was to show the Synod and dash the Matriarch's hopes for your failure. I can project them just for us, if you wish." At Felix's nod, the Farwalker once again reached out and touched his chest. A wave of light was released, solidifying into a series of patterns above their heads. Felix saw the outspread wings of the Endless Raven, now highlighted in his vision. In fact, all of them were.

[Mark of the Endless Raven]
[Mark of the Maw]
[Mark of Vellus]
[Mark of the Archon]
[Mark of the Cantus Sodalus]

Both Vellus' and the Maw's Marks were faded, though in entirely different ways. The Maw's was sunken, like it was barely emerging from the darkness. Felix instinctively understood it was because he had absorbed and incorporated so much of the Maw into himself that it was now inert. The Mark from Vellus was basically obliterated, the pattern of light scattered like far-flung stars, all save for a single branching shoot of crimson at the very center. Just as the crimson growth in his core space; the only surviving remnant of his connection to the Goddess of Storm, Tide, and Blood.

The others were more concerning.

"Do you need me to explain these to you?" the Farwalker asked.

Felix's heart raced as he pointed at the fourth Mark, one of red-yellow energy infused with flashes of bronze-like rigidity. "This one. What can a Mark accomplish?"

"It is a tool of recognition, an accolade in most cases. That is how the Raven treats them. To the unscrupulous, it can be used to subvert one's Will and Mind."

"Can it track location?" Felix asked, careful to keep his voice level. He initiated his Mediation, breathing slowly and purposefully.

"Perhaps. But to do that, it must first overcome the Will of its target," the Farwalker said. "Do you fear such a thing?"

"Fear is a bit of an understatement," Felix said. The Mark of the Archon pulsed regularly, like a heartbeat or a tumor. "How do I get rid of a Mark?"

"Troublesome, especially in the case of one put in place by those of greater power. If it were someone of your level and advancement? Such a thing is easily broken. The difficulty only increases with each advancement Tier above your own, and in the case of Urges or… or gods," the Farwalker's eyes widened a bit as he stared at one Mark in particular. "In that case, it is all but impossible."

"Hrm," Felix said, focusing inward. Had his Will been compromised? His Bastion was secure, its walls as high as ever. His Mind, while strained by his spell, was sound. He was safe, right? The Archon couldn't find them. So absorbed was Felix in the search that the Farwalker had to clear his throat quite loudly.

"*Ahem.* That Mark… the shattered one." The Farwalker licked his lips, and Felix realized the man had dropped his face shadow. He looked nervous. "Can you tell me who bestowed it upon you?"

Felix's eyes flicked up to the array of Marks. An idea wormed into his head, and he bared his teeth. "Perhaps we can trade for it."

The Farwalker's eyes narrowed, but a small smile thinned his lips. "Oh, and what do you wish to trade?"

"Knowledge of this," he pointed to the Mark of Vellus. "In exchange for items of equal value."

The Henaari regarded him carefully. Based on what Felix knew of the Henaari, knowledge of Vellus' existence and location should be worth quite a lot, provided they didn't know about it. Felix was worried he'd turn down the deal, but the man's curiosity got the better of him in the end. "Very well. An equal exchange."

"In addition to the boon you already owe me," Felix clarified. The Farwalker flashed a smile of large white teeth. Amusement warred with excitement on his face.

"As you say, Felix Nevarre."

Felix immediately pointed at the shattered Mark. "That is the Mark of Vellus. Goddess of the Storm, Blood, and the Tides."

"*What?*" The Farwalker's hissed exclamation came at the exact same time as Wyvora's panicked yelp. The toughened warrior looked suddenly terrified. "*How?*"

"Ah ah, you first," Felix said. He pointed at the last Mark, the one called the [Mark of the Cantus Sodalus]. "What's this?"

The Farwalker visibly collected himself. It was like he was reining in a dozen lunging dogs on leashes, all of them straining to reach the treat of Felix's knowledge. "Ah, that. That is of less concern than the others, I imagine."

"Why?"

"Because, unlike the others, I can see the Tier of who placed that Mark. Master Tier, but that is quite the step below even the one you are concerned with," the Farwalker said.

"What is the 'Cantus Sodalus'?" Felix asked. He pointed at the Mark that looked like a collection of strands all gathered into a complicated knot. "That sounds like Latin."

"Latin? I have not heard of that language, but the words are an ancient dialect from the Interior," the Farwalker said. His brows drew down in remembrance. "Cantus means Chanter, unless I miss my guess."

Zara. Felix felt a knot in his gut. *She's Marked me? Why?* He tried not to assume the worst, but first the Urges, Primordials, Gods, and assholes. Now his friend? His teacher?

"Felix?"

The Unbound looked up, away from his own spiraling thoughts. The square had filled with people at some point, and all of them were frozen with expressions of fear, while at their feet, the ground *writhed* with blue-white electricity. Felix could feel the heaviness of things pulling into him, like a bowling ball on a mattress, and small stones collected at his feet. Gasping, he cut off the Skill and tried to apologize, yet every Henaari fled the moment the Skill deactivated.

"Felix, are you alright?" the Farwalker asked.

Pit warbled and pushed his head up under Felix's right arm. The Unbound licked his lips and absently scritched his Companion before looking guiltily at his hosts. "That was… I'm sorry about that. The Skill got away from me."

The Farwalker shook his head. "None were harmed. But you seem out of sorts, and I am realizing it has been quite some time since you last ate, yes?"

In answer, Pit's stomach gurgled loud enough to startle several nearby birds into flight.

"We could eat," Felix said in an attempt at dry humor. "But what about your questions?"

"We'll talk over a meal. I promise it will be delicious."

Felix grinned. "How can I say no to that?"

CHAPTER THIRTY-FOUR

"Blood and ash," Kelgan cursed. "Look at the size of 'em."

"Makes your skin crawl," Karp said with a shiver.

"I once found one the size of my fist in my cupboard," Thangle added. His face was pale, almost matching his white beard. "That one nearly killed me with fright alone. I cannot even imagine..."

Before them was the Iron Gate, not three hundred strides away, a wall and gate twice the size of Tin Gate. However, its defensive structure had nothing to do with the horror that had stricken many of their company. Giant, finger-thick webs coated the Gate, sealing it shut among a gossamer nightmare. Huge spiders crawled atop it, creatures twice the size of avum, busily hunting and killing any monster that roamed too close to their nest. Already, hundreds of bundled shapes were suspended atop the webbing, packed away in a funnel formation at the center of the wall itself.

"How are we gonna get through here, Lieutenant?" asked one of the guard.

Kelgan swallowed before turning around to his men, all of whom were transfixed by the sight of the arachnids. "Just trust that we will, Guardsman Klemin. Zara will see us through."

With fire. Lots and lots of fire, he silently hoped. He left his men and Thangle at the edge of their lookout position and returned to the center of their temporary encampment.

After the terrifying journey in the Dark Passages, Zara and the Hand had pushed them hard overland. It had taken them an entire day of ceaseless riding and Stamina Potions to get them here so fast, yet still they were too late. As before, the Inquisition had placed a high-quality monster lure on this Gate and fled onward. Kelgan feared they might have already reached the next Gate. If they had, there was little chance of them catching the redcloaks without Zara's Night-cursed Passages.

The thought of it made his stomach do backflips. The insidious voices within that place had lingered in his ears for glasses after they'd fled, and even now, the mere thought of it brought its sibilant cadence back. Kelgan shuddered and picked up his pace.

He found Zara at the very center of camp, sitting atop a mossy stone and stirring a long-handled spoon in a large iron cauldron. Whatever was inside bubbled, though there was no fire to heat it nor stands upon which the cauldron sat. Her bird, the weird one that talked, perched on her outstretched finger. The Naiad raised the bright bird up to her ear and nodded once, twice, before her face smoothed into an unreadable expression. "Kelgan. How may I be of service?"

Kelgan swallowed, muscling past his fear. "Ah, well, Lady Cyrene, the boys and I were all wonderin' how we were supposed to get through all… that," he said, gesturing back toward the Gate. "We've managed so far, but there's little chance our Iron Ranks can cut into those webs."

Zara exchanged looks with her bird—*weird*—before allowing it to flutter off into the trees. "Keru was just informing me on the situation we find ourselves in. The Inquisition has lured a slew of Tier II monsters here, including a single Tier III beast." She stood up in a single smooth motion, her robes without a single rumple or stain. "Meanwhile, they have fled farther and farther ahead."

"I cannot sense them beyond the spiders," said a voice. Kelgan started, only to realize it was the Hand looming in the sunset shadows. "The redcloaks have left us long behind."

"All the more reason to chase after them now," Zara said.

Kelgan shifted his weight. "You mean… fight the Tier II spiders? Lady Cyrene, my people will be slaughtered. I can't—"

"No no, not fight. I'll not lose your people on something so frivolous. Darius and I could clear the creatures, but not without disturbing the several hundred Tier I spiders lairing below." She shook her head. "No matter how we approach it, an assault leads to unacceptable losses on our side."

"Are you suggesting we make a run for it?" the Hand asked. Kelgan couldn't see his face, but there was a sneer in his voice. "Our mounts are blown. They're worth little without more rest, and most won't survive the strain of more running." He barked a short, guttural laugh. "We'll lose half our force."

"That is likewise unacceptable. I need all of you for when we've caught up to the redcloaks. I cannot hunt them all down myself, and none must be allowed to report to the Waystone. But the crux of our issue is this: Keru has told me that the Inquisition have not only pushed beyond the Iron Gate, but they've passed the Bronze Gate as well."

"What?" the Hand roared. Birds and chittering lizards fled the nearby trees. "How?"

Kelgan wondered the same thing. Had reports on their original positioning been off?

"Somehow, the redcloaks have gotten hold of two minor Mana-ships. Weak, Iron-Rank craft, but it means they are racing toward Setoria as we speak."

The news was like one of Felix's grenades had been dropped in Kelgan's stomach. "Then we've failed."

The Inquisition would reach Setoria, the Waystone, and communicate with their great leader. Haarwatch would be lost beneath the burning light of their holy judgment. His friends, what little family remained to him, would all be killed by either the Path-less' zealots or the monsters looming in the Foglands.

"No, but we have reached the point of difficult decisions," Zara said. "You will not like it."

Kelgan's eyes snapped to hers. "Explain. Please."

She did and was right. Kelgan didn't like it.

But they didn't have much choice.

Less than a half glass later, the entirety of their force had gathered in a sheltered dell farther away from the Dire Spiders and their nest. After discussing the options with Zara and the Hand, Kelgan had carefully rallied all of his guards, promising them a way forward through this mess.

"The Iron Gate is lost to us," Zara said.

That's *how you start this?* Kelgan stifled a groan, but others weren't so subtle. Frustrated growls and low shouts spread throughout, loud enough that he was thankful Thangle had erected a sound ward before they had begun. Zara lifted her hands in a calming gesture, and his guards settled down. A little.

"The Inquisition has too much of a head start, and their little tricks have turned us aside," she said, gesturing with some heat toward the Gate. "But we can still stop them and save Haarwatch from the cleansing fire of the Grandmaster Inquisitor."

"How?" someone asked.

"A gambit," the Hand said in his powerful baritone. "We walk the Dark Passages again."

"Thought there wasn't one this side of the Gate," Thangle said. Kelgan couldn't even see the Gnome in the crowd.

"There isn't," she agreed. Muttering began, but Zara spoke over it. "This time, I will shape the road myself, from here directly to the Gold Gate."

"Wait, wait! I thought we couldn't stay in there too long? Wasn't that why—" the guard talking stumbled, her voice thick with fear. "—why it… went bad?"

"The Dark Passage destabilized because the Inquisitor upset the path with his fear and hatred. The passage must be held, grasped firmly by a singular Will that—well, the details aren't important. What is important is that the passages are a delicate balance my spellcraft must maintain."

Zara pressed a hand to her chest and gave all of them a look of earnest conviction. "I will hold this longer Passage the entire time, but it will take all of my concentration and power. I will not be able to save any who stray or who cannot contain their thoughts. Those who fail to do so will end the same as the Inquisitor."

The guards paled, and the muttering continued, increasing all the while.

"The solution is this," she said and pulled out a singular vial filled with a thin, yellow fluid. "Those who have a Willpower score of less than one hundred will drink an alchemical potion of my own design. It will put your waking Mind to sleep, leaving your

Body awake to be piloted by your Spirits. In this way, the dark will pose you no more danger than an evening's walk down the boulevard."

If anything, that merely increased the unease in the crowd. Kelgan knew Zara was aware of it, but she didn't seem to care. Or, perhaps she simply didn't have time to care.

"We shall protect you with all that we have, and we will all leave the Passage together. I promise you that." She put the vial back into her robes and pointed to three different cauldrons, none of which Kelgan had noticed previously. "Those with a Willpower less than one hundred, line up at the cauldron and receive your dose. We shall be leaving within the hour."

The crowd milled about, murmurs and indecision giving way to a few full-blown shouting matches. The officers stepped in, Rory, Thangle, and others, each of them dispersing those involved but doing nothing for the rising tension. For his part, Kelgan moved through the crowd, taking the time to listen and speak with his guards. Most were afraid. They'd seen the things in the black below the earth. None were keen on going back to that place, especially without control of themselves. They saw it as jumping into the beast's teeth instead of waiting to be bitten.

"Listen, you might not know me well. The Haarguard hasn't been around long enough for that. But I know Zara, and I know the Hand. They are both of them powerfully invested in seeing this work out. They wouldn't put out a plan doomed to fail, see?" He blew a breath through his mustache and gave the guards a lopsided grin. "Sides, the Fiend trusts ‘em both. That means I do, too."

That moved a few hearts, as he'd hoped. Kelgan liked Felix—thought he was a good kid—though he didn't share the hero worship that had started up. Didn't mean he wouldn't use it. After all, good lieutenants used whatever they could to get results.

"I don't trust that Sorcerer overmuch, Lieutenant," said one of his men, an older one who seemed more afraid than most. He scratched his jaw and wouldn't quite meet Kelgan's gaze. "But I trust you, sir. You fought with everyone this whole time, and before that, at the Battle of Haarwatch. We're behind you, sir."

The sentiment was echoed by a good number of the Haarguard, most of them veterans of the brief but intense fight for

Territorial Authority. Each and every one of them walked to the cauldron, picked up the ladle, and drank down the potion.

Many followed, but not all.

"This is a dark power!" A bald man with scars criss-crossing the top of his head stood at the front of the line and shouted out to the group. His voice was loud enough that Kelgan feared it'd push beyond the sound wards. "And this! This is an evil concoction!"

With a surge of movement, the man kicked over the nearest cauldron. The pot, suspended by nothing but air, tipped easily and splashed a large portion of its mixture onto the dirt before one of Kelgan's men stopped it. Scar-head—Jiron Kale, by his Analyze—scoffed in the faces of the guards who crowded closer.

"I am not going back there. I would rather die a clean death against a thousand Dire Spiders than to disappear into the dark! Those pathways are evil, and none of you can deny it."

"He's right!"

"Don't drink it!"

Jiron stood taller, his equally-scarred chin thrust upward as he gathered support from a handful of men and women, Humans all.

"None of you are required to drink the potion," Zara said from behind him. The bald man jumped in fright, as did the six others near him. Not even Kelgan had seen her approach. "Those who do not have the requisite Willpower to take on the challenges ahead are welcome to leave."

"Leave?" asked one of the guards with Jiron, a man with shaggy sideburns and two short swords at his hip. "And go where?"

"Wherever your two feet can take you," Zara said. Her face betrayed not a hint of emotion, but her eyes blazed with aquamarine light. "Your avum stay with us."

"What? Outrageous!" Three of the guards pressed closer, and Kelgan motioned to his own men.

This has gone on far enough.

"If you dare touch your weapons, you'll be dead before they clear the sheath," he growled. His spear hovered a finger span away from Muttonchop's throat. "Try me."

"Kelgan, it's fine. If they wish to stay, they can," Zara said. "But they will be forfeiting all rank and standing in Haarwatch, and they will walk from here, alone."

All seven dissenters blanched, though Jiran's face soon flushed with belated fury. Yet, even the idiot could read the lay of the land as all of the company stared him down. With a shaking, unwilling hand, he picked up the ladle from the ground and took his dose. The others all followed suit.

Kelgan didn't relax his grip on his spear until his people were organized into a formation four deep. The potion was starting to take effect, which was rather eerie to see. His guards were moving and responding to commands just as they did normally, but their faces were curiously empty. It was like watching a pitcher of ale being slowly poured out, until there was nothing left. Kelgan, Thangle, Karp, and Vivianne all passed the prerequisite for Willpower, as did a handful of common-ranked guards. Those got the privilege of marching at the front of the line while the upper ranks took the rear. Kelgan was insistent about that.

I'm not losing anyone again, he promised himself. *I'll stab the monsters in their giant eyes first.*

Unlike before, Zara led them to a cliff face riddled with small crevices. She let out a sound that was a mixture of a falcon's cry, a distant babbling brook, and the cold certainty of the coming winter. Parts of him he never knew he had cringed and exulted at the sounds. It was like his ears had taken a bite of a kellfruit, and they puckered at its sour rind before sighing at its sweet interior. He was not a fan.

The cliff face cracked open, thunder on a clear night, and the usual earth-scented darkness yawned before them. Yet, as they marched within, the Passage crackled and howled. It felt like they walked into a storm. The dark swirled, black on black, as writhing aquamarine light lashed it into submission. Chaos, followed by sudden, absolute order.

"Keep moving," Zara said. Her voice was light, but there was sweat on her brow. "We must move as fast as we are able."

"You heard her," the Hand said from the front. "Double march."

CHAPTER THIRTY-FIVE

The meal ended up being substantially more than just breakfast.

Felix was led into a large, open air pavilion twice the size of the Farwalker's yurt. The roof was festooned with greenery, like vines and hanging moss, all built upon the backs of carved, Human-sized ravens. A huge spread was laid atop twenty-two tables, steaming in the slight morning coolness in a way that had Felix's mouth watering. His friends were already there, the injured as well as the hale, all digging into the bounty before them. Soon, more Henaari from all over filtered through the streets and into the pavilion.

"What is this?" Felix asked.

"A grand feast for one who has been Blessed by the Raven," a robed member of the Synod declared. She had emerged from among the tables and spread her arms before pointing at Felix and Pit, gathering the attention of the growing crowd. "We celebrate Felix Nevarre and his Pact Companion, Pit! They brought back a Feather from the Raven Herself!"

The crowd cheered, but the rhythm of their Spirits was confused and skeptical. There was a hesitance to their joy. The Farwalker nudged his elbow, and Felix understood. Without comment, Felix lifted the Feather of the Raven up into the air for all to see. This time, the cries were deafening, and shock pervaded the Spirits closest to him.

"Few are they who earn a Blessing directly from the Endless Raven's body," the Farwalker explained to him. To those gathered around them, he raised his voice. "By Right of Wander does this man come before us, and by Right of Wander, he is accepted!"

The cheer that followed put the last to shame. The feast began, and music struck up in the corner. Henaari shed their stoic exterior and reveled in the food and song. It was a dramatic and surprising transformation, enough that Felix barely resisted when he was led to the head of the main table where he sat alongside members of the Synod, the Matriarch, and the Farwalker himself.

"Won't someone hear you all?" Felix asked. Wyvora shook her head.

"The wards keep sound and light within our camp. We Henaari are Blessed by the Raven's own concealment," she said.

Translating in his head, that meant "big magic bird did it; we're fine." And Felix let it lie. Maybe he'd ask to see their wards later.

After a quick meal to ease his ever-present hunger—braised ribs and odd, frond-like leafy greens—Felix checked on his friends and allies. As he'd noticed before, they were all there, and even Vyne was back on his feet. Whatever treatment they'd received, it had worked wonders as their Status Conditions were cleared and their Health was back up to full. Harn had even taken off his helmet and was eating his fair share of the platters near him.

The Farwalker asked his questions and got his answers. Of Vellus, of Felix's relationship with the Lost Goddess. It was all very juicy to a man who collected the unheard and unknown. The Farwalker penned much of it in a thick book he carried, one very similar to the old journal Felix held in his pack.

"I'm afraid you have me at a disadvantage," the Farwalker said after a long moment of contemplation. "The knowledge of the Lost Goddess, alive but mad, is worth far more than what I have offered you."

"What, then, would be appropriate?" Felix asked. A big part of him was urging caution, but something about the Farwalker put him at ease. He wasn't sure if it was the man's irreverent attitude or how much he disliked the Matriarch, but the old man was growing on him.

"I will have to think on this," he said before returning to his drink.

So it went. The morning became afternoon, and the afternoon stretched into shadows long and dark enough to usher in the night. Torches lit, and the songs became bawdier. Laughter flowed as much as wine, and Felix learned the Henaari were not only excellent warriors but also adept performers. Knives were juggled and elaborate tumbling routines performed, though it all felt for themselves rather than for their guests. As if all of this was simply the way these nomads entertained themselves, and Felix was just lucky enough to watch.

More than a few times, Evie attempted their hypnotic acrobat routine, and she was really getting the hang of it by the time Kylar and Davum were encouraged to try as well. The swordsman put on a bit of a show, having invested in Agility fairly heavily, but the Orc axe fighter had little bend to his bulky frame. Regardless, they both tried their best before it all devolved into a gale of laughter and delight.

Henaari men and women rushed to congratulate the outsiders, plying them with drinks and more food as they all poked good-natured fun at their failures. Kikri and Nevia both ended up in deep conversations with Vess, though with all the commotion, Felix was hard-pressed to say what they spoke about. He could have listened, forced his Perception or his Affinity through the white noise, but he shied from that. He tried to let his friends have their privacy, even if the Elf and Dwarf kept looking over at Felix every couple minutes.

Not my business. It had become his mantra as he'd sipped his water. The water everyone else was drinking was nice—rich and a little fruity—but it did nothing for him, despite the Henaari boasting of its Journeyman Tier fermentation. His physical stats burned through it all so fast, he didn't feel the slightest buzz. After the first cup, he'd switched to simple river water. Felix had noticed his friends and the Haarguard had also switched to water. He almost wanted to tell them to enjoy themselves, but thought better of it. As nice as the Henaari were being now, as much as the Farwalker seemed congenial, Felix had little trust left to give to people that had pointed spears at him only a day ago.

Now that the gymnastic entertainment had fled the floor, it was soon repopulated by a small stage that built itself. Dark swirls of violet, black-gray, and green-gold vapor swirled on the ancient courtyard, and in their wake, wood and leaf flowed and bent. The stage formed of these pieces, a wide, semi-circular structure that rose to eye-height before shaping columns that met above the stage in a series of graceful arches. Felix watched, enraptured by the dance of Mana, almost missing the mage that was hidden in a doorway not twenty feet beyond. They gestured, and a screen descended from the first arch, made of a thick paper.

"Ah, is it so late as that?" The Farwalker appeared surprised, despite his shroud of darkness. "The night does sneak up on us all."

"What is it?" Felix asked.

"All Henaari festivities end with a story. A thought upon which to ruminate for a night and a day," the Farwalker explained. "Shh, shh! It starts."

A voice spoke, whisper-soft but easily heard by all in attendance. "In an Age before this, beyond the reach of Memory and the scale of Time, there was a people."

From behind the paper, bright, orange-yellow lights ignited, and shadows swirled to life atop the screen. The shadows resolved into a series of figures, silhouettes only, yet detailed enough that Felix could tell no two were exactly alike.

"This people, though strong, were beset by the teeth of a far stronger nation." The shadow people writhed and fell, cut into by armored foes and vicious arrows. "The leaders of this people despaired, for they believed this meant their end. But the pleas of a child woke the Will of Creation itself, and saviors were called upon from beyond the Void."

A child of shadow wept in a field of the dead, and from the sky came a beam of terrible energy. It struck the battlefield, sending friend and foe high into the air, as if a meteor had touched down. From the impact, two figures emerged.

"The Unbound had come."

Felix sat up, and Pit stopped gnawing on a piece of bone. Surprise and interest echoed across their bond, quickly followed by suspicion. *Who chose this story?* Did they know about him? And did that matter to the Henaari?

Felix tried to cover up his sudden interest, instead folding his arms and leaning back in his chair. Before him, the shadow figures moved on. The two Unbound walked onto the battlefield and began slaying the armored enemy with impunity. The man picked up two massive greatswords and wielded one in each fist, while the woman unleashed a dark fire among the gathered armies.

"Together, the Unbound shook the earth and flooded the mountains with the blood of their enemies. Pledged to the cause of the troubled people, they were creatures of pure destruction, eradicating first one army and then another. The immortals that opposed this troubled people sent monsters, Behemoths and Giants and Dragons, but the Unbound slew them without pause or mercy. The troubled people were troubled no longer, but instead gathered beneath them a great and powerful legion of their own. Led by the two Unbound, they were unstoppable."

The paper itself shook, rippling as if the world was affected by the Unbound's supremacy. Figures, wreathed in smoke and flame and blinding light, appeared at one end of the screen. The Unbound stood tall before them, even as the skies tore open, and the figures poured their might atop the conquering heroes' heads.

"Until, inevitably, the immortals came to oppose them. They were called to stand down, to let the people they served fall. The Unbound refused."

Depicted in silhouette and shadow, Felix nonetheless got the perfect impression of lightning and flame savaging the earth while the Unbound fought back like demons. Water and smoke dropped from the skies, only to be bisected by blades as large as mountains. Until, one-by-one, the figures fell. And the Unbound emerged victorious.

"The immortals proved mortal after all, and from their vanquished bones, the Unbound built up the once-troubled people. They became a nation in truth, an empire that spanned the Ages. It grew, guided by the glory of their victories and the kindness that resided in the bloody hands of the demon Unbound."

The shadows grew somehow luminous as the people were lifted from the depths of their defeat, dragged upward by the relentless momentum of the two Unbound. The whispered narration continued, unabated.

"Compassion and empathy, two terms foreign to the Continent's tradition of slaughter, yet they proved a lasting legacy. The empire expanded, lifting all that it touched up into the Golden Realm, where power was shared and grown. Together."

Hands reached out, neighbor helping neighbor, people raising others by word and deed.

"But it was not to last."

The luminous quality was struck from the paper screen, and a number of Henaari cried out. Felix started, so caught up in the tale that he'd forgotten where he was, But his wayward attention was quickly snagged again as dark shapes began marching from among jagged mountains.

"An Age passed, but eventually the other nations came against them, jealous of their power and despising how they sought to raise up the weak. The weak, as we all know, simply line the Path the strong walk on their way to greatness. That the Golden Empire sought to deny this fundamental truth was perversion! And so the greatest, oldest of monsters came to destroy all that the Unbound had built."

The dark shapes became a flood, surmounted by immense and terrible forms of claw and scale and blade and hammer.

"The Unbound had long since passed, long since traveled beyond the Realms Corporeal, but even still, the Golden Empire was mighty. It fought back and could not be defeated by mortal hands."

The black tide crashed against a bulwark of golden stone and steel. Blades snapped, and claws were shattered upon the Golden Empire's fortifications, and the wash of magics ravaged the opposing armies.

"The war waged for many centuries, but it would have ended with the Golden Empire victorious, had the gods not been roused." Storm clouds rolled into the scene, and from behind them emerged seven brilliant moons. "The war was escalated into the heavens themselves, as magi from the Empire fought against the might of the old gods. The Empire strained, unable to hold out, and in the depths of their desperation, made the Choice of Folly."

The scene shifted until the battle in the sky was in the far distance, and instead Felix could see a mountainous landscape that seemed oddly familiar. "Two Grand Magi found a power source unlike any other. Convinced it would end the war, they tapped into it and used its potency to fuel their great ambition."

Things, segmented and oddly mechanical, surged from the

mountains. Each was twice the size of the people, and as they hit the battlefield, the tide began to turn. The Golden Empire rallied.

"Using this magic, they forged great creations of impervious flesh, things that would serve the Empire and cast out their enemies. Warfare raged, unlike the Continent had ever known, and hundreds of nations were struck from the face of the world.

"The empire was winning. Finally.

"But Folly dogged them and their cursed Choice. The magi were twisted by the power they sought out, and too late, they found that all might comes at a cost."

From among the magi, something else rose from the earth. It was a blur, a bulk as big as the mountains around it, all teeth and destruction. It rushed forward, tearing into friend and foe without distinction.

"A darkness was unleashed, staining the Continent with the blood of an Age. Then the grand creations turned against their makers, against the Golden Empire and the gods alike."

Shapes that looked like massive, armored creatures fought off armies on both sides. Spears and blades shattered against their dark silhouettes, and mortal forms were shredded by their fury. A figure appeared among the Golden Empire, one that banished the creations and the mountainous monstrosity with a great and powerful weapon.

"The Golden Empire stopped the betrayal, but it was too late. A mortal blow had been put in the Empire's side, and the gods did not hesitate."

The moons shimmered and crackled, and the screen rippled again and again.

"A weapon was summoned, a great and terrible one that even they feared. A weapon that could kill the gods themselves."

Another moon rose, this one dark as the others were luminous, and from it oozed a foul and terrible haze. It dropped from the heavens and struck the earth like a hammer blow, and where it landed, the Golden Empire failed and died.

"Not even the greatest of Magi could face this creature, for it was the antithesis of life. Of existence. Jealous and hungry, it could not be stopped."

Darkness enveloped the entirety of the paper screen.

"The Golden Empire, the last bastion of Harmony, was silenced."

Vigorous applause filled the pavilion and the homes nearby as the Henaari cheered. All of them had been caught up in the tale, and Felix could feel their Spirits quiver with quiet relief. Relief that the tale was not about them. That it was simply a story.

But was it? He wondered at that. Apart from the beautiful method of storytelling, pieces of it felt similar to what Zara had told him of the Unbound. Figures of destruction and terrible power that people had conflated with demons.

"That was about the Nym, wasn't it?" Felix suddenly said, voiced pitched to the Farwalker. The man nodded, face shrouded as usual.

"Indeed it was, though few remember the name." He looked at Felix.

"Because of the Ruin. That's what the thing was, at the end."

The Farwalker nodded. "They still teach such things in your land?"

"Apparently," Felix said. The others all knew what the Ruin was, back when they had met. "I think most know." Felix thought a moment. "Why did you tell this to us?"

"I did not choose tonight's tale. That is the work of the storyteller and their Blessing," he said. "Yet, must there be a reason?"

Felix gave him a look. The Farwalker laughed and put up his hands. "It is only a story. An evening's diversion before the real work can begin."

"Real work?"

"You wanted information, no?" A tired-looking Wyvora pulled the Farwalker's chair out. "Come. This time, you should bring everyone."

"Everyone?" Felix looked at Harn, and the man was ready and waiting. He nodded and snapped his helmet back on.

"I suspect they will want to hear this, too, Felix Nevarre."

CHAPTER THIRTY-SIX

Felix led his team after the Farwalker and Wyvora. Harn had gathered the lot of them, and Vyne and Davum were still holding food in their hands as they walked.

"Can't we stay just a little longer?" Atar asked. "That play they put on, the sheer magical skill involved… Remarkable."

"You can go make eyes at the illusionist later," Alister said. "I saw her, back in one of the houses. Quite pretty."

"Burnin' gorgeous, for Henaari," Evie added, then in a quieter tone. "Too much forehead for me, though."

"Can we focus, please?" Vess asked brusquely. Felix looked back at her, and her cheeks darkened slightly. "They may have feted us, but I still do not trust the Henaari's intentions. We must keep our wits about us."

"She ain't wrong," muttered Harn. "But, all of us are in fightin' shape now. It'd be right stupid for them to attack us after goin' through the trouble of healin' us."

Felix held out a hand, low and insistent. "Caution isn't a bad idea. But let's not get too aggressive. The Farwalker, at least, seems to be willing to help." He smirked. "Plus, he can hear all of this."

"Indeed. I had just thought it rude to mention that," the Henaari wise man said.

Evie and Davum barked a laugh, the Orc looking a touch more

drunk than the rest. Felix would have to watch out for that. The others seemed sober enough, but he questioned how much they'd all had to drink before switching to water. Only Harn had Vitality enough to burn through booze so quickly, and that's if they had been drinking the weak stuff.

"It's just ahead here," Wyvora said.

"Where are we going?" Felix asked as they traversed the many free-standing arches. They were near the center of the camp, but the pathways were winding and in slightly confusing ways. Felix could recall their path exactly, but that just meant he could get back to where they were before. If he had to run, he'd have to get above the rooftops, then he'd be a sitting duck for any jerk to pepper with arrows or Skills. "Seems a long way to go for a talk."

"We go to the Clan Hall, dear guests," the Farwalker said. His wheelchair rattled against the bits of ancient flagstone that poked from the earth. "This conversation will involve more than just us, for better or worse. There is much you must know."

They came to a larger structure, around the same size as the pavilion they'd spent the day within, but built more along the lines of the structure they'd found in the outpost. A high, pitched roof dropped all the way to the ground, while panels of carved designs flanked the large door clearly built for taller people. Stairs lead up to the clan hall, but there were wide, flat planes to either side of the steps, and Wyvora simply pushed the Farwalker up and onto the porch.

They've even designed their temporary housing with wheelchair-accessible entrances? Felix was definitely impressed with their strange building magic. That they could create things so fast—like the stage for the shadow play—it was remarkable. It felt a lot more complex than his Stone Shaping, which just moved around dirt and stone with earth Mana. *The stage-builder was using at least three types of Mana, plus whatever techniques were required to make something so complex. Wooden beams, planks, even paper screens. Crazy.*

When they walked through the doors and into the Clan Hall, Felix was struck by the similarity to the outpost. The majority of the space was open with seating around the edges, and on the far end was a Shrine to the Endless Raven. *It's built exactly the same, as far as I can tell.* He hadn't gone around taking measurements, but his memory suggested an identical construction. *Maybe their building magic is more of a preset than spontaneous creation. I almost hope so. It'd make me feel better about my lack of imagination.*

The Synod and—unfortunately—the Matriarch filed in through separate doors to the side, filling the seats at the edges of the Hall while Wyvora wheeled the Farwalker to the Shrine itself. Felix and his team lingered near the exit, stepping just at the edge of the wide-open central space.

"Felix Nevarre! We greet you in the manner of our ancient ancestors, with food, story, and song among the warm regard of our peoples. By Right of Wander, we welcome you," the Farwalker said without preamble.

"As the Raven wills," muttered the others in the room.

Felix looked at Vess, but she just nudged him forward. "Yeah, thank you," he said as he stepped into the center. "I'm glad we've been able to reach a peaceful resolution to our… rocky introductions." Felix felt the Synod's general air of agreement, Wyvora's detached amusement, and a sense of thready anger from the Matriarch. She sat in a chair near the Shrine, her outfit and hair impeccable with silver ornaments and robes of green and purple.

"You have earned a boon from us and from myself twice over," said the Farwalker. There was some muttering at this, surprise and curiosity mainly. "And for the first boon, you have asked us for information on your foe, the one we call the Master of the Mountain Below." This time the murmurs were considerably more agitated. "But first, you will need information on before and on our purpose here in these mountains."

The Farwalker wheeled himself to the front of the Shrine of the Endless Raven. There, he reached up and touched the foot of the carved bird, wings spread in flight. "We have long had a presence in the Foglands. It was where I met my Companion, and the ground lies thick with uncovered mystery. No less now that the fog has somehow lifted. But our return at this time is to seek out a specific person. The former Matriarch, gone into the Wilds by Right of Wander and never returned."

A'zek, across the way, shifted and settled his long, barbed tail around his paws. The harnoq looked intently at Pit, though why was lost on him—the Chimera's Spirit was as occluded as the Farwalker's. The Matriarch was also staring in their direction, her gaze switching between the Farwalker and Felix with a measured intensity.

"The Matriarch—former Matriarch, that is," the Farwalker corrected himself smoothly, and the woman's face darkened in anger the same time her Spirit boiled. "The former Matriarch had set out to uncover a secret so powerful it would change much for our people. An ancient discovery, one long buried by the Golden Empire."

So that's *why you told us that story.* Felix kept his emotions from his face with a flare of Deception, but his thoughts began to gather speed. *The Nymean Temple, then. It has to be. And the former Matriarch...*

An image of bones trapped beneath a nest of wildflowers and vines on the bank of a thundering waterfall.

"Our people draw power from our compact with the Endless Raven. The Blessings we enjoy come from Her munificence and only grow stronger as She is fed from the font of the Unknown." The man's hand traced the base of the Raven's statue. "Curiosity satisfied but never satiated."

"So, you're here searchin' for this person?" Evie asked.

"That is exactly right. Our search was stymied by the emergence of the Mountain Below," the Farwalker said. "This is where my information grows thin. I do not know how, but the creature you seek to avoid broke open its Domain only a few short weeks ago."

Felix clenched his jaw and felt his Spirit reel. It was exactly what he'd feared. His friends let out a few curses.

"That's why there's so many Reforged out and about, and the Wurms and Hoarhounds, too," Alister said.

"That also means more Arcids are gonna be out there," Evie pointed out. "And all of 'em seem to be boosted by that Bloodmoon ritual they did."

"Bloodmoon ritual?" Wyvora asked.

Felix shook his head. "The... Master of the Mountain Below performed a ritual around a month ago. It directly empowered his soldiers with greater Strength, Vitality, and Endurance. And it had something to do with Vellus' Bloodmoon."

"We were aware of the Bloodmoon's appearance. A rare phenomenon. And it vanished right after the Domain broke," A'zek said contemplatively. "This creature has harnessed divine power to shatter the liminal barrier?"

"Intriguing, and yet terrifying," the Farwalker said. "You face truly monstrous foes, Felix."

Felix grunted and forced a smile. "My life in a nutshell."

"Indeed," he replied. "The Reforged, as you call them, they attacked us. We had been tracking their movements, but somehow they slipped past our defenses and laid siege to our outpost. It was a failing on our part, hubris, even. We expected bestial Intelligence from the ice warriors and had not set our best wards." He gestured around them. "Now we shelter beneath a significant array of wards and Blessings, all to keep us hidden while we search."

"Is that what Wyvora was doing out there? Searching for the former Matriarch?" Felix asked.

"Yes. And scouting our enemies' positions and relative strength," Wyvora answered. She drew herself up. "They may have a decent Intelligence score, but their Perception is no match for our Blessings. I have mapped out much of the surrounding area, a challenge in and of itself even without the fog. Though the Reforged keep moving, they are still centrally located around a single point."

"Shelim," the Farwalker said. Felix and all his friends groaned. The Haarguard looked at them in confusion, joined by the Henaari. "You are familiar with this place?"

Evie laughed.

"Yeah. We're familiar," Felix said.

"Is that where you found your blade?" the Farwalker asked. His shadowed face was fixed on Felix's left hip, where the khopesh-style sword hung. "It is a strange design I've not seen before. And quite old, unless I miss my guess."

Share, yes. Pit nodded to Felix's unasked question. *Trust. A little.*

Felix unsheathed his Crescian Blade and held it up. The sigaldry on the blade lit with a momentary flare before disappearing against the bronze finish. "I found this blade several months ago, when I was alone in the Foglands. This, too," he said and pulled a battered journal from his pack. It was far larger than the one he'd given to the Raven, filled with Henaari script and his own messy scrawl. "They were both discovered with a body. A Henaari body."

A few gasps rippled through the Synod. The Matriarch actually paled, before two points of color began to gather on her cheeks. The Farwalker seemed unsurprised, if saddened. "And what of the body, Felix Nevarre? Where does it lie now?"

"I buried it. Her, I suppose." Felix lowered the blade. "I didn't really know what sort of rites you may use, but I buried her in a shaded grove near a beautiful lake. And I found her killer," he added. The Raven had confirmed that for him, at least. "I tracked them down and killed them as well."

Echoes of approval swept through the assembled Spirits, aside from the Farwalker and Matriarch. He was unreadable, and she was simply cold. Suddenly, the Farwalker bowed, bending completely at the waist. Wyvora and members of the Synod paused only a moment before joining him.

"This one thanks you, Felix Nevarre, for the honoring of our dead."

Felix swallowed. "Finding her saved my life. It was the least I could do."

There was a moment of silence for their fallen Matriarch—the Favored Daughter, as the Raven had referred to her. A solemnity and grief plucked at all their Spirits, an emotion that Felix realized had been there all along, but banked like the embers of a fire. Now, it surged. Clearly, the former Matriarch had been well loved.

Felix eyed the current Matriarch, but the woman was stone-faced. She even met his eyes, as if challenging him to call her out on it.

Suspicious, Pit sent. He, too, was watching the leader of the Henaari. Felix agreed, but it was just a feeling.

"Felix Nevarre, you have given us a great gift. The Raven asks that we search for knowledge, and there has been little else more important than finding out the fate of our own. I will have Wyvora draw up maps for the location and disposition of their forces, as best we understand them."

"That would be exceptionally useful," Felix said. "Thank you."

"That is but the first boon owed. To the second, we offer you supplies to ease your journey. Food, water, and a selection of healing salves and potions." A general murmur of agreement rose and fell around them as the Farwalker continued. "And for the third… do you plan to leave soon?"

"Tomorrow, I suspect," Felix said. "We do not have much time to… achieve our goal."

"Speed is recommended. Your foe has been consolidating his power since our encounter, and he seeks mastery over the Foglands. That is without a doubt. His forges are busy, and he is building something. From the way the earth quakes near his citadel, it is nothing pleasant."

"Citadel?" Harn asked. "What citadel? In Shelim?"

"No. Shelim is where the majority of his forces have gathered, but he has built a fortress atop the pass leading to the Bitter Sea," the Farwalker said.

"Well there goes that idea," Atar muttered.

"It is not the only way," Wyvora suggested. "I have mapped several routes through those mountains. But they are dangerous. Far more dangerous than the simple Tier II beasts you've seen so far."

"Can you include those in your maps, then?" Felix asked, and Wyvora nodded. "I do not seek to engage with the Archon. I'd rather avoid him entirely, and I'd suggest you do the same. He is dangerous."

"Our Blessings will keep us safe," Fyszal said, one of the Synod. "The layers of our current protections cannot be penetrated."

The Farwalker's head snapped up. He looked off into the distance and gripped the sides of his chair.

"Farwalker Qzik, what is it?"

For the first time, Felix felt a quiver of the man's Spirit through the dark shroud he wore.

"Our border's breached."

It was the rhythm of fear.

CHAPTER THIRTY-SEVEN

Felix peered over the lip of the ridge, down onto the river valley on the other side of the Nymean ruin. The Henaari had built some temporary stairs that were cleverly hidden by more of their Urge Blessings—however those worked. They had ascended up and over the ruin, able to view the river and crevasse with a bird's-eye view. It was a goodly distance down, and the night was dark, but all of their Perception stats were high enough to make most details clear.

And of course, the river was teeming with Reforged.

"Shit," Felix muttered.

There were twenty that he could see, all of them boosted by that ritual they'd performed weeks ago. Just as the ones they faced days before. It was apparently a permanent increase in power, though it made them more unthinking brutes than capable tacticians. That was enough to pummel their way across the river, fighting and killing the monsters within it, but they'd never pass the illusions ahead of them.

That's what the Arcid's for, Felix supposed. The thing looked like it was made of crude iron, dark and jagged, but its limbs flowed in the same graceful design as the other Arcids he'd faced. It's chest was huge and wedge-shaped, with large, dark slots bored through it, for some reason. Its head, by contrast, was a triangular stump atop its overdeveloped shoulders and chest.

Voracious Eye.

Name: Arcid - Number 55597
Type: Archonic Construct
Level: 72
HP: 7853/7853
SP: 8199/8221
MP: 6045/6045
Lore: Arcids are twisted creations of sigil, flesh, and metal. They are somehow built by the Archon and enjoy a greater amount of power and autonomy compared to his other creations.
Strength: More Data Required
Weakness: More Data Required

Strong, just like the ones in Haarwatch. Felix quickly relayed its details to the others with him. Evie only narrowed her eyes, while the two Henaari guards and Wyvora gazed at him in horror.

"Level 72? And its Health is above seven *thousand*?" Wyvora swallowed heavily. "That is monstrous."

"Wait 'til it pulls out the stops," Evie said. "These things got magic enough to scare Adept Tiers."

"Look," Felix said, nodding down into the valley.

The river began to freeze as more and more of the Reforged entered it, their heavy limbs manifesting axes and clubs of pure ice Mana. Their weapons lashed the water, turning it to slush as it passed through clawed and finned monstrosities hidden below their waists. Then the Arcid followed them across, and its furnace-like body ignited in a storm of orange Mana vapor and black smoke. The openings in its front lit up with white light before belching a five-foot-wide column of magic flame.

Monsters screeched, wet burbles from the water as it boiled away before the Arcid's onslaught. Even the Reforged leaned away from the light and heat, which stripped the river bare enough for the creature to simply walk across its expanse. Behind it, from the shadows of the forest, Hoarhounds and Wurms followed.

"That's… less than great," Evie said.

"Power like that, that thing'll burn right through the Nymean traps." Felix crouched back down and turned to the Henaari. "We have to run. All of us."

The guards traded a look before glancing at Wyvora. She nodded, slowly. "First, back to the Clan Hall."

The trip back down was much easier, fueled by gravity and a distinct sense of panic. Felix pulled Pit from his Spirit, and the tenku brought the lot of them down to the encampment as fast as falling. Pit was getting stronger, and he barely balked at the additional weight. They landed at the clan hall less than thirty seconds later.

The Synod, Matriarch, and Farwalker were already waiting for them.

"What did you see?" the Matriarch asked. The second set of eyes painted on her forehead were smudged slightly, but her face was otherwise immaculate and her poise unbroken even by news of their boundary being breached. "I do not understand why all of you had to go. Our guards are more than capable of handling some rogue monster."

"It's the Reforged. There's a whole battalion coming for us," Felix said.

Shock and fear flowed over the Synod, and the Farwalker nodded as if his fears had been confirmed. "How many, exactly?" he asked.

"Twenty of the ice warriors, half that of their hounds, and a number of the earth-tunneling Wurms. They were obscured by the ground, so an accurate count is not possible," Wyvora said. "They were led by a much stronger creature, what Felix calls an Arcid."

"They're like lieutenants to the Archon. We've run into them a few times, and they're nasty customers," Felix said. He took a steadying breath. "I suggest that you run. They're not gonna be stopped by illusions and a two-star Nymean ruin."

More of that fear washed against Felix's senses, but he was glad for it. It meant they were taking this seriously.

"Ridiculous," scoffed the Matriarch. "The Blessings of the Raven are no trifles to be torn apart by a simple fire mage."

"I'm not saying we can't fight back," Felix said, while inside he wanted to scream. They needed to *move*. "I'm saying all of your people won't survive the encounter. Trust me on that."

"The Arcid alone is at least Tier III, as are the Reforged," one of the guards said, ignoring the uncomfortable looks from the higher-ups. Tier III was the monster equivalent of a Journeyman, and more than many could handle. She stood at attention while speaking to her clan's leadership. "My Analyze could not confirm, but they are stronger than any among the guards."

"Then the decision is made for us," the Farwalker said. He turned to include everyone present and raised his voice. "We will flee. Synod, if you will set the signals."

"Yes, honored Farwalker," one of the women responded. The Matriarch stood there, mouth open and brow furrowed, before an explosion sounded. It was muffled and distant, but it set several tapestries waving.

"They've already reached the ruin," Wyvora said.

"What can we do to help?" Vess asked.

"It is under control," the Farwalker said calmly. "Instead, please gather your supplies and meet us at the southern end of the valley."

They did, though there was little enough for Felix's team to gather. He went over their packs, checking supplies, and found that their water and rations had all been replenished at some point. And the promised healing potions and salves were already distributed as well. They didn't kid around when it came to promises.

The lot of them took off, heading south around the big tree and the tower that held it aloft, through the ancient paved streets and newly erected arches. It was a shame, having to abandon the work the Henaari had put into their structures, nomads or not.

"Siva's Chords, look at that," Kikri said with a point back at the central tower. The Clan Hall had begun to shimmer with traceries of orange and yellow. In seconds, the high-peaked roof crumbled to ash. And it wasn't the only place. All over the encampment, the buildings were falling apart rapidly.

The earth shook again.

"Keep moving, everyone," Felix said.

The earth kept trembling intermittently as the Arcid bulldozed through traps and tunnels in the Nymean cavern. But it took less than a minute for Felix and his team to reach the southern end of the valley. There, they found a large collection of Henaari, and every single one of them was wearing a large pack of supplies, children and the elderly included. The moment Felix arrived, there was no conversation or meaningless chatter; the entire group of approximately fifty people took off toward the cliff face.

Felix found Wyvora in the crowd. "Where is everyone else?" Unless it had been illusions the whole time, there were far more than fifty people in the camp.

"They took the other exits. When a camp is broken early like this, we have a system in place," she said. "We leave nothing behind, and we always have multiple ways to escape."

Felix huffed a breath, impressed.

They kept up a rapid pace that was punishing for those without a focus in Agility. Soon the mages, Vess, and the Haarguard were all puffing along. None of them slackened their pace, focusing instead on keeping together and putting one foot in front of the other. Harn was fine, his Body well used to the exertion, even if his Agility wasn't up to snuff. Evie and Pit took to it easily, and the rapid pace they maintained didn't even exceed Felix's Stamina regeneration.

The path steepened, cutting sharply behind a jagged escarpment in a way that hid it from casual view. There was no taste of the Raven's magic in the air or the kind Felix was used to; it was simply a trick of the land itself, and it hid a series of switchback trails that led up into six different caverns. Their pace never slacked, a few members of the Synod and the Farwalker leading the group up and into the second cave on the right.

The evening's gloom gave way to further darkness, and it was accompanied by an earthy musk. The air was thick with shadow and earth Mana, thick enough to distract, were Felix focusing on his Manasight. He wasn't, though. Instead, his senses were pitched backward, toward the valley. His Perception and Affinity could just barely discern minor details, and he felt it when a blast of fire Mana erupted out of the Nymean cave.

"They've reached the valley," Felix said in a low voice to Harn.

"We'll see if this is enough to give 'em the slip," Harn said. "Otherwise..."

Harn didn't finish his statement, but he didn't have to; they were always going to be walking the edge of constant battle with the Reforged. And that was before he knew the Archon's Domain had broken.

The cavern wound its way through the cliff face. The Henaari disabled a number of traps that Felix had felt only when they came closer to them, smoothly resetting them as the group passed. The ground lightly shook all the while, heat and fire blooming in the back of Felix's Perception, dimmed by the press of earth. Eventually, they emerged into the open night, surrounded by more of those giant redwood-type trees. Moonlight filtered through the thick canopy, enough to see by, and Felix noticed that they were all alone.

"Are the other groups meeting us out here?" he asked.

"We are to rendezvous at a designated location, Felix. It would do us little good if we were to meet up again so soon after splitting." The Farwalker, who had been carried this whole time, turned his seat around. He seemed more agitated than before. "Bzen, scout the area. A'zek, a sweep, if you please."

A male Henaari wearing their odd, lacquered armor nodded and scurried up one of the huge trees like a squirrel. The harnoq, however, took off into the woods, headed north.

"Something is wrong," Vess said. She looked at the Farwalker then at the trees. "The wind is troubled."

The sound of a hundred ravens cawing took all of them by surprise. It was massively loud, but gone in seconds, leaving only a ringing in their ears. A surge of Affinity and Intent had accompanied the sound, but it was too much for Felix to unpack quickly. Flashes of sense images had assaulted his Mind in a blur, the only constant among them the smell of earth and a fetid heat.

"No," the Farwalker gasped. "No."

"Ergh. What—what was that? What's goin' on?" Evie asked. The others on his team were similarly affected by the noise, but it had hit Evie, Vess, and Felix the worst. All the rest hadn't unlocked their Harmonic stats.

"Elder?" Wyvora asked, concerned. "What did the Raven show you?"

"Death. She showed me terrible death this night." The shroud had fallen away from the Farwalker's face, and the man looked shaky and pale. "The others will die."

"The children," someone whispered in horror.

Hissed breaths filled the glade, and the Henaari around them clutched tightly to one another. Felix looked between them, confused. "You saw the future?"

"The present. The Raven brought to me visions of what my Companion seeks. The other groups will not make it beyond their tunnels." The Farwalker clenched his jaw. "Wurms await them."

Felix cursed. "Okay, then we go save them. Where are the tunnels?"

"It is too far away, you'll never make it in time, even if you fly atop your Companion," Wyvora said. Her own voice was hoarse with grief.

"As fast as you might be, Felix Nevarre, you will not stop a death already coming," the Matriarch said. Her face was streaked with tears, and her hands shook, but her voice was steel as she addressed the group. "The Raven does not lie, not to us. We must move now or else share their fate."

"No. That's bullshit," Felix said. He glanced at his team. "Evie, Vess, Alister, Atar, and Harn. I need you all with me."

Evie nodded, uncharacteristically sober. "Good."

Felix pointed at the four Haarguard. "You four, stick with the Henaari. We'll catch up."

"Sir, I think we could help," Vyne said.

"Can't let you go into danger without us," Davum agreed. "Wouldn't feel right."

The others all agreed, but Felix didn't care. "And what if the Reforged gets through us? Comes for these people?" The guard were silent. "I need you here to keep them safe."

Kylar, who had been silent through this entire ordeal, spoke up. "I'm no match for the Reforged, I know that. But we can work with the Henaari, fight them off if they get this far. We'll stay, as ordered. Sir."

Felix nodded at Kylar, and the man almost saluted before nodding back. "We'll return soon enough."

"Felix Nevarre, you are choosing a fruitless Path," the Matriarch said. "The Raven showed us death in those tunnels."

Felix didn't reply, only gestured in handsign to his team. They split, Pit taking to the air with Vess, Evie, Alister, and Atar on his back, while Harn took off running back up the slope. Toward the tunnel they exited. Felix himself angled toward where A'zek had disappeared only minutes prior.

"The secondary tunnels are too far to reach in time. You'll never—"

"Lady, you've never seen me run," Felix said.

The ground beneath him exploded, shattering in concentric circles as his Body surged forward. In a blink, he'd left them far behind.

Captain Ifre of the Dawnguard caught the signal flashed from her subordinate's bracer.

Last one made it into the tunnels. Good. She turned, making sure to keep the lead. "Everyone move quickly and quietly. Everything will be fine. The Raven provides."

Murmurs rolled back through the crowd of fifty, but their Spirits were firm, if tired. Her people were tall and lanky, but they were hardy, used to the sudden abandonment of their settlements time and time again. It was all they knew, as their Pledge drove them ever onward for the old and undiscovered.

At that moment, all Ifre cared about was getting her people out alive. She may not fully trust the outsider, especially not after that stunt with his stone crafting Skill, but she trusted the Synod. Danger was coming.

The earth shook again, though a little more violently than the last few times. A flash of sourceless light flitted through Ifre's Mind, but it was gone in an instant. People behind her stumbled slightly, blinking their own eyes, and the captain knew it wasn't just her. *What was that?*

A child near the front—Eigo's youngest, she believed—let out a sob, and Ifre knelt down. "It will be just fine, little one. You are too young to remember, but we have survived far worse than this."

"I heard it," the little boy said. He looked up at her. Snot and tears competed to run down his face the fastest. "The flashes. The Raven said we're going to die."

"What?"

Someone screamed.

The tunnel ahead burst open, revealing the gasping maw of an enormous Wurm. Ifre frantically Analyzed it, and it came back as a level 52 monstrosity, easily Tier II. Its mouth opened, a four-way jaw filled with barbed teeth and a bright orange glow that began to rapidly intensify.

Blessing of Berm!

The tunnel twisted, the earthen floor lifting until it formed a seven-foot-tall embankment before them. A moment later, fire washed over the top of it as the Wurm let loose its attack. The tunnel filled with smoke and the scent of baking earth.

"Defensive formations! Children in the center!" Ifre shouted backward, but couldn't spare the attention to see if they complied. Just on the other side of her berm, two more Wurms slid from the earth, smooth as if it were water, and pivoted toward their group.

Raven protect us.

Fire flooded the tunnel.

CHAPTER THIRTY-EIGHT

"Stygian Shadow!"

Isyk, her junior, thrust his spear forward. The area around Ifre's berm darkened to pitch, the light ripped so violently away that the tunnel around it began to frost. Yet still, Ifre could see a dim orange bloom on the other side.

"Isyk, take everyone, turn them back!" She licked her lips, though her mouth was utterly dry. "We have to use another way."

"As you will, Captain."

The shadows exploded, torn asunder by another burst of hungry orange flames. Isyk reeled, his nose bloodied, as the Blessing was rebounded upon him. But Ifre hadn't the time to worry about her subordinate. All three Wurms slipped through her berm like water, not even so much as slowed down by their workings.

Wander's Prowl!

Spear of the Second Flight!

Ifre zipped ahead, taking the lead Wurm under its segmented jaw with her suddenly flexible spear. The metal and wood of it bent and twisted to her Will, easily slipping into the spaces between the Wurm's rocky carapace. It screamed in pain and fury. She twisted her spear before ripping it back out. Dark ichor spouted onto the earth, but she kept moving.

Stab. Feint. Thrust. Dodge. Fighting the Wurms was straining her Stamina and pushing her Agility to the limit. They were fast, slippery, and Night-cursed strong. Her spear found the gaps in their segments, again and again, bleeding them by tiny bits. Yet they were relentless, so she couldn't stop. She had to give her people time to escape. If she could—

Screams arose behind her. A wash of heat and light pulled a gasp from Ifre's chest. Wurms emerged from the tunnel, midway down their group.

"No!"

Two more rose ahead, too, pushing out of the stone and dirt, and their gaping maws joined the others. Five mouths filled the tunnel with orange light, enough to flood them all with hungry flame.

Blessing of Berm!

Blessing of Berm!

Blessing of Berm!

Ifre spun her spear, each whirling thrust tearing walls from the earth. She poured her Willpower into it, reinforcing her creations with all the Mana and Stamina she could spare.

The liquid fire tore through it all, and vicious heat cut short the screams all around her. Ifre braced.

And waited.

Yet... *nothing?* She expected flames and pain. Yet all she felt was... cold.

Ifre opened her eyes. A swirling field of frozen clouds lingered among the crumbled remnants of her Blessings. A terrible, dire chill assaulted her Body, forcing Ifre a step back, but she peered into its depths. Blue light flickered among the fog, illuminating the outline of the five Wurms.

"Captain!"

The shocked voice of Isyk pulled her attention back. The two Wurms in the rear had frozen as well, entirely subsumed by blue-white flames. Her people shied away from the heat, wincing and crying in alarm.

"What's happening, Captain?"

Ifre felt Mana moving around her, so much that it felt like her people's wards gathering momentum. It hummed through everything.

The outsider!

He emerged from the clouds of frost, his eyes lit like the blazing fire all around him. He rolled his shoulders, and each arm was outstretched toward the five Wurms around him, as if he were holding them back. "Give me, like, thirty seconds."

What? He didn't even sound strained.

The thrum of Mana increased until a visible vapor joined the frozen, swirling fog around him. The blue-white fire redoubled and, for a moment, Ifre couldn't see anything except a shimmering haze of incandescent light.

When it cleared, the Wurms were destroyed. All of them. Pulped into a purple mess against the stone walls.

"All of you, come with me!" A familiar voice called from beyond the outsider. A shape in the dark resolved into A'zek, the Farwalker's Companion. "More are on their way, Felix."

"I know." With a curt gesture, the earth folded over itself, grabbing and dragging the remains of the Wurms down into the stone itself. He looked at her and his blue eyes flashed again. "Go with A'zek… Captain Ifre. He'll lead you all to the Farwalker and others."

Ifre gestured to Isyk, and her people started guiding the remaining folk onward. The outsider ran his hands across the walls, as if he were searching. Some tried to stop and stare or offer thanks, but gentle prods kept them all moving. A slight tug at her gambeson pulled her attention down. Eigo's youngest was there, looking at the outsider and biting his lip.

"Did the Raven lie?" he asked.

Ifre swallowed, unsure how to handle the question. The boy had said they were going to die, but the Raven never lied. It wasn't in its nature. She ushered the boy ahead of her, joining with him as they moved further down the tunnel. Away from the outsider and whatever else was coming.

"The Raven—"

"The Raven only showed the Farwalker death in the tunnels," the outsider interrupted. He glanced at the boy before looking harder at Ifre. "But that's not happening. Not today." He looked past them, past even the stone itself. His eyes gleamed. "Go. Run now."

Her people began to run into the dark tunnels, following the harnoq's lead. An explosion echoed abruptly down the path, but when she looked back for the outsider, all Ifre saw was cracked earth. The outsider was gone.

The Raven had not lied. Death had come to the tunnels.

Just not for them.

Pit forced his wings down, hurling air Mana beneath him and his passengers, fighting against the pull of the earth. It was hard, but he could do it. He'd been training for this, after all.

Flight is level 47!

"You can do it, Pit," the Dangerous One said, rubbing at his neck. The feel of her was warm and vibrant, a whirlwind contained, while the others were a collection of conflicting sensations. A cold nimbleness, a rigid heat, and a steady, heavy pressure. The Pretty Killer, the Firebrand, and the Stabby One. He knew their names, the ones they used among themselves, but Pit preferred to think of them this way.

"It's probably Atar, weighing us all down!" Pretty Killer shouted as they ascended, narrowly missing a protruding, scraggly tree. "I saw how much you ate today!"

"Oh, shove it up your aaaa—" Firebrand screamed, nearly unseated when Pit had to kick off an annoyingly protruding crag. Only the quick hands of the Stabby One and Pretty Killer together kept him in place.

"Evie, shut up, if you please," the Dangerous One breathed.

Pit screeched, putting them out of his mind as he climbed the mountain. The four of them were shifting now, jostled by Pit's movements, a far cry from Felix's in-sync motions while riding. Yet, with another furious burst of effort, they shot up and over the lowest peak. Air Mana shot off beneath him, Wingblades fired for good measure to boost them up and over. They surged upward into the star-filled sky.

"Blind gods," the Pretty Killer gasped.

Below them, the valley was awash in flames. It lit up the night, sending huge plumes of smoke into the sky. Hovering momentarily in the thin air, Pit wanted to cry out, but that would ruin their task. Felix had sent instructions as they parted, and Pit knew what to do. Even now, the tenku could sense his Companion speeding toward one of the tunnels. He'd reach it in seconds.

Pit tilted his body and tucked his wings. He dove.

The Humans on his back almost screamed, but they held onto control, burying their fear and exhilaration into their grips and breathing. Two hundred feet below, Pit snapped open his wings, letting the rising air currents lift him up and away from the mountain's slope, pushing him out into the valley.

Flight is level 48!

Silver spears manifested around them as they flew, keeping pace despite Pit's increasing speed. Something ignited between his wings amid the gathering crackle of heaviness and cold fluidity.

"There," the Dangerous One whispered. Pit's eyes followed her pointed gauntlet, zeroing in on three huge, ice-bound warriors trudging heavily through the burning forest. He angled himself in their direction, but not before noting the placement of six other groups of Reforged slowly spreading through the valley. Searching.

I will fly low. You all drop. Attack in the dark.

Pit sent the thought at his Companion's friends—his own friends—but only the first two looked at him in shock. The women both nodded at him, and the cold one grinned.

We begin.

Felix burst from the mossy earth, his arrival heralded by a great shaking and booming of explosively displaced rock and dirt. As he was hurled into the air, Felix's hands were wrapped around the neck of a segmented Wurm, dark with purple ichor, and it was not happy.

"HISSSS!"

Cloudstep!

Unfettered Volition!

Twisting in mid-air and kicking off a panel of solidified Mana, Felix pivoted all of his considerable weight downward. The Wurm, attached to him by his indefatigable grip, had no choice but to follow. Its rocky body crackled and snapped as it bent farther than it was ever meant to, and Felix hit the ground with its mandibles directly under his fists.

The Wurm's face disintegrated into a fine mist of purple gunk.

Before its body cooled, another surged from the earth, this time directly beneath him at speeds that rivaled Felix's. It emerged, jaws agape, only to find a curved blade held horizontally over the top of its form. It tore itself apart as its momentum drove it helplessly upward and through the razor-sharp bronze sword. Its two sides spun off to either side of Felix, raining hot offal all over him.

You Have Killed A Wurm (x2)!
XP Earned!

God, that stinks.

Aloud, he said, "That all of them?"

"Yes," came the deep voiced reply. A'zek emerged from the ragged hole Felix's Body had blasted through the earth. "I am surprised. I sense no more in the surrounding area."

Felix cracked his neck. That last fight had been a doozy. The Wurms hadn't hurt him too badly—only knocking about 10% off his Health and Stamina—but it had been a surprise that his Stone Shaping was worthless against them. They simply swam through it. Wispfire and swords, on the other hand, worked just fine. "Why aren't you with the group?"

The harnoq leaped atop a large, solitary stone. It was at least thirty feet up. "They are being met by my Companion and the… Matriarch."

Felix grunted in surprise. "She decided they're worth saving?"

An unreadable emotion flashed across A'zek's Spirit. "We must find the last flight of Henaari. They are no doubt in as much danger as this group."

Felix bent over and wiped his Crescian Blade against some plush-looking moss before resheathing it. The night was growing lighter and… smokier.

"Over there," A'zek said. He nodded to the northeast. "The other tunnels are this way."

"Into the fire, huh?" Felix asked, but the Chimera was already running. "Good thing I've got resistance."

Having Agility and Perception as high as Felix did was a

curious and wondrous thing. When he moved, *truly* moved, it was like nothing he'd experienced. It was like dashing through a world on pause. His Perception fed him ten trillion bits of information, and his Agility moved his Body fast enough to make use of that information. Enough sensory details to make a lesser man's head explode from the pressure flooded in.

But, because his Intelligence was even higher than Perception and Agility—and he'd Tempered a powerful Journeyman Mind—Felix had no issues with processing any of it. The result was a Felix-shaped blur that tore through the trees and gathering smoke, plunging straight into the raging fires.

Abyssal Skein!

A'zek was behind him, somewhere, but once they started moving, all Felix had to do was stick to the sides of the valley. As the Void crawled out of his core space and enveloped him, Felix became like a ghost flitting through the flames. He could somehow feel his own presence vanish, cut off by the skin of Void-stuff around him. Or maybe just… spread out into the world around him. Faded.

Abyssal Skein is level 46!

Hm. So not separated, but spread thin into my surroundings. Less active camouflage and more like...I dunno. Magic, I guess.

He saw the Reforged first. Huge and—to him—ponderous, they each carried conjured ice weapons and swung them with a steady monotony that cleared through redwood-sized trees and low hills. They didn't give any indication that the raging fires bothered them at all, often wading through patches of smoldering under-brush in their relentless sweep outward.

Felix ran up the side of the cliff, his feet sure and powerful. It was hard not to crack the stone beneath him, but he managed, letting his presence mostly get eaten up by his Skein. Felix could sense that others were out there, moving farther abroad. Before him was not the only place on fire, and the Reforged gave off such a glimmer of ice Mana that they were, ironically, like a torch in the night.

Pit. Have you begun?

Yes. A flash of sense images filtered through their bond. Fire. Ice axes swung. Impact and pain, but not Pit's. *Six fight.*

There are another eight to the northeast of you. Be careful. I'm going to save the last group now, he sent.

Stay safe.

You too, lil' pig.

Felix crept along the cliff face, his uncanny Dexterity keeping him balanced atop ledges thinner than a finger, while his Strength supported his considerable bulk. It wasn't much farther, the tunnel, just around another two bends, and he could see a grove of tightly grouped trees and thorns. Similar to the illusion that hid the encampment, this had clearly once hidden the tunnel's entrance, but the Mana of the array was shattered. Burned. Four Reforged stood close by, ranging between fifteen and twenty feet tall, while among their feet, almost a dozen Hoarhounds prowled.

Ten hounds. Four Reforged. And, Felix narrowed his eyes. *One Arcid.*

The fire-attuned Arcid hunched at the entrance to the tunnel and was shouting something in a guttural language into its depths. Felix didn't understand the words, but the creature's twisted Spirit rippled with aggression, anger, and a deep, unsettling *craving*.

"Tua effrata! I give you until count of ten, little wanderers!" It's furnace-like body creaked and groaned with every shift, and a white heat flared up within the grates on his chest. "Ten counts,then I will be not so merciful!"

"The creature baits them," a voice said behind him, and it took all Felix had not to jump. "What does it aim for?"

"How do you keep sneaking up on me?" Felix asked. A'zek didn't reply, only stared at the Arcid with hate in his dark, liquid-seeming eyes. "He probably wants to know where your Companion is, or the other leadership. You've all been a bit of a thorn in their side, right?"

"The Farhunter has needled them to discover their purpose, yes."

"Needled too much, maybe." Felix didn't say what he feared. That his Mark had led them there. He swallowed. "Whatever the reason, we're here to stop them. Without the Wurms, they're hampered by the tunnel sizes; they can't get in, but for some reason, the Henaari can't just leave the other side."

"Tunnel may have been collapsed," A'zek suggested.

"That'd make sense, and would explain why all the Wurms were at the farther exit rather than this one first." Felix bit the inside of his cheek. "They collapsed this one and moved on. Okay. Okay, I think I've got a plan."

"Tell me."

CHAPTER THIRTY-NINE

The Reforged thundered through the undergrowth, paying little heed to things like trees and hillocks or the cloying mix of ice fog and woodsmoke. They swept their ice-shaped weapons in grand arcs, delivering destruction upon the green valley even as it burned alive. Despite their great Strength and Endurance, their size and their fury, they could not touch Vessilia Dayne.

"RUAAAH!"

Dragoon's Footwork!

An axe bigger than her entire body slammed sideways into a tree, but Vess was simply not there. The steps of her movement Skill had her flicker before the ice warrior's perceptions, there and gone, and the giant could only rage impotently.

Evie also danced around her opponents, though she faced two Hoarhounds as well as one of the Reforged. Her new chain proved its mettle as it tore into the hounds, flensing flesh from bone and metal with every rotation. But it did not stop the remade creatures. The Hoarhounds were as fast as the Reforged were strong, and worse, they operated in packs and used tactics. Were it not for the mages, Evie would have died within minutes of their first engagement.

"Imbued Sparkbolt!"

"Grand Impetus!"

Crimson flame and a cobalt lance of power came from opposite ends of the fight, but each one found the legs of a hound, fouling their steps and sending them sprawling. The fire even dropped them into squealing bouts of pain, something that the blazing forest couldn't do. Ice might have been their element originally, but the creatures all seemed inured to normal flames. More hounds lunged forward, snapping for the mages, but a trio of blue pillars from the sky drove their bellies to the earth.

"Thanks Al!" Evie shouted mid-air, already between the tree trunks. "I got the dogs! Can you two kill the big guy?"

"I have it," Atar said. His curls tumbled over his forehead and were slick with sweat, but there was nothing but determination in his eyes as a crown of molten flame ignited above his head. "Crown of Ignis! Imbued Sparkbolt!"

No less than twenty orbs of fire spun out of his crown, zipping toward the Reforged in a volley of light. The former giant screamed in agony as an explosive firestorm wracked its body.

Focus on your own fight!

Vess stepped into the wild swing of the ice warrior, using two of her floating spears to deflect it up and into another charred tree trunk. The woods were thick and close, despite the razing hunger of the wildfire. She thrust her partisan in a flurry of strikes, each one fouled by the beast's icy armor, but her Strength was not to be denied. Cracks crazed the ice of its form, worn ever thinner by the intensity of Atar's fields of flame.

Spear of Tribulations!

More spears were conjured around her, manifesting in a tight net above her head. They blocked the Reforged's first strike and parried the second before the giant's enormous Strength sent the lot of them flying outward. Vess grunted in pained surprise, but wasted no time. Tethered to her Will, they spun back around, each of her seven spears surging forward to rejoin the battle—

—and tangled in trees and brush, held a breath too long to block the Reforged's next attack. Vess desperately dove aside, caught flat footed by her Skill's failure. The blow sundered the well-packed dirt and ancient flagstone beneath their feet, opening a small chasm that crackled with remnant frost.

"RUAAAHH!" The Reforged screamed at her, full of spittle

and fetid breath. Its innards smelled of rot and putrefaction, neatly curdling Vess' stomach. "DIE!"

It flipped its axe into an overhand chop, too stupid to know its end. Vess darted forward and aside, flaring her Dragoon's Footsteps and Pierce the Sky so that the weight of their might rested behind her spear. She closed in, too fast to avoid, too deadly to survive.

Her spear took its head.

You Have Killed a Reforged!
XP Earned!

"Vess! Help!" Alister hollered, his voice rising in a panic. Through the smoke and ice fog, two more Reforged joined against the mages, and Evie still hadn't defeated the Hoarhounds.

Tch. She gathered her spears to her again, careful to maneuver them around the tangled growth on all sides, before leaping high up into the air. Her Skills were designed to be used mid-air, among the skies, not snarled upon the earth. Here, the silver-seeming spears, crafted from the very winds, soared.

Dragon's Descent!

Hurtling downward, Vess' form flickered with streamers of green-white vapor. They burst from the tip of her partisan, chased along the edges of its hidden array, spiraling outward until they enveloped her completely. Her Seven Steps of the Dragoon guided the air Mana instinctively, No longer a Human warrior, nor a Dragoon, but a judgment sent from on high.

The verdict was death.

Pierce the Sky is level 59!
Spear of Tribulations is level 70!
Dragon's Descent is level 57!

You Have Killed a Reforged!
XP Earned!

You Have Gained A Level!
You Are Now Level 45!
You Have 3 Unused Stat Points!

Without pausing, Vess dumped two points into Strength and the last into Willpower. Vibrant, white-green energy flooded her mountainous core space, filling the skies with light and power as her muscles grew just a touch denser. She whipped her partisan into a horizontal slash. The leaf-shaped blade met icy club and rebounded—but so did the Reforged.

"Evie! Now!"

"Reap the Maelstrom!"

Her best friend's chain, spiked and bladed, spun and rotated in ways too fast for Vess' Perception to follow. It howled through the air, snapping fire-ravaged trees and Hoarhound legs in equal measure. With a ripple of movement, Evie sent the chain hurtling toward the remaining three Reforged. They went down, legs swept, and grisly wounds opened across their thighs and calves.

"Raze!"

Twin bolts of silver fire dropped from above, and a vast presence unveiled itself. Harn, armored and impervious-looking, unleashed the full force of his Spirit, stunning the weakened Reforged. Before they could recover, he landed, and the blazing light of his metal Mana cut all three of them to the quick.

They were dead before he stood back up.

"...where'd you come from?" Atar asked, looking up. Vess followed his gaze, only to find an expanse of dark wings patterned with crimson.

"You got ahead of me. Pit came back and gave me a lift," Harn said. He jerked his silver axes from the ancient flagstones beneath them—they'd sunken down to the haft. "Dropped me off."

"Dropped you—from how high?" Atar asked.

"Dunno. Wasn't countin'." Harn looked around. "There are more. That way. They heard the fight."

"Good, that was the point," Evie panted. She was fast, but her Endurance needed work.

Reforged were strong, but dumb. Their Minds… Vess was beginning to sense snapped threads to their beings. All of those she had faced felt incomplete, torn. Like a ship ripped free from its moorings, leaving gaping holes in its hull where once meaning and identity resided.

"Do you sense the Wurms?" The Reforged had almost no grasp of tactics, not by themselves. She was thinking the Wurms acted as their minders when there was no Arcid present. They'd yet to see a single Wurm, however.

Pit squawked as he swooped above them. As before, when he'd communicated with them, it was more than a squawk to her Affinity. It was the tenku's Spirit, singing out toward her, packets of sense memories thrumming across the invisible threads that connected all things.

Felix killed all Wurms. First tunnel safe. Second in danger.

"Noctis' tits," Evie cursed. Vess winced inwardly at the blasphemy. "Dunno if I'm gonna get used to hearing a bird talk."

"Doesn't Zara have that familiar of hers?" Alister asked, but no one paid attention to him.

"I heard nothing," Atar said. "How come you did?"

"I'm special," Evie said, batting her eyes at the mage.

"Wurms are dead. Felix took care of them," Vess translated for the others. "First group of Henaari are safe, but the second is having problems. Danger."

"Bet that's where the Arcid is," Alister said.

"Not takin' that wager," Harn grunted. "Boy draws the strong like moths to a flame."

"Moths get burnt up that way," Atar noted.

"They do, don't they?"

"I am counting down!" Number 55597 warned with a flare of heat, but the tunnel was silent. Save, perhaps, for the hitched whisper of muffled sobbing. *Pathetic.* "When I reach zero, I shall be burning all that you are! Fire of such incredible strength will flood your blocked tunnel, and that will be the end of you! If you come, now, this instant, I will be merciful. In exchange for telling me the location of your leaders, I will only kill the weakest among you."

More sobbing. *Ugh.* The Master had demanded the nomads' deaths, and he would deliver them. Finding them had been difficult. They were more elusive than the Chimera—not that he'd seen any. Regardless, if the Henaari had wanted to survive, they wouldn't have killed his patrol and left their stinking blood behind. Hoarhounds, even the altered ones, were excellent trackers.

Still, the silence and the sobbing continued. 55597 let a rumble start in his cavernous metal chest.

"Fine!" He'd changed his mind. There would be no counting for these pathetic wretches. Fire Mana gathered in the empty chambers of the Arcid's chest, igniting its low burn with a magnificent swell of energy and power. "Choose death, then!"

He could find the Farwalker without their help.

Pyroclast—!

Just as the Mana of his Master-forged Skill reached the cusp of release, a slab of thick, obdurate stone burst from the ground before the Arcid. It blocked his access to the tunnel almost completely!

"Wh-what is this!?" He whirled, his thick, powerful limbs slamming into the earth. "Who dares block one of the chosen?"

At the far end of his servants, a lone Human appeared from the accumulating woodsmoke. The Arcid was as disgusted as he was confused. A Human was a base mortal. Weak, but many. Yet this one was alone. It didn't even attempt to armor itself, paltry though such efforts would be. Instead the Human was bare of limb and wearing *cloth* of all things.

Two weapons glinted at its side, however. At the very least, it thought itself a threat. 55597 would have to disabuse it of that notion.

"*Human*. Why do—"

"Arcid. You're all kinda jerks, huh?"

The Human spoke out of turn, off-hand, and it *insulted* him! The Arcid could not let a single one of those insults stand, and he vented his rage. Twin plumes of fire shot to either side of him, setting more brush aflame. "You wander alone into my presence and insult me? Do you know who I am? Who I represent?!"

"Yes, no, and yes," the interloper said. "In that order. I mean, I know your number. 55597 right? Kinda bland." He spread open his disgusting, fleshy arms. "Plus, you're kinda weak, huh? 55389 was a lot tougher."

The Arcid's eyes, twin fires in their own right, narrowed. "How do you know that designation? Who are you?"

"You don't know? I figure you would. Archon must not like you," the Human said. Its voice was disgustingly smug, and it just about sneered at him. Him!

"The Master trusts me more than all others! Who else would be tasked with ridding his lands of the Henaari pests?" Number 55597 drew himself up, pushing out his burning chest. "None of the others were even considered to hunt them down!" Then his eye fires widened. "How do you know the Master's name?"

"If I told you, I'd have to kill you," the Human said.

"And if you do not, I'll kill you where you stand," the Arcid threatened. No, *promised!*

The Human shrugged. "You can try."

All of a sudden, stone spikes shot from the earth on every side of the Arcid's force. The spikes stabbed through many of the Hoarhounds' heads, killing them instantly, and those that dodged were followed. The spikes bent and twisted. In less than a moment, all of the Hoarhounds were dead.

"Huh," the Human said. He seemed surprised. "That was easier than I thought."

"KILL HIM! KILL HIM NOW!" The Arcid was already charging, filling its chest with a raging, infernal heat. It roared to life, a living flame that melted the rocks around him into puddles of magma. "BREAK HIM!"

Gargantuan, metallic-edged screams shook the tunnel, and a sudden, terrible heat bore down on the huddled group of Henaari. Yet, for some reason, the heat did not bloom into flame.

"What is happening?"

"Has the monster fled? Captain Eskr?"

"I—I don't know," the captain said. His nerves were as shot as all the rest, though he tried to hold onto the dignity of his people. "Perhaps we should—"

There was an abrupt slamming to the side of the gathered Henaari, and without warning, an entire portion of the tunnel collapsed again. Except, instead of cutting them off as the Wurms had done previously, there was a rush of cool, musky air as a new shaft appeared beside them. From the darkness of its mouth, a welcome figure appeared.

"Come with me if you want to live," A'zek said.

Though the Harnoq was ferocious-looking, the entire group

brightened immediately. Cries of "Farwalker" and "Companion" lilted through the passage, and the harnoq had to encourage speed and silence multiple times.

"Move. Faster. The death you avoided still survives. Run!" A'zek hissed the last, striking at the floor with his barbed tail in emphasis. The Henaari took the words seriously and began to hustle, until they were loping down the curiously smooth tunnel he'd traversed.

"You made a tunnel for us?" Captain Eskr was confounded. He never knew the Chimera had such a Skill. "Raven preserve us. How much Mana did this take?"

A'zek regarded the Captain of the Dawnguard with a single, earth-toned eye. "I did not make this. It is the plan of another, one which I do not approve."

"Another...?"

The harnoq sped down the tunnel, forcing the captain to keep up. Yet even as they ran, he did not miss that the opening to their tunnel had somehow seamlessly sealed itself closed.

"Then how—?"

"Questions are for the living. Run. One day, you may hear the answer," A'zek said, before blurring forward too quickly for the captain's Perception to follow.

CHAPTER FORTY

This is working well, Felix thought as the Reforged and Arcid charged his position. *Too well, maybe.*

Distantly, dozens and dozens of feet thumped across the stone he'd shaped. Once the vibrations faded a bit, Felix flexed his Will and burned yet another chunk of Mana to close up the tunnel before dropping the shaping. Hopefully, everyone had made it out.

The problem, however, was that creating then maintaining the tunnel—even for a short time—ate up a large portion of his Mana. His regeneration was kicking in, but it'd take at least a few minutes to get him back to full, and Felix didn't have that long to wait. It was time to get physical, and as the enormous enemies closed, Felix grinned. He was fine with that.

The world slowed as his Perception and Agility flared. He flipped the Femur of the Envoy from his belt, feeding Essence into it and letting the metallic weapon become a six-foot war club more like a Japanese tetsubo than a mace. The Mana of the earth and air sang to Felix as he pushed down then burst into inevitable, unstoppable motion.

You Have Killed A Reforged!
XP Earned!

The first sweep of the war club took a Reforged in the jaw, knocking its head back and into the path of his ally's axe. The ice-forged weapon chewed through the warrior's neck like the sharpest of blades, foiled on its path toward Felix's heart.

Felix leaped up and over the living Reforged's strike, using his recovering Mana to form a single Cloudstep that he rebounded against. Twisting about, Felix hooked the length of the Femur across the brute's neck and let his weight drop. For all their size, Felix was almost as heavy as they were, and its eyes bugged as it found itself pulled backward and off-balance by the Unbound's dropping mass. His feet hit the ground just as the Reforged's back did, and with a powerful, straining twist, he snapped the bastard's neck.

You Have Killed A Reforged!
XP Earned!

More came, brandishing clubs of their own, all of them spitting in fury. Their Spirits were a painful, chaotic noise that Felix had to actively block out. He couldn't afford the distraction because, while the Reforged themselves were no match for his Strength and Agility, they weren't alone.

"Molten Chasm!"

Orange Mana surged, more liquid than vapor, and the ground beneath Felix's feet opened up into a yawning rift, the bedrock flash-melted into a roiling pond of magma. Two Reforged tumbled in, too intent on killing Felix to pay attention to their footing. Felix unspooled shadow from his core, taking a bite out of his recovering Mana to hurl a tendril around a nearby tree. He dropped, swinging down until he was only feet above the savage heat. Superheated air and noxious gases tore apart his lungs as he gasped, while simple convection baked his lower half.

"Kill him while he flails!"

Felix shoved his foot into the crumbling rock and kicked off. He soared upward in a parabolic arc, still attached to a tree, and at his highest point, he was met with jagged shards of ice. He grunted, his Health taking a beating before his right vambrace lit with orange light. A whip of flame snapped outward, wrapping around the outstretched fist of a Reforged, and Felix yanked hard. Without leverage, Felix soared toward the surprised brute, war club held like a jousting lance.

The rapid blow took the monster in the gut, doubling them over long enough for Felix to land on solid ground again. With a mighty grunt, Felix grappled the Reforged, Strength to Strength. The creature fought, powerfully strong in its own right, but it could not match the Unbound.

With a roar, Felix hurled the Reforged into the lava pit.

You Have Killed A Reforged!
XP Earned!

"C'mon! Is that all you got?" Felix coughed and worked spit back into his mouth. He could feel his Body fighting off the toxic gasses released from the superheated stone. "The Wurms hit me harder!"

Without warning, two tons of metal collided with him, hurling Felix into the nearest tree. The tree, thick as a redwood, cratered but did not fall.

The Arcid pulled his arms back, his entire body steaming. "You talk too much, Human."

Status Condition: Concussion (Minor)!

"Haven't gotten one of those in a while," Felix gasped to himself. He was starting to get the impression that this Arcid wasn't a pushover. "Hold on," he said, a little louder. "I'll be right there once everything stops swimming."

"No, you will merely die."

The Arcid shot forward, and this time, Felix was able to observe his motions. Like an old steam train, the Arcid's legs pumped with mechanical precision and steely power. It was impressive.

Felix supposed he'd given A'zek enough time.

Ravenous Tithe!

As he breathed in, huge swaths of iridescent smoke poured toward him, flooding his channels with crackling potency. Then he burned it.

Sovereign of Flesh!

Unlike many of his other Skills, Sovereign of Flesh relied on Essence, not Mana. His skin burst apart, shifting and hardening to black scales that swept across his entire body. Dark, ebon talons punched from his fingertips, and spikes of bone emerged from his forearms, elbows, and knees. Felix's face twisted and broke, his mouth growing wider to accommodate a bevy of new, huge teeth that pushed out his old ones. Felix screamed.

And jolted forward.

The Arcid didn't react—couldn't react—as his boosted Body kicked off the tree and tore through the air. Felix was at his throat instantly, taloned hands outstretched, and he sank them deep into the construct's metal chassis. The Arcid howled in surprise and pain as the force of Felix's impact sent them tumbling down onto the ground.

They hit hard enough to hollow the earth, their combined weight crushing soil and stone as they rolled into a tangle of frantic claws and forged limbs.

"What are you?" the Arcid bellowed into Felix's face, trying unsuccessfully to dislodge his claws. "You aren't Human!"

"Never said I was, Boilerface!" Felix pushed back the Arcid's arms, though it was a struggle. The thing was *strong*.

Boilerface grappled with Felix, trying to crush him with all his might. "Grm—You cannot hope to face—unf—me in pure physical—gah—combat!"

Felix pushed back, just enough to free up his left hand. "Never said I was!" he repeated.

And slammed his fist through the metal grate of Boilerface's chest.

Holy shit! It was hot in there. The white flame that sparked around the two of them intensified, more of the orange Mana gathering atop the Arcid like a thickening mist. Boilerface screamed in anger and pain as Felix shoved his claws into the maelstrom of fire at his core.

"No! I know you!" Boilerface gasped. He tried and failed to pry Felix off his chest. "Vile Nymean! Pyroclastic Assault! Incendiary Shell!"

The Arcid and everything around them ignited in a storm of

white flame. Felix, at its center, was inundated by a column that rose thirty feet into the air and set fire to the lowest branches around them. Brush and grass and stone itself caught, burning and melting in a show of incredible elemental fury. The still-living Reforged were caught up as the blast expanded. They held on for bare seconds before charring to blackened skeletons. Everything went white.

Ravenous Tithe!

Almost blasted away by the force of it, Felix managed to keep himself anchored to the Arcid's vented chest. The maelstrom of white fire surged and swirled, but Felix's Will was not to be denied. The Mana around him was torn apart, rendered into luminescent smoke that poured unceasingly into Felix's channels and core. Essence and Mana rampaged into him, and his eyes burst alight with a sapphire radiance.

"I'll not be… killed… that easily!" Felix growled, and with a mighty lurch, he broke from the Arcid's hold. His arm slammed shoulder-deep into Boilerface's chest. There was something there, something hard and so hot it ate Felix's scales.

"No!"

Felix tore it out.

A roar of cacophony tore into the air, and Vess' head snapped up, swiveling toward the sound. "What was that?"

Evie, atop a branch, squinted into the fiery distance. "Something—Get down!"

Vess saw it too, an orange-white brilliance that rushed toward them. She thrust all seven of her spears down into the earth and called out. "To me! Atar!"

The blonde mage shoved his partner into Vess' arms and called up a twisting spellform, inscribing several quick sigils into the air with the tip of his blazing finger. It completed, just as Harn snagged him by the collar of his robes and into their bulwark.

White-hot fire washed across them, so hot and fierce that the air became superheated instantly. Atar shouted something, but she couldn't make it out. The spellform he'd constructed flared to life, as orange as the fire outside, and created a bubble around them that deflected the worst of the heat.

Atar screamed as his Mana burned to fuel the shield.

The fire flowed like a river, chewing through trees and the land itself. It was hard to see beyond its intensity, but Vess could make out stone and soil burning up, melting until only char remained.

Then it was gone.

Atar collapsed to the ground, spent and shaking. Alister crouched over him, lifting his head. "You stupid man, why would you risk that?"

"Fire—would have suffocated us all," Atar said. His voice was thin and ragged. He'd pushed himself hard through their fights, and now this. "Had to..."

Alister just hugged him.

"Evie?" Vess shouted. The world around them was one of blackened earth and swirling embers. The immense trees around them had all been turned into vast torches, and the heat had not abated. It was still hard to even breathe, but their Journeyman Bodies could handle it. "Evie!"

Dark wings sent a series of ice spears into the ground around them, and though they began to melt, they carried a welcome chill. Vess glanced up and saw Evie atop Pit's broad back. She waved.

"Pit says to get out, to the southern tunnel. I can see it," she said, swallowing. "The fire is out of control now. We gotta run."

"Wise," Harn grunted. "Reforged are down, so are the hounds. Pit?"

The tenku screeched, and it was filled with both anger and worry. She knew what he would do even before Evie hopped off his back. By the time the chain-fighter straightened, the Chimera had taken off. Flying north.

Toward Felix.

Frost Spear is level 68!
Wingblade is level 64!
Cry is level 55!
Flight is level 49!

You Have Gained 3 Levels!
You Are Now Level 55!

The fire raged in the north.

Pit navigated powerful updrafts as the air and fire Mana mixed, spurred along by the destruction of earth and wood and water Mana down below. He felt as if he could fly into the stars, so strongly did the heat push upward, a thrilling idea that he nevertheless ignored.

Pit was searching.

His Companion was down there, hurt but alive. He could feel it.

But where?

A basin of black, acrid smoke and bubbling rock appeared below. It roiled, churned by the advent of whatever spell had caused that firestorm, and seemed just on the edge of spilling out over the land. Then, as Pit circled in the air, the lava cooled and calmed as fiery orange Mana was pulled from it.

Felix!

Pit dropped into the bitter smoke and still-burning trees, until he could lay eyes on a half-burned man with brightly glowing eyes. Dozens of streams of Mana and Essence were funneling into him as Felix laid claim to the dead. The streams finished in time for Pit's landing atop the hot earth.

"Pit? What are you doing here? Are the others okay?" Felix asked.

Pit nodded and sent a series of sense images. Their friends, all heading south. To the tunnel. Felix seemed relieved.

"Good. And everyone in the Arcid's party is dead," Felix looked around. "Best as I can tell. I just hope A'zek got out with the last of the Henaari."

Pit chirruped in agreement before extending a wing toward his Companion. Felix nodded and made to climb onto his back, but froze halfway.

"Really," he said, and his Spirit spiked in surprise. The Unbound turned back toward a lumpy section of the ground, what Pit had taken for a series of burned rocks. It was the Arcid, shattered and half-melted. "Huh."

Without asking, Felix shared the notification he was reading.

You Have Gained A Memory From Your Enemy!
Do You Wish To View Or Save?

Pit tilted his head, not quite understanding. He recalled the Memories Felix had gathered in the past, though their bond had never been strong enough to include him on those jaunts. What made this different?

"Never been able to save a Memory before," Felix explained. "That's handy. We'll have to check it out when we get outta here."

He climbed atop Pit's back, settling into the saddle.

"Let's ride."

Their flight was short and uneventful, much to Felix's relief. That battle hadn't gone exactly as he had planned, especially not the part at the end. The Arcid had released far more Mana than Felix could absorb, and not even his Crescian Blade could cut it all apart. Now, as the two of them flew over the burning remains of the valley, Felix regretted it.

I should have taken the fight right to Boilerplate. The Reforged weren't the real threat, after all. *I wasted too much time on them.*

If he had gone for the Arcid's throat, maybe the ancient ruins below him would have survived. He looked down. The valley had become a lake of fire and smoke. Boilerplate's white-hot fire had cooled to a still-excruciating yellow-orange as it combusted everything it could. The tower and tree at the center of it all were little more than a faint suggestion of carbonized rock.

Annoyed at himself and the Archon, Felix turned his attention instead to his notifications.

You Have Gained 2 Levels!
You Are Now Level 51!
You Gain:
+4 to PER! +4 to VIT! +8 to END! +10 to INT! +12 to WIL!
+8 to AGL! +14 to DEX!
You Have 10 Unused Stat Points!

Hell yeah. Finally. His vision flickered again, and another window appeared, this one bordered in golden filigree. *What's this?*

Authority Recognized, Inheritor!
For Defending This Holding, You May Lay Claim To The City Of Naevis!
Do You Wish To Establish Your Authority?
Y/N

CHAPTER FORTY-ONE

City of Naevis? Felix looked down into the hidden valley of fire and soot again. *The ruins?*

Pit warbled. *Dead city?*

Apparently. Felix had Pit bank to the right until he was flying parallel with the outer cliffs. *What do you think? Last time I tried to take Authority, it almost killed me.*

Do it. There was zero hesitation behind Pit's thoughts. *If it bites, you kill it.*

Felix grinned. He still had his Tyrant of Choice Title, which meant he could break Oaths as he wished. A nasty power in the hands of someone less scrupulous or more ambitious, and it had come in handy twice now.

He accepted.

Congratulations!
You Have Established Local Authority!
Authority Accessed—
ERROR.

That didn't take long. Felix readied himself mentally to engage his Title.

Unbound Detected.
Primordial Detected.
Nymean Detected.
...
Inheritor Status Supersedes All Bloodlines!
Authority Accessed.

Huh! Some good news, finally.

A sudden series of windows populated Felix's vision, dozens of them opening and closing rapidly as text scrolled and flashed across them. Felix widened his eyes and tried to capture it all in his inviolate memory, until only a single window remained, scrolling through a series of seemingly random numbers.

Abruptly, colorless System energy thundered into Felix's cores, slamming through his rings of molten flame with a ferocity that surprised him. It mingled with the Essence he'd stolen from the Arcid and his Reforged, burning him from within, but not nearly as badly as before. His cores were humming together, [Thunderflame Core] and [Cardinal Beast Core] together in something approaching harmony.

The swirling energy shot up and into his channels—Essence and System power both. It surged higher, into Felix's head before settling at the base of his skull.

TRING!

Local Authority Established!
You Have Claimed The City Of Naevis!

Welcome, Inheritor!

His vision went blue-white and red-gold suddenly as his own cores' energies surged behind his eyes. When it resolved, his heads-up display was different. Typically, there was only the three bars indicating his Health, Stamina, and Mana, and the icons for Quests and Status (one for him and one for Pit). Now Felix could see a fourth icon, this one in the shape of a small, crenelated tower. Felix opened it immediately.

A dozen windows opened, but all of them were grayed out. It was clear why, too. [City Defenses] and [City Resources] were obviously no longer accessible. The City of Naevis was gone, little more than a few charred stones after their latest encounter. But there was one option that wasn't grayed out.

[Access Vault]

"Oh, dang. Pit. We're gonna have to make a landing."

In the light of the Twins, Evie and the Henaari scouts spotted one another at the same time. She waved at them and leaped from the tree she had been traversing, lessening her mass until she touched down with a slight tap. The needle-strewn hillock hardly rustled at her landing, though Alister started.

"Farwalker's group is ahead. Holed up around some statues."

"Thank you, Evie," Vess said with a smile. "Seems they found a more secured position."

"Mm," Evie said. She flicked a piece of char from her armor. She'd have to clean it before long; the Reforged were bleeders. "Statues seemed pretty loud."

"Loud?" Atar asked.

Evie waved her hand vaguely. "You know. Like a group of church bells from a few streets over. Not ear-splittin' or nothin', but loud."

"None of what you said made sense to me," Atar said. "Is this more of that Harmonic mumbo jumbo?"

Evie shrugged and walked ahead. "Maybe."

They traversed the distance rapidly, the five of them reaching a low hill and a series of tall, monolithic statues surrounded by leafy trees and covered in ivy. The statues were vaguely Human-looking, but wore a curious mix of armor and robes, and each were carved holding a large orb. The sound of bells only increased as they drew nearer, and Evie was tempted to shove her fingers in her ears after a while. However, the instant they passed the statues and into the inner circle, the sound cut off entirely.

It was almost disorienting, and Evie spun, looking up at the backs of the weird statues. Behind their backs, hidden from the world outside, were huge, snarling faces. The snouts and teeth and glaring eyes filled the inner circle with the sound of violent fury, a bated hatred so deep it made Evie tremble.

A hand landed on her shoulder, and Evie spun toward her attacker, Ice Spike already summoned to her fist. Only the hurried shout of a familiar voice stayed her blow.

"Forgiveness!" Wyvora shouted. The Ice Spike was a finger's breadth from her wide, shocked eye, and the cold it radiated was alarming even to Evie.

"Evie!" Vess hissed.

The chain-warrior blinked and dropped her Skill as she stepped back. What had come over her? She looked up, back at the monstrous faces above, now completely silent. *Noctis' tits, what was that?*

+5 AFI

"I believe our agile friend has been influenced by the true lesson of this formation," the Farwalker said. The man was bundled up against the slight chill of the night, and that hood covered his face in deepest shadow. Still, she swore she saw his eyes twinkling in that darkness. "The Nym left many lessons for those that came after."

"Nym?" Atar asked. Alister and he both looked up, immediately fascinated. "Are these monsters?"

"Threats," the Farwalker said. "Threats the Nym were said to ward against."

"Thus the stoic guardians facing outside, while abominations writhe within," Vess said. She nodded. "Yes. I see."

Evie stuck a finger in her own ear and wiggled it. A lot of words were being bandied about, but it didn't explain why the statues had growled. "Then why—"

"You all survived?"

The Matriarch swept from the deeper shadows in the circle, hidden before by the press of people. And there were a *lot* of people there, with a few more groups trickling in from the north. The woman's makeup was streaked a bit with sweat, though Evie imagined she'd pretend it was tears. The lady was the worst sorta noble, all sweet smiles and false promises before they tightened the noose.

"Wasn't hard," Evie said. She enjoyed the vein that throbbed in the lady's temple. "Just had to kill everything we found."

Impressed murmurs filled the grove, followed by whispered comments she couldn't help but overhear.

"..the outsiders saved us..."

"...he killed everything. It was brutal..."

"...they don't even look tired..."

Evie rolled her eyes. Maybe she didn't *look* tired, but she felt it. Her Stamina hadn't quite recovered from the fights, never being good at the Endurance thing for all that her Strength was growing.

"Then where is your leader? The—the Raven-Blessed." The Matriarch stumbled over the honorific, which Evie found funny. "I do not see him among your number. I truly hope he is well."

I'm sure you do, lady. Evie rolled her eyes. "He's fine. Probably." Felix was a big boy. He could take care of himself, though he rarely did. Usually got himself near dead or worse and drove all his friends to distraction. Stupid men. "Your little valley is clear of enemies now."

More appreciative murmurs, and the Matriarch smiled widely. "Well that is truly wonderful. We are glad to have trusted in your protection." The crowd around her nodded, and Evie heard the sounds of plucking strings and trilling flutes from them all. It was… weird, but she was increasingly certain of what the sounds all meant.

Emotions. Blech.

"Well, if the valley is safe once more, then we must return!" The Matriarch said, and now her smile turned smug. A real cat that got the cream look. "It was our best redoubt in these lands. I would not abandon it without cause."

"If the enemy found us here once, it will do so again. There is little reason to believe it will remain safe," the Farwalker pointed out.

"Oh," added Evie. "It's also on fire."

"What!"

Evie chuckled at the woman's face, though the worry and anger that swept through the crowd was less pleasing. "Listen, the Arcid and his pet monsters did it. We stopped them, but not before the blaze was already lit."

"It is true," said another voice, deeper by far than hers. A'zek the cat-lizard-thing stepped from the night, at the head of a column of people. "Fires already raged when we arrived. The Fiend took on the Arcid alone so I would have time to evacuate our people."

"Fiend?" asked one of the Henaari.

"It is what they call him, no?" A'zek nodded to the Haarguard nearby. The lot of them were around the perimeter, helping guide the stragglers into their protective circle.

"Where is Felix?" Wyvora asked.

"Pit went after him. They should be back soon." Vess said smoothly.

"And he defeated the Tier III construct? How?"

"Probably hit him with his thick skull," Atar said. There was a measure of fondness there, but it was spoiled by the man's pinched expression. "Does anyone have any Mana potions left? I wore myself out on that array shield."

Nevia finally managed to push her way to the fore, the slight Dwarf even shorter before the lanky Henaari. "Take mine."

"Oh," Atar said. His expression eased as he quaffed the potion, and the mage let out a deep sigh of relief. "Thank you, Nevia. I'm sure you know the pain of Mana drain."

"Don't thank me, just tell me more about the Reforged," Nevia said. Atar regarded her silently a moment before nodding.

"In the morning."

"What was that, by the by?" Alister asked, settling down next to his beau. "You never said you've been working on combat array formations."

"It was, ah, well, experimental," Atar admitted. He withered a bit under Alister's glare and was almost relieved when Evie spoke up.

"Experimental? You never tried that before in battle?" Evie asked. She was impressed. He'd saved her friends with a desperate move, and Evie couldn't help but respect that. "That took balls. Thanks."

"I—Oh, yes. You're welcome," Atar said, a blush of color entering his olive cheeks.

Evie smirked. "About time they dropped."

"You—!"

Felix and Pit made a landing, following the prompting of his Authority.

They quickly found the range and limits of his so-called Local Authority. It extended no farther than the cliffs around the valley, though some of the grayed-out menus indicated it had once spread farther. Deeper, too. After toggling the [Access Vault] option, a light appeared far below, leading them to fly back down to the center once again.

The tower and tree were no more, turned to ash or melted by the unnatural heat of the Arcid's fire, and the entire area was a blackened ruin. It was still intensely hot, though the flames had mostly died away. Former trees abounded, filled with the rippling of emberlight and breathing a heat that would have cooked lesser men. Felix felt vaguely uncomfortable, but it wasn't anything like the Arcid's Magma Chasm. It barely tickled his Song of Absolution, though Pit moaned at the heat on his paws.

We gotta get you some fire elemental cores. Get you some fire resistance. Pit chirruped in agonized agreement. *All right. Get in here.*

Pit vanished in a flash of light, converging with Felix's Spirit once again. The tenku's trilling sigh of relief was almost comical.

Now on the ground, the light that had guided him bathed a specific section, now completely covered by the half-melted, half-tumbled remains of the tower itself. His Mana had recovered from his previous exertions, at least halfway, and a little Stone Shaping moved the lot of it back in a wave of liquified rock.

Hidden beneath it all was a door made of Crescian Bronze. It was heavily carved with a scene of a single, enormous tree rising above mountains. From the location and Felix's memory of the tower and tree, the door had been hidden directly underneath its thick trunk. Now, there was not even the hint of a root system left, the fire having scoured all of it clean.

A window appeared before him as he approached the trap door.

Access Vault?

Felix pulled free his Crescian Blade. *Yes.*

The door swung up on soundless hinges, and Felix could only sense the barest thread of Mana in it. Below were a set of stairs leading down into the earth, spiraling, and carved—or shaped—into the most delicate of lace-like designs. It was dark after only a few feet, a pitch blackness that not even his Manasight succeeded in piercing.

Pit warbled in curiosity, and Felix agreed.

They walked down.

The stairs spiraled into a darkness so complete that Felix felt lost. All he could do was hold a hand to the narrow walls and put one foot in front of the other. After a hundred steps, the walls vanished and Felix's senses told him he was in a far larger room than he expected. Cavernous, even.

A little creepy, I'll admit. He was definitely not used to walking blind.

After another hundred steps, Felix reached a landing, one that sang with the barest hint of channeled Mana. He guided a portion of his own Mana out of his pathways and into the structure he sensed. Suddenly, the darkness fell away like a dropped shroud, replaced by a brilliant, omnipresent light.

Felix squinted against the abrupt brightness and found himself at the bottom of what looked like a huge, dry well. Stairs lined the walls, along with star-shaped archways leading to darkened interiors. The entire construction created a semicircle of man-made wonder, long abandoned, and in the magelight, it appeared as little more than an enormous, alien skull with a thousand empty sockets staring him down.

Felix repressed a shudder. The bottom was tiled, but pools of water collected here and there. They were shallow basins filled with filtered rainwater, clearly dripping in from the extensive root system up above. It was unlikely the original well was filled in such a way. The place had been buried, somehow. Then someone had placed a door above it and turned it into a Vault, whatever that meant.

He had been expecting treasures. But all he saw was empty stonework and wet, star-shaped tile.

Inheritor...

Felix's head snapped up, looking for the notification box in his vision. But there was none. Instead, he heard a voice in his Mind.

Step Forward And Claim...
Destiny...
Itself.

A section of the well, one he'd not even noticed despite his Perception and empowered senses, illuminated. Revealed was a low platform that rose level by level until it became a set of stairs. The stairs vanished into a dim crevasse carved with fluted columns and surmounted by an elaborate entablature. The pediment of it was filled with detailed relief sculptures, depicting large, bulky figures among groves of fruiting trees.

The crevasse *breathed*, as if some great beast waited within. Pit warbled in nervous fear. Felix wasn't much better.

This is feeling like a bad idea.

But they'd committed. Felix doubted they would return to this little valley any time soon, and now was the time to find out what he'd earned. If he was lucky, he'd even survive it.

Fingers crossed.

He leaped to the top of the stairs, landing heavily enough to send dust and stone chips flying outward, but his feet barely thumped against the stone dais. Felix paused, senses extended to their limit.

Nothing. Only the soft, almost wet breeze from within the cave. Still, his Manasight was curiously dulled here, like it was being blocked. He fought against it, surging his Skill, but to no avail. A sluggish sort of earth Mana pervaded everything, but other than that, he was surrounded by inert matter. Manaless.

Which was impossible. Everything was made of Mana in some form.

He walked in, Perception at full burn, his hands balled into fists and various spells spinning faster within his core space. Pit coiled as well, wings and limbs ready to burst forth. The gloom enveloped him, and he took one careful step after another down what turned out to be a tiled pathway through the craggy rock. Fifty steps in, it opened back up, and this time, the chamber was dozens of times larger.

Soft green and gold lights flitted about the space, so many that they created a soft but powerful illumination. They were like fireflies, or seemed to be, yet his Voracious Eye said otherwise.

Name: Sprite
Type: Spirit (Life)
Level: 343
HP: ?????????/?????????
SP: ??????/??????
MP: ????????????/????????????
Lore: Sprites are spirits of nature, elemental Mana given form and function by the Song of Creation. They are as mysterious as they are rare, but their elemental type typically informs their attitudes.
Strength: More Data Required
Weakness: More Data Required

Holy—level 343?

Felix tried not to flinch as the Sprite he'd Eyed landed on his shoulder. It looked like a small person made of green-gold glass. Its body was slender and sexless, and its head empty of hair, only retaining two small, sharp ears and large glowing eyes. Around its shoulders was a collar of crystalline spikes rising high behind its head like some sort of Victorian mistress. The Sprite stepped lightly, but each felt like a tiny stab at Felix's Spirit. His Aspects were tougher than they looked, however, and it took the jabs easily. Didn't feel great, though.

"Hello," Felix said. The Sprite looked at him and tilted its tiny head. Felix slowly, carefully waved.

It waved back.

"I'm looking for the Vault," he explained. He felt foolish the moment he said it aloud, but well, the Continent was weird. If he had to talk to some magical life spirits to get some treasure, he'd do it with a smile.

The Sprite suddenly beamed, revealing tiny, jagged teeth. Then it flitted away into the cloud of its fellows.

"Wait!" Felix shouted before thinking better of it. The cloud of Sprites, all of them over level 300, swirled and shifted, moving like a murmuration of birds in a fluid dance. It was mesmerizing, but Felix held his Skills at the ready, waiting to run at the first sign of aggression. He wouldn't survive a direct attack by that swarm of Sprites.

The swarm spun until a space was opened up at the center, and the Sprites pushed up and away from the cavern floor. It revealed a gargantuan tree—filled with more of the same green-gold glow—and, at its base, a towering figure in armor.

Felix's hands blazed to life, crackling with acid and lightning.

"Archon," he gasped.

CHAPTER FORTY-TWO

Wait. That's not the Archon.

Felix's heart was ready to seize in his chest, but its thundering slowed as he took in the creature before him. It was a massive construct, similar to the Archon in size and general design, but made of weathered stone and covered in greenery. Literally. Ivy, mushrooms, and small, bluebell shaped flowers adorned the thing, as if it hadn't moved in hundreds of years. A large glyph glowed upon its chest, a combination of *growth*, *guardian*, and *eternal*.

Voracious Eye!

Voracious Eye Failed.

"Whoa. That doesn't happen often. What the heck are you?" Felix murmured. Eyeing the swirling cloud of Sprites, he carefully stepped forward. Pit growled caution at him, but Felix was increasingly certain this room meant him no harm. He had Authority, right?

The ground was tiered here, descending by a foot every dozen yards in a series of concentric circles. The overgrown Golem was at the bottom of the tiers, at the lowest point where the massive, green-gold tree was emerging from the cavern floor.

It was as thick as a skyscraper, and the roots at the bottom were matched by the distant branches at the top of the cavern, almost lost in the gloom. Were it not for his Perception-enhanced sight, Felix wouldn't have even made out the roof of the cave he found himself within, easily several miles tall. There were no leaves, just a glorious green-gold trunk filled with a luminescence that dwarfed the light of the Sprites.

As Felix stepped down, his feet rang with a certain tonality, like a wine goblet being played by deft fingers. Shudders of energy spun outward from his steps, ripples in a pond that had remained still for a very, very long time. Each tier down added to the song, until by the time he reached the bottom, the air was filled with a complex, weaving concerto. It tasted of silvered springtime and smelled of the high heat of summer, flush with life in a way few things ever were. The song was but an echo, however, to the thrumming contained within the tree itself.

Voracious Eye!

Name: Caryatid Anima
Type: Spirit Tree
Lore: Spirit Trees are a rare and powerful organism imbued with elemental Mana dependent on their growth cycle. The one before you is attuned to Life, Water, Light, and Shadow.
Herbalism is level 34!
...
Herbalism is level 43!

Felix stumbled as the influx of System energy tried to bowl him over. His cores sang as they spun, exuding light and power as nourishing as any spring rainfall upon his Herbalism Skill. Felix could feel it growing, changing as the pattern flexed under the surge of energies.

"Whoa."

Closer now, the Spirit Tree wasn't tree shaped at all, but formed into a humanoid figure draped with green-gold moss and cascading lights. Its feet melded seamlessly into roots taller than houses, as its lifted hands converged perfectly with the branches far, far above. It was a pillar holding up the earth itself and smelled of age, soft breezes, and new growth. It felt primal. Vital.

Then Felix noticed that the Sprites still flitted about not just the Spirit Tree, but the strange Golem as well. Standing on the same tier as it was intimidating, though in a way that was different than the Spirit Tree. The Tree was huge, a presence he couldn't quite encompass. The Golem—if that's what it was—exuded an air of ancient patience and time-worn strength and, while certainly bigger than him, it didn't approach the majestic form of the Spirit Tree.

He walked closer and inspected the Golem with all of his senses. His first assessment was correct: it was made of stone, but there were traces of metal in there, as well. Moss gathered in the crevices and joints, adding to the flora that sprouted from all over the overgrown sentinel. Small, almost invisible creatures crawled through it all, like insects but translucent. Its eyes were empty, a void where its helmet opened to the air, save for the colony of mushrooms that had taken up residence along the left side of its face.

"What do I do here?" he asked the Sprites. The little creatures didn't answer, only circled the Golem before spiraling up the Spirit Tree and back into the swarm. "Okay, cool. Thanks."

What do you think, Pit?

His Companion was silent for several seconds, before sending him the mental equivalent of a shrug. *Authority?*

Dunno. Let's check.

He accessed his Authority again, the little tower icon expanding into the same grayed-out menus. The option of [Access Vault] was still there, however. He selected it, and a new series of options arose.

[Drain Well]
[Fill Well]
[Access Belais Crystal Array]
[Commune]

All but the last were grayed out.

The well?

"I mean, it was a big, empty well, right? Maybe it was meant to water this Spirit Tree?" Felix had no idea, but something like the Caryatid Anima probably had exotic needs when it came to nourishment. "I'm more interested in the array. Belais Crystal is the same mineral we saw in the Revenant Nest."

Ooh, Pit said as memories of that encounter flashed in his Mind. Felix could see them, taste them, as they flickered through his active memory. *Shiny.*

"Big and shiny. And magical. The fact that it's grayed out suggests it's either broken or inaccessible. The only thing there is Commune." He considered the tree and the Golem. "Commune with what, though? The tree?"

Worth a shot?

"I suppose," Felix shrugged, trying to ignore the slow growth of unease in him. He selected the option.

[Commune]

The green-gold light of life Mana flared into blinding brilliance as a series of glyphs appeared in mid-air before him. They were complex, a melding of several sigils as all glyphs were, but also more. The green-gold symbols thrummed with a potency that emanated from the Spirit Tree itself, and for a second, Felix thought he'd guessed right. Power welled, gathered from the dripping Mana in the Spirit Tree...until it shot outward, directly into the stone Golem.

Eidolon System Engaged.

"Oh no."

Liquid Green-gold light splashed onto the Golem, spraying upward into a corona that smelled of a dewy spring dawn. The flora growing from it, far from being knocked off, flourished and expanded. Mushrooms ballooned, ivy crawled farther, and those dangling bluebells sprouted and opened. The stone itself rumbled, cracking and creaking, while within its dark helmet, two green flames burst alight.

"Who-wakes-me?"

Its voice was like a stretch of sandpaper overtop a lion's guttural roar. The sound of boulders grinding against scree, tumbling down a mountain.

Voracious Eye!

Name: Eidolon Exult
Type: Construct
Level: 6E48-$
HP: ?????/?????
SP: N/A
MP: N/A
Lore: An ancient construct built as guardian for this place, the Eidolons were creations of the Nym. Little else is known.
Strength: More Data Required
Weakness: More Data Required

Damn it, I really hope this thing isn't hostile.

"Who? I-I see naught but golden life! Who-stands-before-me?" The Eidolon's voice didn't get any better, and in fact stuttered over words, like a scratched record or glitching audio file. "Declare yourself. Who seeks to commune with the Spirit Tree?"

Felix licked his lips and squared himself up before the Eidolon. "I do."

The flames in the Eidolon's helmet pivoted, focusing on him. "I see, a new Authority rises. I-I cannot move. How long has it been since your predecessor?"

"Uh, several Ages, I think," Felix said.

"S-several Ages—!" The Eidolon's voice, rough and deep, trembled with anxiety. A stuttering, staccato chord progression. "I have slept so long?"

Wait, no. That's its Spirit. Felix blinked. *It has a Spirit?*

"What are you?" Felix asked. "You look like... are you an Archonic Construct?"

"I am an Eidolon! Sworn to s-serve those who rule the great city of Naevis, and to guide those who wish to commune with the Spirit Tree." It jolted very slightly, but enough that the plants on its frame shuddered. "What manner of—I appear to be immobile. The joints, the fixtures, the array itself is corroded. But, if it has truly been Ages, then it is remarkable I am still here at all." The fires of its eyes swiveled toward Felix once again. "Thank you, Authority-bearer, for waking me. Let me perform my duties. To begin with—"

A beam of green-gold light shone onto Felix, sweeping over his form in a single swift instant. "A life scan. You are as expected. A—A Primordial?"

Shock and alarm flooded the construct's Spirit, and Felix flexed his knees, gathering his power to run. The Eidolon creaked again, as if it were trying to moved toward him. "No, more than that. Primordial. Nymean, as well. And—"

It stopped rocking, and those eyes flared brighter than ever, enough that Felix had to squint.

"Unbound."

Unlike before, there was no alarm or beginnings of fear. Instead, Felix was surprised by an absolute avalanche of *joy*.

"An Unbound has returned! Oh glorious ancestors!" Its voice rang from the cavernous chamber and set the Sprites to flow away in waves. "And what is this? Not only Unbound, but an Inheritor? Will wonders never cease?"

Myriad, mirthful noises erupted from the empty chest of the stone Eidolon, and Felix started to relax. It seemed it liked Unbound enough to overlook his Primordial Race.

"Ahem, yes. I am Unbound," Felix said. "And you're a guide construct? Why do you have a Spirit?"

"I am an Eidolon, not some simple guide. The effort of thousands went into my forging, so complex was the process. My Spirit and Mind taken from my mortal Body, placed in this holy receptacle, so that I might be of use for Ages to come." Its voice faltered. "Ages already past."

"You were mortal before? A Nym?" Felix asked.

The Eidolon's Spirit shook as if rousing itself from slumber again. "Yes. I was a humble servant of the Empire long, long ago. My final reward was to continue that service, to live on and aid the city I loved."

"This was… a common occurrence?" Felix asked. He hated the idea of being shoved into a golem, bound to serve others for an eternity. Or as close to one as he could imagine. "Wait, are all Golems people?"

"Golems? Those mean creations of steel and orichalcum? No, those were never more than children's playthings. Idle projects of a few brilliant but bored Minds. The Eidolons were one of our artificers' greatest accomplishments. How do you not know of this?"

"Things change," Felix said. "So being put into an Eidolon was a reward?"

"An honorable and voluntary service, one that would raise a House to exalted status within a generation!" The construct-that-was-once-a-person cut itself off. "Or it was a desolate sentence for the most depraved of criminals."

Felix's eyes widened in horror. "People would be sentenced to have their Minds and Spirits ripped out of their Bodies? Forever?"

"Only the truly heinous. It was not a punishment often enacted."

"How do I know you're the former and not the latter, then?" Felix asked. He was careful to keep out of melee distance with the creature, for all that it appeared immobile.

"My word," said the Eidolon. "And the array on my chest should clear up any confusion."

Felix raised an eyebrow. "All I see is a glyph."

"Yes, that is it," it said. Its voice rumbled and scratched, as if catching on some internal mechanism. "C-can you not read it?"

"I—" Felix frowned. "Gimme a second."

Felix focused, flaring his Manasight and Theurgist of the Rise together. The glyph rippled, meaning teasing slowly from its shape. He already identified *growth*, *guardian*, and *eternal*, but now he began to see more.

Title: Architect of the Rise engaged!

Manasight is level 57!
Manasight is level 58!
Manasight is level 59!

Much more.

The glyph just about exploded, its details unfurling like a thousand, thousand folds in a piece of paper the size of a dinner plate. Within each wrinkle there was *meaning*. Not scribed or engraved, but embedded in the glyph itself. It was an array, the simplest and most profound array he'd ever seen, with minimal effort put into the sigils and their permutations while still achieving something utterly remarkable, packed with Intent instead of scribed notations. Modern inscription used a longhand version of something the ancients apparently did with their very Will.

Theurgist of the Rise is level 66!

...

Theurgist of the Rise is level 70!

Wow! Already Felix could see the ways he could use this technique, were he to grasp it. Small nodes of Intent were bundled along the shaping of the glyph, all of them lit with Mana but the bundles shining brighter still. *Amazing. It's—huh. They're not just Intent. They're Memories.*

Without warning, Felix felt *pulled* by a sudden and inexorable gravity. Between eye-blinks, he found himself elsewhere.

What the hell?

Felix stood in a large chamber, smaller than the Vault but far nicer. The floor was polished marble, a blue kind veined with white and gold. Hexagonal pillars lined the hall, each made of gold or at least painted that way, and between them were a large crowd of people. Folks of many Races, but mostly Nymean, all wearing clothing that was part drapery and part armor. They all looked weary and saddened, as if the sun weren't shining brightly through twenty-foot tall casements down the length of the chamber. It felt like a funeral, though he saw no coffin.

A dais stood at one end of the chamber, and atop that was a dark throne upon which a woman with dark hair, icy eyes, and a crown with nine tines sat. She spoke, and it was like a whip crack of thunder.

"Paragon Karys, come forth."

He recognized the flavor of things. The odd clarity and sudden, disorienting transportation. He'd been pulled into one of the Memories in the glyph array.

A man who looked remarkably similar to the Eidolon stepped carefully out of the crowd. It was as if the image of the Eidolon were superimposed over his stooped, aged form. He had dark skin marred by wrinkles and age spots, and his tightly curled hair had more gray than black in it. His eyes, however, were as bright as any in the crowd—a shade of summer grass. The man—Nym—came to attention before the regal figure.

"Paragon Karys, you have proven yourself in a thousand ways over the course of your career. You are a man of impeccable standing and stalwart virtue. You stand before us, ready for the final—and longest—chapter in your service. Do you have anything to say?"

Karys stood taller, his aged stoop unbending for a moment. "Only that I wish all could have the opportunity to serve the Empire as I have, as I will."

The queen—empress?—straightened upon her throne, and her mouth curved into a sad smile. Her eyes glittered with unshed tears.

"We shall remember you, Paragon Karys. This War will not stop until we have more heroes such as yourself step into the fray. Your surviving family will be elevated among the greatest of Magi." The empress gestured, and figures of stone and glittering orichalcum strode forward. "We bid you fondest farewell."

The figures, Eidolons all, took Karys in their gentle grip.

"And welcome to the final battle."

The Memory twisted. The world turned incandescent—

—and Felix stumbled back, his heels hitting a stone step. The Eidolon loomed over him, still festooned with flora.

"I was once Karys Taiv, Paragon of the Golden Empire. I am now your servant," the Eidolon's eye fires flashed. Knowledge and wonder flitted across the Eidolon's ancient Spirit. "Inheritor of the Herald's Hook."

CHAPTER FORTY-THREE

"Herald's Hook?" Felix asked. He looked down at the sword at his waist. "That's what this is called?"

The Eidolon, though immobile, somehow gave the impression of a kneeling man. "It is the blade of the Herald herself, used in so many countless battles that I would never forget its look or the distinctive Mana signature upon the Ethereal."

Felix had heard of the Herald before, from the Maw and elsewhere. He knew that it was the Herald who chained the Maw to the Essence Anchor originally. She had been strong. Beyond strong, if she was able to defeat the Maw at the height of its power. He held out the Crescian Blade. *This was her sword?*

Voracious Eye!

Voracious Eye Failed.

Ever since he'd earned the Blade—and gotten the Inheritor Title—Felix had been unable to glean anything from the weapon. Before, it only listed it as an "unknown sword" which had been particularly unhelpful. Only his Manasight had ever detected anything, and that was the hidden array just above the small crossguard, the one formed into the interior of the metal itself. It was what let the sword cut through spellforms, and Felix was certain that there was more to it. Even more so now.

Is that why it could unlock the Temple? To the stone guardian, Felix said, "So you're Nymean?"

"I was. I am now Eidolon. Charged in my final days with protecting the Spirit Tree before you."

"Your Memory... your empress had you fighting a war," Felix said. "What war?"

A melancholy danced across its Spirit, gone quickly. "It does not matter. It has been Ages, and I can tell by my state and the condition of this Vault that it did not end well for my people." It cleared its throat, a stentorian blast that echoed in the cavernous chamber. "Let us return to the task at hand. You have gained the Authority to access this chamber, which means you, and you alone, have the right to its bounty."

Felix wanted to ask more about the Nym, about this war, but the words "bounty" caught him. "What bounty?"

"Why, the Spirit Tree itself," the Eidolon said. It paused, and Felix could sense its own inspection of the tree before him. "The purpose of this Vault is to nurture the Spirit Tree, but it is clear that something has failed. I can sense its death looming above its eternal boughs. Too long this land has been unclaimed, too long the world above was drowned in magics malign to the Nymean sorceries that birthed this miracle."

It sighed. "Typically the ruler of Naevis would enjoy a single spirit fruit each year. Such a thing would rejuvenate their Aspects, strengthening their foundations for further ascension. But the Caryatid Anima has not borne fruit in Ages, I can feel that in the weight of its heartwood. Too light. Too porous to have produced anything."

The Eidolon's attention pivoted back to Felix. "It waits upon a true Authority to bequeath its last bounty, hidden within its core. It awaits you, Inheritor."

Felix wet his lips. "Do I—?"

"Approach the Caryatid Anima, Inheritor."

Enraptured, Felix walked forward. Past the Eidolon and closer to the Spirit Tree. The thing was big, way bigger than the Eyrie had been. It almost defied logic and certainly didn't fit within the space it inhabited. Something about it… flexed at the edges, as if it existed here and elsewhere at the same time. Mana surged all around him, the air and earth and shadows all coming alive in a way that had been incredibly muted before. He drew closer.

"Place your heart hand upon the Tree's flesh and feel its power." The Eidolon's voice was a soothing, mesmerizing rumble. If it had some ill effect, it did not touch him across the enormity of his Willpower, but Felix was certain neither the construct nor the tree itself meant him harm.

He reached out and placed his left hand—the one closest to his heart—directly on the nearest root. Power coursed through it, like a live wire. His hand jolted back, but it didn't burn. Felix cautiously placed it down again. His Affinity and Manasight detected cables of life Mana rushing through the roots of the Spirit Tree, some thicker than himself. Pit cooed in delight.

Beautiful.

Yeah, Felix sent back. *Yeah it is.*

"Open yourself to its power, Inheritor. Open, and so shall its Spirit."

Felix did just that, wrestling down his own caution and believing in the soothing, peaceful power before him. By sheer force of Will, Felix let down his guard, and immediately felt an alien presence press against him. Pit bristled and stood in its way.

Friend? Pit sent. His feathers ruffled in Felix's Spirit. *Or enemy?*

Distantly, though it pressed against them both, a not-voice called back.

Friend...

That was apparently enough for Pit, and the tenku stepped aside. The presence quested into Felix's core space, tendrils like roots flashing forward with no ill Intent. Felix figured he should be terrified, but it was… palliative. Pains Felix hadn't even been aware of, things that his Song of Absolution kept dimmed to almost nothing, they lifted with a deep and abiding rush of silence.

Only to be replaced by the gentle swell of something else. Something he couldn't quite define. Before Felix's eyes, the trunk split and broke, unleashing a stench of dry rot and the crumbled corpses of a thousand insects. The opening widened until it was more a doorway than a knothole, and within, there was a dim light.

I offer… take…

The not-voice was faint and growing weaker, for all that it caressed against the orbit of his two cores. Felix stepped forward, talons already shifted upon his hands, and tore it wider with a single slash. Green-gold light fountained into the chamber, acting more like liquid than light but washing over Felix without sensation. He slashed again, and again, until a shape the size of a watermelon dislodged. It was the source of the gushing life Mana, and it glowed like a tiny emerald sun.

…take… it…

Felix gripped it. The not-voice and his Herbalism Skill pushed at his instincts, informing him with whispers and suggestions. Felix shook his head before ripping the watermelon-sized seed in half.

Green-gold light exploded. It expanded from him in a growing ring, and where it hit, life grew upon the stone. The Eidolon itself was suddenly twice as covered with flora as before, and the tiered steps sprouted a hundred varieties of weeds and fronds and crawling vines. From between the two halves of the seed dropped a single, coarse pit, no bigger than the stone in a peach.

You Have Claimed The Seed Of Remembered Light!

Herbalism is level 44!
…
Herbalism is level 50!
Journeyman Tier!
You Gain:
+5 INT
+5 PER
…
Due To The Influence Of The Caryatid Anima, Your Skill Has Evolved!

Energy thundered through him, swirling from the System and the Spirit Tree itself. Felix could feel the Tree withering as it gave him and the seed in his hand all that it had. His cores spun, the discordant harmony of their contact a jarring counterpoint to the sweet music of the Spirit Tree's final act. Within, the pattern for Herbalism pulsed and *changed.*

Herbalism (Uncommon) Has Evolved Into Aria Of The Green Wilds (Legendary)!
Level Has Been Maintained!
Aria of the Green Wilds (L), Level 50!
Embracing the Untamed Chords, you have found accompaniment to the Songs of War! Coupled with eyes to see and ears to hear, you have begun to see the Wilds with the senses of a true magi! Mana cost decreases slightly per level.

Song of War… Wild Threnody?

The Eidolon rumbled beneath its new green covering. "The Treasure of the Vault… is yours."

Voracious Eye!

Name: Seed Of Remembered Light
Type: Consumable (Ancestral Seed)
Lore: Spirit Trees are rare, and they can live for thousands of years. Even more rare are their seeds, within which is contained an exact copy of its Essence, ready to begin anew.
Alchemical Properties: If consumed, regain all Health, Stamina, and Mana and permanent bonus to Vitality and Endurance equal to one's level.

Voracious Eye is level 56!

..thank… you...

The presence inside him vanished entirely, and the room went dark. Sprites vanished, flitting off into the dark like snuffed fireflies.

"Whoa!" Felix blinked into the sudden gloom, and put the Seed into his satchel, tucking it into an inner pocket where it'd be safe.

Manasight is level 60!

He focused, drawing on the faded Mana in the room. The scenes of life that had filled the space just moments prior were dying as he watched, and even the Eidolon's covering was withering to nothing. He drew deeper, pulling at the earth and darkness held within it, until the chamber appeared lit by a too-distant sun.

"What happened?" he asked.

"The Caryatid Anima has passed, leaving you with its Ancestral Seed." The Eidolon's voice seemed faded somehow, though it still sent small pebbles skipping near its feet. "It was all that kept this Vault sustained. Now it, and myself, shall fade into whatever lies beyond the Corporeal Realm."

"What? You're dying?"

"Mm," it rumbled. "I sense your distress. I have died once already. What is one more time?"

Felix clenched his jaw. He had a lot of questions for the Eidolon, last remnant of a Lost civilization and all. "You don't have to die. I can take you out of here."

"You'll never lift me, Inheritor. You may be strong, but I am more than simply stone." The Eidolon's voice was heavy, slowing with every sentence. "Leave me, and let the earth reclaim this place. I am glad to have seen one such as you, an Unbound, returned to our Continent. I am glad."

The tree behind him cracked and snapped, its trunk withering as the plants around them had. Felix looked up, and the branches in the impossible distance quivered.

He ran back to the Eidolon.

"This is stupid; let's go," Felix said. He grabbed the construct around the legs and pressed his heels into the floor. The Eidolon groaned.

"Indeed. You are strong. But it is impossible." More creaking cracks sounded from above, but Felix ignored it all. He pulled. "You cannot—"

"RUUUAAHAHH!"

With an almighty roar, Felix tore the Eidolon from the earth, along with an entire foot-thick root that had grown up into it. Felix kicked it once, twice, and it snapped off in a spray of dust and fibrous strands.

"W-What are you doing!? Set me down!"

"I'm saving you, man," Felix grunted.

He started running, just as the first, mammoth branch hit the earth. The ground *rippled*, and a wave of force sent Felix and his Eidolon flying.

Adamant Discord!

The world blazed electric, reversing Felix's potentially terminal velocity and sending him up instead. The Eidolon bellowed atop his back as it was lashed with violent lightning.

"Sorry!"

Adamant Discord!

Up in the air, Felix reoriented for the exit. But now he had to avoid rivers of wood and stone and darkest loam as the chamber fell apart all around them. Pit screeched in warning, and Felix lashed outward with his Crescian Blade, bisecting a six-foot-thick branch. The two halves fell to either side as they rocketed forward.

Almost… there!

Felix and his hollering payload shot through the narrow tunnel leading to the well on the front end of a wave of earth and woody debris. Lightning wreathed them both, and Felix flared his Skill and those steel cords for all they were worth. He *pulled!*

Until his shoulder clipped the jagged edge of the crevasse, and both of them spun wildly out of control.

Cataclysmic thunder snuffed his lightning, and everything went dark.

Due To Your Tempered Essence of Manes, You Feel A Connection!

Felix woke to groans so loud and unsettling, he was immediately annoyed. He realized they were from him only seconds after waking, and blinked into a haze of Mana streams. Shadow and earth predominated, but the tell-tale hints of water and ice lingered at the edges of his Perception. He could breathe, so he knew he was alive and unburied, and as the tangle of Mana sorted itself, he realized he was at the bottom of the well.

He'd made it.

But the Eidolon hadn't.

"You...are awake," it said. The construct was planted in the earth, surrounded and pinned by an avalanche of stone and dirt and desiccated wood. "I am… pleased you have… survived, Unbound."

"Yeah," he said with a cough. He rolled to his feet. "What about you, though?"

"I… am," it stated. "But not for very long."

"I can dig you out, bring you topside," Felix began, but the Eidolon stopped him.

"No. No, the debris pierced my core." The Eidolon gestured with its one free arm, and Felix saw a steady trail of steam pouring from the construct's chest. "And even then… I feel myself fading without the… power of the Anima. Whatever brilliant arts the Magi placed upon me, they have faded… in truth. I am at my end."

"No, goddamnit," Felix growled. He strode forward. "I got more questions for you—"

Due To Your Tempered Essence of Manes, You Feel A Connection!

Felix swiped away the notification, but the Eidolon's eye fires widened.

"I felt that," it said. "What is—"

Due To Your Tempered Essence of Manes, You Feel A Connection!

"You've a Body Essence… intrinsically tied to ancestral Spirits," the Eidolon continued. New strength had entered its voice. "You… My true form was lost to time's relentless turning… but the stone construct you see before you was imbued to be my new Body. I can grant you what potency remains within its shell."

"Wait, what about you? If all you are is some Aspects bound to this rock robot, then what happens if you give those up?" Felix asked.

"I will pass on, released at last from the Corporeal Realm to find my final reward in the Ethereal."

"Desolation," Felix said. "You think there's something beyond that maelstrom?"

"There is, though it takes proper eyes to see it." One of the green-gold fires shrank rapidly before expanding again. It had *winked* at him. "Perhaps I shall meet you there one day, Inheritor."

Felix just nodded. He figured the Paragon wouldn't take kindly to Felix's thoughts on gods and religion. "What do I do?"

"Simply accept," the Paragon said, and with a last gasp, he was filled with a brilliant, green-gold light.

Eidolon Exult Karys Taiv Has Given You Access To His Experience, Essence, and Memories!
Do You Accept?
Y/N

Felix swallowed, but selected *Yes.* Nothing happened, at least at first.

"Thank you, Felix Nevarre."

"For what?"

"For choosing to become a Nym. For granting me this final wish." The Eidolon creaked and crumbled at the joints, enough that its stone form began to buckle just slightly. It stopped once it had tilted ever so slightly forward in a bow, despite being sideways. "Go, with the Herald's grace, Last of the Nym."

There was a swelling in Felix's cores, and the steam that had been pouring out of the Eidolon's chest pivoted toward him. Its eyes flared bright, twin green-gold lights that shimmered brightly. Felix could feel the power of it, just as he could feel the dimming remnant of the Eidolon, a ghost that would depart once it had given this final boon.

CAW!
The Endless Raven Smiles Down Upon You!
Titles: Thief of Fate and Stigma of the Chosen Engaged!

Ravenous Tithe!

Without his conscious will, Felix felt his Primordial hunger pulse and pull. The Eidolon's flames widened in sudden terror, before everything—power and ghost alike—vanished into Felix's channels.

CAW!
You Have Been Blessed!
The Raven Gifts You The Eidolon's Soul!

CHAPTER FORTY-FOUR

The sound of joyous, gleeful cawing faded as Felix's *everything* erupted with potency. Green-gold radiance surged into his channels and core space, spearing through the dark void between his spinning Skills, drenching it all in its sap-like consistency. It swirled, even as it spread, pulled inexorably toward his center until it reformed into an orb of brilliant, vibrant fluid.

Felix's core space shook, twisted with a hollow pain that made both him and his Companion startle. Pit's screech was accompanied by Felix's shouts.

His hunger, the dread abyss that dwelled between his stacked cores, called for the Eidolon's power. The sound of gnashing teeth, of rumbling guts filled the space. The abyss had locked onto it, and there was no stopping its momentum. It flashed forward, a bullet into the dark, already stretching and pushing into the inky maelstrom at his center. The orb of power shredded apart, too fast and too slow, like a predator enjoying its meal.

No! Not this!

The dark pulled, but Felix pulled right back. Steel-like cords of connection formed between his consciousness and the orb, blinding in their radiance, and his cores sang in a cacophony of discordant harmony. As Felix raged, so did they.

You are mine! And you! Will do! As I say!

Title: Tyrant of Choice Engaged!
You Have Rejected The Rest Of The Eidolon's Potency!
The Endless Raven Is Amused!
CAW!

Invisible claws slipped free of the green-gold power, and whatever lay within that abyss howled with an impotent fury that Felix no longer cared to hear. It cut off as easily as a door shutting in a room, his Bastion of Will blazing in the near distance.

Bastion of Will is level 71!

Nymean Artifact Detected!
Substitute For Sacrificed Potential Found!
Potency Rerouted!

What?

Above the dark abyss, the root-like branch of Divinity resonated like a struck tuning fork. Waves of power hit and were enveloped within his [Thunderflame Core] and [Cardinal Beast Core], before being flung back out, this time a blue-white and red-gold arrow that shot toward Felix and his captured orb.

He and the Eidolon's power, its dang soul, were hurled out of the core space. They traveled backward, spinning through his channels at a breakneck pace until they hit and burst from Felix's left hand.

The same hand that held tightly to his Crescian Blade.

Inheritor Status Acknowledged!
Array Unlocked!

Suddenly himself again, Felix watched his hooked sword ignite in a storm of green-gold light and sloshing liquid Mana. It spun around the hilt and blade itself until it coated it entirely, and the array near the guard lit up, followed by a second one just above it. A new one. It sang to Felix's senses, almost overwhelmed by the vibrations of Mana and his own cores.

The liquid Mana sank into the weapon and disappeared entirely.

As if strings had been cut, Felix sagged, and his arms fell limp. Blinking rapidly, he saw his Stamina, Mana, and Health had all been reduced to just below ten percent. The remnant Status Condition that blinked immediately away told him why.

Status Condition: Aspect Drain (Major)

Aspect drain? To say that was alarming was putting it mildly. Felix felt at this Aspects, but Body, Mind, and Spirit all felt hale and unchanged. His internal snapshot of his condition matched his current reality. *So what drained?*

A flash of emerald radiance called his attention to his Crescian Blade. There, above the hilt, were two elaborate glyphs etched into the metal. They glowed with an intense light that lasted only a few more seconds before the light and the glyphs themselves faded from the blade.

Voracious Eye!

Hoping for something, anything from the glyphs, instead Felix was surprised by an entire block of text he'd never before seen from the weapon.

Name: Inheritor's Will
Type: Weapon (Long Blade) (Enchanted)
Lore: A weapon known by many names, it was once an instrument of the Herald herself, used to defend the Golden Empire from those that would wrong it. It is made of Crescian Bronze, a material stronger than orichalcum and mithril, yet lighter than both and more welcoming to enchantment. Its function as a key to access Nymean Temples is known, but all else is a mystery.
Etheric Division - The first of several arrays. The blade may cut through spellforms and Mana formations at the Inheritor's request, but it is gated by the advancement of the Inheritor.
Etheric Unification - Nymean power resonates with the

Blade, drawing other sources of Nymean sorcery toward itself.

Aside from the fascinating bit of history and strange enchantments, the substance of the weapon had been refined in some small way. It looked cleaner, sharper. Newer, almost. There was a vibrancy—just the faintest blush—and on the pommel of the sword was a crystalline shape, a two-pronged star that looked much like an elongated diamond.

*Two-star ruin...*Felix looked up and around at the broken well. *Did I absorb the power of the settlement?*

He checked his Local Authority, and it was still intact, and there were still grayed out commands and inaccessible sub-menus. Only now, the [Access Vault] option was entirely absent. Pit let out a curious chirrup.

"Hm? What do you mean, 'you feel something?'" Felix asked. But then he *did* feel something, the supremely satisfying and borderline painful sensation of waking after a very, very long sleep.

Who... where am I?

The Eidolon's voice was strong and deep, if not quite as deep as it was within the construct. Felix froze, as at first, he thought he'd gathered another companion in his head, a new, far less menacing Maw for him to deal with... until he realized the voice wasn't coming from his core space at all.

It was coming from the sword. It wasn't *his* Aspects that drained.

"Hey there, Karys Taiv," Felix said and smiled tentatively at his faintly glowing sword. "How're you doing?"

I... am alive?

"Technically speaking, no, probably not," Felix said. Pit chirped his agreement. "But you're not dead, either. Or consumed to fuel the hellbeast that may or may not be living inside of me."

W-what?

"Not important right now." Felix lifted the sword—Inheritor's Will, apparently—until it was eye level with him. "Somehow your... everything got transferred to my sword. The Herald's Hook, as you called it. I don't know why, exactly, though I have an inkling on the how."

The Eidolon was quiet. *You took everything. No... No, I recall the voice, the absurd crowing. Something interfered when I attempted to gift you my Aspects. I can see it now. You*—somehow, Felix could sense the ancient warrior looking at him in surprise—*You rejected my power, for all that it would have elevated you even more. And the System found your blade instead. That is… I had heard the Unbound could be the greatest among us, but to pass on such power… I am humbled, Felix Nevarre. Truly.*

Felix found himself gritting his teeth as the Eidolon went on. Of course, his efforts at decency, at *not* eating another person's soul had caused him to lose out on more power. Except that wasn't entirely true. He recalled bits of the guardian's power draining into him. As if the System was waiting for him to make that connection, he received a notification.

You Have Absorbed A Portion Of Eidolon Exult Karys Taiv!
You Have Gained The Following:
+5 Levels To Any Mind Skill
+5 Levels To Any Spirit Skill
+5 Levels To Any Body Skill

Memories accessed!
Eidolon array consumed!

A burst of sense images flooded Felix's Mind and Spirit, each one a vibrant punch in the gut. Battles gone by and terrors faced down, each one worse than the last. Until it ended, and he found himself kneeling again. Felix's eyes bulged. *How...? What would I have gotten if I'd taken all of his power?*

The sword thrummed, as the Eidolon—Karys—considered itself. *I have become one with the Herald's Hook, the Inheritor's Will. For saving me from the oblivion that…* Urge… *intended, I promise to serve you as I had served my empress once before. I give you my Oath, bound upon my Mind, Body, and Spirit.*

Brilliant silver threads were conjured at those words. Invisible to those without Affinity, they were nevertheless real, and bound Karys in unseen chains that were fastened firmly around Felix's own heart. He felt the sudden weight of it, far more than his friends' Oaths had put upon him, and it took the Unbound a long moment to shrug off the sensation.

"That is... I'm honored. But you don't even know me," Felix objected.

I have seen enough. Bound as I am to this weapon, I also see a portion of its nature. You will need my help harnessing its true power.

Felix couldn't help but be intrigued by that statement. He could use all the power he could get against the Archon. "How so?"

Inheritor's Will is riddled with openings, places where the Crescian Bronze can pull in Mana from the outside. They are so small that not even your senses could detect them. Now that I am part of it, I can feel the grooves. The voice paused. *It is tied to the array for Etheric Unification. It can absorb power, much as you yourself. Astounding.*

Felix eyed the sword. Karys had somehow garnered a more complete understanding of Felix's nature during his journey. "Any power?"

Karys pondered that. *No. It seems limited to sources of power you have gained Authority over.*

Felix grunted. So he'd have to claim another city to power the thing up again. It raised... interesting possibilities.

"Okay, that's a problem for another day I think." Felix looked up, noticing the spiral staircase that had guided him down into the well had been shaken loose by the collapse of the Spirit Tree's grotto. "If you are set on hanging around, then we have to get moving. I've got friends waiting."

We seem to be trapped.

"Hardly," Felix said.

A lone figure crawled from the press of bodies. Its ice armor had melted, but its metal-plated flesh still thrummed with the potency of its terrible master. The corpses had protected it from the intense heat and deadly flames, shielded its Vitality from the senses of that horrible nightmare creature. It had survived.

Now it must flee. Reach the city. Find the Master, its dread Father.

The Nym was alive! It was coming! It—

—a geyser of liquid earth and cascading lightning were the last things it knew.

You Have Killed A Reforged!
XP Earned!

Huh! Felix thought as he rode the solidified connections to the night sky. Lighting hung around him like a shroud or perhaps wings of electric blue. *Didn't think there were any left.*

With a flash of light, Pit emerged from his Spirit, coalescing beneath him in full barding and saddle. Felix cut off his Adamant Discord and gripped the reins.

Remarkable! Karys hollered in his Mind. The sword pulsed with green-gold light with every word. *How did you accomplish that?*

"How else?" Felix asked, urging Pit forward. "Magic!"

They exited the valley in record time, soaring above the still-burning landscape and utilizing the powerful updrafts it provided. Due to Pit's size, the way he flew was less physics and more magical power, but the warm columns of air still helped quite a bit.

From above, Felix's powerful eyes and Manasight had detected no other living creatures, at least not anything overtly hostile. He'd been lucky catching the last Reforged as he'd emerged from the underground well. Hopefully that meant the Archon still didn't know Felix was close, though the presence of his Mark made him question that.

"Karys, what do you know about Marks?" Felix asked over the wind.

The making of them, or their general nature?

Felix's eyebrows rose. "Making them?"

It is a simple technique, though one usually needs the power of at least a Master Tier to form the foundation of a Mark. Karys paused. *Despite your impressive power, you are not even an Adept. In my time, a child was not allowed out into the wider world until they had Mastered their chosen Skills.*

"Really?" Felix looked ahead of them as they approached the peaks. "Most people I've met are either Journeyman or lower. The number of Adepts and Master Tier folk I've met can be counted on one hand."

This...this is a strange Age to have returned to, Karys said after a brief pause. *Yet I find myself no stronger than a Journeyman myself. The bulk of my power fed into your Will.*

Meaning his sword. "Does that mean it's stronger now?"

I would imagine so, yes. The former Paragon's voice was dry. *Stronger than the club at your side and… is that a lance?*

"I mean, basically, yeah," Felix said. "But tell me what you know about Marks."

Generally speaking, they are an imprint of your Aspects upon another creature. A simple process, though as I said, the significance required would not congeal until Master Tier at the earliest.

"What about breaking them? Removing them?"

An interesting question. It can be done, but the cost is great. As a Mark is imposed on your Aspects, you must damage your Aspects to remove the Mark. This can lead to a plethora of problems, not the least of which is a shattered foundation. The sword buzzed at his side. *It is not a procedure I'd recommend you attempt yourself. I have personally seen the results of Marks inexpertly applied and removed. It is… grisly.*

"Thanks for the warning," Felix said. He dug his hand into Pit's soft mix of fur and feathers. "I'll have to find another way."

The surest solution is to destroy whatever dared Mark you, Karys explained. *Who had the audacity to Mark an Unbound, anyway?*

"Easier to make a list of who doesn't have the audacity," Felix muttered. "I'll tell you about them later."

The Twins shone blue above, while the jaundiced light of Yyero shone slantwise from the horizon. They climbed over the peaks with a swirl of air Mana beneath Pit's black and crimson wings, rising up, up into the clear night sky. And with a giddy chirrup, they dropped.

Felix's heart leaped into his throat, but he trilled at the fall. He was riding a free-form roller coaster, banking left and right around the tops of particularly tall trees, even managing a barrel roll at one point. If Felix weren't so concerned with stealth, he would have been whooping for joy. As it was, their descent was so rapid that they soon came within sight of several Henaari scouts.

And beyond them was a curious ring of monolithic statues. Nymean statues.

CHAPTER FORTY-FIVE

"Local Authority. Huh." Harn looked up at the night sky, thinking.

Felix had gathered them close, and they ended up seated around a piece of splintered statuary—a hand, closed around a broken sword—between the tall Nymean sentinels. Those monstrous insides were glaring down at them all, the Henaari having decided to spend the remainder of the night in the shelter of its wardings. They were minor but were clearly driving away wandering beasts and unwanted eyes.

Handy, that, Felix thought while his friends grappled with the information he'd shared.

Built to celebrate our people's pact of trust with the folk of the Continent, offered Karys, unprompted. *There are a number around the land. The Guardians face outward with orbs of power, while within are contained the horrors that would ravage the world.*

"What horrors?" Felix asked.

"What?" Evie asked.

Many kinds. I know that you've encountered some already, though how you purified the Primordials' flesh curse is remarkable.

"What flesh curse?" Felix asked.

"Hello? Felix? Are you talking to the sword guy now?" Evie said, waving her hand in front of Felix's face. He blinked and looked up at the others around them.

"Oh. Yeah, Karys was telling me some… things." Felix smiled, banishing his concern for later. "Now's not the time." He refocused on his team, all of whom were spread around in the shadow of Pit's extended wings. Evie, Vess, Atar, Alister, and Harn were to his right while the Haarguard were to his left. All of them were looking at him with confused expressions.

"A sword spirit," Kylar said with a breathless sort of glee. "I never thought I'd see one."

"Still haven't," Nevia reminded him. "The Fiend—sorry, Felix said it was a ghost he bound to the blade. Not the blade's own spirit."

Felix considered correcting her wording, but decided it didn't matter. "Karys is a boon. He's helped me a bunch, and we've only known each other for an hour. But more to the point, this proves I can take Authority."

"How? Didn't the System try to kill you last time?" Atar said. Too late, he glanced at the Haarguard and snapped his mouth shut.

"What? Why would the System try to kill you?" Vyne asked.

Felix waved his hand. "Not important. My friend here tells me it's because of… circumstances, that I was able to take this location."

"What about other Nym ruins?" Harn asked. "Can you take those, too?"

Provided you take proper control, yes, most likely, Karys said.

"Should be able to," Felix said.

"We can see that as a win, at least," Vess stated. "It means that, maybe, we can secure Authority over the Temple before the Archon reaches it."

Who is—

"How far out are we?" Atar asked. He had wrapped his cloak tight around himself as the night had grown unseasonably cool. "A week or two?"

"Thereabouts," Harn said. "Should only be a couple days until we reach Shelim, provided the way's clear."

"And the Farwalker said the city is occupied by our friends," Evie said. "So we go around the city?"

Felix nodded. "I think that's for the best. We'll circle the city and head directly into the mountains. Hopefully, we can find a way through them without alerting the Archon."

Felix found the Haarguard staring at him. "What will you do?"

"Do, sir?" Vyne asked.

"It's gonna get even more dangerous in the coming days. If you all want to return to Haarwatch, now's the time to do it."

Vyne and others opened their mouths, their Spirits all flashing with denial and no little bit of fear. Felix held out a hand, forestalling them. "Think it over. Let me know in the morning. There's no shame in admitting if a fight is beyond you."

The Haarguard gave him thoughtful nods, even Kylar. "Let's all get some rest while we can. We'll set off at dawn when the Henaari pack up." Felix stood and stretched. His muscles actually felt tight and a bit sore after his fights.

The others spread out, grouping up and chatting. They didn't have to worry about doing any sort of watch as the Henaari more than had that covered. The nomad people had insisted his team relax after driving off their would-be murderers, giving them the rest of the night to rest before they set off in the morning.

The Henaari and Felix's team would part ways then. When he'd arrived on the back of his Companion, the Farwalker and a surprisingly subdued Matriarch had welcomed him with open arms. The gathered Henaari had cheered—in Spirit, at least—and the Farwalker explained their plan. The wandering people would head for one of their nearby redoubts to the north, near where the Hoarfrost abutted the Foglands. There, they hoped to escape the Archon's creatures.

Felix understood. This wasn't their fight. As the Farwalker put it, "the Great Raven empowers us to challenge the dark for the thrill of the unknown, but she does not send us to death." And to face the Archon directly was… well, it was toeing that line.

Felix wandered the area.

Quite a few gave Felix deep bows of appreciation for what he'd done, often clutching close their loved ones at the same time. Felix could feel the shaky relief in their Spirits, like someone told they had days to live only to have the diagnosis reversed. It was nice, the recognition, he could admit that to himself. But it was far more rewarding to see a few of the faces he recognized from the first tunnel, now reunited with family members and children.

They would have died, had you not acted. You have done a good thing, Inheritor.

"Thanks Karys. Always nice to be reminded of that."

Felix settled in against the back of one of the monoliths. A snarling creature with too many eyes and an upsetting number of mandibles loomed above him, but he paid it little mind. The echo of their growling had been unnerving at first, but Felix had seen weirder stuff. He'd followed the threads of sounds, hoping he'd find an illusion array buried in the statues or ground, but the traces of it simply vanished. At the same time, the vicious snarls had cut off completely. Whatever he'd done, it meant that he could settle against the statue without anything louder than the wind in his ears.

They fled. I had thought them only hiding.

"Who did?" Felix unsheathed his sword and placed it across his lap. It felt odd talking to it at his side, considering it had once been a person. "Who are you talking about?"

The horrors I mentioned. Those growls you heard through your Harmonics were not illusions. That was a spellwrought connection to another place, a Vault much like the one in which you found me. Karys sounded agitated. *And now, I can find no sign of that connection, as if it has been severed.*

"Not by me. All I did was trace it backwards," Felix said. "The thing disappeared the closer I looked." Felix looked up at the statues and the monstrous visages. "I've been told the Nym collected monsters, hoarded them like a CEO hordes cash. Is that true?"

What is a CEO and what is cash?

"A rich guy. Money."

My people did not hoard monsters like gold, Felix. They protected people from the worst the Continent had to offer. The Golden Empire was one of peace and learning, free of the strife inherent in our neighbors. The sword buzzed, wisping slightly with green-gold vapor. *Threats were hunted down. Where something could not be eradicated, it was contained and restricted.*

"Okay. That gels with what I've learned about them. But why even forge a connection between some distant Vault and these statues? What's the point?"

Goodwill is transient, unless people are reminded of what is done for them.

It clicked. "So these are political statements." Felix could see it. No wonder the outside looked so heroic while the inside was designed to scare the crap out of people. "And they upped the wow factor by setting up an audio feed directly into the cages. Dang. I'm impressed."

Except now that connection is gone. The threads have snapped.

"Weren't they just something to bring the monsters' Spiritual presence here?"

Yes, to my knowledge. But even still. It is worrisome.

Felix looked around the area, feeling with his Affinity and Manasight. Shadow, life, earth, and water laid thick in the night, while each monolith was a pillar of spiraling colors. Those colors spread outward, forming the wards he'd noticed before, and they were just as strong as when he'd arrived. The only difference was the easing of subconscious terror that everyone within the statues had felt.

"At least people will be able to sleep better," Felix said. "We'll deal with the possible consequences later." A thought occurred to him. "Karys, do you have an idea of where these Vaults were all located?"

I knew the cities in many parts of the Empire. The Vaults specifically were not my purview, but as a Paragon, I would often find myself traveling along the Wayward Path.

"We'll have to take a tour sometime." Felix had a feeling that Karys would keep him asking questions for the rest of his life. He flagged the words “wayward path” for future reference and settled down to meditate. "Wake me if something bad is happening."

I shall do so.

Felix sank into his core space.

He did not often take the time to meditate, not actively at least. As a result, his Meditation Skill had taken forever to reach Journeyman because, while he used it passively during his waking hours, it was rarely ever more than a simple, calming exercise that boosted his regeneration rates. Cal and Harn had told him that it was rarely a Skill people received and more a mindset for enhancing and evolving one's core. Felix hadn't done much in the way of advancing his core since he'd formed two of them, and they were due for a check-up.

He sank through the darkness, floating casually through the glimmering lights and swirling storm of Mana and Essence that made up everything. The two cores, blue-white and red-gold rings of flame, burned and turned below him while dozens of blazing Skills revolved around them in a slow, endless dance.

Felix shaped his Intent, honing his vision of what his core space resembled. Lights burned brighter while the dark clarified and deepened, as if it truly were an infinite expanse. The ribbons of light flourished, twinned sets of blue-white and red-gold, snagged about his Journeyman Tempered Skills. Below his cores, those ribbons twisted together in the tightest of weavings, still not that much more advanced than weeks prior.

Felix wasn't sure how to proceed from there. He'd thought tightening the weave or increasing the amount of monsters he absorbed might help, but it looked the same as ever.

I'll talk to Harn later about it. And Karys. That guy knows a lot.

But that wasn't his purpose tonight.

Instead, Felix pivoted through the cloud of Essence, senses stretching outward. It was easy enough to find the Memories. They drifted through his store of Essence like bright knots in a diffuse mist. There were four Memories Felix could immediately see, and he breathed a sigh of relief. They were points of heaviness that drew Essence and Mana both toward them, and unlike any Memory he'd ever had, Karys' Memories were anchored, like stars in the sky.

Previously, the dark abyss through the double rings of his cores would devour the Essence he brought into his core space. Including, naturally, any Memories. Why it did so was unclear to Felix, though the indiscriminate nature of the hunger was familiar to him. The abyss frightened him, nearly as much as when it had its claws in Felix properly. He had thought he'd rid himself of it when he'd conquered the Primordial remnants left in the city. At least, he no longer felt those physical pangs anymore.

He could sense a terrible vastness beyond the circular aperture of his cores, a whirlpool-like pressure that wanted to consume everything. Karys' Memories were fixed, boulders in a stream of Essence, but they weren't the only Memories there.

Felix's eyes widened. A burning orange light, a Memory from the Arcid, tottered on the edge of his abyss. Felix seized it, flexing both his Will and Intent, yet the hungry dark only redoubled its efforts.

It was slipping away.

We need this Memory! We have to see what the enemy knows! Let go! Felix was yanked closer to the abyss. *Pit! Help!*

An insidious bellow—felt, rather than heard—shook through him. The hunger dug in its heels.

If you let it go, I promise I'll get you something much bigger and more powerful to eat! Okay? Just! Let! It! Go!

Felix could feel Pit approaching, but before the tenku could converge with him, there was a sudden slackening of the abyss' pressure. Surprised that even sort of worked, Felix didn't hesitate: he hurled the Memory straight into the liquid flame of his [Thunderflame Core].

The world pulsed, and Felix was somewhere else.

Felix stepped into the Escher-like mental space of the Arcid's Memories and saw before him the expanded existence that was Boilerface.

He focused his Intent, his need, spearing through the convoluted mind space without hesitation. He needed to know what the Archon was up to, what he knew. In a flash, he'd reached a more pristine version of Boilerface and collided with him.

The world shattered.

He was standing in Shelim, though it looked strange without the fog. He was among a number of other Arcids, all of them looking like armored humanoids but with a strange twist to each. One was a pale, white-green color and had blade-like wings emerging from its back. Air-attuned, clearly. Two appeared as almost liquid, one covered in a viscous black goop while another was literally armor floating in a gel-like body of virulent green.

Between them all, were dozens and dozens of Wurms, Hoarhounds, and Reforged warriors.

"The Henaari are interlopers in my realm. They are not welcome, and neither is their foul godling." The Archon stood tall before them, resplendent in golden armor. He was bigger than any of the Arcids, though many of the Reforged dwarfed him in size. They could not, however, approach the strength of his presence. Felix could feel the construct radiating power like a damn sun.

"More importantly, they have the key to the Temple. Find them. Find the key, no matter what."

Felix tried to keep himself small, despite it being a Memory. The last time he tangled with the Archon, the guy somehow realized he was in a Memory, likely because of his Mark. Felix didn't want that happening again. He watched, but out of the corner of his eyes, careful not to focus too much on the Archon.

"What does the key look like, Master?" the winged one asked.

"You will know it when you see it. We have no idea what the key should be, just that there is one, and that Henaari's corpse radiated traces of the key's power." The Archon growled the last. "That such a pathetic creature thought it could steal my birthright… well. Worse shall happen to its kin."

Felix shuddered at the sense of unhinged hate and bile that brushed against him. The Archon was insane.

"What if they don't have it, Master?" The gel-like Arcid cringed as it asked the question, clearly expecting displeasure. Yet the Archon's mood merely twisted toward a dire glee.

"If the Henaari do not have the key, then we shall take them to the Forges. There, we shall bend them to my Great Purpose, and the Henaari will find it for me."

Dread sank into Felix's gut as the assembled horde raised its voices in exultation.

"Nothing shall stop my ascension! You hear me, Herald!" The Archon jabbed a finger into the sky. "I'll tread the Broken Path! I'll conquer it!"

Felix snapped back to his body like a recoiling rubber band. He gasped, panting for breath and sweating like he'd run a marathon.

Pit was there immediately, pushing his beak at Felix in concern. Felix clutched at his friend's feathers, fighting to stabilize the sense of terror and hate that had almost overwhelmed him.

"What the hell was that?" he panted.

You were influenced by the Memory you examined, Karys said. *I would have warned you, but I did not know you were capable of accessing such things.* He paused. *How did you gain a Memory from this creature?*

"...Ate him," Felix said.

Oh. Oh! Then that explains this next part.

"What?" Felix asked, before his vision was inundated with notifications.

You Have Fully Consumed Your Opponent's Essence!
Thief of Fate Title Engaged!

You Have Learned A New Skill!
Incendiary Shell, Rare, Level 1!
Channel fire Mana in a burst attack that damages all foes around you for thirty feet.

Synergy Detected!
Incendiary Shell (R) and Mantle of the Long Night (R) Are Compatible!
Do You Wish To Combine And Evolve?
Y/N

CHAPTER FORTY-SIX

Felix paused, unsure. He used his Mantle often enough, and it was closing in on Journeyman Tier. But Incendiary Shell was the Skill that had inundated the entire area in deadly flame. And aside from his wispfire, he had little in the way of burning attacks, though they worked against the Reforged really well. If they could get stronger....

Yes.

He'd roll the dice.

Evolution In Progress.

His insides hollowed out as nearly all of the Essence he'd gathered drained from him rapidly to fuel the creation of this new Skill. The pain spiked, stabbing through his core space like a lens flare. With a brilliant, whirling flourish, a new pattern appeared in his celestial array.

New Skill!
Mantle of the Infinite Revolution (Epic), Level 47!
You have discovered the balance between extremes and all the violent potential therein. Shroud yourself in bitterest cold and boiling heat as the world itself turns

about your person. Damage increases moderately per Skill level, range increases minorly per Skill level.

It glowed, fresh and vibrant upon the velvet black, an interplay of shimmering lines and jeweled tones. A sound drifted to Felix, one that was both a crackling inferno and a riotous crescendo of horns. And beneath that, hanging in the gaps, was the blissful silence of a glacial plain, and the slow steady turning of a cold, bitter winter.

It was as if the Skill encapsulated the turning of seasons in the most violent of ways.

Mantle of the Infinite Revolution is level 48!

Got it in one, apparently.

Felix lifted himself from his core space, a sensation that was like rising back into his body though he never moved. Exhaustion teased at the edges of his senses, though his Stamina was full, and flashes of a migraine joined in, reminders of how hard he'd pushed himself today. Multiple castings of Adamant Discord, Stone Shapings galore, and getting very nearly burned alive.

"Been a busy day," Felix muttered to himself.

Indeed. I am impressed by your resilience, Felix. Though my memory is choppy, I do not recall many who would remain awake after joining and evolving two Skills together.

Felix leaned back on his arms and stared up into the night sky. Thousands of stars covered the expanse, filling the blue-black sky with rivers of light. He felt empty, achingly so, and he'd have to hunt down some monsters in the morning to keep his core in balance. Between Essence and System energy, it was a narrow ledge he had to walk. "I've had some experience with it," he said at last.

Karys let out a wordless hum of thought. The Eidolon-turned-sword seemed pensive, and Felix let him be. The combination prompt had set his mind turning. His Mantle was now an amalgamation of a fire and ice-element Skill. It was clearly not a common Skill, as it was literally ranked Epic.

Why did some people focus only on a few elements? Atar and Alister were fire and force focused, respectively. Evie had her core devoted to ice and, to a lesser extent, water. Vess was wind or air. Felix, on the other hand, had a core based in flame and lightning, but he felt no greater affinity toward those elements. He'd gotten the impression that his Unbound nature meant a wider array of abilities and Skills... but was it more than that?

If he had one Skill that was a dual element, could he make more? His Shadow Whip, for instance, was very similar in form and concept as the enchantment array on his vambrace. Smoldering Lash was a fire Skill, meant to burn and cut, while Shadow Whip was a bludgeoning and clinging tool. Could he make a shadow that burned? That clung and cut?

It was something to think about.

He wanted to test out the Mantle, but with so many people around, Felix instead accessed his notifications once again.

You Have Absorbed A Portion Of Eidolon Exult Karys Taiv!
You Have Gained The Following:
+5 Levels To Any Mind Skill
+5 Levels To Any Spirit Skill
+5 Levels To Any Body Skill

"Any advice on what I should advance, Kerys?" It was his power, anyway.

I am happy to offer advice. Will you show me your Status?

Felix willed his Status to show to the sword, which was, frankly, a weird sensation. Weirder still that it could see it. His sword made several humming noises as it looked things over.

This is... You are an Unbound, of that there is no doubt. Your primary stats, resource pools, and sheer number of Titles and Skills are monstrous.

"I try my best," Felix said dryly. "Any advice?"

You have ten unused stat points. I would suggest you place them into Endurance, then focus upon your Perception, Dexterity, and Agility in that order. You are getting close to crossing the Third Threshold.

"Thresh—" Felix picked up the sword and stared at the blade. "You know about the Thresholds? And the Third is when all stats are at one thousand, right?"

Yes, that is the next stage. And, of course I know of them. As I said, my memory may not be entirely complete after my long sleep, but the Thresholds are common knowledge.

"Not anymore," Felix said. "I don't even think Humans can reach the First Threshold without some serious luck. They get so few extra stat points."

You are not incorrect. Humans were… they were… Hm. The sword rattled in his grip, agitated. *The holes in my memory rear their heads. I recall only that Humans were the weakest of those within our Empire, as even the Gnomes and Elves had greater range on their advancement.*

"Humans have been around since your time?" Felix said with some surprise.

The arrival of Humanity was celebrated in the Halcyon Concourse well before my birth. They are old upon the Continent, yet weak. Their survival beyond the ending of the Empire is nothing short of incredible. Felix had the impression Karys was shaking his head. *Our enemies wanted nothing more than the death or enslavement of all those our Empress protected. What could have happened that stayed their hands?*

"Enemies. Who were the enemies of the Golden Empire?" Felix asked.

The gods. Who else?

Felix couldn't help it. He started laughing.

It was a long belly laugh, rising from the depths of his soul. He felt his fatigue and aches carry away with it, drifting up into the sky. After a long few minutes, he looked at the moons, the blue Twins and a sliver of jaundiced Yyero. "There's about five hours until sunrise. You and I, Karys, we've got a lot to talk about."

As you wish.

The morning came quickly, or so it seemed to Felix.

He'd spent the dark hours talking with Karys and petting a snoring Pit. Their conversation had ranged from the mundane to the magical, and the former Paragon—a stage that was apparently above even the Grandmaster Tier—he gave Felix solid advice on his own advancement and Skills. Enough that, for the first time in a while, he felt like he had a good grip on where he wanted to go.

First, he boosted his Endurance, adding his extra ten stat points. It was now sitting pretty at 666 points. The sensation of growth felt like his skin and muscles and bones were all tightening. It wasn't painful or even uncomfortable, not like when he hit the Thresholds, more like he could feel himself growing denser while at the same time his Stamina pool widened just a fraction.

Next, he focused on his Skills.

Wild Threnody is level 61!
Voracious Eye is level 61!

The Body Skill he chose was the one that he'd been neglecting for far too long. Wild Threnody allowed him to channel his Mana Skills directly through his weapons, whether that was his swords, club, or fists. It was strong but required him to split his attention while activating it, which had gotten him struck more than once. The higher leveled it got, the easier it became to use, and Felix had a feeling it would be a powerful and versatile Skill once it hit Adept.

The Mind Skill was harder to decide upon, but he'd had a hard time leveling his Voracious Eye previously, and the information it gave had always been useful. Deep Mind or Manifestation of the Coronach had been close seconds, but he had plans to raise those, in any case.

Several Skills would have reached Adept Tier had he applied the five levels to them, but Felix suffered from a distinct lack of good Essence Draughts or Motes. Even if he brought his Bastion of Will or Ravenous Tithe to Adept, he'd be unable to Temper with them. True, he could have gone and hunted down some rare beast and eaten it, likely extracting some sort of Essence Mote from it, but that would cost them precious time. Time they had already squandered.

No. Not squandered. Their visits with the Henaari and his finding Karys were definite boons, but if the Archon was as close to the Temple as they feared, then they had to hurry.

Felix had also toyed with the idea of saving the levels for later use, but like with Tier-up messages, he only had a day to use the boosts before they vanished. According to Karys, they would simply imbue a Skill at random.

The final choice was one he deliberated the longest on. Between interrogating Karys, he would mull over the choices. He had many Spirit Skills, ranging from Manasight and Oathbinding to Adamant Discord and Arrow of Perdition. Powerful, useful abilities. Again, he wanted to avoid bringing anything beyond level 74 and into the Adept Tier, but that only removed his sigaldry Skill from the list of options. The rest were all well below.

The answer didn't come to him until the first blush of dawn had shown itself. Karys was describing some of the benefits of planting a Spirit Tree in an area under one's own Authority, when frustration mounted. The former Paragon had repeatedly told him that Felix should hold to his personal vision of strength and power. *Who do you wish to be?* the spirit had asked him. *What dream does an Unbound dream?*

What was his dream? Who was he? Felix had worn a lot of hats in his time on the Continent. Hero, Fiend, student, and friend. He wanted to protect people, but was that who he was? If Felix were honest with himself, he wanted to explore the Continent as well, to see the far-off places the others had described to him. He loved the struggle for strength—much as it pained him—he loved besting his opponents and, if not always winning, at least surviving.

Were he given free reign, Felix wasn't sure what he'd do.

So, while he could have pushed any number of Mana Skills higher, he chose one of his lowest ones. Because, if nothing else, that Skill intrigued him. Its effects were mysterious, even to Zara. Kerys also had no idea what the Skill was meant to do, though he was duly impressed by its Transcendent rarity.

He chose.

Unite the Lost is level 13!

There was a tightening in his core space as the last of Karys' stolen Essence was doled out to the Skill. The pattern, situated in the farthest corner of his core space, was smaller than it had a right to be. Less than half the size of even Tracking, his Common-ranked Skill lay barely into Apprentice Tier. When the Paragon's Essence hit it, that changed.

Felix's eyes bulged as a fiery explosion erupted in his center; he fell onto his hands and knees. Within him, the steady, sedate Skill had blossomed to twice its former size as it sang with such crystalline perfection that it startled Karys.

T-that sound! That music!

As quickly as it had begun, it faded. Unite the Lost was now larger than ever and had jumped closer by half to his two core rings. At level 13, it should have remained in the back orbits; only the highest leveled and Tempered Skills crowded near his cores.

Shaking his head to clear it, Felix collected himself and his sword. He had forgotten the rush of change that overcame a Beginner Tier Skill once it hit level 10. This, though, was way more intense. *Maybe because of its high rarity,* he mused.

Felix Nevarre. That Skill... watch it carefully.

"Why?" Felix asked, staring down at his sword. "What do you know?"

Only that the strains of its song are... exotic. I do not know what it will become, should it reach Apprentice Tier or higher. I simply... urge caution.

Frowning to himself, Felix breathed softly through his nose. "I'll keep it in mind." He looked up and around as the Henaari changed their sentries for the morning. They were the only ones still up and moving, but that was slowly changing. "About time we woke everyone up. Sun's barely up, and daylight's already burning away."

His friends had alternated between sleeping and meditating themselves, though most of them grumbled quietly when Felix shook them awake. The sun was already inching above the horizon by that point, so he figured he had given them at least a few extra hours of rest. Evie, among others, didn't appreciate it.

"I was havin' a dream I found a giant sandwich," she said, before going on to describe it in such detail that several among them began drooling. "And just as I was about to take a bite? Some blue-eyed brute comes and shakes my dream apart!"

"A travesty if I've ever heard one," said the Farwalker. Wyvora wheeled the man into their section of camp A'zek followed closely behind in the shadows of the statues. "While I have no sandwiches here, I hope this, at least, will do you in good stead."

The shrouded man snapped his fingers, and several Henaari carted in packs of salted meat, bread, and a bevy of berries and nuts. "For you, as a weak thanks for all you've done. Please, eat your fill and take the rest with you on your journey."

After a nod from Harn, his team fell on the offering with gusto.

"Thanks for this," Felix said. He shook the Farwalker's hand

and let out a relieved laugh. "I'm sure you know how hard it is to feed this many Tempered fighters."

"I'm familiar, yes," he said, and his voice dripped with amusement. "I wish only that we could do more."

"You've helped a lot, and your information on the Archon and his forces is more than I expected," Felix said. "We're not looking to fight the thing head-on, not yet. Stealth is the priority. If we don't, then a couple extra bodies aren't going to slow down the Archon when he comes for us."

"He is mighty, that I can sense. A'zek has tasted the aura of his Spirit, and it has the weight of Ages to it." The Farwalker shook his head slowly. Sadly. "I do not envy your Path, for all that you have yet to choose it. But I can hopefully make it a touch easier." He gestured, and Wyvora and A'zek stepped forward. "My apprentice and my Companion will go with you, see that you make it to your destination. Whatever that may be."

Felix looked at the Farhunter and harnoq, fighting to keep suspicion from his gaze. The Farwalker had only helped them so far, and though Felix couldn't read the man, he felt he could trust him. He lowered his voice, so softly that he barely made a sound. Yet he knew the Farwalker could hear him easily from so close.

"We seek a Nymean Temple. It will be dangerous. I," Felix licked his lips. "I will be opening a dangerous door."

The shroud dropped from the Farwalker's face, revealing the old man's shocked expression. Then his eyes crinkled in excitement. "Truly?" he whispered back.

"Cross my heart," Felix said.

The grin that burst across the old man's features was almost worth the anxiety of telling him their goal. He clapped his hands, twice. "I give my Oath, upon dark unknown, that me and mine will not endanger you. I swear on my advancement and levels, upon the Raven Herself, that they will do all they can to assist your task, Felix Nevarre. I swear."

The Farwalker clasped Felix's hand. Not missing the cue, Felix engaged his Oathbinding Skill, locking the old man into his words. Taut cables of silver tightened between them, with lesser threads extending outward into the Henaari camp.

Oathbinding is level 35!

"Farwalker, you gave your Oath?" Wyvora asked in shock.

"Indeed I did, apprentice." He flashed a smile at her and his Companion. "Be sure to follow the letter and spirit of its Intent, aye?"

She bowed her head. "Yes, sir."

"You too, you old sourpuss," he said to the regal-looking harnoq.

A'zek threw his head back. "Worry for yourself. Who will watch over you when I am gone?"

The Farwalker's grin turned harder, sharper. "I'm sure the Matriarch will take care of me," he said. A'zek snorted.

Unwilling to get involved in more of their internal politics, Felix thanked the man and got his team moving. Without avum to saddle or many supplies to secure, they were ready within minutes. The Henaari themselves were also packing, though they were far quicker about it. By the time Felix started off, they had mostly cleared out of the monolithic circle.

"Well, we ready for more adventure?" Felix asked.

"I could use a nap," Atar said with a supportive nod from Evie. "Maybe we could sleep in a bit more?"

"Onward!" Felix declared.

CHAPTER FORTY-SEVEN

Kelgan walked with his spear out, arrayed at the forefront of the column of sleepwalking guards. It felt quite strange, leading the blank-eyed stares of the alchemically-adjusted warriors, but far less strange than the path through which they walked. The ground, stone-like at first blush, glowed like a moon made of the sea. It was firm, unless they thought about it too much. But Kelgan had learned his lesson there. He kept his eyes firmly forward, and his Mind thoroughly focused.

That made it far easier to deal with the *other* things that inhabited the Dark Passage.

<D-do you t-think they can see us?> Karp signed to him. The Archer was on the inside of their vanguard, one of the safer positions in their company, but his fingers twitched unsteadily as he formed handsign. It was like watching someone stutter. <Or j-just hear us?>

<Unknown,> Thangle signed back, his slight form one of the only ones still riding atop an avum. His handsign was crude, as he'd only ever mastered the basics of the language. The Gnome was an entertainer, once upon a time, not a soldier. <Focus. Do not stray.>

Good advice, Thangle. Kelgan had been about to say the same. While the majority of their company was drugged out of their Minds, there were a handful of them who did not have to drink the potion. Could not, it turned out. When Karp had expressed concern about entering the Passages again, he'd asked to go under. Zara had then informed them all that the potion did not work on those with stronger Willpower.

"Apart from that," she had said, "an ample Will is all that you need to stay safe. That and focus."

Kelgan was a bit relieved when he saw the effects of the potion. Dead-eyed and slack-jawed, the men and women of his company were like Golems. They moved at their command, their steps slowing or quickening as needed, and even held securely to the blindfolded mounts.

How much will they remember after all this? He had wondered that many times now. Would it all feel like a terrible dream? Or were they conscious now and simply could not control themselves? He had attempted to ask Zara twice, but the first time he'd been rebuffed, and the second, he'd felt his focus slip enough to soften the stones beneath him.

He didn't bother worrying again. It was, and all of them had to deal with the consequences. He just had to make sure his people were as safe as he could make them.

Now Zara walked at their head, with the Hand trailing slightly behind and the rest of the awake vanguard leading the blank-eyed horde behind them. There were thirteen of them who had the requisite Willpower to withstand the pressure the creatures in the dark put on them. Said creatures swam around the edge of the path Zara created, kept at bay by her strange power.

The less said about them, the better.

It had been… an unclear amount of time since they had begun this walk. Time faded to meaningless mush between the vault of shadow, and Kelgan was having a hard time differentiating one moment to the next. The things outside the green-blue illumination were growing in number, he could tell that from his peripheral vision. In fact, the longer they advanced, the more he saw, as if his Perception were stretching....

For all his might, he could not avoid thinking of them.

Schools of writhing tentacles moved in fluid groups, swimming in unseen currents. Their mottled gray flesh was hideous enough, even without the fact that tentacles made up all that they were. There was no body, only flashes of iridescent light within their wriggling core, all wrapped in barbed and hooked tendrils. Among them, beyond them, were angular stretches of the Void itself. They moved with a preternatural grace among the thrashing tentacles, visible only when they flew among them and disappeared in the greater dark.

Yet, all of these were possible to ignore. Kelgan had seen such terrible things in the Foglands, in the depths of that Labyrinth, that he'd grown acclimated to their horror. It was the glint of fangs and a body of scales that terrified him, things too large to be allowed.

Immense, dread serpents coiled among the horde, ribbed with fins that billowed like the sails of the greatest of Manaships. Spines lifted among the fins, each trailing iridescence as they wound through the terrors, their eyes bright with nothing less than utter madness. It was enough to rattle anyone, to shake them loose of the Passage.

Beside him Karp stumbled. The ground, so firm for Kelgan, began to deform. To sink.

"Steady yourself!" Zara cried out, her voice resonant yet quieter than a whisper. "The Void cannot touch you if you do not let it!"

Kelgan knew the struggle the archer was feeling, and he supported his friend until the phantom road beneath them solidified once more.

"You're all right, Karp. We can do this."

They got up. They kept moving.

It was all they could do.

Thangle watched as the spearman lifted Karp to his feet, their hands blurring in that handsign of theirs. Too fast for him to follow. Relief, however, seemed to sag the archer's frame, as if someone had shouldered a part of his burdens. The same one all those still awake had to bear.

He was an Illusionist. An entertainer! Why was he here, in this dread place?

It was a question Thangle had been asking himself for weeks. Ever since the world had fallen apart.

The answer, of course, was many things. Survival among them.

But also the look in that boy's eyes when he came to save them from the Arcid and Reforged. A lot of the kids around him looked up to the Fiend for his strength and abilities, but Thangle had seen powerful folk plenty of times in his life. Been ruined by them, more often than not. But that kid cared… about everyone.

Maybe an old Gnome could care just a little, too?

Which brought him here, to the Dark Passage forged by a Naiad Sorcerer who scared him more than any noble. He couldn't even use his magic, not properly. He found that on an earlier jaunt, when his augmentation Mana had attracted *attention* from the things outside the barrier. He shuddered. He'd sat on his hands ever since, marshaling his strength within his core space but closing himself off from energy around him.

Thangle focused on his core, upon the spinning gyroscope that sat within his father's workshop. It was long gone in the real world, of course, but in his core space, it thrived. He'd grown it, detail by detail, over decades as he'd honed his magic and Tempered his Aspects. The bench was scratched, the tools scuffed, but it was solid. Steady. But for how much longer? Closing off his channels meant his Mana was stifled, building atop his whirling device with greater intensity.

Thangle circulated the power, pushing it through his channels before returning it into his core. Each time, he tried to recollect a bit more of his childhood home, but the pain of his closed channels tore at him with every pass. It had worked well on previous trips, but now he felt the pressure pushing at him in ways that were alarmingly different. It felt like being underwater, almost, like he couldn't get a breath of air. Not unless he wanted to let *them* in.

And maybe it was paranoia. They had been traveling this new, extended Passage for what felt like days. Far, far longer than any other trip. Zara's power was keeping them secure. Yet Thangle couldn't help but spot the slight stutter as the path manifested. Did the aquamarine flagstones shine just a touch less? Was that sweat on Zara's brow?

He'd felt the ground shudder beneath him a time or two, and that had been enough to push himself away from those lines of thought. Doubt had no place here, not for the living. Focus on the walk, upon their ultimate destination. That was all there was.

Or else.

Thangle wasn't the only one to notice a waning in the Sorcerer's power, however. Darius watched as the Gnome and a few others eyed the witch, forcing themselves again and again to disregard the signs that had started to build. Darius himself kept a close eye on her and her power, noting each time their Passage grew a touch smaller. Ethereal stones of blue-green Mana faded, almost hidden in the natural rolling cadence of the path she forged, but unmistakable to someone with an Adept's senses.

The Sorcerer was faltering.

<How much time?> he asked.

She didn't bother to lie or befuddle him, and for that, she had a measure of his respect. <Subjective or objective time?>

<Objective, naturally.>

<Unknown,> she signed, and a smile quirked her thin lips. <Time does not move in predictable ways here. Will not, for all the Intent in the world is no match for the gods.>

<We tread in a god's demesne?> Darius wanted to snarl, but had to settle for aggressively thrusting his signs at her. <The gods are dead, and their demesnes are scattered. This cannot be one.>

<Indeed, this merely skirts the edges of a Realm beyond our own, where time and causality intermingle in curious ways.> Zara clenched her jaw, a sudden fire in her eyes. The path flared, and something at the corner of his perception veered off into the black. <I will be fine.>

<You don't look fine. You look as a wineskin, slowly drained. How much time before you collapse?>

<As much as is needed,> she all but hissed.

The floor flickered, but held. Something with long fins dragged against the path on Darius' left side, and a shower of green-blue sparks spiraled into the air.

<What was that?> he asked.

<A danger. Greater than most, but nothing we cannot handle. Even if it were to breach the path, we would be fine.>

<And the guards?> Darius asked.

<They are why I am being so careful, and why I must concentrate, Reed.>

<...Very well.>

The time stretched on, unnaturally elastic, but Zara marked it as she could. The liminal space held markers for those who looked, if only within the throng of beasts clustered at the border. Their numbers increased by a fifth for every glass in that space, though counting them while keeping her focus upon the working was a challenge that even her Master-Tier Mind had difficulty managing. Yet still, she had to check. The path was paramount, but the longer they traversed the dark, the greater the chance of some truly dire creature appearing.

They skirted the Void, after all.

Zara's forehead was slick with sweat, hours after the Hand's irritable concerns were raised. He wasn't wrong, but it didn't matter. None could aid her in this, her order flung about the Continent, and those she had trained were hundreds of miles away. The Song of Harmony was weaker here than almost any other place, which was the true danger of liminal spaces, and it cost her an increasing amount of concentration. Her core felt stretched thin with every line of conjured stone, with each step of the company behind her. Their mindless march was all that saved her, freeing up enough of her power to keep them going.

...neeed...

Zara stopped, and her eyes whipped to either side. *What was—?*

...want...

She flared her power, liquid Mana streaming from her Gates before crystallizing into a hardened shell all around them. Behind her, the thirteen guards stopped in confusion. Handsign fluttered down the line, but she ignored it all.

A presence beyond the others. Far beyond. The sharp needles of its Mind and Spirit assaulted her dome of potency, pressuring it as none of the others had. *The beasts are all scattering in terror. What could drive them away?*

Zara's Affinity flared, and among the ten thousand strands of connection between her and the world, one of the faintest seemed to resonate. She followed it where it flowed back out of the dark, before returning to tangle with something impossibly large above them. The vibration spread, highlighting strands that connected many of the guards with the same distant figure, before they, too touched on this creature she could not quite see.

<Zara! What is going on?> Darius grabbed at her shoulder, but he caught only a spike of shaped Mana. He muffled a pained gasp. <What are you doing?>

<A monstrosity has found us,> she signed.

<You said we were safe,> he signed back. Reed looked at the concerned guards before the drugged company. <Most of us.>

Above, the light of her construct finally shone upon the creature. It was mountainous, so great that she feared they only perceived a bare fraction of its size. It was covered in writhing feelers and paddles the color of rust, while ten thousand eyes the hue of algae-filled water fixed on them. It exuded a bloody, spoiled pressure, a Mana that felt entirely too familiar. Their connection, to Zara in particular, flared with an inevitable revelation.

She knew that Mana. She knew *it*. Felix had told her the story too many times to forget.

But how? How had it found them?

<Zara! What is it?>

Her core quivered as a being surpassing any of them opened a hundred tooth-lined maws.

<Whalemaw.>

CHAPTER FORTY-EIGHT

"Enemy above! Brace yourselves!" Zara shouted.

Her words sent a ripple of terror through the thirteen waking guards. Reed stared up in horror at the gnashing jaws close to a mile long, and those only one of many on the Whalemaw. It closed, dropping with a speed that belied its bulk, and hungry tongues lashed outward to strike at Zara's crystalline enclosure.

"Brace!" she repeated.

The ground dropped out from beneath them all, the conjured flagstones tilting into a sudden forty-five degree angle. Men and avum tumbled and slid as Zara forged a path at an angle, while above them, the gargantuan Whalemaw snapped at a now-empty space.

As if encouraged by her voice, those awake shouted in alarm and pain. They fell like a stone for ten heartbeats, then Zara curved the path and evened them out again. A few among them were injured, but not terribly as they came to their feet. The mounts, unfortunately, had the greatest casualties.

"Move! Everyone run as fast as you can!" Zara shouted. "Kelgan! Bring your people! Reed! We need your sword at the fore!"

Pained and confused, the Haarguard were at least reasonably well-trained. Those thirteen came to their feet and snapped out orders to their own sections of alchemically-dosed compatriots, and what avum that could be saved were brought along. The limping or dead few mounts she left in their own forged bubbles, soon disconnected from their passage.

Reed stomped to the front, greatsword in his one giant hand, and he snarled at her. "What in Avet's black teeth was *that*?"

"That is a creature so powerful not even I could face it," Zara said through a sheen of sweat. They were all running now, full-tilt, and she was building their flagstone path ahead of them while destroying it behind them, a constant effort of recycling Mana that did her strained concentration no favors.

Reed swung his sword as a tentacular beast wormed its way through the front of her barrier, drawn by their fear and blood and wavering Wills. The creature ruptured, its body sliced through easily and releasing a splash of shimmering rainbow Mana. "Why are they getting through?"

"Because I cannot concern myself with the lesser threats any longer," Zara panted. "I've dropped us from the Whalemaw's original path, but we must return to our original elevation so that we can exit this Passage." Beneath them, the angle of the flagstone path tilted upward just a touch, increasing slightly with each layer she reforged. "We cannot deviate too far from the Passage, or else who knows where we will end up."

Reed killed another creature, one his Analyze had issue identifying, she could tell. "It has our scent. Look." Zara spared a look back to see the huge bulk of the Whalemaw turning on itself. It was slow, ponderous, but she wasn't fooled. "It's hunting us now. We have to fight back, or else no one will stop the Inquisition!"

Zara sent spears of crystalline Mana outward, stabbing through dozens of voidbeast that swarmed around their enclosure. It also lit up the dark a touch more, showing thousands upon thousands of them moving for the company. "We have enough to fight! *That* is too much for you, Chosen Hand of Pax'Vrell! It catches us, and we won't have to worry about the Inquisition any longer!"

Reed took the hint, brandishing his greatsword as more voidbeasts assaulted the forward breach. They died with every stroke of his sword, every pulse of his savage wind magic. Still, he glared daggers at her every chance he could, as if the weight of his ire could do anything. Were he stronger, perhaps it could. As it was, Zara put him from her Mind. She had other concerns.

Zara dug deep into parts of her Mind and Spirit she rarely accessed. There, among the wild chaos of her core, she gripped a half-forgotten Skill. Intent and Will she held fast, while her Affinity traced its edges in rapid fashion, until the aquamarine light around her wobbled with the effort. The crystalline enclosure fractured, yet before Reed could even complain, Zara hurled her left palm upward.

"Siren's Song!"

An orb the size of a house shot upward, oozing through the crystalline barrier. It escaped into the liminal space and shot off in a high, powerful arc like a signal flare from an adventurer team. It lit up the dark, shining upon more voidbeasts than ever, a nightmare tide of abominations hungering for them all. Yet, the orb burst alight at its height, singing a song that was alluring as any mind-slaving compulsion. The voidbeasts swarmed it, all of them trying to take a bite of its powerful Mana, until the light was no longer visible under the weight of their dark flesh.

"Keep running!" Zara dropped her arm and did just that. "Look forward and regain your calm! We shall make it!"

A booming roar shook the inky air, so much that the flagstones tilted and tipped, turning treacherous. Men and women stumbled. Beyond her Siren's Call, the Whalemaw appeared, now set to intercept the voidbeasts and their snack.

"Siren's Song!"

Another followed, this time arcing right into its startled, but unharmed head. The orb bounced harmlessly off its massive bulk. It wasn't meant to hurt it.

It was chum in the water.

Zara may not have fought such a beast before, but she knew someone who had. The Whalemaw could not stop itself from tearing into the bounty before it. Voidbeasts died by the hundreds with every vicious snap of its jaws. Mana splashed, and near-soundless screams ripped into the liminal space.

Zara did not stick around to watch. Her team ran off into the dark.

Ten thousand mouths opened in ecstasy as it fed. It was hungry. It was *always* hungry, ever since the burning crimson might had spread across its bulk. It had thought to end that hunger before, when it had chased down its prey, but it had only been hurt by the Light of All Things.

The terrible Light.

After, it had wandered the barren Void, desperately seeking… something.

What?

The rapid growth it had experienced a few weeks ago had slowed to a crawl, despite its almighty power. Its size and shape had not changed overmuch, except the availability of its endless maws and the hundreds of tiny arms that studded its craggy surface. It bore no similarity to its former kin, imbued with such terrible potency, and they fled from its presence.

But they never got away. There was a hunger in it that couldn't be denied, one that sent it ravening after every piece of life it encountered. Hundreds, thousands fell before its razor-sharp appetite, yet none filled the chasm in its center. It had lost the one thing that would make it complete, lost so completely that it could never again be whole. The Light of All Things had consumed it entirely.

And then it heard the Call.

It had been faint at first, but something was skipping across the Void, couched in the greater dark. Enthralled by the Call, the Whalemaw had rolled its monstrous girth and sped after it. The sound would sing and fade before reappearing once again in a far distant location, pushing the Whalemaw to burn its bountiful power to accelerate it across the black. Swarms of lesser voidbeasts followed in its wake, a veritable horde teased from rock crevices and hidden warrens, all of them hungry for the Whalemaw's Mana… yet too terrified to close.

Its power spread outward like a mantle of blood and decay, a rot that ate at stone and flesh with equal alacrity, but the Whalemaw pressed on. It was driven by a Need it could not name, for all that the power within it had enhanced its Mind. A Need. A Want. It followed the thread of that Call until it penetrated the bubble of black on black, rupturing a barrier that screeched in agony at its arrival. It did not care.

The Call was stronger than ever.

Then it had seen it! A glorious light containing such potent Mana that it had never before seen! And the Call led to them, to many of them, strings of connection that tickled at the hollow in its core. One, however, stuck out among the others. This one had a surer connection to the thing it Needed. Would it be whole, finally, if it ate them?

Yet they met its Need with trickery! They fled, faster than prey should, and distracted it with baubles of shimmering Mana. Pathetic attempts to stop its advance. However, the light brought forth the hordes that dwelled in the Whalemaw's shadow. The scavengers that were too afraid to attack were now driven into a frenzy by the plush source of Mana hovering tantalizingly in front of them all.

Wings, tendrils, and serpentine forms tore across the Whalemaw's body, many caught in its grasping arms. But more still surged and gathered in a way that was impossible for it to resist. It had a Need for the Call, but it was so *hungry*.

It ate. Oh sweet glory, it *ate*.

Yet the Call it followed, the one that soothed that emptiness within it, the Call was fading. Fleeing.

Its prey was getting away.

The Whalemaw was coming for them, bellowing out into the eternal dark with terrible force. Her constructed dome shook under the pressure of just its voice. They wouldn't survive direct contact. Perhaps no one could.

All they could do was run, and Zara put everything into that.

The ascent back up to the level of their Passage had nearly been achieved. Her flagstone path had tilted upward at a forty-five degree angle again, but this time, she fashioned the ground into steps. Behind her swarmed the company of dead-eyed warriors and the terrified men and women who led it all. Kelgan and his people shouted terse orders and huffed with Stamina that was too close to being expended.

They weren't going to make it like this. Not all of them.

Even now, the Whalemaw was pulling itself from the morass of voidbeasts. She could see it in the distance. It was only a matter of time before its endless jaws came for them.

"Reed!"

The Hand looked at her, his sword never stopping. Voidbeasts clashed against him like water off the prow of a boat, all of them cut into dark spume by his blade. Zara pointed at the guards. "We are almost to the exit, but they're flagging! I need to open the barrier to speed up our progress!"

The Hand furrowed brow and made a wordless growl.

"More monsters than ever before will assault us. You, and only you can fight them off! Be ready!" Zara said.

"Just get on with it!" he shouted at her.

With a crystalline chime, the green-blue barrier around them shattered into a thousand shards. Zara seized the shards and swept them behind and ahead of them, speed forging a back-and-fore-facing half wall. At the same time, voidbeasts dropped from all directions, coming at them with flashing talons and lashing tentacles. A cyclone of steel met their charge, cutting apart any appendage that dared their platform.

Almost emptying her reserves of Mana, Zara finished her forging. Beneath them, a ship had manifested, conjured and formed from the planes of crystalline aquamarine Mana and her trembling Intent. The ship moved, following her strained Willpower and Alacrity, and her people collapsed to the ground, exhausted.

"Reed! Protect them!"

"I am!" He hurled a net of storm winds at the sky, catching hundreds of voidbeasts in it. Dark ichor rained down on the deck, followed by the splash of rainbow light. That, at least, dissipated into the liminal space quickly. "Kelgan! Get that spear moving!"

A few of the guard stood on shaky legs and retrieved their weapons. Spears and arrows lashed outward, every blow hitting a mark from how impossibly crowded the beasts were; Reed's net of winds held them back, but not forever.

"Aim for the center mass! Don't get fancy!"

Reed was shouting, but Zara let the sound of it drift away. Her eyes were fixed on the Passage they had just reached again. Beneath her, the ship leveled out, straightening and flying with all the speed she could muster. Yet, the Naiad could feel her concentration slipping with every passing instant, and the scraps of Will and Intent were barely enough to hold her creation together. And now, the mass of voidbeasts had started pushing the ship back. They were too densely crowded to push through!

"Damn you! Avet's own! Send me the strength to make it!" Zara slammed her hands into the crystalline deck and sent a shiver of vibrations through its surface. From the prow burst three-pronged blades, each of them slicing deep into the amassed void-beasts. They reeled back, pain and fear overcoming their hunger, and the ship jolted forward again. "Begone!"

They were close. So close. Zara could feel the delicate serenade of the Corporeal Realm, just ahead. They would make it.

An appalling bellow shook them all. It sheared across Zara's senses, interrupting the flow of her magic even as it threw everyone —man or beast—onto the ground. The ship still sped off, her tenuous grip on her Will keeping it aloft, but Zara could not help herself. She looked up into a cloud of gore and viscera to see eyes pushed from behind it all, chasing after them. They were bigger than her ship, blinking at her in a way that made her stomach roil. They rolled and popped, reforming instantly close by like quivering pods of pus. Teeth followed, jagged and curled, pushing in every direction.

"Blind gods," Kelgan whispered. "What is it?"

"That's… that's a Primordial!" Thangle said with a strangled hiss. "That—we have to get out!"

The ship was still moving, still flying forward with all the Will Zara could muster. Yet the Whalemaw kept pace. She wasn't even sure how far away it was, its size distorting perspective more effectively than any illusion. Voidbeasts like specks of dust hit its sides, all of them grasped by tiny clawed appendages littering its putrid flesh. It opened its maws wide.

Zara's eyes widened at the same time Reed shouted.

"Everyone down!"

A beam of heat and corrosive darkness tore through the space above them, punching past with such power it sent cracks spider-webbing across the sky. Sound filtered to them beyond the cries of the Whalemaw, the sound of something immense hissing.

"The abomination cracked the liminal space," Zara said. Disbelief dragged at her heart as the liminal space around them began to erode. The cracks grew wider. The ship shuddered.

We're almost there!

The Whalemaw surged forward, its body wreathed in rotting crimson as if it swam in bloody tides. In moments, it had halved the lead they'd managed to claim, and in moments more, it would have them.

They would die.

"There!"

To their right, the cracks converged on a twisting portal. Normally unseen in the space, the destabilizing nature of the crack had revealed it. Zara wrenched at the ship and screamed. They turned, and the last vestiges of her Mana shot ahead, into the portal.

It burst alight.

The Whalemaw bellowed, high and low notes mixing in agonizing dissonance. Her people collapsed, even Reed, but Zara held on. Fingernails bleeding against the crystalline deck, she *pushed*.

The light consumed them.

And the Whalemaw screamed.

CHAPTER FORTY-NINE

Felix knelt next to a mossy stone. Collection of stones, really. They were on the side of a gentle dell, the trees high and the rocks piled to one side as if excavated in some long-ago fashion. Maybe they had been. Felix wasn't looking for lost architecture, however; instead, he brushed aside some of the Vergris Moss and peered into the small hollows they had created.

The moss clung in dense clumps that kept in moisture and shade, which was the perfect place for a little colony of fungi to thrive.

Aria of the Green Wilds is level 55!

Felix heard the song inherent in the woodlands. It pulsed across every root and leaf, through the soil and the gentle breeze, a lilting melody that had no beginning or end. Each time he inspected a plant or even some monsters, the Skill would vibrate within his core space, feeding on the knowledge he garnered and—in some cases—providing him with more.

Voracious Eye!

Name: Modus Sillcap
Lore: Modus Sillcap were named by the scholars of the

Blue Tower in Levantier. It is a useful fungus that grows only in areas of dense shadow, life, and water Mana, typically in the interior of the Continent.
Alchemical Properties: Soporific, analgesic, useful for Sleep Tonics and Numbing Tonics.

Ooh, useful. Felix reached out and pulled the entire colony from the soft earth, careful to preserve the tiny Mana veins inside their stalks. He only knew to do that because of a few poorly harvested prior plants, and the inexplicable knowledge fed into him from his Skill. At Journeyman Tier, picking the mushrooms was easy, as long as he didn't rush.

"Felix? What's the holdup?"

He stood, his hand still gripping a selection of almost translucent mushrooms. Atar was several steps down the rocks, looking back over his shoulder. Felix held up a hand. "Sorry, found some cool mushrooms."

"Found some—Felix, those are Knockout Stools," Atar said carefully. His eyes widened. "You touched those with your bare hand?"

Felix glanced between the fungi and the mage. "Yeah?"

"Ugh, of course you aren't affected. Put them away," Atar said. Once Felix tucked them safely into his satchel, he continued. "Those knock people out with a single touch. A normal person would have grabbed one and fallen over, likely breaking their skull on these rocks."

"Oh." Felix looked at his hand. "I don't have anything on me. You think it's because I preserved their Mana veins when I extracted them? Hm. Yeah, the power is likely within those, which means I didn't rupture the delivery vessels." He wished he still had his old journal to jot some notes down. Unfortunately, the Farwalker had taken it as proof of the old Matriarch's passing.

"Mana veins? Really? I—wait. No, we have to go." Atar stopped his own curiosity with some effort. Luckily, his Willpower had grown considerably. "C'mon. We're crossing another one of those bridges."

"Excellent," Felix said. He secured his satchel and made sure both his Femur and Crescian Blade were in their sheaths before hopping lightly down the mossy stones. He'd reached the bottom, which was lush with a gray-green grass and deep burgundy flowers called Feverclutch. They were another piece of flora that the Fogland produced, a part of an endless cavalcade of useful and powerful growths all around them. It required him to flex his Will every so often, just so he was not constantly distracted by the singing of his new Skill or the interesting possibilities in the plants and flowers all around them.

If your Will was not sufficient to combat the distraction of that Skill, I'd suggest sundering it immediately. It feels strong, but wild. Karys had begun giving him unsolicited advice after the last week of constant questions from Felix. The sword had quickly realized that Felix was filled with questions, and not all of them were verbalized.

"I've got it," Felix reassured his new, old friend as he walked. "I'm not gonna be pushed around by some Skill, Legendary or not."

Atar landed behind him thirty seconds later, his hop and slide down the stones fast, if lacking in grace. He hurried to catch up to Felix, who had already departed the dell and was well into the shadow of the thicket.

"It's unnerving when you speak to your sword, Felix."

"We all have our quirks," Felix said with a smile. He'd attempted to have Karys speak with everyone else, but aside from Vess and Evie, no one could hear him. The women could only hear a faint whispering, and both found it eerie.

"The idea of being taken out of my body and forced into another is... unpleasant, to say the least. But then to be shoved into a sword?" Atar shook his head and shivered. "A nightmare."

It is an honor, boy. An honor!

"He can't hear you," Felix said to the sword.

"Oh good. I realized what I said was somewhat rude," Atar said with a grimace, assuming Felix's words were directed at him. "That spirit has been through more than I could ever conceive. I wouldn't wish to insult it."

Ahh...that is—that is better. Yes. Thank you, young mage.

Felix smiled to himself as they progressed through the darkened thicket. The thorny bramble had been hacked apart, creating a wide pathway that more than accommodated our larger members, which meant it became an easy stroll for all the rest. Beyond the cleared trail was his team, all of them crowded around the edge of what was one of many jagged ravines that streaked the Foglands. This one seemed just as large as all the rest, and the far end was even hidden by passing clouds.

"What's with all the chasms out here?" Felix asked. They'd climbed in elevation since they'd left the Henaari, but every dozen miles, they'd end up at some eroded gap between the chunks of land.

*It was—ah, if I recall correctly, the-the...*Karys stuttered to a halt, his voice taking on a quality Felix had grown to dread. It was reminiscent of the manner the Paragon had spoken when he'd first awakened. *I—I apologize, Felix. I seem to have forgotten.*

"Don't worry about it," he said, attempting to keep his voice light. "It was just an idle thought."

Of-of course.

It wasn't the first time Karys had forgotten something. He'd mentioned holes in his memory before, but they'd grown to chasms themselves in the last week. It always made the Paragon uneasy, so Felix quickly moved on. Scratching Pit's neck, Felix stepped into the group huddle his team was making. "What're we doing? Thought we found a bridge?"

They numbered fourteen, his team, which felt a little... unwieldy. Practically an army, considering the amount of force each of them could bring to bear. Less force than could be, he was sad to say. Battle had been scarce as they tried to stay stealthy, but Felix had still attempted to get the Haarguard involved in some combat.

Even a few more levels would increase their chances in the fights to come. The main problem, of course, was that monsters were too strong for them this deep in the Foglands. The average level rose rapidly as they moved further west, with almost everything they encountered being a Tier II creature.

He couldn't fault their diligence though. The Haarguard were standing just outside the huddle, watching the forest and the chasm itself for danger. They'd proven more reliable than Felix had expected.

"We did, but that is the problem," Vess replied, and Felix's attention snapped back to her. She stepped aside, revealing the pale, white bridge spanning the wide ravine. If Felix had to guess, it was four or five hundred feet across, and the drop below was at least twice that. "The bridge is guarded."

The bridge itself was just like the others they had seen spanning these chasms, each one almost identical. They were spotlessly white and made of some sort of super dense bone, not stone or wood. They hit one of them once with a sword, and the thing had rang like a bell and hadn't a scratch on it, even from Harn. More importantly than any of that, though, was how they looked. Each bridge was designed to appear to be two immense people, a man and a woman, reaching across the divide to clasp forearms. The thick, stylized arms were the bridges, and the top was so well-designed that water wicked off of either side, and the traction was perfect, even in the light rain they were experiencing.

And across that expanse was a strange… blob thing.

Voracious Eye!

Voracious Eye Failed

"Oh I don't like that," Felix muttered. "My Eye failed."

"That doesn't happen often," Evie said. "What's it mean?"

"That its either too strong, or he's bein' blocked," Harn said. "Either way, I don't like it. Smells like a trap."

"You think the Archon knows we're coming?" Alister asked.

"Felix is Marked. He might," Atar said. He brushed his damp curls out of his face. "I've heard of Marks being used that way."

"Not without us knowing. Mark should burn bright to Felix were he bein' traced, even if it was placed by a Grandmaster." Harn sliced his hand through the air, cutting off that line of thought. "Ain't no reason for the metal idiot to know we're here. And that thing is just waiting, not coming in for the kill. That means someone else noticed us."

"I've never seen its like before," Wyvora added, staring at the thing with curiosity coming off her in waves. "It appears to be made of mud and clay. Could it be a construct?"

"Perhaps. It smells of earth and rotting vegetation, but that could simply be the mud itself. If we were to approach it, I can provide no guarantee it would not attack," A'zek added. His deep voice was cautious, but he showed a similar amount of curiosity as the Farhunter.

"Okay. We can sit around and talk about this all day." Felix took a breath. "I'll go have a chat with it."

"As will I," Vess said.

"I'm comin' too," Evie said. She tapped her chain. "You'll need some capable hands to watch your back, Felix."

Pit let out a wordless, stubborn chirrup as well.

He smiled at all of them. If they wanted to come, he wasn't going to argue. Though, they'd be stuck out on a bridge over a thousand-foot drop, they were the three most likely to survive the fall, aside from himself. "All right. Let's go."

"Careful, Felix," Harn said. "It looks familiar, but I can't place it."

Felix gave the warrior a grin and kept walking, his two friends flanking him. The wind was far stronger out in the open air, and those low-hanging clouds swept across their path, each time obscuring the path ahead and slowing their progress. Felix half-expected the blob creature to jump out at them through the clouds, claws, or teeth or whatever first. But it remained stationary, only its lumpy head pivoting to follow the four.

Voracious Eye!

Voracious Eye Failed

Felix tried his Eye again, now that they were closer, but still was unable to gain purchase. The creature was of medium size, not any larger than a Human, though it was wider at the shoulder than most linebackers Felix had seen. It was also covered completely in a thick, pungent mud. Said mud oozed over its head, shoulders, and down its limbs, like someone was constantly pouring new muck over its form. Hollows in its sodden skull made the barest suggestion of a gaze, but Felix had the sharp sensation of being observed by something dangerous.

Pit trilled. *Caution. Sense danger.*

Your Companion is correct. That is an amalgam of several magics, many of which I do not recognize, Karys added.

They stopped twenty feet away from where it stood at the center of the bridge. The wide, clasped hands were below them while the rain began condensing into actual droplets.

"Hi there," Felix said. "My name is Felix."

The sound of glopping mud and the whistling breeze was all that answered him.

"We want to cross this bridge. Will you allow us to do so?" Vess asked.

Again, nothing.

"Well, this is a waste of time," Evie muttered. "Hey! You! Get outta the way, or we'll knock you off."

At this, the mud monster shifted, pushing one foot forward and raising its hands. Like it was ready to fight.

"Whoa, hey Evie, we don't even know the strength of this thing," Felix said.

"It is unwise to fight it yet," Vess agreed. She stepped forward, her partisan ringing against the bone bridge like a chime. "We will deliver violence, if that is what you wish, but I had hoped we could instead speak."

The mud man's blank face turned, slowly, until it was looking right at the heiress. A voice like a burbling cesspool boiled up from the creature. "Stand aside."

Vess gripped her partisan, and Evie made a gagging noise. "Eugh, gross."

"Stand aside? Do you wish to pass by?" Vess asked.

In response, the creature's leading arm blurred, turning to a whip that crossed the fifteen foot distance in the blink of an eye. Vess was faster, barely, but the spear she conjured to parry it was instead smashed into swirling motes of air Mana. The mud monster's hand turned into a spiked flail, smashed into and penetrated the bone bridge.

"Whoa!" Felix shouted.

Unfettered Volition!

Sovereign of Flesh!

Felix surged ahead, his skin transforming just in time to intercept a second strike by the monster's other hand. The appendage had become a wavy blade, and it hit him harder than the last Arcid. Felix was lifted into the air and hurled from the bridge.

Shit!

Adamant Discord!

Lightning bloomed from him, and Felix gripped the piece of the world that meant "up." He pulled and ascended on a bolt of blue-white lightning.

Just in time to see the monster backhand Evie out of the air.

"Pit!" Felix shouted as he ascended. His Perception flared. Pit was already moving, swooping off the bridge to catch the falling chain fighter. Vess advanced, her spears and partisan joined together to strike out at the monster's legs. Felix pulled harder on his Skill, feeling a burn in his Aspects and core but not caring.

He exploded upward and drove his knee into the mud monster's chest.

Mud erupted everywhere. Vess leaped backward, evading the lot of it, but it got all over Felix. It smelled of rotting flowers and musty water, and it congealed over him only moments later, massive, goopy arms strong enough to make his bones creak. With a crushing pressure, the rest of the mud folded in on itself, trapping him.

It is a construct! Disrupt its artificial core!

"I'm trying!"

Pit swooped back up, crying out, but his paralyzing Skill didn't take. Vess pummeled with her spears and air Mana, but the mud resisted or reformed right after. Evie's chain did even less, only managing to cut furrows in the mud's surface that closed almost immediately.

Felix was dragged down, deep down into it, until all he saw was endless muck.

Adamant Discord!

The lightning burst from him, pushing in all directions, but the mud resisted. Lightning was grounded into the liquid all around him, and the force was somehow absorbed.

Extend your senses! The core is here!

Felix pushed his Perception outward, but it was confused by the swirling contents of the mud Golem. His Affinity, however, snagged on the placid expanse of an artificial Spirit. Only, it felt alive. Felix reached, his hands stretching out, until the tips of his fingers touched a hardened coil of jagged wood. It wobbled from his reach.

Gimme that! He thought, straining his muscles to push him just an inch further.

He grasped it, and he felt his abyss rumble in anticipation. In excitement.

Ravenous Tithe!

The muck around him turned to black, luminescent smoke, and Felix fell. He landed atop gleaming bone, his heavy metal greaves ringing against the surface, and a coil of wood gripped in his hand. Green, gold, purple, and black light swirled around it before rocketing straight into his channels.

You Have Gained A Memory From Vvim!
Do You Wish To View Or Save?

CHAPTER FIFTY

Vvim? Felix's Mind flashed back to the ancient Geist in Shelim. *Did Vvim send this construct?*

"Felix? What is it?" Vess said as she jogged up to him. She grimaced at the pungent muck spread all around them. Not all of it had been absorbed by his Skill, for whatever reason. "Is that the creature's core? It was a Golem?"

"Or something," Felix agreed. He chose to save the Memory for now. He'd have to check it later. *And don't eat it,* he admonished his abyss. A quick check showed the mote of Memory sitting high in his Essence cloud, well away from the hungry rift between his cores. Felix imagined the thing growled at him unhappily, but the Memory didn't move. "I stole a Memory from it, but I don't want to check it here."

"Yes, that would be unwise. We are too exposed." She looked to the side, where Pit and Evie landed with a heavy thump. "Evie, can you signal the others to proceed along the bridge?"

"Yeah sure." She massaged her right forearm as she walked off. "I'm gonna be sore later. That thing hit harder than a Reforged."

She was right. It was strong, a *lot* stronger than Felix had expected. Comparing his memories, it was easily twice as strong as the Orichalcum Golem Felix had faced in Haarwatch. *And Vvim… built this?*

He had a lot of questions.

Felix?

"Yeah?"

Vvim is... a Geist?

Oh! "Yeah, he's an old Geist that has helped me out in the past. Well," Felix amended. "Helped is a generous way to put it, but he pointed me in the right direction. You probably know all about the Geist though, right?"

Yes. I... I did.

Felix raised an eyebrow at Karys' tone. At that moment, Vess stepped close to him and nodded to the rough spiral of wood still in his hands.

"Not to interrupt, Felix," she said. "But I would like to look at this. May I?"

"Sure." Felix handed it over. Just like the splatters of mud around them, the core hadn't been eaten by Ravenous Tithe. Which was strange. "I'm not sure why the core didn't dissolve into Essence and Mana when I used Ravenous Tithe on the rest of it."

"Yes, I am curious about that as well. And how was it able to shrug off our attacks so easily?" She turned the core in her hands, noting several deeply ingrained shapes that almost looked like sigils. "It looks grown rather than built."

"New method of Golem making?"

"Or a very old one." A frown of thought creased her face, but a smile flashed across it when she caught him staring. "We should set camp soon, so you can review that Memory. There is no point in wasting time."

Felix coughed. "Right on that count. Harn!" Felix called, though his voice was mostly eaten by the wind across the chasm. Harn and the rest, however, were close enough now that he heard him fine. "Let's set camp for the evening. We have things to discuss."

What are they doing? Why are they resting? Had the mud monster truly given the Fiend such trouble?

Captain Ifre hunched lower in the mossy stones on the opposite side of the ravine. She had no idea how potent the Fiend's Perception was, and the last thing she wanted was to be caught. They'd kept their distance for the past week, well out of even the Farwalker's effective range. She saw no reason not to be cautious, not if they were to succeed.

"Captain, if they're setting camp, you should get some rest," Isyk said to her left. "I'll keep an eye on them. If they move, I'll wake you."

Ifre hesitated, but it was true she was tired. Both because of the vigilance she demanded of the team, but also for… other reasons. Her eyes drifted down to an item at her waist. Her belt hung heavy; even bound with sealed wrappings, it dragged at her.

"Very well. Wake me the moment they make a move." She crept backward from the ridge and slid down into the secluded hollow they'd found. Tyrk was there, oiling his blades against all the rain. "Tyrk. Relieve Isyk after four glasses. I want all of us rested for the city ruin ahead."

"You really think they're headed there?" Tyrk asked.

"At this point, there is little doubt. I just don't know why." Ifre laid down on her bedroll and pulled an oilskin over her shoulders to ward off the constant misting spray.

"Captain?"

"What is it, Tyrk?"

"Why are we here?" The man was nervously licking his lips. He was a proven warrior of the clan, but he was clearly nervous. "Following that man doesn't feel right. He saved us."

Ifre sighed and sat back up. "He did save us. I would have died had he not intervened. But the Matriarch set us a task, and her word binds us. The Dawnguard serve the Wander, and the Wander is the demesne of the Matriarch."

"Of course. Blessed be the Raven's chosen."

"Blessed be."

Ifre rolled over, determined to wrangle an ounce of sleep, if she could. She tried to let her doubts settle, pushing them aside for the relief of silent dreams.

The Matriarch has her reasons, I'm sure.

Yet the item at her waist pulsed like a heartbeat, and sleep was the furthest thing from her mind.

———

They traveled a short way from the bone bridge, finding a shallow depression to shelter them from some of the wind and rain. Much as they'd seen throughout the deeper parts of the Foglands, there were parts of statues buried in the earth, appearing to be cousins to the Nymean men and women who stretched across the ravine. A large, glowering face tilted sideways out of the ridge behind them, its features unaffected by the passing of time or weathering of the seasons. The head itself was severed, which was a bit of a surprise.

"Huh, what could cut through that bone?" Kylar wondered aloud. His had been the sword to attempt to cut a previous bridge, resulting in nothing more than a strained arm and bruised pride as his sword vibrated right out of his grip. "Has to be magic, right?"

"Hard to say," Nevia said. "Crafting with bone isn't something I'm familiar with, but if it functions like stone, there are a number of enchantments that can be worked into a structure to make it almost impervious to most Skills."

"Could you cut it, Felix?" Kylar asked. He brushed nervously at his thin mustache, one he kept fastidiously trimmed, even out in the wilds. "With your magic, or one of your swords, surely you could."

Before Felix could answer, Atar laughed and smoothed his own mustache, one so pale it was hard to remember it existed. "Likely not. It's a Tempered material."

"Tempered—you mean it's System-enforced?" Nevia asked in excitement.

Atar nodded sagely and adjusted his battle robes. Felix smiled. The man did love to lecture. "It is the only process that makes sense. No bone should be so dense, unless it was once part of a beast that Tempered their Body into something greater. The Nym merely harvested the bone."

"They would have to've been of a greater Tier to defeat it, and the Skill needed to carve it..." Nevia trailed off as she contemplated the hollow-eyed face. To Felix, it looked remarkably similar to a Human, if with a slightly odd tilt to its features. "What Tier would that require?"

"Higher than Adept, I know," A'zek said in his soothing baritone. "My Companion wades in those shoals, and he cannot scratch their surface. He has tried."

"Remarkable," Nevia said in a half whisper.

"Yeah, great. Now help me with this fire," grumbled Davum.

His thick fingers were fiddling with some kindling, but the flames kept extinguishing in the misting rain.

"Oh, allow me," Atar said. A wash of flame followed, sending Davum scrambling backward. "Ah, sorry."

"Atar, stop burning our allies and come help me map out these etchings," Alister said. The man had taken shelter beneath a deeper outcropping that, upon further investigation, was definitely a carved hand. He had a series of parchments laid out on a dry mat. "I've almost pinned down how they modulate the expansion distance."

"Modulate the expansi-what?" Evie said. "You two've been over those sigils for weeks now. What's the point?"

"Knowledge is its own reward," Atar said. Evie snorted.

"Also, if we can understand these, we could push our Sigaldry Skills into Adept Tier," Alister added.

"Also that."

"That, I can square with," Evie said.

Felix let the chatter of their camp wash over him. As much as he wanted to delve into the Relay sigaldry, he hadn't the time. He sat a slight way apart with Pit at his side and let his senses spread out among them all. There were no dangers nearby, but he could feel Kikri, Vyne, and Vess watching the most likely approaches. He also sensed that, deeper down, there were a number of objects and shapes that felt different from the surrounding stone and earth. More bone, most likely. Perhaps he should excavate it?

Distracting yourself?

Felix looked up at Pit's enormous head, larger than any horse he'd seen. The tenku was staring down at him with soft golden eyes and no little admonishment. His Companion didn't think words very often, but his diction and vocabulary were growing fast. Felix smirked. "Yeah, a little bit."

You fear the Memory?

"Not fear, just—" Felix took a breath, pulling in the scents of dark soil, wet forest, and woodsmoke. "It's gonna get harder now."

Pit snorted.

"Yeah, okay. You have a point," Felix said. "It's never easy. But this will be a turning point, I know it. Vvim is… he knows more about the Nym than any of us. Except maybe you, Karys."

Vvim… that is a Geist name, the Paragon said slowly.

"Yeah," Felix said, just as slowly. "We talked about this, already, Karys."

We did?

Felix shared a look with Pit. He didn't know what the problem with the Paragon was, but it was getting worse. "Yes, he's a Geist. Old, though." Felix clapped his hands. One problem at a time. "Okay. Let's do this."

Felix clamped his Will and Intent upon the Memory, still stable within the cloudy expanse of his Essence store. He guided it down, near the rumbling abyss, and pushed it into his red-gold core. His abyss rumbled, a wave of irritation overtaking Felix from within the velvet dark. *Soon. You'll get your meal soon.* The star burst, consumed by the liquid flames of the ring-shaped core, before it spat out a wash of muted gray.

Everything around him froze for a single moment before shattering.

Felix found himself in a familiar room. It was triangular in shape and had two large bas-relief murals carved onto the walls. A triangular depression in the center featured a merrily burning fire, and unlike his last visit to the tower, the place was lit up by magelights. It was also spotlessly clean.

A number of small, anthropomorphic weasel-like creatures walked around dressed in curiously wrapped robes and bearing staves topped with small Belais Crystals. They conversed in small groups, often attended by much larger animals. No. Felix looked again. Not animals.

Chimera.

At least ten filled the sizable chamber, each one close to a robed Geist in a manner that suggested a tight bond. Felix saw several tenku, some harnoqs, and even a dragon-looking creature and a hulking, fur-covered beast bigger than a Shelled Auroch.

Wyvern and a Wendigo, *Felix noted. He remembered their depiction in this very chamber.*

"Felix Nevarre."

Felix spun toward the fire, where a plush bench was built into the recessed center. A single person was there, an old Geist.

"Vvim."

"Do you like this view of the Tower? It is a sight improved from how you first encountered it, I dare say."

"Certainly more occupied," Felix said, gesturing to the Geist and Chimera that walked about. "This seems to be an old memory."

"This one is very old, Felix. These eyes have seen a great many things, this is but one of them. The night we finished one of our greatest works." Vvim looked around the chamber, smiling slightly. The expression crinkled their entire face like tissue paper. "Forgive this one a bit of maudlin self-indulgence. We merely wished to see our family again."

"I can't blame you for that," Felix said softly. Despite the clear signs of revelry and joy, Felix felt an eerie sense of doom. Like an axe was hanging above his neck. He refocused on Vvim. "But how are you talking to me?"

"A clever twist of Spirit added onto your curious ability and carried within the fecund mud of this one's construct. This one assumes you defeated and destroyed the Muckminder."

"It was called the Muckminder?" Felix asked.

"Mhm. This one wished to test the limits of your new Formation. Impressive to have defeated the construct so quickly." Vvim hummed and fiddled with their stave.

"You were testing me? For what?" Felix wasn't sure he liked being tested, especially when it put his friends in danger.

"You have not been quiet, Felix Nevarre. All of the Foglands felt the flare of power when Naevis was claimed. The Archon most certainly did."

Felix's stomach dropped. "Is he moving?"

"Not yet. This one finds the Archon… confusing, for many reasons. More on it we cannot say. Not here." Vvim stood and climbed out of the recessed lounge area. "Come."

They stepped to a door Felix had not seen in his original survey of the room, a door he wasn't positive actually existed in Vvim's Tower. It opened out onto a balcony, and Felix's breath caught.

Shelim spread out before them, lit up and filled with a life that was more than just well-made buildings and neat streets. People were down there, thousands, millions. The city swept outward in all directions, for miles and miles, way larger than Felix recalled.

"The city was all the world to us. Our life. You see how it was in this one's youth, when the Nym were almighty, and the barriers held true." Vvim sighed. "It was not like this, not truly. This is but a reflection of our memories, stretched and held up before you. The reality was more… harsh. Pain and despair still

existed in the Empire, we were simply ignorant of it. Or perhaps inured. No matter." Vvim's small, wizened head lifted to catch Felix's gaze. "What the Archon seeks, what it is, *we must tell you these things. You must find this one's body, Felix Nevarre. There is much you must know and little time to tell it."*

"Why not tell me now?" Felix asked.

"This one cannot. Not even this method is truly safe, and especially not for this. You must find us before the Archon breaches our Tower." Vvim's ancient eyes turned dull as a sharp whistling filled the air. They turned back to the cityscape and sighed. "You have one day."

From the sky, the whistling resolved into the fall of a Stygian darkness. Studded with violet, it fell in comets of shadow that engulfed entire city blocks, leaving nothing behind but ruin.

"W-what is that?" Felix gasped.

"An end. Go, Felix. Find us." Vvim repeated, slamming their stave into the balcony, and the Memory cracked around it. "Before it is too late."

Then the darkness consumed them both.

Felix surfaced from the Memory, sucking in an abrupt, haggard breath. For an instant, he couldn't tell what was real, Shelim or the sheltered camp around him. His skin burned, sizzling with the remembered pain of… of—

When had he come to the bridge?

Felix spun in a circle, confused. The rain was coming down harder, soaking through his tunic and pants, his cloak nowhere in sight. It felt glorious against his skin, but he was concerned. Felix didn't remember walking out to the bridge, and that wasn't normal. Not for him.

Felix focused, thinking back. He experienced the Memory, spoke to Vvim, and then the—

—He had woken up. And… somehow walked five minutes back to the bridge to do… what? Why was he out here?

"Kerys?"

Yes, Felix?

"What have I been doing the last few minutes?"

You ran from the camp after groaning about some sort of fire. You seemed fine, but the cold rain was apparently soothing. You took your cloak off soon after that and came out here.

A fire? There hadn't been any sort of fire in the Memory, and the one in camp was farther away, near everyone else. "Kerys, did you see the Memory I interacted with?"

No. I cannot sense these Memories you access. This one seemed quite potent, however. Your Spirit seems to be in considerable distress.

It was, and for a couple reasons. He tried to put this incident out of mind, at least for now. New problems had arisen. "Let's get back to the others. It appears we're on a deadline."

CHAPTER FIFTY-ONE

"This guy wants us to save him?" Harn said. Night had well and truly fallen, but Felix had returned to the camp and quickly awakened everyone, describing the Memory at least twice as they grumbled.

Technically the Geist are without gender. It is a feature of their Race, Karys offered.

"Yeah, they said the Archon was besieging their Tower," Felix continued. "The same place we holed up months ago."

"The Archon himself, or his forces?" Vess asked.

"They didn't specify." Felix scratched the back of his head. "I didn't ask. Vvim said we have one day before the Archon breaches their Tower. If we leave now, we can get in and out without them seeing us. We can make the tower from our current approach, but it'd be easier to come from the north. I remember the terrain being filled with broken ruins, and the Towers are a little closer to the northern side of the city. Plus, if the Archon is looking for me, that might throw his forces off."

"If the Archon is looking for you, then we shouldn't go to Shelim at all," Atar pointed out. "What exactly can this creature tell you that'd be so important?"

"He has information on the Temple. He says he knows what's inside the door, the one the Archon is after."

"Burn me. Well that's worth it to know," Atar said with a frown.

"Should we all go? Or should this be kept to a minimum? There's a lot of us," Evie pointed out.

"I'd feel more comfortable *not* going, honestly," Alister said. "But this Geist fellow sounds old and knowledgeable. I'm hesitant to skip such a meeting."

"Does the same hold for everyone?" Vess asked. She swept her gaze across their team. No one flinched, not even the Apprentice Tier Haarguard.

"We all go," Felix said, and Harn grunted in agreement. "I'll keep most of you safe with my group stealth Skill, and Evie, Harn, and Kikri can scout ahead."

"And what of us?" A'zek asked.

"I want you and Wyvora with me. The chances of running into problems isn't small, so we need to be able to end any conflicts quickly and quietly."

"I can do that," the harnoq said, flexing the claws from his cat-like paws. Pit let out a growl-chirrup that made the panther-like Chimera grin. "You'll have to race me for the kills, tenku."

Pit's triangular ears flattened, and his golden eyes narrowed in challenge, but Felix felt a nervousness in the Chimera. Felix patted him on the neck.

"We're about an hour outside Shelim, right? A shade longer, if we come around from the north. We should move soon," he said.

"What if the Archon *is* there?" Vess asked.

"We don't stand a chance against him," Harn said, looking at all of them in turn. "If any of you come in sight of that golden bastard, you run. Understand?"

Everyone nodded. Felix had described the Archon's appearance enough that they would know what to look for and what to avoid. "Get yourselves ready. We leave in ten."

"Felix."

He stopped just as he was reaching for his satchel. The rain had soaked him to the bone, and Felix wanted to change clothes before leaving, but he held off. "Vess? What's up?"

"I recognize that this Vvim has important information, but we could do this without you," she said.

"Without me?" Felix furrowed his brow. "Why would you do that?"

"If you are not with us, the Archon cannot capture you," she said. "You said before that he has a hatred for the Nym and you in particular. You saw what he did to the Frost Giants, and—and I would rather you not suffer their fate."

The last was said from behind a curtain of dark brown locks, fallen forward in an uncharacteristic show of indecision. Vess was always sure, or at least poised, so it struck Felix harder than any warning from Harn. He stepped forward and hesitated before putting a hand on her shoulder. Dark brown eyes flicked up at him from beneath her hair.

"I can't sit this one out. Vvim is waiting for me, and I don't know if they'll let anyone else come for them." He mustered up a smile. "Besides, I've survived worse than this. I don't see any goddesses or Primordials mixing in, so we should be golden."

"Please do not jest. The things we have faced… you should not have been able to fight them back. Not as an Apprentice or a Journeyman Tier." She sighed and leaned her partisan against her shoulder, busy adjusting her plate-backed gauntlets. "But fine. If the patterns hold true, you *will* face the Archon, whether we stick you in the back or not. Just remember," she said, jabbing a finger lightly into his chest. "We fight together. All of us."

Felix's smile turned gentle. "We're a team."

"We are." She narrowed her eyes at him in mock anger. "And if you die, I will kill you."

At least, he was pretty sure it was fake.

The camp was packed quickly and quietly after that. By the time Felix and Vess had finished their conversation, most everyone had their packs hoisted, and Davum was gently smothering the fire.

Felix was still soaking wet.

Mantle of the Infinite Revolution!

A spume of chill mist spun out of Felix's channels as his Skill activated, but he restricted its spread with an effort of Will, pulling it closer to his skin. Then, he spun it, rotating the clouds of mist around himself until they became a blur. That blur turned all but invisible as it became a heat haze powerful enough to distort his vision of the others. The ice and water Mana flipped, changed to heat and flame, and Felix felt it work. It prickled a little at his skin, but it wasn't bad, and when he dropped it, he found that his clothes hadn't even been singed.

Huh. It worked. Dried them right out.

Mantle of the Infinite Revolution is level 49!

Felix had used the Skill a couple times in the last week on various monsters, but this was the first time he'd tried that particular maneuver. He was happy with the result. He felt warm and dry, at least for a few moments before the rain started getting to him again. He slung his water-warded cloak back over his shoulders, following it up with his Valderian Satchel, and faced the rest of his team. "All set?"

All of them were staring at him, some in annoyance and others in awe. "Are we all set?"

"Yes, sir," Vyne and Kylar said in unison, and the other guards were close behind. Alister and Evie shook their heads and got walking alongside Harn, the man unflappable as always.

Atar sidled up to him and slapped him on the back. "Was that fire magic?"

"Yeah. New Skill." Felix nodded at the guards as they passed. Pit came after, and Felix gestured to the tenku. "Pit, use Skulk and scout the land ahead."

Pit chirruped and spread his wings. A sharp blast of wind nearly bowled Atar over as Pit took to the air.

"Gah!" Atar steadied himself against Felix's arm. "How's that bird so damn strong?"

"The trick is to fight a bunch of stuff and not die," Felix said and started walking after the others.

"Cute." Atar matched his steps. "Back to the issue, however. You pulled the fire close, too close. It was almost like my Strength Ignition."

Felix tilted his head. "A little, but I think your Skill turns your Mana into a Strength and Endurance boost, right?"

"Yes. But the interplay in your Skill gave me an idea," Atar said. He grinned. "And it's a really good one."

I am curious about this Archon.

The question came suddenly and without prompting. Felix was crawling forward through low brush along with the rest of his team in an attempt to avoid a patrol of Reforged. They hadn't progressed that far before the patrols started, the ice warriors ranging much farther than any of them had anticipated. If nothing else, however, the scenery was breathtaking. Despite the dark of the night, the lands practically glowed with Mana. Even to eyes without Manasight, it was a luminous wonderland, bathed in the silver light of Siva, her surface far less pocked than Yyero's coppery satellite.

Is now the best time to talk about this? he projected at the sword.

I do not believe the abominations will detect you. Your Voidborn Skill is beyond them.

Really? That wasn't surprising, but that Karys knew the origin of Abyssal Skein was. *How could you tell it's from the Void?*

How could I not? You are channeling it through your Spirit, Felix. The Void howls in you.

That was a bit concerning. *Because I took the Skill from a voidbeast?*

I—I do not know. It is clear that it bears the strength of the Void Realm, but how such a thing has sunk into your core space… it is beyond me, Karys admitted.

Beyond a former Paragon? Or just beyond his faulty memory? Once again, the Memories he absorbed from Karys drew Felix's attention. They sat like motionless stars in the dust of his Essence cloud, too dense to crack or even move down to his core rings. If he could only absorb some of those Memories, perhaps Felix could learn some of what Karys was forgetting.

The crunch of dirt and stick grew suddenly louder as one of the Reforged stomped closer. Felix froze in spite of Karys assurances, yet the former Frost Giant didn't even pause. Its heavy tread continued onward, crushing ferns taller than Evie as it ineffectually searched the forest.

Blind to the Void's influence, Karys repeated.

Good to know, Felix sent back.

When the Reforged had all moved on, Felix signaled to his team, all of whom began moving forward as one. It was a long crawl before they slipped into another copse of trees before the unsteady sprawl of Shelim. Felix could just barely see the Tower they needed on the horizon, close enough that they could make it there in a handful of minutes, if he dared to fly. That was a foolish risk, however.

"How long're we gonna wait?" Davum asked after he'd brushed pine needles and loam from his armor. "Can't say as I like being cooped up in these trees, not with those giants wandering around."

"We wait until Evie, Harn, and Kikri return," Vess said before planting her partisan in the earth. It sank easily, a whole foot into rock and root-filled soil. "Sit tight. Evie and Harn know the assignment, and Kikri is quite capable."

Nevia nodded. "Glad she's out there. Girl's one of the best scouts I've ever worked with."

"She's the same age as you," Vyne said dryly.

"Still a child by her Race's standards," Nevia said. "Elves live a long time. Near twice as long as us Dwarves."

"Meanwhile, we're stuck with a handful of decades," Kylar groused.

"Just Temper yourself and live forever," Alister interjected. "You're not destined to a long life if you stay weak."

"Enough chatter," Vess said. "I would rather not have another Reforged patrol on top of us."

They settled in to wait a bit. Felix let his Perception float out from him, taking in his teammates' furtive conversations and the rustling of three hundred industrious insects and a dozen roosting birds. The winds tousled the ferns and leaves all around them, a constant, low murmur. In the distance, at the edge of his senses, a Hoarhound prowled through the ruins of Shelim. It was moving away from them, but it made Felix's gut tense regardless.

He knew there was about ten minutes before their agreed upon rendezvous with the scouts, so he distracted himself. *Kerys. You said you were curious about the Archon?*

Indeed. You say he looks like an Eidolon?

Felix nodded. *I thought you* were *him, when we first met. He is made of golden plates, though, not stone like you were.*

Perhaps a version developed after I'd begun my duty. Aside from the… holes in my memory, there was a time between my first life and this one that has always remained murky. The adaptation period, I believe the Magi called it.

Had Kerys not been a sword, Felix would have sworn he was pacing. *The question remains, however. Was he given this position as an honor, or was it a punishment?*

I'm leaning toward punishment, Felix thought. *Just hazarding a guess.*

Perhaps. Those of us who took this honor were lauded with Titles that carried over to our Eidolon Bodies. They made us formidable, and if the Archon has any of them in addition to his clear advancement, then this will be a hard-fought battle indeed.

Felix repressed the roiling of his gut. *That's what I'm worried about. I don't think we're ready to face him.*

Likely not.

Felix patted the sheath at his side. *Thanks. That's helpful.*

I strive to remain honest, Felix. It is very likely the Archon is too powerful for you or any of your team. The Mark on your Spirit suggests he is at least Master Tier. Kerys paused, and the sword rattled a bit. *But your Transcendent Skills offer you a way to affect him.*

Really? How?

Kerys hummed to himself. *Transcendent rarity typically indicates an ability to affect things and creatures far beyond your own advancement. Not for much or for long. But technically possible. Your Adamant Discord is one such Skill.*

I still don't even know what I'm doing with that one, Felix admitted.

What you are doing is grasping at something larger than any simple Skill. Kerys sounded exasperated and a bit annoyed. *You are doing things all out of order. Only when someone reaches the Master Tier do they begin to approach the fundamental truths hidden within their Skills and Temperings. It has worked for you thus far, but you lack the significance to grapple with them fully. That you have brute forced these connections by virtue of blood and Skill and your Unbound nature… it is both impressive and alarming, Felix.*

You must feel at those connections to everything. Ponder why they exist. What truth is hidden there?

Perhaps you can grasp this, or perhaps not. I suspect you must wait until you've at least garnered more significance in your core before it will truly be your own.

In either case, it is an honor to see you grow, Felix Nevarre.

What can I say, Felix sent with a clenched jaw. *I haven't had much choice. It's been either get strong or die.*

The way of the Continent since Age immemorial. The Empire tried to change that, but it seems we were only a bandage on a wound too far gone to rot. I ache that I was not able to defend my people in their final days.

Felix sent comfort along their connection, almost by habit, the way he would with Pit. Yet Kerys calmed a bit.

My thanks. It is… difficult to modulate my emotions in this state. I do not believe a Mind and Spirit were intended for the matrix of this weapon.

Yeah. Sorry about that, Felix sent.

I was prepared to die, Felix. That… filthy Urge had intended for me to be consumed entirely. That you refused, and I was shunted here? To the ancient relic of my—our—people's hero? Kerys hummed. *There are worse fates.*

Evie and Kikri arrived back first, ghosting at the edge of Felix's senses before dipping in and out like a dolphin leaping above the waves. Their Common-ranked Stealth kept attempting to hide from him, but his high Perception continued to drag them from obscurity and—Felix frowned.

Something was wrong.

They arrived in their dark copse in seconds, startling Vyne and Alister both. Evie was panting, and Kikri had tears in her eyes.

"Evie. Kikri. Where is Harn?" Vess asked. "What happened?"

That was when Felix felt it. A huge surge of ice Mana, deeper in the city. His eyes even picked out the jagged peaks of glaciers stabbing above the far distant rooftops.

"Evie?" Vess asked again.

"Harn's been taken."

CHAPTER FIFTY-TWO

Abyssal Skein is level 47!

The team ran through the tumbled ruins of Shelim, burning their Stamina like kindling. Felix was at the fore, but he wished to zip ahead and leave the others behind. But without his Abyssal Skein, they'd all get found. Felix ground his teeth and couldn't help going over Evie's words.

She'd explained that an Arcid covered in spikes, with hands bigger than her torso, had emerged from nowhere to grapple with Harn. It had been invisible to her senses, slipping in and out again with the warrior so fast she couldn't even give a good description of it. Kikri hadn't even seen the thing.

How did Harn, of all people, get caught?

Felix skidded to a stop, and those behind him did the same. Chunks of ice clung to the buildings here, reminding him of its appearance when the Frost Giants had control of Shelim. Red was splashed about, vibrant against the white and blue, while shattered stone and crumbling ice spoke to a quick, violent struggle.

There was no other sign Harn had ever been there.

"Yyero's withered ass! He-he was taken that way," Evie panted. She'd been running nonstop, but she showed no hint of slowing down. "If we hurry, we can overcome it, maybe."

"No, not like this." Felix said.

"They got *Harn*, Felix! We're not leaving him!" Evie half-shouted.

"Evie. I'm not saying that. We can't go barreling after it without a plan." Felix grimaced. "We know the Arcids are attacking Vvim's Tower, so I have to assume it went back there. Vess, Evie, Kikri: track it if you can, but we'll head straight for the Tower next, unless we see a reason not to."

The others nodded and moved into position. Shortly, they were running once again.

Evie fairly flew forward, her weight lightened and legs kicking hard off the sunken cobbles. She was using Stealth, her outline blurring as it tried to convince his Perception she wasn't there, and Vess was right behind her. Kikri did her best, but her Apprentice Body couldn't keep up with the sheer mobility of the others. He hoped that Harn had been dragged somewhere close by, somewhere they could rescue him without alerting an entire army of their presence.

He was sorely disappointed.

That is a great many adversaries, Felix.

"Yeah," Felix said to the sword. "Yeah, it is."

They'd been forced to the rooftops of the ruins as the streets grew steadily more populated. Hoarhounds, Ghostfire Simians, mantis-like Wretches, and Reforged were everywhere. There were even a number of Wurms winding between the stone, sinking and swimming through it all like water. Around the base of the Tower, however, the horde grew thicker still.

"Has to be at least four hundred monsters down there," Kikri noted.

"Five hundred and forty, give or take a dozen," Atar said. His olive complexion had paled considerably. "Far, far too many to take on."

The assembled monstrosities were tearing into the base of the Tower, fighting against living statuary that peeled itself from the sides of the structure to attack. The white, spectral fire of the Simians and the brute strength of the Wretches and Hoarhounds was doing its dire work, however. One by one, the risen defenders fell to pieces, and the pillars and alcoves beyond were splintered and broken.

"Did you know those statues were all Golems?" Vess asked Atar. The fire mage shook his head.

"Not a clue."

"Why are the monsters all here?" Alister asked. "You said they were after this Vvim person, but why?"

"The Archon's appetites are strange and horrifying," A'zek said. His lip curled from a stark white fang. "No doubt, he planned to use the Geist's ancient body for his dire experiments."

"There!" Evie hissed. She pointed into the rear of the horde, where a series of cages stood out, each of them made of ice so cold they misted in the warm summer air. They were filled with beasts and monsters, but one drew their attention.

"Harn," Felix growled.

The man was slumped in one of the larger cages of ice, stripped of his helmet and weapons. Two Arcids hovered near him, one literally hovering and covered in a haze of green-white Mana, while the other was littered with dark spikes that practically absorbed the silver light of Siva.

"That's the bastard that took him," Evie said. Felix could feel her rage bubbling across her Spirit, ready to boil over in an instant. "I'll tear it apart."

"No," Felix said, as gently as he could. "We can't take them on all at once. Not like this."

"Felix, you can't hold me back. I'm goin' in, and I'll take that oversized anvil's head."

"Peace, Evie," Vess said. She laid a hand on Evie's arm, gently. "We're not abandoning him. We must only be more creative." Vess looked to the rest of the team. "We have two objectives. Rescue Harn is priority one, and reaching Felix's contact is the second. Do we agree?"

Silent, tight nods swept through the group.

"Then, I have a plan. The information Vvim has is crucial to our Quest and perhaps to stopping these creatures' mad master, once and for all. Felix, you and Pit will take to the air and secure your friend." Using her spear, she had scratched a quick diagram in the dirt atop the flattened roof. "Evie's team will split their attention, and my team will head for Harn."

"I'm not doing the distraction," Evie had protested. "I'm heading for the cage. That thing needs to bleed!"

"It will, Evie. But getting Harn out is more important, right?" Vess had asked, and Evie reluctantly nodded. "Then you will cause the distraction. You're one of the fastest here and the only choice."

"*Fine.* But if I get a chance to take that thing down, I'm takin' it."

Felix watched with mixed feelings as his friends risked themselves again.

He had stuck with Vess' group while Evie had split off, and he kept his Abyssal Skein active to keep them hidden. Shaking himself, he pulled his Perception from Evie' progress to his task. Vess' plan. Felix's senses quested forward, burning through his Mana as he sounded Stone Shaping on top of his Skein. It was fine at first, but the farther he traveled from his position, the more Mana it consumed, quickly surpassing his regeneration and stealing away his reserves. It didn't bother Felix—he had plenty to spare—but it concerned him that he might not achieve his goal.

Stone Shaping was one of his best spells, but it had some significant limitations. Primarily it was how Mana-hungry the spell was when he attempted anything wide-scale, though his large reserves were typically up to the task. The other limitation lay in the difference between dirt and stone and ore. The Skill was designed to affect stone, not anything else. Felix had altered the Skill's pattern previously to allow for metal inclusions in the stone, though it had burned through even more Mana. In the weeks since he'd achieved that feat, Felix had done it regularly, but it was by no means easier.

Still, he had little choice. His friend was in danger.

Felix poured himself into the spell, leaving only a small part of himself to maintain Abyssal Skein. The earth liquified before his immutable Will, and he pushed his Intent to shape it all. Mana filled in the rest, providing power and catalyzing the process.

Stone, metal, and dirt shifted and parted.

It took even more Willpower not to attack the Arcids when Felix felt their proximity. Instead, he moved carefully around their positions, mindful to keep vibrations to a minimum, until...*There.*

He pulled himself back and sucked in a deep breath. He swallowed and caught Vess' eye.

Stone Shaping is level 63!

<We're set.>

As soon as they came within a block of the Tower, Evie and her team split off. Each of them had a Stealth Skill, except for Nevia, but the Dwarven mage was slight. Far easier to avoid notice if they were careful.

Evie hopped lightly from the second story roof to the street below. Her Stealth had only recently hit level 52, and she felt like a ghost with it active. Sure, Felix could track her—the jerk—but no one else in their party could, not even Harn. She felt a sharp spike of pain in her chest and sucked in a tight breath.

You better be okay, idiot. I'm not losing you, too.

Evie growled to herself as she pushed through the pain and ran to the nearest set of trees. They were waist-thick and three times her height. They were perfect. They had brainstormed the most efficient distraction they could, and the Haarguard had come up with a great one.

<Here,> she gestured at her team.

Kikri was right behind Evie, but Wyvora had carried Nevia down, much to the Dwarf's embarrassment. They quickly closed.

<Do your thing, archer,> Evie signed, and Kikri nodded.

She reached out and placed a hand on the nearest tree, whispering all the while. Angry as Evie was, she would have had to be deaf not to hear the gentle melody as the Elf's Skill activated. Motes of green-gold and deep blue Mana flickered and swayed among the branches. Evie looked all around. The trees in a ten-stride radius were all... vibrating, ever so slightly. Then, as if on cue, each of the five trees split open.

"Noctis' tits," Evie whispered. The inside of the trees hummed with a gentle song just steps away from melancholy. They were sad but... accepting.

Blind gods, I hate this music thing, she thought with a sniff. *Gettin' weepy over trees, now.*

Task done, Kikri slumped. Wyvora supported her as she rubbed her temples, likely suffering some Mana drain, and Nevia moved forward. The openings were no bigger than her square, Dwarvish hands. A surge of chimes and chill winds assaulted Evie's senses, and the center of the trees all shook at once. The holes had all filled with chunks of ice.

<Back up, everyone,> Nevia warned before following her own advice. They retreated to the other side of the street, and the three others readied their weapons.

<Do it now,> Evie signed.

Ice Mana surged, and with a shrieking blast the five trees *exploded.*

Evie shouted, putting all of her Journeyman Body behind it.

"Come and get it, monsters!"

Vess and the others hunkered beside him, waiting for Evie's signal.

"Did you discuss what the signal would be?" Felix asked.

"I am sure it will be unmistakable," Vess said with a thin smile. She was worried, clearly, but also determined. Felix fitted his hand over hers and gave a brief squeeze.

"It's a good plan. Better than most of mine, in fact," he said.

"That is not a… high bar, Felix."

Felix grinned and let out a soft gasp. "*Et tu, Brute*?"

Vess quirked an eyebrow. "Is that more of your strange native language? It sounds familiar."

"Latin, actually. I've seen it in a few places on the Continent, so far." Felix looked over the edge of the portico they were stashed atop. "I know like three phrases from school and old movies."

They were both crouching, and Felix tried not to notice Vess' nervously bobbing knee. "You think we can do this?"

"It's a good plan," he repeated.

The night was rent by the high pitched scream of explosions, paired with a basso rumble that hit the air like a drum. The horde collectively flinched, and their team hunched lower in the deep moon shadows.

The flying Arcid rose several stories into the sky, peering in the direction of the sounds, before it gestured sharply to the beasts below it. With chittering howls of excitement, several dozen peeled off and tore down the ruined streets. The flying Arcid, glowing brilliantly in the moonlight, followed quickly after.

<Now. Quickly,> Vess signed to everyone, all of them slipping off the roof. She gave Felix's hand a surprising squeeze before she followed.

C'mon Pit. Time to fly.

Harn Kastos was pissed, and he'd just woken up. Not only had he been captured—something Cal would roast him alive for when she heard—but now it was jawing his ear off.

"Why have you come here, Human?" The slippery Arcid said in a voice that sounded like tar bubbling. "What is your purpose?"

Harn ignored it. He missed his axes. These bastards took his axes. If he had them, he could have had a real nice chat with ol' Slippery. And the other one, if he knew where it had gone.

The Arcid moved closer, not walking but *sliding* on its oversized feet around the ice cage. Slippery shook its oblong head at him, and its three eye fires burned bright. "You are being unreasonable, Human. You have trespassed upon my Master's lands and offer no defense save silence. You are blessed that you were not killed outright, blessed by my great Master who desires to see any and all interlopers in his lands."

Harn snorted. "He's claimin' the Foglands?"

"Ah! It speaks! Glorious," Slippery made a weird burbling sound in its metal throat. It made Harn's hackles rise. "The Foglands belong to my great Master."

"Not accordin' to the System, they don't."

"The System has no control over the great Master!" Slippery shouted, and his spiked fists clattered against the ice cage. The blue-white bars turned brownish-black at the contact as something oozed from Slippery's metal body.

Earth and shadow Mana, Harn guessed. He wasn't good at picking out the different types, but he'd seen that combo a time or two. *Makes things slip and slide. Impossible to grapple. That's where I went wrong.* He cursed internally. *Shoulda let it burn instead.*

Slippery, taking his silence for being cowed, leaned back from the cage in clear satisfaction. "You will come to know your place soon, Human. When my Master peels that armor from your flesh, you will learn the Truth."

"An what's that?" Harn asked.

"Only power can fix this cursed world, and we've none of it." Slippery practically hissed the words. "Submit and find peace."

Harn felt the cage tremble, as if it resonated with the Arcids words, but he just grinned. The scars across his face stretched and pulled his expression into a grim specter of a smile. "I was about to say the same thing to you."

Slippery tilted its weird head and weird eyes. "What do you—"

Massive gouts of stone and dirt detonated upward, and with a joyous, bloodthirsty shout, Harn and the Arcid fell into the dark below.

CHAPTER FIFTY-THREE

Abyssal Skein is level 48!

It felt like ten thousand eyes were on Felix as he and Pit ascended into the clear night sky. His Void Skill was wrapped tightly about both of them, singing in discordant defiance of the world around it, as if daring anyone to find them. None did, and despite the cacophony at either end of the Tower, the bulk of the horde did not stop in its assault.

The Tower was crumbling, bit by bit. Spectral flames crawled up its side, followed by creeping ice and the loping advance of stone-swimming Wurms. Lattice-like formations of light, nearly solid, formed around the Tower. It quenched the flames and melted the ice, and even prevented the Wurms from gaining purchase with their stone swimming ability. Statues came to grim life, blades in hand, and cut down all those who came too close.

Faster, Pit! He could only hope the wards would let them in.

Felix eyed the levels, counting upward and trying to remember the floor with the murals. The event was long enough that it was well beyond his Keen Mind Trait, but his thoughts had grown sharper and sharper with every stat point in Intelligence and Temper.

There!

Wurms splashed back through the solid stone, repelled by the flashing wards, up and into their path. Pit dove under and through a trio of the segmented monsters, twisting into a tight barrel roll that had Felix holding on for dear life. His wings clipped the craggy carapace of the Wurms, ripping several pinions straight out before Pit could retract them. Though Abyssal Skein was active, the Wurms still reacted instinctively and unleashed a stream of white-hot flame that engulfed both of them. Pit shrieked in agony as they careened into a lattice of solid light.

The wards parted like a curtain, flashing violet and green-gold. The duo shot through the outstretched blades of dull-eyed statuary and crashed upon the star-tiled flooring of the Tower. Felix was thrown from the saddle completely and hurtled into and through one of the many inner walls.

Status Condition: Stunned for 3 Seconds

The image of a man's head surmounted by a confused spiral flashed in Felix's vision, but he just sat there until it faded. Slowly, he pulled himself from the shattered remains of a wall-sized sculpture of vines and leafy plants, only idly appreciating their craftsmanship. The sounds outside the Tower were muffled greatly, as if the attackers were far away, but tremors shook their way through the walls and floors.

A piteous moan caught his attention.

"Pit!" Felix rushed to his friend's side, finding the massive tenku curled up and nursing several nasty burns across his shoulders and flanks, as well as the damage to his wings. The barding had done its job, preventing a lot of damage, but only where it covered him. His wings and rear had been basically defenseless. Felix checked his Companion's Status and saw he was hovering around half Health. "Take this."

Felix pulled out a Healing Potion and tipped it down Pit's throat. It went to work almost immediately, but it wasn't going to be enough, not immediately. "Bud, converge and rest. I've got it from here."

Worry was reflected in those giant golden eyes, but so was trust.

With a flash of light, Pit joined Felix's Spirit. It was a weight he'd gladly carry.

"Okay. Where the hell are the stairs?"

Felix walked around the chamber, which filled about a quarter of the level, but the only feature, aside from the ruined wall, was a sculpture of a Nymean woman holding a bladed staff. As he watched, the marble woman tilted to the side, as if to let him pass, and the alcove behind her morphed into a deeper recess and a set of stairs leading up.

"Asked and answered," Felix muttered.

He passed by the sculpture, but kept his Perception and Affinity firmly extended. That the Tower's wards had let them in hopefully meant he wasn't considered a threat. Still, he braced himself for an attack as he passed the silent sentinel, but it never came. Felix climbed the staircase.

It was almost nostalgic. The Tower, the wall carvings, even the set of smaller stairs carved into the larger steps. Geist steps. It almost felt like he was going to run into Magda at any moment. Felix stopped midway up the steps to peer out of a small window. In the distance, well beyond the monster horde, the brassy knob waited at the edge of a vast sinkhole. The Labyrinth. Memories swirled in his Mind, plucking at his Spirit, but Felix shoved them down. He didn't have time to linger.

Every thirteen steps, there was a landing. Upon that landing was nothing more than two armed and armored statues. Most were Nym, very tall and with armored robes and staffs, but a few were Geists. They wore similar robes but also had a number of strange objects strapped around their hands and arms. Like mechanical sleeves and gauntlets. All of the statues watched him, quite literally, their heads moving to track his progress. If he paused, they pointed urgently upward, as if impatiently giving directions.

The Tower was alive, in some fashion. He had suspected that months ago, but it was glaringly obvious now. If he concentrated, he could even hear the faint echo of a Spirit animating the stone around him. Shaping it. It wasn't as strong as Karys, but then, it was diffused across everything.

"Do you feel that, Karys?" he asked.

I do. I suspect the Geist is in control of the tower. But he is failing. Look.

Felix saw it, too. Cracks had formed in the walls, and the stairs were sagging through the center. The more he walked, the more he noticed. Hard surfaces sometimes felt faintly flexible, as if they were set dressing, and Felix wasn't sure if that was because of his dense Body or the sheer damage. Pieces of masonry crumbled from the ceiling, streams of dust with every hit the Tower took below.

If this tower is alive, it is on its deathbed. Hurry, Felix.

He didn't need to be told twice. Felix put on a burst of speed, taking two, three, six, ten steps at a time. He split the stone behind him with each footfall, but the Tower was less important than Vvim's life. And Karys was right. Something was wrong. Now that it had been called out, Felix could feel a horrifying chill in the Spirit around him. He flared his Agility and Dexterity, putting everything into speed and blurred up the endless staircase until he reached the final landing and a wide-open, trefoil archway.

Beyond was a slaughterhouse.

Purple-blue offal streaked the floor and walls, while the smoking corpses of bisected Wurms littered the corners. Six more wove through the space, fighting three giant ogre statues. The statues were losing, crumbling with each body slam and bite. The Wurms were too agile, undulating through the floor and walls with a wriggling grace Felix hated to see. It raised too many bad memories. Pit shrieked within his Spirit, anger and hate mixed into the noise. *Kill them!*

He was already on it.

Influence of the Wisp!

You Have Enthralled A Wurm (x6) for 5 Seconds!

All of the Wurms froze in place, Felix's titanic Will overpowering their own. Wurms weren't mental giants, he'd found. The blue-white wispfire of his Skill ate at their stony hide, but it wasn't too effective against them. What was effective were the ogres, which took the opportunity to brain the huge creatures with their immense fists. Stone and dark purple ichor spattered the room, until silence took hold once again.

A slight figure stood at the very center, among the sizzling purple fluid and stained white marble. Their robes were ancient and torn, and they were gnarled around a staff of dark, twisted wood. They smiled weakly at Felix.

"Unbound, you have arrived," Vvim said. "Just in time."

The Tower shook hard.

Vvim crumpled to the ground.

"Alister! Now!" Vess cried and raised her hand. "Before the debris clears!"

The roadway above them had collapsed and dropped twenty or thirty tons of stone, dirt, and monster into the sewers below. Felix's weakened tunnels had primed the ground, and her detonating Spears had done the rest. Alister, Kylar, and Davum all threw small, hand-sized stones into the roiling cloud of rock and dirt, making sure to aim for the far side of the pit. The stones hit with loud *thwacks* and *thuds*, accompanied by no few monstrous howls.

Vyne stepped in front of everyone, planting his tower shield and shouting a battle cry that turned his Human skin into a dull gray. Vess dropped her raised hand. "Atar! Now!"

"HNG!" The fire mage thrust his own arms forward, and tight spirals of Mana vapor burst from his channels. The spirals shot through the clouds, arcing after the stones. Ghostfire Simians and half-broken Wretches lunged at them from the dust, spittle and spectral flames bared. Atar seized up, unable to move as the magic ripped through him.

Vyne's shield expanded and thickened, taking the brunt of the first few attacks. He yelped as the monsters hit his bulwark, and Vess could almost see his Stamina drop. "Do it!"

"Hah!" Atar shouted wordlessly. The spirals of Mana vapor *twisted* before winking out completely, and there was a moment of complete silence as even the monsters looked confused.

Then the tunnels filled with wild thunder.

You Have Killed A Ghostfire Simian (x15)!
XP Earned!

You Have Killed A Lesser Wretch (x6)!
XP Earned!

You Have...

The notifications streamed past Vess' vision, but she let it fade into the background of her Mind, instead focusing on hurling her remaining Spears into the confused fray. The inscribed stones—Felix's *grenades,* or whatever he called them—had done their job. Though they were cast wide, the explosive payload of the lightning stones took nearly half the already stunned horde out. Vess followed her spears with a powerful forward leap, shouting backward all the while. "Atar, to the cage!"

Alister pulled the dazed fire mage forward while the Haarguards formed a defensive net around him. Atar had used a significant portion of his Mana pool, but he should have enough left over to melt the cage. She hoped.

The dust was a swirl of earth Mana to her Elemental Eye, transparent enough that she was not surprised by the sudden appearance of three Simians and two Hoarhounds. Her Spears landed among them, detonating before she even landed and killing two of the giant monkeys immediately. The Hoarhounds were more nimble, but they had to jump away to avoid the blasts.

No no. You do not run!

Dragon's Descent!

Her horizontal momentum shifted, angling her body slightly so that she would land among the scattering hounds. Her partisan hit the crumbled earth first, casting up a shockwave of blasted stone before being followed by a razor-sharp field of air blades. The Hoarhounds yelped and fell, cut to the quick by her Journeyman Tier Skill.

Other monsters met similar fates. Vess' kata, Seven Steps of the Dragoon, had her seizing control of the flow of air Mana all around them, using it against her confused enemies. She had not yet mastered the kata, but she could feel her control edging closer as she guided the air Mana with her deceptively complex movements. Coupled with Dragoon's Footwork, she tore through the battlefield, a deadly whirlwind of blade and crushing force.

"Folly!"

The shout came from within the snarling horde, and its stretched vowels grew increasingly intense as it slipped forward. A large Arcid, easily twice Vess' height and bearing an elongated, wedge-shaped head stomped forward. Its body was absolutely covered in metal spikes that dripped with some sort of viscous fluid. A combination of earth and shadow Mana, according to her Elemental Eye.

"Folly and disdain for the truth!" Its words echoed in the relatively enclosed tunnel like tiny explosions of their own. The Arcid casually batted aside a lance of force Mana that Alister sent its way. The Mana didn't deflect so much as it oozed around the metallic man, in a way Vess had never seen Mana act. "You must all learn to submit!"

"Never!" Vyne declared dramatically. He was the closest to the Arcid, and his massive shield was already planted and growing as it fed on his Stamina and Mana. "We're here to stop you!"

The Arcid laughed, a sound like bubbling tar, and surged forward. "A foolish choice!"

The metallic thing flowed toward them, ignoring terrain and its own allies as it smoothly advanced. Vess rushed to meet it, partisan up to thrust, but it slipped around her spear as if it were made of rubber. With a casual backhand, it swiped at her face.

Dragoon's Footwork!

Her movement Skill saved her life. The deceptive movements pushed her head just a hair's breadth away from the savage spikes on the Arcid's gauntlets, close enough that she felt the tepid heat of the oily substance it exuded. What's more, it didn't stop to properly engage her; instead, the Arcid ran for the Haarguard and mages.

Wyrmling's Call!

A spectral dragon's head formed over her own features and roared with a resounding force. It was almost invisible to her, but she knew to others it was either alarming or simply horrifying.

An Unknown Arcid Is Taunted For 5 Seconds!

Wyrmling's Call is level 53!

Damnation. The Skill had an equal chance to Taunt or Frighten, and while both were useful, Taunt was the lesser option. Fear would have sent it skittering away from Vess, buying them some breathing room. Instead, the Arcid flipped in place and reversed direction, coming straight for Vess again. Its eye fires flared, and its

Spirit raged against the Status Condition she had inflicted. Vess grinned.

Pierce the Sky!

Spear of Tribulations!

Dragon's Descent!

Stamina and Mana were consumed in a flash as she launched herself upward. She flew so high that she cleared the hole above them, able to see the Tower still being assaulted and a furious altercation happening to the south. Then she came down as seven silver spears manifested all around her body, each of them following her fall and angling toward the Arcid down below. They hit, and she triggered their explosions all at once.

"Seven Tribulations!"

A storm of air Mana shredded the ground for at least ten strides, and more green-white Mana flared at the tip of her partisan just before it slammed into her foe. A shockwave rippled outward, hurling two Simians off their feet and staggering a Lesser Wretch.

"Pathetic," it spat, and Vess only had time to see that her spears—all of them—had missed the Arcid completely. Its body twisted, rotating at the waist like a wagon wheel and propelling its spiked fists into her chest.

Vess was caught, blindsided by the blow. The angle of the movement and spikes grabbed at her half-plate, while the sheer force of it hurled her to the ground hard enough to kill an Apprentice Tier. Vess choked off a scream of pain, muscling back the instinct as she rolled to her feet.

Status Condition: Broken Ribs (Minor)

Grace is level 59!

This is bad. Her Health was dropping, and the splintered bone in her chest made movement agonizing. She snatched a potion from her waist, thankful the bottle hadn't broken, and quaffed it back. The Arcid let her, its Spirit burbling with amusement. *It's toying with me.*

"Is that all you have, Human? Spears and a touch of Mana?" It lifted its arms, spread wide as if offering its heart to her. "I stand here, unharmed! This is what my Master offers you! Submission! And in exchange, you will be granted power untold!"

Siva grant me grace. I need help. Vess grimaced as she resummoned her floating spears and leveled her partisan at the slowly advancing Arcid. *Atar, you'd better open that damn cage soon!*

CHAPTER FIFTY-FOUR

"Burn, damn you!" Atar screamed, but the cage held firm.

The world was chaos around him. Growls and explosions, metal clashes, and discharging Mana Skills, it was too much. Atar focused, pushing it away from his Mind. Mana spun, uncoiling from the center of his core space, lashing whips of flame that spun up into his channels with an alacrity he'd only ever accomplished once before: when he'd faced down a horde of Reforged in their final desperate battle for Haarwatch.

His Journeyman-Tempered Aspects pulsed with the effort of maintaining his Imbued Sparkbolts, overlapped so that they created an even greater heat than usual. Still, the cage would not melt. Whatever had made it was strong, the ice Mana in the construct more than equal to the hottest flame Atar could produce.

"This isn't working!" he shouted.

"Get me my axes, then!" Harn snarled. The man's busted and scarred face was more than a little terrifying to see, and the light in his eyes as he stared out at the spiked Arcid fighting Vess...

"Alister! You try! Vyne! You see his axes anywhere?" Atar let his Sparkbolts pull back as his teammate stepped in with a flash of blue Mana. Instead, he set the Sparkbolts flying at the Wretch that pushed against the defender's shield. The Imbued Sparkbolts cut through it, drilling deep into its carapace before lighting it from within.

Vyne sagged in relief, no longer having to push back the insectoid monster. "I'm a little busy!"

"Kylar!" Atar shouted. The man was only ten paces away, but the roar of battle forced him to actually use his Journeyman-Tempered lungs. Kylar spun low, swinging his twin swords in opposing directions and severing the outstretched arm of a Ghostfire Simian. A final flourish ended it completely. "Find Harn's axes!"

"Find 'em yourself!" he cried back, already whirling through another set of dizzying sword Forms. "I've got my hands full!"

"Highest Flame, Urge of That Which Burns, keep me from killing these children," Atar hissed to himself. "Fine!"

Crown of Ignis!

Imbued Sparkbolt!

A coronet of flame blazed above him, showering his body with heat and the heady, omnipotent power of Fire. He felt something open within, as if his core had become an endless wellspring of crimson-touched flame. Sparkbolts manifested around him, fist-sized balls of fire that multiplied into dozens, all of them rotating tightly around the mage's body. He laughed.

"Step aside Kylar! Let me show you how this is done!"

The swordsman had barely dove out of the way when Atar unleashed a storm of fireballs onto the enemy. As if the Highest Flame itself touched the earth, Simians and Wretches charred to husks in the heat and elemental fire of his might. The touch of Primordial power, still tainting him after all this time, merely accelerated their demise. Indeed, it was the primary reason the few Reforged shied back, their ice armor burned by his power.

Then why won't it melt that blighted cage? Atar shouted wordlessly, and the crown atop his head blazed ever brighter. "Find the damn axes, swordsman!"

"A-aye!"

Kylar scurried off and Davum with him as Atar and Vyne held back the broken tide of monsters. A'zek, that terrifying beast, stalked through the enemy like a dark wind and was just as untouchable. The lesser creatures, Tier II Ghostfire Simians and Wretches, fell to every swipe of his claws. The Reforged were another story, too strong and tough to be taken down by much other than overwhelming force. The Chimera was strong, but its claws were not always sharp enough or quick enough to penetrate their altered Bodies.

But Atar's altered fire...that was enough. He fought down the mad laugh that bubbled from within his chest as Sparkbolt after Imbued Sparkbolt whirled outward from his Crown. The Skill, a Blessing he'd received a long time ago, was a dangerous, double-edged sword. It could conjure more Sparkbolts than Atar could ever cast on his own, all of them potent and blazing hot. Yet the power of elemental fire was heady and often threatened to overwhelm his Mind; even more so now that it was in Journeyman Tier.

He firmed his Will, pushing back another wild surge of mixed anger and amusement. He was stronger than his Skills. He was the master of his own power. As Vess danced against the slippery Arcid, and the Reforged charged his position, Atar let fly hot, sweltering death.

The sunken tunnel became a charnel house, an abattoir set aflame, and Atar its mad tender. Still they came, more pouring down from above as they were called to the brutal battle against his team. The heat built until all of them were sweating buckets from the sheer proximity, and the press of flesh alone weighed down their lone guardian.

Beams of blue force relieved the pressure, and Atar followed Alister's strikes with well-placed Sparkbolts that sent enemies convulsing backward from the agony of their insides burning up.

"Your god is potent," A'zek said from atop a pile of monsters. The harnoq had hamstrung and then disemboweled many of them, and his black form stood out against the orange vibrancy of fire Mana. "Such gifts are not given lightly."

Atar frowned. He shouldn't have mentioned the Highest Flame aloud, not around the Raven worshippers. Few people in the north had a good opinion of Urges. Still, he hadn't the time for regret, not when the spiked Arcid slammed Vess back into the tunnel walls. She hit with such force that the impact sent huge cracks spidering in every direction, and the heiress half-sank into the stone itself.

"Vess!" Atar shouted, before drawing deep on his Crown. The

ornamentation flickered and dimmed, but almost fifty Sparkbolts spat out into the air around him. "Burn you, Arcid!"

Atar thrust his hands forward, and every single bolt sped toward the metallic abomination. Crimson light splashed against the monster, turning sections of its gray metal hide black as something caught fire. Black smoke poured from the Arcid, and the thing took a measured step back from Vess to give Atar a considering glare.

"Come and get me, then!" More fire rose at his command, his core blazing hotter than he could handle. Atar grimaced and forced the power through his channels, feeling them scorch and ache. "Field of Flames!"

The Arcid laughed. "You think this is enough? You think *any of you* are enough?!" In a flash, it tore through the area of fire, stomping over any beast that was in its way. It appeared before Atar before the mage had the time to more than flinch, and it brought down a heavy, spiked fist like a hammer.

Strength Ignition!

All of the fire around them was suddenly yanked into Atar's channels, its power rendered back into the Mana which animated it. Immediately, Atar's Strength and Endurance increased massively, determined by how much fire Mana he had spent in the last sixth of a glass.

It had been a *lot.*

Atar's muscles swelled with power, nearly ripping apart his battle robes as he reached upward and stopped the downward strike with nothing more than his bare hands. At least, for a moment—before the Arcid activated some Skill of their own, and his sure grip failed. The metal creature's limbs became frictionless, slipping free and dropping down and away from Atar. Then they thrust forward, faster than Atar could even perceive.

The blow took him straight in the chest, hard enough to send the fire mage flying.

He smashed backward into something that rang like a bell and was cold enough to burn. Dazed, he looked up, only to find Harn glowering down at him.

"Get up, Sparky! Keep fighting!"

Fumbling at his waist, Atar slung back a potion and stood up, his physical stats still bolstered for another few moments.

"Don't bother, mage. You have lost." The Arcid laughed. It casually backhanded Vyne, who tried to Shield Bash the thing from behind. The shield-bearer was tossed aside as if he weighed nothing at all. "Even now, my Master comes. He has heard the sounds of your Spirit, and he grows fascinated. Tell me, why?" The Arcid walked forward, one step at a time, kicking aside Vyne as he struggled to his feet. "Why should the great Master be so interested in you all?"

Atar didn't answer. The mage didn't think—he couldn't, or else he'd have laid down and not stood up again. He ran, his temper stoked by his still-active Crown and pushed by his own rage. Spark-bolts gathered before him in a spinning ring of carmine light. "I am not done yet!"

"Burn bright, little mage. Burn yourself to a crisp." The Arcid's three eye fires blazed in amusement. "You will never—"

"Bindings of the White Waste!"

Chains of frost burst from the ground, wrapping around the Arcid with a speed that brought Atar up short. He snapped his head up.

"BREAKING WHEEL!" Evie screamed as she fell from above, and her heavy chain snapped outward into a massive wheel of metal set on its edge. It screamed downward, ramming into the Arcid faster than it could react. Supercooled metal screamed and popped, and the augmented weight smashed the Arcid flat.

Evie landed nearby, her feet slapping lightly onto the broken earth. "What'd I miss?"

"Evie!" Vess said. She had pulled herself free of the wall and put away an emptied potion bottle. Her armor, much like Evie's, was scratched and dented. "You were to distract the other Arcid! Did you kill it?"

"Not exactly!" Evie shouted back. Metal shrieked as the Arcid struggled against the weight of her chains. "They're really tough!"

"What? What do you mean, 'not exactly'?" Atar yelled. His Crown flickered and faded in the midst of his shout, setting a bone-deep weariness into his Body. He deflated and pushed his stave into the earth for balance. "Where is it?"

"It flew off."

"Flew? Flew where?" Vess shouted. She had leaped forward, landing beside the Arcid with her partisan leveled.

Ice chains snapped and popped, while the Arcid started to twist violently. Atar backed up, his drained Mana and Stamina no match for the creature. The others would take care of it. He needed to get back to the cage. Only his flames had any effect on them.

The sound of pulverizing ice brought him up short. Atar gasped and looked back at the cage to find it shattered into pieces, and a stumbling Nevia holding onto one of the bars. She'd clearly drained all of her Mana, but her power over ice Mana had sundered it completely.

"...I weakened it for you," Atar sputtered.

More ice burst, and this time, the Arcid stood up, slipping past Evie's binding chains as if he were oil instead of metal. Though its face was merely an elaborate, armored helmet, Atar could tell it was angry beyond measure.

"Y-you—" it spat as it drew itself to full height once again. "You dare!"

"Yeah. We dare."

Harn, his helmet and axes returned, stepped free of his broken cage. Silver fire flared along the length of the weapons, as bright as the moon. The Arcid took a single step back.

"Time we had a talk, Slippery." He spun his axes. "One-on-one."

The Tower shook.

"What is that?" Felix asked Pit. He was cradling the small, frail body of the Geist, having lifted him gently from the hard ground. There was a flash of light, and Pit manifested once again, though the stone Ogres took up a lot of space in the room.

Enemy, Pit sent. He sniffed the air. *Smells of… wind.*

"The air-attuned Arcid," Vvim said with difficulty. He hadn't passed out, like Felix assumed, but he was weak. Alarmingly so; his voice sounded like he was pushing mud through a straw. "Your distraction did not hold it."

Evie. Were they all okay? He fought back the urge to rush out and find out. He had to finish this first. "C'mon, Vvim. You gotta come with me. Can you walk?"

"This one… cannot, Felix. The Tower is too damaged."

"Why does that matter?"

They are connected to it, Karys said in realization. *Their Mind and Spirit are tethered to it, like an Eidolon.*

"Your… sword is correct. This one is… nothing more than the Tower itself, and it is falling apart." A wracking cough took them, until they were trembling and even paler than usual. Felix held on, trying to be as gentle as possible. "I… it is how this one has survived so long. This one was—was never so powerful as our relatives. But to escape the Ruin, this one bound Spirit and Mind to the Tower in hopes that its mighty enchantments would survive the ending of our world." They shuddered again, and Felix realized the ancient creature was laughing weakly. "It worked too well. While so many of the family burned away, scoured from the world and memory itself… this one remained. For far too long."

The Ruin. Felix's breath quickened as his Mind shied away from something, a Memory. He realized he was sweating, panting, and the Geist was watching him with rheumy eyes.

"Yes. You saw the briefest glimpse of it. This one's Memory bore a piece of the Ruin when it struck in Ages past. Your Mind struggles to grasp its true nature… even through Memory, it hoards its secrets jealously."

"Is that why I'm missing time?" Felix asked. "Why I can't—I don't remember the ending of the Memory you sent me."

"The Ruin cannot be seen or recalled, not unless it has touched you. And unless you are blessed or cursed by fate, that touch will unmake you, regardless." Vvim shuddered again, this time in fear. "Were that this one was unmade, all those Ages ago. This one had hoped to… convince you to sunder those connections with your sorcery when we first met," Vvim said. Their breathing was wet and thick. "It is not often one's life is ended by irony."

Felix wasn't in the mood for jokes. Instead, he flicked through his Skill list, wondering if any of his abilities could stave off the old man's demise. He had too much information to die here. About the Ruin, the Nym, all of it.

"What if I use Stone Shape to rebuild the Tower? Would that keep you alive?"

"It is more than that," Vvim said. "The Arcids have struck at my connection itself. It's just a matter of time, now."

Felix clenched his jaw, and Pit whined. The tenku shuffled his feet, unsure what he could do to help.

Felix, Karys said.

"Yeah?"

What of your Transcendent Skill?

"Adamant Discord? How would that help?" Felix asked.

No. Unite the Lost. I can see some of your memories. I see how you have used it in the past. It is not a Skill I am familiar with or had any idea could exist, but it is powerful.

"No," Vvim said. "That you have unearthed that Skill is... it is dangerous, Felix Nevarre. To yourself most of all."

"Will it save you?" Felix asked, already eyeing the strange, convoluted pattern of the Skill.

"Un-unknown," Vvim said. "That Skill... it drains significance, Felix. It drains that which you are to fuel that which has been. You... you mustn't use it. Not for this."

"Not your choice, Vvim," Felix said.

Unite the Lost.

The pattern surged with light, spinning into activity like a whirling dervish, and vibrations shook through all of him. Felix felt lightheaded, suddenly, but he didn't stop. He willed the Skill at Vvim, at the connections he sensed between the Geist and the Tower. Something within him locked in place.

Then the pain began.

"AAAGGH," Felix screamed through his teeth. It felt like clawed hands were gutting him, as if a creature had reached into his chest and began scooping out everything that made him *him*. It bypassed his pain resistance, the Song of Absolution utterly ineffectual against its onslaught.

Felix! Pit and Karys cried in unison.

Trembling, Felix directed a stream of Essence down into the Skill. The tendril touched, and instantly, his store was utterly drained. Every ounce of Essence was consumed as the Skill attempted to change Vvim's fate... and it was gone before it could even budge a single connection.

Shaking, Felix cut off the Skill.

Unite the Lost is level 14!

Unite the Lost is level 15!
Unite the Lost is level 16!
...
Unite the Lost is level 22!

He laid there, bent over Vvim's body, for what felt like hours. Felix's stats and Aspects, everything about him, felt strained and raw, as if he'd just barely avoided falling from a precipice at the roof of the world. He clung bloody-fingered to the ledge until he managed to pull himself back.

"It is... useless, Felix Nevarre," Vvim breathed. "Do not burn yourself up for this one. It is time." Vvim put a clawed finger to their temple and pulled back, extracting a brilliant light from inside their skull. It took only a glance for Felix to recognize that it was another Memory. "This is what you need to know. What this one can... give to you fully here. The Archon is—was—a mortal. He was sealed to that armored Body. We were there, this one's family. At the trial."

"A criminal," Felix said.

The worst of criminals, if he were to be bound against his will, Karys added. *A punishment that would be a living torment, the opposite of my own elevation.*

"More than that. His crimes helped unleash the Greater Primordial that you know so well, Felix. And after that? His experiments cost many lives and souls. He perverted the Eidolons, the brave guardians given second life."

Karys gasped in horror. *No!*

"Yes. As punishment, his Mind was shredded, and his Spirit bound to ageless metal of his own design. So that he would serve the Nym forever in the abomination he created."

Such a punishment was too light!

"So he was a Nym, too," Felix said.

"No."

"No? He was—was he a Geist?" Felix asked.

The Tower shook again, and Vvim's expression stiffened. "It... is why his crime was... so heinous. He was the hope of the War. His creations helped turn the tide of battle before we knew what they were. Nothing is so terrible as a hero... turned villainous."

"A hero? So he wasn't Nym, then what—?"

"He is Unbound, Felix Nevarre."

The Tower shook, far harder this time, but Felix barely felt it.

"The Archon is Unbound."

CHAPTER FIFTY-FIVE

Harn came at the Arcid like a storm unleashed. The metal warrior must have truly taken him by surprise originally, because the flare of Harn's Raze Skill beat back the Arcid's strange Mana with every sweeping blow. Vess, Alister, and Atar joined in again, and this time, it was forced on the back foot, unable to bring its dangerous oversized fists into play.

That did not mean it was beaten, however.

"To me! To me!" it cried, and its thickened voice boomed out into the night air. Howls and roars answered, and from the lip of the hole came even more of its horde. Hoarhounds leaped with agile grace, and Wurms swam through the earth to bear their four-way jaws and twisted teeth. Reforged conjured axes and clubs of ice that snapped in the warm air, while ice followed their footsteps like a trail of blood.

"Fall back!" Vess shouted. "Harn! Fall back!"

This, too, was part of her plan. Felix had built most of the tunnels they fought within, though he'd leaned on already-existing sewers for the most part. His gifts were astounding, but he was still only a Journeyman. The plan was to grab Harn and escape down a side tunnel Felix had fashioned, leading out of the area. Yet, as her people headed toward it, the Wurms tunneled across its surfaces and collapsed it.

"We're cut off!" Davum roared. His tusks glinted in the reflected moonlight, same as his massive axe. "Lady Dayne! Where do we go?"

Harn pushed the Arcid, not far away, giving them time to run. But to where? The tunnels were either choked with monsters or stone and debris. Vess wracked her brain, looking for an angle she hadn't yet considered. She Willed her Spears outward, stabbing one after another into the closest Wurms and detonated them. Gaping wounds exploded into the sides of the beasts, and most dove back into the earth to escape.

Atar sucked in a ragged breath. The man was shaky on his feet after wielding so much Mana, but Imbued Sparkbolts still flew from the tip of his enchanted staff. Alister was beside him, his own enchanted rapier providing kinetic counterpoint to Atar's blazing heat. Enemies fell before them, while Kylar and Davum swung their weapons in desperate attempts to stave off disaster. Nevia hung limply in Kikri's arms, the Elven woman only able to brandish her side sword while supporting the Mana-drained mage. Wyvora and Evie bounced about the battle, along with A'zek, each of them taking down dozens of monsters that came to sup on their flesh.

More came, just the same.

"Atar!" Vess yelled. A thought spun at the back of her mind, a hope. "Atar! Do you have enough strength for array work?"

The mage sucked in a shuddering breath. "Yes. I've enough left in me, though my core's dwindling."

"We will make it quick, then," she said. Her partisan spun in her grip, dispersing a Simian's spectral fire and tearing through the chitin of a Lesser Wretch that jumped too close. She explained what she needed from the mage, and he nodded before getting to work. "Alister! Focus fire on the Arcid!"

"As you wish, your Grace!" The force mage smirked at her before conjuring four pillars of blue light, all of which converged on the fluid shape of the Arcid. "Pillars of the Domineering Sentinel!"

Despite its preternatural grace and uncanny mobility, the force of Alister's power hit it like a dropping building. Its arm and leg twisted, turned out of true for only a second—but it was enough.

"RAZE!"

Harn's axe, wreathed in silver flame, cut into the Arcid's joint and severed the creature's left arm entirely. It screamed, more anger than pain, and Vess felt the force of it like a physical blow. Everyone did, and the Apprentice Tiers staggered to their sides.

Spear of Tribulation!

Vess conjured Spear after Spear, guiding them around the battlefield with all the Will she could muster. She intercepted several killing blows aimed at the stunned Haarguard, and she had just enough control that Vess was able to block or parry the majority of them. Only one got through, an attack by a Reforged, but iWyvora stopped it. The Farhunter stabbed her own spear up into the ice warrior's wrist, severing its grip and fouling its deadly strike.

Across the way, Vess and the Farhunter met eyes. Wyvora nodded. Begrudgingly, Vess nodded back.

Damage on the Arcid was accumulating, but not fast enough. Even now, without its arm, it fought like a demon, fending off Harn with its remaining arm and legs. It was all taking too long. The Arcid said its Master was on his way to them. *We have to end this and find Felix. Now.*

"Atar!"

"Not yet!" he gasped. Lines of light flickered at his feet as he scribed increasingly complex forms on the ground. Vess was not sure if the fire mage would complete his work in time. There was little choice.

"Farhunter! Harnoq! Defend our people!" Vess ordered, before she leaped straight into the air.

Pierce the Sky!

Dragon's Descent!

She dropped back down, slamming into the earth just behind the Arcid. It pivoted smoothly and intercepted her sudden thrust.

"Come to die, spearwoman?" it burbled at her.

Vess did not respond, only grimaced as she went to work.

Unbound. The Archon is Unbound.

Felix worked his mouth soundlessly for several seconds. It

was… he couldn't quite process the enormity of what he'd just heard. "Wha—how?"

"Same as you… summoned in great need, to fight the War." Vvim's voice was threadier by the second. They held the wobbling Memory light in their small, wrinkled hand. "Take it, Felix. Before this one fades altogether."

Felix clenched his jaw, cutting off the wild thoughts that rampaged through him. He brought a hand down to the light, and it soaked into his channels like water from a frigid lake. It almost hurt, it was so cold, and it traced a direct path down into his core. Like a rock, sinking to the bottom.

Leave it alone, he commanded. The abyss rumbled, but the Memory sat fixed among the stars of Karys' own recollection, though shining far brighter. Felix hadn't the mental bandwidth to worry about what that meant for the abyss, and he quickly pulled his awareness back up into his body.

The Tower shook far more violently than ever before. Hard enough that pieces of the walls cracked and fell, shattering against the grime-covered floor tiles. Felix swallowed and breathed, steadying his pulse with an effort of Will and the control afforded by his Tempered Body.

"I have it, Vvim."

"Good. It will… tell you more. It will… reveal… all that this one knows." Vvim shuddered, and they suddenly felt lighter than ever before. It was as if Felix held a piece of cloud, and only the solidity of the Geist's robes convinced him otherwise. "The Tower… will fall. That Arcid is close to breaching our… last line of defenses."

Felix was conflicted. He wanted to save the old creature, but he had no idea what to do, and...Vvim seemed so tired. Worn thin, almost. The Geist's Spirit thrummed, held open for Felix's perusal, and he could hear that there was only weary acceptance left.

"What can I do?" Felix asked.

"Bring this one… to the balcony?" Vvim asked.

Felix did so, side stepping the Ogre statues that had already begun crumbling. The far end of the room had a cleverly hidden door latch, one Felix had seen opened in his Memory previously. It was easy enough to unlatch, even holding the ancient Geist. They stepped out onto a narrow balcony, and Felix beheld a night of fire and blood.

Below, the horde raged against the base of the Tower, and beyond a massive hole torn in the earth. Vess' plan was working, as far as he could tell.

"Ah yes… the stars call to us, Felix." Vvim's breathing had suddenly gotten clearer, so much so that Felix couldn't help a sudden surge of hope. "The Geist have a great… many stories about the stars. Each one is an ancestor, a long-lost family member that would watch over us. A superstition this one cannot help but love. Yet the stars are nothing more than flames in the dark, cast into the Void by the act of Creation. It is from there you were summoned, Felix Nevarre."

"Earth is beyond the stars?" Felix asked. "That figures. I always assumed this was somewhere far, far away in space."

"Mm. The Void is many things, often simultaneously. It appears empty, as you know, but it teems with life. No place in Creation is without it, not truly." Vvim grew stronger with each passing word, until their voice didn't ripple with the cloying thickness of pain. "Yet it is an end, of sorts. A last stop before the Ethereal takes us."

"Desolation," Felix said, remembering. The white *fullness* of the hole to Desolation, the grinding chaos of everything all at once.

"Some call it such, yes. It is but the Confluence, where all our Spirits rest before being turned back out into Creation." Vvim looked at Felix, eyes bright and curiously free of pain. Their Spirit was placid. "You do not believe."

"No," Felix admitted. "No I don't."

"You will, child. If you are what this one knows you to be, you shall learn a great many things before the next Song is sung."

Felix looked up into the stars, momentarily lost in the beauty of them. Despite everything. "Why not tell me now, Vvim?"

"It would only delay the inevitable," Vvim said. "We shall meet again, this one thinks. The Song is never over, not really. It is merely the… tempo that changes."

"What do you mean?" Felix asked. He looked down, and his gut climbed up into his throat.

His arms were filled with a fading smoke, wrapped with tattered cloth. Then, even the robes turned to dust in his grip.

Vvim was gone.

The Tower shook, more violently than ever. So hard, Felix felt the entire thing shift to the side. Swallowing, he looked back through the doorway to see the Ogre statues falling to pieces. Whatever magic Vvim's presence worked on the Tower, it was gone now. That meant the Tower would fall soon.

Unfettered Volition!

Felix flipped backward, narrowing avoiding the sharpened edge of shaped air as it sliced through the balcony floor below. His Perception had tagged the approaching Skill and the creature that hurled it.

"Arcid," Felix hissed. Within him, both Pit and Karys shouted their annoyance.

Hovering in thin air, the gangling Arcid looked almost regal wrapped in thick flows of green-white air Mana. Stunted objects clung to its back, like a suggestion of vestigial wings, and a narrow, pointed helmet reminded Felix strongly of a heron or egret.

"You are the one our Master warned us about," it said. Its voice was melodious and feminine, though its form was androgynous. "The Nym. He told us you were dangerous." It tilted its head at them. "You do not seem dangerous, though I cannot Analyze you."

Felix didn't answer. It felt like he was looking at himself from a distance.

"The great Master will reward me if I bring you in," it continued. Hands equipped with metal claws lifted toward Felix. "Do not move, if you value your pitiful life."

"Pit?" Felix said.

"What?" asked the Arcid.

"Your turn," Felix added.

Before the Arcid could grasp his intent, a flash of light and dark feathers made the realization all too clear. Pit's flurry of Frost Spears drove the point home.

Flaring his Adamant Discord, Felix followed them both into the skies.

Beaten and bloody, Vess sucked breath through a broken nose. Everything smelled and tasted of copper and salt, as if the world had been coated in blood. She lingered back, while Harn, Alister, and Atar traded blows with the Arcid.

It fought them like the machine it had become. Though it could be hurt—its severed arm had proven that point—it could beat them in other ways. Its Stamina was bottomless, which while slow, meant it could outlast all of them, given enough time. All of them were running ragged.

Atar had his shoulder torn, and Alister had to drop his rapier when the Arcid smashed his dominant hand. The both of them used their limited Mana pools to harry and confine the Arcid, but they no longer had the leverage to truly hurt it. Harn was hurt, too, but his armor took the brunt of the creature's rage. Only, his axes couldn't find purchase on the thing anymore. It was too mobile, too relentless for even Onslaught to finish off.

Yet they kept trying.

The Haarguard, Harnoq, and Farhunter fought off the horde. Less remained of them than ever, but still a few fell down from above every few minutes, called by the Arcid's thick, bubbling voice. Truly, Vess was impressed with their tactics and commitment. They hadn't been overwhelmed. In fact, they'd fought back waves of beasts that would have taken down lesser combatants. They had proven themselves brave and reliable, even the Henaari, she could admit.

But it wasn't enough.

Vess skidded backward, her partisan warded off by the whirling spikes of the Arcid's form. Her hands buzzed, almost numb from the vibrations of her many assaults. She needed more power to pierce its defenses, to end it. They had so little time before the Archon would arrive—they could not afford to assume it was a bluff.

Desperate, Vess cast her mind up, ascending to her mountain temple in the heart of her core space. She fairly flew up the ten thousand steps, each one carved with painstaking details taught to her by her family's traditions. It was a taxing effort, as each step felt like the space around her was compressing, folding down upon her shoulders like the mountain itself was falling. Still, she took the steps as fast as she could, until at last, she stood at the top, before her Temple of the Winds.

Dragoons do not jump. They do not fall. They ride the winds.

Outside of herself, a spiked fist dropped with cataclysmic finality, but Vess flowed out of the way. The Arcid punched the ground, sending up a spray of dirt and stone chips. Vess' spear flashed forward, thrusting in a lightning flurry. Each hit struck sparks from its metallic hide, but the Arcid grunted in pain and hunched to defend itself.

Within, Vess felt a stillness to her Temple. A curious weight fell over everything as her limbs described strike after strike against her enemy, as if her Skills were dragging against a current. She couldn't penetrate its defenses, no matter her speed or Strength, and the Arcid bashed the tip of her partisan away with an angry swing.

"You do not even harm me, Human!" It smashed another two silver Spears she conjured, not even caring that they detonated against it. "You are *nothing!*"

It flowed around her partisan and shoved its spiked fist into her arm and shoulder. The metal spikes punched through her armor as if it were nothing and tore deep into her body.

Vess screamed and dropped her spear. The Arcid laughed and reached for her with its other arms, fast as lightning, shredding the armor there, too. Vess' eyes were wide, wild with pain, and feverish. The Arcid seemed to breathe it in, to enjoy it.

"It will be over soon, Human," it burbled. "Just surrender."

Vess grappled it. Her bloody hands latched onto the sides of the Arcid's spikes, and she *twisted*. The constructed abomination sucked in a breath of surprise but began to slip away regardless, her Strength not enough to halt its movements. It twisted, sliding, placing its clamp-like hands on her and wrenching her limbs. She screamed.

Without warning, chains wrapped around it, clattering against its metal hide like a warhammer hitting a bell. Both of them, the Arcid and Vess, were staggered as the bladed chains dug in and burst alight with purple-white Mana vapor.

"*You!*" it hissed.

"Me!" Evie shrieked back at it before leveraging her freezing steel core. Power poured through her channels, all but visible to Vess' Elemental Eye, and ice snapped across the Arcid's neck, chest, and shoulders.

Vess pushed its arms back, just a bit. Her Strength surged with desperation.

"Let her go!" The chains increased in weight, enough to drop the Arcid to his knees. It still had Vess though, unable to overcome the heiress still within its grip. "Let her go, or I crush you to scrap!"

"Your magic is weak!" The ice shifted, sliding as if it were melting atop the creature. Evie's eyes widened, and Vess couldn't get a breath in—the thing's grip only tightened on her diaphragm as it lifted her entirely. "You could have had the peace of submission! You could have been part of the Great Work!" It stood, fighting against Evie's chains, dragging Vess forward. The ice quickened along its frame, but it was nearly free. "No longer. The great Master will toy with your corpses before He's through! And I! I will laugh!"

Vess screamed, putting everything she had into a single, final kick. The Arcid's three eye fires went wide with pain and surprise as its knee folded. It stumbled, as if in slow motion, staring at Vess in a fury. It was unable to see its fate, however.

"Here's your peace, Chuckles."

Two axes, wreathed in flame, severed its blighted head.

CHAPTER FIFTY-SIX

Pit wheeled across the clear night, air Mana surging to assist his every movement, yet the Arcid kept pace. It was half as large as him—closer to Human-sized than anything—and its wings were but stumps of metal lattice poking from its back, yet it, too, flew with preternatural grace. It seized upon flows of air Mana, whirling it about itself in a manner that acted both as shield and a source of lift.

He knew it was a shield, because the Frost Spears he kept hurling at the Arcid were turned aside just before they'd impact. Each spear was met with a blade of compressed air, shattering some while the others slipped toward Pit's form. The creature fired Wingblades of its own; many missed, but a few tore bloody furrows in his flanks, while others deflected harmlessly off his barding.

Pit felt the flare of emotion and hardened Will well before Felix's arrival. A flash of electricity and a sense of screaming connections hurled his Companion across the battlefield, an orb of dark acid sent flying as he passed. It, too, was caught up in the circulating shield and sent awry.

"You are both within my realm," the Arcid intoned. Its voice sounded like too much air pumped through empty pipes. "Foolish."

Pit's response was to flank and send more Frost Spears at the creature. The surprise angle caught it at least a little, and a single spear clanged off of its thick metal skin. Pit cried out in frustration, while Felix cut loose his Adamant Discord and dropped from on high. His hand snapped out, kindled with blue wispfire.

Sympathetic wispfire flickered and surged across the flying Arcid, but it failed to take hold. The failure didn't stop Felix. Pit didn't think anything ever could, not for long.

Still, a distraction would be useful.

Frost Spear!

While the Arcid dodged the forest of Frost Spears Pit unleashed, Felix shot upward on a bolt of lightning, blade and bone held in either hand. His body twisted, corkscrewing in a way Pit had shown him once or twice, and both weapons began to glow with a terrible, golden power. They hit, Felix and Arcid, and Mana burst in all directions. Pit had to shield himself with his wings, dropping him like a stone, before he recovered enough to peer up.

The Arcid hung, its shield of air Mana sputtering and depleted, and a large chunk of its torso had been carved apart. Felix was dozens of strides beyond it, above it, twisting his body into a flip that reoriented him back downward. Lightning gathered across his shoulders, and his weapons led the way once more.

"SKREEEAAWWW!"

Arcid Number 55391 Is Stunned For 3 Seconds!

Cry is level 56!
Cry is level 57!
Cry is level 58!

Pit preened as the Arcid suddenly seized and fell from the sky. He hadn't expected his Cry to work, but the creature was hurt by Felix's terrible ability, channeled through his weapons. The one that damaged Skills.

"No, you don't!" Felix shouted, and the lightning around him flashed. He dropped like a spear from the heavens, blade and bone meeting metal spine. The Arcid let out a piercing scream, and Felix drove him into a tumbled roof sixty paces below.

You Have Killed Arcid Number 55391!
XP Earned!

You Have Gained A Level!
You Are Now Level 56!
You Gain +2 PER, VIT, +1 END, +2 INT, +3 WIL, +4 AGL, DEX!

Pit growled in frustration. He hadn't been able to destroy the enemy before Felix got involved. His magic had been too weak, too easily deflected.

He had to get stronger.

Pit circled down, eyes fixed on the punctured ruin Felix had landed upon. His friend seemed mostly unharmed, but Pit had grown cautious. He swept out his Perception, scanning the ground and sky for enemies as he descended. None were near them, but many were still assaulting the Tower or pouring into the deep hole their friends had made. Dangerous, all of them, in number if not in capability.

Friends!

The hole was widening, and a number of brilliant flashes of light came from deep within. Fire and ice and air and pillars of blue force. Pit could feel a tremolo in the Harmony all around him, a scratching, querulous note struck deep in that sinkhole.

And there was an answering cry from the west. In the mountains.

Felix!

Pit dove the rest of the way, tucking his wings for speed. He snapped them out just as he reached the dusty roof, and alighted with a heavy crunch. *Felix! Enemy! It is coming!*

For his part, Felix stood above the shattered Arcid and feasted. Ravenous Tithe pulled its entire form into dark smoke, this time even its metal shell, all of it. It spiraled through his channels, and he split half of it between his stores and his hungry abyss. The dark space between his cores gobbled up the Essence rapidly, greedily, and wanted the rest, he could tell. Felix refused.

I do not trust that thing inside you, Felix, Karys remarked. The blade in his hand still glowed slightly from the Mana and Skills he'd channeled through it.

"Yeah me either," he admitted.

It takes and takes, yet it gives nothing. What exactly does it do with the potency it has consumed?

He had no idea what the abyss was, and had in fact assumed it was some sort of black hole at the center of his little cosmos. Now it had a voice, of sorts, a will at least. Felix was calling it his Hunger now, that portion of the Maw that had sat heavily in his Mind and Spirit before. Now it was separate, sort of. Manageable, maybe. He'd give it what it wanted as long as it listened to him, as long as Felix saw no danger in it.

Who knew when that would change?

There was a heavy crunch above and a large shadow loomed over the hole he and the Arcid had made. *Felix! Enemy! It is coming!*

Felix's nostrils flared, and he jumped. The ruin collapsed beneath him, but he made the roof in time to jump again. Pit fed him a swift collection of sense memories, of what he'd seen from the air.

"Vess," he half-whispered.

Adamant Discord!

Felix hauled back on the connections around him, catapulting himself into the air in a sharp, parabolic arc. Pit vanished in a flash of light as he converged, coming along for the ride. The three of them hurtled first upward and then down, chased by lightning all the while.

The horde below them had turned to utter chaos. Where previously there had been an orderly madness to their attacks, now it was all-out carnage. Ghostfire Simians fought Wretches, Wurms ate both the former, leaving only the Reforged to dully follow their former orders. Felix took in a dozen of the ice warriors still assaulting the Tower as it listed to the side and had to fight down the powerful urge to do violence to them. Instead, he focused on the sinkhole, where his friends were even now.

He flashed across the sky with such swiftness that he barely had time to prep his Skills. Yet, before Felix and Pit could land amid the horde, a large ring of sigils lit up the night. Fire and metal Mana stabbed upward, geysers of power fueling an array that brightened from campfire to inferno in the space of a blink. Felix shielded his eyes as he fell toward, just as the array burst outward laterally across the bottom of the sinkhole.

Hundreds of monsters burned. Howls of pain and fear filled the dark, a terror that shook Felix's Affinity so hard it felt like a physical blow. Felix peered down, still falling, an orange-colored shell of light surrounding his friends. Around them, devastation.

Adamant Discord!

Felix flared his Skill, dragging on the connections he could still sense among the char. As he struck the broken earth, he *pushed*, cratering the ground to the tune of thirty feet while all around him, the field was swept utterly clean. Lighting chased the enemies upward as they were launched directly into the air, stabbed and burned and crushed by the deadly force of his Transcendent Skill. Felix screamed with the pain of it, but he did not stop.

Ravenous Tithe!

Gripping their connections tight, Felix tore all of them apart. Hundreds turned to luminescent black smoke, and their Essence was ripped straight into Felix's channels. His store was quickly replenished, even with the tiny amount he allowed into his Hunger. The thing in his abyss roared in primal triumph.

Manifestation of the Coronach is level 47!

Among his friends, a golden glow proliferated, his Rallying Cry status affecting them. Felix leaped up, relying only on his physical stats, and landed a few feet shy of their fading shield. It flickered away moments later, and Felix got a better look at his allies.

"Atar, Alister, all of you," Felix gasped. They were a bloody mess. "Pit."

A flash of light had his Companion step out to help everyone to their feet. What quick tonics and potions they had were quaffed quickly, and Pit encouraged those hurt the most to climb atop him. That meant Atar, Nevia, and Kylar. The mage had spent himself too much on that inscription array, and from the way Harn was holding his head, the axe warrior had to put in some of his Mana as well.

Thankfully, the effect of his Rallying Cry meant their regenerations were all doubled. It would, hopefully, go a long way to healing the lot of them.

"Vess!" Felix finally saw her, leaning heavily against Evie. Both of them were covered in blood, but Vess' armor was punctured in several places along her arms, shoulders, and chest. Felix rushed to their side, but was terrified to jostle her wounds. "What happened?"

"Arcid was a beast," Evie grunted. "Hard to pin down, so this idiot decided to keep it in place by skewerin' herself!"

"It was… not entirely my choice," Vess said. Her Spirit was exhausted, but victory sparked along its surface, all but hiding the deeper fears and worries. "Felix, is—did you succeed?" Vess asked with a strangled cough.

Felix only nodded. There'd be time later.

"We have to leave now. The Archon is coming, and I've no idea how soon he'll arrive." Felix looked at everyone else. "Can everyone move? Swiftly?"

"We will," Harn grunted. "Ain't got a choice, do we?"

Ifre and her Dawnguards had given the ruined city a wide berth. They had watched as the Fiend and his team ran headlong into its streets, dangerous as they were, and shook her head. No matter their orders, she wasn't bringing her men into the city. It was packed full of monsters, all of them beholden to that creature under the mountain.

No, Ifre instead circled the outer limits, keeping to the shadows all the while. She needn't have bothered. There arose such a cacophony in the city that no amount of stick-snapping and rock kicking by her small party would have alerted the beasts. Lights of fire and discharged Skills flashed deeper within, followed by the near-constant roar of monstrous voices. Once, Tyrk was certain he saw something flying above the clouds. Lightning he said, but no storm.

Ifre silenced him with a glare. They kept moving.

Beyond the city now, the Captain of the Dawnguard waited with her men. It was not an ambush, though it felt that way, skulking as she was beneath the auspices of the Raven. The item at her side kept up its continuous pulse, active despite her fiercest wishes. It was a desperate move, devout as it may be, and the longer it went on, the longer she felt more uncomfortable.

Now, seeing the shape of the Fiend resolve out of the darkness, after having clearly battled a city's worth of monstrosities, Ifre was reconsidering their course of action. This man and his team were not ones she wished to trifle with, no matter the justifications.

"Captain?" Isyk asked.

"Hold," she ordered. They were around a half league from the Fiend's team, running at full speed up into the western mountains. They were avoiding the creature's citadel, thankfully, but that meant they were going over the peaks in far less hospitable places. Places she would have to follow.

"We maintain distance. I've no idea how much they can sense. Not any longer." Ifre looked back at the ruined city, now aflame. One of the massive towers had fallen, taking several others with it.

"How—?" Tyrk asked, staring back at the burning ruins as well. "They slaughtered their way through that city."

"And paid the price for it," Ifre noted. A number of them were bloody and afflicted with a series of status conditions. "They are likely weaker now than ever before."

"Then... we strike?" Tyrk said, but his voice trembled with barely restrained unease.

"No," Ifre said with a frown. Tyrk jerked back from her expression. "That is not our task, Tyrk."

"Would it not make it easier to accomplish?" The unease in his voice resolved into something harder, if brittle. "They're dangerous, just as the Matriarch said. They do not deserve the Temple."

"We are not assassins, child," Ifre admonished with a gathering ire. "If that is the role you seek, then you have faltered in choosing the Dawnguard. Still your tongue before I cut it out."

Tyrk sank lower into the brush, but Ifre could only hope he'd taken her warning to heart. They were set a task, but she would not be responsible for the death of the man who saved her. Who saved so many of her people.

"The Temple is beyond these mountains?" Isyk asked. Ifre breathed a sigh of relief at the offered change of subject.

"So it would seem," Ifre said. She climbed up from her belly and motioned to her men. "Come. Or else we'll lose them."

CHAPTER FIFTY-SEVEN

Light and sound swirled in a mad, unrelenting cacophony. The skin of the world stretched around them, filled with radiance and utter nothingness, extremes that threatened to tear sanity itself from their Minds. All that held them together was a whisper thin glimmer of power, a construct in the vague shape of a ship, wrapped around them like a cocoon.

Without warning or fanfare, they burst from the skin between Realms. Zara's ship of light turned to smoky shadow within seconds of touching the Corporeal Realm, and the Haarguard collapsed to the sodden earth. A scream shook the portal behind them, enough that ears and eyes began to bleed, and Zara made a final effort of Will and Intent. The portal unraveled, also becoming as smoke then as nothing at all.

Zara fell back into the mud and let the rain wash over her.

When next she awakened, it was to the muffled groans of the guards. The rain still poured, and she found herself in a shallow pool of mud water and her clothes soaked through. Metal clanked, and leather scraped softly against itself as the others shifted or stood. Zara came to her feet, though not without struggle; it felt as if her stomach wanted to turn itself inside out, and her head felt liable to explode if she so much as breathed incorrectly.

A pair of feet tromped through the mud, splashing it carelessly toward her.

"Reed," she whispered, playing gentle with her head.

"Sorcerer," the Hand growled back. "What in Avet's name was all that?"

"An unexpected visitor," she admitted. "A denizen of the Void that found its way into the dark between Realms."

"You speak of the Void again, as if it were true and real. This *creature* was a monstrosity on par with nothing I've ever faced. Yet, I recognized its stink." The Hand stepped closer, his huge body dwarfing Zara's. Heat steamed from him in the chill rain, and thunder rolled in the distance. "That was a Primordial, Sorcerer. How? How could two Primordials cross our path within a span of months?"

Zara closed her eyes and looked up, letting the cold water sluice some of the grime from her face and hair. "Ill times come for us all, I'm afraid." She peered at the Hand. The man was sporting two cuts across his lips and nose, though they were closing slowly. Perhaps with his advanced Body, they'd heal without a trace. Perhaps not. "Worse comes if we do not move."

"So you say," Reed growled.

"So it is," she shot back. "Do you think I'd have risked all that for a paltry threat? Hm?"

Reed grunted and looked away.

"No. I'll not have discontent at my back. If we are to save Haarwatch and everyone associated with it, your *ward* included, then we will work together." Zara let some of her power sing through her channels, a rhythm that even the Hand could recognize. "Or not at all."

Reed ground his teeth, so loud she could almost hear a molar break, and he nodded before swiftly marching away. She watched him, eyes still bright and Spirit still stoked with irritation.

Fool of a man, you'll have us waste ourselves against one another. Zara checked her senses, extending them as far as she dared. They were close, and she could not detect the redcloaks' particular brand of power. "We must all of us move on, quickly. Setoria is but a half-day away."

"Half a day's ride?" Kelgan asked. His left side was a mass of bruises from their dangerous journey, though he still held his spear with a sure grip. "We've lost most of our mounts. And that potion… It still addles the others."

He was right, of course. Zara should have addressed that first, but her Mind and Spirit felt muddled. The Long Passage had taxed her more than she had anticipated, especially at the end. "The mounts, we can do nothing for, but the potion should wear off in a few glasses."

"And until then?" Thangle asked, somewhat meekly. His beard was matted with mud and rain, and his eyes were rimmed with dark circles.

"Until then, we march. Mount those we can, and we take to the road." Zara's voice was a whip crack, louder than thunder. "Move!"

Those who could snapped into action, securing their still-drugged allies to avum and pulling the thick cloth blindfolds from the birds. They weren't nearly as frazzled as on shorter jaunts, but their Spirits quailed for moments before they recognized the firm earth beneath them. The potion-dazed guards, on the other hand, were as murky as the puddles. They merely followed the commands of the others with rote movements and a survival instinct buried in all mortals.

They'll be fine, she reassured herself. *The potion was a low dosage. I only fear for the distance we have to cross yet.*

They had not emerged where she wanted.

For much of the day and well into night, they traveled, having emerged in the early morning. Zara had little clue how many days had passed or how few, but her senses assured her that Setoria was close, and the redcloaks hadn't yet overtaken them.

They had gained time, that was clear, yet what little they had felt squandered as the company was forced to a steady half-march. The guards who were fully aware were bedraggled and sore, aching in places they had no names for and which they could not properly explain, even to themselves. Aching feet and pulled muscles were the least of it.

The flight across the liminal space had strained their Minds and Spirits beyond what most would consider natural, and she was lucky they hadn't lost anyone. It was a risk that was as likely as the beasts reaching them through her defenses, but it existed. A part of her felt ashamed at her deception, but the greater portion knew it was necessary to keep them going. They were given a Choice to enter the dangerous Long Passage, and that had been enough.

Still, every one of them had a strained core and bruised Aspects. Skills were not used overmuch, and those with Mana pools had trouble regenerating them. On top of it all, the rain never once let up. A steady, cold drizzle seeped down collars and into boots, driving an unseasonable chill into their bones. All-in-all, a miserable march, one that extended well into the night.

They rested, barely, but a sense of urgency let none of them sleep longer than a handful of glasses. The stakes of their mad flight to Haarwatch's sister city was known to all of them, their fears shared equally. For her part, Zara couldn't rest at all, and instead spent her time staring into the wet dark, as if her Will alone could bridge the distance to Setoria.

The drugged guards had yet to wake, all of them still dazed beneath the work of her potion. That confused Zara. Alchemy was an exacting tool, one that did not change based on the whims of chance. Yet, that made it all the more worrisome when the guards did not stir. She kept that from her face and words, however, merely assuring Kelgan and the others that the same fatigue affected the dozing guards. The explanation was accepted readily, if not happily.

The early morning had them moving again, but by noon, inevitable exhaustion dogged their bones. They rested again, this time for several glasses. The Aspect strain they all felt was not something potions and tinctures could heal, or else she would have brewed up a dozen different benedictions. Instead, they were at the mercy of time itself, as their cores attempted to fix what their journey had bent. An agonizingly slow process, even in the best of times, and that did not describe their current situation in the least.

Despite their convalescence, Zara roused them before three glasses passed. Her gut twinged, vibrating along with strings of Affinity that did not let her sleep or even close her eyes. The Inquisition was drawing close. They could already be there.

"We must move faster," she said.

"The guards are exhausted. Even those still sleepwalking,"

Kelgan said. Beside him, Karp nodded in weary emphasis. "We couldn't move faster unless we were carried," he joked.

"Fine."

Zara and the others turned to Darius Reed as he pressed his thick-fingered hand into the rain. White-green Mana tinged with the faintest of oranges seeped from his channels. The Mana Gates in his left palm and elbow opened wide and spat forth a liquid stream of power. It shunted aside the rain, kicking leaves up from the soaked ground as it swirled and fused. With a sound like a thousand errant breezes, it solidified into a half-invisible platform of thickened air.

"Get the guards onto this; I'll carry their burden from here," he said.

The other guards quickly guided their groggy and confused compatriots onto the platform. It was enough to hold them all, if only just. For all his show, Reed was clearly straining with their combined weight. When he caught Zara watching him, he flushed and growled.

"What are you gaping at? We march on!"

Glasses drifted past upon greased tracks, so smoothly and fluidly did the time move. Glasses that were a rush of tree and leaf and rain-soaked moss. The flora of the Verdant Pass were just as massive here as back in Haarwatch, more so in some cases. The level of insects and small animals steadily rose, buoyed on the higher ambient Mana in the air and earth. But all of that was information Zara hadn't the time to contemplate. There was only the movement, only their advance.

Then they were there.

The forest ended, massive trees and roots twisting the ground before it opened into a flat, rain-trampled field of wild grass. More than rain-trampled.

"Haah… haahh… blind gods," Reed panted. He was shaking from the effort of holding onto the drugged guards. "An attack."

The field, easily a mile in either direction, abutted a massive wall of gorgeous blue stone that rose of a height equal to Haarwatch's orichalcum masterpiece. Gold details decorated the crenelated tops, bas relief sculptures of beasts and the defenders fighting against them. Actual defenders stood at the top, bows and spears and swirling Skills brought into play as they beat back a monster horde at the gates. Above it all, Setoria's standard flew tall and proud, a golden lion atop an unbroken field of blue.

The monsters were everywhere, crowding up against the entrance to the city as if they knew that was where ingress was promised. Hundreds of beasts, all the same type, crawled atop one another as fire and ice and arrows clad in either slammed into their bodies. Many of the Skills broke against their hides—they were Tier II, all of them, a creature called a Shriek that she had encountered once or twice in her life.

They resembled nothing so much as massive, avum-sized hounds covered in heavy muscle and festooned with spikes. Their faces were humanoid skulls, with dull red lights burning in their deep-set sockets, and they possessed a massive, bulging throat that rippled as a ululating sound was struck up in fury.

Tier II they could handle, and if they were at their full strength, it would have been a simple issue to wade toward the front gates. Now, hurt and reduced to so few, Zara did not like their chances. Even worse was the leader of the horde, a creature twice again as large as the Shrieks with not one, but two skeletal faces atop its thick neck.

Analyze...

Name: Twice-Cursed Shriek

...

Zara let the rest of the information wash away. It wasn't important, not truly. She could tell the leader was easily Tier III, well beyond any of her people save the Hand himself. Not that any of them were up to fighting, at the moment.

She extended her senses again, scanning the skies... and breathed a shaky sigh of relief. Zara could sense no lure, nothing drawing the horde to attack. She had to assume it was merely an unfortunately timed side effect of the wards in the Pass being down for months.

"We have to break through," Zara said.

"With what strength?" Reed motioned to the rest of the team, all of whom were collapsed against trucks ten times wider than themselves. "Every one of us is exhausted. Had I not carried these men, I would simply wipe these pests away." Reed panted and mimed a slashing gesture at the horde. "As it is, I'm not sure I could take on all of those Tier II's, let alone the leader."

Neither could the guards atop the wall. Their spells and Skills were proving ineffectual against the toughened hide of the Shrieks, and the Twice-Cursed ignored anything they tried. Zara licked her lips, considering.

"I could… but then I would be spent," she said in a low voice. "The crossing cost me more than I care to admit, but this?" She sucked in a tight, firm breath. It was time to roll the dice once more. "This must be done. We must reach the Waystone before the redcloaks. Darius, I will need you to lead them, once we're in the city. Stop the signal, stop the Inquisition, by whatever means necessary."

The Hand considered her for a long moment, his Spirit shifting through so many moods it was almost dizzying. In her state, Zara was not amused by his mercurial emotions, but soon thereafter, he settled. Solidity reigned through his Aspects, like the stout trunk of an oak. He nodded.

"I will see it done, Sorcerer."

She extracted no Oath, not for such a thing. The Hand knew where his best interests lay, and he would follow their plan for Vess' sake, if nothing else. Zara turned back to the horde and called upon her power.

"Stay back. When the giant falls, make for the gates," she told the guards. The Willful few gave sharp nods of acceptance and stood, reaching over to help their fellows as well.

A song built within her. Outside of her. In everything it was, a Harmony that could not be denied. Zara paced forward, moving further than such simple steps could account for and rose up into the air. As if a set of invisible stairs had been erected, she climbed higher with every step, and the song rang out all the louder.

Silence fell among the horde and atop the walls, as everyone and everything turned to look at her. Aquamarine liquid surged from her Mana Gates, enveloping her feet and palms in a shimmering fluid that drowned out the cloud-choked sun above them all. The rain itself swirled around her, seized from the skies and forced to spin wildly around her form.

The Twice-Cursed Shriek rounded on her, and its massive throat ballooned. Air Mana gathered within its throat, and a massive, ear-shattering howl exploded from between its jaws. The ululation swept its own minions apart, splitting them like grisly logs and hurling grass and sundered earth into the air.

Zara grimaced, pelted with the sonic vibrations. Little else could have threatened her, but the overwhelming sound had, just briefly, drowned out the rarefied vibrations of Creation. A discordance that fought reality itself.

No. I have control. She flared her Intent, gripped hard upon the skein of the Realm, and reminded herself of her purpose. *I will save this Continent, whether it likes it or not!*

With a desperate cry, Zara spent the last of herself. Her Intent solidified, a howling razor of crystalline power that speared into the Twice-Cursed Shriek's open throat. Harmony sang, and its fevered blood answered.

She ripped it out.

All of it.

"Run! Now!" Reed bellowed.

Kelgan snapped out of his daze enough to see Zara fall from the sky. A sky that was utterly excised of rain.

Instead, it was filled with blood.

"Now people! Push your Bodies or die!" Kelgan shouted, and the few who remained awake stumbled into a loping run. His legs burned, and his chest felt afire, but Kelgan didn't stop. Not even when all that blood fell back down onto the fields in a gruesome downpour.

The fields were rough terrain, torn by the giant Shriek's outburst, but of greater concern were the hundreds of lesser Shrieks around them. Yet, as their company approached, the Shrieks fled. But not from them.

None had gone near where Zara had landed.

Kelgan could only get a glimpse of the Sorcerer before the Hand picked her up, but it was enough to know she was alive. And then they were at the gate. Kelgan's vision had begun to narrow into a dark tunnel, but he caught snatches of the Hand shouting at the gate guards. And of the doors slowly, agonizingly opening for them.

They had made it.

CHAPTER FIFTY-EIGHT

Climbing the mountain was a struggle. Felix hadn't expected that, but it was. Even his powerful Body had trouble, though that was in part because he'd strained it again and again in the last battle. His Mind and Spirit were in disarray, still reeling from the revelations set before him.

The Archon is Unbound.

The words were vivid, his Keen Mind holding them exactly as they were said, down to Vvim's thickened inflection. They haunted him, turning his thoughts down unfamiliar paths and avenues he'd rather not explore. Who had summoned the Archon, originally? Who had summoned Felix? Would he ever know?

Would *he* end up trapped in a Domain for three thousand years?

Felix. Help them.

The Nym glanced to his left, startled by Pit's intrusion. Below and behind him, at least fifty feet down the cliff, were the rest of his team. All of them were red-faced and grim-eyed, and some bore wounds far worse than Felix's.

They need your help, Pit said from within his Spirit. *Help them.*

Cursing himself for being a fool, Felix sent a whisper of power into the stones and they… resisted. Though he detected no strong metals or oddness in it, the rock simply refused to move. *No. You will listen.* He sounded his Skill with his Affinity and Stone Shaping shone in his core space, reverberating with the echo of its power. He molded his Intent, hardened it, used his Willpower to sharpen its edge until it gleamed. *You will* move.

Stone Shaping is level 64!
...
Stone Shaping is level 66!

With a lurch in his gut, the cliff changed. It transformed from a treacherous incline to a set of simple stairs, blocky but even and solid. There was no gelling or liquid-like interim, simply instantaneous alteration. Below, his friends reacted with surprise and delight, though heavily muted by an exhaustion that dogged them.

Felix stared at his hands, then again at the stairs below. He had put more Mana and Intent into that spell than any before... he hadn't even used the System to activate it. That was great, exciting even, but for one thing. He looked over at Harn, just topping the new staircase. Fear almost clenched shut his throat. "Would the Archon have heard that?"

"There's wards on this range. Stronger than I've seen so far from the Interior," Harn grunted. "If he had the power to hear anythin' over the noise of them, we'd be in far worse trouble." The warrior stepped up to Felix and gripped him by the shoulder. "Thanks for the stairs. I'm surprised you got your magic to work on this stone."

"No problem," Felix muttered. There was plenty of climbing left to do, all of it as awful as their current approach. There was a reason a pass existed through the range, as they were all finding out firsthand. Pit had been coiled within his Spirit for a while now, though Felix didn't recall it happening. He had been in a fog since their escape from Shelim, and his typically prodigious memory was hazy with their frantic flight. "Any sign of pursuit?"

"Not that I've spotted," Harn said. The sky was lightening with dawn's fast approach. "But the wards are messin' with my senses. I can't be sure there ain't somethin' out there."

Felix nodded wearily. His Stamina was more than half, and his other pools were full, but the straining had left him worn thin. Even his store of Essence sat strangely inert within his core space.

His gaze drifted down to where Evie and Vess labored. "I'll open the way farther up. We need to rest."

The next hour was an exercise in discomfort as Felix Stone Shaped a way up the mountain. He would have simply stone shaped a cave for them to rest and hide within, but the rock would only accept so many changes. Even the stairs began to fail as they climbed higher and resistance mounted. Each step up was like a weight placed on his shoulders, and he wasn't the only one to feel that way.

Wyvora, Atar, and Alister all struggled, while the Haarguard could barely keep their feet, and Harn swore almost constantly under his breath. Vess was still unconscious, as she had been since they reached the mountain, and Evie had her slung over her shoulder like a sack of grain. Only A'zek was moving normally, but half his attention was on the Farhunter and trying to keep her from falling down the cliff-face.

Eventually they came to a horizontal stretch of the peak, a rock shelf well-worn by the elements, but enough to rest. At least for a moment. The spot was high up on the mountain, one of a dozen in a range that pushed up into the clouds. Felix hadn't ever climbed it previously, instead risking it through a cave system below. That had, of course, resulted in his capture and desperate escape from the Archon's clutches originally, which was one of the reasons they knew not to take that path again.

"Beautiful," Kikri whispered, looking out over the sprawling valley where Shelim was located. It was thick forests, a heavy morning mist, and the gray-white shapes of ruins in the distance. "This far away, and I can almost forget we nearly died down there."

"I can't," Nevia said. Her arms were literally trembling, a combination of Mana depletion and sheer exhaustion, no doubt. "Those monsters are one thing. The Arcids, however..." She shuddered.

"Damn near killed us," Davum agreed. He stood nowhere near the edge, and instead had his back against the mountain as if he could glue himself there. Sweat beaded atop his dark green skin. "Now the mountain takes its turn."

"Don't be dramatic," Kylar said. His face was pale, though, and he didn't venture any closer to the edge, either. "It's simple stone. Steep, sure, but that's all."

"I'm not certain of that," Atar said. Felix had watched him and Alister running their hands over the coarse granite of the cliff, whispering to one another. Now they both walked toward the group, both of them looking concerned.

"What is it?" Felix asked.

"The wards… there is something more than some arrays cast onto this mountain range. Its power is not like any I've seen," Atar said. He raised a hand to forestall Harn's open mouth. "I've seen the wards of the Continent's Interior. My old master would show me records of them, and they weren't half as complex as these, nor as sturdy."

"We can find no holes in its design, no place to exert our Wills and perhaps bypass them." Alister huffed a breath as he sat down. "They're as solid as the mountain itself."

"You saying we can't climb over this peak?" Evie asked quietly. Beside her, Vess stirred but did not wake. "Can't Felix just fly up over it, anyway?"

"Not unless he can bypass the wards," Atar said. "And not even Felix is strong enough to do that, especially not if they keep getting stronger than this. No offense."

"None taken," Felix said. "I'm more worried about our speed. The Archon could be after us even now, and we've barely made it a third of the way past the foothills."

"Well, we could always try the pass," Kylar suggested.

"Don't be a fool," A'zek growled, and the swordsman jumped. Strange as it seemed, it was easy to forget the Great Dane-sized Chimera was there at times. He prowled out onto the ledge, spearing everyone with his dark eyes. "The pass through this range is death. We all saw it."

Indeed they had. Among the last few, hazy hours, Felix recalled climbing within sight of the pass. He focused, and the memory sharpened, of an immense structure built of metal and stone. Walls pulsing with yellow-red sigils and towers sharpened like spears. The sigladry—Profane Sigaldry, the Archon's own dire invention—it had pulsed with a malevolence that none of them dared test. There was no way through the pass; the Archon had planned too far in advance.

The only way was up and over.

"We will make it through," Vess said in a strained voice.

"Vess, you should rest," Evie said.

"I have rested long enough," she said with annoyance. A conjured spear formed from the air, slapping into her palm as she used it to sit up. "All of us have. The Archon is coming."

"We're as hidden by this damn mountain as a leaf in a forest," Harn said. "He ain't findin' us."

"I do not care to find out what exactly the Archon's limits are," Vess said.

"Vess is right," Felix said. He let his sight roam upward along the sheer cliff face. It bowed outward above them, and climbing it would have been impossible for him back on Earth. Now, pressured by whatever was going on with the range, Felix was not confident they'd all be able to scale it. "We've got rope. If I can scout ahead and secure some lines, then we can make it."

The others nodded, though he half-suspected some of it was simply a chance for them to rest longer. Felix couldn't begrudge them that; they had fought a hard battle before he'd finished with Vvim. Fighting Tier II and even a few Tier III was getting easier for Felix, but all of them lagged behind him in power.

You can't coddle them forever, Felix.

Zara's words surfaced in his thoughts once again, and his breath caught in his chest. Felix turned and started climbing, putting it out of his Mind. Time enough to think when they were beyond the mountain.

Wyvora watched the Fiend climb up the cliff as if it were a simple ladder. While she was more than adept at climbing up sheer rock, the suppression she was under made her insides quail at the thought of free climbing in such a way. Not for the first time, she wondered at Felix's stats and Temper.

He is wearing thin, A'zek sent.

Perhaps, she replied. A quirk of her apprenticeship to the Farwalker was a closer connection to his Companion, tied to Title and Skill. *From what I have learned of this man, he has surprised everyone time and again with his strength.*

So I have gathered as well. Yet, he has not yet revealed what he learned in the Tower, only that his contact died. What was so important that a Geist under siege would send a message through enemy lines? A'zek rested his great head on his lightly patterned paws. *All for a conversation. And now he returns to us, and we run into the mountains. Toward this Temple.*

Do you not trust him? Wyvora quirked an eyebrow at the harnoq. *The Farwalker does.*

It's not that. I am simply worried. A'zek lifted his head and stared out into the gathering light. *Things are changing, Wyvora. Shifting into something new. Or perhaps something very old. Either way, I fear what may come with the dawn.*

The Farhunter had little to say to that, so she rested a hand gently atop A'zek's pelt. They rested, while they could.

For once, Felix's plan was working out. Using Stone Shaping and his Intent and Willpower, he was able to create loops of thick stone to anchor the ropes and dangle them back down the side of the mountain. They only had approximately two hundred feet of rope, but it was enough to get started.

So it went, traversing from one section to another, the others resting a bit while Felix and Pit climbed ahead. The higher they went, the harder it was for him to affect the stone at all, with Stone Shaping or otherwise. By the time the sun was high in the sky, they had moved beyond the halfway point and onto a sunny meadow that spanned miles.

Grateful for the respite, Felix plopped to his rear the moment the rest of his team was atop the cliff. Tall trees surrounded them, thicker than most but not nearly the behemoths they had seen in the forests below. Wild grasses, thistle, and a smattering of white and yellow wildflowers filled the meadow. These were as tall as the grasslands near the edge of the Foglands, but Felix's senses detected no Kaltraps lying in wait. Or any beasts, for that matter. Certainly, there were small creatures and insects, much as anywhere, but none of them possessed the sort of aggression they would need to worry about. It was peaceful.

"Down!" Harn hissed.

Without questioning, all of them dropped to the earth. Felix landed on his belly in the long grass, enough that it extended well above his head. He scanned the skies, unsure what Harn was so worried about, but then he heard it. A buzzing of wings. The creature zipped up the cliff side and into the air, wobbling with a frenetic need to keep moving. It was more metal than flesh with four buzzing wings, and Felix knew it. Or rather, he knew what it had once been.

Voracious Eye...

Name: Core-Slaved Skink
Type: Lizard/Construct
Level: 62
...

Felix let the information wash over him. Other than the changed name, it gave him nothing new. The Razorwing Skinks had once been a bane of his, so he was familiar with how they fought. He focused his attention on the Skink as it jerked about in the sky, searching for them. His Affinity surged, catching hints of something, and Felix bore down on that sensation. Then he felt it: a solid thread of yellow-red light, wrapped about the Skink's metallic chest and leading back down the mountain. He didn't touch it with anything other than his eyes, but Felix knew what—or who—lay at the end of that thread.

Carefully, without using the System, he sounded the strains of his Abyssal Skein. Will-honed Intent grabbed hold of the dark vibrations within him, pulling it like taffy through his channels. It felt awful, were he being honest, but it worked. Slowly his Skein spread outward, beyond his channels and along the thin loam of the meadow. One by one, his friends were cloaked in it, until Felix was certain they were all covered. Then he simply held on.

The Skink did three more circuits of the meadow before it flew onward, the whisper of dissatisfaction evident in its Spirit. Or the Spirit of whoever was controlling it.

They did not rise up for another fifteen minutes, and when they did, Felix kept his Abyssal Skein active. It was a stroke of luck they hadn't been found yet, but he wasn't willing to tempt fate by standing in the bright sunlight. At least with his Skein running, they stood a good chance of avoiding notice while they kept moving.

Yet Felix soon learned he couldn't keep that Skill going all day. It wasn't the Mana cost, but the extreme amount of discomfort he felt the longer he used it. Upset stomach, dizziness, it almost felt like he had a tiny fever. Still, he pressed on.

Felix this seems dangerous, Karys said. *The touch of the Void is ominous.*

Just a little longer, he said to the sword. To Pit, too, who was whining somewhere in his Spirit. *I can do it a little longer.*

They climbed. Quickly, if not as carefully as before. Skinks returned, flitting about as if they knew his team was around, if not where. He held onto the Skill, tooth and nail, and forced himself ever higher. The pressure of the mountain increased with every inch, and his friends were failing against its pressure. The Haarguard especially, as their Apprentice Tier Bodies were in no condition to resist the wards that inundated the stone.

As the day pushed into afternoon, Felix and Harn were reduced to dragging the others behind them. Below, a barely recovered Vess and stubborn Evie were pushing the Haarguard up a craggy incline, while the two mages held tight to their own robes. Atar and Alister both looked peaked, pale from the pressure, and flushed from the incredible exertion.

More Skinks flew up. It seemed they were scouring the entire mountain now. How did they find him? Or… or were there so many Core-Slaved Skinks that the Archon could blanket an entire mountain range? The temptation to tear them all from the sky was extreme. He could do it, too. He felt their connections to the earth, to the wind and sky, even to the blazing sun. He could fight.

And the Archon would know exactly where they were.

He turned from the sky, from the temptation of violence. He focused. Within his core space, it felt like the Void was leaking into him. Pooling in the swirling darkness between the stars of his Skills. Or had it been there all along? Since his time in the Void? Did it matter?

He focused. He pulled his team along, inch-by-inch.

He climbed.

Time passed. The sun dimmed, and shadows grew long and cool atop the stone. They didn't stop, couldn't stop. Concentrating was harder, the nausea greater, yet strangely, holding the Skill active grew easier and easier. Like a muscle that was slowly cramping. A muscle that faded the world around him in a way he knew that the others didn't experience. It covered them, but it didn't invert the colors of their sight, or set their cores to boil.

Release it, Felix!

No! He'd hold until they were safe. Until—

Something inside him spasmed, the dark contracting inside his core space. It was a pain he'd never felt before, and distantly he felt a… presence. It brushed up against his Mind, huge as the mountain itself, and Felix forgot about the pain completely.

Release it!

Abyssal Skein dropped, and Felix felt the attention of two hundred Core-Slaved Skinks pivot on him immediately.

"Felix! What're you doin'?" Harn growled. "They've seen us! They'll return to their master!"

His vision cleared, returning the skies to their gorgeous sunset tones, and Felix heaved two quick breaths. Already, the Skinks were dropping, diving not toward him but back down the mountain. Back to the Archon.

"No. They won't."

Adamant Discord.

Those connections he sensed before shifted, twirled about in Felix's hands as lightning played between his fingers. Nebulous at first, they hardened to steel and all of them, every single one, was seized. His Body, Mind, and Spirit screamed with the strain of so many. Felix sharpened his Intent, honed it with a Will more powerful than all of the Skinks combined. He slammed his fists down into the stone of the mountain.

The cliff shattered beneath him, then detonated as if struck by hundreds of falling meteors.

You Have Killed A Core-Slaved Skink (x210)!
XP Earned!

Adamant Discord is level 62!
…
Adamant Discord is level 65!

You Have Gained A Level!

CHAPTER FIFTY-NINE

You Have Gained A Level!
You Are Now Level 52!
You Gain:
+2 to PER! +2 to VIT! +4 to END! +5 to INT! +6 to WIL!
+4 to AGL! +7 to DEX!
You Have 10 Unused Stat Points!

Abyssal Skein is level 49!

Felix gasped, the nothing of the Void within him crackling and gelid against the heat of the System energy that surged from without. Red-gold and blue-white sizzled and popped with tiny explosions in his core space. Skills spun, revolved around his cores, hurtled away from the now-screaming pattern of Abyssal Skein.

Felix clenched his teeth against the pain. Aspects strained, Skill pressurized, he felt things would simply snap. A sundering from which there was no return.

But the Skill held. He held.

"Everyone," he grated. "Run."

Felix collapsed. The last he knew was the bloody remains of a Core-Slaved Skink.

He rose, held aloft by unknown hands. Coarse hands, hard and sharp, digging. Clawing. Felix screamed, and blood flowed. It flashed.

He fell. Hands and knees, he swung outward, scattering his enemies. They became as smoke, as water that crashed to the ground and tried to wash him away.

He stood. A key was in his hand. Crystalline and clear, glimmering in its own light. In his other hand was a large feather, enveloped in its own darkness. He watched that darkness, and it enveloped him, too.

Nothingness surrounded him, an infinite span of shadow. The Void. Swirling shapes in it resolved into creatures, deadly shapes he'd once run from in the black. Monstrosities that now chased… Zara, of all people, as she rode within an impossible ship of pure light.

He reached for them, but the darkness fled into a door surmounted by a blazing, eighteen-sided star. It resembled nothing so much as an immense, glaring eye of verdant lightning. Beyond the threshold was a green murk, thick and viscous. Without hesitation or control, he plunged through and it splashed like water.

He was subsumed in the murk. Cloudy green surrounded him, covered him, tried to creep up his nose and down his throat like it had a Will of its own. He fought. He felt *things* touch him, terrible horrors no worse than the Void. Different in features, but familiar. They grabbed at him, tore, not hungry but desperate in their wants. Their needs.

Freedom

Revenge.

Revelry in blood.

They dragged him deeper, ever deeper, and the green pressed in. Through eyes and ears and mouth, they clawed within. He screamed, and it was drowned by thickened muck.

KAW!

Wings of darkness swept them aside and descended on him. Feathers made of birds made of feathers shielded him and dragged him up, away, into the light that shined just beyond the dark.

NOT YET.

The screams of a million birds shattered the dark, and Felix resurfaced into the fading light.

His Mind was cloudy, but Felix could tell he was draped over the back of his Companion. And they were running, racing even through a forest of thin pines. The incline was sharp, not quite forty-five degrees, but high enough that every rock and needle tossed by their relentless sprint hurtled off into the air, off the mountain, most likely.

There was a screech above them, a powerful sound, and Felix arced his head upward. Massive flyers followed them, not Skinks but monsters with bat-like wings and dozens of sharp legs. More centipede than serpent. They dove through the branches, hissing and clacking, but bolts of blue light sent them reeling backward. Others flew among them, bird-like creatures of feathers and leather skin, bolted with panels of dull iron.

Great. More constructs. And, according to his Eye, all of them were at the high end of Tier II. They were *fast*, but his team wasn't defenseless.

Arrows shot through the thin canopy in a constant barrage; Kikri conjured and fired arrows almost simultaneously as they ran. Vyne was beside her, the shield warrior guarding them both from the retaliatory spines and spikes shot by the constructs. Each step brought her to a thin pine, which she pulled arrows from with her Green Shaping and imbued them with tight knots of force Mana. The arrows were mostly distraction, as the Elf didn't have the Strength to penetrate the constructs' defenses. But each arrow scratched their hide just a bit more. Felix saw her hit the same spot over a dozen times in rapid succession, dimpling the thing's chest.

Monsters came for her, spines shot from the flying centipedes like arrows of their own. They hissed and melted where they landed, and the Elven archer barely avoided them. Vyne's stone skin and metal shield weren't enough, but the kid was clever. He didn't so much as stop them as deflect the projectiles, using their own momentum against them. Spines skittered from his shield and embedded in the very trees Kikri was pulling from—the plants exploded all around them, half melting from the impact alone.

Luckily, the Journeymen were also on the offensive. Silver

spears skewered monster after monster, while a heavy spiked chain slapped one out of the sky. Crimson balls of fire and more columns of blue light splashed and slammed against their bodies, torching their feathers and crushing their segmented legs in equal measure. The wounded beasts that fell were quickly dispatched by Nevia, Kylar, and Davum. Ice and sword and greataxe rose and fell as they fought to keep pace with the rest of the team.

His friends were taking the enemy apart, the only issue being numbers. So many monsters littered the sky, too many. Felix's eyes flicked down the slope, and he could spot plumes of black smoke rising like a cloud of pollution into the sky. Mounds of bodies lay strewn behind them, carpeting the forest floor.

How long have they been fighting? How long was I out?

Felix? Pit sent. *Are you okay?*

Aching and sore, but okay, Felix sent as he leveraged himself into the saddle properly. Pit warbled in concern. *I'm good to fight. Probably.*

His sword buzzed and glowed green-gold. *If you are not certain, do not try, Felix. Pushing yourself is well and good, but too much will cost you.*

Felix grimaced, feeling a pain in his chest that radiated to his limbs. *I appreciate the advice, Karys. But I don't have a choice. They need help.*

Do they? Karys asked.

A screaming sawblade of sound cut through his senses. Affinity pinged it, a sound like an anvil ringing, like a hundred blades condensed into one and hit with a hammer the size of a house. Silver flame burst above them, consuming at first one, then two, then all of the monsters in a cluster. Harn laughed, already falling from where he'd leaped out of a tree. He landed along with dozens of still-burning corpses.

Above, storms of wind swelled and burst, the air Mana whipping like knives through the centipedes and birds. They died by the score, spear after glittering spear detonating atop their wings and chests and heads. Vess herself fell atop another, spearing it through its metal plating and into a third, skewering them all atop her partisan. She rode their flailing bodies to the earth, smashing through acid-burned boughs and Green-Shaped trunks alike.

Others screamed in rage and fear, the former overcoming the latter, but were met with a punishing length of spiked chain. One that was so heavy, it smashed their bodies to the ground hard enough to crater it. Evie swirled among them, a tornado of icy metal and cold precision, her normal smiling face replaced with a seething grimace.

Behind her, flame and force followed, each burst of Mana ending a monster with pitiless grace. And still, the Haarguard finished all that they could, arrow, axe, sword, ice, and shield all doing their part.

I may have… judged too quickly, Felix admitted.

Indeed, Karys said. Pit chirruped in agreement.

Felix could admit when he was wrong, but he still felt sour. Not at his team, but at his own decision-making. They'd been fighting together for months. How had he misjudged their abilities? The sour, bitter sensation compounded and concentrated, no longer emotional but physical. Immediate. Felix checked his core space and found his Abyssal Skein Skill chipped and faded; not broken, but not whole either. What's more, his Essence stores were empty again. The hard light of Karys' and Vvim's Memories were all that hung above his cores and Skills.

Was this you? he asked the abyss. He half-expected an answer, but none came.

Back to himself, Felix raised a hand and twined it into the expanding black smoke of the murdered beasts. He gripped it with his Will, it and all the rest it mingled with, and he breathed it in.

Ravenous Tithe!

He fed the power directly into his cores, letting equal amounts flow into each. His [Thunderflame Core] and [Cardinal Beast Core] belched out ribbons of light, streamers that hurtled wildly into his core space until Felix seized them as well with the force of his Willpower. Utilizing his honed Intent, he sent the refined Essence into his damaged Skill where it pooled against the pattern and shook with sympathetic vibrations. The stress fractures eased and settled. Not fully healed, but mended.

He needed more Essence.

Pit, he sent. His head felt woozy again, and the already-inclined ground tilted oddly. *Pit, I need to get closer...*

Felix blinked. Again, slow and steady.

When he opened his eyes at last, he beheld rough stone walls lit by flickering flame. He was in a cavern and no longer on Pit's back. Felix pushed himself onto his elbow and it felt far easier to do than before. The trembling weakness he'd felt earlier had almost completely abated. Beside him, a fire burned merrily while sigils around them warded sound, light, and smoke. Something else, too, but he couldn't tell, not without looking closer. In the distance, outside the cave, he heard the faint cawing of birds.

A steaming bowl of stew was shoved before his face, the steam tickling against his skin. Vess stood over him, still bandaged and currently frowning. "Eat."

Felix took the bowl wordlessly. Vess watched him take a few bites before she nodded to herself and stomped off, toward Evie and Wyvora of all people.

"What are we doing? Why aren't we moving?" Felix asked.

The Haarguard stared in disbelief, but Harn snorted a laugh. "He wakes up from nearly cripplin' himself, and he asks why we stopped. You don't got quit in you, do you Felix?"

Felix finished the stew in three more bites and sat up fully. His muscles protested, but it was the honest burn of too much use, rather than his Aspects. "I don't appreciate being a sitting duck, no. You kill all the beasts following us?"

"Most of them, those that didn't flee," Harn said. He nodded at Atar and Alister. The mages were huddled by the edge of the warding script, discussing something in low tones. "Those two managed a working that sent a familiar sort of lightning down the mountain, to the north. Said it was a lure or somethin' like it." He spat into the fire. "We found this network of caverns shortly after. Enough pathways in here to confuse the best trackers, Human or otherwise."

"More have come, more flying beasts and stranger things," Kikri added. She, like all the Haarguard, looked more than a little exhausted. Her fingers were covered with inscribed bandages in white and green. "I tracked them, just enough to see. To the last, they were following the trail north."

"It'll give us some time, at least," Alister said, sitting down around the fire with a groan. "Best we could manage at short notice."

"Took half the monster cores I've been collecting just to power that array," Atar complained. His fingers were bandaged, as well as his left thigh. He sat gingerly. "Copying your Mana signature is tricky, Felix. Still not sure I did it right."

"My Mana signature?" Felix asked.

"Mhm. Thing is, it changes depending on the Skills you're using, which is—" Atar cut himself off, not quite glancing at the Haarguard. "Makes it difficult, is all."

Felix nodded. *He's saying it's because I'm Unbound. I can use all sorts of Mana types without restriction.* His eyes widened. *Is that why the Archon was able to create his Profane Sigaldry? It's based on the Dissonance that runs counter to the Grand Harmony, as far as I can tell. He can use it because he can use all types of Mana, all types of vibrations.*

To the others he said, "So where is this place? Are we close to crossing these mountains?"

"Through here, we should be able to avoid the mountain peak completely. Cavern goes a ways back, not down or up, simply straight through." Harn ate his stew with big, lip-smacking bites. "Evie and the Henaari did some scoutin'. Looks promisin'."

"Ah," Felix said. "Good."

"We got time, is what I mean," Harn said, finishing his stew with a loud slurp. "Time for all of us to get some needed rest. I figure the last bit will be the final leg of this particular journey, eh?"

Felix estimated the distance from the mountains to the Waterfall Temple. It was not far at all. "Just about. After we climb down this mountain, we're less than a day from our destination. Then we finish this Quest."

Excited murmurs fluttered among the Haarguards, but Felix didn't bother to listen. He let them be excited at the prospect of the Quest rewards, both this one and the potential reward for the Territory Quest Cal had given them all, and that Felix had shared with the guards. *No need to tell them how hard it'll be. Not yet.* Felix patted his Companion and received a low rumble of pleasure from the tenku. *Time enough in the morning.*

As the others settled to sleep; however, Felix found himself increasingly alert. His nap had done him wonders, and he had things to address before they moved on. He summoned his notifications.

Armored Skin is level 73!

Unfettered Volition is level 58!

...

Unfettered Volition is level 60!
Deception is level 25!
Apprentice Tier!
You Gain:
+5 INT
+5 DEX
+5 PER

Exploration is level 48!
Bastion of Will is level 72!
Meditation is level 56!

Fire Within is level 66!
...
Fire Within is level 70!

Much of his gains seemed to happen during his murkier memories, when the Abyssal Skein was truly straining him. He must have taken quite a bit of damage from the Skinks during their flight, or perhaps his own carelessness, to push his Armored Skin up four entire levels. Deception had even Tiered into Apprentice, likely due to his fooling the Skinks. That his Mana Manipulations and Bastion increased was easy to understand, along with Meditation and his Fire Within. Without any of those, he wouldn't have held his Abyssal Skein together at all, or had the wherewithal to mend it.

The System sent power into his core as his Skills increased in size, complexity, and position within his celestial array. And it truly did look like an array, now that he thought about it: it was circular and studded with symbols etched in light and power, all fueled by a bright pair of cores. Strange.

Before he'd passed out, Felix had earned a new level as well, along with 10 more bonus stats. He quickly assigned those to Perception, bringing his total to 808. He'd found his Perception to be increasingly more important as he progressed. Being able to anticipate an attack was just as vital as being strong enough to withstand it, if not more so were he given time to avoid it altogether.

That left Perception, Vitality, Agility, and Dexterity as the four stats below a thousand. At the pace he was going, Felix was unsure how long it'd take to reach the Third Threshold.

You are moving quickly, Felix, Karys assured him. *I'd be more concerned at just* how *fast you are developing.*

"What? Why?"

Strength invites challenge, so it ever was. Your strength above all. The Unbound, it is said, were creatures of the gods once, before the Founders aided our nation. Now, I fear, even the gods would take umbrage at your continued growth.

Felix chuckled, but there was no joy in it. "Already have." He frowned in thought. "The Founders. You mean the two Unbound. The husband and wife?"

You have heard the story. Ah. Yes, I see it in your Mind. That is... broadly accurate. Karys glowed softly in contemplation. *I was not there. It was Ages before my time. But yes, my—our—ancestors summoned two Unbound to aid them in a desperate time. We flourished with them at our side, conquered those who would enslave us all. I... I have sensed some of your thoughts during the past day.*

Felix clenched his jaw. "I don't suppose I need to guess at what you mean." He sighed. "Vvim told me that. Gave me a Memory, in fact, that would answer all my questions. Or so he said."

The Geist were too clever by half, but they were an honorable people. They alone held the line at Mendaat's Gate, when the Absolem fell to the Inferii, and the Fires of Dawn were routed. Each unfamiliar word sent a wave of conviction and green-gold light from his sword, the blade almost vibrating out of its sheath. *It disgusts me that an Unbound would betray us at the close of the war. Unconscionable. You must access this Memory, with all haste.*

"That's the plan," Felix said. He pulled the Inheritor's Will from its sheath, eyeing the blade and the two glyphs that shown to his Manasight. "Will you help me?"

As I can, Felix. I promise you that.

Felix nodded and planted the sword tip-first atop the stone at his feet. Within, the Memory of Vvim dangled above his cores like a star. Banishing his nerves with an effort of Will, he gripped it and guided its light down, down, until he reached the flowing, liquid edge of his [Cardinal Beast Core].

Does it matter which core I put it in? He was fairly certain it didn't, but the decision was taken from him. That moment of hesitation almost cost him everything, as the abyss between his cores surged with a great and terrible need. The Memory slipped, his Will somehow failing against that powerful pull.

Hold!

Karys' voice was a bar of white-hot strength that shot through Felix's Will, and the former Paragon's Intent sidled along Felix's own. The Memory halted, stuck halfway to oblivion.

Pull Felix! Pull!

Felix heaved back with everything he had, fighting against the growling strength of whatever dwelled inside that abyss. It Wanted. It Needed. An urge it couldn't suppress… but one Felix could control.

You can have another meal soon! A powerful one, as before, he shouted at the dark. *I've given you that already! Just let go!*

Without warning, the counter-pull vanished entirely, and Felix hauled the Memory fully into his [Cardinal Beast Core]. It vanished with a red-gold flare of liquid light.

Nothing good will come of that, Felix. Karys was nothing more than a green-gold blob of light beside him, but he could tell the man was looking at his abyss between the stacked core rings. *Nothing good.*

Felix wasn't afforded the time to reply. The world around them pulsed, leached of all color, before it shattered entirely.

CHAPTER SIXTY

Unlike other Memories, there was no convoluted array of Vvim's to choose from, twisting about him enough to drive anyone crazy. No, instead, after the world around him shattered, Felix had the sensation of falling. Not far, and not fast, but he fell into a darkness that turned from black to gray to a burnished gold. He landed with a slight flexing of his knees, though his clothes puffed outward as if he'd really fallen from on high.

Around him, the golden light resolved into blocky shapes, refining by the second until he saw hexagonal columns along tall walls, massive doorways between them, and seven-sided tiles lining the floors. Above, the light resolved into a large, faceted dome, carved until thousands of stars were worked into it, until it resembled nothing so much as a fine, impossible lace.

It was beautiful. The chamber was huge, easily a thousand feet in all directions, and he stood in a large flat space dominated only by two small, chest-high platforms and one larger platform opposite. Further afield, golden light bloomed into tiered seating, splitting and rotating around itself until it filled much of the chamber. Everything was empty, however.

"This looks like a courtroom," Felix said.

"Because it is," said a powerful voice beside him. Felix twisted in alarm, but found a familiar face smiling ruefully at him. A man stood there, a bit taller than Felix, even though he was stooped. His skin was dark and wrinkled, his tightly curled hair more gray than black, but a powerful vigor shone from his grass-green eyes. He looked just as he had in the Memory Felix had experienced a week prior.

"Karys?"

The Paragon smiled at Felix, and his teeth were very white and straight. Tempered, clearly. "An honor to meet you properly, Felix."

Felix grinned. "Right back atcha." Before he could say more, another thump sounded, and an ox-sized creature landed next to them both. "Pit!"

The tenku looked both sleepy and surprised, with the latter winning by the thinnest of margins. He looked around with wide eyes of bright gold, and pawed at the nearby platform. His claws passed straight through it, like smoke.

"It's a Memory, Pit. I didn't think you'd be pulled in, too." Felix patted the tenku on his neck, feeling the surprise give way to a wary understanding.

I am worried. And curious.

"Same here," Felix said. "Karys, what is this? It looks like a courtroom."

"I suspect that is exactly what it is, only I don't—Ah." The Paragon pointed to the stands. "The Memory begins."

Felix followed the gesture and saw more of that golden light rolling down from above, and at each tier of seating, it bumped and burst over shapes that had not stood there before. People resolved out of the light, clothed in odd wrappings and sparkling jewels. Weapons sat at their waists and back, staves and swords and odd oblong things he couldn't name.

Faces emerged last, and those ranged the gamut of ages, sex, and Race. Many in attendance were darker skinned Nym, though a smattering of pale and olive-toned features were there, as well as Dwarves, Elves, Naiads, and Nixies, Goblins, Orcs, Geists. All that and more, as the tiered stands filled as much as any sports stadium back on Earth.

The wave continued on, pushing ever closer as it conjured people from the mists of time. It swept down among them, filling the stands to either side and the larger bench opposite with luminescent smoke. Guards, or something like them, manifested first; they had the look of hard folk, worn and tired but veteran killers just the same. They eyed the stands with hands on more of those oblong weapons, and some with halberds that gleamed with more than just reflected light.

The stands had two figures, a man and a woman, that was clear from their silhouette, but the features took their time in coming. Instead, Felix focused on the bench—judge's bench, he figured—and a tall, statuesque woman with dark hair, darker skin, and eyes of brightest silver. It was a little shocking, despite all he'd seen, even more so as the woman lifted an arm covered in heavy, battle-worn armor the color of bronze and slammed it down upon the bench before her.

"Silence."

Few were talking, but everyone froze, awed and afraid of the woman. She snorted and tossed back her hair. It was cut short enough to fit a helmet comfortably, and a leather band across her brow was darkened with the sweat of many, many days. Those silver eyes flashed as she took in those before her, and for a terrifying second, Felix thought she could see *him*.

"We have come here to bear witness to the crimes perpetrated by one of our own. One of our own, and he who we summoned through the Void." Murmurs stirred the air, most anxious but quite a few eager. "Who comes before us, Eetol?"

A Geist Felix hadn't noticed appeared at the base of the judge's bench, along with two more guards. Minotaurs. Their huge, hairy heads shook, jangling ropes of jade and amber beads even as they tightened their grip on their massive spears. The Geist, Eetol, stepped forward dressed in a complicated robe of intertwining fabrics and small, ceramic plates. They spoke with a sharp voice, a dangerous sound from something so small.

"Before us are the Accused: Lhel, Daughter of Savin, Daughter of Peil, of the Nym. And Merodach, Son of Anatu, Son of Tamzi, of the Nym by Choice, Unbound by Fate."

More whispers and murmurs, the volume rising in pitch. Felix started as the two figures beside him finally coalesced. The man, Merodach apparently, was as dark as Vess and had a nose sharper than most daggers. Dark eyes stared out from heavy brows, and a regal tilt to his chin suggested he was only in chains for the moment. And he was in chains—a lot of them. A collar was fitted around his neck and large links wrapped his shoulders and wrists and waist, all of them interwoven as if they were grown rather than forged.

The woman to Felix's right was chained in much the same way, though her chains did not crawl with glowing glyphs. Instead, she stood with her head down and her eyes cast to the tiled floors.

"Is that the Archon?" Felix asked.

"I imagine so," Karys said. Pit growled at the man, though he took no notice.

Felix looked closer, noting how frail the man looked beneath the chains. He clearly never focused on his Body or physical stats. He tried to use his Voracious Eye, but it was like it didn't even exist in the Memory. Felix was curious what level the man was, what his strengths truly were, but there was no way to find out. Merodach sneered at the murmuring crowd, making more than a few people flinch, only for their jeers to come back even stronger.

"What are their crimes, Eetol?" the judge asked. She stared at the two Accused with an unnerving intensity.

"Merodach stands Accused of High Treason. He has been Accused of developing weapons that steal the very souls of our people, of befouling the Eidolon strictures, and of stealing the secrets to their construction." Angry shouts and gasps met each new charge, but the dark-skinned man only stood taller. "Worst of all, he has been Accused of delving into the vile practice of Dissonance."

The crowd shot to their feet, screaming at such a volume that Felix and Pit both flinched. It felt like they were moments from charging down and murdering the guy. Even Karys sucked in a swift breath, horror written clear across his face. Merodach, however, merely smirked.

Speaking loudly, Eetol continued. "Lhel stands Accused of aiding and abetting his plans and provided his forges with the power she sourced from the project in the Western Reaches. Power meant to be shoring our defensive structures along the front."

More shouting, more hurled threats and dark oaths. The woman cowered under the onslaught, weighed down by it all.

Felix tilted his head, trying to get a better look at her. *Lhel… that sounds so familiar.* Then it struck him. *The Maw.* Felix stepped forward, bending just enough to see Lhel's tear-streaked face. *It is her. She's the one who woke the Maw, the one whose Body was stolen by the Primordial. So this...*Felix's eyes widened. "The project in the Western Reaches," he muttered. "They're talking about the Essence Anchor. About drilling into the Unending Maw. Holy shit."

Felix stepped back, overcome. Lhel had dealings with the Archon? And the Archon was partly responsible for the Maw's release?

"Felix," Karys gasped and pointed to the judge. "Look." The woman stood, her arm leveled at the Accused. In her hand was a very familiar sword. *His* sword.

"The Herald," Karys gasped. "Ancient ancestor of the line of Emperors..."

The Herald? Felix raised his eyebrows. "How's that possible? The Herald was around when you were, right? But also when the Archon was? And you didn't know of this sleazeball?"

"I… My memory strains still. It has holes. But the Herald is ancient… *was* ancient. She was born during the rise of our Empire, when the Founders still lived. She… she is legend, she is myth clad in flesh. It is an honor to see even a Memory of her."

"Okay. So she's really old, was around well after you were put into an Eidolon. And she..." Felix looked at the Herald again. "She has yet to fight the Maw, toe-to-toe. Wait." Felix thought back to the shadow play the Henaari had put on for them. The Golden Empire. It had said the Maw had arisen first, then the mechanical creations went wild. But Lhel died when the Maw was unleashed. *Had the story gotten it wrong?*

Felix's thoughts whirled as the Herald continued to list off the terrible things Merodach had done. Most of them centered around experimenting on living, unwilling subjects and experimenting with Dissonance. Felix had a feeling he knew what that was, too. *Profane Sigaldry. He invented it here.*

Eventually, the litany of charges against Merodach was finished. The Herald regarded both of the Accused with her fierce, silver gaze. "Unbound, you have betrayed the trust of all who relied upon you. Our hope for an end to this War was in your hands, and you dashed it against the Jagged Peaks. I name you, Merodach, for all of time: Betrayer."

There was the sound of a massive bell tolling twice, loud enough that the floor itself vibrated beneath Felix's feet. A small blue window appeared before him.

Merodach Has Been Renamed!
All Shall Know Him As Betrayer!
No Nymean Territory Will Give Him Succor Or Support!
-100% Relations With All Golden Empire Factions!

"Might I speak?"

Felix hadn't expected the future Archon's voice to be so… melodious. It was higher than he expected, too, and Felix began to wonder how old the man actually was. No one objected to the Accused speaking, so he continued.

"I have lived in your world for almost a century, and none of it of my own will. I was torn from my home, my family, my people." He laughed, and it was bitter. "I thought you were all gods when I arrived in your Temple, but I soon realized this was nothing more than the land of weak *fools*." More angry murmurs from the crowd, but he didn't stop.

"Too caught up in what others think and feel to do what is *right*! To make life better for all of those on this Continent, we should seize control of it all, by any means necessary! The only hands that are good enough are our own. But none of you want to see the truth! So I was to make you see the truth!"

Merodach spat more than he spoke, and the fires of madness danced along his Spirit. Felix wasn't sure what else to call the frenetic combination of so much hate and raw desire. A desire for power.

Perhaps because he was watching Merodach's Spirit so closely, Felix was the first to notice when the man's Mana surged, breaking free of his fetters and spearing outward. The power stabbed through windows and doors all around them and was followed immediately after by a series of staccato blasts of stone and metal. Huge, golden constructs ripped through the entries and exits, all of them exact duplicates of the Archon Felix knew.

"Holy shit," he whispered.

Dozens entered, hulking constructs that easily dwarfed the people around them. Screams and shouted Skills filled the air, but the powers bounced from their powerful metal chassis. They waded forward, fists rising and falling, people hurled to the ground covered in their own blood.

"The truth comes for you all! I will raise this Empire up! I will claim that which you are all too afraid to embrace!" That madness was there again, brighter than before. "I will make this Continent kneel before an army that can never die!"

The Archons tore through the crowd, though they gave a powerful showing. Lightning, flames, ice, air, colors and sounds burst around Felix like a fireworks display. Karys looked sick, his wrinkled mouth taut at the sight. Pit warbled in dismay, pulsing with a need to help but knowing it was impossible. It was a Memory; they could do nothing to affect it.

Then, in the center of the chamber, a blaze of incandescent flames erupted. Tendrils of fire lashed outward, each one striking an Archon, and where they struck, they entangled limbs and bodies. Bindings of flame grabbed each and every Archon, until their violence was halted, and their bodies were lifted into the air, utterly neutralized.

Felix marveled at the precision and power necessary to do such a thing. Karys whispered a quiet prayer of thanks. Felix sympathized. He had no desire to witness any more bloodshed, not now.

"You think to conquer, Unbound? You do not know the meaning of strength," the Herald scoffed. She twisted her sword, and the lashes lifted and pulled, drawing the Archons to the center of the chamber. "Did you intend to kill us all? It was a pathetic attempt. You cannot even touch the shadow of our warriors, despite your vaunted powers. I should kill you right now, or let *them* do it."

The Herald pointed at the audience, only just recovering from the attack. People in the crowd surged forward, all intent on the snarling form of Merodach.

"You will all hold! The sentence is not yet given!" The Herald glowed like the sun, sword raised. "We will finish this, as it is intended!"

A deathly quiet reigned in the chamber and everyone halted. Merodach was utterly terrified, his confidence shattered, and his madness banked. He huddled close, hiding from the bindings of flame that held him still. Felix thought he could smell him charring slightly.

"Magi Lhel is to be remanded to the custody of the Family Ssev for the span of a century. There, she may continue her work, but only under the close supervision of the Geist of Shelim." Another bell tolled, so loud that Felix winced. "Know this: that you live is a gift, given only because it is clear you knew nothing of the Betrayer's true goals. If you cross the line again, it will not end well for you."

Lhel nodded, tears streaming down her face, her Spirit a mess of fear, relief, shame, and a dozen other shades of emotion. She clutched at her chains as if that was all that held her up.

"For the Betrayer, I shall grant no clemency. What he has done, what he has attempted—all of it goes beyond decency and well into madness. However, do not let the record show me without empathy. As punishment for violating the strictures of the Eidolon, for defiling the Choices of thousands of innocent souls, Merodach, Son of Anatu, Son of Tamzi shall taste the fruits of his dire labor."

Merodach screamed, and it was a howl that Felix felt in his bones. Flesh and bone was rent asunder, light and power in liquid flows poured among the viscera that burst into the air. Through it all, the crowd watched, sober-eyed and unblinking. This was the price of treachery, the only answer to those who would sabotage the haven they had made. Felix could feel that conviction sweeping through the crowd, so clear it was as if he could read it on a page.

The Memory hazed, and Felix couldn't be sure if it was because of his own agonized eyesight or the Memory itself. The details fled, no matter how Felix tried to parse them. However the Herald accomplished it, the deed was done in moments. Merodach's Body was gone, nothing more than scraps of cloth and red smears atop the tiles. Beside him, within the massive frame of an Archon, the fires of his Spirit kindled, weak and sputtering.

"Merodach, Son of Anatu, Son of Tamzi shall remain within his own work for all of time. His Body sundered, his Mind shattered, his Spirit shall suffer in torment unending, just as all his vile creations once suffered. Do any among you seek satisfaction for his sentencing?"

Utter silence, a silence edged by a hard anger. The Herald nodded.

"Very well. The Empire shall take custody of the Unbound's Archonic Constructs. Perhaps, in time, we might reverse what has been done to them. Perhaps." Suddenly, the Herald looked sickened, and her Spirit flared. "Go. All of you. The War calls, and we cannot afford to waste more time."

Felix watched as the room began to empty, the people all but fleeing the spiking Spirit of the Herald. Then it all froze.

"Whoa, what?" Felix spun, taking in everything. "Is that it?"

"Ah, Felix," Karys said. "We have a visitor."

Standing near Pit and his sword-bound friend was a small, brown-furred Geist. They were young, perhaps equal to Felix's own age, but the eyes that stared at him burned with knowledge too ancient to be real.

"Vvim."

"Felix Nevarre. If you are seeing this, seeing us, then this one has already passed onto the Ethereal. That is good. It is what this one hoped for."

Felix quirked an eyebrow. "Is this a recording?"

Vvim gave no indication he had heard Felix. "There is much to be said, and you've no time to hear it. This one has... placed a great deal of detail in this Memory. You shall likely not sense it all upon first viewing, but there is much to be discovered."

The golden light around them began to fold and compress. Clouds streamed, compressing all into one point as they spoke.

"Think on this Memory, on what you can learn here. Think deep."

Before Felix could get another word in edgewise, everything compressed into a single drop of golden liquid...then it and Felix dropped down into an endless abyss. Felix screamed, yet within moments found himself once more in his core space. Before him, his red-gold core spun as a lazy river of flame, and spinning around within it, a mote of white light.

"It's still there," Felix said. "The Memory wasn't consumed."

It seems this Vvim has more to show you than some traitor's sentencing.

"So he said. 'Think deep,'" Felix quoted. "Think deep on what, though?"

Felix returned his awareness to his surroundings, finding the fire extinguished and everyone asleep. Aside from the thrum of the wards, there was little else in the cave to occupy his attention, and Pit had already returned to snoring. More than a little overwhelmed by what he'd experienced, Felix laid down and stared at the ceiling, keeping his senses tight around himself.

Tomorrow. Tomorrow, they would reach the Waterfall Temple.

Sleep was a long time coming.

CHAPTER SIXTY-ONE

Felix woke them all an hour before dawn. How he knew the time while within a lightless cavern, he wasn't quite sure. He could have counted back the hours to determine it, but instead, it was simply a feeling. A tingle at the edge of his senses when the sun began heating the land.

Strange.

Most of them grumbled, though the worst of it came from the Haarguard. Not that they were mad at him, but every single one of them was still affected by the protracted fights the day prior. Felix felt for them, but there wasn't time. They'd have to keep up.

Felix and Harn took the lead, Pit and A'zek and the rest behind them as they traversed the honeycombed passages. Pit sniffed at the tunnels ahead and let out a piping chirp.

"What's that? What do you smell?" Evie asked him.

Pit twisted his head, tilting it from side to side, as if he heard something he couldn't place. Nothing clear came across their bond, just uncertainty and confusion. Felix patted the Chimera on the flanks, trying to ease his worries.

"Whatever it is, we'll handle it," Felix promised. Pit merely nodded, mollified.

"I only feel the weight of the mountain," A'zek said. He was practically invisible in the dark, even to those with Night Eye or other sight Skills. Felix could make him out, but only because of the Mana in the earth around the harnoq—otherwise, it was as if A'zek wasn't there at all. Even his baritone voice sounded like it was coming from down a deep, dark well. "There is something to these ranges. Something ancient."

"We'll be out of them soon enough," Harn grunted. "Quick now. I'd like to see daylight."

They followed winding, twisty tunnels filled with uneven footing and pockmarked ceilings, as if something had burrowed through it. Soft chittering came to them occasionally, a click-clacking that set Felix's teeth on edge. It reminded him of cicadas, but by the sound of them they were the size of Pit, at least. Felix was tempted to wrap them all with Abyssal Skein again, to avoid any unwanted attention, but the idea of it made him queasy. The Skill seemed to be mended, healed even, but it felt like a broken leg only just recovered; were he to put his full weight on it, he might break it anew. Instead, they all moved carefully, quietly. Some better than others.

That pressure they had felt while climbing the mountain, gone when he'd woken by the campfire, increased with every mile of mountain they traversed. Soon the Haarguard were stumbling, unable to stand straight, and even Evie and Vess were struggling. Atar and Alister were gasping for air, Wyvora too, and she leaned upon A'zek to keep her feet. The two Chimera, Harn, and Felix were relatively unburdened, though the pressure was like a blanket across his senses.

"I was wrong," Harn said. The dark pressed against them like a velvet shroud, and the man spat. "It ain't wards on this mountain. It's natural, grown into the rock."

"The *mountain* is doing this?" Felix asked. "How does that work?"

"Significance builds in all things, Unbound," A'zek said. Felix glared at the harnoq then at the struggling Haarguard. The cat merely shrugged and kept speaking. "The oldest of things have the most significance, the most meaning within them. Is it so remarkable that a mountain as old as the Ages would have garnered this much?"

"That would mean the mountain or the range itself has Aspects to gather that meaning," Felix said. "You're saying the mountain is alive? Sentient?"

"That is entirely dependent on your definition of living, of sentience." A'zek looked upward, and strangely, so did Pit. Both of them stared at the same spot above their heads. "There is... a being above us. A creature of the elements."

Harn drew his axes, and Felix flared his Manasight, hoping to peer through a thousand feet of rock. He saw nothing but Mana, swirling yet rigid in a way that only earth could be, and nothing of a living creature. "I don't feel anything. Does this creature have to do with the mountain's significance?"

"Perhaps," A'zek shrugged. "It sleeps... I can tell that much."

What is it? Pit asked.

"Ancient. More than that, I do not know."

Felix took a breath and set it aside. There was nothing he could do about some old monster living atop a mountain, not with everything else on his plate, and simply accepted it. He had learned, the hard way, to roll with the punches and only fight the battles he could win. His life would have been far more exhausting if he acted otherwise.

He did a fair impression of Harn's grunt and continued on, only pausing long enough to ensure the rest were following.

At the worst of it, Pit had Davum, Kylar, Vyne, and Nevia draped across his back, while A'zek took Kikri and a woozy Wyvora. Evie had taken Vess' arm, and, surprisingly, Alister had to grab onto Atar. The force mage had looked little better than the Apprentice Tiers at one point. But they pushed through it, navigating farther into the maze of craggy tunnels. Now they were angling again, but this time it was downward. Then they saw the light, coming slantwise from a thin crevasse. The tunnels dipped farther, pushing down into the depths of the mountain, but each step down increased Felix's anxiety even as it lightened the pressure from his Spirit. He knew the Archon's Domain was far below them, but Felix could not help but fear drifting blindly closer.

"Stop," he told the others. "We'll exit here."

"Hop-pe you can open that a mite wider, Felix," Evie said. She, too, was now leaning on Pit, and her legs shook like she'd just finished running ten miles. "Vess' got those child-bearing hips, you know?"

Vess smacked her friend, hard enough to send the girl sprawling, which made Vess lunge to catch her. Evie chuckled the whole time.

Harn rolled his eyes, but he also regarded the crevasse with doubt.

"I'll widen the opening. I think we're far enough away from the mountain's...*whatever* for me to shape the stone." *I hope,* he added silently.

Felix turned from his team and put his hands directly on the stone, fifteen feet below the deep fissure. He didn't activate the Skill, but instead leaned against his Will, Intent, and Affinity, as he'd been taught. The shape of his Skill shimmered in his Mind's eye, the twists and turns of it, the vibrations, the...frequency.

His Affinity crooned, catching the song of it, and Felix levered his Intent and Will, coaxing his own Mana through the pattern and into his channels. He held the shape he wanted, needed: of a door, a threshold through which they could walk out of the tunnels. His core space buzzed, rippled, and shook as the song took him, rolling through his veins like an ocean's surf. *Focus.*

Stone Shaping.

The Mana flowed out of him, dusty brown and shimmering with potency. It sank into the stone beneath his hands, and as before, the stone was simply changed. No intermediate forms or gel-like consistency—it was a solid wall one instant, and in the next, it was a threshold without gate or door. It was about ten feet wide and twenty feet tall, more than enough to allow all of them through. Sunlight streamed onto him, hot and too bright after the cool darkness of the earth, but Felix reveled in it.

"There, see? Easy." Felix grinned back at them, but everyone pushed past him, equally as excited to see the light of day. The grin turned into a bemused frown before fading entirely. *Not that I expected a thanks or anything.*

"Thank you, Felix," Wyvora whispered. She had climbed off A'zek's back at some point, and now she stared at him from entirely too close. In a flash, she kissed his cheek, and the sparking feel of her Spirit in his senses was disorienting, to say the least. Before Felix could react, she was gone again, moving down the green slope before them.

"What was that about?" he muttered.

A'zek gave him a long look as he passed as well, and Felix

couldn't help blushing. He could feel Pit chuckling, somewhere ahead, and even Karys somehow gave him sidelong looks. *I didn't ask for that!*

Mhm, Karys sent, while Pit trilled a series of delighted notes.

Great. He hesitated, looking down the incline. *I hope Vess didn't see that.*

It was a silly hope. He'd never been particularly lucky.

The walk down the mountain was entirely different than their ascent. The ground was covered in loam and wild grasses, small plants and stunted, wind-swept trees. All of which only increased the farther they descended. It was an almost leisurely walk, which allowed their people to regain a bit of their Stamina back and shake off the oppressive pressure of the peaks.

The view was amazing, too, though they were careful not to be caught out in the open. Felix scouted ahead, leaving the others to recover, and he found himself atop a thick Kelaar Tree, eagerly plucking the red and white splotched fruits that dangled from its many branches. Amid the greenery, he peered down the mountainside, idly munching on the fruit and fighting off an inappropriate sensation of nostalgia.

Nostalgia? For what? For almost dying? Please. He was at least two miles above the forest, and from his vantage, a familiar forest spread out across a wide valley. At the far end, there were a series of ridges—not quite mountains, but taller than hills—that dominated the western horizon. His twice-Tempered eyes caught a strip of blue flashing in the afternoon sun, and Felix followed it as it wound across the valley floor, disappearing here and there in the forest. *The river. If we follow that, we'll find the waterfall.*

He hopped down and crept back toward his team, eager to tell them the news. Yet, when he reached the dip in the earth where they hid and crossed the simmering line of wards, he found himself interrupting an argument.

"—come this far, and now you wish to set us aside?" Kylar said. His hair and mustache had grown a little unkempt during their time in the wilds, and now it all but stood on end, as spiky as the jarring notes of his Spirit. "You deny us the satisfaction of the finished Quest?"

"We didn't know the Archon was free, kid," Harn said. "Now we do. You saw how it was in Shelim. It's only gettin' worse now."

"We've a right to stay on, see it through," Vyne said in his steady voice. "We've bled just as much to get this far. More so. I almost died fending off that Arcid's blow. I think we should have a choice here."

"Burn me, you almost died, and you want to finish the job?" Evie hissed.

"All Harn is suggesting is that you five stay here to guard the way back," Vess said patiently. "We're not besmirching your honor or calling your bravery into question. Holding the retreat is necessary and vital, and, yes, less risk than engaging whatever the Archon might have waiting for us below. That does not mean it is lesser, or that any of you are, either."

"It's a choice," Felix said, entering the conversation from the shadows. The Haarguard perked up, just noticing him. "Plans fail. Always do. Haven't met one I haven't seen go screwy in the first three minutes of a fight. And make no mistake, this will be a fight. The Archon is… he's driven, maybe insane, but definitely driven." Felix put his hands on his waist and looked up.

The sky was blue, but the west had begun to lighten into a faded white-orange. "He's expecting us—me, at least. This is beyond risky. I don't even know what he's trying to get ahold of, other than it's dangerous. The Quest is clear on that." Felix gave them all a once-over, teammates new and old. "The Quest is for a Nymean Temple. An eighteen-star Nymean Temple."

While Harn and the others knew that already, the Haarguard all went deathly pale. Good. The Guilders from Setoria knew about Nymean ruins: the more points on a star within the ruin, the more murderous the ruin would be. Felix could still easily envision the terrifying door in the Waterfall Temple, warded with a green lightning that had almost killed him the first time he'd encountered it.

"Eighteen stars," Kylar whispered.

"Blind gods," Nevia cursed softly.

The others only shuddered in mute agreement.

"So as I said: it's a choice," Felix said. He looked them all in the eye and tried to convey a calm he didn't feel. Zara was right. He couldn't coddle people, his team least of all. "The river is down below, less than a few miles away, and we only need to follow that to its source to find the Temple. You have until nightfall to choose. After that, it won't matter."

The walk down the mountain was quiet.

An hour and a half later found them off the mountain and well into the thickening forest. He passed out the Kelaar fruit he'd picked before and pointed out the trees to his team, in case they wanted more. They had to eat on the move, but it had been a while since they'd even done that. Days, Felix realized with dulled surprise. He made sure everyone had some food and water as they hiked downward, crossing the distance to the river far faster than he had expected.

Now that they were out of the mountains, even the slight, vestigial bits of pressure had faded, and a spring had returned to everyone's step. Bright, almost neon eels swarmed into the sky as the light faded, like living ribbons of light. All around them, creatures like Mana Voles, buzzing insects the size of crows, and even a pair of sharp-hued Razorwing Skinks sped by them. The creatures hadn't been corrupted by the Archon, but neither had they even attempted to challenge Felix's team.

That's a nice change. Felix couldn't help the wry smile that twisted his lips.

There was wonder and beauty in the Foglands, and all of it had been hidden by illusion. All to keep a Primordial locked away, and a Lost people's secrets hidden. Regis and Holt had said the Nym hoarded monsters, and he guessed that was at least partly true. Karys himself admitted they'd locked up plenty of threats in the past.

As the Haarguard wrestled with their decision, Felix found his thoughts drifting back to Vvim's Memory. The Geist had been right: there was a lot he had missed. Even reviewing it with his Keen Mind picked up strange details he hadn't noticed at first. The constructs had torn through the people in the audience, killing dozens if not more, and the whole time, the Archon—Merodach—

had simply laughed. Laughed and laughed while he had a bloody, cylindrical blade in his coat, hidden from the court.

Felix shook his head at the thought of it. *The Archon was vile even before he was trapped for thousands of years under a mountain.* He shuddered at the thought of such an imprisonment. He might be a violent, probably-insane enemy, but Felix couldn't help but pity the Archon. A little.

Soon after, they came upon the river itself. It was wide, easily a half-mile, and the shallows were dotted with immense green and white flowers. River Lilies, according to his Eye, were useful for eating as well as in tinctures to improve circulation and remove impurities in one's channels. Felix made a mental note of them. They would be useful to clear a portion of the buildup caused by the absorption of monster cores.

Voracious Eye is level 62!
Aria of the Green Wilds is level 57!

Ironically, for all that he recognized the area and wilderness around him, Felix didn't know the name of the river. Or if it even had one. The last people to live here died thousands of years prior.

The River Eile, it is called, Karys said. *The flow of it has changed much, but those enormous river lilies are impossible to mistake. They would only grow on the River Eile back when I lived in the Western Reaches.*

"Really? Why?" Felix asked.

Simple, really. It was because the… the soil? No. No, it was the leaves of...

Felix exchanged a look with Pit, and concern flashed between their bond. "Don't worry about it, Karys."

O-of course, the sword replied. Felix couldn't help but imagine the stooped old man staring absently at his own hands, and a strong thread of confused melancholy drifted from the blade. Unsure what to do, Felix pretended he hadn't noticed. That'd only make him feel worse, right?

"Felix! Look!"

Vess was pointing across the river where a herd of beasts had congregated in the water. They looked like stags, almost exactly save for their moss-covered backs and crystalline antlers. And the fact that they were twice the size of elephants. A buck stood watching, snorting air through his nostrils at them from a mile away, while does behind him drank sedately. There was no question that the creature had seen them, and Felix was thankful it wasn't more aggressive. It seemed like it could have crossed the river in minutes.

"Beautiful, aren't they? I have never seen a Moss-Back Stag before, let alone one so big," Vess murmured.

"They are huge," he marveled. "How?"

"Magic, I suppose," Vess said. She made a face. "That answer does leave something to be desired, though, does it not? I imagine there is a better one out there."

Above them, a bird cried out as it dove for prey, and the water rippled with schools of fish nipping at insects. Night was coming on fast, and already the Twins had risen above the horizon. Felix turned and took in his team as they refilled their flasks. Yet, before he could say anything, Vyne and Kylar stepped forward as if they had practiced it. Vyne spoke up first.

"Sir, we've decided that we will stay behind and guard your retreat, as Harn has suggested," the shield warrior said. The others were a bit behind and nodded along with him. Vyne seemed frustrated, but his Spirit directed the emotion at himself more than anything. "I only wish we could be more help. Stronger."

Felix clasped the man on the shoulder and grinned. "Give it time. I'm told living is the best way to do that."

"Aye, sir."

Kylar shifted as if he were about to speak, but hesitated. Felix narrowed his eyes, only slightly. "What is it?"

"They will stay behind, but *I* choose to go with you," the swordsman said. Only the barest hints of nervousness and fear tinged his Spirit, and Felix wasn't sure if he should be impressed or annoyed. "My sword is your sword, sir."

Felix clenched his jaw, but nodded. "As you wish, Kylar." Felix caught Harn nodding at him, while Vess looked on with a faint smile. He cleared his throat. "Alright. Apprentice Tiers, Harn will let you know what you need to do, while I speak with the others."

Felix hid behind a grin.

"We've an attack to plan."

CHAPTER SIXTY-TWO

The onset of full dark took the Foglands well before they glimpsed the waterfall, but they had been hearing it for miles. Felix crept through the thick underbrush, senses extended. The waterfall was loud, certainly, but he could hear other things over that sound, within it, things that put his back up.

He heard screams.

They weren't Human screams, or Elven, or Dwarven, but they were full of terror. It quivered in the air, more vivid than the scream itself. As Felix stole up a small ridge, he saw why.

Below, the river had been almost diverted into a complicated series of dank, stone-lined pits. Within was a slurry of runoff river water, rotting plants, and the pulped pieces of monsters. Felix fought back his gorge at the sight and smell of it—even with his Willpower, it was a close thing.

Thin walkways had been erected over each pit, and half-starved creatures were being hauled onto them by tall, ice-covered Reforged. The creatures were a mix of monsters Felix had remembered seeing in the Foglands, and each of them fought tooth and nail against the Reforged. As he watched, a large, bear-like beast bellowed before it was clubbed over the head and tossed over the side. It splashed into the thickened goop, sinking like a boulder.

What the hell are they doing?

Pit merely growled in disgust and frustrated anger. Frustrated because he could fly down there and rip the Reforged apart. More monsters were thrown into the vile muck.

The pits are interconnected, Felix. Look, where the nearest one joins its neighbor? Sigaldry. Karys paused, as if uncertain. *Not any sigaldry I have ever encountered.*

Profane Sigaldry, Felix said by way of explanation. *The Archon's own special blend of bad magic. What's the purpose of this, you think?*

I… am uncertain. It is being funneled somewhere, clearly, based on the tiered designs of the… reservoirs.

Felix could see that. As he scanned the Profane Sigaldry he was able to pick up a bit more of the symbols, but they were all tertiary markings, pieces of the whole. They made little sense without the uniting glyph.

Beyond the vile reservoirs, he could see the curve of the lake the river emptied into. It was heavy with willow-like trees, thick roots, and even thicker undergrowth. Due in part to the strange reservoirs, the banks of the lake were flooding over, spreading water several feet deep as far as a hundred yards from the old shoreline. More Reforged stomped through those muddy waters, either carrying beasts to the pits or hunting more. The waterfall pounded in the distance, barely visible through the trees.

<Regroup,> Felix signed to Vess. She was the nearest in their little relay system. She signed an affirmative back at him, and they both disappeared.

It took far less time to cover the same ground, but backward, padding silently through ferns and roots to find the rest of his team. Atar and Alister were marking things out on the ground again, going over their part of the plan, and both of them started when Felix cleared his throat.

"Blind gods, Felix you scared me," Alister said. He slammed home his rapier, which he had half-drawn out of its sheath at the noise. "What did you see?"

"Wait for the rest," he said.

The Haarguard had settled in some miles back, after Harn and Vess had outlined their plans, intent on securing their getaway if—*when*, he amended—things went wrong. Inside five minutes, Vess, Evie, and Harn filed into the clearing, followed closely by Wyvora, A'zek and Kylar. The swordsman looked frustrated, but Felix didn't have the time to ask why. "What did everyone see?"

"Pits. Many of them, all marked up with those yellow-red sigils that hurt to look at," Evie said. Both she and Harn had gone a bit deeper than Felix had, relying on their Stealth Skills, but it sounded much the same. "Nasty things."

"They're disruptin' the river all along this bank, only I don't know why," Harn added. "Monster parts and plants and river water. What's it all for?"

"If it were less chaotic, I would think they were engaged in alchemy," A'zek rumbled. His dark eyes glittered in the moonlight. "As it stands, it looks simply as if they are denuding the area in preparation for something else."

"Something else? What would require such preparations?" Wyvora asked. "We went further afield, halfway to the mountains, and they had cleared large swaths of the forest. Only stumps remained."

"They're clear-cutting the forest?" Felix asked. "Are they building something?"

"So it seems," A'zek said. "We saw evidence of the trunks being shorn and dragged off to the southwest."

"To the waterfall," Vess said.

Felix drummed his fingers on the bole of a fallen tree. "We must get closer. Atar? Is your working ready?"

"We've gone over the script a score of times, but almost. Almost." Atar gave him a considering glance. "Might move faster if you take a look."

"I'll do that. Harn, take A'zek and scout the waterfall. I'd know more of what we're walking into." The warrior nodded and jerked his head at the big Chimera. They both slid off into the darkness. "Evie and Vess, find a path around these reservoirs."

Evie gave him a mocking salute and a grin before she, too, slipped off into the moon shadows. Vess also gave him a smile, though it was threaded with pain. Both of them ignored it, though, and she followed Evie into the dark. Felix sighed.

"What about me, sir?"

Kylar stood to the side, conspicuous now that everyone else had a task. The swordsman still had that frustrated aura about him, as if he wanted to charge something and get some use out of the two longswords at his waist. It wasn't that he was useless, but Kylar's primary function was offense, and he wasn't particularly good at any sort of stealth. Felix wracked his brain for something to keep him occupied.

"Kylar, I need you to guard us," Felix said. He gestured to where Atar and Alister were still going over sigils and drawings on the ground. "We'll be absorbed in this for a bit. We—I—will need your protection during that time. Can you do that?"

The swordsman puffed up his chest, pride and a puppy dog's eagerness rising in his Spirit. "Of course. You needn't worry. My blades will stop any beast from disturbing you or the others, sir."

Felix nodded, happy to have that work. Then he turned to the collection of rubbings and sigaldry his team had been working on.

It was another hour before everyone returned to their hideaway, but by then, the kinks in Atar's array had been ironed out.

Mostly, he amended. There were a few places that it could get… tricky, but Felix trusted the two mages to work it out in the casting.

Your friends are quite clever, given their disadvantages, Karys said.

"Disadvantages?" Felix asked.

Nothing a proper education in the fundamentals of sigaldry wouldn't correct. But then, this part of the Continent is more desolate than what I recall. I imagine institutes of higher learning are harder to come by in this Age.

"Certainly seems so," Felix agreed. "Regardless, our plan is solid. We only have to not screw it up."

Karys laughed, and Felix couldn't help a gallows smile. Something always went wrong. This time, at least, he was prepared for it. The last thing he wanted was to get his friends hurt or killed.

As it was, all of them were battered in some way, even himself. Parts of him wanted to lay down and sleep for a month, for all that his Stamina and Health were at full. Vess was still bandaged, and the most visibly hurt out of all of them. They had run low on Health Potions during their headlong flight through the mountains. More than anything, Felix wanted to ask her to stay behind, to stay safe. But he meant what he'd said to the Haarguard: they all had to decide for themselves whether to take on this fight. Vess had made her choice, and he wouldn't be the one to gainsay it.

Evie punched him lightly on the shoulder, a lop-sided grin on her face. "What's that for?" he asked.

"You're doin' good."

"With what?"

"She expected you to tell her she can't come, you know?"

Felix looked to Vess, who was talking softly with Atar and Alister. She was intent. "I couldn't do that. I just finished telling the others it was their choice to come or hang back."

"You wanted to, though," Evie pointed out.

Felix rolled his eyes. "Of course I did."

Evie grinned.

"What?"

"Nothin'. Look sharp, Harn's got an eye out for you." She was right, Harn was plodding his way to them, but the chain-fighter slipped away before Felix could stop her.

"Felix. Are we set?" Harn asked. His Spirit was flat to Felix's senses, and the man seemed calm as a cucumber.

"Yeah. Get everyone set," Felix said with a nod. "It's show time."

Harn led them along a path that skirted east, deeper into the forest. Felix thought he would recognize the area, but while some of the trees were familiar, the land had been warped and reshaped by the Archon's forces. Hillocks of dirt and stone contrasted with trees knocked down by the errant strike of something far larger, ice on the trunk evidence of a Reforged's weapon. It was decidedly unnerving, like seeing an old, familiar playground overturned by construction equipment.

Not that I'd call what we did out here fun, Felix sent to Pit, still nestled in his Spirit. Sense memories of a small tenku attacking smaller lizards and insects twitched through their bond. *That's true. It's your home more than mine. How's it feel, coming back?*

Sad. I miss her.

Felix knew who he meant even without the image that came along with Pit's thoughts, of a much larger tenku nuzzling her small pup. His mother. Felix sent warmth and comfort along their bond, wishing he could do more. Pit just went a bit more silent, as if thinking.

All Felix could do was leave him to it.

It was largely silent, save for the thunder of the distant river, though Felix sensed a number of beasts and monsters in their dens. None were higher-leveled than 20 or 23, and all of them were scared. Felix thought they were scared of the Reforged and their strange reservoirs, but they soon realized it was the intense Spiritual pressure in the air.

Archon, Felix almost snarled. It felt the same as when the Shelled Aurochs stampeded, or when the horde of avian monsters had fled the Foglands. *He's here.*

The others could feel it, too, and Kylar had broken out into a heavy sweat. Felix was beginning to regret allowing him to come when the word came.

<Waterfall, just ahead.>

Around a twist of land smaller than a ridge but bigger than a hillock, Felix saw the waterfall. Or what was left of it. The land around the cliff and lake had been dug up and stripped bare, with more of those large, stone-lined reservoirs along the shore. The cliff itself was blasted apart and cut into, so much so that the waterfall itself was diverted off to the side, pounding into what was once dry land. An elaborate and oversized wooden scaffold was secured to its side, climbing the open cliff in wide steps not meant for Human tread. What was worse, the cavern that laid beyond the waterfall was exposed, ripped open along with everything else until Felix could clearly see the entrance to the Temple itself, even in the dark of night.

But are the protections still there? he wondered. *Have they accessed the Temple?*

He flared his Manasight and fought back a hiss of pain. The entire place *reeked* of the Archon's power and Profane Sigaldry, his magic just as twisted as his script. It smelled of metal and violence, tasted like isolation and servitude. It burned at him, until he cut off the Skill. He had seen enough.

He pulled back, behind the shadow of the rise.

"They've torn it apart. The Temple is wide open, and its defenses are gone. I think—I think the Archon has cracked it open," Felix explained.

"Twin's teeth," Alister swore as he peered over the rise. "They've denuded the whole area, even worse than downriver. And it's crawling with those monkeys and bugs, and… I count twenty Reforged. Atar, can you make out what that sigaldry is doing?"

"With time, maybe. Profane Sigaldry burns to read, and it's unrelentingly twisted." Atar spat to the side. "It tastes like destruction and madness."

"It tastes?" Kylar muttered to himself. Felix doubted anyone else heard him.

"So, what? We lost?" Evie said with a scowl. "That's not fair. We just got here."

"Is the Quest still active?" Harn asked.

Felix toggled it open.

The Door Of The Lidless Eye!
Seek out the Temple you once took refuge within, Ascendant. Dire secrets dwell within, waiting the Inheritor. It is your duty to prevent the darkness from escaping into the light. Do not tarry, for the Archon is close, and the darkness closer.

"It is. Hasn't changed," he said.

"Then we're in the clear. Either the big metal idiot just got in there, or he hasn't been able to figure out the door thing." Harn rolled his shoulders, unsheathing his axes with the same easy motion. "Either way, it means the plan ain't changed, yeah?"

After a moment, Felix nodded. The plan would still be good. *I just hope it works.*

A'zek growled, a low rumble. "We'll make them pay for damaging such a place. Such history." Wyvora gripped her spear in mute agreement.

"Are we ready?" he asked.

"Aye."

"Yes."

"Mhm."

"Y-yes."

To battle, Felix. To battle!

A chirrup from his Spirit, and they were all in agreement. As one, they split up into separate teams, each one moving forward with determination. Felix ducked low, moving ahead of the rest; he and Pit were moving solo again, and not only because he bore the key to the Door of the Lidless Eye.

He had a feeling, a strong one, that the Archon would ignore his friends. He checked Inheritor's Will in its scabbard, unsheathing the blade for several inches before letting it slide back.

No turning back now.

"They're moving," Tyrk said. "Toward the open cliff-face."

"Then we follow," Ifre replied.

"Into *that*?" Isyk said, his nerves obvious. "Those monsters will kill us as soon as look at us."

"We go to secure the Temple, as we've been charged," Ifre said, her voice iron. "Or did you think this journey would be without risk?"

"N-no, Captain, I just—"

"You are afraid," she stated. Isyk jerked back as if struck. "And that is acceptable. Let fear Temper you, strengthen you, but remember you are beyond it. Above it."

The man tightened his grip on his spear until his knuckles whitened. He nodded, once, with purpose.

"Very good. Now," Isyk said as she padded through the forest, spear at the ready. "Now we go, as the Raven wills."

"As the Raven wills," they both said in low tones.

The darkness rose up and enveloped them all until only moon-shadow and bobbing ferns could be seen. Then those stilled, too.

CHAPTER SIXTY-THREE

Felix took a deep, calming breath, making sure Meditation flared as far as it was able. His Bastion of Will and Deep Mind hummed in the background, distant songs almost out of earshot. After the jaunt up the mountain, he was worried about using his Abyssal Skein again, but they would not make it across the devastated landscape without it. There were no places to really hide except for the stone-lined reservoirs, and there was no way Felix was risking a dive into that… soup.

It should be safe, Karys reassured him. *The burrs in the pattern of the Skill seem mostly smoothed out. You must sound it carefully. Utilize your Intent, as you have been doing. It is the… the truest....*

An annoyed grunt came from his blade. *Another lapse in memory?* Felix asked gently.

In—indeed. I am a leaky sieve, Felix. I worry how much will be left of me in a month's time. In a year?

I'm sure there is a solution. We'll find it, he promised.

Don't waste your time on me. You have a Quest to complete. Go. Sound your Skill.

Felix nodded, though to anyone watching, it would have been at nothing. He felt with his Affinity, pressed close to the strange song of the Skill, and with his Will-honed Intent, brought it to brilliant life.

Abyssal Skein.

The Void, or what felt like it, crept up and through his channels and poured from his hands and elbows, feet and knees, the base of his skull. It enveloped him like a satin cloak draped in oil, drawn from the darkness between his Skills as much as from the Skill itself. Aside from a painful twang in the melody, the Skill was steady, thrumming with a chill implacability that still made Felix nervous. The feel of oil against his skin was unpleasant and constant. He fought to ignore it.

He stepped out of the trees, keeping low despite his Skill. Abyssal Skein melded him with the world, not so much active camouflage as it was an insistence to the world that nothing was amiss. With each level, the effect grew stronger, and now he was like a shadow flitting across the blasted terrain, darting between reservoirs and the plodding tread of Reforged and chittering Greater Wretches. The massive insects, easily as large as the Reforged, were strutting near the cliff and snacking on… something Felix didn't care to inspect. Monster remains, he hoped. He saw no others as he moved closer to the scaffolding, fully intending on climbing its huge edifice—until he did.

A lone Arcid sat atop the lowest rungs of the wooden scaffolding, its body oozing around the crude logs like a tar pit given sentience. The thing resembled nothing as much as a pile of noxious jelly with metal bones inside, all of it lit from within by a venomous green fire. The fire rotated within that jelly, winking on and off as it spun. Felix quickly realized the fires were its eyes, and it saw everything around it, as evidenced by the small Mana Vole that dared come too close. The Arcid shot a stream of itself at it, striking the agile creature and enveloping it in its viscous goo. The creature withered and sizzled away in an instant.

Not good. Felix backpedaled before moving laterally toward the lake. The problem, of course, was that the ground was a squelching morass, filled with thick, pungent mud and ankle-deep water that would prove impossible to stealth within. Even if he was completely and utterly invisible, Felix doubted it would help. *Shit.*

He looked up, gauging the distance to the cave. Felix could jump, that was easily within his power, but landing would be tricky, especially since he'd have to break through the thick scaffolding to access the Temple. It all but blocked off entry from anywhere save the very bottom, where the Arcid waited.

The plan, at least Plan A, was to sneak up into the Temple, open the Door, and deal with whatever was inside. Just him and Pit. And Karys, he supposed.

The others didn't love Plan A and truly doubted it'd work, so Plan B was developed. Felix wasn't a huge fan of Plan B for several reasons, not the least of which wad that it put his friends in danger. He was soundly outvoted.

Resolved to his next step, Felix crept closer, past the Reforged stomping once more across the terrain and under the iridescent bulk of a Greater Wretch. He moved ever nearer the poisonous Arcid. Felix had realized what coated the creature, though his first guess had been acid. No. Pure poison Mana, so strong it was a thick liquid. *A thickquid, if you will.*

A slightly hysterical laugh bubbled up in his chest at *that* thought, and he fought it back. The Arcid turned toward him, its eye fires swirling, but it moved on. Nervous sweat beaded his forehead, his mirth vanished completely, and Felix focused.

One step after the next.

There was only a small gap between the surprising bulk of the Arcid and the damaged cliff, but he could fit. Barely. The Arcid's Spirit was strangely opaque to him, as if it had little in the way of emotions, so it was even more of a gamble that the thing wouldn't move into him, even accidentally. Felix padded closer.

Pit chirruped worriedly.

Please keep me away from that... thing, Karys whispered. *It is foul.*

Felix felt that nervous laughter again. His sword didn't want to get dirty. *Concentrate.* He stepped onto the first log, just another shadow in the night. The Arcid was only an arm-span away. He stepped again, this time bringing himself up and onto the same level. Now, the thing was inches away, and instinctively Felix sucked in his stomach. His body was lean, for the most part, but he was willing to do anything to be thinner at that moment.

Another step. Another—

Something cracked.

It was barely anything, just the slightest scrape of his boots against the shaven log, the faintest of sounds. Yet the Arcid's dozen eye fires centered on it like he'd set off fireworks. Felix froze in place. If he were found out now, reaching the Temple would be impossible without a long, drawn out fight. And if the Archon were here...

The Arcid burbled, its gelatinous casing swirling. The metal bones within, hunks and pieces of an enormous skeleton, jabbed out, still covered by its coating. The bones—finger bones, he realized—prodded the log that cracked. Pushed at it, tested it. The Arcid didn't sense Felix, but it knew something was wrong. Felix cast about, moving only his eyes, thinking furiously for a solution, for a—a scapegoat.

Breathlessly, Felix moved his foot again, this time pushing it closer to the poison-coated hands than ever before. A small stub of bark, mostly shorn, hung from the top of the log. With a deft tap of his boot, the bark snapped. He jerked his foot back, just in time to avoid the lightning-fast slap of caustic poison atop the log. The hand felt at the bark, pulled it and consumed it until it withered into a dark wisp of nothing.

The Arcid moved back, settling into its old position once again.

Felix was tempted, oh god, was he tempted to make a run for it then. But he held his ground, watching the creature, waiting. The Arcids were almost always smarter than Felix anticipated, and more powerful. This one was likely no different.

Seconds passed, minutes. Just as he was considering it time to move, the Arcid snapped its foul tendril outward, spearing the area all around the broken bark… which was a hairsbreadth from his boots. Felix clenched his jaw, but refused to move as the Arcid pulsed and poured itself into that area, twitching like a bowl of evil jelly.

Then it was gone, retreated back to his position again. Its eyes spun about, watching the desolate approach to the scaffolding, satisfied it was alone.

Felix didn't breathe—couldn't—he just moved. Affinity and Intent paired to his Will, he sounded another Skill, layering its song atop Abyssal Skein.

Unfettered Volition!

His feet were the wind as he moved, all but dancing up the logs, across the faint traps laid out on them. Easy to see, easy to avoid with his Manasight flaring along with everything else. Then Felix reached the top, and the stone opened up, revealing the warm, yellow light from inside the Nymean Temple. It spilled into the cavern where once it was utterly hidden, and even from a distance, Felix could tell the sigaldry around the entrance was slashed apart. He had been right. The Archon had entered the Temple, after all.

He crossed the pockmarked cavern with little difficulty. The way was empty, and not even the waterfall was there to detract from his focus, diverted as it was to the west. Even its roar was muted. He stepped over the slashed sigils, hand firmly on the hilt of the Crescian Blade.

The alcoves were all smashed, the murals once depicting various Nym with wild creatures defaced or blown out entirely. Felix slowed down, unwilling to rush, at that point. If an ambush were to happen, it would be now, when there was no place to take cover. He stepped carefully, avoiding the scattered debris with as much care as he could manage.

The Temple was the same as before, minus the damage, a long hall fitted with four doors, each surmounted by a star. The rear of the hall ballooned into a circular chamber, one that was dominated by a raised dais in the shape of a nine-pointed star. As he drew closer, he made out other recognizable details. The dais was made of a lighter stone than the floor and hexagonal pillars, and it was about twenty feet across, tip to tip. The face of it was carved with convoluted lines that criss-crossed the surface in seemingly random patterns. It wasn't an inscription or any sigaldry Felix had ever seen before. It was, as he'd assumed once before, purely decorative.

He hadn't come for the empty dais.

Beyond the raised star stood a massive set of double doors made of dull green metal and covered in carvings of a different sort. On each door, facing toward the center, was a Nymean figure, wearing elaborate robes and holding stars in their hands. Each star had nine points, much like the raised platform. At the center, where they would open up, there was a raised relief of jagged tree-like objects. Lightning, maybe. But there were many, all bursting from one point and surrounded by a much more elaborate eighteen-point star. Sigaldry surrounded these figures, covering every available space on the metal doors. Unlike before, he could actually read them this time, though it was a pain to translate through all the permutations. It said the same thing, repeated over and over.

Secure We Those Below,
Held Within The Gelid Home
Iron Struck And Fire Scourged,
Faster Sank The Stone

Three And Three And Three,
Want and Need and Crave
We Open For The Inheritor,
Neath Thy Metal Stave

Stand Ready, Be Quick, Skill Be Fair
Listen Not, See Not, Speak
Beware.
Beware.
Beware.

Felix swallowed the fluttery feeling in his gut. *Meter is kinda funky. Why does it feel more intimidating when it rhymes?*

A secondary set of symbols lined the floor in front of the doors, inscribed in an arc and leading up the walls and around the frame. At the very top was a single character that looked like a precise 'V' cut with flowing lines and hash-marks.

A warding, and still active. If I'm wrong about this, I don't think I'll have time to be mad. The last time he'd walked too close to these doors, green lightning had almost fried him. He unsheathed his Crescian Blade.

Trust, Felix. This is the key, and yours the hand meant to hold it, Karys said.

Yeah. Well. Here's goes nothing.

Felix stepped over the line of sigils. The ward pulsed, once, and —nothing. No lightning. The ward had immediately gone dark. *Step one, successful,* he thought.

He moved to the door, tentatively reaching out to the dull metal surface. Again, no lightning, and his fingers touched the cool metal, felt at its raised sculptures. There was no handle, so Felix pushed against it. The eighteen-point star above lit up without warning, and Felix made to jump back, but his hand was stuck fast.

"Shit!"

Wards Breached
Temple Defenses Failed
Analyzing…

Unbound Detected.
Nymean Detected.
Primordial Detected!

Countermeasures Deployed.

Shit! Felix flared Stone Shaping, trying to move the metal, but the door was impervious to his spell. The Mana slid off of it ineffectively. He pulled, straining his Strength against the hold it had on him. *Karys!*

I am trying!

Inheritor Status Recognized
Inheritor Status Supersedes All Bloodlines!

The star above him dimmed, and the voice inside his head shifted its tone entirely.

Welcome Inheritor.
Internal Containment Breach Detected
Do You Wish To Access Containment Unit #135?

Almost in unison, Karys and Felix both answered. *Yes.*

With a sound like the groaning dead, the doors opened, pulling away from Felix's now-free hand. Beyond the threshold, the tiles continued, but each one was a complicated design of geometric points. Eighteen-point star tiles, contained within a hexagon. Six steps in, all detail faded to darkness, one that not even his Manasight could penetrate.

Wards. Wards upon wards, Karys said in an astounded voice. *I have never before seen so many layered in one place. What threat does this place hold?*

So involved was Felix with that first step, that it was only Pit's panicked shriek that alerted him to danger. Without questioning his Companion, Felix leaped aside, rolling to his feet in a smooth tumble. He came up holding his sword and lightning crackling in his left hand, but still, he wasn't ready for what he saw.

"You sensed me. I am impressed," said the Archon. He loomed in the broken Temple, filling up the space like a living wall of golden metal. "I suppose the reputation you've garnered is not entirely unearned."

Felix's eyes boggled. *Where the hell did he come from?*

I do not know! Karys sent, buzzing in his grip. *I still cannot sense him now!*

"Thank you for opening the Door, Nym." The Archon's helmeted face deformed, the bottom portion stretching wide in a grim facsimile of a smile. "I have been waiting for you."

CHAPTER SIXTY-FOUR

"Come now, Nym. There is no reason for hostility. Not yet." That smile stretched ever wider, the golden metal deforming. *How was he doing that?* "You have thrived ever more so since last we spoke. Far more than when we met. You were but a mewling worm, come to rob my Domain. Now here you stand, ready to stop me, the mighty Nymean hero." The smile dropped. "How predictable."

Adamant Discord spun through Felix's core space, a bright star begging to shine, but Felix held it back. The Archon wasn't moving, nor was he sounding a spell. He needed time to think. "Been a while, Archie. Last time I saw you, you were beaten bloody and run outta town." He smiled. "Figuratively speaking. Literally, too, I guess."

Where before Felix hadn't even felt the Archon's presence, he briefly caught a hint of murderous rage in the air. The mere thread of it worried Felix, as it hadn't come from the Archon directly, but the entire Temple, as if Felix were submerged within a pool of his Spirit.

You aren't wrong, Felix, Karys whispered. *This one is strong. Stronger even than the Memory suggested.*

Pit just snarled through their bond, still hidden.

Voracious Eye!

Voracious Eye Failed.

The Archon tilted his head, flanged helmet tapping gently against his raised pauldrons. "Haarwatch has been a jewel I could not claim, thanks to you. I found myself angry for that at the start. Furious, one could say." His eye-fires, bright red, creased as if with pleasure. "Yet your obstinance has proven to be my boon. I must confess, I am grateful to you, Felix Nevarre. Had you not repulsed my forces, you would not have had the strength to claim that bauble." He gestured at the sword Felix still held between them. "Crescian Bronze will not calmly go to forge, Nymean. It must be convinced. That willfullness does not degrade after it's worked, whether that is a weapon or not."

Felix narrowed his eyes, but let the creature talk.

"Had you not claimed it, this Door would still lie untouched. My Profane Sigaldry could not even mar the stones around the threshold! And those wards were not gentle to any who approached." For the first time, Felix realized that the Archon's left hand was marred with blackened patterns. Scorch marks where lightning had danced across his metal body. The Archon noticed his glance and held out the arm. "Powerful wards. It makes me wonder what the Nym were so keen on keeping from me. Me, who has more claim on their secrets than any other." His eyes burned, hot and fierce and more than a little mad. "Even you, boy."

Felix didn't reply. He was feeling at the Archon's Spirit with his Affinity, slowly, carefully. His slow steps brought him before the Door again, and the Archon frowned.

"Power has been handed to you, Nym. I have… I have seen it before. Where I—" The Archon slammed at its own head, denting the metal. "I can't remember. The Voice… I woke in the dark, Nym, in the dark where you all put me. Everything was taken from me. I remember that. I clawed it back, as much as I could, but it's not enough. It will never be enough to repay what was taken," the Archon glared, and its helmet snapped back into shape. "Taken by you."

"I'm not Nym," Felix said. "I'm—"

"You're close enough!" The shout rattled the stones at their feet. "I know you've been infected, been turned somehow, into a Primordial. It's impossible that you survived, yet here you are."

The Archon sneered. "Yet still, you are no match for me. No. Never that."

The thread! Felix!

Pit's cry was ice water in Felix's veins. His Affinity snagged upon a thread of connection floating before him, one that was snagged securely around himself. It shot off, straight as an arrow, right into the Archon. The creature's Spirit was disguising it, but the moment it had their attention, it billowed, expanded until it dominated his vision. Yet still, he could see the Archon just as clearly, a snake coiled to strike.

"I see you can feel it now." The Archon laughed again, and it was too high, too ragged. "I've known you were on the way from the very start. I could feel you approaching. How could I not? We are Linked, boy. You, a Nym, and I… someone the Nym sought to control. A threat too great for their vaunted compassion!"

The thread shook, quivered with violence, and that was all Felix needed.

Unfettered Volition!

A beam of white-hot flame speared through the space his head had just been, missing him by only inches and haring off into the thick darkness behind the Door. Felix tumbled, fetched up on his feet in less than an instant, already hurling his spell.

Adamant Discord!

The connections between him and the air outside the Temple firmed up into steel-hard cables, and that very action sent lightning bursting down their length. Thunder cracked, like an explosion in the sky, loud enough to wake the dead. He hoped.

The Archon easily dodged the sizzling bolts, laughing as he did. "Pathetic! All that time to line up a shot, and still you fail!" More fire kindled along his right arm, spiraling up from the Profane Sigaldry carved in his golden limb. "Face me, then! Finally!"

Felix only snarled wordlessly, grabbing at the fire that slashed at him like an enormous claw.

Ravenous Tithe!

The claw quivered before it burst apart, a field of flames that he pulled down into his channels with some effort. It resisted his Skill, pushing back just enough to notice. It slowed him enough that the metal hammer hit him square in the shoulder. Felix all but teleported from the ground to the far wall, his dense Body smashing a whole foot into the Temple's wall.

Felix gagged in pain. So many things broke that he couldn't keep track of it all.

Sovereign of Flesh!

That same broken flesh rippled and stretched, bursting apart as scales as black as night formed across his Body. Spikes of ivory bone thrust out of his knees and elbows, lining the tops of his forearms and shins and shredding the hell out of his clothing. Felix burst from the wall, breaking much more of it as he did. His skin and muscles and bones *screamed* at him—he hadn't used this Skill in weeks. He hadn't *needed* it.

Pit fought to emerge, but Felix shoved back, hard. *It's too dangerous! He'll kill you!*

He'll kill you*!* Pit fired back.

He stood, watching the Archon warily as his arm and shoulder began to visibly repair itself.

"Powerful stats, Nym. Too powerful." The Archon paced, both of them now circling each other. "How? A Skill such as that, Vitality such as that, does not come for free. What bargains have you struck?"

"No bargains," Felix said and spat out a tooth as it was replaced by sharp fangs. His mouth cracked, reshaping itself slightly, becoming wider, more feral. A predator. "Only consequences."

Unfettered Volition!

Adamant Discord!

Felix flared his Skills in addition to his Affinity, and with all the Willpower he could muster, seized the connection between him and the Archon. Lightning streamed between them, searing into his golden armor, and Felix *pushed.*

"WHAT!?" The Archon was thrown entirely from his feet, hurtling twenty feet into the opposite wall. A blinding crack of blue-white lightning hit a second later, once, twice, three times as Felix bellowed in sympathetic pain. His Aspects, not quite recovered from before, shook with the strain. But he couldn't stop.

Wrack and Ruin!

Wrack and Ruin!

Dual-cast orbs of dark acid shot at the Archon, but the creature batted them away with contemptuous ease. The wall fell apart beneath the creature's limbs, still crackling with electricity, and the Archon took to his feet. Felix didn't let up.

Influence of the Wisp!

Stone Shaping!

Shadow Whip!

Enthrall Failed.

Blue wispfire surged up the Archon's form before dissipating, but that didn't stop bands of stone from criss-crossing the creature's chest, stymieing his forward advance. A black whip snapped out, lashing him across the head and shoulders and driving him back into the wall with a resounding *crunch.*

Arrow of Perdi—

A beam of white-hot flame shot at him, spoiling his spell and sending Felix pivoting to the side. Another and another fired at him, but Felix dodged back, Unfettered Volition and his own Agility proved too much for the Archon's aim.

Yet, in that time, the armored creature had broken free of his stone bindings and stepped forward. "I've no clue how you've done that. I should be impervious to spells of force. Impervious to anything you try, Nym." The Archon's Spirit flared, pressing down upon everything around it. "*How?*"

Felix gritted his teeth but remained standing. "Like this."

Adamant Discord!

Lightning flashed, grappled, and the Archon twisted to avoid his hold. But he could not escape. Felix bore down and slammed the creature along the alcoves, shattering column after column with the Archon's face until—

He stopped. The damn Archon stopped himself as if he'd run into a wall too thick to shatter. Red lightning crackled about the Archon, and Felix felt a pulse of foreign, shrieking joy through the air around him.

Felix! Karys warned.

Felix's eyes widened, but it was too late. As fast as his own Skill, yellow-red lightning struck back at him, traveling along the same connection, and Felix was sent flying. He rebounded hard off the open metal Door. But instead of the door breaking, Felix did. His leg, his femur had snapped clean in half.

But that was a paltry pain, not nearly enough to cut through his Song of Absolution. He flared his Sovereign of Flesh, feeding it more Essence as it ran hot. His leg felt like it was being filled with molten lead, and it was a wonder it didn't melt through his thigh entirely. The Archon laughed as he climbed to his feet, having to use the Door as leverage.

"Haha! I've figured out your trick! The connection! How clever, how vile. You use what the Nym of old would consider sacred, defiling it to impress your Will on me?" The fire in his eyes danced while delight and disgust spun end over end through his titanic Spirit. "Well two can play at that, can't we?"

Adamant Discord!

Felix's blue-white force flared just as the yellow-red bolt seared across his vision. Both of them blasted backward; the Archon into a shattered alcove and Felix into the opening of the Door.

He rolled across the star-pressed tiles until his clawed feet slid into the thickened darkness. A jolt of sensation hit him, a chill that near enough froze his feet solid. Gasping in pain and fright, Felix scrambled out of the dark, and his hand secured once again upon the hilt of his Crescian Blade. The cold vanished completely, as did the dark itself, revealing a steep set of stairs and walls carved into lace. Stars and other incomprehensible shapes marched down the length of the stairs, vanished only as the steep steps curved around a sharp bend.

The Song of Absolution is level 71!

...

The Song of Absolution is level 73!

Something is down there, Felix. Something horrid, Karys said in a strangled tone.

Whispers tugged at him, and a soft, wet breeze caressed the skin of his throat. Felix flinched and climbed to his feet, warily eyeing the stairwell.

"I'm not done with you, boy!"

Yellow-red lightning snatched Felix from the edge of the dark and yanked him back out into the buttery Temple light. The lightning bit at him, charring the clothes on his body and chewing through the strap of his satchel. Frantically, he kicked at the ground, rotating his body even as he was pulled toward the grinning Archon. In one smooth motion, he sheathed his blade and grasped his satchel, refusing to let it fall, and engaged his own Will.

Adamant Discord!

Adamant Discord is level 66!

...

Adamant Discord is level 68!

He halted, a mere twenty feet from the Archon, still hovering in mid-air. The Archon's grin creaked and broke, before it twisted completely. Blue-white lightning surged across Felix's chest and arms, fighting back against the Archon's hold, until Felix floated by his Will alone.

"Your problem, Archie, is that you think this is about force," Felix said between panting breaths.

The Archon himself was quivering, his pauldrons trembling with the strain. "Force is but a means! I will destroy you by whatever method I deem fit," the words were a mad growl, torn between a shriek and the basso rumble of metallic thunder. "You're mortal, Felix Nevarre. A powerful one, but destined to die just the same!" The yellow-red lightning crept further between them, almost reaching Felix's face and chest. "I am as old as the civilization you trod upon! The weight of my existence is the crushing behemoth to your paltry Chimera!"

It was true, Felix realized. The Archon's accumulation of power, time, and significance within his golden shell was immense; it easily outmatched Felix's. Yet, his blue-white lightning fought back the red with everything it had, matching it, destroying it. Devouring it.

Ravenous Tithe!

Ravenous Tithe is level 71!

His own Skill cut short; the yellow-red lightning hit Felix almost too fast to activate his Tithe. Almost. His channels screamed as they imbibed the noxious power of the Archon, shredding even as the power dissolved to Mana and was swallowed whole by his abyss. Felix dropped to his feet, satchel spilling, and the Archon stumbled, the force against which they both struggled suddenly gone.

Unfettered Volition!

Wild Threnody!

Green acid Mana bloomed out of Felix's fists as he rushed the Archon, who was so surprised he barely defended himself. Both fists hit, staggering the giant proportioned suit of armor, and setting him up for a flipping kick to the head. Felix's scaled and clawed foot hit, deforming the Archon's faceplate before rotating back onto his feet. He hit again. And again, each time harder and faster than the last. Each time, the metal dented, until it began to tear, until Felix's claws slashed through the metal entirely.

Felix was consumed. Each strike was a strike against the terror the Archon represented, each punch or kick or rending claw was another piece of vengeance. He didn't stop. He couldn't. He wouldn't.

Wild Threnody!

He drew more power, and this time, his fists shone with blue-gold light. Wild Threnody sang through him, and the Arrow of Perdition blazed at its core, fueling the Threnody and captured within his jabbing fists. He struck, once, twice, and the Archon's chest plate sundered.

Wild Threnody!

Blue-gold radiance suffused Felix, driving him forward, as if the light was drawn to the Archon's bloated core. He thrust the flattened edge of his hand out, stabbing like a knife.

He couldn't stop. He *wouldn't!*

CHAPTER SIXTY-FIVE

"No!" the Archon screamed, raw and high. Sigils burned on his chest, within it, a fountain of liquid light. Felix was pushed back, but not for long. He strained, forcing through the deluge of sludge-like Mana. "I AM GREATER THAN YOU!"

Felix's talons scratched at the center of the Archon, just barely, when the Mana around him solidified into a crystalline cage. He was suddenly rooted to the spot, while screaming Dissonance shook his Spirit. The yellow-red *wrongness* of it scraped at Felix, but he'd come to know it well. It was the same Dissonance that had fueled the Maw's madness, the opposite of Harmony, existing in the space between notes.

Ravenous Tithe!

His channels pulled at the crystalline lattice around him, but it didn't so much as budge. Felix bared his teeth at the Archon, who had stumbled back. The creature's huge body was twice Felix's size, and it loomed over him as sparks and clouds of Mana vapor poured from his wounds.

"You-you see? *You see?!*" The Archon slammed his foot down on the tiles, shattering them, cratering the ground for twenty feet or more around them. Felix didn't budge, held in place by the solid bars of the Archon's Mana. "My power is such that I have crystallized my Mana. You, who have just barely condensed to a liquid!"

That unyielding crystal flowed down and over Felix's limbs as the Archon shoved his hand forward, grasping Felix by the neck. He lifted him as easily as a man lifted a pillow. "You are nothing compared to me, Nym."

"I—ugk." Felix tried to speak, but madness raged in the Archon's eyes and howled through his Spirit. He would not listen, Felix knew. "—am not—" The Archon squeezed, his massive hands splintering his scales with excruciating slowness. "—not—Nym. I am—" Then Felix could feel it, something rising nearby, something big. It was all he could do to draw breath. "I—am—Unbound."

The Archon's eyes went wide just as the entire Temple was shaken to its core.

Screams came from outside, bestial ones, but also the distinct hollering of Humans. *My friends.* The Archon twisted, looking through the exit, and the shell around him slackened. Felix took his opportunity.

Mantle of the Infinite Revolution!

A spume of cold Mana surged from his channels, blurring the world around him with icy mist for a half-second before Felix pulled it close and spun it all. It rotated at speed around his body, faster and faster, until the ice and water Mana flipped to fire and heat, and the Mantle ignited. To the Archon, he became a pillar of fire, superheating his metal body and sending a spike of surprising pain into him. The Archon howled in alarm.

Thanks, Atar. Using the Skill like that had been his idea, after all.

Ravenous Tithe!

This time, the Mana around him buckled and was half-torn into Felix's channels before the Archon solidified his hold. It burned as it entered him, tearing his already-worn channels into bloody shreds, but Felix didn't stop. Not until he slipped completely from the Archon's grasp and kicked back.

Felix fetched up against a shattered wall, hard enough to break off a few tiles, and let his Mantle die away. His neck and shoulders were bruised, and he had two deep gashes across his chest. Felix focused on his Sovereign of Flesh, feeding it the abundance of Essence he'd just torn from the Archon. With unsteady movement, he rose from the ground, never once looking away from the Archon's own recovering form. The golden giant stepped from the remains of his crystalline cage, pulling the majority of it back into his own core.

"Tricks," he muttered. "It's all tricks. It has to be. No more," the Archon jabbed a finger at Felix from across the chamber. "No more tricks! You cannot be Unbound! You cannot! They're forbidden to summon more!" He was panting now, and the darkness around his fiery eyes grew wider in obvious panic. "Forbidden. Because—because of me. Because I was..."

The Archon stopped moving. It was so complete that Felix could have mistaken him for a statue, were the creature's Spirit not gone absolutely wild. Discordant song and skewered melodies shook the Temple until dust rained from the ceiling.

"...Because I was the last. I was Unbound. Am. Am Unbound." The Archon looked at his hands in wonder, then at the Temple around them. "I remember. Pieces and shreds, but it's there! The Voice!"

Some of that made sense to Felix, but he didn't care if the Archon was having a breakthrough. He dashed for the Door, hand to his Crescian Blade as he went.

Unfettered Volition!

Red lightning met his charge, but Felix countered with his own Adamant Discord. The two Skills caught up in one another, and Felix catapulted forward and into the doorjamb. He ricocheted from it, feeling a jagged snap at his collar, before he was borne down to the ground.

"I remember, Felix!" The Archon landed on him, a tractor trailer in the form of a giant golden golem. He leered down at him, his golden chest still rent and burning with an incandescent furnace of yellow-red light. "The fog is clearing at last! I can see it, the connection we share isn't just the Nym. Isn't just the Race we'd taken. It is our very nature!" A golden gauntlet shoved at Felix's spine, pressing his broken clavicle into the unforgiving stone. The Archon laughed, and it was so unhinged it made Felix's skin crawl.

"Master! Master! We are under attack!"

The shout came from outside of Felix's vision, but it was a strong, metallic voice. *More Arcids.*

"Under attack?" the Archon rumbled.

"An array! They used the very force of the river to kill our beasts! To sunder the reservoirs! The pits are broken! Number 55778 is dead!"

"*What?* Fix them, you fools! We cannot lose them! Where is 55811?" the Archon asked, but didn't wait for a reply. "Find him and set him to course! Eradicate these pests, or I'll tear all of you back to scrap!"

"Y-yes, Master. As you say!"

Heavy clunking followed the voice, mingling with the screams and howls from down below. Where his friends were fighting for their lives. *Against how many monsters? How many Arcids?* He had to get free. Felix strained against the Archon's pressure, and even managed to rise a few inches before the Archon slammed him back down.

"No no, Unbound. You'll be going nowhere." Delighted, manic satisfaction was tumbling through his Spirit. "We have a Door to explore, you and I." That same crystalline Mana spread down and over him, encasing him entirely in a form-fitting cage of power. He was lifted from the ground, still utterly immobile, until he floated at the Archon's side. "Come now. Let us walk in the darkness."

Together, they stepped into bitter shadow.

All was chaos in the moonlit night. Vess flickered among the lesser beasts, slaying them en masse as they attempted to defend their master's camp. Her spear held no mercy, skewering Simians, Wretches, and even Reforged with an efficiency that she almost wished Darius could have seen. She flowed through the Seven Steps of the Dragoon, her kata executed with a grace she had once found impossible to achieve. A dance of death.

Grace is level 62!
Dragoon's Footwork is level 68!
Spear of Tribulations is level 71!

Suddenly, the sky lit up. The sound of rushing water once again ceased, and in its place a column of blue light speared from the heavens. It was forty paces in diameter, and where it landed, it crushed the land itself… and any creatures unfortunate enough to be atop it. Dozens of lesser beasts expired instantly, ground to foul muck in the wet mud and exposed bedrock. The Reforged caught in its blow were staggered, their armor shattered, exposing cold blue skin and metal hides. But of the Arcid that dogged her, she could see no sign.

"Blighted Night," she cursed. "Not one Arcid taken down."

"That's it! The river needs time to build up momentum again!" Atar gasped from the side. Allister was panting just as hard, both of them wrung out like dishrags. Still, dozens of monsters laid around them, dead as doornails. "Even then, it will be a paltry thing!"

The reservoirs were all sundered, at least those on this side of the river, the earth split and crushed enough to spill the muck they contained. It was flowing across her boots, even now, but Vess forced herself not to think about what was in the foul water. The sigils that ran around the reservoirs were also ruined, cracked, or simply guttered out. It was a victory.

"The spearwoman! Kill her! Kill her at any cost!" a voice snarled, thick and bubbling. Similar to the last Arcid she'd faced. It was an Arcid, of that there was little doubt. She could *feel* it in the air, a rotten, twisted sense of hate and fear and bloodlust co-mingled with the acrid tang of bile.

AFI +1
Elemental Eye is level 51!

There you are. She grimaced. *Poison Mana. An entire Body of it. And beside it…* Beside the virulently green blob advancing on her was a taller form, more graceful but equally deadly. Its Body consisted of hundreds of sharpened points, needles and long blades all angled away from its vitals. Where the Reforged and lesser beasts stalked or stomped, these two flowed at them with a deadly competency. Vess could feel it in the wind.

Evie landed beside her, a whisper even in the knee-high muck. She offered a grim smile. "Which one do you want? Goopy or the blade?"

"I shall handle the poison one," Vess said. Her silver Spears levitated back to her, torn free from the smoking corpse of a Ghost-fire Simian. "Air should be… sufficient to suppress its noxious abilities. Are you fine with the other?"

"Pfah, you kiddin'? It's got blades on chains! It's practically mockin' me!" Evie's grin grew wider, more manic.

"Be careful Evie. I would not lose you."

"Right back atcha, your Grace." Evie's hand found Vess' and gave it a squeeze. "See you on the other side."

"I will head—" The words turned to ash in Vess' mouth as a shape burst from the mire they had created. Vess let out a cry and sent all seven of her silver Spears streaking forward, but four were deflected by unnaturally fast limbs, and the others slipped off its muck-slickened body. It was a horrifying combination of Frost Giant and Hoarhound, an enormous, piecemeal wolfman covered in ice and jagged metal plates. It landed among them, but Vess and Evie were already shooting in opposite directions.

"Another Archid?!" Evie shouted. "This is startin' to feel unfair!"

"Atar!" Vess yelled, ducking under the lunging swipes of the bestial Arcid. "Atar, we need your array again! Fast!" Her only response was a pained groan. "Evie!"

"On it!" The woman was already flipping through the air, slinging her chain forward at the last second to dart away from the beast's leaping slash. The heavy chain yanked her to the side, only slowed when she shifted her mass back from the chain, and threw it again. From the outside, it looked strange and impossible, but Evie pulled it off with a Dexterity that made her seem like a bird on the wing.

"Breaking Wheel!"

The chain dropped, spun into a tight circle, now so heavy it ripped at the air as it fell. It hit the bestial Arcid with the sound of a hundred year oak falling to the earth, and a wave of refuse liquid shot outward in a sharp spray.

"You're not supposed to catch it!" Evie shouted. "Bindings of the White Waste!"

Chains of ice froze the muck around them and attached with cruel hooks into the Arcid's legs. The beast howled into the night, a call so savage and ragged it chilled Vess' bones. Evie dropped on it, new Skills already on her lips, but Vess could not afford to join.

She spun, deflecting a hurled blade with her partisan, driving it into the mud. The Archon had thrown one of its blades, but yanked it back with chains gathered at its back. The poisonous Arcid burbled at its side.

"You test me?" Vess asked, and spun shimmering power from her channels. The winds of her mountain Temple raged, and Spear after silver Spear manifested around her. "Very well. Let us dance."

The darkness persisted for several steps before the wards responded to Felix's Inheritor's Will once again. Being at his hip was apparently good enough, if slow, and the Door recognized Felix. The Archon fiddled with a set of sigils in his metal Body, until he blazed with profane light and stopped shivering from the wards. He stretched the guard along the bottom of his helmet again in a crude approximation of a grin.

Felix could only scowl, barely able to draw the breath needed to whisper.

Down they went, down a tight set of stairs that were designed for a tall man's tread. The Archon took them six at a time, carelessly progressing through the tight, descending spiral.

"I must thank you again, Felix Nevarre. Unbound." He laughed, and that same manic energy danced around its edges. "I have not felt so clear in… Ages, I suspect." The Archon toyed with the broken straps of Felix's satchel. A large pair of fingers fished within, pulling out several rounded stones. Each were inscribed with sigils for *lightning*, *force*, and *fire*, among others. Felix let out an involuntary gasp, and the Archon's laugh continued. "Baubles. More and more. What is this crude working? Is this the result of an Unbound's Skill growth? Tragic."

The Archon upended the satchel, dumping scribbled papers, bottles of ink, broken packages of rations, and a dozen more of his homemade grenades. The contents tumbled off the steps, down and down along the path, while the Archon giggled at the distraught look on Felix's face.

"You have killed my creations many times, Felix. But you cannot kill me. Not by force of arm or trick of Skill and artifice." The Archon sounded saner than ever, but Felix was certain the creature was no longer addressing him at all. "None will stand in my way, not any longer. Not even the gods."

Further they descended. Wards occasionally flashed and flared, glyphs spinning up from hidden niches and alcoves, but each time, Felix's sword buzzed, and they dissipated. Minutes passed before the path finally leveled out, and a new archway appeared at the top of the landing. Through it, a circular room was carved from what seemed like the bedrock of the earth. The moment they crossed the threshold, magelight appeared around the chamber, illuminating an odd place. A set of stairs led down from the threshold, at least fifty of them, but there was so much to grab Felix's attention.

Above him, the dark cavern ceiling was dotted with stars. Or rather, shimmering blue motes of glowing gemstone, half of which were dun save for the light they reflected from the others. The walls were striated with horizontal strata, while atop those complex figures with bestial faces and nightmare forms were carved. These monsters were fighting against men and women in battle robes, each wielding stars of light.

At the highest spot, opposite the entrance, a wide table was depicted. On top of this table,the bodies of a dozen figures were lined in flowing robes and armor. A blade, hooked and deadly, hovered above them, like an executioner's axe. Below the table, smears marred the work, obscuring much of it. Yet, visible near the bottom was the carving of a stone pool… an exact replica of what lay at the very center of the chamber.

Pit quailed at the sight of it, and even Felix's waist began to buzz, like Karys was attempting to move as far away from it as he could. The pool was fifteen feet across and laid with hexagonal stones around its edge, leading to a staggered pattern that somehow reminded Felix of teeth.

Within it, a thick, dark liquid sat flat and shiny as a mirror. It looked like mud, were mud a dark green that reflected oily patterns back at them. It puzzled him, until the Archon began to descend.

Manasight is level 61!

…

Manasight is level 63!

It wasn't water at all. It was Mana, liquid Mana poured from someone's core and deposited into the pool. It seared against his senses, more powerful than even the Archon's crystallized power in spite of what the golden golem had said before.

Ravenous Tithe!

The crystallized Mana around him twisted, pulled toward Felix but refused to break apart. Instead, he was bashed with the bars of his restrictive cage, until they were as knives pressed to his neck. Below, something disrupted the surface of the pool, something far too vast to be contained by such a small opening.

What the hell is in there?

"I believe this is a gateway. The darkness whispered to me of this, the Voice, it spoke of secrets the Nym hid from even him. It is dangerous, yes, that much I can feel. I can hear it." The Archon laughed, and distantly Felix thought he heard the voice of Merodach, high and haughty. It is distorted by the deep burr of the Archon, a metallic tang. "Too right. Too right," the Archon said to himself. To Felix, he giggled. "What do we do with an unknown, hm?"

The Archon squeezed, and Felix felt something wrench in his chest. His collarbone ground against itself as his crystalline prison dissolved once more. Still, he couldn't move, couldn't *breathe*, and something in his core space stabbed him deeper.

"We test it."

The Archon hurled Felix into the pool of dark green fluid, Mana so potent it was a short step away from a true solid, yet it parted before his body like smoke.

He was pulled within, without even a moment to scream.

CHAPTER SIXTY-SIX

Felix sank into murky green darkness. It swirled around him like water or oil, but it didn't feel like it. It felt light, like smoke, and his breath came easy. Yet, when he flared his Manasight, he was almost blinded. Incredibly powerful Mana lay all around him, atop him, restricting him. He couldn't swim, could barely move his arms and legs at all, and he sank like a stone.

Why can't I feel it?

Felix drifted down, farther and farther, until the dim circle of light above him vanished altogether. A muted, ambient light drifted through the green, enough to illuminate his immediate surroundings, yet not enough to reveal what might lay beyond. He still sank, or thought he did, but saw no bottom to the pool. No features of any kind, save cloudy green.

Something moved. Something huge with hard lines and jagged edges, gone in seconds. Legs wriggled, or not legs, but tails. Fins. *Things* were in the dark, swimming through the oily liquid that breathed as easily as if in air. Felix's heart hammered in his chest. His skin was covered in scales and his hands edged with talons, but an unnameable terror welled in him, overflowing into his belly and limbs as if all the energy in the world pumped through him, yet he could do nothing with it. He found he could move, slowly, as if he were truly underwater, but against a creature so massive it wouldn't matter.

"We have a Visitor?"

The sexless voice crooned around him, playing against his ears like the softest whisper. He shuddered, then sharp claws crawled up his back. He gasped and struggled away, but there was nothing behind him. The green shimmered, and the murky depths were filled with confusing details. Steps. Thousands of them in all directions. An MC Escher print gone mad. He'd reached the bottom, and it resembled nothing more than the well, back in Naevis. A huge, mile-wide well filled to the brim with liquid Mana.

More shapes moved, vast things with no more detail than the lantern-like glow of their eyes. Too many eyes. Far too many. They crowded up around him, sharp silhouettes filled in shadow, jagged lines interrupted by the knobby protrusion of leg or claw or fin.

Urges...

The whisper came from his belt, from Karys, who sounded more horrified than ever before.

The Nym imprisoned Urges here.

A giggle. "The sword speaks the truth. A fascinating thing, your sword. So... familiar."

Felix hadn't a clue which creature had spoken to him, as every single one (how many were there?) undulated around him in a dizzying collection of shapes and shadow. They were the size of mountains, yet small as bears or deer, smaller still. Nothing made sense. Eyes burned in the dark.

"A Nym!"

"Not a Nym. The Nym are Lost. And he wears stolen flesh."

"Something old."

"Something new."

The voices broke around him, a new one every time. Was it all one creature, or were there many? He tried his Voracious Eye, but it failed. Felix slowly, so slowly, drew his Inheritor's Will. Light bloomed from the Crescian Bronze, and he heard hissing from their bestial mouths.

"He holds the Hook!"

"Herald!"

"No! No! The Herald is dead!"

Felix's sword shivered in his hands, and though Karys didn't speak, words and ideas jolted through his Mind. Karys knew these creatures, somehow, or perhaps the sword itself did.

Urge of Fratricide, of Dealings in Blood

Urge of Rot, the Vile Touch of the Darkened Earth

Urge of Hollow Bellies, of Famine in Cold and Heat

Urge of Isolation, of Forgotten Letters and Unspoken Truths

Urge of Mayhem, the Madness of Turmoil

Urge of Spite, the Ill Will of Malice

Those names were spun from whole cloth directly into his Mind, as well as the sense that Felix didn't stand a chance against any of them alone.

Six Urges… Six forces that had once toppled an entire kingdom. The last had also been a part of his sword's information. The Urges swirling around him had been captured after a bloody war with the Nym, confined because they could not be killed. How could you kill an Urge, after all? They were forces of nature more than living flesh. Felix couldn't have killed the Raven, let alone these six.

"Ah, not the Herald, but he sees. He realizes our might," one of them hissed in satisfaction.

"Kill him. Devour him and leave not his bones. His strange face bothers us."

"Let meeee, let me bite and tear. I need it so," crooned another, the same who had whispered to him. "It has been too long."

Something struck at him, too fast for even his Perception to track. It passed through his chest harmlessly, but Felix screamed. Bubbles rose as he convulsed in pain, and Mana, torn straight from his channels, swirled in the green depths. Like blood in the water.

The others came.

Unfettered Volition!

Adamant Discord!

Felix flared his two Skills, putting everything he had into them. Barely, just barely, he evaded two converging claws, and the lines of connection around him tightened. He pulled, yanking himself out of the way of another two attacks, these with spines the size of spears. Bubbles trailed him, as did the Urges. They came at him again, and again, each time he was hit more and more. Every hit left him physically whole, but his Stamina and Mana drained so fast not even his regeneration could keep up.

Pit cried out, the first sound he'd made since they'd fallen, but his call was cut short. Something burned in his chest, a warmth that was more than his bond. Painful. "Pit!"

There was no response.

The creatures, all chitinous limbs and segmented bits, struck again with a slashing leg covered in twisted spurs. It passed straight through him, but his Spirit screamed and his Mana dropped by a hundred points.

Karys shouted, though his voice grew fuzzier by the moment. *Felix! Felix… Use the… key!*

Where? Use the… how? It faded, no more than a buzzing at the back of his Mind.

The key? The Omen Key! Felix fumbled at his waist as he dodged, hauling himself through the liquid Mana. He tried to go higher, but each time, the implacable Urges blocked him.

Panting, straining, he pulled out the Omen Key. He'd had it tucked in his waist band along with one other item he couldn't part with, for safekeeping. For when he would be ready to use it, as Regis and Holt had said. Ready or not, he had no other options.

He jammed it into the air, somehow finding a piece of it that stuck, then turned it. A Door in the green nothing around him opened, one that led into a crystalline darkness far more complete than where he resided. The diamond-like Key vanished.

"He flails! He is mine!" cried the hungry voice. A leviathan the size of cities roared from the murky depths, teeth gleaming and eyes of orange and red spinning with madness.

Adamant Discord!

Lightning surged, struck, and Felix heaved with all of his Strength. He shot into the open door, landing barely inside it as jaws swept by his former position. Waves of awful, thickened Mana slapped into him, still touching him, still affecting him, and Felix scrambled backward.

"Where! Where has he gone?"

"What have you done with him!? I'll kill you!"

"Vanished! A trick!"

A wailing scream tore through the green depths, one taken up by five other throats, but none of them came at the door. None of them seemed to even notice it.

"Just like the Raven said. Urges can't even see the Omen Door," Felix breathed. He took to his feet, though he found his legs to be shaking so hard that doing so was a challenge. He dared to take his eyes away from the deadly trap he'd just evaded, to look deeper into… wherever he had found himself.

Behind him, the Door slammed shut.

Felix was in a dark place.

No. Not dark, he realized. *Just poorly lit.* Yet for all his trying, his Manasight could perceive nothing more than his eyes saw. It was a narrow hallway, floored with stone and walled with panels of wide, golden oak. It was simple, unadorned, rustic. A thin carpet covered the flooring, leading the entire length of the windowless hallway—perhaps sixty feet—before ending at a much wider chamber. The light was brighter there.

"What is all this?" he asked.

Your Path, Felix.

"Karys!" Felix only just realized he was still holding his sword. "Are you okay? You were acting strange out there."

I felt strange, that is true. As if the fuzziness in me had grown, multiplying rapidly. I—I fear I was being unmade in that liquid Mana.

"Jesus," Felix said, then jolted in remembered fear. "Pit!"

There was a flash of light, and Pit manifested in the relatively small corridor. His bulk filled it almost completely, but Felix didn't care. He threw himself around the tenku's neck, laughing in relief. "You're okay, too!"

Pit warbled in confusion. *Where are we? Remember pain and burning, then nothing.*

"In the door the Omen Key opened, I guess." Felix glanced around the now-cramped passage. "Wish it was a bit bigger in here, but I can work with it. You sure you're okay?"

Pit thought a moment, then nodded his giant horse-sized head. Or was he bigger than that now? In the cramped confines, the tenku seemed enormous. Felix licked his lips, aware that he was distracting himself. Stalling. He'd used the Omen Key because Karys had said so, but also to escape. Yet...

"Karys, when someone has finished their Path when using an Omen Key, are they brought right back to where they started?"

Yes, of course. Why… Oh.

"Yeah," Felix sighed. He had bought them some time, but how much? "What're the odds I'll be strong enough to fight six Urges when I'm done here?"

I cannot say they are great, Felix. Little can be shared of Omen Keys and their effects, as each of us walks a different Path. The details I cannot share. I am not allowed to do so.

Felix frowned. "The System is stopping you?"

Yes. It is part of the process. One's Path is a personal thing, shaped to you, by you, for you. It cannot be understood by another, not truly. I imagine that is why the System forbids speaking of them.

Pit let out a worried warble. His big, golden eyes watched everything around them in concern. Felix patted him on the neck.

"We just have to move forward. That's all we can do," Felix said, half to himself. "C'mon."

He started to squeeze by Pit, chafing at the lack of room in the hall, when the whole place flexed. That was the only word for it. The corridor bent and shook, flexing like a muscle, and when it was done, the hallway was twice as wide as it had been.

"That's… weird. But convenient."

Now Pit had no trouble turning around and could even walk by Felix's side. Cautiously, they traveled the length of the hall, until it opened up into a wider chamber. As he'd noted, it was filled with bright light, owing to the rotating chandeliers above them. There were three of them, and each one was connected to a series of gears and pulleys, twisting the fixtures into a slow waltz above their heads. The chamber itself was nicer than the hallway, but still paneled with that golden oak from floor to ceiling. A nicer but equally threadbare rug laid here, its designs so faded by footsteps that it could have been roses or the tangled limbs of a horrible beast.

Dominating the wall, however, were three doors.

The First Choice, Karys intoned. It had the smack of ritual to Felix, and he could practically hear the capitals the Paragon was using.

"The First… How many choices do I have to make?" Felix asked.

As many as the Path demands.

"What's the point?"

To find your Path.

"I thought this was my Path?" Felix asked.

Yes and no. It is the manifestation of the Path your destiny lies upon, but the road chosen is your own. At each juncture, a Choice must be made, for good or ill, that will Reveal the true power within your Omen.

"That… is less helpful than I wanted," Felix said with a frustrated breath. He remembered well what Elders Regis and Holt had said to him, and it lined up well enough with what Karys was saying. He stepped closer, inspecting each of the doors in turn.

The first door was a pale white, chipped at the edges of its panels. It looked like any exterior door in any moderately well-off home back on Earth. Voracious Eye told him nothing, other than it was a door and it was made of oak, same as the wall paneling. It had a lever style handle made of shiny brass.

The second door was fancier, with more panels and fluting along the edges. Three windows marked its top in an uneven pattern, but the glass was frosted and scratched to hell. So was the door itself. It had once been painted a dull red, but time and scratching had revealed a grayish wood beneath. The latch and lock were steel covered in chipping black paint.

The third door, the last door, was altogether different. There were no panels, no windows, and no latch save a simple rope nailed to the planks. The door itself was made of six wooden planks crudely nailed together, and some didn't even reach all the way to the top or bottom, leaving gaps that were filled with darkness. Felix peered through those gaps, not expecting much, and he was right. He saw nothing, just unremitting shadow. Pondering, he walked back to the center of the room, where Pit stood warily.

"So I just… pick one?" he asked.

So it seems.

"But I have nothing to go on, just different types of doors," Felix said. He felt frustrated. "I'm not Choosing my Destiny based on which door I think is the least shitty."

I… I think you should think on the doors longer, Felix. I do not know that you have seen them, truly.

Felix tapped the hilt of his sword thoughtfully. His friends were fighting against the Archon's forces as he stood there, looking at doors. Felix had to get out, and fast. Only, when he did leave the Path, he'd be back in the mix with six Urges. He ran his hands through his hair and groaned before slumping into a sitting position.

"All I have are the options in front of me," he muttered. "Everything else I… they'll make it. They're strong enough."

They had to be.

CHAPTER SIXTY-SEVEN

Pit laid about on his back, wings askew and legs in the air while he snored. His tongue lolled, hanging almost in his own eye, but the tenku's rest was complete for all of that. Felix wished he were half so relaxed.

Felix watched the doors. Glared at them, really. As if they would suddenly move, shift, or otherwise give him the answers he sought if only he stared hard enough. How long had he been at it? Time felt… weird in the Path. Stretchy. Felix could recall fleeing the Urges just moments ago, but it easily could have been hours. His Born Trait only muddied those waters, but the point stood.

"Karys, how long have I been here?" he asked.

I… find myself unsure. A shrug, or a suggestion of one from the sword. *But such is the way of liminal spaces.*

"Liminal… what's that, Latin?" Felix asked.

It is the words of magi, Felix. I was never of their orders, but I know enough. Or I did, once. A pause. *A liminal space is a point of transition, from one place to another. A threshold.*

"A Door," Felix suggested.

Quite right. Places such as these pull from the Void, a—

"The same as Domains," Felix said with sudden recollection. The Maw had mentioned such things once, when he'd wandered the Void. "Time moved weird in the Void, too."

My understanding is that it functions as a dream, or perhaps dreams touch upon the Void. I am... I am unclear on the subject. I believe the Paths utilize the liminal space afforded by the Void, peeling it back to create this for you.

Felix looked about at the drab interior. Even the chandeliers slowly rotating above them were wooden and filled with dust. It was not very impressive, and that was reflected in the doors themselves. "So this is like a Domain of my own?"

Of a sort. A Domain, or even a Lair, is not as specialized as this. Paths are catered to those who owned the Omen Key.

"Hm. So are we moving faster or slower than outside?"

There is no way to tell, unfortunately. Not unless you try to tear apart these walls, and that is impossible. You would rip your hands bloody before ever leaving a scratch. It has been tried before... before—it has been tried.

Karys was getting worse. Felix wished he had cared only as a friend—he thought of Karys as a friend, at least—but more than that, Felix feared the knowledge he'd lose if the Paragon's memories dissipated completely. *The advantage lost*, he thought with an inward sneer at himself. *I shouldn't care about that, but it's hard not to, especially here.*

With a frustrated grunt, more at himself than the situation, Felix rolled to his feet. Pit snorted, woke, and watched him blearily through a single half-lidded eye. He took it for granted now, how easily he moved and exerted himself, but not even an appreciation for his physical advancement was enough to appease the sour roil in his belly. He walked to the middle door, the dark red one. Not a single detail about them had clued Felix into their purpose. Was he meant to pick one blindly? What if he chose the wrong one?

Felix frowned, running his fingers over the scratched paint of the door. It was worn down by constant use and none of it gentle. It reminded him a little of the doors to the church off 4th Street back home. The place his family had long attended, well after Felix had grown tired of religion in general. He snorted. He supposed he didn't feel much different about religion now either, though his atheism had been soundly rebuffed. He wasn't a fan, but it was hard to deny the existence of gods when they tried to kill him or worse.

His eyes widened. *What was that?* For a brief moment, Felix had felt something quiver beneath his hands. The door. Or something beyond it, or... *What?*

It was coming from *him.*

Felix placed his hand on the door again, but this time he focused inward, toward his core space. The solar system formed around him, dual cores in the center, abyss and divine sprout, with his Skills arrayed in expanding concentric circles. There, settled in the closest row near his cores, was the origin of the faint trembling.

Ravenous Tithe?

His Skill shook as he kept his hand pressed against the red door, like a starving creature barely restraining itself from a meal. *Why so eager?* He looked at the door, flaring his Manasight once again, but just as before his Manasight was useless in that place. All he saw was a red door. *But what would happen if I ate it?*

He'd done it before, eating objects, though it afforded him very little Essence compared to monsters or the occasional person. But would it mean he was choosing that path if he Tithed the door? Or could he eat each one and then decide? And would eating them even do anything? He hoped it would let him get a glimpse of the Path ahead, but he had no way of knowing for sure.

Felix fell back, thinking. His Ravenous Tithe had grown since he'd first received it. Before, he'd had to "claim" his targets or at least be touching them. Repeatedly now, he'd pulled in Essence from across battlefields, so long as he has been the one to kill them. *Can't kill doors, though. Hm.*

Shadow Whip!

He split the single whip into three easily enough, while the end of each whip became a grabby little hand that would affix to most surfaces. He snapped it forward, and all three hit the doors at the same time. They struck true, but that wasn't a concern with his Perception and Dexterity; that they held fast was the greater relief.

"Pit, stand back. I'm not really sure what'll happen here." Once his Companion backed into the dim hallway, Felix took a breath. "Here goes nothing."

Ravenous Tithe!

It took some doing, but Felix's Will eventually overcame whatever inertia the doors had: with a monstrous roar, all three doors collapsed into smoke and flashing light, pulled inexorably into his channels. Pure darkness laid behind each of them, Void-like even.

"Okay," Felix said slowly, letting his Shadow Whip dissolve back into his channels. The doors were open, and nothing had exploded. He was gonna call that a success. "Okay, I think—"

A Choice Has Been Made.

"What?"Even Pit made a confused noise at that. "I didn't make a choice! That's the whole point."

The Door Is Open.
ERROR
Multiple Doors Open.
Reconfiguring Paths.
Stand By.

The room *flexed*, as it had before, and suddenly, the three open doorways became one single, massive portal edged by chipping wood and peeling paint. Everything rippled, waves rising from solid surfaces in an upsettingly familiar manner.

"Pit! *Converge!*"

There was a flash of light before the long hallway wrapped around Felix's form. Pit nestled breathlessly into his Spirit but was peering curiously out of Felix's eyes.

Why do I keep doing this?

That was the last thought he had before the entire world rippled and shattered into blue-gold light.

The Fool.

Wise And Unknowing, Brash And Kind.

Choices Define Us.

The Path begins.

Felix landed roughly, as if falling from a great height. He stumbled and tripped onto something soft. A couch.

His couch. His apartment.

He swept his eyes around, seeing the tiny studio he'd once lived in, recreated in perfect detail, down to the takeout containers piled next to the overfilled trash can. Outside two small windows, a storm raged in the night sky, the flash of lightning the only illumination in the tiny apartment.

A phone rang.

He fumbled for it, pushing aside dirty clothes and dishes until he pulled the small rectangle from the pile. It flashed and buzzed on silent. His Mind—*mind?*—felt foggy, but he answered it. "Yeah?"

"Bumble! Have you heard from your sister? It's been hours since she said she was coming home, and I haven't heard anything! Please tell me she's with you!"

"Wait, wait, Mom, slow down," Felix said—*Felix?* He rubbed the bridge of his nose. Everything felt… hazy. Had he fallen asleep on the couch again? "Where's Gabby?"

"Where's—she went to that party. The one you were supposed to go to!"

"What? Oh," he blinked and suddenly remembered. The party. The yacht. That had been hours ago. "I didn't go. I uh, I just didn't—"

"Have you gotten any phone calls from her?" His mom sounded at the edge of panic.

"Lemme check." He pulled his phone from his ear and thumbed through his messages. He'd had exactly forty-seven messages from his sister, mostly texts and a few voicemails. They were all about getting him out with her, to the party. To get over his ex. They turned berating after a while, but the last few were concerning.

Gabby: C'mon! My friend wanted to meet you! It'll be fun and if you don't show up I'll disown you!

Gabby: Hey. Where are you? Things are weird.

Gabby: Come soon. Please. I need help.

Gabby: Help. She's hurt! They took her!

After that, the messages were garbled, like the text itself was glitching.

His heart was racing, trying to beat out of his chest. Images of a woman, drugged unconscious, of smug idiots standing over her. *The girl. Her friend. I—what is this?* How could he know what she looked like, or what had happened? He shook his head. He was still groggy from sleep.

"Bumble! Did you? Hear from her?" her tinny voice sounded

on edge. She had always been convinced the worst could happen at any time… and maybe it had. That vision felt so *real.*

"Mom, yeah, I've got some messages from her. Don't worry, I'll take care of this, you just get some sleep and I'll call you with an update in a little bit. Okay?" He put on his calmest voice, hoping he could talk her down a bit. Thunder crashed outside. "It's storming outside right now, but I can make some calls at least."

"Don't go out into it, Bumble. It's a tropical storm that came out of nowhere. I don't want to lose track of you, too."

"I won't, Mom." He peered out his windows. The sky was black but flashed with sheets of blue-white illumination. "But I don't—" Something shifted out there, in the rain. It had the shape of an immense figure, wreathed in… but that was impossible. "I can't wait for it to pass, Mom. Gabby, she's in danger."

How did he know that? Lightning flashed, again and again, and the certainty remained. She was in danger. *She was taken, instead of me.*

Where had that thought come from?

Lightning. Something about lightning. Thunder hit so hard the world felt like it was rocking. He felt his apartment twist, going askew, as something *other* ripped across his consciousness. A force. A Will that could not be denied.

"Bumble? Bumble, are you there?"

A connection to the lightning. A door.

This isn't me! This isn't what happened!

He reached out. He had to find her! He reached out!

Lightning came, and the wall exploded.

The Tower.

Weather The Storm, 'Ware The Lightning.

The Path Continues.

The streets were dark with night, slick with rain. The world was rain, all of it falling, surrounding him. He panted, out of shape with a stitch in his side, but still he ran. He couldn't stop. He *couldn't.*

They took her. They took her instead of me. He knew that, was certain of it. But who had taken her? Where? *I have to get to the marina.*

His car hadn't worked when he'd tried it. Had he tried it? There was a fog in his mind—*his Mind?*—but he had to run. Water poured from the sky, sluicing down the streets like imitation rivers. Yet not imitations for long as waist-high waves crested the corner ahead. 4th Street and St Paul converged, waves crashing in fifteen foot high swells, and all of it was coming at *him*.

He turned down an alley, one still dry enough. The roads were flooding, but he had to make it to the docks. To the yacht. He had to stop it. To stop *what?* Lightning burst in sheets above him, too close, vibrant and blue-white.

His lightning. Something pressed against the backs of his eyes, against his spine.

How could he forget!

His sister was gone, but that's not what happened!

The Path! I walk the Path!

Water roared ahead, splashing through the darkness, and among the cresting waves ran undulating creatures. Too many legs, too many eyes, of smoke and shadow and fire. They shrieked!

Giant icicles ripped from the sky, stabbing down into them all and freezing the waves. Felix skidded to a stop, just shy of a brutalized monstrosity, its flesh half-frozen even as it dissolved into light-streaked smoke. Another shriek, this one of furious victory, sounded from above.

"Pit!" he shouted, the word out of his mouth before he could think it.

FELIX!

"Felix?" he asked, shuddering from the contact of… of whatever that was. "Who is—?"

Behind you!

He spun in time to see more of the nightmares crawling down the buildings to either side of him. Giant icicles came down and skewered many, but more rose from the dark and the water with every heartbeat.

RUN!

He ran. Questions swirled in his brain, so many questions, least of all was the name of that winged thing that saved him. He ran, and the monsters gave chase.

Thunder rocked the city, the streets trembling with every strike, and lightning flashed far above. It was growing, the storm. How far would it grow? He stared up as he ran, unable to tear his eyes away as clouds the size of mountains were wreathed in brilliant lightning and shattered. Yet more clouds always came, all of them of ill Intent and foul Affinity.

He almost fell, the unfamiliar words burning in his Mind. His Body ached, but not as much as he'd feared, his muscles burned but it was a faint sensation. Stronger was the fear. The monsters were right behind him!

Fight, Felix! Fight!

"Fight?" he gasped breathlessly. He couldn't fight! He had never—!

Lightning flashed and thunder crashed. The street buckled, rippled beneath him. He was thrown. Nightmare creatures swirled beneath him as he arced into the air, maws open, claws and mandibles and burning eyes ready. Eager.

FIGHT!

From within him, from somewhere else, he felt an answer. Fury raged, a distant feeling that hammered into the foreground, answered in kind by the winged creature in the sky. He felt it, all of it, everything, and Felix reached to the heavens.

Adamant Discord!

And brought them crashing down.

Wheel of Fortune.

All Things Turn Upon The Tides.

The Path Continues.

The storm raged, but he was among the clouds. Above them. A part of them. Felix surged with the winds, with the lightning itself, riding upon it. He remembered what little there was to recall. Of Pit and Felix and who he was, who he had become. Creatures of smoke and cloud rose against him, monstrous, but his power wiped them away. Others rose in their place, but the power raged to be used, and Felix didn't hesitate.

Gabby! They took her! Why? Because I wasn't there? He had slept through the yacht party, through the violence on deck and the lightning. The one that had taken him from Earth. But that hadn't happened this time. Felix knew it wasn't real, couldn't be, but everything felt real. *Is this what happened when I left? Monsters in Fort Lauderdale? In the sky?*

A shape manifested from the storm around him, one formed of smoke and fire and darkness. It was only vaguely humanoid, but it seethed with shapes that changed with every breath. Spines and fins and claws and teeth, eyes that roiled about the storm, fires burning behind veils of shadow. It screamed, and the whole world screamed with it, deafening him. Nearly knocking him from the sky.

His Perception tangled on an object behind him, a door, fashioned out of dim light. Knowledge stuffed into his brain, words not his own: *The Path Continues, Felix Nevarre.*

He knew he only needed to flee, to run into that doorway. But to do so would be abandoning his home to this… thing. A creature of darkness and jealous endings.

His phone rang, still in his hand somehow. His mother. Felix tried to cancel it, but answered instead, and a tinny voice shouted shrilly over the line. "Where are you? Help! There are things! Bumble, help me! They're coming into the house!"

The beast grinned—*grinned!*—and spread down, toward the city. Toward his family.

"Bumble! Help me!"

Like tearing out his own heart, Felix hurled himself into the door of light.

Felix landed atop a plush carpet that smelled of dust and stale air. Everything came back, all of who he was and what he had done—or hadn't—in the Path was vivid. He didn't move, not for a while, letting the shame of it all wash over him.

There was nothing I could do. Right? I couldn't stay behind. It wasn't even real! Felix clenched his teeth and fists, straining every muscle as if physical exertion would chase away his self-recriminations. *I had to leave!*

A soft cooing came from above, along with the scent of almonds and corn chips. A huge, feathered mass laid atop his head, so light he barely felt it, but warm and soft. Their bond shimmered, but Pit said nothing. They simply laid there.

Notifications blinked at the corner of his vision. Eager for the distraction, Felix toggled them open.

+13 AGL
+11 DEX
+9 EVA
+16 WIL
+23 INE
+21 AFI
+15 ALA

System energy surged into him, met by the Dissonance of his core. Colorless power and dual cores coruscated into a fountain of potency that arched Felix's spine. He convulsed, throwing Pit from him and felt his *everything* burn and freeze, until there was nothing but the struggle to hold onto himself.

You Have Walked The Chosen Path(s)!
Congratulations!
You Have Received An Omen (x3)!

CHAPTER SIXTY-EIGHT

Felix grunted, lifting himself up as the surges of System Harmonics and core-wrought Dissonance quieted. Beside him were three hand-sized cards, each embossed with a gorgeous and intricate design in blue-white and red-gold. They were stylized renditions of vines and stones around a central eye shape. He tentatively flipped them and saw their faces were bordered with white and filled with familiar images.

The Fool. The Tower. The Wheel of Fortune. A figure was in each, someone with black hair and blue eyes, walking off a cliff or falling from a collapsing tower. The last only contained a golden wheel, covered in symbols that weren't quite sigils, but the corners featured a tenku, a harnoq, and what he assumed to be a wendigo and wyvern.

"Chimeras," he murmured. Pit nosed the cards, his hooked beak tapping against them. They rang like steel. "Tarot cards, though? Literal tarot cards?" Felix hefted all three. They were heavy, way more than he expected.

I do not know what tarot cards are, but those are Omens, Karys said. He sounded shocked. *Blessed Ancestors, it is true. The Unbound truly walk a Path above.*

"What? What's so special about them?" Felix paused. "What do you mean, they're Omens? I thought Omens were intangible, some sorta System feature related to people's," he rolled his eyes. "Destiny."

They are. That is what is astounding. The System has granted you Omens, look at them!

Felix did, flaring his Voracious Eye.

Name: Omen of the Fool
Type: Omen
Benefit: +2 AGL, +1 PER, +1 VIT per level gained.
Lore: Omens are indicators of a destiny yet to come, of a potential as of yet unfurled. You may only hold a single Omen.

The others were the same, except their bonuses varied.

Name: Omen of the Tower
Benefit: +2 VIT, +1 END, +1 AGL per level gained.

Name: Omen of the Wheel of Fortune
Benefit: +2 PER, +1 AGL, +1 DEX per level gained.

"If I could find a way to keep these, would they add to my level up gains?" Felix asked, not truly expecting an answer.

Perhaps. But keep in mind what it says. Only a single Omen may be held.

Felix had noticed that bit, but was hoping against it anyway. "What's the point of giving me these, then?"

The System is mysterious, and Paths are stranger still.

"So basically 'screw you, figure it out?' Yeah that tracks." Felix stood, feeling the burn in his overworked muscles. He took in the hall they'd entered, trying to let his latest escapade fade a bit into the background. "This seems nicer than before."

Pit warbled, sniffing at a tapestry that depicted a soaring cityscape, fluted towers among swirling seas. He sneezed, and a great cloud of dust stirred. The same was true all around. The materials were superior than before—blue marble instead of wood paneling—and there were triangular alcoves every ten feet, but it was the same hallway. The same dimensions. Dust coated everything, as if the place hadn't been used in decades.

"Why dust? I thought these spaces were built for the individual?" he asked.

Questioning the System is usually pointless, Felix. Perhaps it does recycle these rooms. Or, perhaps, this is as you expect it to be.

"Old, like a ruin. Dusty because I expect old things to be dusty," Felix hummed to himself. "Perception seems to guide a lot of the System's… weirder bits."

Indeed.

Suddenly, Pit shuddered so hard he bashed into the wall. "Pit?" He smashed into it again, this time driving deep cracks through the marble and toppling an unlit sconce from its setting. "Pit! What's wrong?" Panic swirled in their bond, but also pain and joy and the giddy rush of power. Felix poked at his interface, until a series of rapid notifications came to him, similar to what he'd seen before.

Your Companion Gains:
+31 STR
+11 PER
+22 AGL
+17 DEX
+15 INE
+11 AFI
+31 EVA
+18 ALA

Dissonance had no sway over Pit, not as it did Felix, so the Harmony he heard through their bond was pure and uncomplicated. It was astounding, simply put, and Felix goggled as Pit seemed to pulse with golden-blue radiance that only reluctantly faded. When it was gone, the tenku sank to his haunches and let his tongue loll as he panted.

Tired.

"Me too, bud. What'd you do in there, Pit?" A jolt of their bond answered that, as images of flying through a murderous storm, struggling to reach Felix's apartment, fighting and killing creatures that would not die, merely reformed and advanced again. Felix clutched his friend close, his head to Pit's. "I don't deserve you."

Pit cooed and batted at him with a wing. Felix laughed.

After a time, when they both had the strength to move, Felix and his friends traveled the short length of the blue marble corridor and into a hexagonal chamber. It was twice as large as before, the wood paneling gone as in the hallways, replaced by that polished blue stone. He took it for marble because of the faint white veins in it, though it resembled ice more than anything else.

Thin, hexagonal columns separated triangular alcoves, each containing another hexagonal plinth. Empty vases sat atop them, all of them blue with white scrollwork designed across their tops and bottoms. He picked one up and rotated it. The middle was decorated with figures in robes, each holding stars and battling sinuous, amorphous shapes across a landscape. It looked like a hard battle.

Similar to the mural outside the well, Karys pointed out.

Felix grunted, but he moved to the next, and the one after that. Each vase had a different scene, but all of them were featuring the Nym versus what he had to assume were the Urges. He searched them, hunting for a clue or hint at how they were originally defeated. The closest he came was one large urn depicting the sinuous Urges bound in stars between twice their number of Nym. Useless, unless Felix could somehow duplicate himself. He half-growled as he set it back on its plinth and stomped away.

Except, he must have missed the edge of it, because he heard a loud crash behind him. When Felix turned, he saw the urn shattered into pieces. *Doesn't matter, anyway, if this is my Path. I'm tempted to break the rest, too.* He walked away and toward the doors.

Three again, same as before but different. Each was surrounded by sparkling white stone, the frame and lintels carved into lace-like networks of stars. The first door was a pale wood, old but well-made, and its lock and latch were both formed of a dull iron. The second door was darker, stained cherry maybe, and its corner was burnt. Its latch was a shiny brass. The last door was far more ominous, featuring a iron-bound wooden door more than half burned by fire. Embers still glowed on it, flaring and fading in turns between the crazed cracking of the charred wood. For all of that, Felix couldn't smell a bit of smoke.

"Odd," he muttered to himself. His Perception tugged at him, drawing his eye toward a feature he'd seen but apparently hadn't given any mind. "They're locked."

Every single door had a lock at the latch, varying in shape and composition. *Would that matter to my Ravenous Tithe?* He doubted it, but still. What was the point of a lock here?

Pit chirruped, high and fluting. *Key.*

Felix joined him and found the tenku sifting through the broken remnants of the urn he'd dropped. Within the ceramic chips was a half-tarnished key of silver.

"Huh. Guess I get to smash them, after all," Felix said with a soft laugh. "Pit, you get that side, I'll get this side."

Perhaps more caution should be shown—

Before Karys even finished the thought, Felix was throwing down vase after vase. They shattered on the hard blue flooring, just shy of the plush central carpet. In thirty seconds, all were destroyed and they had found two more keys. And more.

"What is it?" Felix asked. It was a statue—small, only about five inches tall—of a Nymean man holding a star aloft, made of a pale golden stone and apparently unharmed by their enthusiastic vase smashing. Pit warbled and shrugged, but Karys perked up.

I believe that is a focus of sorts. Nymean Magi would use them in their rituals, focusing the Harmonics through them to amplify their works.

"A focus," Felix said. He pocketed it, though his pants were mostly shredded. "Could be useful. I doubt I know enough about the Grand Harmony or Sorcery to make use of it." *Yet*, he added silently. "Why would it be here? And why would keys be hidden, or the doors require keys?"

I do not know, Felix. Karys' mental voice was patient as always, despite Felix's agitation. *Another challenge, perhaps. And a reward for besting the challenge.*

"Not much of a challenge," Felix said. Anyone who'd played an adventure RPG would have sussed out the solution in seconds. "I guess it's not important, and I got a cool magic thing in exchange."

He shrugged and forced himself to move on. He approached the doors again, placing the keys into the locks with slow precision; for all he knew, turning the keys would mean he'd chosen the door, and Felix didn't want that. He intended to do as he'd done before. Three Omen cards received and three doors opened. There wasn't any coincidence about that.

They feel… dangerous, Karys said. *Be wary.*

"More dangerous than before? More… invasive?" Felix said as

he walked back from the last door, key safely placed. He didn't like the idea of more danger, but he liked the scenario it had constructed even less. He'd lived as if his sister had been taken to the Continent, instead of himself, and were it not for his strong Will and Pit, he might not have remembered himself at all. The System had messed with his memories, and that didn't sit well with him. This time, he wasn't going to let that happen. "Were you there, last time?"

I was, and I wasn't. I could see your situation, but I could not speak. It was… unpleasant.

"Hm. Then I'll see what I can do about that. The System doesn't just get to invade my head, not without permission."

Simply walking these Paths gives it permission, Felix. What do you think it meant by Choice?

Felix clenched his jaw. Karys was probably right, though he didn't like it. "Then let's get it over with. Pit, hop in." With a determined chirrup, the big Chimera vanished in a streak of light and settled into Felix's Spirit.

Shadow Whip!

One whip, three strands. This time it was a touch harder, though his Dexterity translated well into the twisting shadow tendrils. Each whip latched onto the latch and key he'd placed, and with a deft click, he unlocked each door at once.

Ravenous Tithe!

The doors burst into smoke and light, and the chamber *flexed* once again. Three doors became one.

The Door Is Open.
ERROR
Multiple Doors Open.
Reconfiguring Paths.
Stand By.

The chamber rippled, followed by a swirling suction and a flash of blue-gold light.

The Hermit.

Silence And Solitude, Fast Friends And Allies.

The Path Continues.

Again, Felix had the sensation of falling, before his feet landed among a buttery yellow glow and hexagonal tiles. The columns and alcoves were instantly recognizable, even if he hadn't seen and heard the blue roar of the waterfall.

I'm in the Temple?

He spun, but the Archon was not there. The entire place was whole and unblemished, untouched by their fight and the Archon's ambitions. In the back, near the raised dais, the green metal door was shut tight. Suddenly, memories flooded him, events of the past and more, of finding Pit and fighting the monsters around him for days and weeks. Foraging for food and fighting to survive. Soon, those memories stretched further and further, piling on in a tale that suggested he had been in that Temple for far longer than he recalled.

Bastion of Will!

Felix knew them for false memories, and he flared his Skill with every drop of desperation he had; he'd not live in a lie, especially when it could kill him. The Skill sang, its complex vibrations beating back the stream of System memories, but it was a struggle. Sweat beaded on his forehead, and a vein in his neck worked, clenching and throbbing with every passing second. Memory after memory, the sensation of years poured across him like a torrent, like the waterfall itself. Unending.

Then it was done, and Felix stood shaking and panting amid the columns of the Temple. He could recall himself, the real Felix, but just over his shoulder was a cloak of thoughts and experiences he'd never had, things that told him he'd spent *years* in the Foglands. He blinked and realized that the Temple wasn't quite so empty as he'd assumed. Pelts and tools were scattered about, weapons fashioned from monsters or found in old ruins among the trees, even a number of scrolls he dimly recalled perusing for hours and hours as he'd attempted to teach himself to read.

All of it was faint, like the ghost of a life, but it was there. Like the last door, this one suggested he had never left the Temple, never gone beyond the eastern mountains to encounter the Archon or find Shelim. He checked his level and goggled at the number.

"Level 94, holy dang," Felix muttered.

There was a clatter in another room. *Our bedroom,* he knew. *Our?*

From out of the door came the hulking form of Pit, though only his head. His shoulders were clearly too wide to fit. He looked at Felix with concerned eyes.

I'm too big. Help. I'm too big!

Felix converged with his friend, letting the tenku jump into his Spirit. The weight of his Companion, however, nearly staggered him, and Pit was almost immediately ejected back out into the main hall. Felix clutched at his chest, the pain overwhelming him, as Pit loomed worriedly above him.

Hurt? Are you hurt? Felix?

The pain passed, but Felix took a bit longer to stand. He rubbed ruefully at his chest. "I don't think this version of us has Tempered all that well."

The earth suddenly shook, heaving beneath their feet. Pit squawked in alarm, his huge body—easily twice the size he had been before—falling over as the Temple pitched forward. Something roared in the distance, a sound so loud it was more of a buzzing in his ears than true noise. Felix ran for the entrance, peering beyond the waterfall and into the forested valley.

Misted by distance and blued by atmosphere, the eastern mountains loomed large, but something else loomed higher still. A… thing… something horrifyingly gargantuan moved, a living mountain, rising from beyond the range. It attacked the mountains, devouring them into a mouth the size of cities and creating another series of noises that were more detonations than anything else. The mountains themselves screamed, surged somehow, attempting to defend themselves but they were not enough.

It was the Maw, unleashed.

"Holy shit," Felix gasped, and Pit was right behind him. "We need to run."

Before him, wavering in the waterfall itself, was a door of pale light. It flickered, disappearing one second before reappearing the next. He didn't hesitate, not when the Maw was coming. He leaped through.

Strength.

Conqueror Or Conquered?

The Path Continues.

The world stuttered, flickered, and Felix was atop Pit while clouds streamed by his face. They were racing through the air with all the speed they could manage. He looked around wonderingly.

The landscape below them was a desolate waste. Mountains had been torn apart, reduced to rubble-strewn hills, while the forests and rivers and meadows were nothing more than deserts of dust and ash. Limp winds stirred, swirling dust devils across the terrain, but nothing living moved. Felix knew, with the knowledge of dreams, that nothing living remained.

"The Maw was never stopped," he realized. He'd once had a vision, when he'd nearly died in the Labyrinth. It had been a world with the Maw unleashed upon it, one that was reduced to a food source for the ever-hungry Primordial. Below, the terrain leveled out, and with a start, Felix realized they were approaching Haarwatch.

Nothing remained. A broken wall, faded and cracked. A tower snapped in two, and a city reduced to rubble and ash. The passed over it quickly, into the Verdant Pass where once a vibrant forest flourished. The trees remained, but they were petrified and withered. All moisture and substance had been torn from the land, and great sharp-edged tears in the earth showed him where a massive mouth had taken a vile bite of it all.

Huge beasts swung out of the sky, creatures of bone and sinew and red corruption. They evaded their first attacks, but there were four against them. Great claws slashed and tore at Pit's feathers, too preoccupied with flying to manage attack spells as well.

Adamant Discord!

Felix's core clenched, painfully. The Skill wasn't there, but it was, and his Spirit screamed at the attempt. He very nearly lost his head for that, only Pit's sudden drop saving him from the claws of the enormous Primordial-spawn.

How did I use my Skills in the first door, then? Felix growled to himself and shook off the pain. He'd felt worse, just not in this life. Forced to rely on the Skills the Path told him he had instead, he conjured an orb of dark acid, a Skill that was both familiar and not.

Wrack and Ruin!

Somehow, he'd still learned that Skill. The orb shot out, but instead of a single, fast moving projectile, it split into dozens. Hundreds. Each with reduced power, but they covered the sky in acid. The Primordial-spawn stood no chance. Acid ate through their bones and sinew, tearing through their cores as well.

It was over with a single shot.

He fell into the next door, barely noticing it as more monsters crowded the sky.

Death.

All Is Dust. Dust Is All.

The Path Continues.

The world flickered once more, and Felix shuddered. He felt the weight of more memories, crowding against his Bastion, all of them suggesting he and Pit had been traveling for months, almost an entire year. More monsters had come at them, twisted things clearly affected by the Primordial's flesh curse. He recalled a loneliness to accompany the hunger and thirst that was driving both of them, and those were hard to chase away.

When the walls of another city appeared, hope kindled within him, only to be immediately dashed. It was destroyed, the walls torn down and whatever structures stomped to pieces. The pair of them landed on a high ledge atop nearby cliffs and surveyed it all. The countryside stretched endlessly in all directions, but everything looked barren. Pit could smell blood. Rot.

"Nothing could stop it," Felix realized. He'd fought the vocalization of it, hoped that some place might still exist, but the Maw was too strong. "It escaped with all its power intact. Did Grimmar release it?"

Did it matter? He swallowed, his throat on fire. *Not for this place.*

Below, in the distance, a group of people could be seen. They were moving furtively, clearly afraid, pulling a wagon of things behind them. The larger of their group pulled the wagon themselves, and he saw no avum. No doubt all butchered for food. Felix was briefly cheered by their appearance, bedraggled or not, until more movement caught his eye.

From between two hills, creatures with too many mouths and

crooked fangs stalked. Monsters of putrid flesh, without eyes or hair, scaled in places but otherwise covered in glistening scar tissue raced forward, a flash of speed the people couldn't hope to fight against.

Before he knew it, Felix was atop Pit, and they were diving. Faster and faster. He didn't want to interfere; he knew it was all fake, a dream at best. Why? Why!

Wrack and Ruin!

His Mana dipped again as countless drops of acid burst before him, flung toward the oncoming monstrosities like a hail of death. Their bodies were peppered by the corrosive, drilled through until they were only pieces, and Pit screamed beneath him. Columns of molten lava surged from beneath the creatures, burning them, hollowing the beasts out at his Companion's Will.

They landed among the dead, and shocked, terrified faces.

"What are you doing? Keep running!" Felix shouted. The people—Humans, all—started and all but leaped to obey. A soft and fading "thank you" traveled back to him, and Felix closed his eyes. He could feel them. More were coming. A lot more. "Ready to fight, Pit?"

Fight today. Kill. Die tomorrow.

Felix grinned despite the situation. They'd been in worse than this. He held onto that thought as the hills boiled over with Primordial-spawn, some the size of a Human, most far larger. The sky, too. It darkened with bone and sinew, and more giant birds came to test them. The world seemed to howl at them, a thousand timbres from a thousand throats, all intent on them.

Felix sat astride Pit, facing the horde, and bellowed right back.

They charged, and Death rode with them.

CHAPTER SIXTY-NINE

The earth ran red, and the skies turned black. Ashen meadows split, torn apart by shifting stone and soil, bored through by drills of acid rain. Tooth and claw, blind but fierce, the Primordial-spawn did not stop. They were unending, impossibly strong, each dig and tear and gnash tearing a wound in his Body. Lightning surged, shredding the black sky and scattering the beasts, but they returned. Again and again, time without end. Felix soon lost track of where he was, of the difference between his limb and the pulpy appendage of a monster. There was only the fight.

In the end, he wasn't sure if it was the door or a monster that swallowed him up.

He hit the floor hard enough that he knocked out a tooth. Fleshy, liquid heat followed him, ichor and worse, and his last thoughts were of how ruined his clothes had become.

Time passed. Felix wasn't sure how much, only that when opened his eyes, there was morning sunlight in them. That, above all else, was strange.

He sat up tentatively, expecting pain from savage wounds, but he was whole. His Health, Stamina, and Mana were topped off, and even his clothes had repaired themselves. Felix let out a soft sound of surprise, startling the snoring bulk of Chimera beside him.

Wha—? Fight! Pit leaped to his feet, wings outspread and scraping against wall hangings and elaborate silver sconces. *Where is the Enemy?*

"We made it back," Felix said, intent on calming his friend, but was distracted by the wide windows along the hall here. Bright morning sunlight shone through the panes, all but obscuring a mountainside vista. Trees were abundant, moving with a soft breeze, but it was nowhere Felix had ever been before. The leaves on the trees were black and gold, for one, and the trunks were a well-worn ivory. "Wherever 'here' happens to be."

Another step on the Path. The last, based on the pattern so far, Karys said. *Are you all right, Felix? The last challenge was… you faced Primordial-spawn.*

"Y-yeah," Felix said, forcing some calm into his voice. "I'm good. I'm probably the only person around with so much experience fighting the bastards." *And even then, I almost died.* He hadn't imagined it, the maws closing over his bloody and beaten form, overwhelmed by the sheer numbers of spawn in that blasted world. He shuddered, but cut it off, clamping his Will upon Body. He hadn't the time for weakness. "We made it through, that's all that matters."

A blue box appeared before him with a trilling sound, half-expected but still surprising.

You Have Walked The Chosen Path(s)!
Congratulations!
You Have Received An Omen (x3)!

Again, three cards sat next to him on the patterned stone. Three tarot cards, backs designed with that same blue-white eye of flame. The steel of them clanged as he flipped them onto the bare floor.

Name: Omen of the Hermit
Benefit: +2 END, +1 PER, +1 VIT per level gained.

Name: Omen of Strength
Benefit: +2 STR, +1 END, +1 VIT per level gained.

Name: Omen of Death
Benefit: +2 VIT, +1 PER, +1 WIL per level gained.

The faces of the cards were as he expected. Himself, shirtless, wrestling a Primordial-spawn to the ashen ground. Himself again, wearing hooded robes, peering out from behind the spray of a waterfall into a dark night. And the last, a dark figure in armored robes, hooked blade in hand and eyes of blue fire. He couldn't help but flinch at the face. It was his sister's. *Gabby. Why? What does she have to do with this?*

He chuckled at himself. Questions were pointless; he'd either figure it out or not. Hopefully before he died. Felix gathered the cards and stood up. Like the others, the cards went into Pit's saddlebags, clattering as he moved. He was forming quite the collection.

Six Omens, now. Karys whispered. *What does it mean?*

Felix's shrug turned into an arcing spasm as System energy thundered into his core. The wild song resumed, Dissonance and Harmony together, a tension driving between the grinding surfaces of his two cores. They sparked and flared, their touching edges shining brighter than the weaving ribbons below. Notifications popped into view of their own volition.

+34 STR
+31 DEX
+22 PER
+25 END
+42 MIG
+17 VIT
+38 AGL

Etheric Concordance is level 72!
Stone Shaping is level 68!
Shadow Whip is level 46!
Bastion of Will is level 73!

Deep Mind is level 61!
Armored Skin is level 74!

Wrack and Ruin is level 46!
...
Wrack and Ruin is level 50!
Journeyman Tier!
You Gain:
+20 INT
+10 INE
+...

Thanks To Your Experiences, You Have Accomplished A Skill Evolution!
Wrack and Ruin (E) has become Rain of Cataclysm (L)!
Level Is Maintained!

Rain of Cataclysm (Legendary), level 50!
All things fall, you are simply there to see it done. Let rain your Will and see that your enemies are washed away. Potency, density, and speed increase moderately with Skill level. Quantity increases with Skill level.

Influence of the Wisp is level 56!
Journeyman Tier!
You Gain:
+10 WIL
+20 INT
+...

Synergy Detected Between Influence of the Wisp, Mana Manipulation, and Fire Within!
Do You Wish To Combine Them?
This May Result In Severe Injury Or Death.
Y/N

Holy shit, he managed among the swirling sensations of potency. His core felt like a rung bell, a spinning maelstrom of sound and fury, worse than at the beginning with only the monstrous load of new stat points. Points of light drove into him, stabbing through flesh into his Mind and Spirit. Pain was dredged up by the power, and it was all he could do to breathe through it.

Felix! Your core is—it's spinning! The weaving!

He gritted his teeth as the ribbons of light, typically as good as immobile, suddenly began to whirl about his cores. Tempered Skills were attached to them, Journeyman Skills all, and their colored ribbons wove beneath the stacked rings of his cores like a maypole.

Seize it, Felix! You mustn't let it coil!

Without thinking, he listened to Karys, hurling his Willpower and Intent at the ribbons that tethered his Journeyman Tempered Skills to his two cores; one from each core per Skill. Their motion shuddered to a stop, and it felt like a mountain was grinding down on top of him. A panicked scream tried to worm its way from his throat, but the pressure trapped it in his chest, where it simply shook his lungs.

Hold it! You must guide the weaving, or else your advancement will—ah! Karys rattled in his sheath. *Your Skills! Fire Within and Mana Manipulation! We need them!*

I... can't hold... these and withstand... a Skill combination, too, Felix thought at the sword. It was like pushing through molasses. *Pit!*

All of it had happened so fast, Pit hadn't been able to respond other than tilting his big head at Felix. But the bond thrummed with his pain, and the tenku knew that trouble was afoot. The world outside flashed with a brilliant white light, and the heavy weight of his Companion joined his Spirit. As Pit's Harmonic stats added to Felix's own, it was like a second pair of hands began to lift the mountain that was crushing him. They might still die, but for a moment, Felix could breathe.

Felix!

Yes, goddamn it! Combine!

Clouds of Essence vanished in an instant, sucked into his cores along with the flood of colorless System energy. Cacophony resulted, wild noise that screamed toward his Skills and igniting each of them in a coruscating fire of blue-white and red-gold. With what Will he could spare, Felix hauled the three Skills toward one another, forcing their proximity in his core space until their vibrating patterns overlapped and surged with potency. Lightning shot up his spine, down his limbs, flame and ice in equal measure tearing at his nerve endings. He screamed.

Influence of the Wisp (R), Mana Manipulation (U), and Fire Within (R) Have Become Cardinal Flame (L)!
Level Is Averaged!

Cardinal Flame (Legendary) Level 57!
Blood calls to blood and flame to flame. Take hold, Ascendant! Take hold! Increases internal Mana control significantly per level, increases external Mana control significantly per level.

The pain—*that* pain, at least—stopped. His bones were jelly, and Felix would have collapsed to his knees had his Will been a mote weaker; as it was, he firmed his joints with sheer desperation. If he fell, the mountain of his weaving would fall, too, and something told him that it would be catastrophic.

Use your Cardinal Flame! Focus on the cables of your weaving!

Karys voice galvanized his attention, and Felix pushed through the fog around his Mind. His weaving shook, rippled wildy with tension, but as his strange new Skill took hold, his grip on it all felt tighter, more sure. As if his hands had been covered in oil, and he'd just rinsed it off for the first time.

Weave them, like so!

Karys flashed along impressions, similar to what Pit could do but less, but still enough to guide Felix. He twisted and braided the ribbons—cables, Karys called them—twining them into a complex weave that was thicker than the giant trees of the Foglands. Within each cable, Felix could feel echoes of the song of his Skills, altering the texture of the weave depending on how they were placed.

Cardinal Flame is level 58!

Karys called out instructions, and even Pit joined in, gripping cables where Felix couldn't. Dissonance and Harmony roared all around him, energies at the opposite ends of the spectrum, yet both streaming from his cores and into the weaving. The mountain grew heavier with every twist and turn, each layer harder to complete than the last.

Felix was barely aware of what he was doing, or whether he had followed Karys' increasingly strained instructions, or if he had simply gone on instinct. His firm grip turned to a precarious balancing act by the end of it, a razor that he walked along, cutting himself all the while. Yet, to fall off meant certain destruction. Felix wasn't sure how he knew that, but the knowledge of it coiled within him, immutable.

Cardinal Flame is level 59!
Cardinal Flame is level 60!

The cables grew thicker the farther they descended, as if each revolution deepened their potency. Felix could barely hold on, monstrous Willpower or no, when the entire pillar finally snapped into place. Sudden music, a song of triumph and fire blared from the heavens. The infinite black of his core space quivered with it, shook to its foundations as [Thunderflame Core] and [Cardinal Beast Core] chimed against one another in perfect Harmony and teeth-grinding Dissonance.

Cardinal Flame is level 61!
Cardinal Flame is level 62!

Felix panted, his Mind and Spirit wrung-out dishrags, and Pit was right there with him. Together, they had built something more than he had expected, a column of brilliant, woven lights that extended downward from the stacked, spinning rings of his dual cores.

A powerful foundation for the start of your Weaving Stage, Karys said at last. *Too powerful by half for someone still in their Journeyman Tier, but then what else could I have expected from an Unbound?*

Due To Vein Of Divinity, All Skills Woven Into Your First Pillar Gain One (1) Level!

Sovereign of Flesh is level 61!
Unfettered Volition is level 61!

The Song of Absolution is level 74!
Bastion of Will is level 74!
Ravenous Tithe is level 72!
Voracious Eye is level 63!
Adamant Discord is level 69!
Cardinal Flame is level 63!
Theurgist of the Rise is level 71!

Felix hadn't the energy to be surprised, but the message still took him aback. He peered at the Pillar, for the first time noticing a threading of black-crimson through the cables of its making. The black-crimson branched and spread like a root or a vein, identical to the same vein-like structure that extended between the abyss and his two ring cores.

You've... you've woven a Vein of Divinity into your First Pillar. Karys' voice was breathless with disbelief and excitement. *Do you know what this means?*

Felix gave his sword a weary smile, lifting himself ever so carefully out of his own core space. "Not a clue."

It means, if you can do the same with the rest of your Pillars, you'll have a Weaving Stage that cannot be bested by anyone short of Paragon status! Karys paused. *That is, as long as you continue to Temper your Aspects correctly. The road ahead of you is not an easy one.*

"Can't say it's been rainbows and sunshine so far."

The hall was just as he'd left it, though it felt larger with Pit nestled in his Spirit. Felix stood up on shaky legs and coaxed his friend out. Pit refused at first, and the worry across their bond made it clear why, but eventually the tenku was convinced Felix was fine. He emerged in a flash of light.

"Okay. That was... that was good, if unexpected," Felix said. He flexed his hands, poking at his Aspects and stats like a sore tooth. He hurt all over, but already it felt like injuries he'd sustained days ago instead of minutes. "One last set of doors, right?"

That is what I expect, yes. Your Path is clearly operating by threes. Three doors. Three omens. Three challenges. I only fear that your last door will be the hardest yet.

Felix opened his mouth to reply, but suddenly Pit trembled with the advent of his own stat gains. He could clearly see them in his notifications, and he was again impressed by the sheer amount of stats they were earning.

+29 STR
+42 AGL
+29 VIT
+19 WIL
+37 EVA
+22 PER

Pit's Bite is level 57!
Pit's Rake is level 61!
Pit's Cry is level 63!
Pit's Wingblade is level 68!
Pit's Frost Spear is level 70!

Pit's Poisonfire is level 50!
Journeyman Tier!
He Gains:
+10 VIT
+10 END

+New Skill!
Poison Resistance (C), level 1!

Pit's Flight is level 57!
Journeyman Tier!
He Gains:
+10 END
+10 AGL
+10 DEX

Pit's haunches quivered, his wings stretched, again smashing into sconces and wall hangings. Somewhere, something broke. When he pulled them back in, Felix realized Pit had grown yet again. He was nowhere near the size he'd been in the last doorway vision… thing, but he'd gained at least five inches of height and an equal amount in sheer width.

"You're massive, bud," Felix said to his friend. "Are you gonna just... keep growing? Is there an upper limit for Chimeras?"

Pit shook his head, tossing the feathery ruff around his neck, and shrugged. *Mother was big.*

Felix nodded. She had been big, but smaller than Pit was now. He felt some hope kindle in his gut. "Maybe... we might be able to get out of this place, after all."

Pit growled wordlessly. Eagerly.

"C'mon, then," Felix said and started walking down the brightly lit hallway. "Let's see what else this place has in store for us."

CHAPTER SEVENTY

As he unsteadily walked the surprising length of the hallway, Felix gave a glance at the pillar now stretching beneath his dual cores. "This is a strange thing. I don't *feel* that much stronger."

You need only wait. The power from this one weaving will—it will surprise you, I am thinking.

"As long as it shows up soon. We've more than a few monsters to kill," Felix said with a displeased grunt. "Still. Weaving done. What's the next stage? Tapestry, right?"

Karys all but wagged his non-existent finger at him. *You have the First Weaving of the First Pillar done. There are eight more to go. Though I warn you, it is harder with each successive attempt.*

"Eight?" Felix blanched. One had been hard enough, but each one would be worse? "Great."

If you manage to weave nine Pillars of the same quality as your first? You might find the Tapestry Stage far lighter work. Your newest Skill, Cardinal Flame, should help with that. I would suggest you focus on leveling it to the next Tier.

"I'll get right on that," he said wryly. "But I can't say it's not a cool Skill." Not only did it help with internal Mana control, such as weaving his First Pillar, but it helped with external manipulation. What's more, the flame in the title wasn't just for show. The Skill hummed, and the song it sang almost contained words, words that told him a bit of how it worked.

He summoned fire to his hands. It crackled, blue-white with red-gold flecks throughout it. Pit cooed in tired appreciation. Felix let the flames fade. It wasn't the only Skill he'd gained, though Rain of Cataclysm had been learned because… because of the way he'd used a high-leveled Wrack and Ruin in the last scenario. He knew it because he saw himself use it. He was tempted to try it out again, but not there.

Felix would be seeing monsters before long, after all.

He reached the Chamber of Doors, as he'd begun thinking of it.

Still tingling and jittery from his near destruction, there was a curious numbness within him as he beheld the Chamber's… oddities. The room was three times the size of the last, and the white-marbled blue stone had been replaced with a red and gold decor, with accents of black and crimson all around. Hexagonal columns were gone, and instead there were massive statues of monstrous creatures, dozens of feet tall and no more than four feet in diameter. At first glance, they appeared to be serpents or eels, but on closer inspection, he saw manes of hair around their heads and stag-like antlers surmounting faces that were decidedly more dog-like than reptilian.

"Dragons?" he asked. Pit cooed in interest.

Indeed. They—have you not seen them before?

Felix shook his head. The closest he had come to were the carvings on Vess' partisan, which, now that he thought about it, did resemble these creatures a bit. "A Primordial called the Ravager King had a draconic look about him, but it wasn't like this at all."

That is a Primordial, that's why. They… follow their own rules. These, if I'm not mistaken, are Dusk Dragons found in—in the lands… It's gone. I had it, but the memory is gone. I know them for Dusk Dragons, but that is all. Karys took a breath he didn't need. *I am sorry.*

"Karys, no. Don't be sorry. This isn't your fault and isn't under your control," Felix said. He was shaky and off-balance, but Felix tried to steady his legs long enough to stare down at his sword. "No more apologizing."

Ah… very well, Felix.

The draconic pillars were holding up the ceiling, which was

carved with ever more wondrous creatures. All four types of Chimera cavorted among winding, stylized greenery, all carved of golden stone and set with rubies for their eyes. In the center was an opulent chandelier made of some sort of glowing crystal, it branched out like an inverted tree, each limb glowing with a soft, warm radiance.

Around the room, those dark tapestries were picked out in gold thread, each depicting mountains and forests and oceans, all of them touched by a draconic figure and various (much smaller) humanoid shapes. What it all meant, he had no clue, but he was amused to find that there were no urns or vases anywhere.

"If this place is built for me specifically, does that mean the System still has a hand in things?" Felix asked.

It must. The Grand Harmony formed the System before the First Age. Before everything, Karys said.

"Why dragons, then? I've had nothing to do with them," Felix said as he stepped further into the chamber. Between the soaring dragon-pillars were deep alcoves holding bronze statues. Each one was of a being with weaponry and scaled armor, though the Race varied. He saw Elves, Humans, Hobgoblins, even a Gnome, all with weapons raised up at the sky while dragons writhed among their feet. "Oh. *Oh.* These are Dragoons."

Dragoons? I have never heard of them.

"They hunt dragons, or fight them, or something," Felix said and fought down a blush. He had a feeling he knew why the room was dragon-themed now. He cleared his throat. "Anyway, it's not important. Let's check out the doors."

Pit let out a teasing whistle before nudging Felix in the side. He grunted and smirked at the tenku. "Shut up."

The three doors before him were huge compared to the last two sets. More like palace gates than normal doors, they were made of metal and worked into fantastical designs, but just as the last, these also had locks. The first door was worked from a bright, silvery material; Mithril, according to his Voracious Eye, and it was worked with swirling dragons, all of them maned and antlered.

The second door was made of orichalcum, red-gold and stamped with a rampaging tyrant, bigger than mountains and possessing twenty arms. The third door was made of a familiar bronze. Crescian Bronze, to be precise, and it only contained a single figure. Humanoid and hovering amid a shattered terrain, it had two eyes inset with gemstones. Sapphires.

"Is this… me?" Felix asked. He ran his fingers over the carving, but pulled it back with a startled oath. The door was burning hot to the touch. "What is this?"

The air crackled, filled with a sudden static that made Felix and Pit both flinch. A voice like ten thousand screaming trumpets surged into their Minds.

One Last Choice, Felix Nevarre.
Each Time, You Have Chosen The Hardest Path.
Each Time, You Have Seen That Which May Have Changed.
The Past, Had You Not Been Atop The Yacht.
The Present, Had You Not Found The Maw.
Now, For the Final Choice, You Must See That Which Could Change.
Which May Yet.
Choose.

The voice, if it could be called that, quietened. Felix looked at the chamber and the doors, but nothing had changed.

"What the hell was that?" he asked.

The… System. It spoke to you. Karys quivered in his sheath. *I've never heard of such a thing… I-I think. Perhaps it is because you are Unbound? Perhaps.*

"It said the other doors..." Felix worked some moisture into his mouth; it had gone dry for some reason. "...The other doors were things that could have been. Which makes sense. Gabby getting yanked instead of me, and then… wait, did monsters attack Earth after I left?"

I wouldn't know, Felix.

"Hey! I'm talking to you!" Felix shouted into the vaulted ceiling, flaring his Affinity for all it was worth. Hunting whatever had just spoken. He felt… something, a soft sensation just beyond his periphery and tried to latch onto it… but it was like grabbing smoke. "System! Harmony! Whatever you are! Did Earth get attacked?"

There was a moment of surprise—not from him, his sword, or his Companion—before they were all hit with an avalanche of sound.

No.
You.
Chose.

The sheer volume of it threw Felix and Pit to the ground. Stone shattered, and cracks ran up the dragon columns beside them. It faded, slowly, but the ringing in his head persisted for long minutes after.

Feli… was not… wise...

Felix got to his knees, working his jaw as if it'd fix his ears or suddenly burdened Affinity. Pit just rolled on the ground, still dizzy.

Felix. Are you alright?

"Yeah, I'm good. Pit?"

Pit shook his head and let out a pulse of shaky agreement. *I will be.*

Felix grunted and took to his feet, though it was even harder than just a few minutes prior. "What the hell was that?"

A miracle. The System answered you.

"It sounded pissed off," he muttered.

As well it should, Karys sniffed. *I understand your fears, Felix. But that was unwise.*

"People don't really accuse me of being wise very often, Karys." Felix felt something pop inside his head, like a bubble disappearing, and his full hearing returned in a rush. "Oh that's better," he sighed. His Affinity still felt burned, though that didn't stop him from reaching out again. Yet the soft presence he had felt was gone, as if it had never been. "It said I chose, and so Earth didn't get attacked by that… cloud thing. But if I had chosen not to go to that party, then it would have? Why?"

It sounds as if you are needed here. From what I have seen, the monsters that would have attacked Earth, or the unleashing of the Maw, none of it has happened because you *have been there.*

Fate, Pit sent.

"Choice. Fate. Seems contradictory to me," Felix said.

Things have truly changed with the Ages, Karys said in dismay. *Choice is the way of the Grand Harmony. All choice is sacred, and to take away that choice is to do a great evil. What you call Fate or Destiny is but the accumulation of Choices. Not even the Prophets of old could truly determine the future, only the twisting, branching pathways that may or may not lead to it. This is a point of change, Felix. The System has told you so. Here, you get a glimpse into what may be and perhaps have a chance at changing it.*

Felix regarded the doors of his four options. Open the mithril, the orichalcum, the bronze, or do as he'd done before. Open them all. "The hardest path. That's what the System called it. That I'd chosen the hardest path each time… yet if I hadn't, I wouldn't have gotten all three Omens."

Risk and reward, Pit sent.

"Tell me about it," Felix muttered. "Well, I'm not stopping now. All three, again. If this thing is gonna warn me about something, I'd rather have all the facts I can. Now." He clapped his hands together. "Let's find the keys."

Smashing giant dragoon statues was, as it turns out, really hard. He started with the Gnome statue, but for all his Strength, he couldn't even dent it. Yet, he felt a curious heat beneath his hands, and though his Manasight refused to tell him anything about these rooms, he swore it was pulsing with magic. The heat was coiling just beneath the surface. *Around a key, maybe?*

What was it the Archon said? 'Crescian Bronze will not calmly go to forge, Nymean. It must be convinced. That willfulness does not degrade after it's worked, whether that is a weapon or not.' The words rolled back to him, perfect, as if the Archon were whispering them into his ear. Felix shuddered. "Ugh, downside of perfect recall."

He placed his hands against the statue and *willed* it to help. He was met, almost immediately, with a flat refusal. Felix blinked in surprise. He tried again, this time forming the image of his Inheritor's Will, of earning it. Still, the statue refused him, but it was less firm. Felix tried again, repeating himself, but the rigidity had reappeared. He almost growled in annoyance.

Stone Shaping!

His Mana poured from his sore channels, dusty brown now flecked with sparking silver as Felix altered the pattern of it. He'd affected metal this way before, and it was far easier to do now. Cardinal Flame burned in his core, aiding the process. Yet the Crescian Bronze was utterly unaffected.

Felix definitely *did* growl, this time. *What does it take to get you to answer me? I didn't know I'd have to debate someone into helping me here. Where's Vess when I need her?*

A connection snagged in his strained Affinity, strong but brief, between Felix and the statue. "What caused that? Mentioning debate? Vess?" Again the connection, stronger this time. "What does she have to do with—right. You're a Dragoon. I know a Dragoon, or an apprentice Dragoon, I think. She is waiting for me, she might be hurt—" Felix caught the thought and banished it. "She is *fine*, but I have to get out of here. Now. Please. Statue… thing. Help me out?"

The connection he felt spread outward, lines of it snaring the other statues. It rang like a bell in his ears, and from the Gnome before him emerged a foot-long key made of ornate mithril. Felix took it, and heard Pit exclaim a few alcoves over.

"Thank you," Felix said to the statue. He wasn't sure why, but it felt right. "I'll make good use of this."

When he stepped out into the main area, Pit was carrying a red-gold key in his mouth, and a bronze one was just a few steps away, floating in mid-air. Felix snagged them all and, as carefully as before, placed them in their respective doors.

Shadow Whip!

Three tendrils, grasping keys and doors. Felix took a breath to steady himself. Plans swirled in his head, ideas for what he could do to survive what dwelled outside the Path, back in the Mana pool. He thought about choices, about the little statue he found, and about the other item he'd tucked into his waistband along with the Omen Key.

Omens. You could only have one. He had an idea, but he'd have to get through the last bit of the Path first. He just hoped he was right.

"Are we ready?" he asked, and received confirmation from both his friends. "One last turn."

Turning the keys were even harder than before, requiring every bit of his Strength and Dexterity to manage them at the same time. Yet he did it.

Ravenous Tithe!

Smoke and light exploded in all directions, before streaming into him.

The Final Door Is Open.
ERROR
Multiple Doors Open.
Reconfiguring Paths.
Stand By.

The world *flexed*, and all things turned to dust.

CHAPTER SEVENTY-ONE

The Moon

The Silver Line Between Two Dreams

The Path Continues.

Felix flared his Bastion of Will and held it tight as the Path shoved false memories and experiences at him. They piled high atop the walls of his Skill, amorphous lights that weren't precisely sinister, but which he knew would consume himself. He'd be lost in the "him" that existed within these alternate realities. His sense of self and proper memories hung on, fully protected.

Feeling safer, Felix relaxed his visualization of the Bastion and found dust forming beneath his feet. He was walking already, his body in the midst of motion as slick roof tiles formed in all directions. It was night and stars wheeled above his head, too bright and too strange, but there were four moons in the sky. He was on the Continent. *But where?*

Felix crept to the edge of the roof, clinging carefully to a line of brick chimneys. He could see the skyline of a great city, far larger than Haarwatch. It was dark, but he could make out the opalescent white, sapphire blue, and emerald green of the buildings all around him, all of them at least six stories. Trees were everywhere, worked into the architecture in some places, often stretching higher than any building and festooned with glimmering magelights. Somewhere in the distance, bells began to toll the hour.

This feels a lot... calmer, than usual. Pit? Felix half-turned and found the tenku standing awkwardly some ten yards back. *Are you okay?*

Fine, just uneasy, he sent. A ripple of disquiet rolled through their bond, and Felix was just as uncertain of its origin as Pit. *Danger in the air.*

I don't disagree, said a voice at his waist.

"Karys!" Felix whispered aloud before stopping himself. *Karys, you're here. That's never happened before.*

Mhm. It is either a sign of progress... or things are going to be worse than usual. The green-gold pulses of life Mana within the sword were dim, and Felix could feel Karys shielding the light as if he shuttered a lantern. *It would do us well to move cautiously.*

"Keep it moving, beefsteak!"

"That's not my nam—yow!"

Felix froze at the sound, but soon realized they were all alone on the roof. He stepped past the row of chimneys and peered over the edge. Down below, the street was paved with wide stones, though stubborn weeds stuck up through their crevices in many places. Lamps on black iron poles marched in a steady procession down the thoroughfare, which was wide enough to be considered a four-lane highway back home. Yet the streets were almost empty.

Except, of course, for the prisoners.

There were seven of them, all manacled and chained to one another, while three dozen armored guards marched with them on all sides. One of those guards, a man in dark crimson and gold plate armor, jabbed at one of the prisoners with a three-pronged spear. The prisoner growled in pain and fear, and Felix's eyes widened. It was a Minotaur. In fact, many of the prisoners were Races he'd never seen before or even heard mentioned.

Voracious Eye!

Failed.

One of the guards jolted. "What'd you do?" he snarled at the Minotaur, jerking his chain. "Did you try to use a Skill?"

"If I could, I'd curbstomp all of you stupid RP weebs," the Minotaur growled. It turned into a pained whine when that trident was shoved into his side.

"Imbecile that you are, I don't doubt you'd try. If the collar isn't dissuading your filthy demon instincts, then maybe we go for a more… permanent solution." The guard held up the bloodied trident for emphasis. The Minotaur, much to Felix's surprise, trembled. "That's right. Fear me. And keep moving."

The group shuffled along, all of them cowed and shivering.

What the hell is this? He couldn't identify them, but the prisoners were a wild array of Races. An ashen-skinned Gnome, two dog-like folk an inch or so taller than the Gnome, an antlered man with heavy forearms, a bipedal crocodile, an Elf with some sort of feathered cloak, and the cowering Minotaur.

Those are elision collars, he noticed. They were devices designed to shut off the supply of Mana to someone's core. Panic gripped him at the thought, but the memories that hovered outside his Bastion whispered to him. False memories of close calls and first-hand experience with them that they only worked on lower Tiers, those beneath a Master. They'd—at best—inconvenience a Master Tier, but not stop them completely. To do more, one would need greater tools, and neither Felix nor his fake memories knew enough to speak on it.

The prisoners didn't need a greater tool, however. Even with his Voracious Eye blocked, their Spirits were easy to read even from four stories up. Three of them were Journeyman Tier and the rest were Apprentice Tier. Regardless, all of them felt strong, and would be stronger still if those collars were removed.

More than that, though, something about each of the prisoners burned in Felix's vision. It was an itch in his eyes he couldn't scratch. He flared his Manasight, his Perception, Affinity, anything to alleviate it. There. He felt it. The thrum of a chord, one so large it should have shaken the foundations of the buildings around them. A glyph, like a complicated halo, manifested around each of them. He'd never seen it before, but understanding bloomed within Felix and Pit at the same time. A kinship.

They're all Unbound? Karys gasped.

"Where'd they come from?" he asked in a low voice. This was supposedly a view of the future. Were *more* Unbound summoned?

Seven of them, but—Felix. The summoning traditionally calls for nine. These—these could be—

"The ones summoned with me." The realization struck him hard. His eyes narrowed. "Are they all from Earth?"

There is no way to tell, except to ask. I doubt it. That ritual… what little I remember pertains to casting a wide net, as it were.

Felix clenched his jaws. He had to do something, right? Isn't that why he was there?

The guards hauled the prisoners down the street, not caring if they walked or were dragged. To a man, they wore dark red platemail, edged in gold, and on both their cloaks and breastplates was an upraised gauntlet, surrounded by a shield overtop a golden sunburst. *Paladins of the Pathless*, the false memories whispered. Felix "remembered" fighting them dozens of times, though the details were foggy. He knew they were strong, which he could read in their Spirit, but Felix also knew he could handle a couple squads without issue. The problem now was that he was looking at an entire phalanx escorting the Unbound to… where were they going?

He soon found out, as an alabaster palace appeared beyond the soaring arches of the city. It was above and beyond any other construction, lit up in the night like a beacon against the dark, glittering like a star fallen to earth. *The Hierophant's palace,* knowledge whispered. *I'm in Amaranth. The capital of the Hierocracy.* Another thought chased the first, like a fox into a rabbit warren. *They're being taken to the Hierophant. If they meet her, it's over. All of it.*

Certainty baked into his bones, thrust on him by the false memories, but it felt true all the same. Felix remembered hunting this group for weeks as they traveled to Amaranth, trying to find an opportunity to save them. His time was running out, now.

Pit chirruped. *We help.*

This is not real. You know that, yes?

"Yeah. But that just means we can find out what happens if I attack a bunch of Paladins in their home city, consequence free," Felix said.

Unless you die. Death here is just as final here as upon the Continent, Felix.

"Then I won't," Felix grinned and padded down the street. While he did, he checked his Status. Just in case.

Name: Felix Nevarre
Level: 52
Race: Primordial of the Unseen Tide (Lesser)*
Omen: Magician
Born Trait: Keen Mind

Health: 3737/3737
Stamina: 4092/4092
Mana: 3449/3449

STR: 1104
PER: 960
VIT: 757
END: 724
INT: 794
WIL: 1322
AGL: 788
DEX: 945

BODY
***Resistances*: The Song of Absolution (L), Level 74**

***Combat Skills:* Dodge (C), Level 54; Heavy Armor Mastery (C), Level 1; Blind Fighting (R), Level 45; Corrosive Strike (R), Level 48; Wild Threnody (E), Level 61**

***Physical Enhancements*: Armored Skin (R), Level 74; Unfettered Volition (E), Level 61**

MIND
***Mental Enhancements*: Deception (C), Level 25; Meditation (U), Level 56; Negotiation (U), Level 21; Bastion of Will (E), Level 74; Deep Mind (E), Level 61; Manifestation of the Coronach (E), Level 47; Ravenous Tithe (E), Level 72**

Information Skills: Alchemy (C), Level 27; Tracking (C), Level 25; Exploration (U), Level 48; Voracious Eye (E), Level 63; Aria of the Green Wilds (L), Level 57

SPIRIT

Spiritual Enhancements: Dual Casting (U), Level 50; Manasight (U), Level 63; Manaship Pilot (R), Level 22; Etheric Concordance (L), Level 72; Sovereign of Flesh (T), Level 61; Unite the Lost (T), Level 22

Spells: Abyssal Skein (R), Level 49; Cloudstep (R), Level 35; Invocation (R), Level 42; Oathbinding (R), Level 35; Shadow Whip (R), Level 46; Stone Shaping (R), Level 68; Mantle of the Infinite Revolution (E), Level 49; Arrow of Perdition (L), Level 40; Cardinal Flame (L), Level 63; Rain of Cataclysm (L), Level 50; Theurgist of the Rise (L), Level 71; Adamant Discord (T), Level 69

Unused Stat Points: 10

Harmonic Stats
RES: 220
INE: 321
AFI: 428
REI: 208
EVA: 285
MIG: 175
ALA: 456
FEL: 410

Name: Pit (Companion)
Level: 56
Race: Chimera - Tenku

Health: 1933/1933
Stamina: 1148/1148

Mana: 1870/1870

STR: 240
PER: 378
VIT: 386
END: 205
INT: 298
WIL: 344
AGL: 714
DEX: 600

Bite (C), Level 57
Rake (C), Level 61
Cry (R), Level 63
Skulk (C), Level 49
Etheric Concordance (L), Level 72
Wingblade (U), Level 68
Frost Spear (C), Level 70
Cold Resistance (C), Level 34
Poison Resistance (C), Level 1
Poisonfire (R), Level 50
Flight (R), Level 57

***Active Titles*:**
Survivor III
Butcher III
Unconquered
Face the Charge
Bulwark of the Innocent
Pactmaker
Work Horse
Blind Pugilist
Hero
Iron Will
Apprentice Magus

The Broken Path
Voidwalker
Indomitable
Unleash the Beast
Blessing of the Lost
Fatebreaker
The Shape of Fate II
Frostbane
Architect of the Rise
Cardinal (Major)
Save The Lost
Thief of Fate
Tyrant of Choice
Against Catastrophe
Tyros of the Unseen Tide
Stigma of the Chosen

<u>Pit's Harmonic Stats</u>
RES: 35
INE: 72
AFI: 73
REI: 68
EVA: 255
MIG: 45
ALA: 78
FEL: 74

Partially because he was holding back those false memories, Felix could see his true stats and Skills. Thankfully. He also saw Pit's, and both of them just about blew his mind. Felix's Strength and Willpower were reaching new, insane heights and many of his other stats weren't far behind. How much longer until he crossed into the Third Threshold? If he was lucky, not much longer at all.

Still, he had enough to handle these idiots.

The Paladins were moving fast, but Felix easily kept pace. His Unfettered Volition made traversing the damp tiles easy, and his Manasight kept track of the Unbound even when he had to break line of sight due to the variety of architecture. Felix bolted over roofs, across bell towers, atop porticoes used by relaxing citizens. He had wrapped Abyssal Skein around himself, and Pit was Converged within his Spirit; there was no chance he'd be spotted.

Somewhere along the line, Felix saw more enemies join into the procession. These wore platemail and cloaks as well, but their armor was white enameled and emblazoned with a sunburst. *Inquisitors*, he sneered. *Good. We can fight them, too.*

Pit almost vibrated with restrained anger and glee. He always was a violent bird.

They surged ahead, leaping over rooftops in an effort to outpace the growing procession. Yet, before he could, they had entered a wide, four-way intersection with a small fountain shaped like a fish. The Paladins slowed, suddenly cautious, and Felix saw why. Men and women were stepping from the other roads, at least three in each street, all of them bearing weapons.

"Halt, dogs," one of the men said, a burly Dwarf wearing a cloak over heavy armor. "Free your charges into our care, or else die."

The leader of the Paladins scoffed. "You dare challenge us? In Amaranth itself? Brigand, you are a fool."

"Only fool I see here is you," said a melodious voice, one he recognized.

Zara!?

The Naiad stepped from the left side, and instead of a weapon, she suddenly blazed with aquamarine light. All around her, every single cloaked figure did as well.

"Sorcerers!" cried an Inquisitor. "All of them! Fire! Trackless forfend, fire if you wish to live!"

Chaos reigned.

Spells and song and burning light shattered the false peace of the night. Screams of hate and pain and fear echoed through the streets as people died by the handful. The six Chanters—for what else could they be—tore into the company of Pathless devotees while weapons and Skills of fire and light Mana bounced harmlessly off the Sorcerers' protections. From above, Felix saw the zealots grow desperate then clever: under the cover of blooming flame, a number of them grabbed the chained Unbound and dragged them off into a side alley, barely wide enough to manage the Minotaur's huge horns.

Felix grinned and leaped across the street, Abyssal Skein still wailing within him. He landed hard on the opposing roof, but no one would notice the noise in the cacophony of battle. He raced ahead, but found himself slammed into the tiles, hard enough to shatter them. A Spirit unlike any he'd felt before pressed down on him, so hard he could barely breathe or even think.

"This is all the Cantus sends? Six meager Master Tiers?" someone said softly, yet loud enough that Felix felt it shudder through his entire Body. "Can you not at least deliver a challenge?"

From his position, Felix could just barely see over the edge of the roof, backward and down into a narrow slice of the intersection. The Paladins and Inquisitors were regaining their feet, and the Sorcerers stood staring off to his right. He could see Zara, and she was paler than he'd ever seen her before.

"Hierophant," she hissed, baring her shark-like teeth at the unseen interloper. "Your plan will not work. Even chasing them as you have has lost time. It is almost upon us!"

"And we would not have chased them had your kind not interfered, heretic!" The Hierophant's bellow was louder than before, so much that the tiles around Felix shook wildly. He felt something wet trickle from his ears, and all sound cut out for several seconds. Paralyzed, Felix could do nothing as he felt his eardrums repair themselves. "—Pathless would reward me! I will end you and all that you represent!"

"I welcome the attempt, Coward in White!" Zara didn't wait, but unleashed a series of green-blue strikes that turned the air itself into a boiling liquid, hot enough that Felix screamed in pain at a distance. The Hierophant fared worse, and the Spiritual pressure on him abruptly dropped.

Felix surged to his feet, Unfettered Volition thrumming manically, but froze. He could help. With his stats and Skills, and with Primordial Skills like Ravenous Tithe and Sovereign of Flesh, he could maybe put a dent in this Hierophant he'd heard so much about. He knew he could take out the other Paladins and Inquisitors, his false memories told him as much.

A door, limned in red-gold light, appeared at the edge of the roof.

Below, that Minotaur bellowed in pain and fear. Others joined in. They were hurting, and Felix could help them.

It's not real! Felix!

He could… he could see more. There was more to find out!

Run! Felix! The Door!

Felix soaked it in, everything he could. The strange harmonic powers being used, the abilities of the Paladins and Inquisitors, the feel of the Hierophant. If only he could see her face! Just a few steps—

"There! Atop the roof!"

Fire followed the call, igniting the night with the heat of a forge. Felix shied away, nearly slipping on the broken tiles. The door flickered.

"Goddamn it!"

He ran, just ahead of another fireball, leaping into the dark.

The Sun.

Beyond The Dark, The Light Awaits.

The Path Continues.

The Bastion shook, assaulted on all sides. Light battered the gates, the walls, burned the forest and the greens beyond the dark stone. It held. It barely held.

More memories, more false life piled atop Felix's own.

He landed in a crouch upon sandy soil. His back felt charred, and for a brief second, he couldn't remember why. His Bastion quaked, and he *couldn't remember.*

"NO!" Felix's Will pressed back, hurling the Path's lies away from himself.

Mind settling, Felix blinked at the heated dust in his eyes. The sun baked him, and even through his resistance, he could still feel the intense heat. Felix stood and was greeted by golden dunes and the red-orange bluffs of windswept buttes in the far distance. Closer to hand, however, was a wild sandstorm that dominated the southern horizon.

"Karys? Where's Pit?" He turned. "Karys?"

His friends were nowhere to be seen, but columns upon columns of crimson-armored soldiers were marching into that sandstorm, polearms and banners raised. Banners that included a crimson fist atop a shield and sunburst, as well as a white tower overtop three sunbursts. *More Paladins,* he thought. The other banner wasn't familiar, and Felix worried too much to search his false memories for clues. One wrong touch, and those memories would overwhelm him, and he'd lose himself.

Atop a dune himself, Felix watched in tired curiosity as the leaders of the army raised their arms up in wild gesticulation. Sunlight streamed down from the sky, briefly focused into a beam of incandescent glory as it fired into the sandstorm itself.

With mute astonishment, Felix saw the sandstorm rip apart as beam after beam fired into it. Then it was gone, millions of pounds of sand drifting back to earth.

"Holy shit," Felix said, his extended Perception almost feeling like ten thousand gritty points of pressure. He recoiled, reeling his Perception in. When the dust cleared, he already saw the columns of Paladins marching forward, but now it was toward a massive, floating city.

He—

The world upended.

Sound and fury scaled his Bastion, reaching grasping claws over the edges of the battlements. Felix strained to keep them at bay.

Lightning from a clear blue sky.

Thunder rolled. An earthquake shook everything.

He stood on streets of a city painted blue and gold. Massive windchimes stirred, struck, resounded to the screams of butcher's work. Red-armored Paladins stalked the streets, putting to sword and flame anyone that crossed their path. Their faces were hidden behind metal, Human-like masks, but no mercy was in their dark eyes.

Felix knew, as the weight of memories crushed his defenses, he knew that he was too late. They had taken Ahkestria. In the sky above, a massive gout of flame struck against a hardened beam of light, and the backwash of their conflict shredded roofs from houses. Felix ran, already summoning his own power.

Cardinal Flame!

Red-gold fire bloomed in his hands, chased by hair-thin tendrils of blue-white lightning. He cast it out, shaping it with his Intent and fueling it with his Affinity and Will. Mana poured from his channels, a torrent of liquid flame that struck the Paladins and melted their armor to their flesh and bones.

A door into a burning hut gleamed. Called to him.

He shaped it again, and it hunted. It consumed them all.

"AH!"

A beam of light hit him. Once. Twice. Claws that rent his back open, hot and wet and achingly cold. Felix lurched away from it, sending fire into the skies, calling down acid, but whatever it was had an Agility far higher than his own. It struck again and again, always at his back, always out of sight. His Health dropped fast. Too fast.

He ran, flaring his Unfettered Volition, burning his Agility, hurtling through the doorway. Into the black.

The World

End It All. Begin Again.

The Path Ends.

Felix landed among dust.

Not sand or soil. A fine dust more akin to ash. He looked up. The sky was blackened and boiling, clouds spinning in unnatural formations, fleeing the rising sun. Fire burned down his back, and he couldn't remember why. His Mind shook, and his Spirit quailed. Thoughts and memories were pouring into his Bastion, unable to be stopped. They were an avalanche, a flood, too much to stop and none of it solid. It slipped past him.

He watched the sky, watched the sunrise on a blasted land, and accepted his fate. This was the end. He couldn't stop it. He had tried for so long, and there was no one left. He was Unbound, and Fate would see him dead.

NO!

The sun burst.

It was fire and greedy tendrils, following in the wake of monstrous figures he could just barely see. Mountains were crushed and seas boiled with their movements. They were more than large; more than physical.

Six moons hung in the sky, and the bloodiest hung closest.

"All is as it must be! Let it no longer be on us! Let us be free!"

Felix heard the voice with his bones, it was so loud, so pervasive. The exploding sun-that-was-not changed, darkening to purple and black, into clouds of hungry darkness streaked with opalescence.

"Let Ruin have it!"

It came for him, and at their back rode the gods. He knew them now, the shadowed giants. Not dead, not dead at all. Free. They pushed the Ruin into the Continent, riding behind it upon chariots of starlight and the infinite cold of the Void.

Fear coursed through his veins, and he tried to run. But lightning burned him, seas of blood drowned him, and the relentless force of the tides pulled at him. He was seized, body and soul.

The Ruin was coming, and he could not move.

"It is but a shadow of itself, but it will end you just the same." A familiar voice said. It hardly sounded mad at all. Then it laughed, and he heard it. The terror. "I wish it had not come to this, Felix Nevarre."

Felix—

"I am given no choice."

—Nevarre—

Her hands were pushed, forced atop his body, squeezing. Other limbs, other figures layered atop her—Vellus'—form. Monstrous creatures, all of them surmounted by halos of immutable power.

Divine power.

"The Unbound cannot be allowed," they intoned. A hammer striking an anvil.

The violet dark took him.

He was unmade.

The World shattered; its flame snuffed out. Screams and cries and joy and laughter and all things that were and could and should have been. Everything that he was, is, could be—unmade. Body, Spirit, his Mind last.

That last of all.

Brilliant lights shone to him, whoever he was, true lights. He knew some were false, some too dim to be real. Memories, he knew. He clung to them. Tightly. Too tightly.

Just let go, the voices whispered. They were legion, one voice and ten billion, all at once. All different. All the same. *Just rest. You deserve rest. Let us in and rest.*

Tired. He was SO tired.

Of fighting

and

hurting,

but Memories sparked, and he recalled,

p e r f e c t l y

the moments that weren't fighting. That weren't hurting, few though they were. Of eating around a campfire with friends. Sitting in the Wall, figuring out sigaldry with that man...Hector! It was Hector! Of a woman's green eyes and laugh. Of another's darker eyes, and a dimple he could never forget.

Of danger. They were in danger. He—No.

He wasn't done yet.

Let go...

NO! I REFUSE!

DO NOT FIGHT! STOP!

A wave of lethargy poured over him, so much that the sparks of light dimmed and faded.

Let go! Release yourself!

His Will engaged, he grabbed at those motes of light, his Memories. And others. Other lights. Things that didn't seem familiar until he held them close, where they clung to each other like constellations. More. More. His Will was iron! Mithril! Crescian Bronze! It was absolute and he would not be denied.

Cores and Skills, sparking sound among a chorus of chaos. Threads, cables of light, he grasped them tight. They shivered at his touch, and clarity surged into his Mind and burgeoning Spirit. A dark crimson vein, a thread within the cables, it *sang.*

He cannot!

It is not allowed!

Words of thunder rattled through him, forbidding him. He —*Felix*—refused.

From that core, he built outward, pulling inward. All that he was once and would be again. False Ruin had struck him, but it was a crucible, a forge from which he would emerge as *more*.

He was *reborn*.

Felix drifted, fell, flew through the doorway.

The final threshold.

The World shattered. The World was remade.

CHAPTER SEVENTY-TWO

After an eternity, his feet touched solid ground.

His—*Felix's*—feet flexed in his metal boots and greaves. His pants were, remarkably, utterly whole, as was his tunic and jacket. Their enchantments blazed, almost overcharged, ready to repair or clean themselves at a moment's notice. Felix held up his hands, saw unblemished skin and flexing tendons. Blunt fingertips, thin with seeming youth, Tempered.

I'm... me.

His Will thrummed into the ground, into the air, and he was no longer alone. A sword belt appeared at his waist in a bloom of green-gold light, the sword tugging his hip down. And from the forest—*forest?*—around him, a massive tenku charged at him. Felix laughed and took the hit straight on, going down in a tangle of fur and feathers and reborn limbs.

Felix! Felix! Safe! You're back!

"Hey, hey buddy," Felix managed between Pit's frantic licking. "Glad to see you, too."

I thought us... that was the Ruin, Felix. Karys' voice was a little muffled, as if it mattered if Felix was sitting on the blade or not. Regardless, he shifted it and cleared the hooked sword from its sheath. *You survived the Ruin. That is so utterly impossible as to be... I have not the words.*

"Not Ruin," Felix stated, thinking of the violet darkness. "Vellus… she may have actually been there. I certainly felt *something* from her. But they called it false. I think it was just a fabrication of the Path."

The Grand Harmony would never create such a Path. Something meddles in your progress, Felix.

"I'm pretty sure I know who." Felix took to his feet, glaring at the placid glade around him. "Vellus… and the other gods, all forcing her hand. But why? It's supposed to be the future, right?"

The future… Not even Seers can rightfully parse the paths of causality, Felix. The System called it "That Which Could Change." I cannot believe any of these are futures we must take as certain.

Felix swallowed, his mouth dry. He could still remember the feel of it, and false or not, it had been horrifying. His Born Trait repeated, in excruciating detail, how he'd been taken apart, piece-by-piece, atom-by-atom. His Mind shied away from it like a hand from a hot stove. He focused on the ground, on the small shoots of green that poked from the dark loam. With exacting motions, Felix took the memories and pushed them down, away, locking them into his Bastion where they could rot until he'd forgotten them entirely. The visions of empty darkness and swirling clouds faded, not forgotten but held at bay. He—

"Violet clouds," he said with a jolt. "It was the same thing that attacked Earth, the shapes, the things in them." Felix took a deep, shuddering breath. "The Ruin would have gone after Earth?"

Pit warbled quietly in concern but still sounded like a bird the size of an elephant. A breeze stirred the glade, making everything shake and shiver, but it didn't touch Felix. He blinked and extended his senses. The trees rustled in a wind he couldn't feel, and the dirt felt… hollow. As if it ended after only a few feet. "What is going on here?"

Felix ran into the woods, burning his Perception and Agility both. Still, he barely managed to stop himself before the terrain simply… stopped.

After thirty yards or so, the forest and blue sky ended in a sheer delineation. Beyond that line was a thick, cloying emptiness.

The Void.

"No, not the Void. If it was the Void, none of this would be here. It doesn't have trees, can't have them, I don't think." Felix clenched his jaw. He addressed the dark around him, the System or Path or whatever it called itself. "What is this? Where am I?"

New Title!

"What?"

Born of Will (Epic)!
You have remade yourself, held together by your foundation and sheer Willpower. You shake the heavens, Ascendant. For what is beyond you, if you have the Will? +100 WIL, VIT, END

Felix barely shivered as the System energy slammed into his core, but when it filtered back out and into his stats, it wrenched out a startled gasp. His Body thrummed with energy—Stamina, Health, and Mana—but more than that: his Vitality had crossed the one thousand mark.

And, dear god, my Will hit 1500. Why wasn't that Title more than Epic, though? Felix felt another shudder wrack his limbs. *I remade myself. That's gotta be worth a Legendary, right? Though that description is… suggestive.*

Felix, I think I understand, Karys said. Pit had followed close behind, but had slowed long before the edge. Now he, too, peered over it into the Void beyond. *This is still part of the Path, but it is… separate somehow. All three Realms are intersecting here, I can feel it. I almost recognize it but—no. It evades me. Yet it hums with importance.*

"Still the Path. But I thought I was done with them now?" Felix tapped his lips, considering. "I didn't see a doorway, though. So am I still in the last Path?"

As if in answer, the voice of the System rocked his microcosm.

Congratulations!
You Have Completed Your Path!
Choose One.

Path of the Survivor (From Survivor Title, Vitality And Endurance Above 500)

+10 Vitality, Endurance, and Perception Per Level

Path of the Slayer (From Giantslayer, Butcher, Frostbane, And Titanslayer Titles, Strength Above 500)
+15 Strength and Endurance Per Level

Path of the Ascendant (From Broken Path, The Shape Of Fate, and Fatebreaker Titles, Core At Ring Stage Or Higher)
+20 All Stats Per Level

The window before him thrummed with power, descending notes that never found bottom. Each one felt potent in a way Felix couldn't explain but understood viscerally. He could sense them, though they were only words, as through a narrow viewfinder into possibility.

Path of the Survivor had him hidden from danger, hardy enough to live while everything around him died, yet smart enough to avoid the obvious fates. Felix was tempted by it, but for what else he saw. Loneliness, bleak isolation, hung about his neck like a weight. He would live through the worst, but be unable to help those he cared for; he rejected it immediately.

Path of the Slayer showed him a blood-soaked battlefield fully embroiled in chaos. Races and monsters came at him, armed and armored to the teeth, and all fell. It was a strength carved from the carcasses of his enemies, and Felix saw his own face radiating such savage glee it shook him to the core. Weapons leaped to his hand, axe and spear and sword and flail, all of them used efficiently. Brutally.

Felix recoiled from that Path of slaughter, quickly refocusing on the last.

Beyond the Path of the Ascendant were gilded cities and soaring archways. Skies of blue and gold spanned the heavens, and a new moon was rising. A red-gold moon wreathed in a ring of blue light. Felix's breath caught as he saw himself filled with light until his eyes, mouth, and fingertips radiated illumination. Wings, Pit's wings, spread from his back, and they were somehow golden, too. Undeniable strength oozed from his pores, a confidence to shake mountains, and a power to back it all up.

Felix pulled back before he lost himself.

"These are my Paths?" he asked no one in particular. "Karys, Pit, did you catch that?"

Yes, Pit sent.

I did, the sword vibrated.

"Three seems to be the System's favorite number, huh? Three doors, three times three Omens. Three Paths. Odd," Felix said. He calmed his breathing and slowed his heart, attempting to still his agitation and unease. He was only partially successful. "Survivor, Slayer, and Ascendant. All based on my Titles, it seems."

Such is the nature of the Omen Paths. Titles, Skills, and stats determine what you are offered at the end of things. Karys grumbled, twitching in his sheath. *Any more I cannot say. Only that... the... Paths should not be as you have experienced them. They are unique, yes, but this... this is beyond strange.*

The last sentences were spoken in a rush, as if he were forcing them out. Karys ended up panting by the end, exhausted.

Felix grunted. "I appreciate that, but it doesn't do me any good now. Is this how Paths were offered at the end of yours?"

Karys made an annoyed sound. *I cannot say.*

"Right. System restrictions." Felix rubbed the bridge of his nose, trying to let his body calm down. He'd run from door to door with barely enough time to think. He'd been torn apart, goddammit! Felix paused, his Mind lurching in pain as the memories tried to escape his Bastion. *Calm. Breathe.*

Meditation is level 58!
Deep Mind is level 62!

He had three Paths, each of which offered him a promise. Survival at any cost, with per level bonuses to his Vitality, Endurance, and Perception to increase his defenses. That one didn't appeal to Felix. He'd had enough of taking a beating and hiding. But did that mean he wished for the second Path? It was brutal and bloody—offense at the expense of his humanity. What he saw through the Path had been too gruesome by far, and Felix had more than once torn into an enemy and exploded them from the inside.

That left only the final Path, one that had more than a little touch of Divinity in it.

The Path of the Ascendant was superior to the rest, clearly. It offered an insane amount of bonus stats per level, and the future it promised—if that is what he saw—was remarkable. Powerful. Beautiful. Neither running nor brutal slaughter, but rising above. How could he choose anything else?

And yet... Felix couldn't make himself choose it. "This feels too easy."

Easy? Pit warbled. *What's been easy about any of this?*

"That's my point," Felix growled. "I've chosen all three doors each time. First, it was because I didn't know what to choose, and then because I didn't want to miss out on the Omens. The System itself said I chose the hardest Path each time. So why only three? If my Paths are based on my Titles, Skills, and stats, then I should have more, right?"

The others didn't answer him, but it didn't matter. Felix knew he was right. Something was wrong. He looked all around him, but the terrain and strangeness of the space was too off-putting. *Everything* seemed wrong on his island of green in the Void. Felix closed his eyes, centering himself, and immediately felt it.

Pressure.

Something was pressing down on... him? On the glade? Perhaps on the whole liminal space itself. *Yeah. That's what it is. And I know this pressure, the taste of it.* He'd felt it, not too long ago.

"Vellus!" he shouted into the dark. "Get away from me!"

The pressure quivered once before redoubling. The trees around him groaned and bent, like a giant hand was compressing them all, and Felix felt a sharp pain behind his eyes. The blue window showing his Paths flickered and glitched, static running across it in waves. When it cleared, there was only a single Path shown.

Path of the Ascendant (From Broken Path, The Shape Of Fate, and Fatebreaker Titles, Core At Ring Stage Or Higher)
+30 All Stats Per Level

"No," he hissed, and lashed out with his Will and Intent. It smashed into the pressure like a hammer into steel, denting it but leaving it whole. The hands of the Divine pressed again, dropping Felix to his knees, all but pressing his face into the Path window.

Convergence!

Pit screeched the word and vanished in a flash of light. His presence drenched Felix's Spirit and sent all of his Harmonic stats rising as they combined with Pit's. With a roar, Felix refused to be bent or broken.

He *refused!*

Tyrant of Choice Is Active!
Thief of Fate Is Active!
Indomitable Is Active!
Against Catastrophe Is Active!

The Vein of Divinity within him hummed, spreading an intense heat throughout his First Pillar and core space. Everything within Felix, all of his Skills and Aspects and Titles, they ignited into a conflagration of furious Will and Intent. He would not be bullied or pressured, forced or coerced into being a slave to the gods. For he saw now what it was Vellus had wanted; she was in danger, had said so herself, all the gods were, and they needed him to survive.

Him and the other Unbound out there.

Once more, he refused. He denied them. His Titles of defiance all activated by Will, shaped by his razor-sharp Intent. He sliced upward, through the pressure, through it all. A scream tore through him like a thousand cut harp strings, like a detonating mountain, like an ocean boiling. It bellowed then went utterly silent.

And in its place, Felix could feel the threads of possibility surrounding him. Enveloping him and Pit both. There wasn't just a single choice, and not three either. So many were there, hidden from them.

An Unbound was not held by the rules of the world—not truly—and Felix was held by nothing unless he Chose it. With a sharp gesture, he tore away the veil of obscurity, baring the System before him in all its majesty. The black resounded, filled with a choral glory. A concerto thundered, pure and powerful enough to shake the heavens. It was there, and then it was gone in a second. Yet it burned in Felix's Mind, indelible.

Another blue window appeared, this one far, far larger.

Congratulations!
You Have Completed Your Path!
Choose One.

Path of the Devourer (From Ravenous Tithe, Thief of Fate)
+20% Essence Gain Per Foe Devoured, +20% Skill Gain Per Foe Devoured, +5 All Stats Per Level

Path of the Unconquered (From Hero, Unconquered, Face the Charge, Bulwark of the Innocent, Indomitable, Iron Will, Work Horse)
+15 Endurance, Strength, Vitality, +5 Agility, Dexterity, Perception Per Level

Path of the Cardinal Beast (From Cardinal (Major), Unleash the Beast, Cage the Beast, Sovereign of Flesh, Voracious Eye, Ravenous Tithe, Race: Primordial of the Unseen Tide (Lesser))
+50% Essence Gain Per Foe Devoured, +50% Skill Gain Per Foe Devoured, +7 All Stats Per Level, +5 Levels To All Primordial-Touched Skills

Path of the Ascendant (From Broken Path, The Shape of Fate, Fatebreaker)
+30 All Stats Per Level

Path of the Bond (From Pactmaker, Etheric Concordance)
+10 Affinity, Alacrity, Felicity, +5 Willpower, Intelligence, And Agility Per Level. Greater Benefits To/From Companion. Decrease XP Penalty By 5%.

Path of the Survivor (From Survivor, Vitality and Endurance above 500)
+10 Vitality, Endurance, and Perception Per Level

Path of the Scholar (From Natural Scholar, Aria of the Green Wilds, Voracious Eye)
+10 Intelligence, Perception, And Dexterity Per Level.

Path of the Slayer (From Giantslayer, Butcher, Frostbane, Titanslayer)
+15 Strength and Endurance Per Level

Path of the Magus (From Apprentice Magus, Iron Will, Spellslinger, 3 Epic Rarity or Higher Spells)
+10 Willpower, Intelligence, Intent, And Resonance. 5% Leveling Speed Increase For All Mana Skills.

Path of the Archmagus (From 3 Legendary Rarity or Higher Spells, Intelligence and Willpower over 500)
+15 Willpower, Intelligence, Intent, And Resonance. 10% Leveling Speed Increase For All Mana Skills.

Path of the Cardinal Theurge (From Cardinal Flame, The Shape of Fate, Fatebreaker, Broken Path, Cardinal (Major), Intelligence and Willpower over 1000, Theurgist of the Rise, 1 Transcendent Rarity or Higher Spell, Cardinal Beast Core, Thunderflame Core)
+15 All Spirit Stats, +10 All Body Stats, +5 All Mind Stats Per Level. Increase XP Penalty To 50%.

Path of the Void (From Voidwalker, Abyssal Skein, Presence Of Void Elements In Core Space)
+10 Willpower, Alacrity, Agility Per Level. 50% Protection From The Void. All Stats Doubled While Within The Void.

CHAPTER SEVENTY-THREE

The blue window hovered before him, shimmering with a golden light at the edges, as if gilt. The Paths were listed there, but they were also in the dark sky of the Void, like stars in the night. He could feel them just as he felt the first three, endless possibilities laid out before a narrow pinhole. A dozen Choices that could change the rest of his life.

Or lead him to his doom.

What to choose?

"This is… a lot," Felix said. He'd figured there would be more, but four times as many was surprising.

Remarkable. I had thought the Path of the Ascendant was powerful, but some of these others are truly mesmerizing. Karys hummed at this waist, even hopping a little in his sheath.

"Path of the Ascendant is a trap," Felix snapped. "Vellus can go rot. I'm not taking the bait."

Pit trilled in furious support, and Felix couldn't help the smile that twitched his lip. "Thanks bud. First, though, let's look at what we got here."

He knew, more than anything else, what he desired from these Paths. He wanted power, strength enough to secure himself and those he cared about, and autonomy to see it done. Despite everything, the Path of the Ascendant was still tempting, yet it was a free lunch in a world where all things had consequences. It fiddled with the Broken Path and gods. The more Felix interacted with them, the more he wanted nothing to do with the Divine, even if they gave *really* good bonus stats per level. That interference just now, what he felt? If that wasn't Vellus putting her hand on the scale, he'd eat his boots.

Felix wasn't aiming for godhood, he simply wanted to survive.

But survival alone was not it. Survivor was gone as an option, as was the Path of the Slayer. The Path of the Scholar, too, unfortunately. Visions of himself investigating and unearthing long lost secrets, cataloging the amazing creatures in the world, the plants, the magic… it called to him with surprising force. But Felix shoved it aside, rejecting its allure.

The Path of the Bond was next. It flared in the distance, the vibrations of its light reaching him in the same instant he focused upon it. Felix was suddenly upon a mountain, a cliff, and Pit was beside him. The tenku was stronger than ever, bigger and heartier, faster. He was closer than ever with his Companion, stronger while Converged, able to not only combine their Harmonic Stats, but their Primary Stats, too. Yet, as much as he loved Pit and wanted to strengthen their bond, it didn't compare to the rest of the options. Felix cut off the light, returning once more to the edge of his liminal forest.

Pit let out a disappointed sigh, and Felix patted him on the neck.

The Path of the Magus was tempting, but it was matched and bested by Path of the Archmagus, which showed him visions of a future Felix hurling spells from atop a Stone Shaped battlement. He wore battle robes and held a blazing staff, thrusting it downward to send streams of solid-seeming Mana into the armies that came at him below. They were obliterated, wiped clean from the field in a daisy-chain of fire, lightning, and roaring earth. It was tempting. Magic was absolutely fascinating, and he'd never tire of it, but his was not a pure magic Path. He had to account for his physicality as well; without his powerful Body, he'd have died long ago. He moved on.

Next came a dark light, barely anything at all, in the black around him. The Path of the Void had a song that was less than a whisper, but potent just the same. Yet it struck Felix as… lacking.

The Path shimmered with visions of him soaring through dark, an army of voidbeasts at his back, of confronting the Whalemaw itself—He jerked back, stumbling from the vision in surprise.

"Whalemaw..."

Path of the Void might make him stronger in some ways, but he knew temptation when he saw it. The Whalemaw was beyond him… might always be beyond him. Yet the abyss gurgled at the thought of encountering it again, of consuming it and the remainder of the Maw's power.

Felix shivered. The Path of the Void was strongest when he was in that Realm, and while he was finding himself in liminal spaces and Void-adjacent areas more often, the Void was not a place to which he wished to return.

He licked his lips. *Next.*

The Path of the Devourer called to mind his earliest incarnations with What Dwells Beneath, the precursor to his Sovereign of Flesh. An incomplete ability that amplified his aggression and hunger. He saw that in the resonance of the Path, a future hinged upon his ability to control himself...or else devolve into something bestial. That too, he rejected. He'd fought his Hunger enough, wrestled into submission too many times to return to such a state.

The power it hinted at, however, that led him to the next Path. The Path of the Cardinal Beast. It blazed upon the list, the potency it heralded undeniable.

Path of the Cardinal Beast (From Cardinal (Major), Unleash the Beast, Cage the Beast, Sovereign of Flesh, Voracious Eye, Ravenous Tithe, Race: Primordial of the Unseen Tide (Lesser), Cardinal Beast Core)
+50% Essence Gain Per Foe Devoured, +50% Skill Gain Per Foe Devoured, +7 All Stats Per Level, +5 Levels To All Primordial-Touched Skills

It boosted the benefits of the Path of the Devourer and added a clutch of extra Skill levels; on paper Cardinal Beast was amazing. Felix's Affinity fixed upon the resonance of its distant song, however, and saw within it a fate almost as terrifying as the Path of the Slayer.

Felix strode through city streets, larger than before, covered in black scales and crackling with blue-white lightning and red-gold flames. Men and monsters came at him, charging him from every alley and thoroughfare, as if to crush him beneath the press of their Bodies. Yet Felix reached out, and with a sharp inhalation, rendered all of them into dust and smoke. Smoke that he immediately consumed, pulling Essence from skin and bone and metal, Essence that he drove into his own cores. His skin burst, scales forming anew, and teeth—

Power. The Path of the Cardinal Beast promised power untold, as long as he was willing to take it.

Felix shuddered and pulled away, too tempted; almost so enamored that he immediately chose the Path. It called to him, and the abyss in his center sang back, a crooning cry that shook Felix's bones. It was the first sound his abyss ever made, but not its first overture of communication; he could tell what it wanted, could almost feel black claws attempting to reach beyond the spinning rings of his dual cores.

Give… Give...

Alarm spiked through Pit and Karys, all three of them now watching the abyss. It churned violently, bubbling, but did not spill over the containment of his ring cores.

"Hoo boy," Felix breathed. "That was… unexpected."

It is hungry, Pit sent. *I do not trust it.*

Nor do I, Karys added. *But it is not wrong. This Path of the Cardinal Beast is powerful, and I see why. It carries the touch of your Race to its next evolution.*

"Primordials," Felix all but spat. "Right."

There were more Paths, others that could draw his attention away from the buzzing light of Cardinal Beast. One in particular hummed with a strong, immutable song, and it leaped to his attention as he fled the Beast.

Path of the Unconquered (From Hero, Unconquered, Face the Charge, Bulwark of the Innocent, Indomitable, Iron Will, Work Horse)
+15 Endurance, Strength, Vitality, +5 Agility, Dexterity, Perception Per Level

Felix beheld a vision that seemed to be a through-line in his

Paths. Him against an army. Soldiers in white armor and red cloaks marched alongside larger figures in crimson plate, but all of them bore swords of brilliant flame and trailed vaporous, golden light. Felix stood alone, covered in his black scales and bearing his Fang over his shoulder. A shield was in his off-hand, seemingly torn from the hide of a massive creature and inscribed with dizzying patterns, and he calmly beheld the charge that began.

He could feel neither fear nor panic at their approach, only the steady, solid realization that he would stand. Faceless others fled behind him, scurrying for safety, but he would stay. Stand and fight and never give in, not ever, not even unto death. At a gesture, stone walls rose from the earth, funneling the zealots' toward him alone. He hefted his weapons.

It was a good day to die.

Felix gasped as the first blade came against him, shattering against his shield, driving him from the vision.

"No no, definitely not that," he said, sharing a concerned look with Pit. The tenku's ears were straight up and his feathers ruffled in alarm. It hadn't been that Unconquered wasn't powerful, it clearly gave good bonuses and drew from some of his most laudable Titles… but Felix wasn't keen on pushing himself toward self-sacrifice. Not again. Not unless he had to.

Which left the final option.

Path of the Cardinal Theurge (From Cardinal Flame, The Shape of Fate, Fatebreaker, Broken Path, Cardinal (Major), Intelligence and Willpower over 1000, Theurgist of the Rise, 1 Transcendent Rarity or Higher Spell, Cardinal Beast Core, Thunderflame Core)
+15 All Spirit Stats, +10 All Body Stats, +5 All Mind Stats Per Level. Increase XP Penalty To 50%.

Numerous Titles, Skills, stats, even the existence of both of his cores had set this before him. "Cardinal, like the Beast Path, like my Flame and Title." He'd gathered by this point that 'cardinal' had something to do with Primordials. "But 'Theurge' is odd." Theurges were miracle-workers, if his memories from Earth were right. Some sort of cross between a wizard and a cleric in old tabletop games. Warily, Felix regarded the light of the Path and opened himself up to it.

Felix beheld himself, standing amid a collection of ruined silver towers. Upon the floor, etched into the stone, were glowing sigils and glyphs, circles upon circles lit with a crackling blue-white Mana. Above him were echoed the same shapes, etched in the air in red-gold light. Felix was wrapped in white robes that trailed down to the earth, dusty and darkened as if they had been dragged upon countless miles of dirt. Wings of black and crimson spread outward, forty feet wide, the tips of his pinions just touching the edges of the working.

Power swirled, gathering. Far above, between the arcing towers, a moon hung in the sky. The moon was huge, taking up all he could see, as if it were falling to the planet itself. A beam of braided light suddenly shot from the arrays around Felix, straight up and directly into the moon's surface. Straining his Perception, Felix could just barely make out a similar array forming there, at the far end.

A scream of dread Harmonics tore across the skies, quaking the silver towers to their cores. Somehow, Felix knew he was the cause, and it filled him with dread and conviction in equal measure.

"As above, so below," he intoned.

A cacophony of sound erupted, shooting up into the heavens along that braided beam. The moon crashed, like a cymbal, like a gong. Ripples spread outward, waves that grew as they traversed the Void above, then stopped. Caught.

Pulled.

A sense of the Divine descended, pulled by his call. A blurred figure fell upon that braided line, wrapped in chains, bound by light and sound. Felix arrested it with a surge of blue-white lightning, cratering the stone beneath him and sending plumes of dust in all directions. The silver towers beside him rang like struck bells, each toll in time with the figure's struggling limbs. Too many limbs. A body that twisted and turned.

A face that wasn't—the eyes—!

Felix's mouth opened, teeth upon teeth. He shuddered. Or the world did.

He—

He staggered back, pulling all that was him away from the resounding light of the Path.

"What the hell was that?" he hissed. Not for the first time, he wondered at the visions the Paths were showing him. Were they all future events, future possibilities? If he chose this Path, would this happen?

Karys flashed at his hip. *Choices define us, Felix. Fate is never certain, but this would begin a Path that increases the odds of this occurring. Of that, I have no doubt. You are at the crux of change. At the cusp of the future. And if these are the futures before us, I fear for what may come.*

You must be ready, Felix.

"Be ready," he muttered. "Who could be ready for this? For any of it? Blood and slaughter, losing myself to my hunger, to whatever trap is in the Divine Path, to… whatever the hell this was." Felix swallowed, but it hurt; his throat was dry as a desert.

Cardinal Theurge was dangerous. Powerful. Very powerful, yes, he was certain of that. The bonuses alone were great, though it came with an increase on his XP penalty. Yet it called to him, just as strongly as the Cardinal Beast did.

Was I about to eat a god? Felix shook his head in wonder. *How is that possible? Or wise?*

He regarded the Paths again, idly petting his Companion. Pit laid his head onto Felix's shoulder, the weight of him a comfort. "What should I do, Pit?"

Each Path was born of his choices, each linked to his being by his actions and achievements. Felix regarded the Paths arrayed before him, like looking at a tank of vipers. His Affinity twitched, shying away from the song of their possibilities, yet Felix tentatively looked again. From all angles he could.

What should I choose? The weaker but steadier Paths, or the more powerful and far more dangerous ones? Risk and reward. *Yet, if I choose the stronger, even avoiding Ascendant, am I just trading freedom for power? Slaving myself to hunger, or to a slantwise connection to the gods?*

His Affinity caught on something. Threads of light, mingled with the vibrations of the Paths, they stretched across the Void and tangled with Felix's core. To his Titles, Skills, stats, everything. *These are…* They were the same sort of threads he manipulated with Adamant Discord, that he could grip and intuit with his Affinity.

Why couldn't he manipulate these, then?

Felix. What are you doing? Karys buzzed at his hip. *This feels... strange.*

"I'm making my own choices for once," Felix growled, and Pit howled into the blank night. He disappeared in a flash of light, joining his Intent and Affinity with Felix's and sending a surge of support. There were no words needed between them, but Felix spoke them anyway. "In it together, eh Pit?"

Always.

Far be it from me to oppose your Will. I doubt I even could, anymore. Karys bloomed with green-gold life Mana, and Felix unsheathed him. *Let us challenge destiny, then.*

Felix bared his teeth.

Adamant Discord!

Cardinal Flame!

The Paths quaked, their harmonics turned askew as the lights in the distant Void wavered. Felix could feel the pieces, the shapes of them all as they sang of his future. He seized them with his Affinity and Will, and shaping his Intent with a razor's edge he lifted his crooked sword and severed those threads.

A tone shook through him, through *everything*. A sound like the end of the world.

Felix grappled with the threads, which even now were attempting to run from his grasp. His powerful Willpower was all that secured them—backed by the thrumming Vein of Divinity within his core—inch-by-inch pulling them together. Closer, as the songs of them all rose to a catastrophic crescendo. Harmony and Dissonance, echoes of his core space, of his opposed rings, they sang in furious competition. Each outdoing the last note as Felix wove thread unto thread, *pulling* with blue-white lightning and red-gold flame.

All of it seared into him, into his soul. His Aspects trembled, convulsing as threads thick as cables secured themselves to his core space.

Felix would not be limited, not by the gods or the System itself. If this was the beginning of his destiny, then he would forge it himself.

He poured out everything he had into it, all his Mana and Stamina, even his flesh and blood. Essence bloomed and was subsumed, power flaring along his cores as they spun wildly, and the abyss screamed out in ecstatic terror.

The touch of the beast within him was there, a basso growl threading beneath the sound. It promised to satisfy his need for conflict and battle and physical supremacy. But there was a mind there too, a power that was beyond even the potency of the Theurge. Its song was a croon, and a baying howl, and a triumphant battlecry.

He knew—*he knew!*—and the knowing made the song all the brighter, the melding melody and shocking, jarring notes of its crescendo almost more than he could bear. Harmony and Dissonance, swirled together as the thrum of all that was crested an impossible note.

He chose.

Path of the Cardinal Fiend (From Cardinal Flame, The Shape of Fate, Fatebreaker, Indomitable, Tyrant of Choice, Thief of Fate, Against Catastrophe, Inheritor, Cardinal (Major), Willpower Over 1500, Strength Over 1000, Theurgist of the Rise, 1 Transcendent Rarity or Higher Spell, Cardinal Beast Core, Thunderflame Core, Vein of Divinity, Born of Will)
+50% Essence Gain Per Foe Devoured, +50% Skill Gain Per Foe Devoured, +5 Levels To All Primordial-Touched Skills, +20 All Primary and Harmonic Stats Per Level. Increase XP Penalty to 50%.

And in the dark, in the unraveling forest, a doorway formed of flickering light.

Felix fell.

CHAPTER SEVENTY-FOUR

The door flashed, and Pit found himself falling free, Convergence failed.

Felix!

He tumbled through the air, seeing nothing but blurring blue streaks all around him. Pit extended his wings, their tips spreading farther than ever, but he scraped and smashed into the sides of some invisible structure, too dark to see.

Felix!

Through their bond, Pit sensed him far below. And getting farther. He tried again, snapping out his wings more carefully, cupping the invisible wind as it buffeted against his feathers. He spun once, twice more, then success!

Flight is level 58!

Steadied, Pit still spiraled down what seemed an endless shaft into nothing. The blue streaks, however, settled into windows that were furiously blinking for his attention.

Your Companion Has Chosen His Path!
Now You Must Do The Same.
Choose.

Path of the Companion - Gain +7 STR, END, VIT, WIL, AGL per level, Skill level gain increased in concordance with Companion's core composition/attunement. Etheric Concordance +10 Levels.

Path of the Berserker - Gain +20 STR, +15 END, VIT per level. Skill gain in offensive abilities increased.

Path of the Void - Gain +10 WIL, ALA, AGL per level. Protection from the Void increases to 50%. All Stats are doubled while within the Void.

Path of the Faithful - Gain +10 To All Primary Stats Per Level. One Time Boost Of +30 To All Harmonic Stats.

Path of the Guardian Beast - Gain +10 STR, AGL, DEX, +5 END, PER, AFI, RES, REI Per Level - All Harmonic Stats are doubled upon acceptance of this Path. Skill level gain increased in concordance with Companion's core composition/attunement.

Pit tried to surge past the notification box, but it arrested him.

Choose.

Felix was falling farther ahead. Pit couldn't care less about the stat bonuses. He understood them, but he needed to catch Felix, he was falling while Pit was hemmed in by the burning lights and rarefied vibrations this Path. He slammed his claw upon the choice he'd seen spoken a thousand times, one which he still did not understand.

And he dove.

Adamant Discord is level 70!

...

Adamant Discord is level 74!

Cardinal Flame is level 64!
...
Cardinal Flame is level 71!

The world became a series of flashing, spinning lights, a vortex of color and sound that hurled Felix along like a rocket. Things—feelings—sparked and bloomed in his chest, his core. Harmonies and Dissonance yowled at one another in unholy noise, and the things that made up Felix resounded with their confrontation.

Path of the Cardinal Fiend Chosen...
Unique Path Forged!
Unique Path Detected...

Core Compatibility 100%
Stat Compatibility 100%
Energy Required For Conversion...
Stand By.

Agony speared through him, but Felix bore it silently as he fell. Pain and him were old friends, and he knew how to handle it all. Yet even his Song of Absolution and insane Willpower weren't enough; a moan of distress squeezed from his lungs as his core space was wrung dry. What little Essence remained was pulled from him, funneled into his new Path, before it began taking his Mana, Stamina, and Health. It was slow at first, nothing his regeneration couldn't maintain, but it sped up. The Path he had forged was powerful—too powerful, it seemed.

It was going to kill him.

Path Conversion in Progress...

Felix clenched his Will, cutting off his screams before they began, and flared his Skills in rapid order.

Bastion of Will!

Cardinal Flame!

Adamant Discord!

Those three would help him, he hoped. Mana swirled and

burst all around him, splashing against him and through him in constant waves invisible to the normal eye. To all others, it would be a featureless black in all directions. To him it was a riot of power—and possibility.

Ravenous Tithe!

Mana was sucked into his channels, through his palms and elbows, knees and feet. It soaked into his core space… only to be ripped right back out by the System. The Path grew, a weighty sun behind his eyes that felt likely to burn out his skull. It was nowhere and everywhere, within him and without.

It drained him even more, but his First Pillar below his double-stacked ring cores burst into furious light. A dark vein among it shuddered to life, adding a piercing, gossamer cry to the hammer of his Will. Even the abyss joined in, its voice a song of absences and buzzing Dissonance that howled into the melody, filling the spaces between glorious Harmony.

Felix screamed again, pulling at the connections he'd forged. Titles and Skills and stats all strained, rooted within him, as the threads to his Path hauled itself together. Lightning crackled across his limbs, chased by red-gold fire that speared through the Path, heating it into a brilliant white. His Will crashed down upon it, his Bastion gates slamming into the blazing Path and forcing into place. The Wild Song—the Grand Harmony, Final Dirge, all of it—resounded within him, showing Felix where the Path should go.

And then it was done.

Pain transmuted to brilliant ecstasy in an instant. The Path lit up his Aspects, his cores, everything that was Felix.

+50% Essence Gain Per Foe Devoured, +50% Skill Gain Per Foe Devoured, +5 Levels To All Primordial-Touched Skills, +20 All Primary and Harmonic Stats Per Level. Increase XP Penalty to 50%.

The benefits and penalties sank into him, changing Felix at a fundamental level. Things blurred and shook, vibrations through the center of his being, hitting his dual cores and redirecting everywhere. Harmony and Dissonance, mismatched pairs, thrummed through his being as he fell on.

Voracious Eye is level 64!
...
Voracious Eye is level 68!
Sovereign of Flesh is level 63!

Ravenous Tithe is level 73!
...
Ravenous Tithe is level 77!
Adamant Discord is level 75!
...
Adamant Discord is level 79!
Cardinal Flame is level 72!
...
Cardinal Flame is level 76!

Ravenous Tithe - Adept Tier!
Adamant Discord - Adept Tier!
Cardinal Flame - Adept Tier!

Felix seized, pushing against the Temper his Path was trying to force upon him. He hadn't any Essence at all, let alone Essence Motes or Draughts. His Intent shaped his Will, while his Affinity sounded out the thrumming signals of the System's notifications. He suppressed them, held them at bay, for just a little while longer.

Yet they kicked back, the System bucking against his manipulation. Not even his incredible Will was enough to cushion the blow of it. Felix spiraled through the darkness, falling ever faster as a sudden an immediate end loomed below. Hard stone and wood, barely visible, manifested from the sea of chaotic Mana around him. Had he the spare attention, Felix would have found it fascinating. As it was, he barely held onto consciousness as he careened into its surface.

At the very last second, a bundle of feathers the size of an SUV caught him by the hips and shoulders. Pit squawked in fear, his wings beating back, but it only proved enough to slow them both. Felix and Pit hit a hardened, stone floor with enough force to shatter bone and stone in equal measure, yet nothing was disturbed. They landed in a tangle of limbs and too heavy flesh, and Felix's sword went skittering across the ground.

"Thanks," he groaned.

Ye-yeah, Pit sent back with equal discontent. The both of them simply laid there for a time.

Then, achingly, Felix struggled to his feet. He was still clamping his Bastion around the processes of his newest Tier Up, and it took almost all of his concentration to maintain it, but he would have had to be blind to miss Pit's sudden transformation.

"You're bigger again, I think," he panted. Pit nodded. "Good. I'll need your help for the next part. My plan went… a little wild there, for a second. I didn't—didn't expect the Paths to be like that."

You have achieved the impossible. Again. Karys buzzed from ten feet away. *Perhaps someone should keep a running score.*

"Sounds exhausting. How would you keep up?" Felix let himself grin as he stooped to pick up his blade. Karys glowed in his grip.

Indeed. Are you—are you holding your Adept Formation at bay?

"Yeah," Felix grunted. "Some Skills I want to use went over thanks to my Path, but I'm fresh outta Essences." Felix was sweating, heavy enough that it was dripping down his face and neck. "Never been this hard before."

That is because you're not supposed to be able to hold off an Adept Temper. I believe you're only managing it due to your utterly ridiculous Willpower.

"Intent and Affinity are in the mix, too," he gasped. "I can feel more, just at the edge of my senses. Power waiting to flood my cores once I've left this place." He looked around, noticed the Mana still swirling in chaotic whirlwinds. Only the stone and wooden flooring was steady. Real. There was nothing else. "Another stop."

The final one, I believe.

Felix could feel it like a draft through an old house. The walls were thin here, as if he could simply push his arm through that chaos and emerge back in the Mana pool. Back among six deadly threats. Felix's breathing was ragged as he strained to hold onto his Skills, but he had to confirm one last thing. One last task before they could leave.

"Pit." His Companion stood, looming larger than ever, and

trotted to his side. "Karys, when the plan starts, I'll need you to distract them. Can you do that?"

I can certainly try. This place has shown me a few new tricks; I simply hope I can manage them from within… this. The sword shook for emphasis.

From Pit's barding, Felix retrieved the Omen cards. "I only need a few seconds. I—" The moment they were out of Pit's saddle bag, however, they flew from Felix's surprised grip. "Hey!"

The Omens slammed into the swirl of chaotic Mana above them, horizontally as if they struck a wall. Each one was face up and perfectly separated from its neighbor, as if… *As if it's a tarot reading.*

Yet Felix had received six Omens so far, and nine glimmered before him.

1. **The Fool**
2. **The Tower**
3. **The Wheel**
4. **The Hermit**
5. **Strength**
6. **Death**
7. **The Moon**
8. **The Sun**
9. **The World**

They were arranged in three rows and three columns. The last row were his recent acquisitions, and his Voracious Eye nabbed them.

Name: Omen of the Moon
Benefit: +2 INT, +1 PER, +1 DEX per level gained.

Name: Omen of the Sun
Benefit: +2 STR, +1 PER, +1 VIT per level gained.

Name: Omen of the World
Benefit: +2 END, +1 STR, +1 VIT per level gained.

If this is a tarot reading, what does it mean?

In answer, the chaos shuddered. An ascending note gathered in the distance, moving toward them in a steady, harmonic whine that set Felix's teeth on edge. It thundered through them all.

First, The Mind, Who You Are
Fourth, The Body, What You Face
Seventh, The Spirit, The Strength Within
First, The Past, What Has Been
Second, The Now, That Which Rises
Third, The Future, How Things May End

The voice was no less loud than before and equally cryptic. Felix had no experience with tarot readings, despite his Aunt Cecelia who loved crystals and astrology. He said the same thing now as he'd heard his mother once say to her sister.

"What does *any* of that mean?"

Remember, Felix Nevarre.
Go Forth.
And Remember.

Then the note was gone, as if it had never been.

Felix grumbled to himself while Karys made "ooing" sounds at another instance of the System directly addressing him. Maybe it was rare and amazing and notable, but it wasn't *helpful.* And people were going to die unless he did this right.

With a gesture, all nine Omens slid together, clanking into a single deck that hit Felix's outstretched palm.

The door manifested before him with a desperate flex of his Will. What little he could spare. He understood this place now, sorta. The door flickered with trapped light, fading in and out as if it were the memory of a door. Beyond, he could see a dark, murky green.

Terror hammered in his chest, and a spike of adrenaline quivered along his limbs. "We ready? Do we all understand our roles?"

Pit's Spirit shook, just as Felix's own, but he stood tall beside him. *Ready.*

Do you truly mean to do this?

"What's the other option? Become Urge food?" Felix growled. "Not me. Not ever. If I'm going, I'm going down swinging."

A warrior's heart. You do the Nym proud, Felix. Karys buzzed with apprehension and slow burning excitement. *Let us, then. Into the heart of the storm. May we live to tell the tale.*

As one, they walked into the murk.

CHAPTER SEVENTY-FIVE

The Temple was eerily quiet as Ifre stepped within. Torchlight flickered within, but she saw no torches, no source at all for the illumination.

"What happened here?" Tyrk said in a low tone. His slender forehead was slick with sweat. Ifre kept forgetting how young he truly was; she shook her head and motioned for silence.

The ground was littered with debris, but they had anticipated that after seeing the butchery outside. The scaffolding alone was a creation of creatures without regard for grace, aesthetics, or the ability to perform fine motor skills. What they had not been expecting, however, were the dozens of crushed alcoves, walls, and murals. Thousands upon thousands of years of history had been shattered and scattered across the floor of the Temple, in some places utterly unrecoverable. Ifre was aghast at the destruction, at the wanton disregard of history and artistry. The Henaari sought such things, reveled in them, and the damage to the Nymean Temple hurt her soul.

She made several sharp gestures and the three of them advanced, toward an open, green-metal door.

The Temple was empty. Her Perception and Skills could detect nothing living, so whoever had committed the atrocities above had left. They padded quickly down the spiraling staircase, its length lit by some sort of clever magic, intent on making their way into the very heart of the Temple.

Only there could they finish their duty.

Eventually the stairs opened up on a massive, circular chamber festooned with sculptural reliefs. Nymean magi, stars in their grips, fought back the noxious forms of several terrible Urges. That was clear to Ifre, she had seen its like before, though never Nymeans. Urges, however, were often depicted in many hidden sanctuaries around the Continent. Not all of them were as altruistic as the Endless Raven.

The Raven would draw immense power from this, she thought. *The clan, we would be empowered many-fold.*

The Matriarch had been right, but Ifre still didn't like it. Felix was an ally. He had helped her specifically, and others, too, when he'd charged into the tunnels to face the Wurms. Then he and his team had taken on the Arcid's entire force. That was not something an enemy of the clan would do.

I will claim this place, for my people. But I will not kill him. Ifre set her hand upon the Dire Talon, still wrapped at her waist. Still pulsing like a heart. *Let the Matriarch punish me, but I'll not do it.*

The defiance had her breathing heavily, and her forehead beaded with sweat near instantly, but she was steady. Ifre would not be budged, not anymore. With a sharp nod, she stalked her way into the lit chamber, making sure to stay low. The Dire Talon throbbed in her hand, a powerful Blessing from the Endless Raven. It was a weapon designed to slay the clan's greatest threats, to end them with a single strike. She gripped it loosely, hoping it would not be needed.

Down the steps they went, until a circular pool of cloudy green water appeared. It was the center, the heart; from there, Ifre could claim the Temple for the Endless Raven.

She crept upon it, her subordinates close behind. She made no sound, her Blessing disguising them all as shadows upon the ground, a power the Raven granted passingly few. The pool of green liquid bubbled slightly, as if something far below had moved or shifted. It struck a sense of dread within Ifre's chest, something primal that caught her breath. Slowly, she unwrapped the Dire Talon, forcing her fingers to cease their trembling.

"What have we here?" said a deep, rattling voice. "What an interesting Skill."

Ifre gasped in astonishment—*where had it come from!?*—but her Body did not fail her. She spun, Dire Talon pivoted into a saber grip and drove its preternaturally sharpened point straight up.

It sank halfway into the golden metal, and its noxious power discharged. The golden giant grunted and grabbed her wrist. With the ease of a parent dislodging a child's hand, it forced hers from the hilt of the Dire Talon.

"No," she whispered.

"A wicked weapon. But useless in the end." Crimson lightning spat out from its joints and tangled all three of them. Tyrk and Isyk both screamed in wretched pain, and only belatedly she realized she was also howling. "But you three… I have a use for you. I tossed something into this pool a short while ago. For a bit, the liquid churned quite interestingly, but now it's all gone still. I'm still not sure what lies beneath." The lightning stabbed and burned across Ifre's chest and face, holding her aloft like burning strings. "Do be sure to find out."

The strings were cut, and Ifre was dropped into a liquid that parted beneath her like smoke.

The moment Felix stepped out of the door, back into the liquid Mana pool, the System redoubled its efforts to reach him. Karys thrummed, his life Mana spiraling around Felix's form before sinking into the base of his skull. It soaked into his channels, boosting his handle on the Tiering Skills, and for a brief, important instance, let loose the notifications he most needed to see.

You Have Completed A Hidden Quest!
Walk The Omen Path!
You have used the Omen Key and survived. You have not only chosen a Path, but forged one yourself! All bonuses are doubled!
Rewards:
+6 Levels
+30 All Harmonic Stats

+2 Titles

50% XP Penalty In Effect!
~~+6 Levels~~
+3 Levels

Congratulations!
You Have Gained 3 Levels!
You Are Now Level 55!
You Gain:
+60 to STR! +66 to PER! +66 to VIT! +78 to END! +72 to INT! +84 to WIL! +78 to AGL! +87 to DEX!
+60 All Harmonic Stats!
You Have 55 Unused Stat Points!

Pit Has Gained 6 Levels!
He Is Now Level 62!
He Gains:
+60 to STR, +42 to PER, +12 to VIT, +54 to END, +18 to INT, +36 to WIL, +96 to AGL, +102 to DEX, +30 to AFI, +30 to RES, +30 to REI!

Beside him, Pit screeched in triumphant agony, his being wracked by incredible power. Felix could barely think, could only notice that Pit grew once more, and his piercing cry became something of a shattering bellow. His own Body, his Mind, and Spirit too, surged with a sudden, terrible potency.

The notifications continued, unabated.

New Title!
Coronation of the Wild Song (Transcendent)!
You've forged a Path from the very threads of Harmony and Dissonance! A crown from the fields of Creation itself. Hope that the benefits outweigh the consequences of your actions.
+10% INE, AFI, ALA, and FEL.
+20% Leveling Bonus to all Skills touching on the Wild Song!

New Title!
Forge Of Cardinal Thunderflame (Unique)!
You have forged a Path of your own and as such are the first to ever use it! The forge of your cores and the hammer of your Will has fashioned a Path, one that will shape the future that you make. Be wary, Ascendant, for naught is set in stone.
+5% Completion Bonus to Fiendforge!
+New Skill!

New Skill!
Fiendforge (Unique), Level 1!
You've proven yourself capable of Forging Paths from the threads of Harmony and Dissonance both. This Skill lets you do the same for others, but the learning curve is great. Dare you tempt fate again? Risk of failure decreases per level, risk of permanent damage to core decreases per level, speed of Forging increases per level.

At the same time, his cores rang with the glory of System energy rushing in. The woven pillar beneath his horizontally stacked cores thrummed in sympathetic vibration, then that thrum became all he could hear. It became the world itself, as the pillar boomed beneath everything, lifting up his cores and providing an ineffable *heft* to the space. An incredible importance hung about it, the woven ribbons of light and power, braided like a Maypole and filled with a dark thread of buzzing Divinity.

The gains are always greatest on the First Pillar. The next comes with less significant boosts, but cumulatively, Karys provided helpfully. *Your significance waxes bright, Felix.*

"Let's just hope it's enough," he gasped back, but clamping his Will upon his Tiering Skill had become vastly easier. He had to move. It had been bare fractions of a second since he'd stepped from the Omen Door, but the Urges had noticed him.

"He comes again! Gone a moment, but pulled back!"

"GET HIM KILL HIM GET HIM KILL HIM!"

"He's mine!"

Nightmare shapes roiled through the green murk, heading for him.

Convergence!

White light blinded the Urges for a critical moment, allowing Felix to hurl himself upward and between the gargantuan maws of two opposing monstrosities. Leviathans both, their forms were hazy and unclear, save their predatory shape. Felix twisted between them, going so far as to push off the immense snout of another as it dove downward at their group. He felt stronger and more graceful than ever before in his life, and his thoughts and senses took in so much that everything moved in slow motion. But it wasn't enough. Felix shoved his unused stat points into the only place they could go: Agility. The last brick in the wall he'd built.

Power soared through him. He felt...

Congratulations!
You Have Achieved The Third Threshold!
All Primary Stats Exceed 1000!

Title Updated!
The Broken Path (Legendary)!
The path narrows, crumbling, but your step is sure and inexorable. Behind you lie the corpses of all those that would follow you, and ahead the grasp of the multitudes in your way. The path is a sword's edge, and the only way forward leads up a mountain of bodies. Ware the fall, Ascendant. +10 Journeyman Tier Bonus (Body, Mind, Spirit), +20% Adept Tier Bonus (Body, Mind, Spirit), +30% Master Tier Bonus (Body, Mind, Spirit)
Requires: All Primary Stats Exceed 1000, Level Below 120, Lost Race (Primordial of the Unseen Tide (Lesser))

Due To Reaching The Third Threshold Before Level 100, You Have Earned A New Title!

The Call of Defiance (Transcendent)!
The Divine and Primordial alike could not stop you, nor the amassed servants of men. When the world pushed at

you, you pushed back. When it bled you, you armored your skin. It told you to fall, and you denied them.
+25% Willpower When Contested By A Foe Of Divine Formation Or Greater
+5 Levels To All Mind Skills

Deception is level 28!
Meditation is level 63!
Deep Mind is level 67!
Alchemy is level 32!
Tracking is level 30!
Voracious Eye is level 73!
Aria of the Green Wilds is level 62!

Negotiation is level 26!
Apprentice Tier!
You Gain:
+3 INT
+3 PER
+3 WIL

Exploration is level 53!
Journeyman Tier!
You Gain:
+7 INT
+7 END
+7 PER

Manifestation of the Coronach is level 52!
Journeyman Tier!
You Gain:
+5% VIT
+Rallying Cry Bonuses To Regeneration Increased By 10%
+A Crisis of Faith Penalties To Willpower Increased By 10%

Bastion of Will and Ravenous Tithe bucked in his control,

fighting against the cage of his Will, and in the fury of the System's onslaught he almost let them. But his stats were so much more, Primary and Harmonic, and he soon clamped back down upon them both.

Primary Stats
STR: 1344
PER: 1177
VIT: 1340
END: 1094
INT: 1197
WIL: 1790
AGL: 1084
DEX: 1162

Harmonic Stats
RES: 370
INE: 615
AFI: 1313
REI: 465
EVA: 542
MIG: 513
ALA: 795
FEL: 1065

A massive tail, wide as a city block, swung through the haze. It took Felix full in the face, sending him hurtling down, down, down into the tiled floor of the Mana pool. Stone cratered, shattered in concentric rings that exploded in waves of catastrophic force. Shards blew upward, moving through the liquid that was like smoke, trailing bubbles behind them. Felix coughed up a streamer of vibrant blood, practically glowing with the System energies that still coursed through him.

Yet, because of those energies, because of his Third Threshold, his wounds knitted before the Urges could reach him.

Unfettered Volition!

Felix shot back upward, a leap or swimming stroke propelling him into the murky depths. Jaws snapped and crashed all around him, claws seeking his flesh and life; but he was too small, too fast, too strong.

Adamant Discord!

Pivoting himself, Felix shot back downward, through the closing jaws of another Urge to slam, meteor-like, into its damn skull. The Urge convulsed in surprised pain, its Spirit blaring it to the world, and crashed into the tiled floor of the well. Smoke and liquid swirled, parted, sloshed until silty debris made vision an impossible thing. For all his stats, terror welled up in him. It was all he could do to focus while the beast below him writhed. He ran along its length, the liquid Mana still parting before him like smoke. Felix held an oversized card in his hand, its face brilliant with golden inlay, a sun that banished the dark to the farthest corners.

"'Beyond The Dark, The Light Awaits,'" Felix gasped.

"What does he say?"

"Only foolishness! He has attacked us! Us!"

"We end him!"

Felix bared his teeth, and from his waistband pulled the other object he'd been careful to keep with him. A feather as long as his forearm, black and night and crackling with potency.

"Mark of the Raven!"

"That upstart!"

"He invokes!"

The sibilant words overlapped, mixed with the rushing of waters as they came at him again. At his side, his Inheritor's Will burst into vibrant, green-gold light.

On me!

A figure of blazing Mana surged upward, looking exactly like Felix and lighting up the strange, dark waters. Green-gold light bounced off bony, bulbous forms, creatures of sinuous strength and terrible, nightmarish shapes. Almost all of the Urges hissed and plunged after Karys' phantom.

You... have... moments only.

He'd make them count. The feather in his hand ignited, bringing a brilliant light to dark depths. The urges that hadn't followed the phantom, the Urge of Rot and the Urge of Spite, convulsed, driven backward by the pure, white light. Holding the Nym statuette aloft, he cast Cardinal Flame through its enchanted substance.

Red-gold flame erupted in a ring around him, worked by his Will and Intent until it formed a series of massive glyphs, each and every one the same as the last. He had seen it before in many places, even among the Archon's twisted works, but his was different. Changed by his experience with the Theurgy of the Rise, a combined form of *siphon*, *life*, and *connection*.

He called it *Devour*.

Driving his sword into the tiled floor, Felix reached into his pocket and hurled a stack of metal cards into the array he'd built. Each Omen card was snagged by a glyph, snapping into the sigils' centers as if magnetized. The cards lit with the same red-gold flame, an incandescent glow that grew all the brighter as the Omens truly ignited.

Affinity seized the threads that connected him to the Urges, threads of want and hunger, and he tied those into the array. His Intent and Will did the rest, directing a massive tide of Mana from his channels out into the well. It flowed from him in waves of almost-liquid vapor, thickened and potent and split into nine different streams in a circle.

The phantom faded, and Karys trembled in the ground, but Felix was ready. The Urges screamed, those closest already rounding on him. Those above charged as well, until all six came at him, maws agape.

CHAPTER SEVENTY-SIX

A raging ring of carmine and sapphire light erupted in all directions, nine alternating pillars of flame and lightning speared up into the endless sea of smoke. The Urges were atop him, even as the array seared their approaching jaws, not slowing no matter the fact that they would all collide. Tendrils of flame stabbed through the Feather in his hands, lifting it up. It burst alight.

"Raven! Do your thing!" Felix bellowed.

The Feather bloomed into a blinding light, and the array caught it all, hurling a wall of power out into the Mana well. Light and something more hit the Urges, fueled by the Endless Raven's gift. The Urge of secrets, of bringing light into darkened places, the Raven's power was multiplied by the carmine and sapphire light of his sigils.

Every single Urge was caught and sent reeling.

"What is this!"

"It cannot be! He is a mortal!"

"No! That light!"

"That upstart bird!"

Above his array, congealing from the blinding light of the Feather, came a vast shape. A hundred thousand wings rustling together shook the Mana around them, and a scream pierced the ears of all who listened. The Urges roared in rage and no little fear; if nothing else, the light itself seemed to scald their ancient forms. These were monsters used to the dark, and the pressure of their Spirits threatened to lay Felix flat. He held on, barely keeping his legs under him while he used his Affinity to sound the Skill required next.

Shadow Whip!

Felix cast as many tendrils into the array as he could, hurling eight from each hand and splitting each of those into four. As each hit the radiant glyphs, they burst forth in all directions, multiplying until they were legion, until the smoke-sea around him became a writhing darkness that *he* could control. Barely. With his Willpower and Intelligence, he held on with the tiniest of finger holds, but he held. The whips tangled against the careening Urges, latching onto scaled flesh and hardened bone, knotting among flailing fins, spines, and slimy claws.

Felix's spell was little more than an annoyance to them, however, as each Urge was instead hunched against the deadly attacks of a different foe. Claws of light were attacking them all, slashing at them with talons the size of skyscrapers and leaving behind bloody gashes that clouded the already disgusting liquid Mana.

A screaming cry came from within Felix as well as without. Above. He could not look, but he knew.

CAWW!

A piece of the Raven manifested, its shape now clear, and its Intent heavy upon the well. The Urges redoubled their fury and violence, rapidly breaking apart Felix's Shadow Whips. The Raven breathed inward, and the smoke-sea drove into its shape, absorbed, condensed until the great avian looked fit to burst.

And then it did.

The detonation hit the well like a bomb, a blooming rose of purest light and ephemeral force. Ephemeral, that is, to Felix and Pit within him. To the Urges, it was a blastwave, hurling every single one of them back into the dwindled smoke-sea. Fissures of radiant shadow rent their wounds even further, until the leviathans that threatened them were banked and convulsed like mammoth fish. Noxious fluids and cloying miasma spilled out into the well.

In that moment of pain and confusion, Felix engaged the full power of his array. Unable to choose them or else lose his Magician Omen, Felix made better use of their latent potential. They were paths not taken, possibilities unrealized and packed with power as a result. The Feather and Omens were a focus, a lens for his Will and Intent to become amplified among the searing glyphs of his own creation. And all of it, the damage and weakness instilled by the Raven's explosion, his connection to the murderous Urges, his own titanic Willpower: it was too much, even for demigods.

He was no longer the man he had been. The Path *had* changed him, but not as he had expected. By dint of his incredible Willpower and stubborn desire to live, to *be*, without the chains the Divinities offered; he had remade himself. Himself and *more*. He summoned all that he had forged from the chaos of Harmony and Dissonance by Will alone. The Mana around him quaked with his fury. With his power.

The power of the Cardinal Fiend.

Ravenous Tithe!

The Skill hit the *Devour* array, and each of the pillars surged with a rapid glissando. Swelling, melodic chords met jarring atonal notes that burst along the length of his thousands of Shadow Whips. Ravenous Tithe screamed forward, amplified by his Path bonuses and the array itself until it was an omnipresent maw, chasing down the tumbled forms of six stunned and wounded Urges. Their Spirits flared—Minds and Bodies too battered by the Raven's onslaught—but the weight of Omens pressed against them. Choices ripped from the Path, consequences of his past, present, and future. Felix couldn't say he understood what the Omens may have presaged, but he understood power. And if Felix couldn't have them, they'd work just as well as a weapon.

They could not last against his Ravenous Tithe, not with the force of the Raven and nine Omens behind it, let alone his Path's compatibility with tearing free the Essence of his enemies.

Screams of unwilling horror and mindless gibbering hate flowed around him as the six Urges were torn asunder by Felix's power. Hideous forms of black smoke were pulled back along his shadow tendrils, their true purpose realized, each filled with a core of dazzling light that flared into gleaming brilliance as they hit his array. Felix screamed himself, barely able to hold it together with his dwindling Mana and split faculties. He held Tiering Skills at bay, the array together, and his Skills blazing to keep it all alight. His Will was split in so many directions, like a man juggling chainsaws, it was all he could do to keep the blades from ripping him apart.

The clouds of darkness and light spun among the array, sending out cascading sparks whenever they struck a pillar of red-gold flame or blue-white lightning. It became a whirlwind, a tornado that tore up the tiles at the bottom of the well, creating such a suction that even the remains of the smoke sea came roaring in.

Hold! Pit cried, his own Will long joined to Felix's struggle. They would either succeed at this or die together. There was no middle ground, and there could be no stopping. *It hurts! It hurts, but hold!*

It felt like wrestling with the sun, or a glacier in the depths of space. A comet, yet ice and fire and darkness and reprehensible filth. The Urges were vile, each of them a collection of the basest of desires and fears. Betrayal, murder, famine, and isolation. The touch of rot, the bile of spite, and the frenzied upheaval of mayhem. All of it howled in the storm, dark winds and vivid, too-bright lights. It was free, shorn of its semi-corporeal shape, and now it sought him. Wanted him with a visceral, palpable *need.* Felix fought them off, kept them to the array, too taxed to consider his plan. Too pressed for regret.

The Omens shattered, their power swirling into the mix, and the weight upon Felix's Aspects was a mountain that sought to crush him utterly.

Felix! Karys screamed. *Now! Raise me aloft!*

With an almighty lurch, Felix gripped the sword's hilt and swung it into the sky. The tempest howled, spinning ever faster, while fire and lightning shot through it all, bending its tumult inward. The array touched the very tip of the Inheritor's Will, a cage of spinning Harmonies and buzzing Dissonance, condensing into an orb the size of his head. It balanced atop his blade, infinitely dense and light as a feather, such power that it bent light. Without warning, it slammed down upon him, its weight yanking Felix up to meet it. The sword pierced it, hilt-deep, and a torrent of liquid power poured over him.

Sigils flared along his sword, but Felix wrestled with the tidal wave of Essence, Mana, and more that flooded every single one of his Mana Gates. Potency screamed along his newly remade channels, tearing them raw as the power hit his core space like a bomb. A storm of convulsing liquid slammed into Felix's dual cores, ignoring the pull of the hungry abyss and instead soaking directly into both his [Cardinal Beast Core] and [Thunderflame Core].

The ribbons of light spun, Skills sent hurtling through his core space at a speed they'd never before attained. Felix burned the power, pulling it into himself as fast as he possibly could, seizing it with Cardinal Flame and all the strength of his ridiculous stats. Beneath his spinning cores and hungry abyss, another pillar formed. Again, Pit and Karys threw their aid into weaving it, braiding thickening cables of buzzing Dissonance and trilling Harmony; all of it fueled by the unstoppable tsunami of Urge Essence.

Cardinal Flame bloomed, red-gold fire chased by Adamant Discord blue-white lightning, the both of them guiding his weaving as much as Karys or Pit. They bucked in his grip, his Bastion audibly cracking as level notifications piled on, fighting against his Will.

Almost! he cried, hoping to hold on. *Almost there!*

Cables twisted, braided, woven under and through, spiraled around a dark red vein that guided the way. The Vein of Divinity aided him, and he was too pressed to be surprised. Felix gripped it all tightly, moving with a deftness that combined his Dexterity, Cardinal Flame, and Adamant Discord into an almost seamless whole.

The second pillar completed, his cores resounding as it snapped into place with a shuddering *boom*, before it tried to start a third. Felix could sense power enough to weave all nine of his pillars right then, such was the immensity of the Urges' bounty that there might have even been some left over. Karys recoiled, pulling ineffectually at the cables as they spun.

Felix! You must stop! You cannot weave so many so soon! Journeyman cables will not hold alone!

Karys' voice came as if from far off, almost drowned in the cacophony, but Felix heard him. His Mind was assaulted by visions of woven Pillars, all of them Journeyman, and a core that collapsed under the weight of its own significance. Pit pulled back, as if struggling with a hose that was spraying both of his cores with unending vigor. Felix joined them both, hauling on the thread that was hundreds of feet tall, cutting at it with his Intent and what Willpower he could spare. It severed, releasing a roar of Essence into his core space.

A solidity weighed him down, as from the Urges' Essence came a dozen Motes of light. Felix suspended them, letting the liquid clouds fill his core space with their chaotic fury. All of it was soaked up by the clarified darkness and spinning Skills, the lot of them becoming abruptly more than they were. As if the light and vibrations that made up his Skills had gained heft and mass; celestial bodies in truth.

All thrummed with a glorious Harmony.

All ached with a gut-wrenching Dissonance.

Felix's Perception and Affinity spiraled inward and outward at the same time, submerged in his core space while at the same time pushing the edges of his crackling array, watching himself as if he were another person entirely. He stood, sword upraised, magic and music and light and shadows blasting in all directions. It sank into him, into his Spirit and Mind and Body. Skin bubbled and regrew, scales emerging and vanishing almost at random, though his eyes blazed a sapphire that never wavered.

And deep within him—from far outside—a golden-blue light flashed.

Bloodlines Detected!
Urge of Fratricide, of Dealings in Blood
Urge of Rot, the Vile Touch of the Darkened Earth
Urge of Hollow Bellies, of Famine in Cold and Heat
Urge of Isolation, of Forgotten Letters and Unspoken Truths
Urge of Mayhem, the Madness of Turmoil
Urge of Spite, the Ill Will of Malice

Processing Bloodlines—!
ERROR!
Primordial Bloodline Devours All Contenders!
New Bloodline 1%

Scales emerged again across his chest and shoulders, heavy plates turning to the smallest of diamond-shaped studs. Traveled down his back and along his legs and arms, accompanied by heavy, brutal spikes at his joints and along the tops of his forearms and shins. Dark, organic armor accented with brilliant cyan and red-gold light, edging his scales in patterns that resembled nothing so much as the glowing magma beneath ocean-cooled stone.

New Bloodline 57%

Talons ripped out of him, and massive, feathered wings burst from his back. Felix screamed as his flat teeth were replaced by long, sharpened fangs. All was pain.

The golden-blue light welled again.

New Bloodline 100%!
Primordial of the Unseen Tide (Lesser) has become Primordial of the Unseen Tide (Greater)!
Primordial of the Unseen Tide (Greater)
The Weight Only Grows, The Mountain Cannot Be Set Down
+6 To WIL, INT, DEX, END, +15 Bonus Stats Per Level!

Within his core space, Adamant Discord blazed the same as Cardinal Flame. The patterns of both curved inward, yet grew and grew, threads of it reaching out to all of his other Skills. Lines of gossamer light and hardened steel, of crimson fire and golden chains. In a flash of deep, primal understanding, Felix knew. Both Skills were intrinsic to who he was becoming, and Adamant Discord was linked profoundly to his Race. Connected in a way that shook him, just as it shook the Mana well all around him.

Felix could *see* so much. Connections that had been invisible were there, so physical he could touch them. The well crumbling around him, devoid now of all Mana and threat. His friends and allies, close but too far, trembling with fear, pain, and exhaustion. They still fought, but hadn't for too long, as if no time had passed since his capture. His enemies were there, too. The Archon was above, he—

Felix surged upward, and he hadn't a clue whether it was his physique or his Skill that did the greater share of work. Lightning shattered the empty darkness of the well, falling with thunderous detonations as hexagonal stone met the far away floor. Felix wove through the debris, lightning and lines of adamant connection sending him flying around crumbling pillars. He shot to the opening, to the falling forms of three Henaari that had somehow tumbled within.

Shadow Whip!

One split into three, each tendril snaring a body, and Felix kept rising. The well was falling apart completely now, but the bright circle of the exit was shrinking. It was being eclipsed by a dark shape, as if—

It's closing! he realized.

Cardinal Flame!

Right palm crackling with lightning and the left with a Shadow Whip, red-gold flame kindled at the Mana Gate at the base of his Skull, surging forth in a roar. Cardinal Flame streamed upward, a dragon's breath, and carved the closing cover in twain.

Adamant Discord!

Flaring his Skill for all he was worth, thunder exploded around him as his Body shot through the demolished opening. The well shattered beneath, behind, all around him, but Felix didn't care. Couldn't.

The Archon stood, staring aghast at Felix's rising form. His Spirit, powerful enough to fill even that chamber, shook.

In fear.

CHAPTER SEVENTY-SEVEN

The crushing stomp of Felix's landing sent a peal of sound through the massive chamber. The crystals above them flared with light and rang like giant bells, and Adamant Discord stormed outward, throwing the Archon from his feet.

Manifestation of the Coronach is level 53!
...
Manifestation of the Coronach is level 63!

The Archon Affected By A Crisis of Faith for 3 Seconds! Willpower Is Reduced By 60%!

"How are you alive!?" the golden giant wailed, trying to stand again. He was annoyingly unharmed. The Archon's chest, where he'd before been torn by Felix's claws, had been repaired. Instead, there was a dark object half-buried in it that Felix thought looked like a vicious dagger. The Archon's eye flames flickered toward the side, where Felix had carelessly hurled the Henaari. "How are *they* alive!? That was pure, liquid Mana! It should have melted the flesh from your bones!"

"Didn't even burn," Felix growled.

Sovereign of Flesh!

His skin rippled and flexed, changing faster than ever before. His muscles swelled, Strength and Endurance growing beyond their already ridiculous limits, and brutal spurs and spikes of bone erupted from his elbows and knees. Scales, small and large, colored the blue-black of midnight covered him instantly. Cyan and red-gold light limned him, edging the scales across his arms and chest.

Sovereign of Flesh is level 64!

...

Sovereign of Flesh is level 67!

Unfettered Volition!

Corrosive Strike!

Wild Threnody!

Felix's fists ignited with virulently green Mana as he rocketed forward, crushing hexagonal stone beneath every step. The Archon was already on his feet, but Felix's movements were lightning. His clawed fist smashed into the golden giant's torso, throwing the constructed man's body back another five feet.

Corrosive Strike is level 49!

...

Corrosive Strike is level 58!

"You've grown stronger, Unbound. How? What lies beneath us?" the Archon demanded.

"Nothing," Felix said and closed the distance. "Not anymore."

The wind roared, displaced, as Felix surged forward. The Archon met him, his own limbs now glowing with yellow-red sigils, the golden giant's speed suddenly increasing to meet his. Felix bared his fangs and struck. Blow after blow, Felix and the Archon traded them, pummeling at each other with strikes strong enough to tear through steel and stone.

Fire bloomed, lightning crackled. Their bodies moved too fast, and more than once, the Archon overshot his mark. Yet Felix, with all the benefits of his Third Threshold, never did. His hits were precise and brutal. The golden armor was dented and split in several places, revealing an interior of shimmering yellow-red lights and wounds the gouted flame like blood.

"You dare too much, Felix! You will die here, along with all of your team," the Archon snarled.

"Touch them, and I'll do more than kill you, Merodach!"

The Archon flinched. "That name? Where—how do you know it?"

Felix only grinned and closed once again.

Adamant Discord!

A net of lines caught up the Archon, hurling him up and into the ceiling atop a bolt of brilliant lightning. Yellow-red sparks attempted to oppose Felix's power, but failed. The Archon may have been a genius, but Felix wasn't the same as before. The weight of his significance had multiplied, and his Transcendent Skill finally lived up to its rarity. It was like… it was like gravity, but more. It was everything, all connections, from the smallest to the largest and Felix could access them. Seize them.

The Archon collided with the roof, shearing off giant, dull crystals.

Adamant Discord!

Another flare, another bolt of incandescent lightning, and the Archon hurtled to earth. He smashed straight through the falling crystals, bursting them all into a glittering rain, and right into the hexagonal flooring with the sound of a mountain exploding.

"Haah haaah," Felix panted. "You… stay down."

Felix! Pit warned.

A beam of white-hot light cut up from the crater he'd made, straight for Felix's face. Felix flinched back and *pulled.* He chomped his teeth over the beam just as it reached him.

Ravenous Tithe!

The heat was incredible, the pain worse. Ravenous Tithe shook, still held in his Bastion, but the Mana streamed into Felix's core without issue.

The Song of Absolution is level 75!
…
The Song of Absolution is level 82!
Adept Tier!
You—!

Desperately, Felix shoved that into his Bastion as well, relaxing his Will enough to see his Skills all but combusting with bated revelation. He clamped down, unable to handle it. *Not now. Hold on.*

The Archon bellowed in rage.

Just hold on.

The golden giant emerged from the ground a fraction of a second later, accelerating toward Felix like a bullet train. A massive, clawed hand manifested above him, spun entirely from flame, and slashed down at his position. Felix dodged, leaping aside then forward, his own Skills burning across his channels.

Dodge is level 55!

...

Dodge is level 63!

Unfettered Volition is level 62!

...

Unfettered Volition is level 64!

Corrosive Strike!

Wild Threnody!

Acid drenched scale met flame-bright metal like two tractor trailers crashing. A wave of concussive force swept outward, scattering bits of stone and crystal that surrounded them.

"You're done!" the Archon howled. His golden body flashed with new yellow-red sigils that appeared in sweeping lines. The pressure of his Spirit and Strength nearly doubled. Felix gritted his teeth, shifted his fist, and gripped the Archon's hands with his long, ebony claws. He tore into them.

"I haven't even started!" Felix shouted and forced his arms up and back.

Mantle of the Infinite Revolution!

Cardinal Flame!

The bestial Arcid howled, its strange fur and metal flesh parting beneath Evie's chain. It tore at the bladed weapon, furious, more animal than thinking creature. Evie was thankful for that. She'd have been dead twice over if its reasoning matched its Strength and Agility. As it was, she was still hard-pressed.

Bindings of the White Waste!

Chains of frost burst upward, snagging the Arcid by the arms and legs. It resembled nothing so much as a Hoarhound mixed with a Frost Giant, then armored a little like an Arcid, and it responded to her restraint by tearing at its own flesh.

Bindings of the White Waste is level 62!

"Disgusting," she hissed. Her chain was twisting, spinning for momentum while she manipulated the mass of it with her Born Trait. With a final flick, she brought it down. "Die!"

Its shoulder snapped beneath the blow, almost shearing off completely. Which should have impaired the monster, but it only freed it from her Bindings. It lunged at Evie, metal jaws agape.

A dark shape slammed into it from the side, bringing it hard into the sludge at their feet.

"A'zek," Evie panted, wiping at the blood in her eyes. "Kind of you to join in."

The massive harnoq tore the bestial Arcid's throat out with a single, savage heave. Dark ichor poured into the sludge, fouling it further, and the Chimera spat. "Vile things, these creatures. They taste of unclean promises."

"Huh," Evie pulled her chain, letting it coil about her arm and shoulder. "Gross."

A huge noise came from up above, and the timbers at the side of the cliff trembled. The sound of combat stilled for a brief moment, before it resumed with even more of a rush.

"Felix's still fighting," Evie said with relief. "I had worried—"

"Come, Chain Maiden, we've allies to aid." The harnoq bounded off, toward the furious conflict at the other end of the encampment. Evie was right behind it, muttering.

"I'll 'chain maiden' you."

Still, she ran even faster than the Chimera, skimming over the surface of the muck and unspooling her chain as she went. Harn and that Kylar guy were fighting the Arcid of Blades, while Vess and Wyvora were caught up against the poison one. As she ran, more Tier I beasts emerged from the forest, all of them looking to hit Harn first before sweeping over the rest of them. She didn't know where A'zek was going, but it wasn't a choice for Evie. She veered off, toward the horde.

You got this, Vess!

Felix! The explosion above sent a thrill of joy through Vess' Spirit, and she was too tired to mask it.

"You hear that, creature? Your master fights for his life at this very moment." Wyvora circled the Poison Arcid before Vess, the both of them with spears at the ready. The Henaari spat at the gelatinous creature. "You will die here, at the base of this cliff, in the mud."

In response, the Poison Arcid simply lashed outward with barbed tendrils. Vess leaped up and over the attack, kicking off the cliff and running along its face for several long strides.

Wall Run is level 62!

As she did, Vess summoned another set of silver Spears from her Skill. Air Mana streamed from her sore channels, congealing with a touch of metal Mana.

Spear of Tribulations is level 74!

She leaped from the vertical face of the cliff, arcing through the air, and sent three Spears speeding downward. They struck, just as Wyvora severed the vile green whip.

"Seven Tribulations!"

They exploded, blasting chunks of the Arcid's body outward and splattering it against the muck. "Now, Wyvora!"

The Farhunter's hooked spear glowed with brilliant green-gold light, life and light Mana woven tightly together, until another spear tip laid atop the old. She thrust, stabbing deep into its revealed chest. The Archid screamed, a sound like a boiling tea kettle.

We can finish this!

Harn bashed the Arcid's blades from the air, trying and failing to sever the chains that secured them. His own enchanted axes weren't enough, and Raze was being deflected somehow.

"Damn thing is usin' my metal Mana against me," Harn groused. "Kid! You still alive?"

The Apprentice Tier swordsman gasped in response, his narrow blades a thin defense against the legions that had emerged from the woods. Ghostfire Simians, Prismatic Wretches, even some Hoarhounds, all coming in for the kill. They had emerged from the only approach, which narrowed their advance, but the swordsman had been their only opponent for at least five minutes. Harn was impressed he was still alive at all.

"I can't hold them much longer!"

"Bindings of the White Waste!"

The advancing horde froze in place as chains of purple-white light speared up from the mud.

"Breaking Wheel!"

A rigid circle of spiked metal dropped from above, crashing into the front lines and smearing their bodies into the earth. Gore and mud fountained beneath its weight, and Evie descended from the air above. She skidded to a stop before the stymied horde, grabbing her chain back. More monsters appeared from the woods, more than they could hold just the three of them.

"Don't just stand there, swordboy! Kill!"

Harn would have laughed, had the Arcid not used his distraction to attempt a backstab. Harn's armor deflected the blow, but it still hurt.

Descent of the Barbarian is level 76!

Rage poured into him, his armor bulking up around the wound, and Harn swung a backhanded blow at the Arcid. The metal construct took it to the chest but skipped back, blunting a lot of the force. Harn didn't care. He advanced, axes blazing.

"You think you know violence?" Harn growled. "I'll show you violence."

Armored Skin is level 75!
Adept Tier!
You Gain:
+15 END
+15 VIT
+200 Health

Strength against Strength, Felix broke the Archon with every blow. With each breath, the Archon repaired himself, those flowing yellow-red sigils burning with power. Adamant Discord smashed him into walls, shattering the murals of the Urges' capture, burying the bastard in tons of rock. But the golden giant would emerge, again and again, ready to fight.

Felix obliged.

Claws slashed. Mana burst and ignited. Everything they had was brought to bear against one another, filling the huge chamber with sound and fury and leaving almost none of it untouched. At some point, Felix spared a thought for the Henaari he'd saved, but he couldn't find them. Then thought of them was driven from his Mind as the Archon came at him once again.

"Enough!"

Felix skidded to a stop, his claws dripping with the red-gold fire of his Cardinal Flame. He regarded the Archon, beaten and battered, hunched over another wound in his metal gut.

"You've grown powerful. Too powerful. Why are we fighting when we could work together?" The Archon glared at him, his eye-fires bright. "The gods have wronged you, just as the Nym have abandoned you, yes? We are Unbound. Together, we would be unstoppable."

"Wow," Felix said through his gathering breath. "You think I'd believe that?"

The Archon's helmet deformed into a grin, and a spray of crystallized power shot forth from the Archon's feet. Felix stepped back, but it had already formed a cage around him, a lattice-work of solidified power that began to *squeeze*.

"I said 'enough,' and I meant it," the Archon hissed. "Goodbye, Felix Nevarre."

A spear of crystalline Mana shot forward, so fast that, had he still been Human, Felix wouldn't have even seen it move. As it stood, Felix wasn't Human. Not by a longshot.

Felix seized the spear in mid-air, stopping it an inch before it hit his chest. With a flex of his enormous Strength, he shattered it and the cage around him.

Ravenous Tithe!

And then he ate it all.

"Im-Impossible," the Archon stammered, backing away. "You cannot break—you cannot absorb solidified Mana!"

"Can and did, Archie," Felix said. He walked forward, flaring his Sovereign of Flesh as his minor wounds began to rapidly repair. "I walk a new Path now."

"A Path?" The Archon's eye-fires blazed brighter, but the Spirit Felix could feel everywhere trembled in fear. "No. No, you can't. I saw no Omen Key!"

Felix didn't care what the bastard believed. They were too evenly matched, even after all the bullshit he had just gone through, the bastard was augmenting himself too powerfully to overwhelm. Not as he was. Felix grabbed the swirling mass of Essence within his core space, that thickened potency from the Urges, and fed it into his cores. His Intent shaped its direction with relative ease, his Will reinforcing it.

Sovereign of Flesh is level 68!

...

Sovereign of Flesh is level 72!

His muscles and scales pulsed, expanding, growing with every step he took. Felix felt the power within him as the significance he'd stolen from the Urge of Mayhem blossomed within his Skill; a revelation of turmoil and struggle. To be Sovereign, one must know turmoil, must be tested by it. Conquer it.

Sovereign of Flesh is level 73!

Sovereign of Flesh is level 74!

Blue lightning and red-gold fire scintillated across his shoulders and chest, down his limbs and across his neck and face. Felix grew until his Body was the equal of the golden giant himself. His eyes were bonfires of sapphire flame.

Unfettered Volition!

"RUUAAAAGH!" The Archon roared as he burst alight with his own strange abilities, flames and sour fumes coiled within his already-repaired armor. He charged at Felix, meeting him halfway with claws of flame.

They met, tooth and claw against profane sigaldry. Golden armor against midnight scale.

The Archon was blasted back, chest torn apart by Felix's upward swinging talons. A conjured Shadow Whip snagged him, however, yanked him back to be met by Felix's thunderous blow. The Archon's right arm was torn completely off, golden metal and strange forged pieces shearing and pinging off the walls. The golden giant screamed, engulfing his entire body in a sheath of white-hot flame. Felix jerked back, scorched by it.

The Archon… ran.

He was so surprised by it that the Archon was able to make it all the way to the stairs before Felix acted. Felix blurred after him, his speed so much greater than it used to be, reaching the stairs only a half-second after his foe. Still, that meant the Archon had already disappeared up the curve of the stairwell, forcing Felix to reach ahead with his senses as he ran, lest the bastard ambush him or—

Felix almost stumbled before he grinned. He reached out, sending his bountiful Mana ahead of him in a dozen tendrils of Intent. The Archon was just up ahead, running like mad, right before a series of rocks on the steps.

Grenades.

Felix detonated them, and the stairwell filled with light and thunder, followed by a crash of metal on stone. Felix rounded the corner and wasted no time. He leaped atop the staggered construct, leading with an overhand blow. It hit him, driving the Archon to his knees.

"You vile boy!" The Archon twisted around, his single remaining arm blazing with Profane Sigaldry in an array more complex than anything Felix had ever seen. The force of it sent Felix back down a couple steps. "You are facing someone who has spent Ages plotting his revenge! My Mind may have been broken, but I'm remembering! You! You have helped me remember!"

The fire intensified until the heat was too much to bear. Felix snarled and backed up more steps.

"I was a living god to the Nym! A being capable of wonders they could not believe nor understand! They trembled before my might, my unrivaled intellect!"

Felix! He draws on unstable power! His core quivers with it! Karys buzzed at his waist. *He cannot hold that much Mana!*

Now that the Paragon mentioned it, Felix could feel it, too. A wobbly buzzing within his Affinity, scratching frantically around the connection Felix could still feel between the two of them. Flashes of what he'd seen in the Memory of the Archon came back to him, of the strange rod Merodach had displayed and of the awful pulses of power he'd used. He could feel something at the Archon's center shudder with every uptempo of dissonant magic, the Mana he gathered opposing directly against the Harmony of the world.

Felix tried Stone Shaping, but the stairwell refused to bend to his Skill, and Shadow Whips melted in the intense heat. He cast about with his senses, looking for something, anything that he could use.

Then he saw it, sitting between the Archon's feet.

On it!

"Pit! No!"

Convergence!

A blinding flash of light filled the air, so bright even the Archon shouted in alarm. But nearly as much as he did when all three tons of Chimera manifested right on top of him.

"SKREAAAWW!"

Emerald fire covered Pit's huge expanse as he bit down onto the Archon's helmet-face. The Archon screamed in hideous pain, born backward by Pit's enormous bulk.

Pit's Poisonfire is level 51!

...

Pit's Poisonfire is level 68!
Pit's Poison Resistance is level 2!

...

Pit's Poison Resistance is level 22!

They both slammed into the stairs, both aflame, struggling against each others' weight and magic. Pit's Health descended rapidly as his Vitality was eaten away by the Archon's terrible, yellow-red power. Felix shied back, the atonal burr of that power too much for his senses.

"Pit!"

The plan, Felix! The plan!

Breath hissing between his teeth, Felix lunged forward, grabbing the object from the steps at the same time he unsheathed his Inheritor's Will.

Wild Threnody!

Arrow of Perdition!

Unfettered Volition!

His Crescian Blade ignited with a golden-azure glow as he channeled the Mana of his Arrow into its edge.

"Pit! Convergence!"

The tenku's weight vanished from the surprised construct, and Felix dove forward, bringing his blade down. Straight onto the dark dagger in his chest. Both of them slammed home, and the Archon howled as the physical core at his center *splintered.*

You do not deserve this Body! Karys shouted while Felix gathered all of the significance he could and slammed it into his Skill.

UNITE THE LOST!

A huge, massive amount of power from the Urges siphoned into the Skill, fueling it. Chords of majestic Harmony clashed against descending Dissonance, both of them bursting against the other, separate but matched in might. Felix gritted his teeth, forcing the Skill and Wild Threnody *and* Arrow of Perdition all at once, his Mana dropping too fast for his regeneration to match.

"No! You—!" The Archon's choked howl met Felix's Will and *shattered* apart, unable to withstand even a second of it. Not when it was backed by the weight of six immortal Urges.

BEGONE!

The golden body rent, split beneath his Blade. Flesh and blood was spun, whole cloth from sheer power, spooling upon the steps just above them. Feet and legs, torso, chest, and arms. A man, full-grown. A familiar face that gasped with his first true breath in Ages. He fell to the stone steps, screaming all the while.

The Unbound that became the Archon was whole once more. Beneath Felix's Blade, the Archon construct fell, finally limp.

"Merodach, Son of Anatu, Son of Tamzi," Felix panted, blood running from a wound on his scalp and cheek. He left his Blade in the construct's chest. "Eat shit."

Merodach's newborn eyes widened in surprise and fear as Felix slammed into him. In his free hand was the object he'd snatched from the stairs, the Seed of Remembered Light. He grabbed the man's face with a brutal, ebon claw and shoved it straight down his throat while slamming a chunk of potency from the Urges into it. Power enough to see it grow.

And grow it did.

Roots exploded from Merodach's gut, branches and bark spiraling upward to smash against the delicately carved ceiling and walls. Felix leaped back, but it wasn't enough, he was caught up in the titanic growth that speared upward into and through the rocky ceiling. Through the entire cliff.

Aria of the Green Wilds is level 63!
Aria of the Green Wilds is level 64!
...
Aria of the Green Wilds is level 79!
Adept Tier!
You Gain—

Felix could only clamp onto his Bastion as he tumbled back, while the Nymean Temple—and the cliff that housed it—were torn asunder.

CHAPTER SEVENTY-EIGHT

Zara jolted awake, the darkness of unconsciousness banished in an instant of blaring Harmonics.

"Lady Zara? What's wrong?"

Several of the Haarguard stood by, clearly watching over her slumbering form. The Naiad swept her gaze around the small room, barely big enough to house two guards and herself, yet nice enough for all of that. "Where are we?"

"In Setoria, ma'am," said the same guard. "We got you to an inn as soon as the gates shut behind us. The Lord Hand's orders."

"I see," she said primly, peering out the relatively small window. It was paned with glass, which meant the inn they stayed at was far more expensive than it appeared, and it looked out onto a wide square that was absolutely teeming with people despite the late hour. All of them were shouting and hollering something, a chaotic mix of joy and frustration. *A festival.* "Have the Inquisitors arrived?"

"No. We have eyes on the Waystone, and not a single Redcloak has shown their face."

That was good. The Waystone, a manner of communication between cities, was the only manner in which the Inquisition could reach their Grandmaster. They had to stop them from reaching it at all costs. Zara stood, dark robes gathered around herself. Her face was serene despite the Mana drain by which she was still afflicted. "Then let us join these eyes. We cannot hope that the Inquisition will simply give up."

At that moment, it felt as if the world quaked, and a massive, dire chord was struck. Zara screamed, unable to help it, accosted by reverberations that twisted Harmonics into knots of discordant chaos.

Distantly, she was aware of feet pounding on the stairs outside her room, of a hand hammering at the door. Someone else entered, Thangle, and spoke, but the words made no sense. Her Affinity soared, trembling from the touch of that chord, and Zara could hardly breathe.

Felix! It's him, it has to be. She looked up, to the west, from where the sound was already fading. *What has he done?*

"Zara? Zara the others sent me! It's the Redcloaks! They're here!" The Gnome was tugging at her robes, his own white hair in wild disarray. "They've landed a Manaship at the Waystone!"

You Have Killed The Betrayer, He Who Has Fallen!
XP Earned!
You Have Gained 1 Level!

You Are Now Level 56!
+20 to STR! +22 to PER! +22 to VIT! +26 to END! +24 to INT! +28 to WIL! +26 to AGL! +29 to DEX!
+20 All Harmonic Stats!
You Have 15 Unused Stat Points!

Your Companion Pit Has Gained 2 Levels!
He Is Now Level 64!
+20 to STR! +14 to PER! +4 to VIT! +18 to END! +6 to INT! +12 to WIL! +32 to AGL! +34 to DEX!
+10 to RES, AFI, REI!

Unite the Lost is level 14!
...
Unite the Lost is level 37!

Apprentice Tier!
You Gain:
+Reduction of Significance Consumed
+10% RES
+10% REI

Claws digging into stone and root, Felix arrested his long fall, clinging instead to the rough bark of a monstrously growing tree. It moved like a serpent, expanding by the second and sending him higher into the Temple, through shattered ceilings and sundered sediment. Around him, in every direction, stone collapsed or was bound by the fierce grasp of hungry roots. The Spirit Tree blazed with Mana and more, almost blinding to his sight even without Manasight, fed on the storm of potential he'd fed into its seed and whatever Merodach had contributed.

Twinges of System energy fluttered through him—Harmony meeting the Dissonance of his [Cardinal Beast Core] and sparking into conflict—but Felix ignored it for the most part. After everything else, it felt more like a love tap than the electrifying jolt it usually seemed. Now, he was more concerned with the feedback he was getting from his external senses.

Voracious Eye!

Name: Atlantes Anima
Type: Spirit Tree
Lore: Spirit Trees are a rare and powerful organism imbued with elemental Mana dependent on their growth cycle. The one before you is in the process of attuning itself.

The Seed of Remembered Light had reached far above him, bursting from the top of the cliff and diverting the river itself. A torrent of water poured all around him as he clung to its bark, a roaring cataract in all directions as the branches above spread out into the night sky. Far above, beyond steam and spray, ten thousand stars were blotted out by rapidly expanding boughs and huge, palmate leaves bigger than his entire body.

As it spread, Felix's awareness spread with it, riding atop the highest twigs as it soared into the heavens and spreading down, down into the earth. Roots as thick as houses smashed through the cliff-face, charging into the slick earth and shattering the vile reservoirs that remained. Winds shook him, clouds wreathed his crown, the rumble of water fed him, as did the ants that struggled among his spreading roots. Felix was the Spirit Tree, and the Tree was Felix—only his immense Willpower, Intelligence, and Perception kept them separate enough that he didn't go immediately insane.

Aria of the Green Wilds is level 80!
Deep Mind is level 68!
...
Deep Mind is level 74!

Felix's friends and enemies battled among one another, their fights only paused the shortest of intervals during the Spirit Tree's ascension. The roots he spread about hadn't killed them—not one—and that surprised him before he felt the Spirit Tree's utter conviction in the sanctity of life.

Of Choice.

Felix? A voice called to him, seemingly from far away. He knew it was Pit, but Felix couldn't pay it any mind.

Below him, he could feel his friends fighting. Evie and Kylar, fighting off a horde of lesser beasts while Harn battled an agile Arcid covered in blades. A'zek weaving among the greater threats in the horde, killing with precision from the moonshadows. Wyvora and Vess, struggling against that poison-attuned Arcid that had both of them covered in burns and weeping wounds. Alister, standing atop Atar's prone form—still living, but severely injured—hurling columns of force at a legion of ice-armored warriors.

More than that, he could feel the monsters themselves, their strange thoughts and alien impressions. Fear and rage threaded with an insistent strumming at the back of their Minds and urging to push them forward into battle. He could even sense the approaching forms of the Haarguard, Nevia, Davum, Vyne, and Kikri all racing toward the sounds of furious battle. Coming to help.

All of it was there, in him, below him. Apart and separate in a way that left Felix dizzy. He was tangled so close with the Spirit

Tree, with its...not Mind, but *presence*. It spoke to him in song, strumming his Affinity so that thoughts and concepts flowed between them with lightning understanding.

He could finally hear why the Tree had not killed, of Choices long torn away. Chains forced on unwilling Minds and Spirits, lashed to carry a burden none of them agreed upon. Marks hung heavy across the battlefield, metaphysical brands that had twisted every single creature the Archon had touched.

He could make it stop.

He could *fix* it.

Unite the Lost!

The Spirit Tree joined with him, amplifying his power through some mechanism Felix couldn't understand. He had no need to, not then, only for the power within his core to spread out through his channels and into the shuddering bole beneath his fingers. Its branches still grew outward, leagues in diameter now, and everything that fell under them was struck by Felix's descending light and song.

Harmonies silenced the night, breaking apart the fighting that had shown no signs of stopping. His friends paused mid-strike as their foes crumbled to their knees or were seized in fountains of brilliant radiance that spun from above. Stolen significance, great swaths of it, fled Felix's core space with a roar of transformed joy. Whatever he'd taken from the Urges had been transmuted in the process, turned from the fetid impulses they had embodied and become something lighter; refined, even. All of it poured out into the Tree, into his enemies.

It washed them clean.

You Have Cleansed The Spirits Of All Within Ten Leagues
All Unwilling Marks Removed!

Felix's core space spasmed, all but empty, as the wide-scale work was almost finished. Almost, but not quite. He'd had enough of those who would impose their choices on others, enough of predators who sought only to use and exploit. He'd had *enough*.

Tyrant of Choice Activated!

All Thus Cleansed Can No Longer Be Unwillingly Marked!

His own Spirit soared, weights finally lifted from it, and within him, he could hear a triumphant cry of a tenku. His Marks, those of the Raven, remnant Maw, even the one Zara placed on him; all of them shattered and were washed clean.

Hidden Quest Completed!
All May Rise!
Compassion is to be lauded, Ascendant. Rewarded. You have spent yourself, the very power you'd use to advance, on those who have sought your death. There are those that would call you a Fool, but it is the Fool who challenges the impossible.
Rewards:
+Title!
+Increased Authority!
+Skill Evolution!

New Title!
Transmuter of Burdens (Epic)!
You have chosen to lighten the burdens of all, friend or foe, by spending your Mana and accumulated significance, returning them the Choices that had been stolen from them.
+5% Reduction of significance and Mana consumed in all future attempts!
+5% Completion bonus to Fiendforge!

Skill Evolution!
Unite the Lost Has Gained An Ability!
Mark Cleansing And Immunity - Use of Unite the Lost on a target will cleanse them of all Marks and make them resistant to further tampering. Effects increase with level.

Aria of the Green Wilds is level 81!

Wild melody shook the Foglands, more gorgeous than he could comprehend, and Felix's Mind went blank. He trembled, Tree and man, as two beasts within him held him tight. One dark and hungry, the other of light and wing, the both of them anchoring Felix as chaos stormed into his channels. A flow of… something flooded back toward Felix from the horde beneath. It hit the Tree —him—and sank back into his channels and core space. Into the dark places between Skills and Cores and Pillars, where the significance of the Urges once dwelled… and restored that lost weight. Restored it and so much more.

"What?" he gasped, jerked free of his communion with the Spirit Tree. Of the two beasts inside. "I spent it..."

Yet significance had returned two-fold. Everything he'd given had been repaid, and then some.

Unite the Lost is level 38!
…
Unite the Lost is level 49!

New Title!
Savant of the Green Wilds (Epic)!
You have raised a Spirit Tree from Seed to Elder Tree! A remarkable achievement seen all too little!
+15% Effects and harvests from all flora attended by you personally.

Vess drew up short, her spear inches from piercing the Arcid's vile form, when it simply… melted.

"What is this?" Wyvora hissed. "What is happening?"

A sound rang out, a chord so deep and powerful it almost turned her bones to jelly, and Vess flinched away. Rays of light stabbed from above, drawing her attention up to a woven darkness that blocked out the stars themselves. Vess was confused a moment, before the light revealed far off branches and leaves, sparking a series of new questions. Yet all questions died, unasked, as the Arcid was subsumed by that light. The entire battlefield was; spears of radiance hit every single one of their enemies and stopped them all in their tracks.

"It is Felix," Vess said, a certainty growing within her. Her Affinity thrummed with the truth of it; she could feel him, somehow. "He won."

Wyvora didn't speak, but stared in commingling fear and hope. Vess felt both as well. Hope for them all, and fear for what may have been lost already.

You Have Been Cleansed Of All Unwilling Marks! Rejoice!

"I was Marked?" she asked in mounting horror. A shape washed away, looking like an unraveling knot. It was gone in moments, faded. "By whom?"

"Vess!"

The Henaari pointed with her hooked spear at the fallen Arcid. The light had vanished, leaving behind a perfect circle of new growth. Moss and grasses rose above the otherwise unending fields of mud, and at its center...

"Siva grant me your grace," she whispered. "Felix. What have you done?"

At some point, Felix had let go of the Spirit Tree. Instead of falling, however, he had simply slid down its sprawling length. The memory of that was hazy, distracted as he'd been. The curve of the gargantuan plant had led him deeper into the earth, past cracked foundations and into chambers Felix hadn't known existed. Now, he was in a deep chamber that had clearly been carved from the bedrock, and in the Nymean style. Far above, the sound of falling water dominated, but not a lick of that moisture was reaching him.

Felix stood, insides still buzzing with the accumulated power he'd received, and had to lean on the Tree for support. Moving felt... weird. He wasn't huge anymore, as he'd been while facing the Archon, and his skin had returned to normal, but he felt alien in his own Body. Like he was simultaneously too slow and too fast; likely a result of his

Agility being a touch lower than his Perception, and the both of them reaching above a thousand points. But the gains of nebulous significance pulled too, an internal weight that drew everything inward.

"Karys? Pit?"

A flash of light manifested in his tenku Companion, now bigger than any horse or ox Felix had ever seen. Still not quite as huge as he'd been in that one vision. Burns marred his feathers and fur, dark patches that oozed blood and charred flesh.

"Oh god, are you okay?"

Pit winced but warbled assurances. The Chimera's Health was increasing slowly from the depths the Archon had pulled him to. Just the thought of that bastard made Felix's blood boil all over again. He breathed sharply through his nose, mastering his anger, taking solace in the fact that the Betrayer would never bother anyone ever again.

Abruptly, Pit perked up. His triangular ear swiveled, tilting toward their right. The Mana glow of the Spirit Tree roots behind him made seeing much else in the chamber difficult, but Felix had reached the Third Threshold. He flared his Perception, accessing the full potential of his stat, and the room shifted into abrupt focus. Shadows became thinner, details more pronounced, and his eyes were drawn to the lone exit from the partially collapsed room. It was a trefoil archway without a door, opening up into another, even darker hall.

Dark, save for a flash of green-gold light.

"Karys?" Felix called out, but he heard no response. His sword had been left, buried in the chest of the Archon when the Spirit Tree had taken root. Had he fallen all the way down here? Pit took off into the dark, and Felix was close behind.

Beyond the archway was a series of interconnected rooms, four or five of them maybe. But Felix only had eyes for a suit of armor piled carelessly upon the flat, dusty stone floor. The Archon's old body, now utterly inert and dark, laid in a broken heap with Felix's sword still stuck through its chest. Felix and Pit reached it in a flash, moving so fast the air clapped like small bits of thunder.

"Karys? Are you still in there?" Felix asked, inspecting his sword. He wanted to pull it out, but their plan had involved the Paragon leaping into the Archon's damaged core to force Merodach out in case his Unite the Lost didn't work. If he pulled it out now, would Karys be damaged? Felix's Manasight caught hold of a vague impression, green-gold and fading, gathered around the very edge of his sword and... and within the depths of the armor.

"Karys," Felix said. "Hold tight."

Unit the Lost!

It took only the barest hint of his redoubled significance, though Felix wasn't sure how he could tell. He felt it leave him, traveling along with his Mana into his Inheritor's Will and the Archonic Construct. Green-gold vapor sparked and ignited, catching along the surface of bronze and golden metal. A flame at first, then a steady fire manifested within the hooked sword and the armor both. He fell back, short of breath and seized with a sudden exhaustion. Pit caught him, strong enough to hold up his bulk.

Felix, the fire spoke, clearly confused. *What happened? Did we—?*

"We did it. The Archon's dead," Felix said.

Glorious victory, Karys breathed, sounding more exhausted than Felix. *I feared your mad plan would not work, but it must have for us all to still be standing here.*

"Yeah. He was a pushover once I got him out of his armor," Felix said. He got his weight back under his own legs, patting Pit affectionately.

But I—I almost perished. I can feel it. Why am I not dead, Felix? Karys voice increased in concern with every word, as if the Paragon were reading a report that set his teeth on edge. *What have you sacrificed for me?*

"Not a sacrifice, man," Felix smiled. "Just a little significance. What else are friends for?"

I... thank you, Felix. My... friend.

"You seem like you're in the Archon's old body now. Can you stand up?"

No, unfortunately. This form was well and truly mangled. I see several repair functions buried deep in this core, but even that is flawed. Broken. It will take some time to repair. Karys' voice shifted, now coming from the sword within his own chest. *But it appears I can split my attention.*

"Oh, that's handy." Felix gripped Inheritor's Will and pulled it free. It rang as he lifted it, a crystalline chime. Green-gold Mana sparked across its hilt and edge. "You're still portable."

An... interesting designation, if apt. I will set part of my Mind to work on repairing this body, if you do not object.

"No, no, repair away."

Thank you. It will be difficult. On the one hand, your Skill cleansed this form of that nasty Profane Sigaldry. On the other, that means I shall have to spend some time inscribing it anew. I still recall much of the Eidolons.

Felix nodded, happy that his friend would have a body once again. Perhaps it might even help with his fading memories. He hoped so.

Without warning, a jolt of pain shot through Felix's Mind and Spirit, echoing only faintly into his Body. It was his Bastion, still containing his Skills but straining. Pressure waxed and waned within it, only occasionally crossing over into pain, but Felix knew he had little time. The Adept Tier was calling for several of his Skills, and there were still vast quantities of Essence and Memories he hadn't yet processed from his Devour Array.

What's this? Pit sent.

The tenku stood atop a glittering series of lines engraved into the smooth stone floor. *Not engraved. Inscribed. It's an array. The most complicated one I've ever seen.* Far and above the complexity of the Eidolon, loops and whorls of inscribed glyphs and sigils spread outward in ever-widening patterns of what looked like silver metal. He stepped closer, yet the moment his foot touched the first line of the array, a golden-bordered window appeared with a trilling note.

Authority Recognized, Inheritor!
For Defeating A Local Threat, Seven Territorial Threats, And Raising A Legendary Ranked Spirit Tree
You May Lay Claim To The Lost Territory Of Nagast!
Do You Wish To Establish Your Authority?
Y/N

CHAPTER SEVENTY-NINE

Felix stared at the notification in a combination of disbelief and outright frustration. He shouted up into the dark ceiling. "Now? You're dumping all this on me *now*?"

The System didn't answer, and he didn't feel the soft bundle of threads that he'd poked at while in the Path. For all Felix knew, getting a direct response from the System was never going to happen again. Mana vapor was condensing and steaming all around him, pulled into the silver sigils in a way that was compacting it into a silver layer that grew more lustrous as he watched. The air hummed and the array gleamed, glowing steadily now.

"Karys?"

It is an exceptional offer. And considering you already hold Authority over Naevis, I do not suspect you will have any issues with accepting this as well. Just...

"Just what?"

This is far more than just a city, Felix. It is a Territory. And different than any you've encountered.

Felix had noticed that. But wasn't that the same as Cal's Authority, then? "I've seen Territorial Authority on offer before. What makes this different?"

It is a Lost Territory. You are reestablishing lines that have faded with time and Ruin itself. I cannot predict how it will go.

He had a point there. So, ignoring the window asking about Authority, Felix focused on what he could see and sense. The array around him was complicated to the point of being nonsensical. Similar in how the Eidolon's arrays were above and beyond any he'd seen on a Golem, these were the same amount of advancement beyond even *that*. It almost hurt to look at, and they covered all of the floor, walls, ceiling, and even extended out into other rooms beyond that one. Pit was still poking around at it, though he hadn't strayed far, and he chirruped curiously.

Felix. Found something.

Wincing at the flare of pain from his Bastion, Felix strode forward to his Companion's side and saw him pawing at a series of carvings circling the central portion of the chamber. They were words, not sigils, in a tongue Felix could somehow read as easily as English. "Enter If You've The Will, Claim It If You've The Right."

The ancient challenge. A rite as old as the Ages.

At the center of the array—some thirty feet away—among the swirling lines inlaid with brightening silver, was an empty space. Right where a central, controlling glyph would go in a normal array, there was only bare stone. It was typically the linchpin or keystone of an array, the thing that provided an overarching meaning to the rest of it.

Felix could hear it call, a link between his hooked sword and the array. Between *him* and the array.

Felix, I think—

"Yeah, me, too." Felix swallowed nervously. "I think I have to go in there."

The Manaship had not landed atop the Waystone, but it was so close as to make little difference. Darius Reed glared at the craft, wishing he could simply send a windblade at it and finish this task once and for all. His ward was likely in dire danger while he dealt with frustration after frustration a thousand leagues away. The urge to let loose his Strength and the tempest within him was strong, curtailed only by the inevitable fallout his actions would cause. The Redcloaks hadn't landed atop just any roof, but the roof of the Governor's manor. As the Duke of Pax'Vrell's Chosen Hand, attacking it in any capacity would be the same as an attack by the Duke himself, and Reed refused to ruin his Duke's reputation on a whim.

Reed scrubbed his hand over his face, clamping his Willpower over the urge to scream. At anyone. Everyone. He remained quiet, however, still and contained. To do less was to be unworthy of his position.

"Four Redcloaks have exited the Governor's manor, sir," one of the Haarguard answered. "Southern exit."

"Two more have exited to the west," said another. "North exit reports another two."

"Stay here. I'll handle the south," Reed ordered. "Keep watch. We let none of them leave that manor."

"Aye, sir. And the west and north?"

Reed loosened his massive sword in its sheath and grunted in approval. "Kelgan has the west, and the north will have to sweep around to the east to reach the Waystone, anyway. Send the remainder of men to the Waystone, now."

"Diurnal Reach!"

"Shatterstrike!" Kelgan hissed in response, his spear glowing briefly before intercepting and bursting apart a volley of light Mana bolts. He spun it defensively, deflecting two arrows that sought his kidneys, and brought the blunt end down hard upon the nearest Redcloak.

You Have Defeated An Unknown Initiate of the Inviolate Inquisition!
XP Earned!

Another flare of Mana followed his own, intercepting two more arrows with projectiles that shone green-gold. Karp fired arrow after arrow, his quiver almost empty, but each one knocked back the two hidden Initiate's shots. Until, with a single bright flash, one of his struck true and the top of the opposing building was abruptly festooned in tangling vines.

You Have Defeated An Unknown Initiate of the Inviolate Inquisition (x2)!
XP Earned!

"Got em, Kel," the archer grunted.

"Good. Meera and Watts. Go and collect our friends. Bring ‘em back here," Kelgan gestured to his feet, where another Haarguard was tying up the Initiate he'd knocked out. It had been extra difficult fighting to subdue rather than outright kill, much as he wanted to—his orders were clear. "Don't rough ‘em up too bad."

Meera and Watts saluted and hustled off, heading to one of the wooden stairways that lined the outside of almost every building in Setoria. *Practically beggin' for thieves.*

"Lieutenant!"

Kelgan jerked in surprise, flaring his Strength. He'd hopped a full eight strides away, spear spun at the ready, before realizing who spoke. "Blind gods, Lady Zara. Warn a man."

Zara stood close by, flanked by those guards he'd set to watch over her and Thangle. Everyone was puffing for breath, the Gnome in particular, but Zara seemed utterly composed.

"Is this all the Inquisition you've faced? Three?" Her bright blue eyes swept over the prone Redcloak at her feet and then, unerringly, found the two above. "That seems a paltry number."

No. Not entirely calm. Kelgan could see sweat on her brow, and her fingers shook slightly before she clenched them tight in a fist.

"Maybe they're afraid of us," Karp suggested.

"Foolish to think so," Zara rejoined without much heat. Her eyes glazed over slightly, a look he recognized as someone accessing their enhanced Perception. "Reed has positioned men all around the Governor's manor, covering all exits. He's captured six himself, and more of your fellows have reached the Waystone to—"

She cut off, ice-blue eyes wide. Kelgan followed her stare, turning to see the monolithic Waystone over the tops of nearby buildings. He'd seen several Waystones in his travels, and this one looked the same as all the rest. It was huge, a white sentinel against the night sky, topped with metal spires shaped into fluted spirals that the operators inside would adjust before sending out messages to another Waystone far, far away.

And, right then, the spires were lifting. All of them.

"They're already at the Waystone! They intend to contact Amaranth!"

"What!" Kelgan gripped his spear and started running. "Everyone! On me!"

"There is no time!" Zara snapped, before aquamarine light bloomed from her arms and legs. "I hope you have not just eaten?"

"Whyyyy—!"

Kelgan, Karp, and the other six guards on the street were lifted bodily by a wave of green-blue Mana. They took off like a shot, threading the empty allies with a speed that forced the breath from his lungs. At the fore, Zara surged, her hands directing the wave so that they banked around a sharp corner, crashing shopfront facades and scouring the cobbles below. The Waystone grew, taking up the horizon as the streets fled rapidly, until they barreled down the main causeway toward it.

"Redcloaks! Northwest and southwest!" Karp shouted.

Ahead of them, Acolytes and Initiates emerged from the buildings around the Waystone, filling the square with a sheet of golden light that slammed down and around their path. Zara screamed, and her Tempered lungs sent cracks through the road while a vibration built along the undulating wave of Mana. The power split, Kelgan and others shifting until they were behind Zara, while the Mana collected at the fore like a plow blade.

They hit the barrier of golden light with the sound of a roaring ocean, a tempest the size of a city. Yet the golden barrier held, if *barely*.

"Burn you! I'll not have this wasted!" Zara was shouting, but Kelgan couldn't make much sense of it. Her voice rose, a crescendo atop another, building until he thought his head might burst. "BREAK!"

Light flashed, golden and green and a deep, enduring blue. Ten thousand shattering glass panes, screaming metal, a titanic bellow that threw Redcloaks off their feet. Kelgan and Karp and all the rest fell to the cobbles in a loose heap, heads clutched tight against a pain barely faded. The lieutenant flared his Perception, afraid of being stabbed while he writhed, but all those around them had also fallen. The Initiates and Acolytes had been dropped, every one of them breathing but senseless.

What happened?

Zara was only a few strides away, but her chest heaved like a bellows, and her sea-green hair hung limp about her shoulders. He was surprised she could even stand. She had spent everything she had on breaking that barrier. His men were slowly regaining their feet, but they had made it. Ahead of them loomed the Waystone… and one other.

A full-fledged Inquisitor. Adept Tier.

"You go no further, heretic," he rasped. His hands bloomed with a golden radiance. "I call to witness, Guardian of the Faith!"

A beam of golden Mana shot from the sky, as if from the Pathless Himself. It wavered and shook, but within its confines, a hulking form emerged. An armored knight, eerily similar to those Arcid things but twice as big… and made entirely of light Mana. The Inquisitor pointed at them.

"Kill them all."

The pain of his held-back Skills intensified, waxing bright as Felix chewed his lip in consideration. He couldn't speak to why, but he felt a terrible sense of *urgency*, both in his Bastion and in the array around him. Like it wanted him to claim it, almost.

Notifications were still there, waiting to be checked. They were half-cloaked by his Bastion, though, so any perusal was painful in super fun ways that he was absolutely looking forward to later. He'd have to Tier up before long. But did he have time?

His vision spasmed, and his notifications flashed again and again, brighter than previously. A soft, insistent trilling grew in the distance, a connecting thread of the System that sought his vision. *A notification*, he mused. *Bypassing my partitioning of them.* Resigned, Felix seized it.

Hidden Quest Completed!
The Door Of The Lidless Eye!
You have discovered a part of the dire secrets hidden within the Nymean Temple, have opened the Door and

prevented the darkness within from escaping containment.
Rewards:
+Title
+Increased Authority

New Title!
Champion of the Halcyon (Epic)!
By fist and fury, you have defeated multiple enemies of the ancient Halcyon Empire so thoroughly that not even their Essence remains to taint the Continent. For this, you are to be commended and rewarded.
+5 Levels To One Body Skill Of Your Choice (Below Adept)
+Evolution Of One Body Skill Of Your Choice (Below Adept)

"What a Title," Felix said. "But that doesn't help right now. Except the 'increased Authority' bit, I guess."

Yes, that is a good thing. More Authority secures your position and ability to claim ever greater responsibilities.

He'd have to take Karys' word for it, as he felt nothing at the supposed gain. With stats, even a small boost, Felix would feel *something*. Even the metaphysical concept of significance was a heft in his core space. Authority was nothing.

Wait, what about my other Quest? Home Sweet Home?

Another thread floated toward him, urging him to connect to its frequency. Felix felt like he was starting to understand the smallest bit about the System. He grabbed at it, secured it with his Affinity and Intent as easily as catching a ball.

Quest Completed!
Home Sweet Home!
You have secured your ancestors' Temple from all threats, internal and external!
5 of 5 Threats Eliminated
Rewards:
+Title

+Home
+1 Gold Chest

Rewards Increased For Defeating Seven-Legged Orit In Single Combat...
Rewards Increased For Defeating Incursion With Minimal Casualties...
Rewards Increased For Defeating Archon In Single Combat...
Rewards Increased Greatly For Defeating Unending Maw Completely...
Rewards Increased For Defeating Caged Urges (x6) Completely...
Title Upgraded!
Home Upgraded!
Chest Upgraded!
Rewards:
+Title
+Stronghold
+1 Platinum Chest

This time, it was like an explosion in his chest as the System sent a pulse of Harmonics into his core. They burst to spume, crashing against the rocks of Dissonance before blending together in a chaotic roil. More than that, however, as threads of terribly distant aquamarine thrummed in sympathetic pain. It stabbed at him, a knife of golden light hurtling through the green-blue—a familiar power he'd come to despise. Felix flared his Affinity, focusing on those distant threads, on a connection he'd partially cleansed from his soul.

A giant of golden light, so similar to the Archon that it blinded him to the fact that it was being fought off by familiar faces. Kelgan and Karp and others among the Haarguard. Thangle! Hands of ochre hue lifted and wove darts of deepest blue that shot off into the giant, breaking panels of light that reformed in moments. Pain and exhaustion echoed through it all, thoughts sluggishly fighting against a hundred accumulated wounds and overtaxed resources.

Fast as lightning, a boulder-sized fist took him straight in the chest.

"Zara!" Felix staggered, almost thrown from his feet despite his stats and significant weight. His footing shifted as the entire room rang, a bell the size of a mountain droning in his ears. He stepped.

The world lit up in silver and gold, the same message once more repeated. It flashed at him, as if pleading.

Do You Wish To Establish Your Authority?
Y/N

Accept Felix! Something is happening! It is far away, but there is danger!

"It's Zara," he growled. "Everyone's in trouble, they—the Redcloaks." Felix growled through the madness in his chest, worse now than it had been in a long time. He fought it down, smothering the chaos with all the power he could muster. He had questions about the Chanter, about her intentions, but he'd not let them die if he could help it. "Yes! Give me the damn Authority!"

CHAPTER EIGHTY

Kelgan dodged a glowing sword larger than most wagons. He cleared it, but its impact against the cobbles hit him with a cushion of air that sent him sprawling. His armor and spear clattered across the ground, crashing painfully atop the unconscious Acolytes.

That thing hits harder than three Ogres! Kelgan thought as he struggled to his feet. *Didn't even touch me, and my Health dropped,* his eyes bugged in alarm. *Nearly half!*

Kelgan leaned against his spear, only to find it give way beneath his weight. He stumbled, catching himself with the splintered haft of his weapon before casting it away. "Useless now."

A high song—like rain and wave against a narrow beach—shook the air. The Guardian's next strike was fouled, pieces of its gauntlet and vambrace peeling off in great sheets of golden light. Yet still, the force of its blow buckled shields and crashed through the screen of defensive Skills, scattering their power and his people. Zara shot out another flare of humming bolts, and these detonated against the Guardian's pauldron and chestplate, taking chunks out of the solidified light. It barely flinched.

She's not enough. They were losing. It was so burning obvious she had expended herself in the Passages, and then spent herself again after too little time recovering. She had precious little left.

Rallying Cry!

All Allies' Regeneration Is Boosted By 50%!
Rallying Cry is level 64!

"Kelgan! Here!"

Spear or not, Kelgan almost threw himself at the voice before realizing he knew it. "Thangle! Where the hell are you?"

The air wobbled, then the wild-haired Gnome appeared at his side. His hand was outstretched and holding a pear-shaped bottle filled with a crimson liquid. "Take the blasted Health Potion, Lieutenant!"

He did. It tasted vile, but then Kelgan had never particularly liked the flavors of alchemy. Combined with the bonus to his regeneration, he could feel it knitting pieces of himself together. There had been leaking, he'd realized, and his Health stopped dropping before slowly reversing the damage. "Thanks."

"It was my last one," the Gnome admitted. "Kelgan. We gotta run if we wanna survive. Sound the retreat!"

"Can you hold that invisibility spell of yours for the whole group?"

"It's not—No. That's too much. I can handle four, *maybe* five people, including myself," Thangle admitted with a scowl.

Kelgan reached down, grabbing another weapon. More a halberd than spear, though it'd do the trick. He'd trained with one before. "If you can't get us all outta here, then we go for the head."

Thangle followed his gesture directly to the tall form of the Inquisitor still on the steps of the Waystone. Trails of golden light clung to the man's armor and hands, like puppet strings that connected to the Guardian of Faith currently stomping their friends.

"We take him out, this fight's over," he insisted.

"He's an Adept! He's fighting off *Zara*!" Thangle shook his head. His white hair quivered. "That Guardian would sense us before we ever get close enough to do any damage."

A flare of radiance was followed by the sound of crashing breakers, a peal of distant thunder, and the massive sword halted. The Inquisitor screamed and the Guardian pressed, all of its bulk behind its huge weapon. Kelgan noticed—and judging by Thangle's pale face, he did too—the unspooling of green-blue light, ribbons that snapped atop the stalled blade. A sharp, tinny scream of sundered metal tore the air, and the Guardian's weapon vanished into golden smoke. His men cheered, heartened as they pressed the attack.

"No! Shields!" Kelgan hollered.

The warning was too late as the Guardian's wild haymaker swept in from their left. Zara, mage or not, squared herself off against it, taking it head-on. She was launched into the Haarguard, the lot of them thrown from their feet as their weapons and limbs tangled with one another.

The Inquisitor laughed, and the Guardian stomped closer.

The array lit up, silver and gold lines that filled the entirety of the large chamber. The light of them revealed its size to be even larger than he estimated, and massive, triangular crystals hung down from a vaulted ceiling covered in carved vines and organic shapes. The array sang to him, notes that shook his core with every wordless verse. Meaning was there, just outside comprehension, and all of it was focused on him.

State Your Name.

Beneath his feet, the blank stone glimmered with the beginnings of a complex glyph. But only the beginnings; it seemed to be waiting on his answer.

"Felix Nevarre."

Why Do You Seek Authority, Felix Nevarre?
Why Do You Seek The Crown?

"The crown?"

The rite! Answer truthfully and do not fear!

Nodding at Karys' advice, he licked his lips and muscled past the pain in his core space. "To help."

Gold and silver light arced all around him, spitting a choral chaos at him from every angle. The force of the Grand Harmony weighed against him like an avalanche, a crushing stone that threatened to grind him flat.

Reason Not Sufficient.
Redefine.

What? He searched for words, to boil down exactly what he was feeling since coming to the Continent. Power was a means of survival, at first. But somewhere along the lines, that changed. Transmuted. Why did he want Authority? What did it even mean? To be a ruler, like Cal? To reign over people like some noble?

His Keen Mind threw back at him visions of people struggling with the burdens this world put on them, burdens that *Felix* inadvertently put on them when he'd landed in the Foglands those months back. So many dead, because the "haves" could not let power into the hands of the "have nots." The partitioning of power and the gluttonous hoarding of secrets.

You cannot coddle them forever.

All of us, them included, have to live with the consequences of our decisions.

Danger abounds on the Continent. You do them no favors by protecting them from it. That is how it always has been, and always must be.

Zara's words echoed in his Mind, accompanied by visions of people lost beneath the claws of Revenants and Wretches, Arcids and the Reforged. His back curled under the weight of the array. Visions of his friends, allies, the random people he could recall with perfect detail, hurt by the Archon or the Maw or the Inquisition. At the mercy of the strong and cruel.

The array shoved at him, burned him. Gold and silver flared and shone enough to blind, to deafen. It begged an answer. A truth.

He recalled the hands of the Divine pressing him, dropping him to his knees. Forcing his decisions, no matter his Choices. Yet then, as before, Felix refused to be bent or broken. "No."

Reason Not Sufficient.
Redefine.

"You—" he unbent his back, shoving with every ounce of Strength he possessed. A sharp whine cut through the Harmony. "You want me to name one thing, but I can't! I have a million! To protect! To thrive! To fight back!" Felix hurled the weight from his shoulders and stood, utterly free of its insidious pressure. "I remade myself, and I can remake this, too. I am me!"

Reason Not Sufficient.
Re—

"I am Felix Nevarre! Born of my own Will! And I bow to no one."

The chamber lit. Gold and silver.

"In the name of the Duke, I condemn you!"

Kelgan gasped as, from above, a man fell from the dark sky. Stormwinds arrived with him, as clouds scudded across the clear night sky. Cloaks and capes snapped taut, and the light of the Guardian dimmed, ever so slightly.

"Your Duke holds no power here, Hand!" The Inquisitor turned his sharp smile up at the falling soldier, and the Guardian did the same. A new sword was conjured from its Mana and was lifted into a high guard. "Kill that man!"

The Hand's own unnaturally large sword was brought to bear, swinging down like judgment descending. His blade, wreathed in green-white air Mana, struck the Guardian's beam of golden light… and sheared right through it.

"No!" the Inquisitor howled.

The Hand hit the earth like a boulder, cracking cobbles and his greatsword continuing through the Guardian's defenses and into its right pauldron. At the same time, a gout of fire shot from the Guardian's wound, and its entire right arm exploded into burning motes of light.

The Inquisitor screamed, a high-pitched thing draped in fear. It was so intense that it pulled Kelgan's attention away from the Hand now facing the Guardian in single combat. He looked, burning his Night Eye to make out details at his distance, and saw the Inquisitor hunched over while liquid dribbled down his gauntlet.

"He's hurt," Kelgan realized with a shock. The white-enameled armor was charred along his shoulder and bicep, and blood welled up from between a savage rent in the metal. "Thangle, make me invisible! While the Guardian is distracted!"

The Gnome followed his gaze, apparently, because he gave little resistance to the idea. "It's called Obfuscation! It simply redirects the eye!" Kelgan felt a warm power settle over him, like a cloak he couldn't see. "And I have to come with you!"

An aftershock of razor-sharp wind tore ahead of them, slicing into the cobbles and through several of the unconscious Redcloaks. Neither stopped it much, and that was only a deflected blow by the Hand. Kelgan hustled forward, uncaring how much noise they made. The Inquisitor wouldn't be able to pick them out in the chaos. He hoped.

Golden flames swept over their heads and Windblades scoured the square with increasing violence. The clash of the Adept Hand and Guardian of the Faith was colossal, each blow shaking the earth and rolling across Setoria like thunder. Time and again, Kelgan was thrown from his feet with only his stolen halberd to steady himself. Thangle didn't even have that, and was far smaller; the man fell many times and was once caught by flying debris across his eye.

Still, the two of them stumbled forward, both bleeding and drained. Redcloaks—alive or dead—littered their path, and the aftershocks of every attack could mean nothing or the approach of Avet's dire scythe.

"ENOUGH!"

Kelgan dropped to his knees, Thangle close behind him, as the Inquisitor lurched forward and down several steps. His face was ashen, and his right arm hung uselessly at his side. "You tangle with forces you do not understand, Darius Reed! Stand down, and the Inquisition shall let you live. Stand down, and Pax'Vrell doesn't get razed next!"

The Hand parried a gigantic unarmed blow of the Guardian yet still managed to bark a harsh laugh. "You think I trust your word, Redcloak? Your people nearly killed my ward in Haarwatch. There was no parley or mercy then. There will be no mercy now."

"Very well! Prepare to die, Chosen Hand! Heretic!" the Inquisitor screamed. Power swirled above them all, the sun appearing in the sky as if it were noon and not nearly midnight. The Guardian raged, slamming into the Hand with renewed fervor. Kelgan and Thangle crept forward, only ten strides away from the base of the stairs.

"Pathless, heed my call! I give unto you those who violate your High Laws! Violators of the truce you've long protected!" The Inquisitor stepped down another two steps, angling his head so that he was bathed in the light of the unnatural sun. "Help me end them! Let us wipe clean the impurity of this place!"

The sun burst, changing from an orb of riotous light to a sword that hung high in the sky above the square. A sword the size of the Waystone itself.

"Skyfall Judgment!"

Kelgan grabbed Thangle by the waist and ran with every ounce of Strength and Agility he could muster. The Gnome flailed, but he couldn't be worried about it. He hit the base of the stairs. *Just four more to go!*

"Reed!"

"Zara!"

A thread of aquamarine Mana swept just above Kelgan's head, scoring the Waystone's walls and igniting an explosion of furious light behind him. Thangle screamed. Kelgan leaped, halberd thrust forward.

The square ignited, and a blast that somehow pulled everything *inward* dominated the space. The earth rocked, pitching upward and hurtling both Kelgan and the Inquisitor from their feet. The Redcloak screeched in pained alarm, finally noticing the spearman almost atop him.

Then the Guardian detonated.

Golden fire flared outward in a ring of refined Mana, vapor so thick it was a half-step from becoming liquid. It scorched Kelgan's back, pushing at him, but he would not be stopped. The Inquisitor writhed, his own flesh boiling, and was unable to stop the spike that stabbed through his skull.

You Have Killed An Unknown Inquisitor Of The Inviolate Inquisition!
XP Earned!
You Have Gained 1 Level!
You Are Now Level 58!
You Have 3 Unused Stat Points!

The System's energy soaked into his core, into him, but he hadn't the strength. He tipped, fell, but rough hands caught him by his jerkin.

"A good job, Lieutenant," the Hand said in a deep, tired voice. Kelgan was put back on his feet with a lurch. "You can stand?"

"A-aye, sir," he managed. Thangle was beside the Hand, looking unburnt but utterly drained. "Is it over?"

"Almost." The Hand bared his teeth at the thick door of the Waystone. "We'll take it from here."

"The Waystone is transmitting!" Zara gasped from behind them. She hobbled up the steps, her gait ruined by a bleeding leg. "Halt it, whatever you do!"

Kelgan gaped at the state of her, then at her words. He'd barely pieced together how to run when the Hand demolished the thick double doors with a single blow.

Light and sound turned to pressure and pain, all of it fused into a single, exalted moment of transcendent song.

Congratulations!
You Have Established Territorial Authority!
Authority Accessed—!
ERROR.

Dissonance reared its head, flitting through the notes of Harmony with an atonal shriek.

Unbound Detected.
Primordial Detected.
Nymean Detected.
...
Inheritor Status Supersedes All Bloodlines!

Harmony and Dissonance met, clashed as they did within his core. And just as within him, they settled, filling in gaps neither had shone before the other's interference. Felix's entire being hummed like a struck key, rising and falling in equal measure.

Lightning and fire tore around him, igniting the gold and silver array. Anointing it. Beneath his feet, a glyph blazed to life, filled with blue-white and red-gold light in equal measure. It depicted a complicated mash of sigils, all of them forming the shape of a single eye surmounted by a crown with nine tines.

Authority Accessed.

Territorial Authority Established!
You Have Claimed The Lost Territory of Nagast!

Welcome, Inheritor!

"Oh," he said, blinking his eyes. The pain and pressure, all of it was gone. "*Oh.*"

A sense of what he'd just accessed filled his Mind, the borders of the once-Territory of Nagast shown clear against a map from another Age. It spread from the Bitter Sea in the west and south, to the Hoarfrost in the north, all the way to—

"Holy crap."

Felix could feel the breadth of it all, like a limb he hadn't known existed. Mountains and forests and swamps and rivers, vague impressions for the most part, but it was there, etched on an ancient map in his Mind. He could even feel the influence of the Spirit Tree on the Territory like a balm.

Due To Reviving A Spirit Tree On The Brink Of Extinction
Authority Has Been Increased!

A large menu appeared, floating in mid-air and glowing with a golden radiance. Like in Naevis, there were several tabs, and much of it was grayed out, but a few pieces caught his eye.

"Mana Relay? Offensive and Defensive Arrays? Is this what I think it is?" Felix asked his sword.

It certainly seems to be. I—I recall a similar display in my own Family's Holding. I think. Look there, under Defensive Arrays.

Felix toggled that tab, and a list of illegible symbols populated his screen, all of them grayed out. All except one.

Mirk Enclosure - Ritual, Defensive Array, Tier IV
Effect: Encase your Territory in an impenetrable fog, invisible to your people within, but a physical and sensory barrier to all those without.
Initial Cost: 10,000 Mana/5,000 Essence

"Ten *thousand* Mana? Jesus. Wait, does that mean Essence is twice as potent as Mana?" Felix asked.

Of course it is.

"Why didn't you mention that before?"

I—because I only just remembered it. Karys went silent, humming to himself. *I remembered something new.*

"I'm happy for you and all, but let's focus." Felix read the description again, but it wasn't too informative. "What does it do?" He focused on it again, and this time pressed with his Affinity and Intent, and knowledge of the ritual swept through his Mind. How to perform it, how to fuel it, and even how to infuse it with a touch of his own potency. He felt at that connection, the one that had set him in such a panic. The fight raged on, inside a large stone building now, the tension still as thick as the fear coming from Zara. He had to help. He could make this work.

"The cost… I have enough, if you can help me, Pit," Felix said, and was immediately met by acceptance. The tenku held wide their bond, and Felix could feel his Mana sitting there. As if he could reach out and grasp it with his hands. Warmth and affection and urgency colored their connection, and Felix didn't wait.

Etheric Concordance is level 73!
Etheric Concordance is level 74!

"Mirk Enclosure."

A pulse of Mana, Essence, and shimmering song bursting in all directions. It was like pure joy spun into threads of music and Intent, a shield woven of the powers of creation; it sent shivers through Felix even as his Mana tore painfully out of his channels. The silver and gold light was subsumed by red-gold flames and blue-white electricity as Felix poured himself into the glyph beneath his feet. *His* glyph, he realized. It was the last thought he had before his consciousness was consumed by the spreading roil of power.

It and he were swept outward toward every border of his new Territory. He could have followed its progression in all directions at once, but instead focused upon the rolling storm of potency that flashed into the east. Toward Haarwatch and beyond.

The Inquisition wants to come for us? Then let them come! Pit sent, a screech of challenge that echoed across the vast terrain of his Territory. Caught up in the frenetic joy of the ritual, Felix couldn't help but howl along with him.

In Haarwatch, a fog wall roared from the wilds like the storm of the century. Blue-white lightning scattered across its face, and the Fiend's Legion called desperately for citizens to take shelter. Yet it rolled past them, harmless as a summer breeze, the thick fog turning translucent as it advanced until it vanished utterly. Gasps of surprise and elation crossed the Legionnaires' faces as notifications popped before every single one of them.

The fog wall rolled on, catching people in the streets, in their homes and slowly rebuilt houses. People shouted at its approach, but every single one felt a jolt of power once it had enveloped them. A surge of potency that left thousands gasping.

Cal stood atop her balcony as it hit and immediately felt the change. Her regenerations were boosted, and her Strength and Willpower increased by a flat 5%, all due to something her Status was calling a Boon. She barely had time to see that before another message superceded it. This one was framed in gold and was twice as large as any other.

A Defensive Array Has Been Activated For the Territory of Nagast!
Lost No More!

A New Territorial Lord Has Risen!

Cal laughed as she read the rest of the notification. "You son of a bitch."

Zara chased after Reed and Kelgan, weakened immensely by the power she had been forced to expend, but she would not trust this to others. The Waystone had to be shut down, and without the proper protocols, it would take either the finesse of a Master to accomplish, or the power of one. She had spent the latter, but the former was always to hand.

Yet she had barely gotten to the relay chamber, noting the redcloaked bodies on the ground, when a shimmering wave of power swept over everything she saw. A pulse that ate across hidden sigaldry in the walls, burning them out as it passed. Popping and sizzling filled the air, and then all was quiet.

What in Avet's name—?

The magelights in the Waystone had snuffed out, so she conjured an orb of aquamarine light. It illuminated the relay chamber, a place where the complicated mechanisms of ancient etheric technology would shift and turn, pumping Mana into the spires above. Kelgan and Reed stood in the center, looking confusedly at everything.

"It all just… stopped," Kelgan said. "It was going, and then —nothing."

Reed shook his head. "Was that you? Why have us race in here if you could shut it down with such ease? You damn near burnt the Waystone out!"

"It was not me," Zara said. She strode forward, keen to hide her weakness from the Hand's angry eyes. "And they had started the sequences already. There is no way to stop it at that point, not short of ripping it apart." She tapped the mechanisms, convoluted brass things that escaped her knowledge. "These are quite whole. That wave of magic disrupted it, somehow. Shut it down."

"Then who did this?" Reed growled.

They were all interrupted by a sudden, golden-framed notification.

A Defensive Array Has Been Activated For the Territory of Nagast!
Lost No More!

"A defensive array? I've never heard of Nagast," Reed said in confusion. His next words were interrupted by another notification.

A New Territorial Lord Has Risen!
All Hail The Inheritor, Autarch of Nagast, Felix Nevarre!

"WHAT?" Reed roared, and Kelgan looked like someone had just saved his life.

Indeed he should. Zara could sense the power of the array that had enveloped half the city. It was a roiling fog that spread out of the Verdant Pass and over the majority of Setoria. Already, guards and other folk were testing it, and finding themselves unable to penetrate the dense mist.

Reed whirled on her. "What has the Fiend done?"

Zara's heart hammered as she heard the threads that sang beneath the System message. She wanted to leap for joy and curse that Felix had ever left her sight. Those threads weren't just transmitting this message to her, but to everyone. The entire Continent.

A new power had arisen, an untested one in a land known to perhaps only the eldest of scholars, but which would soon be beset by those willing to test its borders. To test this new Autarch.

"Avet help us all."

ABOUT NICOLI GONNELLA

Nicoli Gonnella spent his formative years atop a mountain, breathing deep of the world energy and expelling impurities from his soul. Also he went to school and stuff. He always wrote but now he's abandoned everything to do it full time. Readers give him strength, spirit bomb style, and there's no telling how strong he will become. This isn't even his final form.

He lives with his wife, two kids, and a corgi named Cornelius.

Connect with Nicoli Gonnella:
NicoliGonnella.com
Discord.gg/sqQvJQhY8F
Patreon.com/Necariin
RoyalRoad.com/fiction/30321/Unbound
Facebook.com/Nicoli-Gonnella-Author-347428719693359

ABOUT MOUNTAINDALE PRESS

Dakota and Danielle Krout, a husband and wife team, strive to create as well as publish excellent fantasy and science fiction novels. Self-publishing *The Divine Dungeon: Dungeon Born* in 2016 transformed their careers from Dakota's military and programming background and Danielle's Ph.D. in pharmacology to President and CEO, respectively, of a small press. Their goal is to share their success with other authors and provide captivating fiction to readers with the purpose of solidifying Mountaindale Press as the place 'Where Fantasy Transforms Reality.'

Connect with Mountaindale Press:
MountaindalePress.com
Facebook.com/MountaindalePress
Twitter.com/_Mountaindale
Instagram.com/MountaindalePress

MOUNTAINDALE PRESS TITLES

GameLit and LitRPG

The Completionist Chronicles,
The Divine Dungeon,
Full Murderhobo, and
Year of the Sword by Dakota Krout

Arcana Unlocked by Gregory Blackburn

A Touch of Power by Jay Boyce

Red Mage and
Farming Livia by Xander Boyce

Space Seasons by Dawn Chapman

Ether Collapse and
Ether Flows by Ryan DeBruyn

Dr. Druid by Maxwell Farmer

Bloodgames by Christian J. Gilliland

Unbound by Nicoli Gonnella

Threads of Fate by Michael Head

Lion's Lineage by Rohan Hublikar and Dakota Krout

Wolfman Warlock by James Hunter and Dakota Krout

Axe Druid,
Mephisto's Magic Online, and
High Table Hijinks by Christopher Johns

Skeleton in Space by Andries Louws

Dragon Core Chronicles by Lars Machmüller

Chronicles of Ethan by John L. Monk

Pixel Dust and
Necrotic Apocalypse by David Petrie

Viceroy's Pride by Cale Plamann

Henchman by Carl Stubblefield

Artorian's Archives by Dennis Vanderkerken and Dakota Krout

Vaudevillain by Alex Wolf